OFFICIAL BUSINESS

(Lost in Service)

BY

BILL RUNYAN

W & B Publishers
USA

W & B Publishers

For information:
W & B Publishers
Post Office Box 193
Colfax, NC 27235
www.a-argusbooks.com

ISBN:978-0-6923596-4-8
ISBN: 0-6923596-4-8

Book Cover designed by Bill Runyan, based on *A Higher Level,* picture 170387, all-free-download.com.
Printed in the United States of America

Dedicated to anyone's trust in everyone to always do the right thing.

OFFICIAL BUSINESS
(LOST IN SERVICE)

ITINERARY

CONNECTICUT

PENNSYLVANIA

SOUTHEAST

THE NAVY YARD

PATUXENT NAVAL AIR STATION

ASCENSION ISLAND

GREECE

SOUTH KOREA

THE PHILIPPINES

HAWAII

WASHINGTON D.C.

CONNECTICUT

CONNECTICUT

The age-appropriately overweight man leaned far back in the rotating swivel chair and carefully stacked his wingtipped feet on a scuffed vinyl credenza behind the small steel desk. As he slowly raised his arms with interlocked fingers over the nape of a thick, red neck, the youthful onlooker seated nervously in front of the desk thought he had never seen so much dandruff on the back of one head.

"So tell me, Mr. Rossy, why....should I....lend you this money?" carefully projected the assistant branch manager of the Peck & Watts Aeronautics Credit Union, making no move to face his potential client.

"I don't know, sir, maybe because my orientation supervisor said you probably would?" offered Bill Rossy, feeling hot irritation rising through his face.

"Not a reason, young man. We are running a responsible financial services institution here. We've got to account for..... every penny out."

"OK, how about because I don't get paid for three weeks and I'm broke?"

"You don't understand, son. I need assurances....that you will.....repay the loan....in a timely manner and that we can retain payment should you....fail to do so."

"Well, what does that mean? I don't have any assurances, otherwise I wouldn't need a fracking payday loan!" The young man was in the process of going spontaneously stupid. His mind was flashing back a few months when he had to face a pompous board of hypocrite peers for illegally popping a Rolling Rock in the dorm lounge. They made him explain why he shouldn't be expelled from the university for such a blatant rules violation - the same offense they had all committed a lot more than he. *Because I graduate in June and if I'm booted now it would go a long way toward ruining my goddam life before it starts!* No, that didn't go particularly well and he needed help from the Assistant Associate Dean of Student Affairs to be released into the world with lengthy advice on proper responses, causes and effects, as well as, and vastly more importantly, his undergraduate degree in chemical engineering. *And now, here we go again.*

The abm remained silently motionless for a moment and then forcibly leaned forward and spun around in his chair to face the applicant, who reflexively flinched back in his own seat nearly tipping it over.

"Look, boy, I'm going to authorize this for you," whispered the bankster, "but only because I know and respect your boss. You are a dumbass punk and you better get that big ol' board off your shoulder. Nobody owes you anything and you'd best learn that as quickly as possible! Now take this chit to a cashier and get the hell out of my office!"

The new engineer mumbled a reluctant thanks and sidled out the door into the closing moments of his first workday as a professional.

***

Dumbass punk didn't know much about Connecticut when he accepted the job offer from PWA as a development engineer. He had been to Hartford in the early spring before graduation for an interview, but hadn't had time to see anything other than the hotel, the airport and the main plant of the company. It was an up and back trip in two days, in between midterms, featuring the first time he had ever traveled by air. On the return flight to Pennsylvania, one of the plane's fan turbines caught fire, necessitating an unscheduled landing in Allentown. Prior to the spiraling descent the cabin lost pressure and mostly everyone on board was totally or partially deaf by the time the distressed aircraft touched down and led a screaming parade of emergency vehicles to the end of the runway. The surfactant foam fire suppressant was already being deployed as he rolled down the canvas slide to the blessedly safe and stable asphalt tarmac below.

When the aborted passenger received a firm offer some weeks later, after fully losing his temporary hearing loss and certain grounds for lucrative litigation, he researched the engine supplier for the carrier of his near demise and, upon determining it was a competitor, accepted the job. And so here he was, on his own and ready to earn, though without an address and in more debt than he had ever been before.

PWA offered a housing placement service during orientation for newly recruited engineers. It was the classified ads of the Hartford Courant. The homeless hire found a room for rent in East Hartford that was in his low end price range and departed directly to check it out upon leaving the credit union. The room was in a modest, old brick row house in a mixed ethnic neighborhood of unmaintained urban trees and sprawling, potholed streets. The sidewalks were cracked and lumpy with root heaves, but, surprisingly, everything was sort of neat, in a broken down, trashless way. As he tapped on the storm door off the canopied portico, he heard muffled yelling and movement from inside. After waiting too long to not knock again and self debating whether to retry or just forget it and leave, the door flew open and he looked into the faces of four people - a woman, two boys and a girl. His new, hopefully temporary, rental family. The woman was a French Canadian widow, who spoke good, but heavily accented, English and was prone to faking heart attacks for attention. The girl was, well, a fourteen year-old eighth grader. She would quickly develop a crush on the young engineer, resulting in unauthorized entry to his room in his absence to help and impress. Like burning some of the few shirts he had while trying to iron them. The boys were sixteen and seventeen, both in vo-tech and not clearly on track to graduate from high school, let alone go to college as their mom would incessantly urge the new, educated boarder to convince them to do. The room seeker quickly decided this dysfunctional slice of Americana would refuge his needs just fine and he moved in immediately, after emphatically assuring mom, that he was, indeed, a devout believer in Jesus Lord Christ, and paying her a couple of bens cash security deposit.

***

Work at PWA was not easy to adjust to. Following two weeks of mandatory jet turbine school, the freshman was assigned to a special division engaged in research and development for fuel cell power plants. Though PWA didn't make any money from fuel cell technology, since most of the manned NASA programs were disbanded and commercial applications were presently cost prohibitive, fuel cells were considered a viable future energy alternative for clean domestic power. Accordingly, Unified Technical Group, PWA's parent company, wanted to stay competitive in the field. The Fuel Cell Power Research Facility (FCPRF) was located about ten miles from the main plant, in a small town within Hartford's suburban ring. It was basically a two compartment building housing the separate research and testing divisions, which were also segregated by union membership status. Rossy would be with the non-union research group. His first look at the workplace was overwhelming. A maze of tiny cubicles, spread over thousands of square feet, housed a legion of engineering subgroups, each one involved with a specific task in the development quest of efficiently reliable, cost effective fuel cell technology. His subgroup was located near the center of the maze and about as far from the outside egress ways and perimeter windows as possible within the configuration of the open span room. Lighting was overhead white florescent track tubing and the air was statically stifled with the pulsating aura of countless electronic devices. He would share a couple hundred square feet of cubicle space with three other engineers, one of whom was the lead for the subgroup and another a fellow recruit in his orientation class. The third was a few years older than the recruits and looked like a 1960's doo-wop crooner. All in all, a thoroughly rookie work station deeply imbedded in a visually and physically oppressive working environment.

Work attire protocol was half casual - dress shirt and tucked tie with long, waist-belted slacks (khakis or jeans) and tied sneaks or loafers with socks for men and what? for women. The green DE wasn't observing much of a feminine presence. This was consistent with the gender imbalance in his university's engineering program, which trended nationally, as far as he could tell. Why was that? Engineering seemed to be an equally logical career field for everyone, yet only a disproportionately low percentage of the country's engineering force was female. Maybe because ladies are more sociable? You had to be somewhat of an outcast recluse to get through engineering school. How many weekend parties had he missed while in p-chem or unit ops lab or taking some bizarro two-day exam? Anyway, women's half-casual dress criteria were probably the same as men's, sans tie.

The first day of assigned work, and mostly every working day thereafter through his eventually brief initiation tenure, Rossy's subgroup was visited promptly at 9:30 a.m. by two individuals from elsewhere in the network and the six engineers would go to Donna's Deli Diner for breakfast. Sometimes, even frequently, they barely made it back in time for lunch break at the company cafeteria. Of this social group of professional colleagues, or perhaps more aptly, professional group of social colleagues, only the subgroup leader, the eldest, was married with family and did not participate in after work happy time at Gelson's Goodtime Grill. One of the morning visitors was divorced and currently dating the administrative supervisor's assistant. He was, therefore, somewhat knowledgeable about general policy happenings within the research group, FCPRF, PWA and even UTG and was freely willing to share such information during the offsite consorts.

***

A few months after reporting to FCPRF, the rookie and his colleagues were advised at breakfast break of the appointment of UTG's CEO as the national chairperson for the annual United Way fund drive. The heads up was that the CEO was going to mandate participation, via auto paycheck deduction, of 100% of UTG employees, including all affiliate companies in the conglomerate. Rossy was struggling financially. Though his starting salary was relatively decent, he was still on probationary status and not eligible for a raise for at least another half year. He had almost paid off his credit union loan, but would be paying on student loans forever and thereafter and at least half that time on his used car note. He had to rely on libraries and cafes for free broadband to use his pad. His smart phone was restricted to basic minimum voice service with no internet. Cable wasn't a problem, since he had no TV. Gas prices were killing him in his commute from East Hartford, but he couldn't find cost comparable housing closer to work. Food was even more deadly. A burger? Fuhgettaboudit! He could only afford to eat healthy, but it still cost almost one abe for a fistful of turnip greens. He was trying to nonchalantly limit his breakfasts to coffee and happy times to a single draft beer that warmed to skunky undrinkability after about a half hour. So he made a mental note to respectfully decline the forthcoming opportunity for participation in the UW fund drive.

That was a mistake. On the morning after his notification to admin that he would not authorize a UW deduction, he was called in to the supervisor's glass-partitioned corner office for further discussion. "Please close the door and have a seat, Mr. Rossy", began the super. *Uh-oh.* "So I see here that you declined to author-ize a paycheck deduct contribution to the United Way fund."

"Yes, sir. I just can't afford it right now."

"Let me explain something to you, son." Rossy hated when an older dude called him 'son'. It invariably meant he was going to be told what to do or what he had already done was wrong. "You don't have a choice on this issue. When the boss says, 'de-duct', you say, 'how much?' Now, what's it going to be?"

"I'm sorry, sir, I can't do it." The recent 'A' student in *Engi-neering Management Fundamentals* was certain he was good on this. Employers had no right to coerce employees in such manner, even probationary employees. The ACLU or EEOC could squash this illegal manipulation in a few nanoseconds. This was America, not some leftover communist subdivision.

"OK," sighed the super, as if he well knew the drill. "I'll give you twenty-four hours. One last chance. Any amount. It doesn't matter. Just let me know in writing. Leave the door open, please."

The next day, the rebel refusenik noticed a conspicuous void in a nearby cubicle. All furniture and equipment of the work sta-tion of a senior engineer had been removed and the occupant was nowhere to be seen. Upon inquiry, he learned that the man, an ad-amant and unyielding foe of forced charitable contribution, was no longer employed at FCPRF and had been professionally disenfran-chised from the company. He had been covertly canned, less than two years before retirement eligibility, for not authorizing a paycheck deduct to the UW fund! Rossy had about ten minutes before his twenty-four hours were up. He literally ran through the cubicle complex to the little glass box in the corner, where he saw another engineer behind the closed door with the supervisor. Grabbing a sticky pad from an adjacent desk, he hastily wrote, dated and signed a note authorizing $0.25 per paycheck deduction for United Way. He reached over the partition and stuck the note to the inside of the office door with three minutes to spare on his deadline. A short while later, the super called and thanked him, on behalf of the UTG CEO, for his voluntary support of company policy regarding full participation in the United Way fund drive. After work, at happy time, the underfunded recruit spent three years' worth of charitable deduct on beer.

Despite the physical discomfort of FCPRF's harsh working conditions, the new analyst was finding his assigned research activity to be technically interesting. He was supposed to design a test stand for a pilot project to determine varying rates of matrix drying under a range of operating temperatures, pressures and electrolyte concentration. Matrix deterioration in fuel cells was a feared source of hydrogen/oxygen crossover that usually resulted in explosive violence and collateral destruction. Legend had it that many PWA heads were on the block during the ill-fated Apollo 13 abort, until it was determined that a supplier's oxytank gasket, and not the fuel cell, was the culprit for the near disaster. His design was to include safe containment of such an accidental explosion. He was directed to work with a test engineer in the construction and operation of the project stand in the other half of the FCPRF building, but, as a non-union employee, he was instructed in no uncertain terms to never, under any circumstances, touch anything in that section. After construction of the stand and commencement of the pilot program, Rossy found an increasing degree of frustration in trying to regularly locate his TE to change operating conditions and collect data according to the prescribed schedule. Since the procedures were specifically time sensitive, he couldn't afford to wait for the availability of the testie every time an operational adjustment or data collection was required. Therefore, to avoid compromising the results of his project, the brash DE made an unauthorized, unilateral decision to operate the stand and take data readings on his own. Well, jesus fracking christ!! It would have taken an imminent threat from al-Qaeda in Connecticut, to match the ferocious blow back of administration.

"Mr. Rossy," quietly intoned the supervisor behind the closed door of his transparent office, "you have been clearly and repeatedly advised from your first day on board at this facility of the distinct differences between union and non-union employees. You fully understood the restrictions associated with such differences and yet you chose to ignore our carefully negotiated protocol and proceed in a manner that constitutes a serious breach of policy. What the hell is this all about?"

Rossy, cognizant of his seemingly more frequent conflicts with authority, turned a passive side and said he was sorry and it would never happen again.

"Well, sorry isn't good enough, son. And, for sure, it never will happen again. I could let you go as a probationary frack-up, but your subgroup leader tells me you're showing some promise. So what I'm going to do is extend your probationary status by thirty days and suspend pay for one period. Fair enough?"

"Yes, sir," murmered the submissively humbled subordinate, "sounds good."

But, of course, it wasn't so good. He didn't care about the probation extension. That only meant another month without a raise. But losing two weeks salary could send him back to the credit union for another payday loan. He would rather stick his finger in a blender to make a protein smoothie. Quickly realizing neither was a realistically acceptable nor necessary option, the promising frack-up decided to adopt a temporary imposition of relative austerity to get over this minor speed bump in the dirt road of life. He pretended he was back in school and had two weeks to start and complete all his term projects. With this mindset he was able to focus solely on work and eventually develop a sound data base from which he prepared a very conclusive report with viable recommendations regarding the optimal operating parameters for hydrogen-oxygen, potassium hydroxide based fuel cells. He felt really good about this effort and his subgroup leader acknowledged receipt of the report with well deserved accolades. By this time he was getting paid again and his probationary status was approaching closure.

***

PWA had a policy requiring all engineers to become licensed professionals within five years of date of employment. This involved a two part testing process, including a fundamentals exam for new graduates and a practical applications exam for those with working experience. The tests were standardized, except as modified from state to state. Rossy had been scheduled to take the fundamentals exam at the university a week after graduation, but missed it because he had to be at work. To facilitate preparation for the exams, PWA hired a consultant to come in annually and conduct review courses for each of the licensing tests. The courses were held in a facility conference room every Friday afternoon for six weeks and attendance was mandatory until receipt of one's professional registration in Connecticut, or any other state of choice. The consultant was an intense academic with doctorate degrees in applied physics and mechanical engineering and professional registration in nineteen states. He began each training session by playing a recorded audio oration of his personal hero and internationally acclaimed motivationalist, Reverend Doctor Philip Bentley. During the audio, all eyes in the room went closed. With a furrowed brow of total concentration, the consultant silently mouthed each word of inspiration broadcasting from his computer in front of the room, while everyone else zoned out into varying stages of stupefied boredom, or just fell asleep. Rossy always listened for the monotoned words of the speaker, "Remember, people, the only obstacle to fulfillment is refusal to recognize potential. Success and may God be with you." This signaled the end of the taped message and the start of the course review, which was almost as boring but more interactive. It was like when he was a kid and had to go to church, sitting/standing/sitting/standing among heavily cologned and perfumed adults, who sang woefully out of tune while unknowingly suffocating the poor children beneath. He would pray for the preacher's words 'let us pray', meaning the end of the sermon and approaching release from the hell of the church service. The PWA licensing program was very effective as everyone complied as soon as possible, to avoid repeating the review course and to get the incentive pay increase. 100% participation - the watermark of team technology.

***

It was the morning of Halloween when the well rehearsed candidate made his way into the Hartford Civic Center to sit for the engineering fundamentals exam. This was a regional testing site serving most of southern New England and there were several hundred registrants in attendance. Looking around the crowded floor, he observed mostly men, some of whom appeared thoroughly unprofessional in costumes ranging from super hero figures to skeleton jump suits to star trek re-enactors, zombies and beyond. They were obviously programmed to phase directly into party mode in about eight hours, regardless of the outcome of their testing performance. Some things never change. Rossy could have been costumed as an airline passenger, as he was pulling his allowable references in a small, wheeled suitcase and walking in flip flops. He did not see any of his PWA associates, though he knew his fellow subgroup recruit, Ken Booker, was supposed to be there. He noticed the few women in this assembly of prospective professional engineers were very executively attired and thought that one of them would probably someday be his boss. The exam was not particularly difficult, a multiple choice format, though grueling in its scope and length. Being generally pretty good at standardized testing, as were most products of 'no child left behind' public schooling, he was not concerned about the result but had a mind-blurring headache by 'pencils down' time in the late afternoon.

On the way out of the Civic Center, Rossy spotted his colleague and they decided to celebrate completion of the exam by going to Chickenfeets Country Culture Club, a regionally well known night spot specializing in urban country fusion music. The club was on Asylum Street within walking distance of the Center and, after depositing their reference material and test paraphernalia at their vehicles in the nearby parking garage, they arrived as the evening crowd was starting to trickle in. It was difficult to tell whether the patrons were dressed like cowpeople for Halloween or as usual for a normal Saturday night on the town. Either way the engineers did not really blend in, mainly because of their foot, belt and head wear, or lack thereof. The club was divided into three parts. An auditorium, with a wire-screened band stage, parqueted dance floor and rows of fixed, cushioned seats, most of which were stained with bleached over hurl, was adjacent to a massive ell shaped bar with high stools on the long leg and a pool table, shuffleboard and dart board at the far end away from the club entrance. Tables paralleled the bar between the aisle to the game area and the street side windows. The kitchen was behind the bar. Most people coming in went directly to the auditorium where the band was already setting up. Many of the bar stools were filled, but all the tables were empty. The two selected one nearest the gaming zone where a large group of large men were drinking, shooting and betting. Tim McGraw blared from the barside speakers and it was not easy to talk, so they mainly watched the close-by eight ball contest in progress, after ordering a couple of longnecks. The action was so close-by that a player's Levied butt hung over their table from a corner shot. So close they could clearly see every move by everyone in and around the heavily wagered game. They couldn't miss seeing a shooter lining up the cue to sink the winning black ball when his opponent reached across the green felt, snatched the target from the table and bowled it down the linoleum back bar floor into the kitchen.

A moment of disbelieving silence and then all Chickenfeets hell broke loose. In a single fluid motion, one buckeroo grabbed a beer bottle, smashed it over the edge of the bar and followed through with the jagged end of the longneck targeted toward the face of the would be loser. Another cold-cocked the bottleman before he connected, probably saving a messy homicide. Within seconds a full-fledged barn brawl was in progress. It was like a maniacal fury ball of human destruction was activated, a tornado of fists and boots destroying all things vulnerable in its path. As the wrecking machine thrashed toward the general service area, the bar emptied and terrified patrons fled into the auditorium. Rossy and Booker jumped up and moved backwards just before their table and chairs were pulverized. They watched in retreating fascination as the mayhem consumed each table, the chairs and barstools and all dishes, bottles and glassware, in sequence, along the length of the bar. It was almost ten minutes and near the head of the bar at the club entrance foyer, before the violent soiree burned out. The torn and bloodied warrior cowboys slowly picked themselves up and staggered around in a collective semiconscious stupor trying to regain a handle on their confused senses. The floor was covered in glass shards that crackled under the heavy stomps of the aimlessly pacing combatants. Two cops strolled in from the street and stood inside the doorway surveying the scene, tasers in hand. In no time, the ceasefire was broken when someone bawled, **"WHERE'S MY WALLET? WHERE'S MY MOTHA-FRACKIN' WALLET?!?"** And the fury ball started to roll again, but the cops intervened before it redeveloped any serious mo. After a few minutes the brawlers settled down and were meandering back to the remains of the bar to resume drinking, like bees returning to a stick-hammered hive. The band was starting its first set and order was restoring. The police secured their unused tasers and sauntered back over to the entrance area.

"You boys from around here?" inquired one of the officers after a hard look at the still gape-mouthed engineers, who were staring incredulously at what had to be thousands of dollars of purposeless damage.

"I live in East Hartford." responded Rossy quickly, feeling a certain queasiness of alarm roiling in his stomach.

"Got any ID?" the other continued.

The local boy carefully handed over his PWA security photo card and looked at the floor. He did not yet have a Connecticut driver's license and sensed that an out of state license would not work well in this situation.

The officer studied the card for a moment. "There's no birth date on this, Willie," he observed, slowly returning the card.

"No, sir, it's a work ID." agreed Willie.

"You guys gay?" queried the first cop, with a trace of accusatory condescension.

"No."

"Well, I suggest you get the hell out of here, anyway. I don't need any goddam hate crimes on my clock. DOJ paperwork would take 'til Christmas and I can't deal with it. So go on, beat it! And don't drive - you obviously been drinking, if you're in this fine establishment!"

The well-tested engineers obediently exited Chickenfeets and elected to call it a day.

***

The following May, Rossy went on a weekend excursion with three of his working pals. They planned to go to Maine and canoe down a segment of an obscure river from its natural lake source in the vicinity of the White Mountain National Forest. The trip required execution of a tight schedule between after work on Friday and return by Sunday night. They secured the rental canoes and packed the dry food and camping gear on Thursday, so all they had to do in departure was change clothes and pick up beer ice. They needed three cars. Two to each carry a canoe on top and drive to the start point at the lake and one to park at the endpoint approximately fifty miles downstream for transportation back to retrieve the canoe cars. Doo-wop engineer refused to put a canoe on his beloved Alfa Romeo, so Rossy's used Civic sedan was one of the carriers, along with administrative assistant dater's Outback. Booker had a lightweight Yamaha sport cycle, which was useless to the operation and sat this one out. The road distance to the lake was almost 250 miles and they managed to get underway by 6:00 p.m. Because none of the four had ever been to where they were going, the route was not familiar, resulting in several GPS recalculations. Because the cars were not design stable with canoes overhead, the pace was slow, requiring many stops to adjust and tighten the bungee binds. After depositing the Alfa at a public landing selected as a suitable endpoint, the two carrier cars finally arrived at the start point around 2:00 a.m. on a cloudy, moonless Saturday. It was pitch black dark and without actually seeing the lake they knew it was nearby, as they could hear the softly lapping water at the shore beyond the end of the lane where they had parked. Exhausted, they set up tents, crawled into sleeping bags and promptly faded away.

In seemingly short order, they saw the light of day when they were brutally awakened by the blaring horn of a pick-up truck very close to where they lay. They popped out of the bags and then out of the tents in front of a tall, elderly, overall-clad man with a zz-top beard under a battered Farm Bureau ball cap.

"Ya get along a lot bettah in Maine, if ya ask pahmishun before ya set camp!" the man said, matter-of-factly. Glancing around, the strangers quickly discovered their encampment was in the middle of a driveway off the lane, presumably to the pick-up man's place, and was blocking his way out. Embarrassed by their inadvertent transgression, they hastily rolled the little LL Bean dome tents back to the cars and cleared the driveway. Returning to the truck they apologized profusely to the property owner, who eyed them somewhat bemusedly. "You boys move well fast when jostled. What's yer plan?"

"Well, we want to canoe down the river, but don't know exactly where it leaves the lake. Can you help us out?"

"Sure, it's right ovah therrah." said the man, pointing across the lake to what looked pretty much like the featureless far shoreline.

The four quickly packed up, locked the cars and carried the canoes over the low sandy berm to the water. As they started to paddle away under a rising sun, the man assumed a position on a chair-sized tree stump by the water's edge and reiterated his point to the river's outfall. With little breeze and a glassy surface, they rapidly distanced themselves from the embarkment and were soon gliding into the deepening mid-lake channels. Glancing back, they noticed the old guy was still sitting on the stump, pointing with outstretched arm to their destination, like a bird dog on target. With distance, he became smaller and smaller. Finally, approaching the far shore, they could no longer see their de facto guide with the naked eye. But with binoculars, they saw he remained in place, pointing the way.

"That dude's un-fracking-believable!" observed one of the adventurers. But he was accurate, as it turned out when they found the minuscule river outflow under a mass of tangled blackberry brambles exactly where it was indicated to be. Pushing through the overgrowth, they were soon underway downstream, only a couple of hours behind schedule, which they figured would have been lost anyhow had they not been shown the way. To everything there is a purpose.

Rossy had not been canoeing since he was fifteen, when he was at a summer camp in the New York Adirondacks. His mom thought he was developing into a problem boy, because he was growing up without a dad, who died when he was four, and he seemed to be overly sullen in his general teenage demeanor. He knew he was doing fine, getting good grades, future looking bright, but he couldn't convince her. She had heard about the Adirondack Wilderness Camp from a friend's husband, who attended back in his day. He advised that the heavily structured, eight week summer program AWC offered was perfect for troubled young men and boys and he would be more than happy to offer his sponsorship in getting Billy enrolled. When he arrived at AWC, the troubled teen quickly discovered this was no ordinary camp. Two of his bus-mates were plotting to knock off the canteen before they even processed in. It soon became evident the campers were from all over the country and many had been assigned to be there by their respective juvenile courts. One thirteen year-old from Detroit had a felony record for stealing a tractor trailer rig. There were no girls. The camp was directed by an Afghan/Iraqi War vet, the son of the founder, an ex-colonel Vietnam War vet. The heavy structure was militarized in format, though, of course, without weapons. Issued uniforms of logoed, yellow tee-shirts and khaki long trousers were required dress at all times in the base camp, where frequent personal and sleeping quarters inspections for cigarettes and other contraband were conducted regularly and randomly. Days began with early morning reveille and ended with early evening taps. Activities consisted of well supervised bivouac deployments to surrounding mountain wilderness areas for up to a week at a time, via hiking, horseback or canoe. Base camp meals were at the mess hall across the lake from the assigned lean-to quarters and were preceded by line-up, roll call and hygienic inspection by the camp nurse. Young Rossy and another boy often canoed to the mess hall. On one occasion they failed inspection before lunch for having mud on their hands and arms from mooring the canoe on the beach. The nurse ordered them to carry the boat back around the lake to their quarters, properly wash-up and return by foot on the lake trail for re-inspection. It was about a two mile round trip. On the return to quarters, with the heavy aluminum canoe bearing on their shoulders, they were besieged by a younger, much smaller boy, who skipped along side, giggling loud taunts and insults, like an obnoxious, unmannered squib dog yapping at anything that moved. After several minutes of this annoyance, Rossy stopped, hoisted his end of the load over his back and placed it on the ground. Without a word he walked over to the grinning poodle kid and smacked him upside the head. The boy somersaulted off the path and disappeared into a shallow ravine. The rest of the punishment portage was quietly uneventful, but later in the day, the junior pugilist found himself standing in front of the director's desk.

"YOU A TOUGH GUY, BEATING UP ON A LITTLE KID?! IS THAT WHAT YOU ARE?? A TOUGH GUY?!?" bellowed the marine vet.

"No, sir, I was just....."

"SHUDDUP!! I'M TALKING, HERE. MAYBE WE SHOULD FIND OUT HOW TOUGH YOU ARE! YOU WANNA TEST THE BIG BOYS?? YOU WANNA PUNCH OUT SOMEBODY BIGGER THAN YOU?!?"

"No, sir, I just...."

"SHUDDUP!! HERE'S WHAT'LL HAPPEN. IF THE KID IS NOT SERIOUSLY INJURED YOU ARE CONFINED TO QUARTERS FOR THREE DAYS. IF HE IS INJURED YOU WILL FACE ASSAULT CHARGES AND BE TURNED OVER TO THE LOCAL AUTHORITIES. DO YOU UNDERSTAND?!"

"Yes, sir, but...."

"SHUDDUP!! COUNSELOR! GET THIS FRACKIN' PIECE OF CRAP OUTTA MY OFFICE!"

That was the last day before the river trip that the would-be delinquent had canoed. He found his j-hook and steering stroke skills intact and was enjoying riding the current down the mellow waterway. The river was more a flatter piedmont type estuary than a steeper, faster kind of mountain run. Though the water was flowing seasonally high, there were no serious white rapids to negotiate and they did not have to carry around impassable areas. Their speed was good, maybe four mph. They figured to work about six hours before making camp for the night. Around 3:30 p.m. they came upon a confluence where a sizable, but smaller, branch inflowed to the river. In the upstream vee of this fork was a structure that appeared abandoned, yet curiously intact. They maneuvered the canoes to the steep bank by a grassed, level patch in front of the building and climbed out to investigate. The single level, wooden house was obviously an old homestead. Chairs lined the exterior wall on the covered, wrap-around porch deck, punctuated by the entranceway and several fully glazed windows. The hardwood portal was shut, but unlocked behind a rusted screen door held in place by a creaky spring closer, and opened easily. With no hesitation, the four entered into a furnished past that was well before their time. The musty three room interior was like a museum of the rural, backwoods 1930's. Pre-war era *Life*, *Saturday Evening Post* and *Sports Afield* magazines were stacked on a small metal stand beside a dust encrusted overstuffed chair by a massive stone fireplace. Crumbling area rugs covered wooden floors that were in generally good condition. Off to one side of the fireplace area was a bedroom, featuring a once colorfully quilted double bed, a milky mirrored dresser with white porcelain bowl and pitcher atop, and moth eaten remnants of natural fiber clothes on wall hooks around the room. On the other side of the fireplace was a kitchen area with a small table and three ladder-backed, wicker chairs. Cabinets shelved a considerable number of sealed tins, jars and boxes containing long defunct food product brands. Hand painted glass dishware, corroded silver plate utensils, steel pots and a black iron skillet filled some open counter drawers adjacent to a wood burning stove with a thick cast metal cooking surface. Decaying log splits were stacked in a rack beside another door to the outback of the house. Several dark, heavy woolen jackets and leather fedora hats were pegged on the spalling plaster wall beside the front door. On the fireplace mantle were two kerosene lamps and a partially loaded Smith & Wesson cylinder pistol. Above the mantle hung a large framed photograph of a man and a woman seated on recognizable porch chairs in the yard in front of the house. Hatless, they both had long, dark hair, appeared to be in their mid-thirties and were fairly attractive. The clean-shaven man was smiling broadly, revealing an even row of white, upper case teeth. The woman was tight-lipped, with an unsettling expression of fear diffusing from her intensely focused eyes.

"What do you think?" asked one of the canoeists, to no one in particular.

"Looks good to me," responded another.

"OK, let's set up camp. It's gonna be dark in a few hours," agreed a third.

"Isn't this trespassing?" wondered Rossy. "What if they come back?"

"Come back? Are you kidding me? They would have to be a hundred twenty five years old by now. There's no one here to come back, for chrissake, unless they're frackin' ghosts. Besides, we're in a national forest on un-posted property. No way are we trespassing."

"OK, dawg, let's roll."

The night was peaceful except for the intermittent, piercing caterwauling of a large northeastern mountain cat from some distant fold of the darkness. Rossy, in a quasi dream state, at first imagined he was hearing the baleful cries of someone in mortal danger. Soon it was Sunday and time to float on down the river.

They broke camp and departed downstream, leaving no discernible trace of their intrusion on the homestead site. Today's start was much more efficient and earlier than yesterday's and they anticipated no problems in reaching the endpoint landing by noon. In fact, they made it with almost an hour to spare. Leaving Booker with the canoes, the other three piled into the Alfa and headed back to the lake to retrieve the two carrier cars. This would be a hundred mile roundabout, probably taking no more than three hours. They hoped to be on the road home by mid-afternoon. Again, they were slightly ahead of schedule and found themselves fully underway with a good chance of anticipated return to Hartford by sundown. However, they lost a great deal of time in heavy end-of-weekend traffic and it was well after dark when they arrived at the downtown rental agency to offload the canoes. Rossy finally made it to his boarding house room by about 11:00 p.m. and flopped down on the bed, totally spent. Then, sixth sensing another presence, he bolted upright and glanced furtively around. The daughter girl was sitting in the shadows at the kitchenette table, staring at him with the hint of a smile. *OMG*, he panicked. *This is not good.*

The boarder rose slowly from the bed and eased backwards toward the door. "Be right back," he croaked. "Forgot something in the car." Leaving his room door open, he glided quickly down the hallway and the stairs, out the front entrance and around back to his car. He drove down the alley and away from what was no doubt a potentially disastrous situation. His memory drifted to the witless schmucks featured on *To Catch A Predator,* an old TV program he had watched a few times to see profiles of people he was glad he was not. This was actually sort of the inverse of that hapless show, in that the underage bait girl came unsolicited to his place. But he was still fleeing the premises, just like the predator schmucks. Affirming to himself it was much better to run away than to risk becoming an innocently-charged registered sex offender for life, he decided to go to the Motel 6 off I-84 for the night and deal with this problem tomorrow, after work, at a more reasonable time of day. That would give him an alibi, in case the girl was inclined to create a late night scene in his room and express her angry disappointment through outrageously false accusations. Hell hath no irrational fury greater or more damaging than a delusional adolescent rejected by her crushee. He had to get out of this house of shelled nuts.

Time was passing quickly. Rossy found himself revolving in a repetitive schedule of going to work and then going from work, spending both blocks of time in similar fashion day after day. By his first anniversary of university graduation, he was a full status employee and had received a couple of pay increases. His finances were improving, despite the endless debt burden, but since he didn't really do or buy anything, or go anywhere other than an occasional Saturday run to Misquamicut Beach and a few holiday trips to Pennsylvania to see his folks, he was actually saving some money. The highlight of his warm weather free time was playing in the township slow-pitch softball league, for a team sponsored by Benevolent Bonny's Bistro, a popular local pizza pub. He started dating a girl he met there during an after-game beer slosh, but that fizzled after a few weeks due to mutual lack of interest. It seemed life was becoming sort of an automated routine for him, maybe even a boring rut. One day at work, a senior level tech executive came by his station cubicle and Rossy could not help overhearing his subgroup leader receiving a generous string of 'attaboys' for a submitted report they were reviewing that sounded very familiar. Following a short discussion, the report was placed on a work table and the two left for coffee. The reluctant eavesdropper went over to the table to take a look and, sure enough, it was his work, but gone was his name from the cover byline. His superior had placed his own name and authorship credit where the junior engineer's should have been and was now receiving false acknowledgement and likely benefit from top level management for something that he really had no direct involvement with. The rookie was stunned and, after some deliberation, decided to confront his sg boss to find out what was going on.

"It's called 'corporate domain', which means you have no rights of ownership regarding anything you generate while employed by PWA. You signed a waivers during orientation," curtly explained the subgroup lead engineer.

"Well, how come you have rights to *my* work? You're a PWA employee, too. Why aren't *you* domained by the company?"

"Look, son, maybe I can decipher your frustration. It's called inexperience. You have, what, a year? Come back and talk to me after you've got seventeen years. You're not a lone wolf in this organization. We function on teamwork and you better understand what that means if you expect to have more than a fat man's chance in a marathon of making it here or anywhere else. Now I don't want any more shit on this. Do I make myself clear?"

"Yes, sir, I hear you" capitulated the underling. But he would not forget this psyche stinging thwart to his professional development.

***

Happy time at the Grill was a daily ritual that served to transition the engineers from work mode to personal life. It was like an airlock between the inside of an orbiter and free space, or, perhaps more accurately, a halfway house en route from any place of confinement to the real world. The happy time group was not always intact in toto, but there was always at least one representative in attendance to extend the tradition. Not long after the project authorship misunderstanding, Rossy was transitioning with Booker and related his growing dissatisfaction in the big corporate work experience, as well as his uniquely stressful living conditions in the East Hartford boarding house. He thought he was starting to feel trapped. Booker also expressed doubts about how much longer he wanted to stay in Connecticut working for PWA. He revealed that he had recently interviewed with Haas Oil, during a vacation week in the U. S. Virgin Islands. Haas had a refinery in Christiansted, St. Croix, and Booker's friend, whom he met while she was visiting relatives in the Hartford area and had invited him to spend a week at her place in the VI, was a niece of the general manager of the plant. She suggested he talk to the manager and see if they had any jobs available so he could move to St. Croix. Booker thought he could probably adapt very well to the Caribbean lifestyle and agreed to the interview. His friend set it up for the week he was there and the result was surprising, if not entirely compatible with his mission and motive. He was offered a job at a Haas facility in New Jersey. *Really??* He declined the offer and, upon returning from vacation, gradually lost contact with his Virgin Island friend after several calls and correspondences of diminishing frequency.

But Booker had another friend. A dude he went to school with. Seve Smith, an industrial engineer, had taken a different track out of college and went to work for the federal government. Specifically, he was a civilian employee with NAVOSUR, Naval Ocean Survey, a little known agency of the U.S. Navy, under the Department of Defense. NAVOSUR was based at the Washington Navy Yard in Washington D.C. A few months ago, Smith had phoned Booker to see how his bud was doing in the Great Northeast. During the conversation he said that NAVOSUR was hiring and Booker should consider coming down to D.C. The work was easy, base salary scale not that great, but there were lots of pay differentials and always mega overtime, and you got to travel all over the world. Actually, you *had* to travel all over the world, because the job description required a minimum 50% field duty. That was why they were perpetually hiring - few people wanted to travel that much and fewer wanted to go where NAVOSUR sent you - to remote and/or dangerous places. There were no Sandals

Resort beaches in this itinerary. Smith asked Booker to 'smoke' it over and they could talk about it later.

"Do you think I should get back up with Smith?" mused Booker. "It might be a ticket to ride."

"I think that would be a great idea," cajoled Rossy, as he signaled for a second round of special happy time ale.

***

To save money, the thrifty roomer volunteered his car to the automotive vo-tech shop where the boarding house brothers attended school. He got free routine maintenance and diagnostic evaluation and only had to pay for parts, oil and fluids. The work performed on his car by students was presumably closely supervised by the certified master mechanic teacher. Though there was little, if anything, that could go wrong with this arrangement, he had been requested to sign a standard waivers absolving the school of all liability should any case of adversity arise related to the school's interaction with his vehicle. It was a win-win scenario that was of obvious benefit to all parties involved. On days his car was serviced, the boys would ride with their older boarder brother to work and then take the car to school and pick him up after work to go home. They had done this several times without a hitch. The only time there was a problem was the day of the final service. The boys were waiting in the car when their client got out of work and took his place behind the wheel. As he turned the ignition, he heard and felt a horrible clanking sound and the dashboard lit up like a Polish Christmas tree. **"HOLY FRACK!!!"** he screamed as he immediately shut the engine off. **"WHAT THE HELL WAS THAT ?!?"** The boys shrugged non-explicit 'dunnos' and slumped low into their seats. The dismayed driver popped the hood and got out to investigate. He found oil all over the underside of the hood and the engine and no cap on the oil reservoir riser. They had forgotten to put the cap back on after changing the oil and had driven the car from the school to the FCPRF under obviously inoperable conditions that might well have destroyed the engine. Realizing immediately he would be eating this fiasco, he decided to leave the car at work, call a cab to take them home and deal with the problem in the morning. Eventually, the costs of towing, repair and temporary transportation added up to nearly twenty times the amount saved by not using a qualified commercial mechanic for his routine car service. Rossy wondered if Booker had gotten back with Smith yet.

***

Indeed he had. Smith enthusiastically informed Booker there were several openings at NAVOSUR and gave him the phone contact of the agency director. Booker asked about qualification requirements and Smith explained the available position descriptions were classified simply as 'engineer' slots, meaning an engineering degree in any discipline would comply. The only other requirements were no health issues precluding overseas duty and no personal history issues obstructing receipt of a security clearance. No specific work experience was necessary, as all training to perform required duties would be received on the job, according to field assignments. Smith urged both Booker and his pal to call the director asap. He said with all the agency vacancies, he and his coworkers were having to travel almost continuously. They needed more bodies and they needed them NOW!

A few days later, it was decided that Booker would make the call, as he had an indirect contact, through Smith, with the agency. As his colleague anxiously listened in, Booker placed the call on low speaker from a back corner table at the Diner, during breakfast break.

"Paul Blackburn, NAVOSUR. May I help you?"

"Yes, sir, Mr. Blackburn, my name is Ken Booker. I'm a friend of Seve Smith, who works in your organization? He advised me that you might have some job openings for engineers?"

"That is correct, Mr. Booker. Are you interested?"

"Yes, I believe I might be. How would I apply?"

"Well, do you have at least a bachelor's degree in engineering from an accredited school?"

"Yes, sir. Chemical Engineering from Blue Ridge University."

"Excellent. Are you able to travel overseas for extended periods under possibly harsh or unusual conditions?"

"Uh, I guess so. As far as I know."

"Any criminality in your background?"

"No, sir."

"American citizen?"

"Yes."

"Good. When can you report?"

"Well..., don't I have to fill out an application, or take a civil service test, or come in for an interview, or something like that?"

"Not really. All we need is your full birth name and SSN. We can backfill all the paperwork after you're on board."

"Well, what does the job involve? What's the salary? What, exactly, would I be doing? What is NAVOSUR?"

"You would start at GS-7, step 1. Most of what we do is classified, but generally we perform hydrographic and oceanographic surveys in the coastal zones of friendly, developing countries around the world. I really can't be any more specific than that. You would, of course, receive much more detailed information after you're cleared."

"Cleared?"

"Yes, security clearance. We must be able to clear you for 'Top Secret' classification."

"And what if I can't be cleared?"

"You would be released."

"Well, how do I know if I can be cleared?"

"Look, Mr. Booker, if you want the job, let me know when you can report for duty. If not, have a nice day."

"OK, I'm definitely interested, but I need a little time to think about it and I would have to give notice to my employer. How about in four weeks, which is, what, early October?"

"Three weeks. September 28th."

"Really? Uh, well, OK, I guess so."

"Great. Just give me your full name and SSN and we'll see you in three weeks."

"Mr. Blackburn? I've got an associate, who's also interested and I think he qualifies."

"No problem. Give me his name and SSN and we'll see you both in three weeks."

"You don't need to talk to him? He's right here."

"Not necessary, if he answers the questions I asked you the same way you did."

Booker gave Blackburn the requested info, thanked him profusely and the conversation was over. The two engineers could not believe what had just transpired. They high-fived across the table and went back to work.

***

Rossy was ecstatic. He had an escape route from what was becoming an increasingly intolerable dilemma in both his professional and private lives. All he had to do was resign his PWA gig and move out of the crazy boarding house. He had never quit a permanent job before. He had turned down job offers, most memorably from the chocolate factory in his hometown where he worked summers during college as an engineering trainee. He had really liked that job. The head engineer for plant operations hired him following a blurb in the local weekly about his making the freshman year dean's list. Right before he returned to school for his senior year, the engineer proposed that the company would pay his entire final year expense, including tuition, books and equipment, living costs, transportation and even spending money, if he would sign a contract to work for them, at a negotiable salary, for three years after graduation. He declined, since it was never his intent to stay in his hometown after graduation any longer than it took to pack up and leave. As it turned out, that was a lucky correct choice, because the small, family owned chocolate factory was consumed by a large, international candy conglomerate within a year of his graduation. The engineer he would have been working for was fired and he, likewise, would have been plonked into the street in a decaying little town he never really liked. And he had declined a few other offers received during the senior interview season. But he had never resigned a permanent, full-time, on-his-own job. It would not be easy. Nor would be departing the boarding house. He was convinced the chuckleheads living there were truly whacko. But he didn't know if they were dangerous. He didn't want to end up being hacked up in his sleep like a tourist victim of a deranged hostel manager, so he knew he had to approach the situation with diplomacy. He would give them each a goodbye gift.

There were other factors to consider, of course. The analytical one confronted them as counterpoints in a debate against the established premise. *Salary.* He would be taking a cut, about ten grand, but overtime, differentials and per diem should easily make up the difference. Plus, when he was on field duty he would spend none of his own money, except for the never-ending debt payments. The bottom line was a potential net income increase, so salary should not be an issue. *Moving to Washington.* He didn't know much about Washington D.C. The only time he had been there was on a class trip in eighth grade, which had almost resulted in his expulsion from school. The bus left at 4:00 a.m. and, to assure he got up on time, he slept very little the night before. The first stop was Mt. Vernon. The bus parked in the corner of a huge parking lot and student Rossy, the last one off, shambled into the first building he saw, assuming it was Mt. Vernon. He didn't notice the rest of his group moving away down a walking path that led to the mansion and grounds about a half mile away. In the restaurant and tourist shop, he found a booth in a darkened, closed dining section and lay down on the bench behind the table and fell asleep. He was located about five hours later following an extensive search by county, state and park police, during which preparations for an Amber Alert had been finalized. After another two hours were lost in police and media interviews, the trip schedule was blown and all they had time for was a quick walk around the downtown monument mall area, during which the sleeping sluggard was confined to the bus under supervision of the driver. The chaperoning teachers and principal were divided whether he should be expelled or suspended. Fortunately, cooler heads prevailed and he did three days suspension. But he really didn't remember much about Washington. While learning a new city is never easy, he could consider it a belated completion of his class trip. Tying up loose ends. It would be fun. *Clearance.* Another black hole. He knew nothing about security clearances, or what caused them not to be issued. He couldn't recall anything in his past that should pose a risk for national security, but who knew what would trigger a rejection? Something on internet, an obscure surveillance video, wrong place at the wrong time, an unknown terrorist third cousin or anything circumstantially suspect could all be problematic. To what extent was he vulnerable? He had no clue. But, if he quit PWA, gave up a valid home address and once again moved to a city where he knew virtually no one, and then got bounced because he failed a security clearance background review, he would be facing more than another speed bump in the dirt road of his life. That would be a total low light, for sure.

That evening, the fretting roomer was sitting on the boarding house portico still mind wrestling with himself over whether, or not, to commit to his new opportunity. The clearance conundrum was blocking a final decision. It was a cool, clear nightfall displaying a spectacular array of stars in the late summer sky. Conditions seemed so clean that he could discern varying hues and intensities of the star lights, almost to the sense of watching a massive fireworks display. Yes, it was the ultimate fireworks show. He never looked at the night sky much, but thinking of the fireworks analogy made him stare in fascination. He saw several 'falling star' illusions, following the meteorites as they exploded and extinguished in a moment of burnout through the stratosphere. Mars was in place as an orange beacon of the lower sky. The Dippers were visible in orientation with Orion's belt. The moon was reflecting very sharply, though not in full phase. The uncountable other constellations and stars and galaxies stretched away to the end of the universe, wherever that was. He saw the blinking lights of a high jet with its distinct engine rumble lagging far behind. A few helicopters chopped across the dome of the metro night glow. Looking toward the upper sky, he noticed a changing point of light. It started as a faint speckle, like a distant star, and slowly brightened to the intensity of a neighboring planet, while remaining seemingly stationary relative to all objects around it. It was like a missile headed directly toward him on a straight line from the cosmos. The light remained bright and stationary for several minutes and then started to move from right to left across the sky. It moved at a constant velocity through about forty five degrees of vision and stopped. It remained stationary for fifteen or twenty seconds, at the same brightness, and then reversed its course back to where it had first started moving. It stopped again and after another minute, or so, began to diminish in brightness, at a constant rate, until it finally vanished. The star gazer was flummoxed. *What the hell had he just seen?* It wasn't a meteor, or any other natural space object going through the atmosphere, because it reversed direction, an impossibility, according to I. Newton. It wasn't an aircraft. Planes don't stop and go backwards and disappear. Ditto satellites, orbiting labs or even stratospheric data balloons. It was too high for a helicopter. It couldn't have been some kind of conventional earth based light, since there was no beam to ground. A laser? The sky was perfectly clear, so there wasn't anything for a laser to bounce from to be visible. Maybe it was some sort of remotely controlled microwave device. Maybe.

Rossy didn't think too much about *big unknowns*, because it made his head hurt. Was there an omnipotent god, responsible for everything? If not, or even if so, where did all the space come from to contain the universe? How could space be infinite in all directions? If it wasn't infinite, where was the boundary and what was beyond it? Another universe? An infinite number of universes? Was there ET life out there among all the other independent objects in the vast sea of space? Of course, there was. If biochemical, organic life formed on earth, it formed everywhere else conditions were right. It would be irrational to think this process only occurred on one tiny dust speck in the entire multiversal ecosystem. It should also be irrational to believe that a mythological, all purpose god is a reality. Unconditional god has always been the simple answer to questions beyond human comprehension to understand. The imaginary existence of god is easy to embrace. It unilaterally addresses all the *big unknowns*. But the concepts of infinite time and space make no sense whatsoever, because infinity has no points of reference, no beginning, no end. And what if there was no readily conclusive explanation for the strange sky sights he had just seen? The only alternate plausibility was deep space alien intrusion. Now there is a whole new subset of *big unknowns*. How could any biolife from somewhere beyond our own star field overcome the key restriction of relativity, the limitation of mass to achieve a velocity greater than the constant speed of light, to be able to traverse the vast distance to our planet? Or, was the speed of light, in fact, an arbitrary barrier, beyond which mass actually could exist in state? Or, could some new classification of energy exceed the speed of light? Or, could life exist as pure energy? The big thinker was getting a headache. He realized his own minute being was so insignificant in the grand scheme of the *big unknowns* that it made absolutely no difference whether he took the new job in Washington or remained where he was with PWA. He decided to go to Washington and worry about it later.

***

Booker had not struggled at all with his decision. He knew what he was going to do while he was still on the phone with Mr. Blackburn. He was outta here and not lookin' back. If Washington didn't pan out, he figured he still had a bailout in New Jersey. But he wasn't sure about his colleague. The bro was too analytical. Over thinking an option could easily lead to confusion and brain freeze, which invariably resulted in regret. It didn't matter, though.

He was making the move with or without his bud. And soon, like tomorrow, because, at this point, time was money and neither should be wasted.

The next morning, the secret short-timers collaborated at delidiner time, like inmates plotting a prison break during daily yard exercise. They were both elated with their respective acceptances of the hopefully positive opportunity availed to them. Now it was time to develop and execute an exit strategy. Obviously, the first item on the agenda was resignation from PWA. This would trigger everything else in the sequence and the sooner it was accomplished the more time there would be to deal with the logistics of relocation to Washington. They decided to advise the administrative supervisor right after lunch. But who would go first? Both wanted to be first to avoid the certain rain of shit on the one who went second. They agreed to a best of three rock-paper-scissors. On the first go, Rossy threw paper over Booker's rock. Booker then scissored a second paper from Rossy. Tied. Booker calculated that Rossy would think that he, Booker, would probably think Rossy would throw a third paper and try to win with a scissors, so he, Rossy, would throw a rock. On the third go, Booker threw paper and won. Rossy would have to go in second to resign.

"What, is this some kind of joke? Are you assholes fracking with me? If you are, I'll put your butts back on probation faster than you can say, 'I'm an idiot'," snapped the reddening supervisor.

Number two squirmed in his seat inside the glass box office, which seemed to be heating up like a summer green house. "No, sir, not a joke. We have a chance to do something different and thought we would give it a shot."

"Well, you know, the way you're going about it is highly unprofessional. PWA has invested a lot in your training and development and your compensation has always been fair and competitive. Maybe we don't expect you to spend your whole career here, but we do expect some period of reasonable service return, certainly more than a year."

"I'm sorry, sir. I appreciate the opportunity PWA has given me, but I can't ignore other opportunities that come by. That's nothing against this organization. I've enjoyed working here and will always value the experience."

"Actually, as I think about it, maybe this is for the best. You never really seemed to be much of a team player, here. I think you're inclined to resist policy and are not interested in understanding how it works in the corporate world. I'll start your out processing. By the way, do not use us as a reference in the future. We'll only confirm your employment dates. Consider this your exit interview. Good luck, son. I think you'll need it."

"Thank you, sir."

***

Rossy skipped happy time after work and went to the East Metro Mall to purchase bye-bye gifts for the boarding house people. The mall was nearly empty as there was no holiday and no special theme attractions. It was still summer, but Labor Day was over and most kids were back in school. Since there were few people to dodge or get around in maneuvering through the maze of atrium retail corridors, the infrequent shopper observed the rows of kiosk stands between the store fronts. Each one had a single attendant on duty to sell almost anything you could think of you didn't want or need. Electric vapor cigarettes, ice cream pebbles, finger nail art decals, next year's calendars, wrist watches, futuristic fantasy posters, profane tee shirts, plastic plants, cheap and cheaper jewelry, smelly candles and much, much more, including, of course, Christmas decorations. Only a hundred ten shopping days left. No one was buying, or even looking at, anything the kiosk vendors were peddling and it didn't seem really clear how they were making a valid living sitting there all day wired for tunes, playing with internet phones and selling nothing. Not his problem.

First stop was Wanda's Wines to get a bottle of New York red merlot for mom. Rossy knew she liked wine, because he had seen her drinking it. And, since he often saw empty green bottles in the recycling bin, he figured she liked wine a lot. The wine probably contributed to her intermittent loony behavior the kids warned about right after he moved into the house. He had witnessed one inexplicable incident that pretty much validated their portent. About four months ago, he was downstairs in the living room watching television and mom was in the adjacent dining room, seated at the table poring over some end of year correspondence from the high school. All at once she let out a low, throaty rasping sound that quickly escalated into a high pitched wail. He heard a loud, dull thump and ran into the dining room to find her laid out on the floor, nearly under the table, clutching the middle of her chest with both hands. He yelled out for the children, who were upstairs in their rooms, or, more likely, in his room. Mom was moaning about her sick, breaking heart and the pain, the horrible pain. He didn't know what to do. Was this another bogus heart attack the kids had told him about? It looked kind of real to him. She didn't need CPR, as she wasn't unconscious or dead, meaning her heart was still ticking. But shouldn't they call 911? She seemed to be in genuine medical distress requiring professional help. By this time the kids had shuffled into the room and sat down at the other chairs around the table. They stared down blankly at their mom and said nothing, as if they were waiting for the expected next scene in a movie rerun. Rossy thought of the old *Sanford and Son* show he had seen on cable a few times, remembering how Redd Fox would call up 'the big one' whenever he was upset. Is that what was going on here? He had no idea, but didn't want to take a chance. He reached for his pocketed phone and started to call emergency, punching 9..1.., when mom slowly sat up and climbed back into her chair. Canceling the call, he re-pocketed the phone, while anxiously awaiting whatever happened next. He had not seen this movie. She glared at the boys and tearfully accused them of trying to kill her, of trying to evict the life from her very heart. Had they no respect for their *mere*, who had given them everything? Why had she received such a disturbing and disgraceful letter from the school informing her of the impending failure of their respective grades? This is the second year in a row. Now they would have to go to summer school again and there was no money. No money. *Pourquoi,* oh why, do they treat her with such cruelty? Such dishonor? She now feels only deep sadness and pain. *Sweet Jesus Lord of Blessed Mary's Sacred Conception, s'il vous plait,* please help us! The boys closed around her, kissing her gently, and promised to do better and make things right. She lavished in the attention for a moment, then chased her children away and went to the corner cabinet and removed a green bottle. Glancing over at her brainy boarder, who was still standing by the table, she again implored him to please talk to her sons about the importance of going to college. Oh yeah, mom liked wine a lot.

Next was Student Locker to get the daughter a backpack. Rossy had noticed hers was looking a little worn and raggedy. The store had about a thousand units displayed on shelves covering an entire long wall of the showroom. Scanning through the selections he had no idea how to decide which one to buy. Then he saw a pack that was covered with pink elephants on a lime green back-ground with blue straps. It was a hideous piece of work, but should be perfect for the girl, because, evidently, ... she loved elephants. Her room was filled with stuffed elephants of all shapes, sizes and colors and elephant posters were pasted over most of the wall sur-faces and part of the ceiling. She even had a plastic elephant bobblehead on her homework desk. Typically, girls her age would have pop star posters plastered all over their rooms, but elephants? What the hell was that about? One of the boys said she had been to every regional circus since she was three, specifically to see live elephants, and has always wanted her own real elephant as a pet. No one in the family could explain her strange fixation. Maybe she was a natural born Republican, though the outsider had never de-tected much of a political inclination in this household. Mom sometimes ranted that Quebec Province, as the most important French cultural center in the western hemisphere, should have in-dependence from Canadian oppression, but he had never heard any discussion of American politics. More likely, the girl was either a couple of putts off par, or simply an undiagnosed OCD case in need of specialty drugs to keep balance. That might also explain her creepy compulsion with the older roomer engineer. Neither obsession made any sense if she was mentally plumb, but it didn't matter, as long as she was happy with the gift and he would soon be gone.

Last on the list was Sears, where the gift shopper intended to score a couple of Craftsman ratchet wrench sets for the boys. De-spite the hard proficiency lessons learned from the failed servicing of his car, he surmised their aptitude, such as it was, resided somewhere in the realm of automotive mechanics. Perhaps they would grow up to become the anti-Click and Clack Brothers, ad-vising anyone with a flat tire to stab the side walls of the remain-ing good tires with an ice pick so the vehicle would roll more evenly. *If it ain't fixed, don't break it.* He knew they would not be working with chemicals, or doing custom welding, so car body retrofit and repair was off the table. Likewise diagnostic maintenance and troubleshooting. They would be limited to simple, tightly supervised mechanical repairs for which the wrench sets should be useful. Sports was not a gift option. They definitely had no viable athletic ability or work ethic to develop a skill. The younger one had apparently been interested in parkour a few years ago, but that often involved illegal trespass on abandoned private structures to practice and there was no locally organized instruction for properly learning the basic techniques. He gave up this activity when he misfired a double flip from the alley side roof of their row house and broke his arm and collar bone. No sports. The wrench sets would be just fine.

On the way out of the mall, the goodbye shopper approached Techways, a mega outlet for the latest tech devices, accessories and supplies. This store had been the scene, about six months ago, of the local, limited introductory release of a major new device called a 'phad'. It was the hybrid of a smart phone and notebook pad, featuring all the elements and capabilities of both devices, including voice and facial recognition and solar recharge. It looked like a phone, but the screen could be unfolded like a map into a slightly larger size of the standard pad. So it was like having a pad that could be carried around in clothes pockets, or small purses, like a phone. And it could be used as a phone with or without unfolding it. It was not noticeably bigger, bulkier or heavier than a phone, and when unfolded, the screen was much thinner than a pad, though stronger and more rigid. This was afforded by the application of super efficient, graphene nano-conductors embedded in high-strength, titanium alloy wafers that were less than a millimeter thick. The screen wafer sections were joined by a flexible, synthetic fabric, of very high fatigue strength, through which the nano circuitry was also embedded. When extended, the sections locked into impossibly rigid joints that formed a seamless screen. A bonus feature of the advanced electrical efficiency was extended battery recharge life, though no specific performance data on this issue was yet claimed or provided by the manufacturer. Since the device exhibited new, so called 'cutting edge' material applications, the introductory retail price was very high, like *27 bens high!* Rossy had been extremely interested in the phad, but no way would he buy at that price. Many, many others, though, were more than willing to shell out whatever it took to be proud, early owners of this latest tech 'phad'. The night before they first went on ultra publicized sale at 5:30 a.m., thousands of customers were camped outside the mall, in subfreezing temperatures, to save a place in line to make the purchase. There were fights and arrests, even some injuries. The scenario was simultaneously replicated all across the country and the first day sales tallied into the billions. The manufacturer's stock soared, as well as all the stock indices. Everybody made money. It was like a tsunami of cash washed over the economy and roused it from a coma of stagnation. The sideline consumer was confident the power of the mass market would eventually pull the price down and he stopped in at Techways to check it out. Phads were now selling at $989, which was still more than he would pay. When it went south of five bens, or if they could reliably claim a 24 hour battery capacity, he would consider being a serious consumer.

As he returned to his car, the development engineer thought about the mass market and fuel cells. If the two could ever converge, there would be a world-wide energy renaissance. But too much had to happen for such a convergence anytime soon. Carbon based power generation had to dramatically increase in cost and fuel cell power generation had to correspondingly decrease in cost. Currently, a kilowatt-hour of fuel cell power cost a hundred times more than a kilowatt-hour of carbon fuel power. No mass market appeal there. Also, conversion to fuel cell power technology was not exactly a plug and play proposition. It was not like purchasing a phad. Entire new industries of suppliers, installers and technicians would have to be developed to accommodate the ease of access and use for the consumer. Eventually, it would happen, if not by natural progression, then by circumstance and politics. Carbon based energy supply was a dead end street. UTG knew this and, at some point in the future, PWA would be a premier place to be employed. The resigner found himself starting to second guess his change of professional direction and had to check up before he fell into a crisis of confidence. Obviously, quitting PWA was grossly irreversible as he had virtually nuked all bridges behind him. His only immediate mission going forward was to get out of the boarding house and move on down the road. He had to stay focussed.

***

Later in the evening, Rossy wrapped a wide red velvet ribbon, he had saved from last Christmas, around the wine he had just bought and cautiously went downstairs to talk to mom. She was in the living room reading the paper and listening to Clifton Chanier, her favorite cajun zydeco artist. In *la mere's* world, it was all things *Francais*. He sat down and filled her in on his plans to leave the area and go to another job in Washington. She looked directly at him with an aura of rising emotion but said nothing. Sensing an impending outburst, he handed her the gift wine and waited for a response.

"So, William, does this mean you will be moving out?"

"Yes, it does. It would not be feasible to stay here and commute to Washington, so I'll be leaving in about two weeks."

"What, do you think I'm an imbecile? Of course, I know you can't live here and work in Washington." Mom was visibly angry, now. "But don't expect any rebate on your rent or deposit!"

"What? What do you mean? Why, not?" Mover man was counting on that money for gas and incidental expenses in his relocation.

"Because you broke the water faucet in your lavatory and I'll have to get it repaired before I can rent the room again," she retorted in a loud, screechy voice.

"What are you talking about??" shouted the toggled tenant. "There's no broken faucet in my room. I didn't break anything!"

He noticed the kids filing quietly into the living room from the hallway. They probably heard the yelling and thought mom was having another 'coronary'. Rossy asked everyone to stay where they were and went back upstairs to get the other gifts. When he returned, mom had already uncorked the wine bottle and the kids were sitting cross legged on the floor watching her to make sure she had re-stabilized. He repeated his going away story for the children and proudly distributed their gifts as tokens of his appreciation for having had the opportunity to meet and know them. He would always remember them as good friends.

"This is totally the grossest thing I ever saw!" said the girl, with razor sharp acidity. "Do you seriously expect me to wear this to school? I would be laughed off campus, for sure! They might even expel me!"

"But it has elephants on it. You love elephants," defended her good friend. He was starting to feel confused, maybe even a bit frightened. This was not going well.

"Oh, man, get real," she shot as she stomped out of the room, leaving the backpack behind. The gifter shook his head in disbelief and looked questioningly at the boys who remained on the floor with the new wrench sets stacked between them.

"Yeah, these are cool and stuff, but guess what? We already hiked better sets out of the school shop. No problem, though, we can pawn 'em for some stash cash. Thanks, man," said the older boy, rising and extending a fist. Mom had inattentively returned to her paper, while slowly sipping the merlot directly out of the green bottle. Clifton's staccato accordion riffs still refrained in the background, pleasantly breaking an otherwise dead silence.

"You people are fracking goofy!!" muttered the distraught appeaser, in departing the living room to go back upstairs. That night he slept restlessly behind his locked door with a chair back jammed up under the knob.

***

The next couple of weeks were hectic and awkward, both at work and at the boarding house. The runaways didn't have any project deadlines on the docket, but their departure was going to punch a large hole in the subgroup. It wasn't like anyone could move up into their slots, because they were still pretty much at the bottom of the totem, meaning the vacancies would probably not be filled for some time. They weren't concerned about any special hassles this would force the lead engineer to deal with. He had long since revealed himself as the dickhead he was, so frack him. But they felt bad about doo-wop engineer, who would probably be forced to work about a hundred hours a week to take up the slack. Actually, they had asked doo-wop if he, too, wanted to go to Washington, but he declined. He was a native to Hartford and his family ties were all in the area. Moving away to see the outside world did not appeal to him. Maybe he would one day, after the energy renaissance, score an executive position with PWA. That would be good.

The boarding house people were icing their roving renter. Mom and the girl were quietly hostile and the boys seemed to be avoiding him in a timid, guilty sort of way. A few days after the farewell gift disaster, Rossy came home from work and found his lavatory faucet hammered out and the water turned off. The porcelain sink was cracked below the point of destruction. Mom had obviously instructed the boys to perform this idiotic deed to validate keeping his deposit and over rent money, just as she had predicted, but it looked like the repairs would cost more than she was withholding. Meanwhile, he noticed, the girl had cut the pink elephants out of the new backpack fabric and tacked them to the outside of her room door. She was still using her old, worn out pack. He decided to just forget these disturbing incidents, eat the deposit and keep aligned on looking ahead. He was not yet adequately trained nor sufficiently experienced to confront raw stupidity, even in its purest form.

On early Wednesday evening of the last week, Rossy started moving his belongings from the boarding house room to his car. He was making lots of runs up and down the stairs carrying out boxes, clothes bags and anything he didn't immediately need. He was hoping everything he owned still fit into his car, just as it had when he first moved in. Not being much of a consumer, he really hadn't accumulated a significant amount of new stuff in the past year, so it shouldn't be a problem. While he was engaged in this activity, he saw mom open the front door to a tall African American man standing on the portico. He knew she had already advertised the vacancy of his room and this was probably the first inquiry. He ducked into the front room to listen. She told the man she was very sorry but the room was no longer available. She was obviously lying to cover her prejudice, which was a surprise to the overhearer as he had not previously detected bigotry among her many lunacies. He briefly considered catching up with the man to advise him the room *was* available and he should file a complaint with the fair housing authority. Then he thought the best thing for the rejected man, or any other applicant, would be to not move into this house of halflits and that was the compelling argument for saying nothing. He continued his moving out task at peace with his silence.

On the last Thursday morning, promptly at 9:30 a.m., the social group of professional colleagues made their way to the Diner for what would be The Last Breakfast together. Rossy and Booker sat in the middle of the large family table, flanked by their friends and associates of the past year. Even the subgroup leader was there, though shunned in sort of an ostracizing position of betrayal at the far end of the table. Rossy broke with his self imposed tradition of austerity and ordered the Loggerman's Bellybuster Special, featuring unlimited blueberry pancakes, with eggs, bacon or sausage, fried potatoes, a fruit cup and coffee, all for $7.99. The order became super special when Donna cheerfully announced that the last timers' tabs were on the house. This in appreciation for their loyal and steadfast patronage as daily regulars during their PWA tenure. The young waitress seemed especially attentive to Rossy, refilling his coffee cup every few minutes, while repeatedly hovering if 'everything was ok?'. She finally asked him if she could 'ask a question?'. He said, "sure", and she said she had always wondered if his teeth were real or fake. They seemed too perfect to be real, but he seemed too young for false teeth. The goodtoother exhaled a small sigh of exasperation and confirmed that, yes, they were real. This was not the first time he had been asked this particular question and he always found it curious that anyone would make such an inquiry of a stranger or someone they didn't know very well. He, himself, would never ask this of anyone, even someone he knew well. It just didn't seem like something you would normally say, nor have any interest in. It was no different than asking someone if their hair was real. Who would say that? Yes, his teeth were real and they looked good. But they weren't born that way. When his dad was dying from Hodgkin's lymphoma, he instructed his younger brother, the dentist, to "fix Little Billy's teeth". Little Billy Rossy had a terrible overbite as a child, which no doubt would have caused severe problems with the emergence and alignment of the permanent teeth. He spent years visiting his uncle's dentistry every two weeks to painfully get the braces tightened and adjusted. He was forced to wear taut rubber ligatures every night causing his whole head to feel numb and cramped in the morning. The only good times associated with this process were the waylays at the club on the trips home from the dental office, where his uncle would drink, while Little Billy played video games. The treatment was eventually successful, his teeth looked good and his uncle had fulfilled his older brother's deathbed command. Rossy got in the habit of proper dental hygiene and had maintained his teeth in excellent condition into adulthood, even allowing his wisdom molars to be immediately extracted according to routine professional recommendation right after they started to peep through the back gum line. Good teeth did not come easily, or naturally. They involved considerable trouble and pain and he did not particularly like to talk about them.

Maybe the waitress was just making a clumsy hit on him. He didn't care - it was still a stupid, invasive question. Besides, it was too little, too late. Today was their last visit to the Diner and the group of colleagues had to leave shortly if they were to make it back to the office by lunch.

On the last Thursday evening, right after work, the professional group of social colleagues reconvened at the Grill for The Last Happy Time together. The farewell tour was happening on Thursday, because the quitters were each using his one remaining 'sick' day on Friday, tomorrow, their final official day of work at PWA. This, so they could get an early, pre-weekend start on the long trips into the next phase of their lives. The Last Happy Time quickly devolved into an impromptu going away party for the two departing engineers. It was also very likely the swan song for the HT group, which everyone knew in their hearts would not survive without its two youngest charter members. As the special happy time ale flowed through the bittersweetness of impending separation of friends, the conversation became increasingly incoherent, nonsensical and loud. The attention of other Grill patrons, including a couple of families with children, turned toward the source of what was becoming a minor disturbance. Some were thinking of complaining to Gelson behind the check-out counter near the bar area. Concurrently, the administrative assistant dater, now ex-dater, whispered to Rossy that the occasion warranted a special 'BO Salute'. He said to check him out, particularly his fly zone, when he returned from the rest room. A few minutes later, ex-dater emerged back into the service area and Rossy scanned his crotch. Good lord of the flies! His hairy bare balls were hanging out of the zipper of his pants! Ex-dater winked, placed an index finger over his lips and strode across the floor to the bar to get another pitcher of ale. As he walked deliberately back toward their large round table in the middle of the dining area, a woman at a nearby table, presumably the mother of the kids in her group who were now running around making more noise than the HT colleagues, looked up at him and glowered. Then she saw the BO and started screaming, **"SEX PERV!! SEX PERV!!!"** She pointed wildly at ex-dater's groin and frantically tried to round up her children into a protective covey behind her. Everyone else in the Grill immediately fixated on the BO and several people had phones up taking video. A few old regulars at the bar broke into applause and bellicose laughter, as Gelson ran into the dining area to see what was causing so much commotion in his normally quiet establishment. When he spotted the broadly grinning joker, turning in a standing slow circle of x-rated exposure with arms extended like a runway fashion model, he went into a rage.

"YOU FRACKING ASSHOLES, WHAT ARE YOU DO-ING!?! THIS IS A GODDAM FAMILY RESTAURANT!! GET THE HELL OUTTA HERE BEFORE I CALL THE POLICE!!"

He started grabbing at the colleagues, pulling them out of their chairs and herding them over to the front door. Everyone else stood up from their places and yelled epithets of either humorous encouragement or angry derision while the children started whooping like crazed banshies. A scene of confusion exploded, that probably could not have been precipitated any faster by a shrilling shout of **'FIRE!'**. The colleagues found themselves abruptly outside and quickly regrouped away from the lighted entrance in the darkening shadows of the side of the building, where they fell into a collective fit of uncontrollable giggling guffaws. "Now that was a sick kickin' 'Balls Out', baybeee!!" hiccoughed ex-dater, adjusting his pants to normal status. Rossy thought he understood why the former 'dater' dude was now 'ex-man' and silently marveled at how long out of school some people behaved as if they were still in school. Amazing, but it really was an absurdly comical stunt. After a few minutes the silly levity started to subside and a serious realization of finality overcame their mood. This was it. The rooks were leaving and this posse would never ride again. They vowed to stay in contact, via media, phone or whatever and to get together again sometime soon. With handshakes and bro hugs, maybe a few tight throats, they dispersed. The escapees had the next week off and were going home to see folks before reporting to NAVOSUR, in Washington, the Monday after next. The others had to go back to work at PWA in the morning. *Adios, mi amigos. Keep your sails to the wind.*

***

Rossy did not sleep well his last night in the boarding house. At first he worried about the phone videos taken during the 'balls out' episode at the Grill. Though he wasn't the object of the videos, he might show up in the background and, if they were uploaded and went viral, he would forever be associated with a lewd internet moment. What if this affected his security clearance background review? *Oh, god.* Then he worried about his whole life changing. Sure, there was no shortage of problems and disappointments, not to mention dangers, here in Connecticut, but at least he knew where everything was and what to expect. Now he was rejecting all the familiarity he had gained and leaping into the blind unknown without a safety net. He flat out had no idea what he was getting into. And what kind of job is it that no one talks to you before throwing out a third person offer? What the hell is that!? Finally, he worried about checking out of the house tomorrow. He hadn't spoken to anyone in the family for days. Shouldn't he try to say goodbye, or something? That would seem to be the civil thing to do, regardless of the zany cranks they had put him through. Hell with 'em, he decided. He'll never see those turkeys again and, for sure, he doesn't owe them anything. Tomorrow morning he'll just leave the key in the room, go out to his tightly packed car and drive away from the sunrise into the future. He had played his cards, laid out his hand and there was no point worrying about anything out of control. With that thought he slowly drifted into a light doze and disturbingly dreamt of slogging alone through a seaside swamp filled with invisible leeches, where each step resulted in a deeper sink down into the muck, until halfway across he was mired to the neck, couldn't move and the tide was coming in. *Oh, well!*

On Friday morning, his last day in Connecticut, Rossy had one final logistical task to complete before hitting the road. He had to close his accounts and cash out at the credit union. He arrived about fifteen minutes after they opened and approached the reception desk with a slight sense of trepidation. While his association with this institution had been functionally useful, it had not been particularly pleasant. After explaining his request for account closures and providing proper identification and personal information, the receptionist advised it would be a few minutes and directed him to the waiting area. He retrieved a cup of coffee from the concession and sat down on the couch with the morning paper. Turning to the sports section, he noticed the Red Sox had swept the Phillies in a late season interleague series, winning the last game 11-2. This really sucked, especially since the series was in Philadelphia and yesterday's loss knocked the home team into last place in their division. Rossy was a lifelong Phillies phan. As a kid he and his older cousin often took Amtrak from their hometown in Lancaster County to Center City Philadelphia, go to a game and return home, all in the same, long, glorious day. Back then he knew all the players and their stats. A few players in the Phillies organization always came from a central or eastern Pennsylvania farming community where every boy played ball at some point in his youthful development. Rossy would never forget hitting a Little League home run off a kid who eventually went on to journeyman success as a sidearm relief specialist for the Phillies, but blew his arm out after a couple of years and was no longer playing. In Connecticut, he never picked up on following the Red Sox. Probably because Red Sox fans were so overbearing. They acted as though their team was genetically entitled, maybe even divinely ordained, to win and when they lost, it was not their fault. The phan thought it would be great to go to a ball game again. Perhaps he would get a chance to see the Nats when he got settled in Washington. Soon the receptionist interrupted his baseball daydream announcing the paperwork was ready for pick-up in the assistant branch manager's office and he may go right in. *Damn! Why do I have to deal with this reprobate again?*

"Good morning, Mr. Rossy. Please have a seat." The abm gestured to the same chair in front of his desk that the tyro had been insulted in by this larded buffoon more than a year ago. The man was about twenty pounds heavier than then and came across every bit as spurious.

"Thank you, sir," said the familiar young patron, settling uneasily into the un-cushioned hardwood seat.

"So, you want to close your checking, money management and CD accounts, ...why?"

"Because I'm leaving PWA and the area and I would rather have my accounts in proximity to my new location."

"OK, but you know, of course, ...that with electronic banking it really doesn't matter where your institution..... actually is," explained the CU official, leaning back into the swivel and raising his arms with interlocked fingers behind his neck. "We can continue to provide services for you...... wherever you are."

The account closer saw massive, yellow sweat stains in the armpits of the fatso's white shirt and, for no apparent reason, imagined the guy was sitting there, spread-legged nude. He stifled a belch that erupted with this mental image and repeated his desire to keep his accounts close.

"And..... where might 'close' be?" inquired the finance man.

"I don't think that's any of your business," retorted the impatient foreseater. "Look, can we just get this done? I have a long drive ahead of me and I need to get going."

"I see you still have a punkass attitude problem," hissed the bankster, as he dropped his arms and shot forward in the swivel. "Yeah, boy, we can get this done." He sloppily signed the documents in front of him and more or less threw them at his newly former client. "Now get the hell outta my office!"

Rossy gathered up the paperwork and left the office with no further discourse. He had a strong impression of ugly deja vu as he returned to reception to cash out his accounts. Upon receiving a little less than the final balances due to penalties for early withdrawal of the CDs, he exited the credit union and returned to his car.

After picking up a lunch hoagie, he was soon on the interstate and headed away from his first post-undergraduate working engagement. Driving into the open country the slightly experienced engineer never felt more free in his entire life. Nothing but net - it was exhilarating. The way out of Connecticut reversed the way he drove in. West on I-84 from Hartford, through the heel of New York, across the Hudson and the Delaware and on into Pennsylvania. As he sped over the seemingly endless track of noisy concrete pavement, he thought it highly unlikely he would ever pass this way again.

PENNSYLVANIA

The freedom rider liked driving on interstate highways, because of limited access and no traffic lights. It was the only place he could use cruise control. He wasn't a fast driver, never trolling at much over sixty-five, and generally went left just to pass. He hated when someone passed him and cut over in front at a lower speed. Then he had to brake to slow down, which disengaged the cruise and he had to reset. It happened all the time! It wouldn't be so irritating if he had adaptive control, but his older car wasn't so equipped. In defense of some of the offending drivers, he noticed they were often being chased by a giant semi-rig hanging within paranormal distance of their back bumper and had to cut him off to avoid being overrun and plunked. It was tough out here on the big road.

Interstate driving had a love-hate relationship with radio. Since the roadways were mostly in remote areas of quickly varying terrain, radio reception changed faster than a politician's flips on partisan compromise. Rossy preferred deejayed radio music over programmed streams and always searched for anyone playing blues, reggae, or ethnic roots. This was typically found on university stations in the public radio bands of metropolitan areas he might be passing through. Out on the open road, he usually could only get Jesus rock or hard country honky-tonk. Occasionally he might receive a clear frequency of blue grass, but it never lasted long, maybe a hill or two, before phasing out. When the FM music died, he switched to AM for talk. Mostly this would be a hyper-voiced evangelist extolling the power of prayer or the horror of eternal damnation. It was fascinating how these guys could stretch 'god' into a two or three syllable word with half-octave inflection. They reminded him of political comedian Bill Maher, who sardonically defined prayer as 'telepathic communication with an imaginary friend'. It seemed the 'godsters' could always broadcast the strongest. Maybe because they had more money for bigger transmitters. Sometimes he fell into a financial advice show, where a caller would need to be told why he shouldn't buy the sixty thousand dollar boat when he had an underwater mortgage, thirty grand in credit line debt and had recently lost his job. With luck, he might find a live promotional broadcast from the sidewalk in front of Kleinfelter's Hardware at town center, where they were giving away free tickets for the upcoming carnival to anyone who could eat twelve hotdogs in three minutes. Or, he could always listen to an Atlanta Braves baseball game, which the Turner Group continuously aired all over the world through all available media. AM radio could be bizarrely entertaining, but was, more often than not, a lost wasteland of fringe Americana. The buzzed out listener finally turned the radio off and watched the scenery go by.

Pennsylvania could not be considered a rich state. It had boundless natural resources and lush, productive farmland, but it never regained the pivotal economic status it enjoyed during its manufacturing zenith and was still suffering heavily from the recent great recession. Unemployment remained above average, the aging state population was declining and public facilities were decaying. But, visually, it was always a beautiful place. Homes invariably featured bright green, manicured lawns, colorful blooms and precisely edged walkways and curbs. Everything was so very neat. Rarely would a farm or homestead have any significant accumulation of junk surrounding the structures or scattered through the yard areas. Even abandoned businesses and commercial buildings were maintained in good and orderly condition. Litter along the roads consisted mainly of easily retrievable bags of empty beer cans and bottles tossed by pick-up drivers to avoid an open container violation should they be stopped by the police. Among the discarded beer empties were little ditch bank cross shrines testifying to the futility of the drinking drivers' attempted riddance of evidence. Seen from the higher elevations of the ridges of the Poconos, the spectacular Susquehanna Valley stretched to the distant central highlands like a vast rolling quilt of unmethodical patchwork of varying patterns, shapes, sizes and earth toned hues. Shadows of moving cloud masses offered the illusion of undulating motion through the still life of the static vista. The colorful valley blanket was laced together on both sides of the mighty river by curvy ribbons of roadway that meandered from town to town via the scenic routes. Specks of cattle dotted many of the open patches like scattered pepper. Countless church steeples, water towers and barn silos pierced the picturesque fabric as minuscule needles to the sky. Uncleared areas of forest land appeared as broccoli head buttons randomly sewn into the quilted cover to tack it down. The consistently meticulous appearance of the Pennsylvania landscape was likely rooted in the efficient German ancestry of its inhabitants, who certainly would never be mistaken for sloven custodians of a squandered past.

Rounding a widely spiraling curve descending into the valley, the safe driver saw a pedestrian walking some distance ahead in the grassed strip adjacent to the paved right shoulder of the roadway. It was unusual, if not illegal, for anyone to be walking in the interstate right-of-way, without a vehicle parked or disabled nearby, and the bypasser slowed slightly to get a look. The man was very thin and carried a giant, plastic bag filled to bulging capacity on a makeshift tree branch rack tied to his back with fraying rope. He had long, tangled hatless hair that wove into a wild beard of the same color and texture, so his whole upper body and head looked like a thick, furry blackish-gray pole with no discernible features. His shirt and pants were torn and filthy and his worn out sneakers had no laces. He wore fingerless, dark leather gloves, clasping a long walking stick branch in each hand. This poor soul looked like a lifelong derelict and Rossy thought briefly about pulling over to see if he could be of assistance. Then he thought, more cognitively, that might not be a good idea, maybe even a fatal idea, and he resumed speed. No doubt the next state patrol coming through would take care of any problem that was going on here. But he wondered about the dude. Here it was, mid-afternoon, miles from the nearest interchange to nowhere, cold temperatures and maybe bad weather just hours away. Where was this guy going to and coming from? How did he stay alive? How did he get in this condition? Harshly, it occurred to the wondering wanderer that the only real difference out here on this remote highway, between the hiking derelict and himself, was a car and maybe a phone. The used car was mostly not his - he still owed three-and a-half years' payment, after which it would be essentially worthless. And it could break down at any time. He had no idea what was happening under the hood, or through the power train. He could be mere minutes away from a wheel flying off. Who really knows what will go haywire? The phone? Check it out - no service! So, really, there *was* no difference between him and the derelict. What did it all mean? In musing such a metaphysical *big unknown,* he contemplated the thought process of Francis of Assisi—the 13th century patron saint remembered from a religious history course he took for required liberal arts credit—who doffed his clothes, gave away all his possessions and ran into the mountains to figure out the purpose of life. Evidently, FOA never accomplished his mission, because people still puzzled over the same issues today.

The road tripper didn't drive long distances without breaks, stopping every fifty miles, or so, at the highway rest areas. After walking around the premises to stretch and loosen up, he would sit at an empty concrete picnic table to relax, drink some water and watch the people. It was interesting to see who was in the vehicles that had been passing and cutting him off for the last hour. Americans came in all ages, types, tones and sizes, but the dominant size looked to be xxxl and nearly all had a phone in hand. Many were noisy, yelling obnoxiously back and forth to friends or relatives they were traveling with, who were somewhere else on the grounds. *Was there some empirical correlation between largeness and loudness?* He usually saw quite a few elderly folks, helping each other up the walkways to the rest buildings from their oversized sedans in the parking lot, many with Florida plates. He wondered why these people flocked to Florida to retire and then hit the road to spend all their time driving around the country. And sometimes not very well. It seemed a disproportionate number of cars that tailgated, drove too fast or slow, or deviated from the prevailing traffic patterns, were Florida tagged, operated by tense, popeyed looking old men, who often could barely see over the steering wheel they held tightly at the top, with both white knuckled paws, in a stiff-armed death grip. They did not really appear to be having a good time and it wasn't exactly clear why they drove so much if they didn't have to. Children were running around everywhere, making annoying squealing sounds as they broke from the confines of a vehicle. The rest stopper didn't dislike children, but he didn't particularly like to interact with them, or be where they were. His happiest birthday was when he was eighteen and no longer had to be counted as a child. Why *were* there so many traveling children? Shouldn't they be in school? It was a mid-

September Friday and summer vacation was way over. Possibly they were on home-schooled field trips?

And the dogs! God, it seemed every car bound party included at least one. Seeing all the others, some went into grand mal seizures of yelping frenzy, as they strained at their leashes while pissing and shitting all over the picnic area. Nice. Rossy probably disliked dogs a lot more than children. His only direct experience with the critters was when his mom decided to get one as a positive family influence for him and his sisters. They all quickly lost interest when it grew out of cute, funny puppyhood and turned into a canine sociopath. It was some sort of terrier that, for no known reason, would ankle bite anybody wearing long pants, so they had to keep him tied up. This devolved him into a complete lunatic. He spent most of his time chained to a stake under a rose hedge in the backyard with a grapefruit sized rock in his mouth, drool oozing grossly to the ground in front of him like a junior Cujo. It was not much of a disappointment when the animal succumbed to an asthma attack one day after a daily run, though a little sad he had spent such a miserable existence. In hindsight, the little dumbie should have been euthanized when it was evident to be a crazy liability, rather than a good, normal pet. Since then there had never been any thoughts of getting another dog.

At one stop, the highwayman parked in the truck area to take a break. This was an entirely different world than the car sector around front. Much less hyper, with no incessant, undirected noise and activity. The sweet, dirty smell of diesel exhaust and constant drone of idling engines were all that permeated his EN senses. He couldn't even hear the sounds of the highway. There were few people walking around and no kids or dogs. Several serious looking xxxl men were sitting at a canopied picnic table, phones in front of them, talking in low voices. Truck drivers were kind of like a secret society, or subculture, who might act insanely aggressive on the road, but otherwise were reserved and quietly unobtrusive, not unlike ultimate MMA fighters. He wondered whether the separation of cars and trucks at the rest stops was for reasons other than safety. Maybe so trucksters could conduct a remunerative interstate drug and smuggling trade in the privacy of their own seclusion? *Hey! C'mon, man, that's just pop speculation.*

The last break was at a state park south of Scranton, to eat the foot long Italian lunch sub. The park was a little run down, in need of basic maintenance and repair, but was, of course, neat and un-cluttered. It was also deserted. Not another car in the lot. The af-ternoon picnicker thought this somewhat odd, considering all the people he had seen at the interstate rest stops. Apparently, most people on the road were destination orientated and not interested in enjoying the peace of a forest park on such a beautiful, late summer day. Rossy appreciated parkland areas, especially those that were unoccupied. But it was, of course, a bit of a paradox. While parks were reserved for public use and enjoyment, if they were heavily patronized they would not be the serene places eve-ryone loved to enjoy.

***

By the time the native son arrived in Lancaster County, the sun was starting its descent and the dusk light was dimming the sight lines ahead. He knew that special careful caution was neces-sary driving through this area, particularly in the early evening. This was when the Amish farmers were coming home from their fields, or their neighbors' fields, or church, the store, work, or wherever. They were on the roads in their black, horse drawn bug-gies and difficult to see in the fading daylight. Some had large or-ange triangular reflectors on the back, but not all. You had to as-sume there could be one right over the crest of every hill ap-proached, clopping along at about eleven mph. It was not unusual to see a long string of cars stacked up behind a carriage in a no passing zone of a two lane highway. Sometimes a motorist would yield to impatience and pass around a curve or over a rise with no clue what was coming from the other direction. **BAM!!** There were several of these types of serious wrecks every year, but noth-ing would ever be done to rectify this road safety problem. In fact, the buggies were no more dangerous than non-Amish tractors and equipment that had been forever allowed on public roads, operated by twelve year old boys and with no registration. It was all part of the regional farming culture and would never change. Local driv-ers were inured to the situation, knowing these slow moving vehi-cles were not on long road trips and would be exiting out of the way soon. The Amish coaches were often pulled by retired harness racing horses. These standard-breds needed no training in trotting a rig and were available at the end of their professional careers through low cost claiming race options. Two things the Amish knew were horses and how to get them cheaply. Occasionally—and Rossy had seen it a few times—a car would attempt to pass a buggy and the horse would speed up, thinking through its instincts that a competitor was pressing for a stretch run. Yes, it could sometimes be a unique driving experience, through the Garden Spot of America.

The Amish religious order and their distinct lifestyle had always confounded the nonsectarian engineer. He couldn't believe they thought they had to live in the seventh century to properly impress and deify the Lord. Didn't most Christian teachings instruct people to strive for their highest potential in realization of God's intent for humanity? What was the point of rejecting the modern accomplishments of civilization in humble service of God Almighty, the quintessential imaginary friend? *"Remember, people, the only obstacle to fulfillment is refusal to recognize potential. Success and may God be with you."* But wait! The Amish didn't *really* spurn modernity. Rossy remembered a summer job in high school when he worked on a chicken egg farm. During the day he assembled the racks of little two cubic feet wire cages the chickens spent their productive lives in, manually banding the parts together with a crimp pliers. Prolonged periods of this activity would quickly lead to permanent ligament damage in the crimping hand, so he had to break every few hours to do other tasks, such as cleaning the shit troughs under the laying cages, or breaking cracked eggs into vats for sale to bakery companies. At night he earned mandatory overtime by catching young chickens, in dark, open floor raising houses, for vaccination and debeaking. Basically, it was just about the worst job that even the most cynical of sadists could devise. The inescapable smell, dust, dirt and heat made him feel like he had been dipped in hot, wet chicken crap and feathered for exile by the blessed end of each long, long day. But the Amish dudes he worked with loved it! They piled out of the van the boss farmer's son transported them in each morning like a bunch of imported migrant workers just happy to be there. Some he recognized from school, though he hadn't seen them since eighth grade, the Amish senior year.

Through the course of that chicken summer, the coworkers revealed much about their lives that conflicted with the popular

image. Evidently, many of the Amish farms had generator powered electrical systems they used for all sorts of conveniences, including computers, power tools, water wells, irrigation systems,
refrigeration equipment and most modern household appliances,
including, even, TV, for chrissake. They loved riding in and driving automobiles, though few, if any, had operator licenses, or actually owned a legally registered car. Growing Amish enterprises
utilized the internet to market and promote their products and way
of life to a worldwide consumer and tourist pool, resulting in revenue streams rivaling the Native American casino industry. Apparently, limited education wasn't a hindrance. All they needed to
know was basic, money counting arithmetic. While the front of
biblical sacrifice seemed contradictory to their success, maybe
they truly were deeply religious, seeking to bear the opus of a hard
life in the name of the Lord. Rossy surmised the truth lay somewhere between, but he didn't care. Live and let live. Everybody is
listed in the roll call. He certainly had no problem with Amish
folks - he rather liked and admired them. They made super great
buffet food and their men's dress style was dope, too. Black Zorro
hat, Stooge Moe haircut, Lincoln beard, high-water woolen pants
with suspenders, combat boots and a blue cotton work shirt. A retro farmer grunge look. He might try it in Washington.

***

It was after dark when the road runner arrived at his mom's
house in Ebbottown. She was in her study working on cosmic predictions, listening to pan flute and whale ping music. By day she
was a legal secretary for the local, small town barrister. On the
side she did astrology charts for people, at a couple of bens per
pop. *Cash only, please.* The educated engineer was amazed that
anyone would pay that much for such unmitigated nonsense. But
then he recollected the story about the group in Arizona, who gave
up ten grand each to overheat and die in a special, holistic, hot
spring sauna, and realized there could be a viable market for anything. Especially when new age hippies were involved. He considered his mom a *resourceful* new ager. She did not seem overtly
pleased to see him, wondering why he was showing up at such a
late hour. But he knew the real reason she was out of sorts was
that he had quit a perfectly good job and knowingly clouded his
future with uncertainty.

"Do you know how many people coming out of college can't find any work at all in this economy?" she had reprimanded him when he informed her of his change of direction. "Your so-called new job sounds like a scam to me. I think you've been set up and you're going to find yourself on the outside looking in. Well, don't believe you can come back and live here. Since you and your sisters have been out, I've discovered this place isn't big enough for more than one adult and that would be *ME*! So don't even dream about moving back!"

Of course, mom's boy knew he would much prefer living on the slumdog street before he would ever try to rebound into his mom's place. Hell, he would *die* on the street before slinking back home. He just hoped she wasn't anywhere nearly right about his new gig. Time would soon tell. "Nice to see you, too, Mom," he said giving her an affectionate hug and peck on the forehead. She warmed immediately and offered some left over chipped beef and gravy toast that was still on the stove from dinner. "Welcome home, Billy."

***

Ebbottown was way past its prime. The decline began decades ago with the closure of a large Air Force base in the mid-state area, putting tens of thousands of people out of work. Then a nearby nuclear power plant, within the dreaded, but arbitrary, ten mile radius, almost melted down, resulting in prolonged closure and another several thousand lost jobs. Most recently, a Black & Decker small tool plant closed up shop and went to Honduras, axing more than five hundred jobs. When Billy and family arrived in Ebbottown, moving from Chambersburg to be closer to relatives following his dad's death, there wasn't much left. An Amtrak station on the Pittsburgh-Philadelphia railway, a Masonic Home for Children, a small liberal arts church college and the chocolate factory. Never enough jobs to replace the losses and nothing new ever developed.

Today, Ebbottown was struggling to renew its image in the same fashion as thousands of small towns across the country, but it was an uphill battle. Giant franchise retailers, surrender of manufacturing to the cheap, low quality global economy and persistent slow growth were killing the American town. Typically, the focus of revitalization was attraction of tourists, starting with establishment of a town center Historical District. Every town had a history, so anything could be deemed historical. The HD zones, streets and features were marked with brown and white signs, projecting the illusion of a quaint park-like environment. Any HD house or structure over fifty years old received a distinct historical plaque to mount by the front entrance. Heavy gray metal signs with black lettering were strategically placed throughout the district to provide National Historical Register narratives about sometimes forgettable events and persons from the town's past glory days. Such a sign in Ebbottown's square explained how Harlan Lionel Ebbot migrated from Europe in 1752, at the age of 34, to start the first Lutheran Church in the region. He profited enough money from the church to open a provisions store and later a post office, hotel and stage depot. His enterprises eventually made him one of the most influential men in the county, a major supplier of the Revolutionary Army, and led to high appointment in the Commonwealth following independence from England. Ebbot died at the age of 75 after being kicked in the head by a horse he was trying to get out of a burning barn on his farm near the thriving town he founded.

Many redefining towns enhanced their HDs with old style street lamps adorned with hanging blooms, cobbled brick sidewalks and colorful banners proudly boasting a 'unique' theme. Ebbottown's contrived theme was 'corn', claiming more temporary summer jobs for unemployed young people, manually detasseling corn stalks on surrounding farms, than any other town in America. It was never really clear exactly why corn had to be detasseled, or why machines couldn't do it. Possibly, the explanation was something inanely simple, like the lost reason you always cut the end of the ham off before roasting was that somebody's great-great-grandmother had to do that to get it to fit into her pan. The annual Corn Fest at the town's fairgrounds celebrated the best corn in the world from the heart of America's Garden Spot. This two-day August event offered specialty foods, crafts, music, rides and games, pathetically capped by a grand finale 'Miss Queen Corn' beauty contest, in hopes of drawing folks from all over willing to sheck up an abe per head to witness another desperate reach for attention by the local chamber of commerce. Perhaps their efforts could be better applied in finding ways to seduce people, looking to spend their disposable time and money, into town on a

regular basis, like daily or weekly and in the evenings. Good restaurants, interesting shops and markets, free broadband wi-fi and
diverse, modern entertainment will always trump a tanning salon,
bridal gown shop, video rental parlor, flea market junk stores and
a plethora of empty, boarded up building fronts, as downtown attractions. And for godsakes get rid of the so-called art gallery
filled with comically overpriced paintings of bowls of fruit on a
table and silhouetted trees on a hill. Rossy was not a community
redevelopment planner. He just knew he didn't want to spend any
time in Ebbottown.

***

The next morning, Saturday, the homecomer unloaded his car
to sort through and reorganize his stuff, and maybe get rid of a few
things he didn't really need. He also didn't feel like driving around
town during his bye week with the car filled to the gills. That
would be inefficiently uncool. Later, he would clean the car and
repack it in a more orderly manner for the trip to Washington and
his new future. His mom thought he was trying to stake a move
back in and reminded him of the nonnegotiable ultimatum regarding rebounds. He assured her there was no danger of violation of
her edict and he would make sure to leave nothing behind when he
departed next week. She accepted his avowal of compliance, but
requested he also remove a bunch of his stuff that was still stored
in the attic. He couldn't exactly remember what might be there
and, out of instant curiosity, went up to check it out. He found his
old space helmet—a clear, hard plastic sphere with a red stripe
over the top and circular ear and neck openings—that he had used
during his astronaut days when he roamed the ether, traveling to
the moon, Mars and beyond, into deep space. His weather station
was intact with barometer, humidity and temperature gauges, wind
meter, rain collector and all the other incidentals needed to observe and record weather patterns and, ultimately, make forecasts.
He recalled consistently being at least 50% correct in his weather
predictions. The old model automobile engine was there, all million plastic parts that took him months to assemble. It was a transparent replica of a V-8 engine that actually ran with a small battery
operated servo motor showing all moving parts of the engine in
operation. He had learned a lot about engines from the model and
remembered the special thrill of accomplishment when he first

fired it up and saw it successfully running. After that all he could do with it was watch it run, seeing the eight little cylinders go up and down with the rotation of the cam shaft. That obviously got old very quickly and the engine soon became an artifact. His worthless internet stamp collection and Harry Potter books were there, along with his old baseball glove holding a Scott Rolen home run ball. Without a doubt, that game, during which he some-how managed to retrieve the ball from a corner of the center field stand deck amid a hundred other phans trying to do the same, was the highlight of his spectating career. He looked around for his card and comic collections and was dismayed to discover them gone. Over the years of his elementary school youth he had bought and traded for a fairly decent compilation of baseball cards and a little known series of military aircraft cards, all available from fif-ty-cent bubble gum packages at the long gone Raymond's Candy Store on High Street. And he had loved his avenger comics, wherein the artwork was fantastic and the story lines were mysti-cal twaddle. He often thought these collections might appreciate in value with time, but not now, since his mom had obviously chucked them. So, as far as he was concerned, the ball was the only item worth keeping in this pile, though with no signature or identifying features, it would never appreciate above value zero. It would always be only a worthless memento, but one that was easi-ly stored and transported. Everything else was going to the land-fill. He went down to get a trash bag and ask his mom why in hell had she thrown his good stuff out and left something as useless as the space head?

***

After dealing with his personal debris from the past, Rossy called his old bud, Cambaugh, to see if they could hook up to catch up. Cam was the visiting homeboy's longest running friend in life. They had been pals since kindergarden, but hadn't really hung since high school. He webbed Cam last week to let him know he would be in town and to reserve some time for them. To-night was good, around six. The two had gone different ways after graduation. One was off to the university and the other enlisted in the Air Force. College man couldn't understand anyone volunteer-ing for the military, especially with all the scuffling Middle East 'wars' going on, but Cam played his own options. As it turned out there was no risk. During basic-t at Lackland AFB, he re-injured an old ankle break from his football days and was released with a medical discharge. Then, as a 'vet', he was qualified to legitimately include military service on his resume and landed a decent job as a mortgage adjuster for a local savings and loan company. He still lived in E-town with his parents and showed no signs of seeking anything more motivated, or independent, in life, at least not for now and the immediate future. Rossy thought it odd for Cam to be so satisfied with such a mundane existence, in that he had always seemed to walk a little on the turbulent side. After all, it was Cam who devised and organized the air gun battles in the woods surrounding College Lake, which went on for nearly a whole junior high summer before all twenty, or so, 'bb warriors' were captured by the police one afternoon and turned over to the custody of their parents following several hours detention in a town jail holding cell. They tried to tell any of the furious adults who would listen, that it was not a recklessly dangerous activity, because they wore plastic football helmets and swimming pool googles during combat operations and no one was ever seriously hurt. Collectively, they logged about three years 'grounded' time. And it was Cam who led by example in scaling an impregnable 'no trespassing' fence around an abandoned sand quarry and swan diving thirty feet into an opaque pool, with no telemetry on what was beneath the pea green water surface. Others in attendance at this convergence of fools followed like lemmings once they saw his smiling face bobbing below. Cam, again, in the middle of a pile up of stacked sleds at the bottom of a snowy slick hill street, resulting in a steel runner through an eye of one of the winter funsters and plenty of blood on the ice. And who could forget the bone rattling pea shooter sorties, for six consecutive Halloween midnights, on the windows of houses around town? This harmless fun provoked at least three live shotgun retaliations - fortunately, no casualties. Yep, the Camster had always been the exemplar wild and crazy guy, but the times, they were a changin'. Or, maybe they were a switchin', 'cause safeside Rossy was possibly heading into a clear and present danger, while Cam was living low. They would probably redefine their roles tonight.

***

There was invariably a list of to-do tasks awaiting the wayfaring son when he came home to visit his mom and this trip was no exception. He started with cutting the grass, a chore he had been doing since he was old enough to see over the handlebar of the Lawn Boy power mower that still resided in the garage. After checking the oil and gas, cleaning the air filter, scraping the old moldy clumps of cuttings from the underside and file sharpening the blade, he was ready to make some noise. VRROOOM! The LB's Briggs & Stratton fired up with one pull of the rotor rope and it was off to the back yard. He liked to cut in a clockwise direction, starting from the outside perimeter, so that everything was ground up and thrown to the inside and he didn't have to catch the grass or rake. Rossy didn't mind cutting grass. He found it relaxing. There was little extraneous noise audible over the rhythmic purr of the machine and he could basically let his head go blank, or, think about whatever he wanted, without distraction. Like singing in the shower. Passing along the rose hedge at the back edge of the yard he approached the bare spot that seemed to be permanently contaminated by the spirit of the idiot dog that once resided there. While walking through the dust cloud created by the mower whirling above the dirt his mind swore it heard a low growl through the whine of the engine. Suddenly a sharp metallic sound when the blade spun on a rock and he immediately felt a stab of pain from a stone shard biting into his right ankle. *What the hell?* he thought, raising his jeans leg to see a reddening welt.

Continuing around the landscape, the yardworker noticed some changes from the last time he had cut grass here. A large new patch of something growing in the bed along the split rail fence beside the garage entrance pad appeared to be thriving and well kept. He guessed it might be ginseng, recalling mom had long said she was going to start a ginseng operation, claiming she could get more than a grant per ounce for the herb from her astrology associates. The thought of other, easier cash crops, that might sell even better with her clients, came to mind, though at greater inherent risk. The grossly messy crabapple tree was gone and so were all the flies, gnats and birdlife it perpetually harbored. He remembered the sour odor of mower mashed crabapples and how difficult it was to clean the apple gunk from the LB after cutting under the tree. Why anyone would voluntarily allow a crabapple tree in their yard was beyond figuring.

When the back yard was done, lawnboy man moved to the side strip between mom's house and the neighbor's driveway. The three oak trees he had long ago planted in this area from acorn sprouts were now at least twenty feet tall. He was very proud of these trees, which always reminded him of the large pine grove he and his cousin had started on his nearby uncle's farm when he worked there on weekends and during the summer as a young kid. His uncle had paid him one george an hour for doing some fairly heavy duty farm work, including cutting grown over-fallowed fields with a rotary mower pulled by a full-sized, bright red Farmall tractor. He would never forget the solitary thrill of driving the tractor on the public road between the barn and the fields when he was only twelve years old. In retrospect the job probably violated many wage and labor laws, on a variety of levels, but he never knew anything about that. He only knew that working on the farm made him feel something in common with all the real farm boys he went to school with and gave him a little bubble gum and video game money.

The front yard, rectangularly shaped with few obstacles, was simple to mow. He cut this in straight lines, alternately pulling and pushing the mower parallel to the house so the grass always blew streetward. In pushing toward the neighbor's yard, he noticed it was just as perfect and neat as ever. Golf green smooth and so evenly textured that the guy manicured it with a manual reel mower, catching all the cuttings, that he carefully placed in the composting bin in the back beside his immaculately designed and tended vegetable garden. In contrast, mom's yard was rife with dandelions and other undesirable growths that re-bloomed an hour after cutting. Rossy always thought the neighbor lived in constant fear, though he never complained, that his property would be infiltrated by invasive weed spores carried by the winds of entropy from the inferior adjacent plot. Actually, he was a good dude, often helping the drifty widow lady next door with outside maintenance after her children were launched. Probably, someday, both lots would be perfect.

Next on the list was cleaning the roof gutters. This was a nasty job offering dubious risk-reward incentive. Certainly, the highly trained engineer understood that clearing gutters and downspouts was necessary to efficiently get water away from the roof and house during heavy downpours and normally the best way to do this task would be from a ladder. But here the thick growth of fire-thorns and holly trees around the house meant he had to get up on the roof and squat waddle on the thirty degree slope along the gutter line, cleaning from one end to the other with a small scraper. The mucky, ant, beetle and spider infested material, with masses of embedded leaves and twigs and even some live vegetative growth had to be manually removed between the gutter spikes. There were also accumulations of crud pushing up underneath the shingle overhangs that had to be reamed out. It was a slow tedious process that could result in being hideously shredded if he slipped over the eave and dropped the ten or twelve feet into the spiny, prickly shrubs below. Why his mom never had gutter guards installed was indefensible from a basic house maintenance consideration.

But if she had, son Billy would not have been able to play the endless series of 'roofball' games he so much enjoyed during his little league era. Roofball was throwing a tennis ball up on the roof and then trying to catch it as it rolled back down and bounced out into the yard. Depending on how high it went up on the roof and how it reversed back down, the ball could go anywhere. If it fell to the ground uncaught, it was a hit. If caught it was an out. To the street was a homer and singles, doubles and triples were in evenly spaced zones of the yard between the house and downtown. The return of the ball was affected by where it was thrown and how much spin it was released with, just like in real baseball. But the high long balls, the four baggers, had to propel from a certain bounce off the lip of the gutter. Such a play would never happen if gutter guards were in place. In fact, the whole game would not have been possible with gutter guards, because every play would have been an easy out. With unpredictable bounces and careens of the tennis ball facilitated by the open gutters, the roofball wizard was able to simulate complete ball games and whole seasons of fantasy baseball with standings, stats, playoffs and world series. He had killed a lot of time playing roofball and sometimes wondered, thinking back, what it must have sounded like inside the house. **Bump...bumpity...bumpity...bumpity...bumpity...bump..** Over and over, for hours. It must have driven his family nuts, but no one ever demanded that he cease and desist. His mom probably thought it kept him out of trouble, or at least where she knew he was and what he was doing. Plus, it was good exercise, better than playing video games. With completion of the gutter work, but not nearly the work list, it was time to clean up and get ready to go out.

***

Cam's parents' place was directly across the street from the high school. They had lived there for as long as the cross-towner had known them. During the past ten years, Mr. Cambaugh suffered three coronaries, received bypass surgery and was medically retired from the Postal Service. He was on a waiting list for a heart transplant that he would forfeit in a jumping jack flash for one last cigarette. Mrs. Cambaugh worked part time at the Masonic Homes as an alternate house counselor. So, considering their circumstance, it was probably good for them that Cam still lived at home and commendable that he was willing to help his parents out. Such an arrangement would certainly never work in his best friend's case. After a few minutes of exchanging pleasantries with Mr. and Mrs. C., the boys headed out for the evening. Rossy offered to drive and Cam offered to buy the first round at The Intown Inn. Over beers, Cam related he had won quite a bit of cash betting on last night's county schoolboy football games, including the Ebbottown Panthers. The financial conservative didn't know you could bet on high school sports. Cam explained you could bet on anything and apparently he did, going into some detail about his triumphs at the track and in playing several pro sports pools. He said he had even won money betting on political elections. Was he into anything illegal? "Hell no, man, I only pig on-line through a registered bookie." *Whatever that meant.* Had he ever bet on high school games while he was playing? "Hell no, man, that would have been illegal!" Actually, back in the day, Cam was a fairly good running back and really enjoyed the game...and winning. His good crony believed him if he said he didn't bet against himself.

Rossy never excelled much at team sports. He had not really been hefty enough for football and never considered trying out for any organized play in the sport. Soccer was always available for football rejects, but he was not particularly drawn to that activity. It involved too much effort for hardly any points, mostly bringing the ball back into play from out-of-bounds. He had some success in baseball at the Little League level, making two all-star teams as a pitcher, and then played in an intermediate Rotary league for early teens. The high school coach had told him for a couple of years to make sure he showed up for tryouts when he got to ninth grade. So he did and he made the team, but after a year and a half of bench duty without a single inning of play, not even a warm up call, his frustration boiled over and he walked out during a mid-season home game, returned to the locker room, showered, dressed, threw his uniform in the waste can and went home. That was his last baseball game as a 'player'. Basketball? Average height didn't get it in b-ball, without speed and some natural ability. Not a chance. And then a strange athletic opportunity developed. EHS had hired two teachers, Mr. Thompson and Mr. Thompson, who were fraternal twins and alternate NCAA wrestling champions from Oklahoma State. The Thompson brothers were interested in starting a wrestling program at EHS and conducted a clinic to attract prospective participants, shortly after the would-be pitcher parted ways with baseball. He knew nothing about wrestling except that he should not try at home what the WWE superstars did on TV. He attended the clinic, mostly out of curiosity, and found himself recruited by default, along with the other nine or ten boys who showed up, to be members of the inaugural EHS Wrestling Panthers. Coach Thompson and Coach Thompson immediately began rigorous training sessions to teach the 'team' how to wrestle and get the novice matsters in shape. They quickly learned that a three period wrestling match was the longest, hardest six minutes in all of high school sports. It could leave you gasping for air and nearly paralyzed from total muscular exhaustion. And if you were not in some semblance of shape, it might leave you unconscious or dead. For months they trained like Rocky Balboa preparing for a title bout and when their first scheduled conference meet finally occurred, they got universally clobbered. No one on the team won his match and several boys wanted to quit. But the Thompsons were master psychological manipulators of young minds and held the team together with a projection of guilted self pride. They trained and practiced even harder. They lost again and again ramped up the training. Another loss and more work. Finally, during their fifth dual meet, several guys won their matches, including Rossy, much to his own astonishment. The Thompsons celebrated by taking the team for pizza, which they had to burn off with an extra half hour of weights the next day. After the breakthrough of match wins, a few spectators started to dribble in to watch the home meets, though attendance never rose much above the sparse number of fans, parents and girlfriends who figured out how the matches were scored. More individual wins followed, but they were not really instinctive wins. They were more the result of following the explicit instructions of the Thompsons to exploit observed weaknesses in opponents' style or execution. No one had yet developed sufficient wrestling skill to apply their own spontaneous innovation and creativity and win by themselves. By the end of the season, Rossy won four of twelve matches and thanked jesus god in heaven that wrestling was over. No more spitting into jars and doing weird sweating exercises in the steam shower to make weight. The next year, as a senior, he enrolled in a couple of AP courses at the college and was not at the high school very much. He intended to scrap wrestling in lieu of concentrating on his university prep. When he informed Coaches Thompson of this decision, he found himself slammed up against a locker wall in the hallway while being called a loud string of profane 'gutless coward' slurs. A large group of students and teachers witnessed this outburst, some of whom recorded it on phone cam. Within minutes the video was streamed to the police and media and the story led on the local evening television newscast. The ex-matman refused to talk to any of the school administrators, the police or the press about the incident, but the Thompsons were subsequently suspended and eventually fired after their arrest for endangerment and misdemeanor child abuse based on the video evidence. That ended the wrestling program at EHS and Rossy's involvement in organized sports.

The E-Town homies ordered a large pizza and continued filling each other in on their respective post graduate lives. The visitor recognized Dottie Gramheiser working behind the bar and Cam said she was down on hard times. Dottie had been a prototype high school social elite, one of the privileged 'specials', with killer blondie good looks and a 'ME' central attitude. She was the quarterback's girl and had once tried to make an unwitting ass out of nobody Rossy, by faking coming on to him in front of a group of snickering incrowders. He remembered deflecting the faux flirt, jokingly saying he was not interested in time wasting with a 'los-

er-in-training' such as herself. This impropriety earned him a rather sharp slap across the face and a blast of insulting obscenities
that continued via social media assault for two more days. Cam
said she was divorced with three kids and no money and had to
work shit jobs to make ends meet. Quarterback man was long gone
into the underground, where non-payment of child support was a
virtue. The ex-classmate saw she had lost her looks somewhere
along the way. He felt a little sorry for her, not prescient correct-
ness, because it was not in his nature to glut over anyone's misfor-
tune. He was relieved she had not recognized *him*.

Cam seemed happy with his job at Penn Central Savings &
Loan. As a loanster he was responsible for managing failed mortgages in accordance with federal guidelines for recovery to avoid
foreclosures. PCSL held a huge number of unproductive accounts
and was not permitted to write them down if it was to receive capital infusion funding from the Fed. Managing the mortgages involved sitting down with clients, who were hopelessly in over
their financial heads, and working out household budgets that
might facilitate some sort of payment schedule. He was stunned by
how inept and utterly stupid many of his clients were. He said it
was a real crapshoot whether they would be able to sustain payment on their modified mortgage plans. Rossy realized why Cam
liked the job so much - it was just another pig to him, albeit with
house money. The engineer didn't have much to report about his
new job in Washington, in that he didn't know much about it. He
said he would know more after he got his security clearance, but
he probably still wouldn't be able to tell anyone, if it was classified. Cam said it sounded like a lame bunch of bullshit to him,
some kind of scam. *Oh, Christ, same take as mom.*

***

After pizza, Cam suggested a change of venue. Earlier he had
called Shelby, an old war buddy in Millton, and said they might be
down later to play some nine ball. Shelby had been at Lackland
with Cam. The two met and became friends during basic when
they discovered they had regionally close hometowns in common.
Shelby decided he, too, wanted out of the Air Force after Cam was
booted on a medical. He conjured a mental breakdown and, following a month of psychiatric evaluation, was released with a

'nonfunctional' general discharge. This classification did him no good in finding a job and he had been pretty much unemployed ever since. Rossy had driven through Millton a few times, but didn't know anyone who lived there, or why anyone would want to live there. It was a little larger than Ebbottown, but much more broken. Once a booming steel town along the river outside of Harrisburg, it died with the industry and never had a Plan B to save itself. Steel had been very good to Millton for more than a century. But the unions had jacked wages way out of scope of the global economy and the company could not afford necessary upgrades of its ancient capital assets needed to stay in production. It couldn't even afford to relocate to cheaper labor. And so the executive officers cashed in their stock options and shut 'er down. Now the borough was essentially falling into ruin, with deteriorating infrastructure, no tax base and a dwindling, unemployed population. Sort of a microcosm of the state, except Millton was not neat and clean. It was a trashy, dirty dump. It had no historic district and no marketable tourist theme. The only marks the steel mills left behind when they closed were about two miles of unusable waterfront structures, resembling a bombed out, post war manufacturing district in Europe, and a heavy residue of black soot. And, of course, chronic unemployment. People living in Millton were edgy, angry and trapped. A large majority were on whatever form of welfare and public assistance they could qualify for and a growing contingent of the population was homeless. No one had ever stepped forward to try to clean things up and lead the town into any kind of new prosperity. In fact, they often had trouble getting candidates to run for the elective offices governing the local jurisdiction and there was constant talk of un-incorporating the borough township back to the control of the county. The most prominent municipal employees were those of the police department and incidents of conflict between the citizenry and law enforcement were occurring with increasing frequency. It was a potentially dangerous situation that could blow at anytime, over any insignificant issue. Millton was not a happy place.

But Leonard's Lounge was a reasonably happy oasis in the desert of Millton's despair. A hole-in-the-wall dive off the river side of Front Street, Leonard's offered cheap beer and drinks, packaged bar snacks, a soul rapping juke box and pool. It was

grimy, never properly restored after the last flood and had a perpetual, musty uriney odor mixed with embedded tobacco reek
from the pre-no smoking era. The once black and white tiled floor
was an oily colored gray with many chipped, broken and missing
squares. Darkwood wall paneling was moldy and rotting beneath a
leak stained ceiling. The only interior lighting was from overhead
pool table lamps, blinking neon liquor lights, the juke and either
daylight or streetlight sneaking in from the usually open front
door. Many male patrons did their beer pissing outside along the
river facing building wall rather than use the unbearably filthy rest
room. If you drove to Leonard's you almost needed an all terrain
vehicle to get down the driveway and across the parking lot, a
crater infested dirt and gravel access that became an undrained
mudhole on wet weather days. Rossy wasn't sure his low riding
Civic could make it through the lot, but he carefully followed the
high points, avoiding sparkling piles of broken glass, to a spot
along the front near the open entrance door. His headlights caught
a pack of brown river rats scurrying away from an overflowing
dumpster in the far corner as he maneuvered to a stop. There were
about six other cars parked in the lot, all of which could easily
qualify for the old 'cash for clunkers' stimulus program. As they
walked from the car, the night owls could hear loud thumping music, talking laughter and the distinct crack of colliding pool balls
spilling out from inside. Cam detected Shelby's over amped voice
and silently smiled at the cultural shock his homeboy was about to
immerse in.

    "**MY MAN, CAM!!! WHATCHU DOIN', MAN!?! WHAS
HAPPENINNN'??**" Cam and Shelby embraced and bro handed
greetings like they hadn't seen each other for years. Actually, it
had only been about a week, because they both spent most Saturdays at Leonard's. "**HEY, MAN, WHO YO' SIDE DUDE??
YOU FINE HIM ON DA STREET? HA!! YOU BRINGIN' IN
A STRAY?? JUST JIVIN', MAN, YOU KNOW DAT!!**" Cam
introduced Rossy, who was looking around the room, trying to get
a bearing on the surroundings. The place was a dive bomb. He
instantly knew, without trying to remember, that this was the worst
looking and smelling interior space for human occupation he had
ever been in. Much worse than any dorm room or frat lounge he
had seen in college. Besides the lastcomers, everyone in the room,
at the back pool tables, seated around the rectangular bar and

Leonard, inside the bar - maybe fifteen men and three women - was African American. Rossy was not in the least bit a prejudiced person, but he flat out didn't have any social experience with black folks. He had only seen one black student in all the years he attended school in Ebbottown - an older boy he never knew, who, oddly enough, was named Jonel White. White's father was an economics professor at the church college. There were certainly no black Amish or black Mennonite kids from the outlying farms he went to school with, as no such people existed. At the university he saw quite a few black students, but they were mostly from Africa and generally stayed among themselves at the International Student Union. In Connecticut, the only people he routinely associated with were his PWA colleagues and the boarding house loonies, and they weren't black. So, standing here in Leonard's, he found himself in a totally new and alien element for which Cam had given him no preview, whatsoever.

"**HEY, MAN, NEW BROTHA BUY DA BEER!!**" shouted Shelby, glancing at Rossy with a split toothed grin.

"Nah, Shelb, I got it", said Cam. "I pigged sweet last night. Pulled double bens on the Panthers, man."

"**WEEOOO!!! YOU DA MAN, CAMMY!! LEONARD!!! THREE BREWS OVA HERE, MAN!!**"

Leonard brought three longneck Buds over to the trio and squinted hard at the stranger as he placed the bottles on the bar in front of them. Leonard was sort of a Chuck Berry looking dude, with slicked back processed hair and a pencil line mustache. He wore a green silk shirt featuring an oversized pointed collar and open chest, where a bunch of gold link chains hung from his neck like a gilded wreath. He appeared to be some kind of disco throwback, but he was a shrewd and successful businessman. "I'm going to need some ID for this, son," he said softly. "LCB been up and down this street all month and I can't take no chances, even if you with my boy, Cammy, here."

"No problem, sir," said Rossy, as he pulled his Connecticut driver's license from his wallet and passed it over the bar to Leonard.

"This ain't Pennsylvania, man. It ain't phony, is it? If you dekin' me, I'll call the cops."

"No, no, it's good, sir. I used to be from Pennsylvania, but I moved to Connecticut and had to change licenses. It's real."

"He's good, Leonard, same age as me. We been homies forever," vouched Cam.

"OK, man. Enjoy," said Leonard, passing the license ID back across the bar.

"HEY, ROSSMAN, YOU PLAY TABLE BALL?"

"Yeah, a little. Mostly eight ball. I'm no good, though."

"WHOA! SOUND LIKE A HUSTLE TO ME! LESS GO, MAN!!"

They all moved back to an empty pool table, where Shelby threw an abe on the bumper and Rossman matched. Cam fed in four quarters and racked for eight ball, while the players picked sticks. On lag, Rossy left the cue less than a foot off the return and Shelby double bumped. Rossy's break sunk three balls - two stripes and a solid. There were no straight-in striper shots, so he took solid and proceeded to run through the eight.

"WHAT DA FRACK, MAN!!?? YOU AIN'T GIVIN' ME A SHOT?? DOUBLE IT UP, MOTHAFRACKA!!!"

Shelby slapped two more abes on the table over the unpicked two and Cam racked again. No balls dropped on break and it was Shelby's shot. Rossy was a decent eight ball player, especially on the smaller pay tables. He had cued up many, many hours from high school through Connecticut and knew how to strategically miss, which is what he did on the break. He noticed a bunch of other dudes in the back had circled around to see what kind of game this new boy was bringing. This was not the time to rerun the table. Shelby dunked a couple of stripes and missed a cross-side bank. The defender was lining up a long three ball to the corner, when a boisterous commotion directed all eyes to the front, near the door.

"SHELBY!!! WHERE YOU AT, SHELBY?? I KNOW YOU IN HERE!!!"

A large white guy with protruding midsection under a disheveled, gray sweat suit was making his way along the bar toward the back of the room. In the darkened environ he stumbled into a bar stool, noisily knocking it over. He nearly went down himself as his feet got tangled up in the metal legs. Angrily kicking the stool away into the adjacent wall, he spotted Shelby behind the corner table.

"I TOLD YOU BEFORE, BITCH, TO STAY AWAY FROM MY COUSIN!! SHE DON'T WANT NUTHIN' TO

DO WITH YOUR BLACK ASS!! NOW I GOT TO GIVE YOU SOME CONSEQUENCES, ASSHOLE!!!"

Off duty Millton Police Corporal Bryan Henke was very drunk. And he was obviously in a state of high dudgeon. He made a beeline around the end of the bar and headed directly toward the target of his mission in long, lunging steps of furious determination.

"I AIN'T SEEN YO' BUTT FACE, HO' COUSIN, HENKE! AND IF YOU DOAN BACK OFF, I'M GONNA CALL ME SOME *REAL* COPS!!!"

As a wide-eyed Shelby came forward to confront Henke, Cam stepped between the two and pushed Shelby back into the corner with one hand, while extending the other in Henke's face like a traffic cop signaling 'stop'.

"Whoa, slow down, cap! What's the problem, here? Chill, man!"

"THE PROBLEM IS IF YOU DON'T GET OUTTA MY WAY, I'LL RUN YOUR ASS IN ALONG WITH THIS FRACKIN' BOZO!!" His reddened face contorted in rage, Henke took a quick step backward, reached around behind under the sweatshirt, and shined his 9 mm service issue from a back holster beneath the waistband of his pants. **"NOW, YOU GOT A PROBLEM WITH THIS!??"**

Cam saw the gun snub pointed at his chest and froze in place. Rossy eased slowly over from where he was watching to stand between Cam and Shelby, never taking his eyes off Henke's threatening weapon. Shelby, emboldened by the two bodies buffering him from the raving cop, hollered, **"YOU BESS PUT DAT SHIT UP, MAN, OR MY ATTORNEYS, HERE, 'LL RIDE YO' ASS DA HO' WAY UP DA RIVVA TO LEWISBURG!!!"**

"WELL, WELL, WELL! WHAT HAVE I GOT HERE??! THREE PEAS IN A POD?? THE THREE MUS-KETEERS?? OR MAYBE JUST THE THREE FRACKING STOOGES WAITING TO GET HOOKED UP FOR OB-STRUCTING AND RESISTING ARREST!!"

By this time many of the bar patrons had slipped out of the door and vacated the premises. The situation looked like it might not end well and they wanted no part of it. A few others in the back remained, though they had carefully retreated to the far wall and tried to be inconspicuously attentive to the bizarre drama playing out before them. At least one man had his phone out recording video of the incident. Leonard had a hand on his own semi on a shelf under the bar and was intently watching the developments in the back to see if his intervention was necessary. He hoped he would probably only lift his piece if his own life was in danger. He did not want to be a player in this game. Then he thought he might have an obligation to the well being and safety of his customers, including Cam and the new kid he came in with. And maybe Shelby, too, though Shelby rolled in a trouble bubble and what happened to him, as often as not, could well be classified as self-inflicted. But the Lounge proprietor knew if he shot a cop in this town, no matter what the circumstances, he would never see the light of day again. It was all insanely complicated and he just wished everybody would leave so he could close up and go home.

Arrest?? I can't get arrested. Even wrongfully. That would kill my security clearance and my job!! I would be unemployed and homeless. Is this really happening to me?? What the hell's going on here?? And OH, CHRIST!! Look at that dude over there taking video!! Jesus fracking christ - I'm toast!! Rossy didn't think Henke would actually fire his gun, at least not on purpose, but he knew the wasted cop couldn't be safely agitated any more than he already was, so the best thing they should do is whatever the jackass wanted.

"OK, CHILDREN, LET'S MOVE!! SINGLE FILE! C'MON...HUP!!..HUP!!" Henke waved his gun arm in a circular motion in the direction of the door and waited for the trio to get past him, so he could fall in behind to funnel them forward along the bar and outside.

"WHAT DA FRACK YOU DOIN', MAN?!? YOU CAIN'T TAKE US OUT!! WE DIN DO NUTHIN'!!"

"SHUDDUP, CRACKHEAD!! MY LITTLE BUDDY, HERE, SAYS I CAN DO ANYTHING I WANT!! NOW MOVE IT!!!"

Shelby decided he couldn't immediately talk his way out of this fix and went uncharacteristically silent. He followed the attorneys, as ordered by the krazy keystone kop, deftly snatching the four abes from the end of the table as he shuffled past. He thought briefly about picking up a cue stick and whacking Henke into early retirement, but then figured it wasn't worth getting popped over.

So he just stayed in line and moved on by. When the odd little parade passed the onlookers still standing along the wall, Henke glared at the video taking guy and grabbed the phone out of his hand, threw it on the floor and stomped it into oblivion with his duty boot clad foot. *Thank you, jesus, thank you, lord!* Rossy felt a gushing relief that at least one record fragment of this freakish nightmare was destroyed. He guessed Henke realized there might be a lot to lose if video of his conduct reached the viral media. That showed rational thinking, meaning reason was somewhere nearby and with it a harmless settlement of any contrived dispute that was in progress here. Then all parties could go their respective ways as though nothing this weird ever happened.

Not so fast. First, Officer Henke had to whip it good. He shoved Shelby roughly forward into Rossy, who ricocheted into Cam, and the three nearly piled up on the floor in front of the juke box. Henke screamed at them to quit farting around and get their asses moving like they were told! When they reached the front, Henke directed them to go outside and 'assume the position' of hands and faces up against the wall to the right of the door. As soon as the four had cleared the room, Leonard ran out from behind the bar and over to the door. He slammed it shut locking the deadbolt as the latch engaged. Motioning for the remaining patrons in the back to get down and stay silent, he listened for any sound of activity outside. If he heard a gunshot he would call 911. If not, he would just wait until it seemed like the problem had possibly dissipated so he could take a peek to see what was going on. He did not want to open the door as long as that lunatic cop was still on the premises.

There was only one car in the lot. Henke knew Shelby had no ride, so he focused on the E-Towners. **"WHICH ONE OF YOU DICKHEAD ATTORNEYS IS DRIVIN'?!?"** The Civic man meekly raised a hand and Henke yanked him away from the wall by the back of his shirt. **"GET OVER THERE AND OPEN IT UP..... ALL FOUR DOORS, WIDE OPEN, BOZO,"** commanded Henke, **"AND THEN COME BACK HERE AND GIVE ME THE KEY!!"** As Rossy followed instructions, he started to feel lightheaded and out of breath. His pulse was accelerating and sweat was oozing out all over his body. All the classic symptoms of a major anxiety attack. And why not? He had never been forced to do anything at gunpoint before. He was in uncharted territory and stressing more than ever he could imagine. More than twice every negative experience in his life all rolled into one giant stress ball, threatening to flatten him like a freight train. Upon handing Henke the key, the obedient operator was ordered to go sit in the driver's seat and close his door. Henke then told Cam to get in at shotgun and close his door. He put Shelby in the back behind Cam, closed that door and scurried around and got in the back himself, behind the driver. After closing the last door, he ordered lock down and returned the key. **"LET'S GO, GENIUS!!"** shouted Henke, holding the gun up and waving it in a visible arc between the other three car occupants. Rossy asked where and Henke almost fired a round off through the ceiling of the car. **"TO THE GODDAM PRECINCT, NUMNUTS, WHERE THE FRACK DO YOU THINK?!?"** The wheel man said he didn't know where that was and Henke nearly ruptured an artery. **"JESUS CHRIST, ARE YOU PLAYIN' ME, BOY??! ON FOURTH AT MEETING PLACE!! NOW MOVE!!"** The out-of-towner still didn't know where that was and felt his anxiety stress start to upgrade to panic. Cam quietly said to calm down, not to worry, that he would give him turn by turn directions. The unstrung driver started the car, backed around and eased across the lot to the driveway. As they pulled out onto Front Street, Shelby started singing a grossly pitchy rendition of *Nobody Knows The Trouble I've Seen*. Henke told him to **"SHUT THE FRACK UP OR I'LL PLUG YOU RIGHT HERE, RIGHT NOW!!"** Meanwhile, Leonard hustled his sequestered loungesters out of the bar, secured the register, pocketed his handgun, turned off the lights, locked the door and disappeared into the night.

Rossy blocked off the outside world and concentrated only on following Cam's turning directions. He felt almost like he did during the emergency landing in Allentown, when the air seemed heavy, sounds were distantly muffled and everything was moving in slow motion. He wasn't sure he should be driving a car under these conditions. After what had to be hours, but was really only a few minutes, they approached the Millton Police Precinct Headquarters, in the Public Safety Center. Situated between the Town Hall and a General Municipal Services building, it looked like a converted motel with a canopied driveway at the main entrance. Henke ordered the car parked in front of the entrance and the engine turned off. He then told the front seaters to get out and go stand by the door. With his gun on Shelby, who was mumbling continuous conversation to himself in a strangely whispered voice, Henke unwedged from the back seat of the car and loudly ordered Shelby to slide over and get out on the same side. He marched Shelby over to the waiting twosome and directed them all inside. They entered a small office, that was the modified lobby and check-in area of the old motel, occupied by two uniformed officers and a civilian dispatch operator. The officers looked up at the incoming group of men and instantly fixated on Henke and his weapon pointed at the three in front of him.

"Whatcha got, there, Bryan?" inquired one of the officers, glancing nervously at the other to confirm his gut that they might have a situation on their hands.

"I GOT ME A HALF A SIX PACK, BROTHER BLUE, AND THIS ONE'S GOING STRAIGHT BACK TO THE COOLER!!" shouted Henke, roughly pushing Shelby in the direction of a heavy steel door, with barred plexiglass observation port and keypad lock, in the corner of the back wall.

"YOU CAIN'T LOCK ME UP, MAN, I DIN FRACKIN' DO NUTHIN'!!!"

"HARASSMENT, THREATENING AN OFFICER OF THE LAW AND RESISTING ARREST, FOR STARTERS, ASSHEAD!! YOU GOT THE RIGHT TO REMAIN SILENT AND I WISH THE FRACK YOU WOULD!! NOW MOVE!!" Henke poked Shelby in the back with the nose of his gun and again shoved him toward the security door.

"Whoa! Whoa! Whoa! Bryan! Hold up, there, man. You know you can't take a weapon back into housing. Give me your gun, man!" yelled the lead uniform, jumping from his desk and running over to the secure area access.

"OH, YEAH, YOU RIGHT! I FORGOT!" conceded Henke, handing his weapon to the duty cop. **"BUT DON'T LET THOSE OTHER TWO GO!! I AIN'T THROUGH WITH THEM!! I BE RIGHT BACK!!"** Henke punched the key code and the lock clicked. He opened the door and plunked Shelby through to the holding cell area, which used to be the motel's breakfast dinette. The regular cells, through another sally port door on the other side of the room, were the old guest rooms that had been converted to various degrees of secure housing as specified in the recent modification project. This project was managed by the county, under consent order of the U. S. Department of Justice, to replace the 19th century county detention center declared to be in violation of hundreds of provisions of modern federal statute pertaining to correctional facilities. The project had been wildly successful in that it satisfied all the requirements of the consent order at a fraction of the cost of a new facility. The motel had been a downtown franchise unit of a national chain that used to serve visiting clients and business people associated with the steel company, whose office headquarters was next door in the four story building now utilized by municipal administration employees. When steel bailed, the motel eventually went under and both properties became available for next to nothing. The retrofit of the motel into a detention center, housing primarily pretrial inmates booked by both the county and the borough, attracted national attention for its innovative reuse of commercial 'brown zone' property. Officially dedicated as 'The Millton Public Safety Center', it was locally dubbed, from the beginning, as 'Hotel California'.

Henke called the control center on an intercom box and and requested HC-A door to be opened. The control operator, in the County Sheriff's office at the other end of the building, verified the intercom request through video surveillance and unlocked the cell door. Shelby entered quietly, but began a loud, ranting stream of obscene protest as soon as the cell door closed and locked behind him. Henke smiled to himself and walked over to the sally port door and punched the key code to exit back into the precinct office. Rossy and Cam were still standing where they had stopped after entering from outside, not having said a word to anyone, not even each other. They could hear Shelby screaming from the holding cell when Henke opened the sally port door and then abrupt silence when the door was re-closed. Henke sauntered slowly across the room to his remaining detainees intending to explain how he was going to ruin their day. He did not recognize them and had no idea who they were or where they were from, but he just plain out didn't like their wimpy-assed looks and wanted to let them know, in no uncertain terms, whose town this was. He wanted to scare them shitless and maybe lock *them* up, too, depending how they reacted. Before he could get a word out, the duty officer-in-charge appeared on the other side of 'beavis and butthead' and motioned for Henke to follow him over to the desk.

"We'll take it from here, Bryan. You're off duty and you've been drinking. Go on home and get some rest."

"WHAT ARE YOU TALKING ABOUT!?? THEY'RE MY COLLARS!! I BROUGHT 'EM IN, SO LET ME BOOK 'EM!!"

"No, can't do that. Do you need a ride? We'll be happy to drive you over to your place."

"NO, I DON'T NEED NO GODDAM RIDE!! GIMME BACK MY PIECE!!"

"Bryan, I think we'll just hold that here until you come back on. You don't need a gun right now, you need to get some sleep. So, we'll see you, Monday, OK?"

Henke scowled at the OIC and knew he had no choice but to comply with the more or less direct order to leave. Without a word, he spun around, walked across the room looking straight ahead, went through the door and was gone.

The OIC exhaled a deep sigh of *thank god that's over* and turned toward the silent statues. He looked at them for several seconds and asked them to come over to his desk and take seats in front of him. "Names, please, and IDs," he said, in an official, administrative processing tone. They each recited and spelled their full names, while reaching for their wallets and driver's licenses. The OIC wrote their names on a pad and compared them with the IDs. He handed the IDs to the other officer and requested him to run them through central data check for any outstanding warrants or other irregularities. Facing back to the implausible pair, he asked them to relate exactly what had transpired to bring them before him this evening. Cam took the lead and provided a detailed account of the events preceding their arrival in the precinct. He tried to stick with facts without sounding overly biased against Officer Henke's woefully illegal behavior.

"Mr. Rossy, do you concur with what Mr. Cambaugh has said?"

"Yes, sir, I do."

"OK, gentlemen, I believe we have a misunderstanding, here, and I apologize for any inconvenience you might have experienced. But let me offer a bit of off-the-record advice. I don't think you need to be coming down here from Ebbottown for your Saturday night's entertainment. As you are probably aware, Millton has its unique problems and is going through harder times than most places right now. The people here are struggling and prone to poor judgement when interacting with non-locals they might perceive to be, shall we say, less unfortunate. It's a bad mix and could easily lead to serious trouble. So, in a nutshell, unless you have legitimate business here, stay the hell out of Millton." The OIC returned the licenses and dismissed the E-town infiltrators with a generic 'have a nice evening'.

The would-be-collars simultaneously muttered, "thank you, sir", exited the precinct and got into the Civic. Rossy was starting to regain his emotional stability as realization set in that he was not going to be arrested. He thought it odd that he would feel elated relief over escaping this potentially disastrous predicament unscathed, rather than being furious for having his basic constitutional rights so throughly macerated by a drunken purveyor of the law. Maybe he could do outrage under different circumstances, but right now he had to stay under the radar and not make blips...not until he got his clearance and settled into the new job. Cam did not seem at all scathed. He acted like it was just another Saturday night on the town, no big deal that they almost got shot, or falsely arrested and jailed. Cam had always been a 'nothing-to-lose' kind of guy. He would probably have made an excellent combat military man, had they let him stay in. "What about Shelby? Are they just going to keep him locked up for nothing?" wondered beavis, thinking about violation of rights. "Nah, Shelb'll be fine," advised butthead. "They'll give him something to eat. He'll get a good night's sleep and they'll turn him out in the morning. Don't worry about Shelby." In leaving the precinct, they retraced the incoming route. Approaching Front Street they saw a large collection of people, maybe fifty, or more, congregated about a block away from Leonard's. It did not seem like a party crowd, nor one, Cam surmised, that should see the two E-townsters driving around free, while Shelby was still in the hole. He told Rossy to duck down a side street, rather than go past the gathering mob on Front. *Oh, yeah, Shelby will definitely be better off staying at the Hotel for right now, because it looked like Millton was in for a long, hard night.*

Soon they were on the two-lane highway back to Ebbottown and clear of the turmoil left behind. They rode in silence most of the way, Cam eventually speaking to observe how slowly his pal was driving at the literal speed limit. He said the real limit was about twenty mph faster. Seemingly on cue to emphasize his point, an eighteen wheeler glided up behind and followed so closely that the headlights couldn't be seen over the trunk of the little car. The truckster started blinking his high beams and blasting the air horn to urge the turtle to go faster. Rossy slowed down because he didn't want the semi-rig running through them at full speed, if that was the driver's end game. With nowhere to pass, the big boy put his lights on full high and laid on the horn, as he loudly and angrily down shifted to slower speed. Cam sunk low in his seat, afraid the dude might open fire in a fit of road rage. Right when it appeared they apparently were destined to become pavement plop, they entered the reduced speed zone of Ebbottown's city limits. The cautious one immediately slowed to the posted limit forcing rigman to brake, while he downshifted, high beamed and air horned about two feet off the Civic's back bumper. This was how they passed the EPD roadrunner parked behind a hedge along the property line of an out-of-business drive-in restaurant. In the mirror, Rossy saw the cruiser fly out onto the road behind the truck, blue strobes flashing, and then saw both vehicles pull off at the end of the restaurant lot. He continued into town, smugly mentioning to Cam that had he been going faster, he, too, would have been yanked by the speed trapping cop. Cam didn't say anything, thinking it strange how, sometimes, last guys finished first. When they got to Cam's place, the two old friends said their good byes and good lucks, vowing to stay in contact and look each other up whenever possible. The survivor drove back through town to his mom's house, already feeling considerably lucky in escaping the night's potential for career or life ending catastrophe.

Mom was still up, working in her study, or, more likely, feeling instinctive parental duty to maintain vigil until one of her own was safely back in the fold. "You're coming in a little late, Billy. Did you have a good time?" she greeted with false complacency.

"Yeah, mom, Cam and I just had a few beers and a pizza at The Inn. Nothing special. We caught up on what's going on, saw a couple other guys we knew, shot some pool. You know, just hangin' out. I'm whipped, though, so I think I'll turn in. See you tomorrow."

"Night, Billy."

***

Rossy planned to spend the next couple of days working around the house and relaxing before repacking his car and shoving off for D.C. about the middle of the week. He had not really thought much, at least not continuously, about the road ahead, but knew, as the day of reckoning approached, he would start to go into major stress mode. There had been no contact with Booker since leaving Connecticut and, of course, there had never been any direct contact with his alleged new employer, the U.S. Navy. *Jesus christ, what kind of corner have I boxed myself into??* he wondered during weak moments of impure thoughts. *And no back-up plan! No way out!* Then he would readjust by remembering there was nothing, at this point, he could do about the future. It would be what it would be. He could only deal with unanticipated adversities as they happened, winging it as he went. But, goddam, until then, please stay out of problem situations that could cause hassles or ruin everything. *Just lay low the rest of the week and don't take chances.* At least he could control failure *before* the future did him in.

On Sunday afternoon, Rossy's mom mentioned that he should visit his grandfather before he left for Washington. He considered this, wondering what possible jeopardy it could lead to. Such a diversion was not on his immediate no risk agenda, but he didn't see any harm in it. Besides, it seemed important to his mom and he hadn't seen the old guy since graduation. So, sure, he would go see grandpap, no problem.

Grandpap Rossy lived in a public housing apartment in Harrisburg. He received supplemental social security benefits, intermittent support from his surviving son, the dentist, and whatever welfare resources he could score as a poverty level citizen of the commonwealth. Grandpap had essentially gone through life as functionally unemployable, never holding any kind of a career resembling job. He was extremely intelligent, in a PhD orientated way, having completed a hodge-podge itinerary of courses at a variety of institutions and universities, including a history and philosophy curriculum for two years at Juniata College and a year of language study at the University of Munich. His study in Munich featured courses in Russian, conducted in German, in which he had been fluent since high school. He took several continuing education courses in basic business and investment fundamentals at Wharton School of Business at the University of Pennsylvania and even took a course in bay fishing at Chesapeake Community College, in Easton, Maryland. But his education never added up to a marketable degree and he bounced from one temporary gig to another, half expecting to be drafted into the military, deployed to Viet Nam and killed while on some futile, night patrol to hell. Fortunately, his draft board didn't do much drafting, possibly because its constituents were mostly religious pacifists, and he never got the call. He wasn't religious, not necessarily a pacifist, definitely not a volunteer, but he evidently was lucky. So he settled on flea marketing as his vocation of choice. He always knew in the back of his mind that he would find that one forgotten Monet or Picasso, or maybe an early government document signed by George Washington, or an autographed Beatles album, stuffed in the side batting of an old storage trunk he would buy for less than a jack. Basically his livelihood and retirement plan were always akin to winning the lotto, which, predictably, never happened. He spent a lot of money buying and selling junk, ultimately at a net loss, eventually leading to a failed marriage and a hoarding psychosis. Grandma had left grandpap years ago, when she accurately concluded their financial bus was speeding toward a fiscal cliff. She moved to Albuquerque to live with her maiden sister, a modestly successful artist of high desert scenery. After the divorce, grandpap's collecting obsession reached critical mass and Rossy's mom and uncle finally had to help him clear his apartment to avoid eviction. Grandpap had been very helpful to Rossy's family following his dad's death, doing considerable repair and modification work on their house and giving little Billy extra attention in guiding him through the loss of a parent. The boy's mom had really appreciated the assistance during this rough period in their lives and had kept in close contact with grandpap ever since. And she wanted her son to do the same. It was a family thing.

Actually, Rossy was looking forward to the visit. The last time they had spent quality time together was the summer before the Adirondack juvie camp banishment. They made several two or three day trips to the Allegheny National Forest in north central Pennsylvania, where grandpap had membership in a hunting and fishing club called 'Red Bear Lodge'. The camp, accessible only by old logging roads, was in a remote wilderness area above a small village along Pine Creek, in the heart of Pennsylvania's prime fly fishing country. And that was the purpose of the trips -

to teach Billy how to fly fish for native brook and brown trout. Grandpap had been fairly well known through the mid-state area as an expert angler. He tied his own flies and, back in the day, made a little money guiding fishing trips for urban indoorsmen. The young student learned basic techniques of casting and rigging on Pine Creek before they went up into the little trout runs to fish. The streams were too small for drifting wet flies with the current, so they only used dries, a much more difficult fishing genre. The trout always faced upstream, so you had to cast the fly, usually an impossibly tiny black gnat, from downstream, to land softly on the water, ahead of the leader and above the fish. This required an extremely careful approach to a hole, to get into position to be able to cast, under and through overhanging bushes and tree branches, without the fish detecting any intrusive presence. If the cast was good, the trout would hit as soon as the fly touched water. If not, it was time to move on upstream to the next hole. Grandpap had explained he sometimes spent more than an hour preparing for a single cast, getting situated and waiting until lighting and wind parameters were exactly right. He said no matter how diligent or skilled one was in presenting a fly, the result was, way more often than not, zilch. A perfect cast drawing a strike was only half the battle. The fish would reject the fake fly immediately upon striking, so reaction to the strike had to be almost simultaneous. The object was setting the hook without whipping the fly out of the fish's mouth and sending it up into a tree, where it would irretrievably lodge forever, or until it corroded into dust. If you were fortunate enough to get a good hook, you then had to very attentively navigate the furious thrasher through a fast water maze of rocks and crevices to a point where you could either net it, if you were going to keep it, or unhook it, if you wanted to release it. Most people fortunate enough to catch a wild trout wanted to keep it, not only to show someone else, but to prepare as a pan fried delicacy.

Up in the bush, grandpap would drop his grandboy off along an unnamed dirt road and tell him to meet him about a mile upstream in six hours, or so. The youngster would then have to scramble down a deep ravine a few hundred feet to get to the run, where he would be completely isolated in the middle of nowhere, with no communication to the outside world. The only sounds were the cascading rill water and maybe a rustling breeze through the trees. Sometimes these sounds were indistinguishable from each other. There were no traffic or engine noises of human activity. He couldn't even hear any birds. He had his lunch and water in a backpack, the Cortland #7 graphite fly rod, leader and flies grandpap had given him and a fierce determination to catch a fish. He had no idea where he was, but knew he could not get lost if he stayed with the water and followed the stream. The first few excursions Rossy spent most of the day untangling his line from itself and surrounding vegetation. He rarely even landed a fly in the water. There was nothing to show grandpap when they rendezvoused, though the old master would always have at least a couple of half pounders. So it was fresh trout for dinner every night, hand cleaned by Billy and sautéed by the beer buzzed mentor.

On the final day of the last trip of the summer, with pure, unobstructed early morning sunlight filtering through the forest canopy from a glorious weather high, Rossy found himself ready to make a perfect cast. The target pool lay in a swath of shade about twenty yards in front of him, below a relatively sizable falls. He knew, feeling to the deepest sense of his consciousness, that he could light the fly onto the surface about an inch from the cascading white water at the top of the pool. Already anticipating the violent hit about to consume his little micro gnat, he swirled the line forward and back, forward and back, paying out length each cycle from the small spindle reel at the end of his rod, until there was exactly the right amount of line in the air to make the cast. On the final loop he let the line arc forward, like a pitcher delivering a blooper change-up, and waited for the fly to flitter down from behind and above to the water below. But then he saw the line go over a tree branch and knew his perfect cast was about to become a snarled, irreversible mess that would probably end up in loss of leader and the fly. He cursed loudly and splashed angrily through the water, reeling in line as he moved toward the point of entanglement. Upon reaching the overhanging branch, he couldn't reel any more slack, as the line was hopelessly entwined among the leaves and sprigs of a branchlet high above his head. He grabbed a lower portion of the branch to pull it down so he could access and free the line, but noticed it was taut on the other side of the snarl. Assuming another area of complication he followed the line out of the foliage and saw that it went into the middle of the pool, where it was moving through the water in jerky, random patterns. Sud-

denly a large fish leapt at least two feet out of the water and headed downstream when it fell back in, taking the line as it swam. The
neophyte flyman realized he had somehow hooked a trout with the
errant cast. Tossing his rod aside into the bushes below the snag
tree, he went sloshing after the bobbing line. He pulled it back
hand over hand and finally got to the leader, which he eased over
to the bank so he could retrieve the catch in the flat gravelly shallows. It was a beauty - a sixteen inch brownie, speckled with gray
ringed red and black spots around a bright amber underbelly. His
first fly fishing trophy. Trembling with excited pride, he put the
trout in his backpack, unraveled the tangled rigging from the tree
branchlet and headed upstream to find grandpap. In reviewing
what had happened so he could get the sequence of events straight
in his own mind, Billy knew he had not performed a perfect cast.
But if there was a strike, which obviously there was, the fly must
have landed perfectly on the water above the fish. And since there
was a hook, somehow there must have been a perfect reaction to
the strike. None of these components of the catch would have occurred had he not made the cast, perfect or otherwise. So, when it
was all considered in context, he had actually made a perfect cast,
because, if the end result, the trout in the backpack, is the only
criterion that mattered, there could be many different paths of perfection. That was his story and he was sticking to it.

That evening the area forest ranger, a good friend of
grandpap's, stopped by the RBL to say hello. Grandpap told him
about Billy's breakthrough angling success, showing off the evidence laid out in the cooler, and marveled at how quickly the boy
had picked up on the fine art of fly fishing. The ranger praised the
accomplishment and asked if they had seen any timber rattlers,
advising that the snakes were unusually prolific this year. He requested they shoot any they came across in the bush. After the
ranger left, grandpap gave Billy a beer, saying if he was old
enough to gun down a rattlesnake, he was old enough to drink a
beer. Rossy had really enjoyed those fishing trips, though he
hadn't much continued his development as a fly fisherman since
then.

***

Monday morning, Rossy set out for Harrisburg to see
grandpap. He called yesterday to coordinate the visit and planned

to take him to lunch and spend the afternoon just hanging out and talking, or doing whatever the old man wanted to do. Maybe helping with some chores or running errands. He took the interstate from north of Ebbottown, even though it was further than the parallel old highway through Millton. Having been thrown out of Millton, he would never go there again. *What the frack was that all about, anyway? How can you get run out of a town? That's like the old west, or something, a hundred fifty years ago. What a shithole. Why in hell does Cam hang there? Guess because E-town is worse? Whatever.* He got to Harrisburg about eleven o'clock and followed the GPS directions through the downtown area to Harris Heights, the public housing complex for seniors where grandpap resided. Harrisburg looked like a big Ebbottown. There had recently been a major revitalization effort to upscale the downtown, but it fizzled with the great recession and the city's subsequent bankruptcy. Now there were mostly boarded up buildings, many in various stages of incomplete rehab or upgrade. There was some commercial activity, though few people on the sidewalks. He drove by a couple of pawn shops, a tattoo and tanning salon, a Chinese carryout, a state store, a gun and knife mart and a tobacco and newspaper stand, en route to HH on a large property at the end of the wide street he was on, which tee'd with another boulevard heading uptown. Harris Heights appeared as dismal as its name might suggest. A six story, flat roofed brick box, that never looked better than the day its construction was completed, the facility was about as inviting as a depot warehouse. Rossy parked on the street, in the only available space he could find, under a large Bradford pear tree filled with squabbling birds. He walked through the driveway opening in a rusted wrought iron perimeter fence surrounding the site and across a circular patio littered with flattened old gum wads and cigarette butts. A bevy of rough looking elderly women in night robes and slippers sat smoking on a trash filled concrete planter in the middle of the patio. They eyed him suspiciously as he strode by toward the front entranceway. Adjacent to the corroding steel framed glass doors, a security attendant sat in a transparent booth with a small brass speaker box over a transfer tray at about waist level. The guard asked his purpose and for ID. Rossy leaned over to give grandpap's name and apartment number as destination info, while slipping his driver's license into the tray. After a moment and return of the license, the door clicked and he passed through the weather foyer into the lobby. He was immediately stifled by the heat. It must have been 85 degrees inside the large square room - much hotter than outside. The center of the lobby was furnished with a cluster of torn and taped black pleather easy chairs around a cracked glass covered coffee table. A floral patterned settee was placed along the middle of the similarly floral patterned wall on each side of the room, flanked by small wooden stands holding urns of dusty, plastic ivy plants. On the walls above the settees were huge, gaudily framed prints of painted bowls of fruit and vases of flower bouquets. The far corners were occupied by a massive artificial fern plant on one side and a giant replica of a large leafed tropical shrub on the other. Dark, open hallways to the interior stretched straightaway from either side of the entrance doors. The worn, olive brown floor carpet was badly in need of replacement, or at least steam cleaning, and the suspended ceiling was missing about ten acoustic panels, windows to the building's ducting, piping and conduit infrastructure. Despite the overwhelming depressing character of the decor, several people were sitting in the lobby, mindlessly passing time, when the stranger entered. They stared at him with squinting intensity as he nervously glanced around, looking for an egress to the upper levels. Grandpap was on the fourth floor. Spotting elevators on the far side of the room, he started across the open lobby area, aware of all eyes following his every move. He felt like a foreigner in another country where he did not blend in, like when he went into Leonard's Lounge the other night. While waiting for the elevator, he noticed a greasy paned doorway into a small courtyard that was overgrown with grass, weeds and dead blooms around a dried up garden pond. Beside the courtyard door was a crumbling cork bulletin board tacked with emergency contacts and scores of residential 'dos and don'ts' posted by building management, as well as a torn and yellowed copy of federal regulations pertaining to public housing facilities. What a slag of a place to live, he thought as he entered the ostensibly seldom cleaned elevator cab. Tapping '4' with his elbow, he wondered if grandpap was okay here.

The heavily smudged and dented black metal door of 437 opened shortly after the first knock and Rossy stood face to face with his old grandpap. "Well, how you doin', Billy Boy? Great to see you! C'mon in! C'mon in!" greeted the elder with a broad, warm smile. He looked about the same as last time Rossy had seen him, maybe just slightly older. Still had the same gray, jaw framing beard and mustache, trimmed to precision, and longish gray hair, combed back from the sides and his balding front pate to fall over the collar line.

"Doin' fine, grandpap, how're you doin'?" Rossy grabbed the old man's extended hand and gave him a strong hug and pat on the back. "Good to see you, too. Been a while, hey?" They moved in from the hallway and grandpap shut the door. They stood in a fairly sizable living room, well lighted from many lamps and an undraped glass slider to a small deck balcony directly across from the front door. The caller noticed a tiny kitchen off to the left from the balcony and a short alcove, presumably to the bedroom and bathroom from the right. But what really caught his eye was the stuff. Everywhere, stuff. Newspaper and magazine stacks three or four feet high, amid piles of what almost looked like collected debris from a natural disaster. Old tools, toys, dishes, furniture, knick-knacks, collectibles, glassware, metalware, books, sporting equipment, machines, gadgets, clocks, jewelry, clothing, artwork, pottery, records, electronics, boxes, storage trunks and a million other unidentifiables were scattered in random order throughout the room and into the auxiliary areas. Even the little balcony was filled up to the railing. Narrow strategic pathways through the junk provided the only way to move around the apartment.

"Yeah, sorry about the clutter. Haven't had a chance to straighten up for a while," said grandpap, noticing the boy's dropmouthed look-around. "We can sit down over here." Along the wall on the right side of the room was a clear, open area covered with a magnificent Turkish carpet rug, featuring a circle of fierce blue dragons spewing red and yellow plumes of jagged flame. Two hickory branch rocking chairs, with thick pillowed seats, perched on the carpet facing the wall about eight feet away. A hand carved teak low table, with a small ceramic lamp in the center, separated the chairs. On the wall, above a long, narrow buffet cabinet, was a 60" curved screen, hi-def TV. A pedestal lamp stood at each end of the buffet. Further down along the wall, toward the bedroom hall alcove, was an upright piano that appeared to be in decent shape with an attractive, well polished black walnut finish. Rossy sat in one of the chairs, while grandpap retreated to get a couple of PBRs. *Jesus christ, how can he live like this? He must be losing it. What a fracking landfill!*

They spent the next hour talking about incidentals, updating each other on what was happening in their respective lives. Regrettably, neither had been fishing in some time, but that didn't mean they had hung up their rods. They would get out there again. Grandpap was wondering about the new job Billy was interested in, mentioning that his mom had some concerns. "Well, I'm a little more than interested in it, grandpap", said Billy. "I actually accepted the job offer and I'm supposed to report for work next Monday." He went on to explain why he couldn't be very specific or talk about more details related to his new career endeavor.

"I dunno, son, sounds like it could be a scam, or something. You know how the government is. They lie all the time and then just duck into some kind of camouflage cover so you don't know what the hell is going on. I'd be very careful, if I was you."

God, everybody I talk to about this calls it a goddam scam! Are they all being controlled by remote? I'm not going to discuss it with anyone else. That's it!! Rossy changed the subject and asked how grandpap liked living here. He didn't know exactly how to bring up the obvious elephant in the room - the junk. Or more specifically, how much more junk could he accumulate before facing eviction again? And, how will it be removed if and when it came to that? The collector apparently didn't recognize the possibility of a problem, if he thought his apartment was only a little 'cluttered'. He said he liked it here, but the tenants drove him nuts. They were always spying on each other, watching everything everybody else was involved in. He felt they sometimes acted like little grade school kids, tattling to the manager whenever someone did something out of the norm or what they perceived to be against the rules. And then they were forever trying to get him involved in their activities that he had absolutely no interest in. Like their ridiculous card and board games. Bid euchre, mah jongg, hand and foot. What the hell were those? And monopoly, for chrissake! When was the last time you played monopoly, when you were eight? But the worst were the women! They thought every apartment should have a wreath of fake flowers on the hall door, to brighten the place up. So far he has removed at least three unwanted wreaths from his door. He was also perturbed by their politics, saying they were mostly republican bigots. This was a puzzle, because every last one of them took social security and medicare, which republicans were on an eternal mission from god to abolish. Speaking of god, many of the residents considered 437 some kind of 'other', a special agent of the devil, because he didn't subscribe to their biblical fantasies. If they wanted to believe that religious palaver, fine, but don't try to force it on someone else. He also wished they would keep their medical conditions to themselves. Everyone he talked to somehow drifted to a chronology of personal maladies and medications within a few minutes of conversation. He didn't give a damn about any of that crap! They all ate prescription drugs like candy and were obviously crock cooking their brains into taupe mush. But, yeah, grandpap *did* like it here. It was near a nice riverwalk park. The people on the street were interesting and friendly and all the stores and shops he needed were in close proximity.

All of a sudden a cacophony of clock gongs, from various unseen sources around the room, signaled the twelve o'clock hour. Rossy started in hearing the unexpected discordance and checked the time on his phone. Lunchtime, and he was starving, since he had skipped breakfast. He suggested they go out somewhere to get something to eat, adding it was his tab. Grandpap said sounds good and they both rose up from the comfortable rockers. Before they left, the boy asked him if he played piano, gesturing toward the old upright. He said a little, but not very well. Rossy requested a sample, but grandpap demurred. "C'mon," pressed Billy. "Alright," said grandpap, reluctantly, as he slid onto the bench in front of the keyboard. He cut loose with an astonishingly smooth riff of jazzy blues improv that left Rossy dumbfounded. "Wow, grandpap, that was sweet," he spluttered. "Can you sing with that?" There was nothing cooler than an old bluesman, the older the better. Steven Tyler trying to rock at sixty five years old was not very pretty, but B. B. King harmonizing with Lucille at eighty five was beautiful. Mr. King never made his move too soon. "No, Billy Boy, I don't sing. Let's go to lunch."

As they exited the elevator and went across the lobby toward the entrance foyer, the same contingent of oldsters who had stood sentry earlier, when Rossy arrived, were still on duty. They didn't miss a step as the two made their way through the doors and out of the building. "Watchy, watchy," said grandpap, contemptuously. "The old fools are always watching!" Outside, he guided the direction to the right onto a sidewalk paralleling the front of the facility around to a parking lot off the north side. They were walking through the well shaded parking area toward the uptown boulevard, when Rossy saw an old white Dodge Ram truck parked by itself in a remote space along the far edge of the lot. "Is that your truck, grandpap?" he asked, zagging over for a closer look. "Yep, same one, Billy," said the owner, with a hint of embarrassment. "Fraid it's seen better days, though." Approaching the vehicle, Rossy noticed all four tires were flat, so he didn't ask if it still ran. He saw the familiar faded decal on the rear window proclaiming "A BAD DAY FISHING BEATS A GOOD DAY WORKING" over a huge rainbow trout arching out of the water with an oversized fly hooked on its lip at the end of a high taut line from the rod of a minuscule, grinning fisherman way in the background. This was the same truck that had carried them through the wilds of Allegheny about ten years ago. Grandpap said he had not driven in some time because he refused to pay the exorbitant insurance premiums and the registration had consequently expired. Plus the cost of gas was just "too damn high". He said he really didn't want or need to drive. There were too many crazies on the road and everything he had to get was within walking or bus distance. However, there was a problem with HH management. They notified him, via certified letter a few months ago, that the truck had to be removed from the lot by the end of the year, or it would be towed to auction impoundment. He was debating whether to get the insurance, reregister the truck and repair it back into useful condition, or, try to sell it as is, or, just let the apartment goonies steal it. Rossy suggested a fourth option would be to donate it to the Salvation Army. They would come and take it away, fix it up and give it to some worthy, needy person, like an out of work plumber or contractor, who could use it to get back on his feet. The old man instantly liked that idea and decided that was what he would do. On that note they turned away from the dead truck and continued down the parking lot, passing a stately row of towering willow oaks, and exited the HH grounds toward the uptown district. Rossy couldn't help but wonder to himself how grandpap ever got all that stuff to his apartment without a truck.

After a couple of blocks they came to a relatively appealing pedestrian plaza off the boulevard. There was a variety of shops and cafes around the plaza and a significant lunchtime crowd was meandering about, relaxing in the midday sun. A central fountain pool was spewing water high into the air, projecting a colorful myriad of refracted sunlight, and a muffled drone of classic elevator music issued from hidden speakers. Grandpap pointed to a small restaurant adjacent to a service alley that looked like the back end of a caboose car on an old railway train. Fryin' Freddy's was the name of the place and they took an outside table near the narrow entrance boardwalk across the front of the vivid red building. "Best burgers in town," declared grandpap. "But not as good as your dad's." Rossy's dad, with his partner, Badler, had a hamburger house in Chambersburg. They had perfected a unique oven rotisserie procedure for cooking specialty burgers, they called 'chamburgers'. The burger patties were impaled on an open drum, consisting of a circular horizontal configuration of six, eighth-inch diameter steel spears. They were continuously spray basted with a proprietary marinade sauce as the spear drum slowly rotated. The drippings were caught in a sump below the drum from which they were vacuum pumped to a centrifuge, where the fat was drawn off and the marinade recycled to the spray baster. They had three oven centrifuge assemblies, each with three drums, and each drum could hold ten patties. So, they could simultaneously cook ninety burgers using up to nine different marinade recipes. The raw burger patties were prepared with lean, grass fed beef and a secret blend of seasonings and egg whites to maintain consistency while cooking. The result was essentially fat free burgers that were moist, coherent and delicious. The chamburgers were so popular they could charge nearly four times the price of fast food joint burgers and still have people lined up out the door to get in. Rossy's Rotisserie was quickly overrun by demand and plans were initiated to open a second, larger house. They also had patent pending on the equipment, which was custom designed and fabricated, under contract, by an engineer friend of Badler's. Then dad got sick and died and mom's half share of the business was bought by Badler. At a huge, coerced discount, always thought grandpap and his surviving son, the dentist. All of this was ahead of Rossy's memory arc. He didn't have much reminiscence of the restaurant and had never gone there as an adult. He knew there was now a whole chain of Rossy's Rotisserie restaurants in the south central area of the state and assumed Badler was probably very successful. He often wondered what would have happened if his dad had not prematurely passed away. He couldn't imagine he would be working in a burger place, but who knew? Following lunch the two took a leisurely stroll along the river greenway, before returning to the apartment, where grandpap said he had something he wanted to show Billy.

As they settled back into the rocker pad with another round of PBRs, grandpap pulled a touch pad from a shallow drawer of the buffet under the big screen. He sat down, brushed a control on the pad and the screen came to life. A huge still of a star spangled eagle in flight appeared over a backdrop of the Milky Way. Quarter sized icons lined the bottom of the screen. Rossy recognized most of them, but some were unfamiliar. Grandpap moved a two inch curser from the pad control and clicked on an icon showing an old style TV with little rabbit ear antennas sticking up behind it. The big screen blipped and CNN was on, reporting the top story of the current news cycle - yet another flareup between Israel and the Palestinians in Gaza. Revolving video showed rocket damaged concrete buildings surrounded by people picking through the rubble. Emergency vehicles, klaxons blaring, were meandering their way through the confusion, as a field reporter excitedly told the camera what was going on. Grandpap clicked again and the screen blipped to another news channel, reporting the same story. After a moment a commercial came on for a biotic medication to help you shit better and he flipped back to the opening screen. He clicked on the WWW icon and there was internet.

So, the old guy had a full service, big screen TV computer. Rossy was impressed, though instantly concerned, knowing the unit likely cost upwards of ten grand. Grandpap recounted that he got the TVC about six months ago and it literally changed his life. Confirming it was very expensive, he proudly reported it was fully paid for and his new most valuable possession. His old most valuable possession was a prefaced and autographed limited first edition copy of an obscure Thomas Hardy novel, in excellent condition, that he had found in a bin of books, for fifty cents each, in the back upstairs of a local thrift store. The hand written preface, dated June 15, 1895, urged the 'dear reader' to "enjoy the book, because it might be one of the last available pleasures in a world destined for church inspired damnation and ruin". Grandpap had the book, note and autograph authenticated and assessed, at a retail value of $15,000 - $18,000. He was able to sell it on net auction for $12,500, enough to buy the TVC with several grand to spare. He was using this money to pay for cable and internet services. Good deal! The old man had finally gotten a piece of the pie in junk lottery world.

Grandpap asked if Billy knew his heritage, expecting, of course, he probably couldn't even recite his great grandpap's name. True enough, confirmed Billy, and grandpap proceeded to tell him who he was. Native American. They were all Indians! He had researched the Rossy family on MyAncestors.com and found the original Rossy in America was one Jierre Rossineau, who fled France in 1690, with a boatload of fellow Huguenots, for the new world. They first touched ashore on the southern beach of what is now the Delmarva Peninsula, near a dual settlement of escaped African slaves and Lenape Indians. The Huguenots got on well with the people of the settlements, but found the area too desolate and opted to continue southward. Except Jierre, who didn't want to spend any more time at sea and decided to stay. His compatriots departed after a few weeks and eventually drifted into the Gulf of Mexico, settling in the bayou wastelands of Louisiana. Jierre was a hard worker and assimilated well into the village fabric of life, though it took some time to learn to communicate effectively with his new friends and neighbors. In the course of this mutual learning curve, his name was shortened to the easier 'Rossy'. He developed a strong friendship with a young Lenape woman and they became known as 'together'. At some point Jierre and his Lenape 'wife' set out to make their own way in a different milieu. They headed north along the eastern shore of the Chesapeake Bay, ultimately finding the Susquehanna River, which they followed into Pennsylvania. They finally settled in the Laurel Highlands, in an area that would be known as Nine Mile Run, and built a homestead, where they farmed and trapped and started a family. They were befriended by a tribe of nomad Iroquois who frequented the region, as well as a clan of Scottish families settled nearby. They had a son, who took an Iroquois woman as his wife when he was of age, as did *their* only child and son, Temuk. It was from Temuk that half the modern lineage of Rossys derived, so Billy's tenth, or so, pre-generation grandpap was nearly a full blooded Native American. "That doesn't make us Indians, grandpap," said Rossy. "The connection is too far back."

"Sure, it does, Billy. Look at you. Dark hair and eyes. Dark complected. High cheek bones. You could be an Indian if you wanted. Hell, you *are* Indian."

"Well, look at the rest of the family. My sisters have green and blue eyes. Light skinned. They don't look Indian. And neither do you. You've got blue eyes, too."

"You don't understand, Billy. If you have the blood, you are what you are. It doesn't matter how far back the link. You should be proud of that. And maybe use it as a plus. There are all kinds of special benefits for Native Americans. You should check it out."

"Look, grandpap, at some point in the future everybody in the world is going to look like a Brazilian. So what difference does it make where we came from, if we're all going to end up at the same place?"

"Be proud, Billy Boy. If you need any record of your history, I've got it right here." Grandpap brought up a file with all the genealogical documentation he had downloaded so far. "I'm still working on it, though, trying to fill in the blanks. Now, there's something else I want to show you."

Returning to the home screen, grandpap clicked on a black circle icon with tiny red lettering, reading "narp", inside it. The screen turned completely blue and Rossy thought the system had crashed. Then he entered two typed inputs that did not visually display. Up came a screen titled "Correspondence Board", below which were groups of date and time identified messages under subheadings of names. In its simplistic white text on blue backdrop appearance, it looked like the ancient 'wordperfect' screen. Grandpap explained this was a special chat program of the National Association of Retired People, that protected subscribers from spam, ads, intrusion, solicitation, hackers, fraud and any other unwanted garbage that bombarded the mainstream internet mail and social media services. It was like a separate dark net, that was completely impenetrable by unauthorized sources. NARP had developed the program, called 'Narpcom', to shield vulnerable, elderly retirees from scammers and identity thieves, while providing a safe, reliable means of electronic communication with their selected correspondents. Only NARP members could apply to participate in the program and, upon approval and payment of an annual dues surcharge, were registered with an assigned five character alphanumeric code ID. This code was needed to access a user's

Correspondence Board. Users were also issued ten correspondent IDs, each consisting of a seven character, alphanumeric code in a format of the user's selection, that was activated by providing the correspondent's name and basic background info. Up to ten additional correspondent IDs could be obtained at an annual cost of one jackson each. A Narpcom user could access the Correspondence Board from any internet device by clicking the black circle 'narp' icon on the NARP webpage and separately entering name and user code ID on the blue screen. A correspondent could contact the user from any device by separately entering name and the assigned ID on the blue Narpcom screen, at which point only that portion of the Correspondence Board pertaining to the accessing correspondent would show. If the correspondent name and ID did not correlate with each other or the user, the access would be terminated back to the NARP website and any further attempt to access from that correspondent would be denied for twenty-four hours. Messages both ways were limited to a thousand words, with no attachments, and could not be forwarded or copied. It was impossible to track Narpcom traffic from the outside, as records of access to Correspondence Boards were internally encrypted and could not be detected and retained by any device or software currently on, or off, the market. Even the record of access to the NARP website was abolished with use, or attempted use, of Narpcom. Not to say no one was trying to hack into the dark net. There were plenty of would be intruders, but so far no successes, because it was virtually impossible to follow anyone into the program. So said NARP, confident in their claim of infallibility to the extent that they guaranteed payment of 100% reimbursement for damages, plus $100,000 reparations for inconvenience, to any client victimized by a Narpcom hack.

Grandpap said he enrolled in the program, because he was terrified of contaminating his most valuable possession with viruses from the regular internet media services. He still had his e-mail account, but didn't use it much. So far he had assigned eight of his basic ten correspondent IDs. His most active correspondence was with a former client from his fly fishing guide days, with whom he became good friends and maintained contact over the years. Bobby Waintrow was a retired Air Force general living in Florida. His final active service post had been chief of the Air Systems Command, headquartered at Joint Base Andrews, in Camp Springs,

Maryland. ASC was not only involved in special high tech weapons, surveillance and defense systems development, but was moving toward establishing a military presence in high atmosphere and space research operations. ASC consumed about two thirds of the entire Air Force budget and most of what it did was ultra classified, thus publicly unknown. It had black ops going on inside of black ops. Gen. Waintrow served in a highly charged and pressured capacity that required periodic total disengagement to maintain sane ability to command. He chose isolated mountain fly fishing as his getaway of choice and connected with grandpap through the ranger's office at the Allegheny National Forest. Their similarly near genius intellects were immediately compatible and they formed a quick and lasting friendship. Grandpap had another correspondent, a German friend he met while a student in Munich. They, too, had stayed in communication over the years, which seemed to be intensifying as they got older. Hans Mueller was still an anarchist, maybe somewhat of a conspiracist, and he closely followed the activities of governments around the world. His theory was that nobody did anything in a vacuum. There was a reason for everything and he wanted to find out what it was. So he continuously sailed the cyber sea, looking for any intel that could make the pieces fit. His paranoia was akin to the annoying behavior of the HH people, but grandpap found Hans very interesting, as well as entertaining, and he immensely enjoyed their discourse. His other correspondents were family, including his ex-wife, grandma, and Rossy's mom, and a few junkster friends he kept in contact with in continuous search of the ultimate deal.

The old man asked Billy if he would take one of the remaining correspondent IDs, so he could report what was happening with the new job and his life in general. Rossy didn't think he had a problem with that. *Just lay low the rest of the week and don't take chances.* It was ultra secure and it might be fun, at least different. But he wondered about NARP. He knew they were an allegedly non-profit advocacy organization for retired and senior citizens, but they seemed to be involved in everything. And they constantly advertised everywhere, for all kinds of stuff, like insurance, discounts, drugs, security and alert systems, travel venues, legal aid, a variety of services catering to the elderly and always for themselves. They were arguably the most powerful lobby in Washington and one of the most voluminous solicitors in the country. Rossy got several pieces of mail a month from NARP and he was only twenty four years old! They must send something weekly to everyone in America. That did not seem like non-profit. It seemed more like conglomerate. Somebody was making a lot of money from all that activity and much of it had to be coming from social security revenues. Assuming the average social security recipient paid NARP an annual ben, for whatever, then NARP was raking in four billion a year! The more he thought about it, the more NARP came off as a provocative, maybe even subversive, organization. Who was the real scammer, here, anyway? Oh well, what the hell? If the old guy wanted to communicate with him through his secret system, so be it. He recorded his Narpcom correspondent ID, *ROFLY09*, on a note paper and put it in his wallet. Grandpap said he would submit it for registration and it should be activated in about five days. He instructed Billy to enter his full name, williamarlorossy, with the ID, to access the chat board.

It was starting to move into the later afternoon and the visitor said he better soon leave to get back to Ebbottown. He hoped to jump ahead of rush hour traffic and there were a ton of things he had to do before heading down to Washington. Grandpap said he wanted to give his 'best grandboy' something before he left and walked through the maze across the room to a desk table near the kitchen. He pulled out the pencil tray of the desk, removed a small plastic box and carefully handed it to the curious onlooker. "What's this?" asked the favorite, with genuine interest. "Open it," commanded grandpap, and the obedient recipient snapped apart the plastic clasp. Inside was a ticket stub on a bed of cotton gauze. It was for Section 59, Row L, Seat 11, in the Hershey Arena, for The Philadelphia 76ers vs. The New York Knickerbockers, March 2, 1962. "What's this?" repeated the confused ticket holder.

"That, Billy Boy, is proof of attendance at the greatest event in the history of professional sports. There were probably only a few thousand live witnesses and your grandpap was one of them."

"Witnesses to what?"

"To the legendary Wilt Chamberlain scoring a hundred! You never heard of that game? It's a record that will never be broken, even if the NBA plays basketball until the end of time."

"Oh, yeah, I think I remember reading something about that. You were there, grandpap?"

"Yessir, buddy! And let me tell you it was unbelievable. I remember it like it was yesterday. Wilt was never any good at foul shots, but that night he was 28 for 30, or something like that. And it was before the three pointer, so he made 36 regular buckets. So he's on the floor with 98, still a couple of minutes in the game, and here comes rookie Wayne Hightower off the 76ers' bench. Young Hightower is more interested in getting his 2, than Wilt getting 100, and Wilt finally steals the ball from his own teammate and slams in the century! The whole arena went ballistic and live pandemonium broke out. It took about fifteen minutes to clear the court and restore order so the game could be completed. The final score was Philadelphia one sixty something to New York one forty something, I don't remember the exact score, but I think that's still a record, too, for most total points in a game. It was incredible. The only pro basketball game I've ever gone to. And the reason the record will never be broken is the game is no longer played the way it was then. With the three pointer, they don't feed a big center under the basket like they used to. No one has anywhere near the opportunity to turn in that kind of scoring number in the modern game. It just won't happen. So hold onto that ticket stub, Billy. It could be a valuable artifact. There are a million people who claim they were at that game, but, like I said, there were really only about three thousand of us."

"Well, gee, grandpap, are you sure you want to give this up? It sounds like it's pretty important to you."

"No, no, Billy, I want you to have it. It's a genuine piece of Americana. You obviously can't claim to have been at the game, but you can tell the story of someone who was. That makes you special and I want you to have it."

"OK, grandpap. Thank you very much. I'll take good care of it."

"I know you will, Billy Boy."

The two old fishing buddies started wrapping up their visit and moved slowly toward the front door of the apartment. Both honestly thought they had spent a very enjoyable afternoon in each other's company. Billy Boy promised to stay in regular contact, through Narpcom, phone, internet media, snail mail or, best of all, in person. He really wasn't worried anymore about the status, or result, of grandpap's hoarding obsession. The only important thing was that the old man seemed happy with his life and appeared to be in decently good health for his age. Everything else would work itself out. He would report to mom that about 40% of the entire vertical space from the floor of the apartment was filled and she could decide what, if anything, had to be done. It was not his problem. It was somebody else's problem and he did not do SEPs.

As he exited the elevator and started across the lobby toward the foyer, the intruder saw the same whiteheads sitting there watching him, who had monitored his other three passes through the room during the course of the day. *Wow! They must be hammered. No one could stay there that long without helpers.* Outside, the patio was empty, so at least the smoking ladies had more than one station in life. He walked over the driveway to the street and stepped onto the sidewalk along the iron fence. In approaching his car, he was dismayed to see it covered with blobs of white bird shit. What a fracking mess!! He had to clear the windows to be able to drive. No wonder this was the only empty parking space on the street. Next time he would park in the HH lot. For right now, though, he had to get this crap off the car. He remembered a car wash at the interchange where he exited the interstate to the downtown area. That would be his first stop. Then maybe he would get another burger and a beer somewhere before returning to E-town. It had been a long, tedious day and the best grandboy was mentally wasted. He felt that nothing had been particularly easy the past few months and the strain seemed to be bearing on him a little like a light, wet fog. But better days were coming, so he just had to keep on slogging.

***

The oddjobber spent the next few days completing mom's chore list and repacking his car. He cleaned the garage and the basement, trimmed the shrubbery around the house, pruned some trees, raked and bagged leaves, put all the vegetative material out front for collection by the town, repaired the breezeway screening between the house and the garage, installed a handrail along the basement steps, cut the grass again and made several runs to the landfill to dispose of collected debris from the clean-up work. He figured he did at least ten bens worth of work, but all he got was temporary lodging while visiting fabulous E-town. Also, a happy mom, so that was good. There was nothing more dangerous, to an adult son, than an unhappy mom.

***

On Thursday, the day before he was to leave for Washington, they went out to the farm to visit his aunt and uncle and have dinner with them. His aunt was mom's sister and his uncle was from a family of three successful boys and one sort of slacker boy. Billy grew up calling them all 'uncle', even though, technically, none of them was his bona fide, genetic 'uncle'. They were, more accurately, uncles-in-law. But since they were all related to the same person, a cousin, it seemed natural they were all, in fact, related for real. One of the uncles was a surgeon, who had removed 'nephew' Billy's tonsils, when he was in second grade, to mitigate a chronic bronchitis problem. He remembered waking up from the anesthesia and crying because his pillow was covered with blood and he thought he was dead. The nurse chided him for being a baby, pointing out that the other boy in the room was very brave and not crying at all. He later learned the boy was unconscious under an isolation tent and couldn't cry if he wanted to. The slacker uncle was his Little League coach. He always paid a george to anyone on the team who hit a home run. Everyone remembered one game the coach uncle got into a furious argument with the umpire and was ejected. He had to leave the field and, for the remainder of the game, stood in the parking lot shouting crude obscenities. The farmer uncle owned a Purina feed mill with his brother and they were quite successful providing livestock services throughout a multi-county area. He was also on the board of directors of the largest independent bank in Ebbottown. Farmer uncle was instrumental in lining up some supplemental loans to help finance the 'nephew' student's college costs. These bank loans, with the federal loans, financial aid and some dean's list scholarship support, were the only way he could stay in school through graduation and he really appreciated his uncle's assistance. And he liked the guy, even if he seriously underpaid for legitimately hard work around the farm. Hell, that's why he was a bankster.

***

Before dinner, the former farmhand took a swim in the pool, a mammoth in-ground concrete reservoir between the two hundred year old, stone house and the smaller, white brick summer house. He knew every square inch of the rectangular pool's interior surface area, as he had cleaned it with muriatic acid and roll painted it a pastel blue tint at least twice. Working in an empty, unshaded concrete pool under a hot spring sun was not unlike spending the day in a huge walk-in oven, and he roasted accordingly. Fortunately, he tanned more than burned and ended up darker than had he gone to the Jersey Shore for a week. But that was then. Now, he could just enjoy the cooling water and relax in the peaceful country poolside setting with no concerns about uncompleted maintenance issues. He didn't know who did the yard and pool work today, possibly undocumented immigrants, but the grounds around the house were in top condition. Better than he recalled ever seeing it. Everything was perfectly trimmed, cut and mulched and autumn blooms were coming into full splendor. The place looked more like an estate than an old farmstead.

Later, during dinner, conversation turned towards the young man and his future. His mom went into the familiar twirl about giving up a good job for some kind of government scamming nonsense. She reiterated her prohibition of him coming back home to live, saying he was a grown man and had to be responsible to take care of himself. Auntie said not to worry. He could come and live with them if things didn't work out and he needed a place to stay. The real aunt's nephew pondered that for a moment, thinking it might not be a bad life living on the farm, here, working for room and board and a george an hour. *Stop it! That is not going to happen.* He didn't say anything. He was over talking about his future. All he wanted right now was another plate of teriyaki turkey and fried brown rice, because it was really good. His aunt was always a much better cook than his mom.

***

The next morning Rossy got up early. This was the big day he had been waiting for from the moment Booker allegedly brokered him a new job in Washington. God, that seemed like eons ago, but it had actually been only a few weeks. Today, he would return to Washington for the first time since the ill fated junior high class trip that, for some reason, seemed like last week, but actually *was* eons ago. He felt like a returning conquistador, ready to take his rightful place over a city state that had spurned him, some might say defeated him, in the past, but was now ripe for the taking in the dawn of a new age. Today was his to seize in a fresh genesis of hope, direction and opportunity and he felt fired up and ready to go. Nothing was going to bring him down. Nothing could ruin his mood. He would resist the dreaded stress of change and emerge victorious. His mom had already gone to work after they hugged their goodbyes and wiped away a few tears. She said she was sorry, but there was a bad vibe about his venture, an adverse premonition. His celestials were not aligned for good fortune right now and he should be very careful, if not afraid. He must call regularly to let her know he was okay. Then she gave him an empty Starbuck's coffee bag, reading on the side it was redeemable at any participating franchise store for a free grande latte. He would stop at the Giant Eagle, that had a Starbuck's cafe, on the way out of town. A nice, sweet freebie should neutralize the negativity his mom had just laid on him.

With the last few small things loaded into the re-stuffed Civic and a final check to make sure nothing was forgotten, the good son departed for destiny. Arriving at the GE shopping center, he pulled into the supermarket lot and was able to park near the entrance. Inside, he went directly to the cafe, where there was a small line queued in front of the only order lane open. After a few minutes, it was his turn and he requested the grande latte. When the barista returned with the order, the empty bag was offered in payment and ignored. "That'll be $9.89," said the clerk. "No, no. The bag is for the latte. It says right here, a free grande latte with the bag," explained the patient patron, pointing to the fine printed offer on the side. "I don't know anything about that, sir. We aren't participating in that program. That'll be $9.89, please." *What the hell!?* Rossy couldn't believe he was being diddled by this dropout coffee grinder, but he realized there would be no gratis grande latte today. He placed a hamilton on the counter beside the empty bag, picked up the drink and walked away. "Thank you, sir. Have a nice day."

***

Back in the car, the latte lover's hand bumped the emergency brake lever as he tried to put the involuntary purchase into the drink holder, knocking the plastic lid loose from the cardboard cup. About a quarter inch of coffee sloshed out all over the console components between the seats. *Jesus christ! Is this the kind of fracked up day it's going to be?* The returning conquerer forgot his earlier euphoria, while he mopped up the hot spillage, and settled in for a drudge drive to the so-called capital of the free world. First, a twenty-five mile ride on secondary roads through the country side, and then onto a southbound interstate. The only discernible thing on the radio was a confederate sounding broadcast revelator admonishing him for being a hopeless sinner. The indefatigable mood had gone dour by the time he jumped the Mason-Dixon line and left Pennsylvania behind.

SOUTHEAST

Rossy was supposed to meet Booker around 3 p.m., at C-14 of the Avery Garden Apartments, off Suitland Road in Maryland, a little over a mile from the D.C. line. They coordinated this yesterday, by phone. Seve Smith had sent Booker a key set to his apartment and that is where they could stay, at least to start off with. Smith was on TDY, temporary duty, out-of-country and wouldn't be back for another couple of months. It worked for him to have someone in his crib while he was gone and it certainly worked for the new kids on the block to not have to find a place to live right away. Rossy pulled into the apartments a little after two and easily found the rendezvous unit. There was no sign of Booker or his Yamaha bike. He parked in the lot adjacent to building 'C', got out of the car and stretched, glancing around at the surroundings. The AGA complex didn't look too bad. The low rise buildings were an attractive amber brick and natural finish wood trim with gray shingled roofs. The grounds were nicely landscaped with a variety of shrubs and mid-sized trees. There was a lot of open lawn space and everything seemed to be well maintained. He could see a fenced swimming pool facility further down the access road. He followed a sidewalk from the parking lot up and over a short berm into an open stairwell entrance in the middle of building 'C'. Apartment 14 was on the first level facing the lot. There was no answer to his several knocks and he stepped up a half flight of stairs to a landing with a bay of mailboxes inlaid into the wall. The box for #14 was labeled S. Smith, verifying he was at the right place. The earlybird returned to his car and got in to wait for Booker. He soon felt himself nodding off.

A tapping on the window startled the dozing drifter from the beginnings of a grim dream about clinging to a barrel sized cork that was accelerating around the perimeter of a massive maelstrom of sea water, each revolution descending further into the fathomless vortex. He looked up into the round, mustachioed face of a large African American man peering into the car from under the visor of a black ball cap. The inparker opened the window and straightened up in the seat, feeling somewhat disorientated from the abrupt and unexpected awakening. On the front of the man's hat he saw 'DCA SECURITY' emblazoned over two x-crossed keys in gold braid. The same logo was on the left breast of the man's black pullover crew sweater, above a name tag pin identifying Donald Trevair, as DCA #238. Then Rossy recoiled slightly in noticing a holstered handgun on the man's belt. *What is this? Am I going to the precinct again?*

"Sir, may I ask what you are doing, here?"

"Yes, I'm just waiting for a friend. He should be here anytime." Rossy saw it was a quarter to three.

"Are you a resident, here?"

"Yes, sir, I'm at C-14."

"Sir, I know Seve Smith at C-14, and you are not Seve Smith. Please step out of the vehicle."

"No, I don't mean I'm a resident, I'm just staying at Smith's place, but I'm waiting for another guy who has the key." Rossy got out and leaned up against the side of the car in front of Trevair.

"Smith is not here right now. You are trespassing on private property. I must ask you to leave the premises immediately, or I will call the police."

"No, please, Mr. Trevair. Really, I'm a new employee at the same office where Smith works and he said I can stay here until I find my own place. He sent a key to my friend, who knows Smith and is also a new employee at the same office, and that's who I'm waiting for now. He's supposed to be here around three."

"OK, let me see some ID."

The trespasser pulled out his driver's license and handed it to the security officer, who jotted down the identifying information and returned the license. "OK, Mr. Rossy, you may wait here, but be advised you are under video surveillance. If I see any suspicious activity on your part, or, if you are still sitting here in the lot an hour from now, I *will* call the police. Do you understand?"

"Yes, sir." Rossy waited until Trevair drove away in the black Jeep Cherokee, that had been idling nearby, before getting back into his car. Dammit! *No matter where I go somebody wants to mess with me!! This shit is getting old!* The first comer settled in to continue waiting for Booker, wondering how he would arrive. He certainly couldn't be on the bike with all his stuff. He probably rented a U-Haul, or something. Sure enough, at about ten after three, a U-Haul half truck lumbered down the access road. It pulled into the lot, parked beside the Civic and out jumped Booker. "My man, Rossy!! You made it! How're you doin', man?" greeted Booker, putting up a knuckleball. He was actually a little surprised to see his colleague, in that he never really was totally convinced the boy was 'all in' on this gambit. But here they were and it looked like all systems were go. The engineers exchanged debriefs on their homecomings, while sidling up the walk to the apartment. Rossy scanned about for a surveillance camera, but didn't see one anywhere.

Smith's apartment looked like a Dick's Sporting Goods store. There were sports equipment and accessories everywhere. Balls of all shapes and sizes, footwear for any game or activity, ski sets, hockey sticks, bats, lacrosse nets, golf clubs, helmets, numbered shirts, specialty gloves and goggles and a host of ancillary athletic gear dominated the first visual impression as they entered the front living room from the entrance breezeway. "Jesus, is Seve some kind of superstar athlete?" wondered Rossy, gazing around the room. "No, I don't think so," said Booker. "He didn't even play intramural sports in school. Maybe I don't know him as well as I thought. But he did tell me they call him 'gameboy' at work. Guess this is why." In getting past the conspicuous, they discovered the apartment was actually pretty nice. It had two good sized bedrooms, a bath and a half, a separate dining room sunken in a two step-down pit from the living room and the adjacent kitchen. The living room featured a gas log fireplace and another doorway to a flagstone patio under a picture window overlooking the parking lot. A utility and storage closet was accessible from the patio. The interior wall between the living room, dining room and kitchen was brick, as were the exterior dining room walls. The entire apartment was carpeted, except for the kitchen, bathroom and lavatory, which had attractive terrazzo flooring. The non-brick walls were flat painted, eggshell white, and the ceiling had a matching textured finish. Posters of travel scenes from around the world were tacked up everywhere. All the rooms were adequately furnished with a lot of functional, Ikea-type pieces. There were large, wall mounted TVCs in both bedrooms and the living room and an expensive digital sound system with speakers throughout the apartment. They also noticed an impressive archive of game and music cds stacked on a shelf under the living room TVC. In checking out the available space, it was obvious there was not much room for any more stuff. Rossy contemplated whether Smith might have the same collecting disorder grandpap had, but then figured it was different, because Smith's inventory was predominately sports themed and new. Grandpap's things were random and old. The interlopers both thought, but did not say out loud, that Smith must be making some decent mazuma. This place was not cheap and neither were the furnishings and possessions in it. They decided not to immediately unload anything other than overnight necessities and worry about where to put their belongings later. Maybe they would have to get a storage cell somewhere.

After hanging out a bit, the two walked up the road to a place, on top of a small knoll, they both remembered passing on the way in. 'Gino's Green Grotto' beckoned from a green neon marquee at the entrance driveway. Odd, they discussed, that a grotto would be at the crest of a hill, but there were cars parked on the premises, so there must be some attraction. They went inside to a thoroughly unexpected scene. Initially, flashing darkness and a driving techno-rock wall of sound required some orientation of the senses. In adjusting, they saw a perimeter mezzanine around an expansive open area to a square, polished hardwood floor at least ten feet below. Dimly lamp lit tables were spaced on the mezzanine adjacent to a railing overlooking the pit from all four sides. The gym-like floor below was illuminated with inlaid green lights and several rigid plastic tube poles extended from the floor to the ceiling above the mezzanine. Blinking green strobe lights inside the poles and on the ceiling punctuated the darkness in precise sync with the music. Intimately entwined with each pole was a nearly naked girl, suggestively moving approximately in sync with the music. Three other nearly naked girls were rolling around on the floor, no where close to in sync with the music. The engineers shuffled over to an empty table, circumspectly peeping at the activity in the green grotto beneath. Within seconds a waitress appeared out of the shadows and approached their table, order pad in hand. The first thing she said was a request for ID. Rossy was becoming quite skilled at submitting ID and reached reflexively for his wallet. Booker, not as experienced, reached hesitantly for his. Legal ages verified, the waitress asked for their order. Going into a 'Gino' named establishment, they had been thinking pizza and a six pack, to carry to the apartment. They just wanted to kick back and relax

this evening, watch a little TV and turn in early. Both were exhausted from their past week off with family and time on the road.
While waiting, they each ordered a draft. Checking around the
mezzanine, they noticed about eight other patrons, all men, alone
at separate tables. They were mostly middle-aged indoorsmen,
with buttoned down shirts and loosened ties. Office men, leaning
with elbows on the railing, unabashedly gawking at the 'dancers'
on the green floor. Especially provocative moves prompted the
release of currency into the pit, which took a few seconds to float
down. Upon landing, one of the floor dancers would roll over and
snatch the donation up, seductively stuffing it under her thong
strap, while smiling luringly at the generous contributor from
above. The music never stopped. It was a continuous, pulsating
beat of electronic syncopation that evidently ran in conjunction
with triple G's operating schedule. It was too loud to talk over, so
the engineers just sat and watched. Eventually, their order came
and they paid the waitress lady. Rossy dropped a george over the
railing as they stood up to leave, observing a roller girl getting into
position to retrieve. When she picked it up, she frowned at the low
roller, dabbing her eye in a mock pout, then crumpled the bill into
a wad and threw it back up towards him. Apparently, she was expecting the portrait of a more recent president. He wondered how
much those other dudes were pitching in. Oh, well, he didn't think
he would be returning to this place anytime soon, especially if the
pizza was not reasonably good. On the way out, he looked up, directly into a surveillance camera over the door. *Oh, that's just
fracking great! Faced on video coming out of a smuthouse!!
Christ, what if this somehow gets to the net, or some police data
base? Can you please, please not take chances, goober??* Rossy
was discomposed, but nothing he could do about it now. Only
hope there would be no fallout. Booker did not seem to be concerned. He was essentially oblivious to risk management issues,
sort of like Cam. By the time they walked into the AGA entranceway, traffic had picked up considerably, as Washington's afternoon rush was out of the gate.

Later in the evening, the engineers were watching
'Smackdown', on *WWE Network* , when they heard soft raps on
the front door. Rossy eyeballed through the peep and saw a short,
young white dude, with long, brown scraggily hair hanging down
from under a dark woolen skull cap, wearing oversized sunshades,

a fully buttoned pea jacket, green and black madras bermuda shorts and unlaced, red Converse hightops over white knee socks. *What the hell?* He cracked the door to the limit of the security chain and doubtfully surveyed the jughead standing before him.

"Yo, man, is Seve there?" husked the visitor.

"No, he's not here."

"Well, who are you, if he's not there?"

"A friend. Who are you?"

"I'm a friend, too, man. Let me in a sec."

"What do you want?"

"Let me show you somethin'."

"Don't open the door, dawg," cautioned Booker from behind.

"Wow, there's two of yous?" from the breezeway. "C'mon, open up. I got somethin' for bofe of yous." The stranger spread apart his jacket, revealing rows of small plastic baggies fastened to the inside liner on both sides. "Whatchu need? I got the best. Sugar, spice, everything nice. Got weed, dust, crack, snow, acid, meth, oxy, molly, whatever. Even sudafed, if that's your thang. You call it. I got it cheap, my brothers. Best quality."

"WHAT THE FRACK? GET THE FRACK OUTTA HERE, OR I'LL CALL THE POLICE!!" Seve's new friend slammed the door shut and turned the deadbolt. He was visibly shaken by this freakish episode and went directly to the kitchen for another Heineken. "Can you fracking believe that??" he asked Booker, who was settled back into a beanbag easy chair, chuckling to himself. "Don't worry about it, Rossy, chill, this is the big city. A different world." But the small town farmer boy couldn't help worrying about it. He had never heard of anything so blatantly illegal as a door-to-door drug slinger. What kind of neighborhood were they in? It looked like a nice area driving in this afternoon, but, now, he wasn't so sure. Where the hell was Trevair? And was Smith a crackhead, or something like that? How could he be, if he played all those sports? Druggies can't do anything except hallucinate and pass out.

It had been a long day. They tossed for bedrooms. One, the larger of the two, was a total wreck and obviously where Smith laid his head. The other was a little less jumbled and appeared to be not normally occupied. Booker got choice and opted for the smaller, more habitable looking room. Rossy couldn't believe Smith would go away for three months leaving his apartment, at least his bedroom, in such deplorable condition. As he climbed into the unmade bed, he had to clear a football, a volley ball and a basket ball from under the rumpled afghan. Who sleeps like this, with official Wilson game balls? He was beginning to wonder about gameboy Smith. Soon, the room guest was falling asleep at the wheel, driving recklessly into REM territory. He found himself outside a turnstile gate of an enormous baseball stadium, filled to deafening capacity for the seventh game of the World Series between the Phillies and the Yankees. Tied score. Last of the ninth. Bases loaded. Two outs. Full count. Mike Schmidt in the box. The elderly gate keeper asked for ID, but the young phan couldn't find any. His license was gone from his wallet where it usually was! No, no, only seconds until the final pitch and he couldn't find his ID to get in and see what was surely going to be the most famous home run in the history of baseball! The crowd was berserko. Roger Clemens was circling the mound. And then he found an old ticket stub in his wallet and thrust it toward the attendant, who took it with little interest. "What's this?" he asked.

"That's a ticket stub for the greatest basketball game ever played, when Wilt scored a hundred."

"No way! I was at that game. Remember it like it was yesterday! You're in, young man, go, go!"

The ecstatic boy vaulted over the turnstile and sprinted for the nearest section tunnel to the stands. Clemens in his stretch, left foot high in the air, right arm rocketing forward. The high heat delivery......

***

The next day, Saturday, the engineers decided to make a dry run to the Navy Yard, so they wouldn't get lost on Monday morning and be late for their first day of work at NAVOSUR. The packed Civic did not have room for both of them and they didn't want to drive the U-Haul through the city, so the only ride was the Yamaha. After unloading the bike from the truck bay and retrieving head gear from the cab, they went out the AGA throughway to Suitland Road. First stop, McDonald's, for a happy meal breakfast, from which they gave the super hero action figures to a kid at a nearby table. They checked the phone map app to determine their route, because Booker's portable GPS was deeply packed.

It looked like a straight shot down Alabama Avenue to the 11th Street Bridge, and over the Anacostia River to the Yard. Initially, they rode through about a mile of cemeteries on both sides of the road before crossing the line into D.C. *Christ, there's a lot of dead people in Washington,* thought Rossy, looking to the flanks from Booker's back at the endless rows of graves. Down and up a lengthy hill, through a complicated five street intersection and continuing on..., what the hell? Good Hope Road? What happened to Alabama? Not knowing exactly where they were anymore, Booker kept straight as the street narrowed and became more congested, with cars parked tightly on both sides. Traffic crawled to nearly a standstill in trying to work through the long red lights at every block and the air was thick with the intermittent clangor of revving engines, blurting horns and screeching brakes. Pedestrians constantly meandered slowly back and forth across the street in front of the bikers, sometimes staring at them bemusedly as they passed by. Rossy noticed the people were all black and he reflexively tucked his white hands into his pockets. *Why did you do that, hayseed?* The neighborhood, while well populated, did not seem particularly upscale. There were a lot of dilapidated, empty building fronts and a general aura of unswept trashiness prevailed. But there was also a significant number of open shops, stores and cart stands, most with their own overloud music blare, to attract the people wandering about. Amid the kinetic sidewalk activity were many static panhandlers, sitting on the concrete in grimy jeans and rasta dreads, trying to beg an honest abe, or two. One yelled out to the engineers, as they waited for a light in front of him, demanding some 'cash for the cause'. They looked directly ahead, not acknowledging the verbal barrage. Finally, they came to a tee intersection with Martin Luther King Avenue and had to choose whether to turn left or right. Unable to orientate on the map app before the light changed, they went left.

MLK was wider than whatever street they had just been on, but there was still a lot of traffic and pedestrian bustle. At the *Divination Temple of the Final Prophecy,* a gathering of chain smoking men paced the sidewalk, anxiously awaiting the next AA meeting. A little past the storefront church an impromptu Saturday reuse market was attracting a throng of people as well as an accompaniment of food vendors. Up ahead it looked like the avenue started bearing to the left towards a complicated interchange with

a major thoroughfare. Booker didn't see a river or a bridge anywhere and decided they were going in the wrong direction and had
to turn around. He made a right onto a very tight, one-way street
going up a long, fairly steep hill, through an area of unsightly,
mid-rise housing facilities that were long vacated and falling into
ruin. Windows were broken out, doors torn off and abandoned car
shells rotted away in the contiguous, weed-grown parking lots.
Trash, litter and garbage overflowed from a forgotten dumpster
and were strewn throughout the vicinity. Garish graffiti covered
the spalling, spectraglazed walls of the structures and open spaces
between the buildings were empty dirt bowls. A small playground
near the center of the complex featured several corroded swing
frames and a tipped over slide, beside a half basketball court with
a badly bent and netless hoop. A few more then ten noisy boys
were scrumming around on the cracked asphalt pad for an old,
partially deflated soccer ball, in some variation of a pick-up basketball game. They ceased their frantic activity and stood goggling
as the cyclers rolled cautiously by. Rossy's weak wave was ignored and he self-consciously felt like an over-exposed intruder.

Once through the defunct housing projects, Booker turned into a small side street with a deformed, bullet riddled 'Dead End'
sign turned parallel to the curb. Ascending a slight rise, they approached a cul-de-sac atop a high bluff overlooking a dual highway, a railroad and a wide strip of barren, brown marshland along
the river below. A number of tiny Cape Cod style cottages surrounded the circle, two of which were burned out and obviously
empty. The others were in serious disrepair, though possibly habitable. These were the only structures on the street. An old Cadil-
lac and a couple of other junkers were parked at the curb and several more were up on blocks in the dusty, debris cluttered yards. A
large pit bull lunged from the limit of a collar chain connected to
an iron ground peg in front of one of the houses, snarling fero-
ciously at the alien vehicle descending from the rise. Near the
middle of the cul-de-sac were six men, sitting on rickety folding
chairs facing a low, makeshift backstop of concrete bricks, against
which they had been shooting craps. They forgot the game, at the
dog's alert, and rose to watch the slowly advancing visitors. Rossy
tensed in seeing the black men, not necessarily at the color of their
skin, but more at the sight of the colors they wore. These dudes
were gangbangers! And here they were, coasting right into their

front yard! *Holy jesus christ!! We are fracked!! I don't have to worry about any goddam background check for a security clearance! I'm gonna be checked out right fracking here on the street!!* The gangsters circled the bikesters with tattooed arms folded across orange, plaid flanneled chests. Booker tried to turn the bike around, but was blocked by two of the homeboyz. No one spoke for at least ten seconds, as the situation formed perspective. The frenzied pit dog was on the verge of ripping loose.

"Demar, I doan tink no crackerheads bin down Mule Circle inna hunnert fifty years!"

"Shit, man, dey ain't nevva bin no honkie kongs up here, man."

"Mebbe iss Batman an Robin comin' te save ar sorry ass."

"Doan tink so, man. Batman wouldn't be ridin' no toy bike. Robin, dough, he might be ridin' anyting." The gangsters broke into loud laughter.

"Mebbe dey busted outta wunna dem crazy boxes ova Sane E's."

"Dat it? You white boys from Sane E's?"

The engineers had no idea what or where Sain E's was and didn't know what to say, but they knew they had to say something. "Uh... actually, we're a little lost? We're trying to get to the Navy Yard?" stammered Booker.

"Da Navy Yard? What da frack you wanna go dair fo? How 'bout you come ova heah an have a taste wit us? Mebbe tell us 'bout yoselfs." The oversized gangster, who seemed to be the boss, gestured toward the chairs. Booker motioned for Rossy to get off the bike, while he cut the engine and kicked down the stand. "OK, sure, why not? We'll have a drink with you." *Oh, sweet jesus! Just fracking shoot me and get it over with!! We are so dead!* As they walked across the cul-de-sac, the frantic dog made a vicious thrust forward and yanked the anchor peg out of the ground. It was in full-bore attack gallop, chain and peg whipping wildly behind, when the front man commanded, **"STILL, CLINTON, STILL!!"** But Clinton charged on, his snarl almost a roar. Just before he reached the chairs, the big dude stepped forward and uppercut the dog directly under the jaw with a haymaking closed right fist. Clinton's head snapped back and he squealed an ear piercing yelp of stunned pain, then dropped like a bad joke, out cold in a quivering heap on the street about five feet from the engineers. They gaped in disbelief, neither having ever witnessed anything as singularly outlandish as what they had just seen.

"Don't worry about Clinton, he'll be fine. It's all part of his training regimen. Have a seat, gentlemen. Try this." The host offered a clear glass mason jar, partially filled with a colorless, slightly oily liquid, to each of them. "The purest 'lightning' you'll find in D.C. Enjoy." Rossy and Booker accepted the jars, sat down and wondered silently about the strange change of vernacular, from street patois to educated English, in the boss gangster's speech pattern. "God bless America," he said, raising a jar toward the engineers in an apparent toast. They half-heartedly raised their jars in acknowledgement and the three each took a hit of the maximum proof liquor. To the uninitiated, ingesting 'lightning' feels like the blast of a solar fusion flare from the tongue to the stomach and the honored visitors reacted accordingly, in a spate of reflexive, spasmodic coughs. Again, the gangsters broke into loud laughter.

"I sense your surprise at my house English," said the patriotic toaster, with an amused smile. "I am a cum laude graduate of Howard University. I have a bachelor of science degree in information technology and a master's in business administration. 'What's a college man doing here on Mule Hill?', you ask yourselves," reading the engineers thoughts verbatim. "Because, after I got out of school, I couldn't find a job and I owed over fifty thousand god-trusted dollars in education debt. Good jobs in this town flow with the politics and I wasn't properly connected. The Mule Hill Crew had been recruiting me since I was nine, so I said 'why not?' and took the oath of orange. Our territory includes about half of Southeast and we have nearly two hundred associates. While we still make considerable profit from drug sales, primarily to Saint Elizabeth's staff and outpatients and other distributers, we have diversified into computer cracking operations and enjoy gainful returns from identity theft and unauthorized cash account transfers. The internet is an infinite resource, my friends, filled with limitless bounty there for the taking." *Hmm...maybe NARP's dark net is a worthwhile service after all.* "Fortunately, I've been able to pay off my debts much sooner than working a conventional job, so at this point, as far as I'm concerned, it doesn't matter if the system wasn't kind to me." The boss took another swig of 'lightning', ignited a humongous blunt and carefully eyed his guests for any response to his personal brief.

Rossy was pretty sure he never had the opportunity to join a gang and pay off his college debts early. There weren't any crews in his hometown 'hood, unless there was some religious posse, like, maybe, the Amishboyz, or the Mennonite Mob? Uh-huh. "So, are you going to bust us?" he choked, now thoroughly resigned to a lost fate up here on Mule Hill, beyond the middle of nowhere.

"Oh, goodness, no. We are not violent. The modern gang culture is much different than how it has traditionally been portrayed in the media. We work with the police. We help our families and our neighbors. We peacefully negotiate territorial agreements with competitors. No, you will not be harmed for your inadvertent trespass. We do, however, ask that you pay for your drinks. 'Lightning' is a very expensive commodity and not easy to procure."

"Sure, no problem, how much do we owe you?" asked Booker, seeing a positive spin evolving in their predicament.

"Well, how much do you have?"

"What do you mean?"

"Let's see how much you have. Empty your pockets, please."

Seriously?? We're getting jacked?! OK, that's a hell of a lot better than getting killed! Rossy and Booker took everything out of their pockets, placing the items on an empty chair. The educated boss reached over and plucked the wallets from the small pile of effects. He smiled approvingly while removing more than three bens' worth of cash from the bill folds, leaving them empty. Returning the wallets to the chair, he stood up, extending an open hand to the now insolvent engineers. "Thank you very much for coming to visit us. It has been a pleasure, and if we can ever be of assistance to you, please don't hesitate to call. I'm known on the hill here, and around Southeast, as 'the graduate'. A word of caution. You should never carry more than cab fare when sightseeing in the ghetto. Have a nice day, gentlemen." The biker boys shook hands with the graduate, recovered their pocket possessions and walked over to the Yamaha. They could hear loud laughter behind them as they wheeled back up the rise and exited Mule Circle. With the sound of the whirring motorcycle engine, Clinton roused from unconsciousness, whimpering in residual pain, and dazedly sat up on the pavement in the middle of the cul-de-sac. The gangstas resumed their craps shoot.

In concluding it would be futile to report their misfortunate loss to the police, the engineers decided to stay on plan and continue their surprisingly difficult journey to the Navy Yard. They took another one-way street down the long hill, through the old ghost projects, right onto MLK and across the bridge. Exiting to M Street, they followed a high brick wall to the main gatehouse into the Yard. A marine guard MP, in full dress uniform, asked for ID and purpose of the visit, and waved them through. They thought that was rather lax security for a military installation, particularly remembering the horrific shooting incident that had occurred here a while back, but soon concluded the Navy Yard was not as much a base as it was a park. They passed by a grassed quad area where a large marine honor guard was practicing parade cortege maneuvers, as an assemblage of spectators watched from the peripheral. The tourists were heavily equipped with cameras, eagerly recording the precise marching moves of the colorful marines. Further toward the river, was a voluminous, brick industrial building identified as a naval museum. They parked the Yamaha and went up to the entrance to check it out. The museum was open, but there was a fee to get in. Being cash free, and with no accounts for ATM access, they reversed back to the parking area and decided to leave the bike and walk around. Certainly it was safe with all these marines nearby. A broad concrete and brick paver walkway bordered the entire waterfront strip along the mighty Anacostia River. The view down stream to the mightier Potomac was quite scenic. In the other direction they could see the tops of the Washington Monument and the capital dome dominating the distant panorama. Rossy thought the Navy Yard looked like a really nice environment to work in and detected the start of a feeling of positive anticipation displacing the dull, burning stress he had become accustomed to the past several weeks. Booker was immune to stress and had never succumbed to any negative thoughts regarding their joint venture.

The riverwalk was obviously an attraction, as there were many people strolling in both directions and relaxing in the sun by the water. But something did not look right with the water. It almost resembled a dried up bed of olive green muck that could be walked on. Closer inspection revealed the river was filled with a long, stringy aquatic plant growth that seemed to float about half a foot below the surface. An informational placard by the water's edge explained the growth to be hydrilla, a super oxygenating, submerged aquatic vegetation introduced to the Washington waterways decades ago to mitigate pollution. At the time, the Anacostia was so toxic that some thought it was flammable. The hydrilla worked well to clear the water up, but was very prolific and had to be periodically cleared to maintain navigability. The engineers saw the water was, indeed, nice and clear, but it looked like hydrilla harvesting time. At the end of the walk was a large, gray naval ship, decommissioned and permanently tied to the bulkhead. If not the mooring cables, the hydrilla would hold the ship in place. This vessel was never going to move again and, as far as they could tell, was the only boat at the Navy Yard. Civilians were moving up and down the gangplank, so the ship was apparently open to the public. Rossy had never been on a big ship and assumed it would be interesting, but probably cost something to go in, like the museum. That tour would have to be postponed. Anyway, right now they were more concerned with locating where they were to report for duty on Monday morning, which was, in fact, their mission of the day.

On the other side of the end of the riverwalk was a crushed stone parking lot, below a cluster of buildings in the northeast corner of the Yard. A sign identified this area as the Navy Yard Federal Center. Smith had advised Booker that NAVOSUR was on the second floor of the Nathaniel Bowditch Building, within the NYFC. The engineers started out across the lot to find their new workplace. Being the weekend, there were not many parked vehicles. But there was one, near the sidewalk to the buildings, from which loud music was throbbing out of the open windows. As they passed by the car, the unmistakable scent of funny smoke wafted through the air and they saw four heads inside, randomly bobbling behind the rhythm of the beat, reminiscent of the Kia gerbils. They couldn't help but notice the gerbils were well stocked with Coors beer. Booker and Rossy walked quickly past the party car, thinking it a little unusual to see such conduct in plain sight, on government property, in the middle of the day. Entering the NYFC campus they observed the buildings, scattered under an impressive and well tended stand of grand old oaks and maples, to be in much worse condition than they appeared from a distance. They seemed to be World War II vintage structures that had not received much maintenance and upgrade attention since. The Bowditch Building was a large, three story institutional looking affair, with white clapboard siding and a clay tiled, pitched roof without soffits or gutters. A conspicuously oversized, vented wooden cupola, capped with a corroded brass spire pointing skyward, sat on the middle of the roof ridge. The rectangular boxlike edifice was wrapped in rows of evenly spaced factory windows on each floor, some of which were broken out and covered with plywood. The siding had a severe rotting problem and was urgently in need of repair and painting. There was an entrance at both ends and in the middle of each long side, accessed from small, uncovered concrete landings about four steps above grade. Black iron railings bordered the steps and landing at each entrance. One middle entrance had a long handicap ramp from the sidewalk at the end of the building nearest the parking lot. A faded sign on the wall adjacent to the unglazed double doorway, identified the building and the offices within. The engineers confirmed Naval Ocean Survey on the second floor. The first floor was Naval Maritime Service and nothing was listed for the third floor. Rossy was rapidly losing his good working environment vibe as he walked around the shabby rattrap housing his new office. He wondered about the empty Coors beer cans and hundreds of cigarette butts littering the grounds at the base of the building near the end entrance steps. *What's up with all* **that**? Truth or dare, there was no denying that this was a hovel house of a workplace, a lot worse than the FCPRF facility at PWA. But, then, so what? He would be away on TDY most of the time and, hopefully, making good money with few expenses. He didn't really care what the condition of his home base was as long as he got paid.

The sun was starting to lower deeper into the afternoon and the engineers decided they should think about heading on 'home' to Smith's apartment. They returned to the museum parking area and found the Yamaha undisturbed and intact. The marines were gone from the practice quad, as were most of the tourists. They saddled up and motored slowly back towards the gate. Outside, waiting to turn on M Street, they noticed a large, concrete kiosk, with a brown, circled 'M' on top, further down the street in the opposite direction from the 11th Street Bridge they had crossed coming in. They decided to investigate and turned left away from the bridge. At the kiosk plaza, they saw escalators moving people to and from the underground. Parking the bike nearby on the street, they walked over to the kiosk and stepped onto the very long downward escalator. At the bottom they discovered they were in a subway train station. Under a huge archway to a cavernous opening beyond was a wide row of ticket gates opposite twenty, or so, ticket vending machines against the wall. A large schematic of the entire 'Metro' subway system was on the wall beside the machines. Looking at the map, they determined they were at the Navy Yard station of the Green Line. Further study showed the Green Line extended out through Suitland, with a station at another federal center near the AGA, within easy walking distance of their apartment. Fantastic! They would not have to drive to work. They could take the subway. With this revelation, life immediately seemed a whole lot simpler. A rate schedule posted beside the station diagram showed the round trip cost between Suitland and the Navy Yard was probably less than the cost to drive. Sweet! All of a sudden the lights started blinking and people on the other side of the gates moved forward on the red clay tile platform they were standing on. They heard a ding, ding, ding sort of bell sound and felt a rush of air. Then a bullet train came whooshing out of a tunnel and glided silently to a stop at the platform. Doors slid open, people got off, others got on, the doors closed and the train was gone. The engineers were impressed. They hadn't been aware of Washington's world renowned 'Metro' system and were certainly looking forward to using it. Returning to the street, they retraced their route over the bridge, onto Good Hope, through the congested 'street emporium', past the cemeteries and finally back into their new home base, at AGA.

It had been another long day. Yes, they were mugged and lost a lot of money, but at least they weren't mauled by a deranged fight dog, shot by gangsters and left to die in some remote storm culvert. Both hated when *that* happened. And they learned a lot. About D.C. About the new workplace. About Metro. All in all, it had been a successful, productive day. They decided to unpack some vital stuff from their vehicles and go get something to eat. Then maybe look around for a storage cell facility. Shouldn't be hard to find. Those things were everywhere, like pawnshops near a casino. Next week they had to get new bank accounts to deposit what was left of their cash resources. They remembered seeing a Navy Federal Credit Union branch at the Yard, which should suit their banking needs conveniently. And Rossy wanted to line up a dentist as soon as possible. He was almost due for a biannual check-up.

***

Sunday was a rerun of yesterday's beautiful, sunny weather. Booker suggested they use Metro to go downtown and do a little sightseeing at the National Mall. They would also educate themselves in riding the subway, so there would be no screw-ups on their first day of work. Rossy was hesitant. Only one more day. Why should he take a chance risking another potentially disastrous exposure to some absurd situation that could ruin his still developing background and over which he had no control? Booker persisted. What could go wrong? They would be out in the well policed public the whole time, enjoying one of the best and most famous parks in the entire country. Despite his better instincts, the timid tourist relented and off they went. It was about a ten minute walk to the Metro at the Suitland Federal Center. The massive parking lot was almost empty, but they surmised it filled up on work days. Easily locating the 'M' kiosk, they found the station configuration similar to that at the Navy Yard, so it wasn't like they were two incoming barats, fresh off the tour tram from Connecticutstan. They boarded the first thing smokin', after a wait of only a few minutes. It took about fifteen minutes to arrive at the Navy Yard, through several stops between. The schematic showed Archives should be the station on this line nearest the mall area and that's where they exited, up and out onto the street in the heart of the 'big dawg' capital city. But it didn't look like the mall Rossy vaguely remembered from his confinement behind the tinted bus windows, when he was here before. Rather than a huge open grassy area with monuments and pools, they were surrounded by enormous concrete and marble buildings between wide boulevards with heavy traffic. It seemed more like Wall Street than a park. Glancing around, they saw the peak of the Washington Monument pointing skyward from behind, probably, the archives building? Following this most famous of landmarks, they quickly found their way to the mall that was the crown jewel of America's national parks.

People were aimlessly rambling around everywhere through the precisely laid out expanse between the capital building and the Lincoln Memorial. And vendors were likewise everywhere trying to sell whatever people at leisure would buy, which was almost anything. The overall atmosphere was akin to the look and attitude of a gigantic state fair midway, including specialty attractions throughout. Frisbees and balls of all shapes, sizes and colors missiled through the air in random trajectories, sometimes retrieved by slobbering dogs, but mostly run down by shirtless, young white men. The azure sky above the mall was dotted with scores of escaped helium balloons rising to the stratosphere from the slippery fingers of crying toddlers below. A lot of picnics were in progress, with people of all shapes, sizes and colors sprawled on ground blankets or lounging in portable quiver chairs. Pedestrians continually streamed in and out of the surrounding museum buildings and to and from the Smithsonian Metro station, in front of the greatest museum of them all. The engineers deduced they didn't get off the subway right here in the mall, because this station was for a different train line than they rode in on from Suitland and would have required a transfer. They walked slowly past the WM toward the Reflecting Pool, in which a large number of children were noisily and happily splashing about behind signs prohibiting entry into the pool. The supervisory adults smiled from in front of the signs, with video cams rolling. *Typical*, thought Rossy. Americans just aren't very good at obeying rules. Or enforcing them, either, for that matter. But then, the water wasn't much more than a foot deep, and it was getting hot, so why shouldn't kids be allowed to slop around in the pool? It was a park, for chrissakes. He recalled seeing old video, on the History Channel, of hippy Viet Nam War protestors cavorting nude in this same pool and they apparently weren't breaking the rules. At least they weren't shown getting busted on the film. A sizable crowd was congregated before a bandstand along the south side of the Reflecting Pool, from where a Beach Boys impersonation band was adding their contribution to a scheduled park event celebrating American heritage music. *Little Surfer Girl* absorbed quickly into the background noise, as they made their way toward the Lincoln Memorial at the far end of the pool. A hippo-large Clydesdale plodded by, effortlessly dragging a wagonload of mini-U.S. flag waving Japanese tourists being loudly lectured to about the landmarks by the 'Uncle Sam' costumed driver. In watching the mall people, Rossy concluded the most common hand held item, besides a smart phone, was a beach ball sized swirl of cotton candy. The spun sugar mess was literally all over the place. On the ground, on faces, in hair, on clothes. He had always hated the stuff, but had to admire anybody able to sell such a glob of useless crap for at least one abe a wrap. Cotton candy vendors were making a fortune! Maybe even more than the graduate up on Mule Hill.

But not everyone was at the mall to relax and enjoy the day. Some were there to protest. Or to warn. And since Americans were incessantly terrified of the status quo, the National Mall was never without demonstrations, and often impromptu counter demonstrations, of any special interest imaginable. On the steps of the Lincoln Memorial stood a man with an electric bullhorn, amplifying his dissatisfaction at the District government's suppression of his 'second amendment' rights. He had a plywood replica of a Glock semi-automatic pistol attached to his belt, a cardboard Bushmaster AR-15 automatic assault rifle, with an extended ammunition clip, slung over one shoulder and a cardboard Barrett 50 sniper rifle on the other. He was protesting District law prohibiting him, as an ordinary citizen, from openly carrying these weapons in D.C. In point of fact, he was on national parkland, where carrying was legal, but it would not be possible to bring actual weapons through D.C. jurisdiction to the park property without being in violation. The man proclaimed his intention to strap on his *real* arsenal as soon as he got back across the river to *real* America, in Virginia. He urged everyone to arm up against a government that was becoming increasingly tyrannical every day. Another man yelled from the plaza below the steps that if 'gun nut' didn't like America, he should **"get the hell out and take your goddam guns with you!"** Gun nut bullhorned the other guy to **"keep it up and I'll come down there and kick your communist ass into the pool!"** The spat died a natural death as the heckler's wife hustled him away and the gunster continued his rant.

Further on to the other side of the Reflecting Pool, a group of people were in dramatic protest against abortion. They marched in a wide circle carrying signs affixed to one surface of wooden Christian crosses. The signs were lettered in running red paint, presumably to look like blood, condemning abortion as child murder, an abominable sin too horrible to be redeemed by Christ. Anyone performing or receiving an abortion was guaranteed to spend perpetuity in the last rung of hell. Outlaw abortion NOW! On the other side of the crosses were blown up sonogram photos with pictures of children's faces over the apparent heads of the shadowy pre-fetus images. The flock of very intense men and women, in long, hooded druid robes, sang *We Shall Overcome* as they shuffled in slow rotation around a central stationary cross holding a lifesized cardboard Christ figure. Over Christ's anguished head was a sign reading, 'Forgive me, Father, for I cannot forgive the sin of abortion'. Quite a few non-participants watched in curious silence for a moment and ambled on. But Rossy wondered about these ban-abortion activists. They weren't thinking things through. First of all, Jesus didn't know anything about abortion, because the procedure did not exist during his time. So, how could he not forgive something he never heard of? Second, if Jesus was free to decide he couldn't forgive the sin of abortion, what other sins might he not waive? The whole premise of Christianity was that Jesus took a whack for all of every imperfect person's sins, no questions asked, giving everyone the opportunity to start over with a clean slate. Then you could do much better the second time around and end up living with big daddy God for the rest of eternity. But if Jesus decided some things he couldn't, or wouldn't, erase, how could anyone ever be sure they had a zero sin, born again restart? Under the cloud of such uncertainty, what was the point? Finally, the protestors were likely exceedingly conservative in their political persuasion, meaning they probably supported abolishment, or acute reduction, of social programs aiding children born into blinding poverty, or malformed disadvantage. To put forth so much vehement vitriol in protection of a microscopic cell union and then abandon such protection following birth to a screwed up life seemed to be a gross contradiction of values. Rossy knew, of course, there could be no rational discussion of such issues with the demonstrators, because they owned absolution in the Bible, their indisputable, all purpose 'reference manual'. He also knew there could be no such discussion with Booker, because Booker had no alternate opinions on anything. He didn't even vote. The two moved on by the abortion circle, without comment, focussing on another diversion up ahead.

A young man in spandex shorts, tee-shirt and bare feet, wearing a colorful mini-umbrella beanie hat over his shaved head, was holding a black Hefty trash bag open to anyone who walked by. "FILL THIS BAG WITH MONEY!!" he shouted every fifteen seconds, or so. "SAVE OUR PLANET!!" The dude's black shirt displayed large silk screenings of the flat-tailed ass end of a beaver going into the back of the shirt and the buck-toothed face of the beaver emerging out of the front of the shirt, with "SAVE THE PLANET" emblazoned on both sides. The engineers watched in fascination as people actually threw money into the bag while strolling by. *Washington is a fracking clown show*, thought Rossy, in total disbelief of what he was seeing today in the heart of America's epicenter.

Across the mall from the Tidal Basin were a couple of sizable coteries of young people facing off in obvious, serious disagreement. They appeared Mediterranean or Arabic in feature with black hair, dark eyes, or dark sunglasses, and cocoa complected skin tone. The men were well groomed in pressed white linen shirts, pleated woolen slacks and European leather slip shoes, though some wore sneakers. They all were hatless, displaying stylish, anchorman haircuts and several sported some sort of orthodox looking beards. The women wore richly patterned blouses and long skirts with sandals and a lot of gold bling. Many had colorful silk head scarves. All in all, a visually appealing convergence of ethnics, but in resolute contention with each other. The two parties stood about twenty five yards apart and were lobbing emphatic, sometimes profane, insults back and forth like explosive tennis balls. "AMRIKAN JENDE KHIABOONI!"...... "BISHARAF KALE KHAR"!...... "KHAR TOO SARET!" ..... "SHOMA FRACK!" ...... "BE MIR TAA KASI NAMORDE!"..... Fortunately, the slurs were mostly in a farsi dialect and no one in the general propinquity had any idea what they meant or were about. But the signs they were waving up and down, in English, offered some explanation. Apparently, one contingent supported the ayatollahs and their imposition of fundamental Islamic law on Iran, along with a never ending quest for 'death to America'. The opposition spoke for Iranian progressives supporting American sanctions against the ayatollahs until death of religious oppression freed Iran into the community of the modern world. The adversaries were all Iranian nationals, sons and daughters of the Shia elite and full-time resident students attending some of the most prestigious universities in America, right here in Washington. They demonstrated regularly at the mall in hopes of raising American public awareness regarding the complicated issues Iran was grappling with. The average American didn't know much about Iran. It had a lot of oil, possibly some nukes, didn't play very well with its neighbors and was a long time unfriend of the U.S. It might not be a bad bet that a remarkably small percentage of Americans could even find Iran on the map. A much larger percentage didn't really give a poot about this loco Arab country, nor its internal conflicts, nor its location and standing in the world. There were those, however, structurally imbedded within the policy framework of the American government, who were very aware of the nuances of Iranian society and the potential impact they played on regional, even global, geopolitical stability. But here on the National Mall in Washington D.C., on a beautiful September Sunday? Nah. No one was paying any attention to yet another war of words and certainly there was no raising of awareness, about anything, going on.

Rossy and Booker could hear the spirited diatribe as they approached the confrontation. They stopped to watch when they were nearly proximate to the neutral zone separating the disputing factions. Abruptly, the anti-ayatollahs broke laterally and were directly in front of the engineers. The pro-ayatollahs immediately followed and fell in behind the bystanders, snaring them in the middle of the shifted 'no man's land' between the two groups. Without warning, Rossy felt the pelt of a projectile bouncing off his shoulder and turned to see a salvo of rocks arcing through the air! Booker hollered to get down, as rocks started to hail from everywhere. Evidently, the students had brought sacks of throwing rocks to escalate their tirades against one another, Middle East style. As people started getting nailed by the crude bombardments, shrieks of pain overrode the disparaging defamations that had been zinging the mood just moments ago and the demonstration rapidly began taking on the characteristics of a howling street riot. Within seconds the sounds of police whistles and sirens added to the boisterous confusion and large numbers of mallsters started rushing toward the disturbance from all directions to see what was going on. The first responding police quickly surrounded the combatants and pressed inward, scrunching them all into an inescapable knot, with Rossy and Booker trapped right in the center. Some of the students were injured, including one woman with blood streaming down her face. A fleet of emergency medical vehicles, red and white flashers spinning wildly, promptly arrived on the grass and set up triage within the control boundary established and held by the increasing numbers of multi-jurisdictional police forces flooding the scene. In short sequence, there were capital police, park police, metropolitan police and even mounted police converging, in predetermined protocol, to activate a command center system for safely restoring and maintaining order, securing the medical zone for tending to the wounded and injured, sorting out exactly what happened and processing arrests, as necessary. They also had to control and restrict the spectating crowd that was building in a broad line between the Reflecting Pool and the Washington Monument. A bomb squad was en route to address any explosive threats that might be involved. Homeland Security and both the Maryland and Virginia guards had been contacted in case a terrorist issue was detected requiring special national reaction. Constitution Avenue, between 14th and 17th, rapidly became a parking lot of blue strobing police cruisers and motorcycles and fire trucks blocked access to the busy thoroughfare at both ends of the controlled area. The sounds of emergency riposte dominated the setting, with walkie-talkie static, dispatch transmissions, klaxon siren burps and bullhorn barks replacing the diminishing chaotic screaming of the subduing demonstrators. In the distance, on the other side of the mall, Rossy could see portable satellite transmission towers rising out of mobile news vans, from which reporters and camera techs sprinted toward the developing story like ball players pouring onto the field at the start of a game. CNN, Fox News, and all the local network affiliate stations were represented. He shook his head in dismay.

The Iranians and the engineers remained confined in detainment by the ring of the law, while those requiring medical attention were treated and escorted back into the custodial detention sector. Everyone was ordered to sit on the ground, keeping their hands in front of them and in plain sight. The police began to separately search and interview each detainee, after which they were moved to another area of the sector. A prison bus idled nearby to remove anyone designated for arrest. As the students were processed, it became obvious that very few of them would, in actuality, be arrested. Most produced documentation resulting in some kind of immunity. Not diplomatic immunity, because Iran had no active embassy in the U.S. It had to do with a special student visa status stipulated by the State Department to promote normalization of relations between the two countries. Such status was facilitated by receipt of payment of a large sum of money from the students' influential parents. But not all of them had special papers. Those few that didn't were eventually boarded onto the bus. Rossy and Booker were the last ones to be interviewed and they had no papers. All they had was their trusty old driver's license IDs. *Here we go, again! This time will do it. I am now totally fracking screwed. Yeah, Booker, what could possibly go wrong? What a joke!!*

The police believed their story that they were not Iranian, but the engineers could not immediately convince the field interrogators they had no involvement with the students, nor their demonstration, cum riot. They were merely passersby, trying to enjoy a nice day on the mall, and got inadvertently boxed in by events. Finally, the authorities decided the two were not complaisant to the disturbance and they were released. But the ordeal was not over. As they made their way out of the detention zone and away from the restricted scene of controlled, official activity, they were spotted by media hounds, who darted forward like a school of news seeking piranha to seize the first available morsel of information emanating from the breaking event. The fair gamers saw them coming and ran as fast as they could to escape the onslaught. They pulled their shirts up over their heads as they ran to avoid being caught on video and were able to draw away from the lagging reporters and their equipment toting techs. They didn't stop running until they got to the 'M' kiosk of Metro's Smithsonian station, where they ducked into the underground and melded with the subterranean fray of Washington's weekend tourist traffic. "Wow! That was close!" huffed Booker, once they were safely on a train out of the mall. "Ya think?" retorted Rossy with some frustration. But he was relieved that he had dodged yet another bullet of disaster in this long and troubled path to wherever he was going. Typically, Booker seemed good with the fiasco they had just survived and looked alertly around the cab in calm anticipation of whatever next misadventure awaited. Certainly there was no danger out here in this *well policed public.*

***

The engineers spent the last evening before the start of their new careers relaxing in the apartment playing *WarpRove*, a popular video game they found in Smith's extensive inventory. This game involved players starting from earth on a sojourn through the galaxy, where they travelled from one solar system to another, stopping at planetary checkpoints along the way to log in and re-stock. There were varying degrees and types of difficulty and hos-tility encountered at the checks, related to terrain, environment or populating lifeforms. Points were awarded for each successful planetary log in, based on distance from earth and on-site hard-ships overcome. Players could plan for distance and hazard with the resources they stocked at each checkpoint. The more resources carried the further a player could travel and the easier obstacles could be overcome. Distance could also be planned by use of speed and space-time warps facilitated by the varying gravitational slings of system configurations relative to each other. A player could choose a shorter route and try to make a greater number of lower point checks during the journey. Some checks had known conditions, but others were blank, as far as information was avail-able. Some solar systems had life supporting planets, others didn't. The game lasted for a pre-selected time, in minutes, and the win-ner was whoever had the most points in returning to earth within the game time. Or, a player could win by annihilating all the other players in space, within the game time. If no players returned to earth and more than one were still in play at game over, the player with the most standing points won. Up to eight players could par-ticipate in one game. Each player's orientation in the galaxy was continuously displayed on the split TVC screen, but players' re-sources were not shown. It was an interesting game requiring planning, execution and some applications of basic principles of astronomy, cosmology and astrophysics. The possibilities were nearly endless, in that there were an estimated 17 billion solar sys-tems in the galaxy with potentially life supporting orbs. There was a wildly popular on-line version of *WarpRove*, played in real time by people all over the world. In order to log into this game, a new player had to pay a one ben entry fee and fill out an application that included an exam, of sorts, to determine technical proficiency. Based on testing results, a new player would be assigned a starting rank. The higher the starting rank, the more resources a player would initially receive. The second step in logging in was to estab-lish an avatar, which could be any form or definition specified. With the avatar, a player could embark into the game and try to advance in rank and amass as much territory and power as possi-ble, ultimately becoming Topremica, the most dominant force in the game - the one to knock off, the big kahuna. So far, only six players had held the Topremica title, one of them twice. The top twenty five players in the world, below Topremica, held the rank of general, numbered according to standing. They controlled the most resources in weaponry, territory and life essentials, as well as hierarchies of other players working for them. A new player started on earth and could send the avatar wherever desired to begin building status. The avatar could go to work to increase resources, or it could join on with one of the generals' forces to be dispatched to any assignment given. Maybe the avatar would form an alliance with others, maybe it would operate alone. The scope of possible courses of action was unlimited and the loci of operation, the entire universe. When not active, the avatar could be placed into dormancy, during which, if threatened, the player was signaled, via media message. Failure to respond to a threat might result in loss of resources, if precautions were not taken, but an avatar could never be killed. The only way an avatar could be removed was if a player logged off by resigning the game, in which case all resources and territory would be revoked and all employees would be released. If an avatar was dormant for more than thirty days, or the annual membership fee was unpaid, the player was automatically logged out of the game. *WarpRove* was a game of wits, of adaptation to new and unknown environments. There was constant strategy required to execute plans for advancement. It was a game for 'type A' personalities, big egos clawing for success, of which there was obviously no shortage in that there were currently over four million participants. In its first three years, *WarpRove* was exhibiting nearly exponential growth. But an increasing number of players were reportedly becoming obsessed with the game and essentially never logging into dormancy. There was some evidence of behavioral anomalies among such obsessions, but no clear indication of dangerous fallout, at least not yet. Rossy and Booker were not among the on-line 'wrovers'. They had neither the time, nor the temperament, and were content to play the static version of the game for a few hours, turn it off and turn in.

THE NAVY YARD

Monday morning dawned with a hard rain. As expected, the parking lot at the Suitland Metro station was full and there were long queues at the underground ticket dispensers, despite the availability of a heavily advertised phone app to beef up pre-purchased passes and avoid the lines. It was a pedestrian rush, taking nearly a half hour to muddle through the throngs of commuters on the embarkment platform and board a downtown train. But the engineers had given themselves an early start and were not concerned about time. They arrived at the Navy Yard station well before eight o'clock. At the main gate on M Street, the marine guard asked for ID and purpose of visit. They showed their driver's licenses and Booker stated they were going to NAVOSUR, at the Bowditch Building. The marine MP said he was "sorry, sir, but you must have a security pass for that purpose of entry." Booker quickly recanted, "OK, we're going to the museum." The MP said, "Yes, sir, have a nice day," and waved them through. *How fracked up is that?* thought Rossy, while mentally congratulating Booker for playing the guard. They retraced the route they had followed on Saturday, past the quad and the museum to the riverwalk. At the end of the walkway, abreast of the nearly beached tourist ship, they entered the federal center parking lot, which was now filling with vehicles and had become a considerably muddy morass in the rain. At the upper end of the lot, they passed by the space where the party car had been parked the other day. Rossy was a little surprised to not see it still in place. How in hell could anyone in that car have driven it out of there? They were all so totally blitzed they couldn't even have left on foot, let alone drive. Maybe, hopefully, they were arrested and the car was towed off. But no! A pile of Coors cans by the curb in front of the space meant the party boys had, indeed, driven away. *Oh, man, do not drive in the District!*

Rossy was fighting back unwelcome feelings of misgiving as they stepped up to the Bowditch Building entrance. The condition and appearance of the structure had not improved under the wet weather and a waterfall of rain runoff from the roof dumped onto the entrance landing. They quickly opened the door and slipped inside to a dingy, musty smelling corridor foyer that extended across the building width to another set of exterior doors on the other side. The empty foyer had a high ceiling with three light fixtures casting a dim yellow glow to the closed space below. The cracked, pale green plaster walls extended to a dark wood wainscot, four feet up, all around, from the tiled floor. There were several closed, solid wooden doors on both sides of the hallway, one of which identified entrance to the Naval Maritime Service. Another door, right inside the entrance, was labeled Naval Ocean Survey. Everything was incredibly dirty, looking like it had never been painted, waxed, cleaned or repaired. Rossy thought it was worse than grandpap's building. It was downright distressing! He remembered the Safety Center, in Millton, had been the opposite, spotless with shiny, reflective surfaces. Of course, they had unlimited inmate labor, but, Jesus, you would hope the federal government could take better care of its property. Is it that hard to perform basic cleaning and maintenance functions? They swiped their shoes on the large rubber mat inside the entrance and walked over to the Naval Ocean Survey door, opening to a stairwell. There was no elevator and, as they climbed up the steps to NAVOSUR, Rossy wondered how anyone needing the outside handicap ramp for access would ever get upstairs.

"Good morning, gentlemen. I'm glad to see that you made it. No problems in finding us, I assume? Welcome aboard." Director Paul Blackburn motioned, in settling into his chair, for the engineers to have seats in front of the desk, in a small, cluttered office next to the stairwell. Blackburn was a thin, borderline elderly appearing man, with graying hair and no abnormal features, except popeye huge forearms and vividly blue, but friendly, eyes. He also had a small digital amplifier embedded in each ear, though they were not obtrusively noticeable. He shuffled through some papers for a few moments, without saying anything else, and finally looked up, over glasses perched at the end of his nose, and back and forth between the two. "Mr. Rossy?" said Blackburn, looking at Rossy. "Yes, sir, I'm Bill Rossy," said Rossy, nervously extending a hand. Blackburn reached across the desk and shook hands with an almost painfully strong grip. "And you are Booker." "Yes, sir, I'm Ken Booker," said Booker, confidently extending a hand to also receive a painful grip from Blackburn. Rossy wondered how Blackburn identified them, since all they had submitted, so far, was their names and SSNs and they had not separately introduced themselves before he greeted them right after they had walked in from the stairs. *This is a little freaky. What else does he know about me that I did not tell him? At least he didn't say I was disqualified for clearance on an internet technicality. Not yet.*

"OK, gentlemen, I have to get to a meeting and don't have time to talk right now, so if you'll follow me, I'll turn you over to administration and get you started on in-processing. This way, please." Blackburn stood from his desk and walked down a short hallway, into another small office on the other side of the stairwell. "**Tom...Tom**," he snapped in a sharp tone, before the engineers entered behind him. On the other side of the room facing the door, they saw a heavyset man lifting his head from crossed arms on the desk top, revealing a bright red face, with swollen red eyes under slightly reddish, unkempt hair. The dude had been sleeping! And he looked grossly hung over. Maybe still drunk! *What the hell?!* "Tom, here's our new engineering recruits. Remember, we were expecting them today?" Tom McCarven offered a listless wave as he creaked back in his swivel, huge stomach ballooning outward and upward. "Yeah, sure, mornin'. How you doin'?" The recruits murmured 'hellos', wondering what kind of organization they were allegedly joining. Even Booker looked a little stunned by the abnormal introduction they had received thus far. Rossy didn't know how he looked, but he was starting to feel uneasy, maybe a little frightened. *Is this place for real? Do I really have a job here?* "Go ahead and get their paperwork and PI going. Then show them around and return them to me, if I'm back from department, OK?" instructed Blackburn, as he retreated to the hall. "Yessir, no problem," obeyed Tom, reaching into a desk tray for forms. He handed each of the recruits an employment application, Standard Form 171, and directed them to a work table against the wall, at the far end of the office. As Rossy sat down to begin the paperwork, he noticed his name was tagged on the upper left corner of the document. *What the hell? How did Tom know me? Blackburn hadn't introduced them by name!* He looked at Booker and pointed to Booker's name in the corner of his application. Booker shrugged, equally perplexed, but seemingly unconcerned.

He was already transformed into 'go with the flow' mode. But Rossy felt like he was peeping into some kind of an illusional chimera, like Alice looking down the mystical rabbit hole, and he did not feel fully comfortable. He started working on the questionnaire, finding many, no, most of the blanks already filled in. The job title, classification, federal identification and personnel office and his full name and personal information were all printed out, and correctly, as far as he could discern. His educational and work resumes listed appropriate summaries, with dates. Birth data, medical background and administrative history were accurately reflected, even showing documentation of his treatment for temporary hearing loss after the near plane wreck he almost went down in. His immediate family relatives were listed, with current contact info, including a 'deceased' indication, after his father's name. His cell phone number was printed, as was today's date, at the bottom of the form. Basically, the only things missing were his current address and signature. He wrote "TBD" in the address slot, signed at the signature blank and leaned back in his chair, feeling like he had fallen into the rabbit hole and was floating in a nightmarish 'wonderland'. *How in god's fracking name could they have compiled all his personal data? Did the government know everything about everybody!? Holy shit!!* Rossy noticed his hands were shaking and he was starting to perspire. He sensed a slow roll of surreal terror advancing through his awareness and had to re-orientate himself to reality before engaging any further interaction. He glanced at Booker, who was also leaning away from the table, having completed the form. "Wow, that was easy enough," whispered Booker, grinning back at his fellow inductee.

The recruits collected the paperwork and stood up, turning toward McCarven's desk. The admin supervisor was awake and upright, reading the morning *Post* spread over the top of his desk. "All done?" he asked, closing and folding the paper while rising from the swivel and retrieving the completed 171s. "Yes, sir, but I have a question," said Rossy, with some apprehension.

"Shoot," offered the supervisor, replacing the forms to the desk tray.

"Well, most of the application form was already filled out and I was just wondering how you got all that information. A lot of the stuff I thought only I knew about myself. So I'm a little curious about what's going on here."

"Oh, I don't know, Mr. Rossy. I just process the paperwork for the files. Mr. Blackburn gives me the forms and I get them processed and recorded. I really don't have anything to do with actual data."

"But how could all that personal stuff about us be pre-compiled? All we submitted so far was our names and social security numbers."

"Well, like I said, we receive the forms from personnel. I think they probably go through DIS before we get them, but I really don't know anything about that, or what their procedures are."

"DIS?"

"Yeah, Defense Intelligence Service. They review all the applications for security clearance."

"Is that part of the Navy?"

"No, I think it's under Homeland Security, or the CIA, or some central group like that. I'm not sure."

"Well, how do they get all this background info about us without us telling them?"

"Look, Mr. Rossy, I told you, I don't really know. If you have any questions about our procedures, please take it up with Blackburn. I just don't know. I have nothing to do with setting policy. Now, if you're ready, let's get your physical ID work out of the way." McCarven opened a cabinet behind his desk, retrieving some small equipment kits, a pair of latex gloves and a 3D camera.

"What's this?"

"This is for scanning your fingerprints, taking a DNA swab and your security photos. Nothing to it and it won't hurt a bit, trust me." Rossy had never been printed or swabbed before and asked why they had to be treated like they were going through a prison intake procedure. Tom explained they needed to return this info to personnel as part of their security clearance background investigation. "So, do we get a pillow, blanket and jumpsuit?" joked Booker. Tom ignored him as he began the print scans of their hand digits, which were uploaded through an encrypted transmission to personnel. The saliva swabs were preserved in airtight tubes for delivery to a contract lab for DNA analysis and digitized record. The photos would be used for their security badges as well as for integrated biometric comparison. This physical identifying information would be match searched through national and international criminal data bases. If there was any type of hit, clearance would be rejected and the recruits would be demoted out the door. *Ouch!* Rossy felt like he had been convicted of something, though he was certain he was innocent and his rap sheet was clean.

Upon completion of the PID processing, Tom put the equipment away and said he would now take them around, show the facilities, and introduce them to the other folks they might be working with. "Unfortunately, mostly everybody's in the field right now, but there are a few here in the office. OK? First, coffee?"

"Yeah, thanks, I'll have a coffee." *Might be working with? What the hell does that mean?*

McCarven walked out of the office with the recruits in tow. They followed a passage between a concrete block wall and opaque, corrugated plastic partitions to a large room on the other side of the floor. Inside the room portal, they turned into a tiny vestibule, accommodating the office coffee concession. The three coffeed up with styrofoam cups and McCarven offered some scone looking biscuits from a box on the table beside the pot pads. He said they were made by the processing supervisor's granddaughter for his birthday. *That's nice,* thought Rossy, as he reached for one of the baseball sized treats. Jesus christ! The thing must have weighed a half pound and was hard as granite! He knew there was no way he could eat it, but neither could he put it back in the box. And he didn't want to throw it in the trash can right there by the concession. So he waited until McCarven was looking the other way and shoved it into his front pants pocket for disposal later. Booker didn't have this problem, because he wisely passed on the leadball scones.

Emerging from the coffee closet, they entered the open office the recruits had glanced at going in. The square room was filled with high table desks, divided into two parallel groups of abutting rows that were lined up facing each other. A rotating bar stool chair sat in front of each mylar covered work table and each table was equipped with a detachable, mobile hinged task light. At first look, the furnishings seemed to be old style drafting work stations, but they were actually flatbed autocad units, with integrated computers and plotter screens to produce full-sized, navigational survey charts. There were four people seated at various work stations in the center of the room and a fifth behind a low admin desk in the far corner. Undraped windows lined the two exterior walls and a single door under a red 'EXIT' sign was at the end of the interior wall. A short, stocky forties-something man, in jeans, striped, long-sleeved Arrow shirt and deck shoes with no socks, arose from behind the corner desk and strode quickly forward to meet the incoming group.

"Hey, Dick. Mornin'. Got some new engineers for you to meet, here," said Tom, hitching his thumb at the recruits, behind him.

"Great! We can never get enough new people," chuckled Dick Whittberg, the engineering supervisor. As he got closer, Rossy thought that Dick's puffy round face, like Tom's, had a crimson alcoholic glow, though his squinty little eyes were clear and lucid. "Nice to meet you, Mr. Rossy, welcome aboard," smiled Whittberg, offering a hand to Rossy, who received the gesture with concluding realization that, somehow, everyone here already knew him. "Mr. Booker, welcome aboard," continued Whittberg, shaking hands with Booker. "Let me introduce you to some of the guys."

Rossy looked out into the room at the other four dudes, who were not paying any attention to the strangers. They all seemed to be in the same age bracket as the recruits, but not very professional in appearance. TV reality fringe people, like the redneck duck callers, or the swamp dwelling alligator rollers, came to mind. He wondered, but did not ask, if any women worked at NAVOSUR. Whittberg led them over to the nearest 'engineer', Peete "doubleman" Andersson, an obviously very tall, and correspondingly large, Scandinavian type, with long, straw hair tied in a ponytail down his broad back and a scruffy yellow beard. Doubleman glanced briefly away from an online video game he was playing on his phone and nodded acknowledgment to Whittberg's introduction of the newmen. They moved further down the row to two other 'engineers' at facing comp desks engaged in table football, where players, in turn, tried to finger flick a small folded paper wad through the other player's hand formed 'goalpost'. Manny "groob" Silvera, a Portuguese descent native of Fall River, Massachusetts, laughed from under a full head of dark curls after he placed a shot dead center through the upright thumbs of his opponent. "That's game, man! Break beer's on you, bt." Jesse "blacktongue" Cain ejected a deep-south, Mississippi "frack you, Silvera!", and threw the paper wad football across the room.

They both mumbled 'how's it going?', to Whittberg's presentation of the recruits, as they got up from their stool chairs and headed toward the exit in the back of the room. At the end of the row, the orientation tour encountered a blank-faced, Afamian 'engineer', wearing a neatly trimmed goatee beard, a navy blue beret and very dark sunshades, almost as dark as his skin. He was reclined in a regular desk chair with heavily booted feet propped up on the edge of a work table and headset muffed ears linked to his personal music stream. Without moving, Rokko "rocko" Limeweaver might have looked up from the current issue of *NASCAR Illustrated* he was reading, or not. It was hard to tell. He sliced a crisp salute from his right eyebrow, in silent, expressionless response to meeting the recruits, and returned to the magazine, or maybe to sleep. Whatever. The trio reversed back to the front of the engineering room, where McCarven was waiting to escort the recruits to the next segment of their initiation walk-through.

Lawrence Lockbark cut a dapper image, in a professional, grandfatherly sort of way. He was neatly dressed in gray, gabardine suit slacks, short sleeved business shirt, with a tightly-knotted red bow tie, and shiny brown, tasseled loafers. His grayish white hair was combed away from a precise side part, though a stubborn cowlick protruded behind one temple. His desk sat in the middle of a small, open-ended, bunker-like room, beside an ominously closed, solid metal door to the cynosure of his responsibility. Lockbark was the data processing supervisor and he took his duties very seriously. Behind the overwide, unidentified door was NAVOSUR's automation center, where field data was digitally received, compiled, processed, formatted, transmitted, encrypted and stored. While no unauthorized personnel would ever get past Lockbark's diligent observation, the classified data center was also protected by a handprint scan pad, recognizing only those with registered clearance to enter, and by high frequency perimeter attenuation, which blocked any random transmission of microwave spectrum energy through the envelope of the shielded space. A small red status light above the entry pad indicated no one was inside the secured area. The light was green when the area was legitimately occupied. The recruits did not yet have any level of security clearance, and Larry, of course, would not allow them entry into the center. He wouldn't even let them past the red tape line he had installed on the floor, five feet in front of the entrance wall, over which only authorized personnel were permitted and no unwarranted approach could illicitly reach the print pad. But he described the facility to them, proudly overviewing the custom, high speed, high capacity super computers that were interfaced for selective closed satellite communication with more than five thousand fixed and mobile service points around the globe, including the international space station. They could, nearly instantaneously, receive, process and distribute real-time field data to any place on earth and it was completely dark. The system was open only to restricted frequency bands and was unpenetrable , unless there was a security breach. And that's why Larry felt such a special responsibility. *Nothing* would ever be compromised on his watch. Rossy was impressed, but silently wondered how the center was properly guarded when Mr. Lockbark went home at 5 o'clock.

Further on down the floorway were two oblong office areas shaped by portable partitions. The first one, the tech work space, in a large, central part of the floor, held a bunch of task tables and a gray metal desk. Two technicians were at one of the tables and the tech supervisor sat at the desk. All were watching a TV, mounted on the partition at the end of the enclosed space. *The Price Is Right* was blaring the obnoxious squeals of hyper-excited contestants vying to win some useless prize, like a patio furniture set. Rossy hated the show and could never understand how it remained on the air for fifty years, or however long it had been broadcast. Mickey Green got up from the desk and quickly muted the TV when he saw McCarven and the engineering recruits entering his 'tech zone'. Green was a retired navy enlisted man, barely honorable and undistinguished, who never had much use for military officers, or educated civilians. His disdain for authority evidently motivated a secondary career in union advocacy. He was NAVOSUR's local representative of the Federal Government Employees' Union, of which he was the only agency member. Green had been stuck in step ten of his grade for years, with no hope for promotion, either by merit or reclassification. He had pissed enough people off during his tenure that no one in a superior position would ever endorse his advancement. Consequently, the only pay raises he got were cost of living adjustments, which were few and far between, as well as minuscule, in the flat, debt ridden economy. A while back, he lost a suit, filed through FGEU, claiming discrimination against his Lebanese heritage in being passed over for a higher grade job. Since then, Green maintained a calendar by his desk featuring a large 'X' over each past date with a small, circled number indicating how many days until early retirement, on his fifty-fifth birthday. He was literally time tracking the passage of his life. Seeing the two new 'engineers' entering his domain, Mickey could barely hide his contempt, knowing they would soon, if not already, be making more than he was without knowing a fracking thing about what they were doing. All they had was a goddam college degree. Big, fracking shit. But he managed a minor smirk, handshakes and a few smalltalk words for the recruits when introduced by McCarven, the useless, asshole drunk. During the brief discourse with Green, the techs got up from the table and left the t-zone, in the direction of the stairwell exit at this end of the floor. Rossy figured those dudes probably already knew him. If not, he would likely meet them later.

The other partitioned work area on this section of the floor was for party chiefs, the engineering supervisors of operations in the field. There were six desks in this space, only one of which was occupied. Trent "redeye" Bergle was tending to the monstrous L. A. Times crossword puzzle from the Sunday paper. He had just returned from a survey project in Palau, where a helicopter had gone down over shoal water, losing nearly $2M worth of specialized NAVOSUR equipment. Bergle was awaiting scheduled debrief at a SECNAV division office, where he would report no deviation in operational protocol contributed to the loss, despite the requirement that floating, waterproof containers were to be used at all times when transporting classified equipment over water. Redeye was a staunch, far right conservative. He espoused his perception of government as a liberty confiscating, tax leaching scourge and loved to endlessly argue this postulation with his 'socialist' colleagues way past happy time over far too many rounds of beer. His eyes were permanently bloodshot, but he was an amiable sort and enthusiastically welcomed the recruits into the organization, emphatically stating he was looking forward to working with them. He offered assistance with any aspect of orientation he could help them with. Rossy appreciated redeye's upbeat attitude, thinking maybe there were others, in the agency, with whom he could possibly develop a good working relationship. McCarven described the end portion of the floor as caged storage for equipment and supply inventory and led the recruits back toward the front office. They had only met a fraction of the staff so far and, quite frankly, Rossy thought they pretty much resembled a collection of disconnected lazers. He hadn't seen anyone doing any work, but was willing to give them the benefit of the doubt and assume their production was primarily contributed while on field duty. So, for now, he would keep an open mind and reserve judgement until some point after a few hours of the first day. Booker looked bored and totally unconcerned.

Paul Blackburn had returned from the early morning meeting and was seated at his desk when the recruits returned from the walk-through. He asked if they had any questions and Rossy responded, "Yes, sir, I was just wondering exactly what are the duties here in the office?"

"Well, like I told Mr. Booker a few weeks ago, we perform hydrographic and oceanographic surveys, primarily in coastal belts, around the world. I'm sorry, I can't be more specific until you are cleared to work with classified information."

"But it didn't look to me like anybody we met in the office was doing much of anything. Do they have work assignments when they're not traveling?"

"Again, Mr. Rossy, since you are not yet cleared, you cannot be exposed to any classified material. It might have seemed like no one was occupied, but that's because they were protecting the parameters of the mission. I think you'll understand after you are fully integrated into our system."

The inquisitor was not convinced. The people he saw weren't hiding classified stuff from anybody. They were sitting there fracking off and not doing anything that could be even remotely mistaken for work! But he had another question. "Mr. Blackburn, I also was wondering, earlier, when we got our application forms from Mr. McCarven, most of the background info was already filled in. How do you know all that about us?"

"It's all part of the process, son. We deal with highly sensitive issues here and our resources are extensive. All you need to know right now is the investigative process for your clearance is engaged and, when satisfactorily completed, you will be fully instated."

"How long will that take?"

"It depends how straightforward your personal history is. If there are any complications, they must be addressed and it will take longer. I really can't say, because I'm not directly involved."

Oh my god! I'll never get cleared! I'm sure I have complications!! "So what are we supposed to do until we're cleared?"

"We'll put a table here in the hallway and you can work there."

"What work are we allowed to do?"

"I'll get you each a copy of *The American Practical Navigator*. You can read that and educate yourselves on the principles of navigation. That's our bible, the basis of all our modern survey techniques. Nathaniel Bowditch published it more than two centuries ago and it is still highly relevant today, though obviously with extensive revisions and updates. Every vessel in the United States Navy has a copy of Bowditch on board."

The rest of the day passed quietly. There was very little traffic in proximity to the recruits' temporary work station and phones rarely rang anywhere on the floor that they could hear from their sequestered vantage point. In reading the Bowditch manual, Rossy actually found the science of global positioning quite interesting. He learned the earth was not spherical, but more elliptical, in shape, but not a perfect ellipsoid. There were different mathematical ellipsoids defined to most accurately establish a point position at different locations on the earth's surface. A geoid was the actual imperfect shape of the earth's surface, which could not be mathematically defined, like the ellipsoid. It represented a surface the seas would conform to if there were no land masses, a surface of equal potential gravity. The difference between the geoid and the most accurate ellipsoid applicable to any given point was defined as the geodetic separation. Latitude was the angle between a perpendicular line at a point on the geoid or ellipsoid and the equator, or long axis, of the geoid or ellipsoid. Astronomic latitude could be measured for a point on the geoid, with a sextant, as the elevation of Polaris, the north star, and geodetic latitude could be determined mathematically for a corresponding point on the ellipsoid. The measurement of the geodetic separation was called the deflection of the vertical, which was the angle between the astronomic and geodetic latitudes. The smaller the deflection of the vertical, the more accurate the determination of latitude. Similar considerations were applied to the meridian of longitude and together they defined a geodetic position on the earth. Modern positioning techniques used doppler wave data through orbiting satellites to establish positions points, but they still had to use one of the defined ellipsoids to map and compute the points. Booker did not find much fascination with the reading material and eventually dozed off, quickly awakening when admin Tom popped out of his office and issued them each a temporary security pass for getting on base through the Navy Yard gate.

At about ten minutes before five o'clock, everyone on the floor, at least the non-supervisory personnel still remaining, congregated near the exit to to the main stairwell, which was also near the work table set up for the uncleared recruits. After a few minutes of milling about in the hallway, a whistle sounded from McCarven's room, like a football referee blowing a play dead, and they all bolted through the door and clonked noisily down the stairs. Quitting time. The first day newbies got up from the table, said 'goodbyes' to Mr. Blackburn, who was on the phone and waved, and admin Tom, who didn't see or hear them and didn't respond. They went cautiously through the door, down the steps and out of the building. In leaving, Rossy noticed there were no steps in the stairwell to the third floor. He did not remember any mention of the third floor during their orientation walk-through. Strange, he thought, but maybe it was a classified thing.

Outside they began their trek to the main gate when they were intercepted by redeye coming down the walkway from the end of the building. "Hey, you guys wanna grab a brew?" He was already holding a can of Coors and Rossy started to ask "where in the hell did you get that?", when Booker said, "sure, sounds great!" Redeye threw the can into a small shrub. "Super! Let's go! Follow me." The three moved together toward the gate and redeye provided a tour guide brief of everything they passed. He seemed to be somewhat of a Navy Yard archivist, explaining that the big gray ship they passed at the riverwalk, the USNS Beecher, was a decommissioned navy tender that had been reincarnated into a retrofitted NAVOSUR survey unit, operated by the NMS. The Beecher, renamed for a Maryland U.S. senator instrumental in establishing NAVOSUR as a separate agency within the Navy superstructure, was permanently retired after an inebriated master ran it aground during a domestic survey operation near Charleston, South Carolina. Rossy continued to wonder where the party chief got a can of beer within minutes of leaving work at the Bowditch Building, but never got the chance to ask. Soon they were out along the wall on M Street approaching a crosswalk to the other side of the wide avenue. There didn't seem to be very much of significance in the vicinity - mostly large, old, empty looking warehouse and industrial shop type structures. Maybe a few office buildings, a parking garage. No stores or residential houses or apartments that were obvious. They came to a small intersecting side street, more like an alley, on the corner of which was a long, narrow two-story, white brick building, projecting a slightly historical character. "Marcie's M Street Mashup" read the hand-painted driftwood sign above the prominent green, gold and black entrance. Redeye led the way up a one step brick veranda and opened the door. They entered into a comfortable barroom and cafe lounge, awash in the rich reggae trip beat of Peter Tosh's *Legalize It*. Though the lighting was appropriately low, augmented by shuttered casement windows across the front, they could see a long, mirrored, cherrywood bar along one wall and a row of round tables, surfaced with red and white checkered vinyl cover cloths, lining the opposite wall. A pool table was in the middle of the well-waxed hardwood floor at the far end of the room, beyond which were the slatted, swinging doors to a small kitchen. Almost life sized, mahogany flat-carvings of palm trees, marijuana boughs, banana bunches and other Caribbean icons adorned the speckled brick walls. Evenly spaced paddle fans, hanging from the high molded tile ceiling along the centerline of the room, rotated slowly and silently through the afternoon heat. Air conditioning was pending. The NAVOSUR engineers and techs were seated at a couple of tables pulled together in the front corner of the room, accompanied by a strikingly beautiful black woman with yard long dreadlocks streaming thickly to her waist and four inch gold hoops dangling from her ears. They all watched as the recruits approached behind redeye to join the ensemble.

"What ya bringin', redeye, mon?" purred Marcie, in a lilting, island cant. She was the Jamaican born owner and proprietor of The Mashup, who often sat with the NAVOSUR 'sailors', as she called them, until happy time picked up and more after-work customers drifted in. Marcie had been married to a marine who was killed in action during a late tour of duty in Iraq. She used her $500,000 military death benefit to open the place, across the street from the marine police unit that had redressed her husband's burial at Arlington, hoping to support herself and her 'likkel piken'. The Mashup started as a bar and social lounge, but was rapidly gaining cred as a good jerk joint, attracting patrons from the Yard, as well as the nearby Metro station. A recent, positive feature in *The Post* was helping to draw residents from the contiguous Adams-Morgan district and establish a neighborhood clientele. Business had picked up to the extent Marcie was able to employ three people and she was thinking of jettisoning the pool table for live music on the weekends. She liked the sailors, recognizing them as her earliest, most reliable and probably most frequent supporters. "Got some new sailors for ya, Marcie," answered redeye, pulling up more chairs from another table.

"Ooh, dis one bwoi, ya know, him got som biggi junk in him trunk, mon", smiled Marcie, looking directly at the bulging pants standing beside her. *Shit!* thought Rossy, gazing down at the round protuberance knobbing out from the front of his trousers. He had completely forgotten about the concrete scone he stuffed in his pocket this morning! Now it felt like he was hiding a watermelon and he could feel his face reddening as all eyes at the table converged on the object of Marcie's jesting scrutiny.

"Well, I believe you right, Marce, this boy fo' sho' is packin' a 'biggi johnson', snickered rocko. "Matter of fact, his 'johnson' so big, I believe he need to buy a round of troggs for the table! Whaddup, bj? You the **main**!" Marcie happily got up to refill the pitchers as the table erupted in raucous laughter and applause. And from that moment forward, Rossy was known among the NAVO sailors as "bj". He sat down at the table not knowing exactly what to do. He couldn't pull the scone out and have everybody muse on what kind of a dipshit new guy are they going to have to work with that carries a scone around in his pocket. Who the hell does that? He decided to not say anything about it and after a while go to the restroom and throw the damned thing away in private. Then, if anyone wondered where his 'biggi johnson' went, that was their problem.

***

The next morning the engineering sailor recruits did not feel well. They had stayed far too late at the Mashup, redeye and bj arguing every conceivable point-counterpoint associated with solving the worldwide climate change problem. Redeye was all for climate change. He didn't care if summer daytime temperatures in Phoenix were higher than the recommended setting for domestic water heaters. He planned to buy land at the cooler climes of upper elevations and sell at a huge profit as the lower piedmont regions became uninhabitable. Global warming, apocalypse now, end of the world, whatever! Bring it on! Redeye was ready. Rossy thought maybe humanity should try to mitigate some of the adverse impacts of civilization and keep the earth livable. Clean, alternative energy systems, yes, like fuel cells, should be optimized and implemented, while polluting combustion of carbon based fuel sources should be phased out. Redeye was against policy change, predicting it would only inspire government to smother everyone with tax-heavy regulations and send the economy into permanent depression. Booker, now aka "shiner" in accession to his southwest Virginia roots, had no opinion on any of the topics debated by the verbal jousters and entertained himself watching TV and gabbling with a couple of incoherent dread heads at the bar. He felt a Caribbean alliance with them in that he had almost moved to St. Croix. The other sailors had long since pulled anchor and floated home.

Bj and shiner each carried several thousand dollars in cash with them as they walked up to the Suitland Metro station to go to work. They intended to deposit the cash, their respective life savings, in opening accounts at the Navy Yard credit union branch. Rossy was thinking about the graduate's advice to never take more than cab fare into the ghetto, but eased his concern a little by rationalizing that the Metro was probably, hopefully, not the ghetto. Booker was not worried - he hadn't considered the potential danger of bringing a large amount of money into the city, nor thought about their recent experience on Mule Hill. If he had, he would say the odds were astronomically against being mugged twice in four days, like a double lightning strike, and forgotten about it again. So when they boarded the train, Rossy felt like he was wearing the cash pinned to the outside of his shirt and everyone was staring at him, plotting their attack, while Booker was mesmerized by the tunnel wall zipping by a foot outside the subway cab window.

Arriving at the M Street gate from the Metro, the recruits were relieved to find their temporary security passes were good with the guard and they would not have to visit the museum on the way to work. After checking in at the office, they asked to go to the credit union to open their accounts. Rossy wanted to get this done as soon as possible so he wouldn't be carrying his net worth around any longer than necessary. No problem. They were gladly excused to take care of personal 'settling in' business and were pleasantly surprised at how smoothly it went. The Navy Federal Credit Union people were professional, efficient and friendly, unlike the grinding hash of pifflebunk the PWA credit union chunked out in Connecticut. But then again, they were now *giving* the banksters money, rather than taking it, and that made all the difference. Money was always the difference. There were really only two kinds of people in the world - those with money and those without. On the money team, everyone was civil and got along reasonably well with each other. On the other side, all you got was a bunch of helly hokum and a hard way to go. If there was no such thing as money, like how it would be after a cataclysmic collision of earth with a rogue planet, everybody would be trying to rip what they needed from others and no one would be happy. So, no matter what the cliches to the contrary, money *was* the key to happiness, or at least to not having to constantly take shit in blumbering through life.

On the way back from the credit union, the recruits observed groob and bt leaned up against the parking lot end of the Bowditch Building, in the sun, swilling beer. It was, like, nine-thirty in the morning! The engineers waved the recruits over and invited them to take a time out. They followed the breaksters up the steps to the single doorway. Inside was a nearly empty concrete deck, an enclosed porch-like space, reeking of stale smoke. Against the blank far wall stood a large vending machine. Groob put a george into the currency slot and out popped an ice cold, ten ounce can of Coors! He handed the beer to Rossy, while feeding another bill into the slot releasing a second Coors, which he gave to Booker. They had a fracking beer machine in the building! Rossy had never heard of, nor seen, anything like this... anywhere, not even in liquor stores. They had to be totally illegal. And this thing wasn't even secured. Apparently, those dudes in the car did their party shopping here, as did a lot of other people, judging from the large rubber container, overflowing with empties, that was placed across from the machine right inside the door. This also accounted for the beer cans strewn at various places around the outside of the building. And the cigarette butts scattered everywhere in and out of the unorthodox break room. A five gallon bucket of sand beside the can bin was filled with the gross little stubs, looking like it rarely, if ever, was emptied. This was unbelievable! Hell, an eight year old kid could come in here and get snockered and nobody would have a clue how it happened. Groob noticed the surprised look on the initiates' faces and offered an explanation. The machine belonged to NAVOSUR. They had all pitched in and bought an old *Pepsi* dispenser they cleaned up, repaired and painted to a generic, nondescript appearance. They worked out a sweet, undocumented deal, with a beverage supplier for the Navy Yard service clubs, to keep the unit filled at a tad over cost less salvage value of the empty cans at a nearby Alcoa recycling trailer. The proceeds from the operation went into the office 'sunshine fund' for special events, like going away parties that occurred with unusually high frequency, since few field people worked at NAVOSUR for more than three to five years, or, until their TS security clearance expired. *But how the hell can you drink while you're at work?* wondered Rossy, as he quaffed another slash from his break-time coldie.

Returning to the office, the recruits assumed their stations at the hallway work table for the 'uncleared'. The Bowditch manuals were still there, along with their orientation notebooks and a cupful of black, '*Property of the U. S. Government*' pens supplied by admin Tom. Rossy continued his navigational studies, choosing geometric geodesy as his topic of interest for the day. This involved the determination of precise positions of points on the earth's surface, using the principles of triangulation and trilateration, or the measurement of angles and distances through a traverse from known geodetic coordinates on the defined ellipsoid of use. The field data had to be adjusted to mean sea level, or the geoid, to be as accurate as possible. Because the ellipsoid deviates from the geoid away from the original area of adjustment, the error must be distributed through the traverse via a La Place observation. GPS technology, developed by the Air Force, did the same thing utilizing reflective wave data, but was not sufficiently accurate for precision positioning. Back in the Bowditch day, or at least back in the pre-microcomputer day, geodetic calculations had to be done by hand and were so tedious and would take so long that several sets of field data were required to verify the technical surveyor did not suffer a mental meltdown during the process and frack the whole thing up. Booker failed to last until lunch break without falling dead asleep, upright in his chair.

At a little after twelve, redeye stopped by with groob and bt to pick the recruits up for lunch. They went across the Yard to a large, sand colored concrete building at the waterfront, below the museum. The NCO Club or, more commonly, the Chiefs' Club. Inside the simple entrance foyer, they faced a small purser's office to the left and double glass doors to a long corridor straight ahead. Through the astro-turfed, windowless corridor, they passed elaborately framed prints, prominently mounted on the enameled cinder block walls, of some of the Navy's most legendary fighting ships. The Enterprise, The Independence, The Constitution, The Nimitz, The Eisenhower. All were displayed in full, battle worthy glory, each the master of the sea in her own unique way and time. They also passed by restrooms, a mechanical room and a fire exit near the end of the hallway, where the wall to the left opened into a short tunnel-like cloak passage to the main service area and a closed door at the end led to the kitchen. A small, square table with a couple of chairs sat in the corner between the egress ways. "This is where *you* mothafrackers have to sit until you're frackin' cleared", chortled blacktongue, pointing to the table. "Then you have to pay some dickhead chief to bring your frackin' lunch." The recruits started to protest with misgiven dismay, when they realized bt was just fracking with them. They were all chuckling as they entered the ballroom sized dining room from the coat alcove. A long buffet paralleled the inside wall to the right. In the center was a massive rectangular bar. The far wall across the room was entirely glazed with floor to ceiling fenestration, including several doorways to an outside deck service area overlooking the Anacostia. Rows of ornate chandelier clusters hung from the high ceiling, refracting too much extraneous light into the already brightly sunlit room. White clothed tables were everywhere on the floor around the dining hall, many of which were occupied, as were most of the bar seats. Even the outside deck tables were nearly filled and there was a considerable line at the head of the buffet, as people seemed to be swarming in from all directions. The recruits looked around, astounded at the volume of activity. There must be three hundred people in the place - a mix of civilians and uniformed military - all talking, or yelling, at once. The reflected noise was deafening, echoing from the hard surfaced decor with little attenuation. It looked like some kind of a special banquet party, but the engineers said this was just the normal workday lunch crunch. The sailors turned toward the buffet line where the most obvious feature was the broad *Golden Paddock* sign hanging above the tray track. Evidently, the food service was franchised out. Rossy had never been to a *Golden Paddock* and wasn't sure a fifty yard long buffet could offer high level cuisine. But, it cost under a hamilton, so what the hell? Besides, how bad could it be, if all these people were here? Then again, he noticed everyone was drinking, possibly a negative indicator of the food quality. *Jesus, it seemed like everyone at the Navy Yard was **always** drinking. What the hell is that all about?* The perennial worrier fought back familiar vestiges of foreboding and grabbed a tray.

After noshing a monster mediocre lunch, Rossy felt overstuffed and got up from the table to return to the office. Booker likewise started to rise and, when he noticed no one else was budging, sat back down. Redeye said they had plenty of time for another round of brews and urged bj to "relax, we're professionals - we're not on a clock!" But bj couldn't drink anymore and just wanted to get out of there and away from the unyielding clamor of the dining room. He was developing a headache. So, he exchanged 'laters' with his coworkers and exited the club. Walking along the riverway, soothed by the harmonious symmetry of the beautiful weather and the buena vista, he slowed to enjoy the slight beer buzz accumulated from the strange itinerary defining his day so far. Christ, at this rate he would be sozzled by quitting time, but right now, in the present, he felt pretty good, maybe even a little mellow. He sat down on a sun drenched bench facing the water and gazed at the peaceful, attractive surroundings, again thinking this was not a bad place to work. Listening to the gentle lapping of the water against the bulkhead, he felt his eyes starting to close as he went into a nod, but then something detected in his lateral vision caused him to abruptly turn his head. Down near the end of the riverwalk, close to the parking lot, he saw two figures standing in conversation. Squinting against the brilliance of the sun, he recognized one man as processing supervisor Lockbark and the other, much larger man, was....what the hell??...the graduate?! Rossy couldn't believe his eyes. What the frack were those two doing together? As he watched, slumping below the bench back, he saw them exchange battered, government issue briefcases, shake hands and turn away from each other. Larry crossed the riverwalk and went up the gangway ramp to The Beecher, disappearing into a hatchway off the side deck. The graduate, dressed in Navy camo fatigues, followed the fence along the parking lot and headed toward the upper Yard area in the direction of the main gate. The reluctant witness sat on the bench, now widely awake, and tried to process what he had just seen. He couldn't make any sense of it, because no explanation computed. The two were from different universes, they had nothing in common. What could possibly be their connection?? And how could he find out? Booker knew the graduate, but he wouldn't know anything about Larry and the graduate. He couldn't ask anyone else in the office, because then he would have to explain who the graduate was and why *he* knew the gangster dude, and that wasn't going to happen. He obviously couldn't ask Larry what the story was, because he just didn't know the supervisor yet and, if he was getting into something he shouldn't, it might jeopardize his clearance. It looked like the only option was to do nothing, at least for right now. He decided to not even discuss it with Booker, since Booker would be prone to repeating the conversation to his new pals, which would reveal their embarrassing Mule Hill encounter that he did not want publicized, ever. Rossy was done feeling mellow and was starting to get a headache again. He stood up from the bench and walked quickly back to the office.

Similar to yesterday, the afternoon was uneventful. The Chiefs' Club lunchsters mozied back into work around two-thirty and Booker had trouble staying awake until break-time, at a little after three. Rossy passed on break and tried to concentrate on the mathematical relationship between eccentricity and flattening in the definition of a geodetic ellipsoid, but his mind kept straying to the peculiar scene he had witnessed earlier. He knew this was going to be a real problem for him and, until he got answers, his professional enthusiasm for this new job was certain to be critically sidetracked. Something was not right in the organization and he needed to find out what, if he was going to satisfactorily settle in and thrive here. Otherwise, the whole deal would be a bust. At quitting time, the engineers again congregated around the stairwell door awaiting admin Tom's whistle, only today they were somewhat incapacitated from the day's strenuous break schedule. They moved slowly down the stairs and took nearly twenty minutes to make it over to the Mashup for happy time. Rossy barely stayed for one beer and then departed by himself to catch the Metro back to Suitland. He never knew when Booker returned, just that it was long after the witching hour.

***

The remainder of the recruit's orientation week brought more of the same. They seemed to be essentially on their own to do whatever they wanted, as long as there was no violation of security protocol. There weren't any specific assignments other than a suggestion from Dick Whittberg that if they wanted to do something useful, maybe a little different, while awaiting clearance, they could clean up in and about the downstairs break room, which was getting a bit unsightly. Rossy surmised this was probably some kind of rookie initiation task, like being sent to retrieve a left handed monkey wrench, and thought nothing about taking an hour, or so, improving the appearance of the building purlieu. Booker grumbled that he didn't spend four years and a fortune at engineering school to pick up trash and basically took a beer break while his running buddy worked. Their responses were noted by the covertly observant engineering supervisor.

On Friday, redeye advised the recruits that everybody was headed to Kelly's OK Klub, on K Street in Georgetown, after work, rather than The Mashup. Doubleman was leaving Monday, on TDY, and it was a loose office tradition to give everyone a Kelly's TGIF sendoff before departure. Every Friday, from three to seven, KOKK offered a mighty spread of free, five-star hors d'oeuvres and half-priced drinks, creating one of the hottest end-of-week destinations in D.C. One just might see the speaker of the house, the senate majority leader, some superstar media politico, anybody's chief of staff, a brigade of first-year law students, or any number of nobody federal workers, all jammed in together, shoulder to shoulder at the wrap around bar, sloshing down Norwegian oysters with one of more than a hundred imported draft lagers and stout ales. It was quite a madcap mise en scene and not a place for the claustrophobic, nor the impatient. The sailors arrived about five-thirty and the place was totally, probably illegally, packed. After showing proof of age ID to a greeting hostess, they easily spotted doubleman from the elevated entrance gallery overlooking the open service area, who needlessly waved as he like-

wise spotted them standing at the balustrade. He was in a far corner of the room, seated at a raised, round drink table with a borderline elderly woman, who glanced furtively around while clutching
a large, canvas tote bag. Doubleman lived with his nearly equally
oversized mom, in a townhouse off 21st Street, and had left work
early to run a few pre-travel errands and pick her up to join the
group at KOKK. He was lucky to get a table where they could all
at least have a place to anchor their drinks and plates amid the
overflowing confusion of this super happy time crush.

The sailors worked their way slowly through the horde, eventually reaching the table of destination. Following greetings and
introductions to doublemom, they maneuvered their way back
across the room to the self-service food ensemble, where an extensive and eclectic display of award winning gourmet eats was
available. Bacon wrapped venison meatballs, crab cake and burger
sliders, sautéed wild goose and mushrooms, smoked mountain
trout, bison meat loaf, quail pot pies, oysters, sushi, free range
chicken tots, roasted pepper sauce and pasta, chocolate covered
fruit berries, cakes, tarts, cheeses, veggies, papaya and mango salad, pizzas, salsas, chips, nuts and on and on and on - much too
much stuff to fit a sample of everything on one plate. And the
busy, efficient staff kept every item well supplied and the serving
area orderly and clean. It was truly a stunning, culinary offering
and well worth the crowded hassle to experience. But KOKK did
not tolerate 'feeders', those who would partake of the free fare
without buying a drink. Accordingly, within seconds of leaving
the food service area with a plate, every patron would be accosted
by a floor server taking the drink order. Most people immediately
paid or tabbed their drink transactions, plus tip and including a
charge for water, via phone or video ID charge, so there was essentially no cash flow happening in support of this at once chaotic
and systematic process. Not surprisingly, their drinks arrived at the
little round table nearly simultaneously with the sailors. They
forewent this cycle five or six times, while doublemom held their
place sipping hot Indonesian tea from a hand cast pewter service,
and eventually were able to score the equivalent of about a ten
entree meal. Saweet!

After toking to fulfillment on the excellent aliment, the
NAVOSUR reps decided to depart KOKK and go to a quieter, less
congested venue. There was no point staying in this teeming envi-

ronment, where it was impossible to conduct even a rudimentary conversation about nothing, let alone any deeper discussion of anything, over the throttling din of the TGIFsters. As they got themselves together and prepared to fjord through the shuffling stream of compacted humanity to the exit, Rossy saw doublemom remove the expensive pewter tea service items and salt and pepper shakers, as well as the silverware and linen napkins, from their drink table and cram them into her tote. *What the hell?* he thought, watching the conspicuous swipe unfold. The group did not get five steps away from the table when they were intercepted by a tuxedoed maitre d' type accompanied by two, larger, security confreres. Doubleman looked down at the md' and asked what the problem was. They were advised to turn around and move toward the management office between the restroom passageway and the kitchen access. Away from the press of the jostling swarm, the manager asked to see doublemom's tote bag and she refused, drawing it in tightly against her prodigious chest. He promptly raised his phone, spoke a few quiet words aside and directed them all to remain against the wall beside the office, where they were more or less pinned in place by the manager's burly associates. In a few minutes, two police officers entered from the street and made their way down the steps to the open service room. *Oh, no! Not again!!* Rossy couldn't believe he was trapped in yet another engagement of potential fatum ab doom with the law. He was obviously recorded on the omnipotent surveillance video in party with this crazy old lady klepto-thief he didn't even know. As the cops made their way across the floor in the direction of the detainees, the multitudes parted before them like the Red Sea for the fabled crossing of Moses. At the same time, there was at least one well known congressman hastily leaving his bar seat, from tightly beside a much younger blonde aide, to discretely exit the premises before the media cams started their panoramic vigilance. Police, infidelity and video were never a good recipe for re-election.

The officers approached the manager, who briefed them on the situation while pointing to the alleged perpsters lined up at the wall. Rossy lowered his head in noticing all the phone cameras extended by the gawking happy timers on the floor. The police extracted the tote bag from doublemom's grip and verified the contents as KOKK property. They suspected they had a crew of restaurant rip-off specialists on their hands and proceeded to initiate arrest protocol, starting with ID checks. Rossy submitted his Connecticut driver's license in lieu of the WNY security pass, though in his experience a non-local ID generally compounded the potential for trouble, sort of like for the only dude with no pants in a lineup. Sure enough, "A yankee, huh? You got a record in Connecticut, Mr. Rossy?"

"No, sir. I'm new to this area and haven't had a chance to get my license changed yet."

"Hmm....well, let's just run this through ampol and see if you've been busy anywhere else."

Beautiful!! Here I go into a criminal data base. I'll be fracking gone by Monday! Rossy started to feel the creeping clutch of apprehension, but forced himself to relax and relent. He was really tired of being blindly whacked by crazy circumstances he did not create, but even more tired of stressing about it. From now on, it was Booker-think for him. Don't worry. Be happy. C'est la vie. By this time doubleman was in isolated parley with the manager and the other cop. He explained that his mom suffered from a form of bipolar disorder that has been aggravated by her recent divorce. She feels an irrational sense of loss that she inadvertently tries to compensate for by stealing. He reluctantly disclosed she is receiving professional treatment, and is making good progress. But, unfortunately, she sometimes relapses into bad behavior, like what just happened here at KOKK. Doubleman emphasized this is strictly a problem with his mom and the other people in their party have no play in the incident. After conferring with the cops and recovering the lifted property, the manager consented to not press charges. Doublemom and the sailors were released and departed into the evening. Out on the sidewalk between K Street and the Klub entrance, doubleman broke into a mordant laugh and apologized to his colleagues, saying that his mom does not usually get caught. *What the hell does that mean?* wondered Rossy, though he was certainly not interested in any further detail. Maybe everybody had problems with their moms. Who cares? Right now, he just wanted to go home and crash in peace.

***

Paul Blackburn was gone from the office, during normal working hours, about 95% of the time. He was at his desk early every morning, but generally left, shortly after everyone else arrived, for nonspecific 'meetings at The Pentagon' lasting most of the rest of the day. Sometimes, but usually not often, he was back in the office by quitting time. Rossy wondered how someone could efficiently spend all that time in meetings, but certainly didn't have enough operational information to question the bossman's activities. But on Monday morning, Blackburn remained in the office and, after all who were coming to work were in attendance, requested admin Tom call everyone together for a special staff meeting. This was somewhat unusual, in that, because their activities were so thoroughly and separately classified, they seldom had any group discussion about anything related to work. Save the director, there was essentially no one among them who had a routine need to know everything about what anyone else was doing. As the engineers, technicians and supervisors passed by the uncleared recruits' work table and crammed into the small front office area, Rossy and Booker found themselves visually blocked from seeing the speaker, but they could hear what was being said. Blackburn advised that the SECDEF was launching an initiative to get 100% involvement of DoD personnel in the annual United Way fund drive. His good friend, the CEO of UTG, had signed on for another year as national chairman of the United Way Campaign and the unequivocal, unwavering goal remained 100% participation, nationwide. The Pentagon did mega-business with UTG and the secretary wanted to keep his contracts solvent and on schedule. While Blackburn acknowledged no one could be legally forced to contribute to the UW fund, he strongly urged the staff to comply. He had a form on his desk whereon everyone was asked to sign, date and fill in an amount to be deducted each pay period. Rossy had not yet received a paycheck from NAVOSUR and wasn't entirely sure he was actually employed here, but he knew exactly what to do. After waiting in line behind the other employees, he dutifully authorized a quarter george deduct for UW. Noticing there were no dissenters, the prudent donor figured it could be safely assumed there were, indeed, consequences for non-participation and he wasn't about to test the system. Even though the system was probably way fracked up. Since the UW fund issue was the only agenda item, the meeting quickly dissolved and most of the engineers and techs went on break.

When his office area was depopulated, Blackburn called Rossy and Booker in and told them to sit down. He looked carefully across at Rossy and said, "Mr. Booker, I'm..." "No, I'm Rossy, sir," interrupted Rossy. "Yes, yes, of course, I'm sorry. Mr. Booker," continued Blackburn, looking at Booker, "I'm pleased to inform you that your security clearance has gone through and you are duly instated as a full capacity engineer for NAVOSUR, though you are still on routine probationary status as a new employee. You will be able to commence with training and administrative preparation for field duty. Go ahead and see Tom and he'll coordinate you into Whittberg's section." As Booker exited both the director's office and his 'uncleared' restriction, Rossy felt his pulse accelerate, maybe even palpitate. *This is not positive. If we were both good, he would have told us together. Booker's in and I'm sacked. I knew it! I knew it!! I knew it!!!* "Mr. Rossy," resumed the director, not looking up from some documents he was pretending to examine on the desk in front of him, "I'm afraid we have a small glitch in your clearance investigation."

"Yes, sir, may I ask what the problem is?" *The problem is this whole thing is a bullshit bust and now I'm out on the street in a goddam place I don't know fracking dicks from dongs about.*

"To be honest, I have no idea, son, but I don't think it's anything insurmountable."

"Well, w-what do I do now?" stammered Rossy, in a noticeably quivering tone.

"Ok, you'll have to go over to DIS headquarters to answer a few questions. I'm sure it's just clarification of some minor issue in your background check." Rossy thought he detected a sense of indifference in the director's demeanor, maybe indicating he was already written off as 'damaged goods'.

"How do I do that?"

"DIS is at Joint Base Anacostia-Bolling, which is right across the river from the WNY. You can't miss it. It's the biggest facility on base. You can take a shuttle van from the District Commandment building, here at the Yard, right down from the gate. They are expecting you at DISHQ this morning. Just give your name to the reception guard inside the main entrance. Good luck, son. I hope this works out, because we are really shorthanded right now."

*Good luck?!? What's luck got to do with it?? If luck is a factor, I'm **totally** fracked!* Rossy felt like he had just been issued a diagnosis of professional death and Blackburn's empathetic tone seemed as if he was, indeed, given up for dead. But he pulled him-self together and pogoed down the steps in singular determination to vault this hurdle and get on with the program. After all, what could the issue in question be? Nothing that he did with Booker, including Friday's KOKK bust, because Booker was approved. So, it must be something from before he knew Booker and there was nothing in his past he could think of that would preclude be-ing okayed for clearance. It's got to be some kind of misinterpreta-tion, an erroneous assumption on the part of the investigators. In a face-to-face, he should easily be able to dispel whatever false im-pression they had perceived in his character and then he would quickly be fully and legitimately employed. Life would be good by this afternoon. Outside, he passed by the breakineers, who tried to deflect him from his DIS appointment with a cold morning Coors, but he deferred and hustled on across the Yard to catch the JBAB shuttle.

The DIS headquarters building was a visually imposing struc-ture. Perched on the high middle of a spectacularly landscaped oasis of flowering greenery inside a broad circular accessway, the facility consisted of a series of connected glass and granite mod-ules stepped in order of increasing height. The shuttle drop-off at the main entrance was in front of a one story section, beyond which could be seen the top of the highest six floor module at the back of the site. A forest of antennae towers spiked over huddles of ferris wheel sized receptor dishes from the sectional flat roofs, apparently out of the flight lanes from nearby Reagan National Airport, yet a host of strobe lights atop the towers protectively blinked their elevations. Rossy got out of the van and ascended a half flight of cobbled steps to a wide concrete terrace featuring a row of flagpoles parallel to the building front. A U.S. flag was in the center, ruffling higher than the adjacent DIS and flanking ser-vice branch flags. Though DIS was the military arm of the CIA, and technically subordinate to the CIA, there was no CIA banner in the flying flag group. There was probably no Consolidated In-telligence Administration banner flying anywhere, because that organization mostly did not overtly exist. The flag runners, rattling noisily in the breeze off the hollow aluminum poles, sounded like a loud, discordant wind chime dominating even the traffic drone from I-295 along the eastern bound of the base. The nervous arri-val entered into a broad, open lobby, with gleaming terrazzo flooring and, off to one side, a small, bubbling fountain surrounded by overstuffed sofas and easy chairs. A TV beamed Fox News down from an overlooking corner into the empty waiting lounge area. The wall directly opposite the entrance foyer was gold streaked black marble upon which the DIS mission statement was mounted in gray metal relief:

THE DEFENSE INTELLIGENCE SERVICE IS COMMITTED TO THE PRESERVATION OF THE SECURITY OF THE UNITED STATES OF AMERICA, THROUGH PREEMPTIVE DETECTION AND ELIMINATION OF HOSTILE ACTIONS, FOREIGN, DOMESTIC, CIVILIAN OR MILITARY,AGAINST THE COMMON PEACE, PROPERTY AND LIBERTY OF THE AMERICAN PEOPLE.

Rossy read the statement and, for reasons he couldn't quite nail to the post, felt a little less safe than before he entered the building. The reception bench was to the right of a bevy of stand mounted American flags fringing the worded wall. He tentatively approached the guard and stated his name and purpose. The guard asked to see ID, handed him a secure, clamp-on visitor's pass and directed him to the waiting niche. Settling into a big soft chair, he noticed an assortment of publications on an adjacent end table under a heavy brass eagle lamp. *Defense Initiatives, Weapons Policy Review, Strategic Security, International Affairs and Policy, Vigilance.* Rossy had never heard of these magazines. They certainly were not sold at any drug store reading rack he had ever seen, nor were they available in any typical county library he remembered. In leafing through a couple of the glossy print issues, he felt like he was in a different world. A place of perceived danger where threat and preparedness were the cause and effect of order. He had never thought much about national security, but now, in this alien environment, he might have sensed a pang of paranoia creeping into the hidden reaches of his under psyche. Then he saw a full page ad for UTG, showing an angry Uncle Sam caricature pointing at the reader, imploring, "I NEED YOU", and underneath clarifying, "To participate in your local United Way Campaign. If we all help, we all benefit. Give today!" *God, it never ends*, thought the unsettled citizen, wondering if the ad was paid for with UW contribution money, including his paycheck deduct.

"Mr. Rossy, please come with us." Rossy looked up in surprise at the stealth appearance of two secret service looking suits. He stood up quickly and followed the youngish agent dudes, who were already walking briskly away toward a skylit court, around the corner from the reception desk, that discharged to a long narrow corridor through the interior of the building. The block corridor walls were painted in various semi-gloss shades of tan, faded yellow and milky green and the ceilings sported perforated, off-white acoustical tile around a centered row of florescent light insets. A rather depressingly retro institutional motif in what looked like a modern building from the outside. The engineer had to force himself to keep pace, a few steps behind, as the trio moved, without conversation, through a series of double doors and eventually arrived at a bay of elevators. The permeance of paranoia cut a little deeper when he noticed the tiny wires from underneath the lobes of his escorts' right ears to inside their collars. So far, he hadn't seen any other people, though they had passed by countless closed, windowless doors, presumably to offices, where, maybe, thousands of DIS employees worked. *Doing what? Protecting America? Dumping on my security clearance?* "Coming up," said one wire in a low tone, to no obvious party in particular, as they entered an elevator. The door slid shut and the cab started moving upward, though the well escorted visitor couldn't tell how far, as there were no controls or level indicators. He was not going to have any idea where he was in this facility.

After about ten seconds, the elevator slowed to a silent stop and locked in place with a slight bump. The door opened to an elevator foyer identical to the one they had just lifted from. Rossy followed the leaders down a familiar looking hallway for about two hundred feet, where they turned right into another corridor, forward thirty steps, or so, left, another short walk and finally stopping in front of an unidentified, featureless solid door. The apparent senior agent, the only one who had spoken anything so far in this procession, opened the door, turned on the lights and gestured for the subject to enter into a small room with a metal utility table and three chairs. One of the chairs faced a blank, black window and the other two were across the table. It looked like a good cop/bad cop interview set used by a million movies and TV shows, so he sat down at the single chair, figuring he was the in-terviewee. The suits left the room, with no instructions to their charge, and closed the door. Rossy pulled his phone out to check the time. No service.

OK, let's assess. I'm alone somewhere in a big building, somewhere in Washington D.C., where no one I know, including myself, knows where I am and I have no phone. So what are they going to do? What can they do? I'm not guilty of hostile action. Don't worry. Be happy. The isolated security candidate assumed he was being observed and tried to look frosty by leaning back in the chair, folding his arms, closing his eyes and ommming out, just like when he was tortured by the motivationalist during his engi-neering licensing prep days at PWA. He was prepared to stay in neutral, revealing nothing, for hours, if necessary, for as long as it took to outlast them, whoever they were. But the door reopened in a few minutes and his two muted friends entered carrying a bulky equipment case and loose coils of coaxial instrument cabling. "What's that?" asked Rossy with considerable unease.

"It's a polygraph unit."

"What for? What's going on?"

"It's to find out if you're a liar and I'll ask the questions."

"I'm not a liar and I'm not taking a polygraph test."

"Fine. We'll close the file on your clearance review." The agents started to put components back in the case to repack the equipment unit.

"No, wait. OK, I'll take the test. Whatever you want."

The lead DISser gave the recruit an irritated glare and reo-pened the case. They proceeded to attach finger, neck and arm pulse sensors connected to a digital analog convertor that was routed to a touch pad computer. The set up and calibration took about five minutes. When they were ready, the potential liar was advised he would be asked a series of not necessarily related ques-tions to which he should only respond 'yes' or 'no', with no elabo-ration. Did he understand? "Yes."

"What is your full, legal name?"

How the hell can I answer that yes or no? "Yes."

Wiseass. "Is your full, legal name William Arlo Rossy?"

"Yes." The interrogator went through several logistical ques-tions related to his subject's identity and irrefutable record of background and then, "Are you a sociopath?"

A sociopath?? Whaaat!? "No."
"Are you a pedophile?"
Jesus fracking christ!! "No."
"Are you a sexual predator?"
Wow! "No."
"Have you ever considered carrying out acts of public terrorism?
Whoa! "No."
"Are you a homosexual?"
They can't legally ask me that! "No."
"Are you now, or have you ever been, suicidal?"
This is getting really weird. "No."
"Do you believe in god?"
Uh-oh. Trick question. "Y-yes."
A long pause as the interrogator studied the output display. Again, "Do you believe in god?"
Holy shit! "No."

There were a number of other questions pertaining to incidental personal preferences, phrased as likes or dislikes, eventually ending in an extended silence while the polygraphers pored over the results. Finally, the speaking agent arose from his chair, turned and started toward the door, while directing the other to dismantle the assembly, re-pack the equipment and bring it back to the office. The apparent subordinate jumped up and quickly strode after his departing associate, grabbed him by the shoulder and spun him around, loudly exclaiming, "Hey! You're not my supervisor! We're the same grade, so don't tell me what to do!!" The acting boss roughly pushed his agitated partner away, firmly instructing, "Get your goddam hands off me!" And then they went into it, like a couple of feral tomcats in a darkened alley. The interviewee watched with amazed disbelief as the instigating underling landed a crunching roundhouse punch to the side of the interrogator's face, resulting in both of them collapsing to the floor, directly in front of the door. The puncher landed on top, straddling the slightly larger of the two, and started pulverizing his colleague with both fists. The seated spectator saw that the underside agent was bleeding profusely and seemed to be close to unconsciousness, but the enraged attacker kept swinging. Unless there was some kind of intervention, it looked like the big guy was going down. Rossy leapt from his chair, ran over to the lopsided slugfest and pulled the thrasher backwards, off and away from the distressed dupe writhing on the floor. The aggressor immediately turned to his collateral antagonist and, from a half kneeling position, whomped the sailor recruit flush in the grille, knocking him clumsily back into the chair. He then got fully to his feet, kicked the injured agent out of the way and exited the room. The big, bleeding dude rolled over to his knees, managed to slowly rise in groaning pain and, likewise, staggered out of the room, slamming the door behind him. The interventionist sat dazed and alone, wondering what the hell just happened. The polygraph equipment remained on the table in front of him and he thought, briefly, that maybe he should disassemble it and pack it up. *What, are you crazy? Frack the polygraph! You're bleeding, too, for chrissakes!!* Thick red drops plopped on the table from his split lower lip and Rossy felt a shooting pain from an adjacent tooth. *No way*, he agonized in discovering one of his frontal incisors, maybe #26, was cracked, but luckily not loose. Now it was priority number one to get to a dentist.

As considerable quiet time elapsed, maybe ten or fifteen minutes, the sullied sailor didn't know whether to flip or fly. The door wasn't locked and, presumably, he could just willfully leave at anytime, but he really didn't feel like wandering around alone in this creepy building, with a bloody shirt and a big fat lip, trying to find a way out. Some idiot DIS agent would probably shoot him on sight as a terrorist infiltrator. But, then again, he didn't want to stay in the little interview room much longer. He was starting to feel seriously closed in, slightly panicky. Suddenly, with no indication from the outside, the door opened and a smiling, middle-aged man entered carrying a rigid briefcase. He was well attired in an expensively tailored Armani suit, starched white shirt with a solid blue silk tie and black wingtip shoes. He looked like a White House economics advisor. "Mr. Rossy, my name is Special Programs Agent Murphy. How are you doing, today?" greeted the new DISser, extending a hand. *How am I doing, today? Are you fracking kidding me?* Rossy wiped his right hand on his soiled shirt and cautiously accepted the agent's introductory gesture. "I've been better, thank you."

"Yes, yes, of course. I'm sure you would be interested in an explanation regarding your condition, but first here's some tissues and a glass of water for you to straighten up a bit." SPAM retrieved a covered plastic cup and a small box out of the case and placed them on the table in front of his swollen subject. The battered engineer dabbed at his crushed lip and took a swallow of water. *This must be the good cop,* he figured, never taking his eyes off the new suit, who had assumed a relaxed seat on the table facing toward his subject and away from the observation port. "Mr. Rossy, I'm your clearance review case officer," continued SPAM, removing a file folder from the briefcase. "I've been overseeing your background investigation from the beginning. Generally speaking, everything about you is fairly straightforward, though we do have a few questions pertaining to some data bits we reviewed."

"What's the problem?"

"Well, we received a video clip of you at a rest stop near mile marker 134, on southbound I-81 in Pennsylvania, let's see, on this past September 18th, at about 1600. Does that sound familiar?"

Jesus, were they following me? "Yes, I could have been there."

"OK, the clip shows you watching people in a way that, quite frankly, raised a huge red flag for us. We specialize, here at DIS, in visual profiling through digital comparison integration, and, I must tell you, the expression on your face in that video was very similar to that of a typical suicide bomber right before detonation. We have hundreds of case study photos and videos of bombing sites from around the world and they all show a distinct look of bemused contempt, a resolute and foreboding peace, in the features and demeanor of the terrorist about to unleash his, or her, hell. To anyone, or any camera, paying attention, almost invariably the clear signal would be impending death and destruction. You had that same unmistakable look, except there was, obviously, no bombing. So, I have to ask you, what were you thinking that day? What was going through your mind at that rest stop?"

"Uh, I don't know. I was just tired from driving and taking a break. I guess I was just sort of tunneled out, not really thinking about anything. I can't exactly remember what I was thinking. I didn't talk to anyone and I sure wasn't planning to set a bomb off." *Is this guy for real? I can't believe my future is up to this buffoon!*

"You know, Mr. Rossy, that's not a bad answer, because it collaborates well with your polygraph indicators. We didn't detect any sociopathic or predatory tendencies in your responses, which was also reinforced by your reaction to the RAPE exercise."

"Rape exercise?"

"Yes, role activation participation event. The altercation you just witnessed was staged to observe how you reacted to an unexpected and escalating negative situation. You moved quickly to assist a person in possibly deadly danger. In real life, your actions would have been called heroic. But for our purposes, they showed you have a high quotient of human valuation capacity, which perfectly supports your polygraph responses."

"Well, what does that mean?"

"It means, I'm happy to tell you, that we can approve your clearance for task specified top secret security."

"So, the fight was fake?"

"No, the fight was real. The effect was a false impression. There are many causes to a desired effect."

More than one way to skin a cat. Many ways to catch a trout. "Well, what would have happened if I hadn't done anything? Would the one guy have gotten killed?"

"No, no. The agents are highly trained professionals. They know exactly how far to extend the exercise without permanent injury."

What?? They looked like a couple of out-of-control mugheads to me. There wasn't anything professional about them. "So, I didn't have to get blonked? I could have just waited a little longer and it would have been over?"

"Technically, yes. But then we would not have had conclusive information regarding your character and I could not have made an immediate determination on your clearance approval. Sometimes, son, you have to take a punch backwards in order to progress. Nothing is easy, or without a price, and you should always be aware of that, going forward. At the end of the day, it's those that sacrifice the most who achieve the most."

Flush that shit. I didn't sign up for this job to be bushwhacked! "OK, I hear you, Mr. Murphy, but I'm going to have to get my tooth fixed and who's going to pay for that?" Rossy could feel his paranoia morphing to anger, as it started to sink in how much he had been played in this whole DIS approval process.

"Yes, of course, Mr. Rossy. Your exasperation is understandable. We will make a dental service appointment for you first thing tomorrow morning at Bethesda Naval Hospital. Just check in at main reception off Jones Bridge Road, at 0900. Give them your name, under my coordination, and they'll take good care of you. Now, I assume you've had enough evaluation, so let's get you out of here." SPAM slid off the table, closed his case and moved to the door, with the newly cleared sailor in tight pursuit.

They took a different route in leaving than what the visitor remembered coming in. There seemed to be more turns through shorter corridors with a sense they were not going in the direction of the elevators. As they veered into one hallway, the recruit saw the flash sideback profile of a vaguely familiar individual rounding the corner at the far end. Dick Whittberg!! Even though it was only a split second glimpse, he was sure he saw Dick Whittberg! *What the hell was the engineering supervisor doing here, at DIS? Had he been watching the bullshit crappery going down in the interview room?* Paranoia started creeping back, like a crow to roadkill, and Rossy sensed an overwhelming downpression of inexplicable issues he knew were way out of his reach and control. The personal history pre-compiled on his 171 form. The video analysis from some obscure stop in boonyland. How does a military intelligence program uplink with a random highway surveillance system? Is everybody being watched, all the time, through a vast network of interlocked, real-time data points? Has modern tech finally regressed to the worst case scenario fictionally predicted for 1984? Larry and the graduate?? Too many brand new *big unknowns*. But he didn't start with a headache. Actually, he was becoming euphorically lightheaded. His clearance was approved and he was going to be certifiably employed. *Got a job! Got a job!! Good god almighty, I got a job!!!* And so the rookie engineer was feeling pretty topside as SPAM delivered him to the lobby guard for check-out. Much better than earlier. Yes, life *was* good by this afternoon, but what an emotional roller coaster he had ridden today. He was well ready for Mashup happy time!

***

Booker was still pissed at Rossy the next morning as they wordlessly waited for the shuttle. No matter how much he ferreted, his roommate and colleague would reveal nothing about his fissured face. In point of fact, the last thing Mr. SPAM had said in discharging the ruptured recruit from DISHQ was explicit instructions that everything that had occurred during his clearance interview was classified and he was not permitted to discuss it with anyone not directly involved, except his organization director. That left out Booker and the other engineers. Even Mashup Marcie, who, as an experienced bartender, should normally be reliably confidential with sensitive information. But Rossy was convinced *they* could watch everything he did and he wasn't about to violate a specific classified order. He wasn't even sure who *they* were. Maybe, probably, the whole higher government. DIS certainly wasn't the top rung of the ladder. There was no way of knowing how many people were watching him. So, while Booker and the others had to be mushroomed, he advised Blackburn what happened during his DIS review that had resulted in his morning appointment at BNH. The director decided to kill three birds with one stone and arranged for the new engineers to get their required physical exams, including drug and infectious disease testing, and preliminary travel shots out of the way on the same run. They could have taken the Metro red line, but the WNY shuttle was free.

During the ride to the medical center, Booker finally broke the verbal impasse and mentioned that he had received an e-mail from Smith. Booker texted him several days ago, saying they had arrived and were orientating into the office and that all was well in the apartment. Gameboy had a proposal. Since they would all be on frequent TDY status, it was unlikely the three of them would be in Washington at the same time. So why don't they all stay in the AG apartment and split the rent and utilities three ways? Rossy thought that was a great idea and immediately said he was good with it. Booker agreed and spent the rest of the shuttle run texting their acceptance back to Smith. Sweeet! Now they wouldn't have to worry about finding their own place, or places. They had never really talked about whether they would get separate pads, or share one. They also decided, at least for the time being, to just keep their stuff in the apartment rather than use a storage cell. With this arrangement, they could be one big, happy, low-cost 'family'! What could go wrong?

Rossy came out of the dental clinic feeling like he had been smacked a few more times in the maw. He received a bonding procedure to repair the cracked incisor and had his teeth cleaned and x-rayed. To alleviate painful aggravation of his split lip and bruised lower jaw area, he was novocained for the treatment and still had the puffed numbies effect. For all this there wasn't even a freebie goodie bag, like with a brush, floss wheel and paste tube. A little disappointing, but considering the no-charge service, it was cool. He found Booker in the waiting room at the general practices clinic. "Di ya ga in yeh?" blabbered bj through the paralysis. "Yeah, man, and wait'l you see the rpa," smirked shiner, holding up ten. "Best physical I ever had, dawg. No lie!" Rossy went over to the window counter, checked in and returned to a waiting seat. Within moments the receptionist motioned for him to come forward and he was led into the other side. A corpsman went through a schedule of background questions, collected urine and blood samples and took his vitals. *155's not bad - still within ten pounds of my wrestling weight,* thought the former grappler. All the data was entered into a pad form to be uploaded for permanent record. He was then placed in a small examination room and told to strip to his underwear. Sitting alone on the cold bench, he pondered how much recent time he was spending in little rooms. Hopefully, this time, he would not be assaulted. Just as his eyes and head started drooping into a fugue, the door burst open and in rushed what looked like the white frocked starlet of a critically unacclaimed doctor movie. Booker was right - she was absolutely stunning, in a sexy kind of way, maybe a double ten. Rossy had never been alone in a room before, with a woman he didn't know, wearing only his Hanes. He sensed his face reddening as he tried to cover up with his arms. The rpa began immediately with stethoscopic lung and heart checks, followed by eye, ear, nose and throat visuals. She took his temperature, observed reflexive joint reactions and pushed, poked and squeezed all through his mid and abdominal core area. With completion of each examination routine, she entered observational data into the automated record. There was no extraneous conversation, only terse instructions to accommodate the procedures. Then she went over to the small sink, thoroughly scrubbed her hands and extracted a pair of surgical gloves out of a box on an adjacent supply shelf. Rossy was directed to stand up, lower his shorts and lean over the bench with his feet wide apart. *Oh, no! She's not going to do this! No waaa...* "Aaaahhh!!" He involuntarily lurched forward trying to escape the greased rectal invasion, but she pulled him back and ordered him to relax. After what seemed like an interminable period of agonizing prostate probing, she withdrew the attack and retreated to the sink, telling her victim to stay in position. The rpa rescrubbed, regloved and returned to the scene of the crime, where the whimpering rookie sailor was desperately trying to keep it together. Then, without warning, he felt his jellybeans rolled, kneaded, tugged and pressed by her latexed fingers searching for testicular tumors. He also felt 'biggi johnson' rising to the occasion, like a breadstick in the oven, causing him to break into an embarrassed, all-systems sweat. He again tried to duck forward and again she jerked him back, demanding that he remain still. Finally, she released him, went back to the sink, discarded the gloves and rewashed her hands. After completing the final data entries, she offered some sanitized wipes to clean up, saying he could get dressed. And then she was gone. The examinee slowly regrouped, gingerly reinstalled his clothes and sat on the bench in a shaken stupor. He wasn't sure what just happened, but was fairly certain he had been thoroughly processed.

In short order, a dowdy, middle-aged nurse lady came clumsily through the door pushing a small, stainless steel tray cart, upon which was an array of variously sized syringes and cylinder serum vials. She requested he take off his shirt and drop trou and proceeded to inject him with one shot after another. Diphtheria, left arm. Yellow fever, right arm. Typhoid, left. Hepatitis A/B, right. Avian flu, right. Gamma globulin, right ass. Tetanus, left ass. Tuberculosis test, left forearm below the earlier blood sample perforation. Finally, the dart game was over and he was covered with little pads of gauze taped across each point of attack. The nurse told him he was finished and he believed her. With a curt 'have a nice day', she wheeled out of the room, again leaving the new government engineer alone. Taking a few moments to collect his composure, Rossy started to stand up to get dressed yet one more time and discovered he could barely move. Pain shot everywhere, like a pinball off hyperactive bumpers, and he fell abruptly back onto the bench. He removed all the bandages, massaged the shot sites and slowly stretched out to the point he could function. Eventually, he managed to put his shirt on, pull up his pants and stumble carefully to the checkout desk, where he was informed the clinic would hold his record until he completed all the required inoculations. Still to come were rabies, meningitis, cholera and encephalitis, though he didn't think he could take another shot anytime soon. He was also instructed to keep an eye on tuberculosis to make sure it didn't form a positive, 'bullseye' red welt, in which case he must return to the clinic asap.

Back in the waiting room, Rossy found Booker deadfast asleep, with the TV remote clasped tightly in his hand. Several other patients-in-waiting stared angrily at the dozing drowser, apparently not interested in watching supercross racing highlights. Rossy removed the remote, placed it on a nearby table and woke Booker up. As they left the clinic, bj thought he probably wouldn't be any worse off had he taken a broken bungee dive off the Washington Monument. Or, if he had gone as far as consciously possible in a round with Poco Ramirez. He absolutely felt hoary horrible, especially with the novocaine wearing off. "But, dude, it was totally worth it, don't you think?" yukked the shiner. "Man, I'd let Doc Xena, back there, give me a physical all day, everyday! I mean, she made me proud to be an American! *Daimmm*, was she hot, or what?!!"

"Booker, she didn't give a shit any more for us than she would for two frogs on a lotus leaf. We were just a burp in her schedule and I'm glad it's over. All I want to do right now is get the hell outta here." The engineers shuffled down the hallway in the direction of the elevators when they encountered a floor sign beside an open portal into a lab. The sign indicated an urgent blood drive had been initiated and all personnel were requested to participate. A free meal pass at the main mess was offered as incentive. 'Chow chit for a pint!' Booker was immediately hooked and started swerving into the lab, trying to herd a resistant Rossy along. "C'mon, man. Let's do this. I'm starving!"

"Jesus, Booker, we just got fifty cc's of seven contagious diseases. There's no way they'll take our blood. And there's no way I'm taking another needle."

"A free smorgasbord meal pass, dawg!! We won't have to grub for a week!" Booker pushed Rossy through the entrance, where they were greeted by a beaming, young nurse, who motioned for them to sit down by a small gray metal desk in the corner. She verified IDs and robotically breezed through a few general health questions in filling out the registrations. Rossy asked if their blood was any good, with all the inoculations they had just received. The nurse said she didn't think it mattered, because they comprehensively screened all donated units. *She didn't think it mattered? That doesn't sound right.* Soon they found themselves laid out on adjustable recliners, squeezing hard rubber balls, as dark red oil oozed from their veins through flexible, translucent tubing to the receptacle pouches. Rossy had offered his only unpunctured site, his right forearm, and was having trouble assimilating the new burning pain into his current repository of discomforts. Booker was again dozing out. After what seemed like an unreasonably long period of time, they were disconnected, bandaged, given cafeteria tickets and released with silly, cartoon blood drop decals, proclaiming a happy faced 'I gave blood today', stuck to their shirts. They went directly to the dining hall, where they discovered another massive *Golden Paddock* buffet offering. *Jesus christ! Does GP have a contract for every Navy facility in the world?* wondered Rossy, feeling instantly qualmish in recalling the probably less than two star lunch experience at the Chiefs' Club. Christ, if he had known what the meal ticket was for, he would never have given blood. On the bright side, Booker astutely observed, they now had less serum in their systems and should have milder reactions to the shots. Maybe a good point, conceded Rossy, gagging down a pressed cube steak that was far too chewy for the condition of his mouth. He felt like he was, indeed, chowing shit for his pint. They left well short of all they could normally eat and went directly to the main reception lobby to wait for the shuttle back to the Yard.

***

Over the next few days, working conditions changed dramatically for the recruits. Rossy joined Booker in the engineering room and was assigned a computer desk near Whittberg's corner. The supervisor had not spoken to him about his clearance interview at DIS and Rossy was convinced that Whittberg had monitored the whole freak show through the one-way black window. But why? Booker was not being subjected to this kind of scrutiny. The shiner didn't have to take a polygraph. And the reason for the special interview seemed ludicrously bogus. *I looked like a suicide bomber? Really??...c'mon, what the hell was that all about!?* Another NAVOSUR mystery and no way to find answers. Rossy was dying to talk to someone about these puzzles, but calculated he was better off maintaining radio silence, like a nuclear submarine in unauthorized territorial waters. That way no one would know what he was thinking. If he asked questions, they would immediately realize what was going on in his head and he would no longer have any cover. The secrecy of his thoughts was the only resource he had in this situation, because apparently, unbelievably, he could be visually tracked everywhere he went. Somebody, maybe many, once said you would learn a lot more by listening than by talking and that might well be true for him at this particular point in his status. Besides, he should at least wait until after a successful payday before making waves.

One morning, there was considerable commotion in the stairwell and entrance way between admin Tom's room and the front office, as two dudes Rossy had never seen before lugged several fiber glass shipping containers up the steps from outside. They were immediately met by dps Larry and redeye and the four of them disappeared with the containers into the restricted access processing center. The green 'occupied' light went on simultaneously with the door closing behind them. Rossy and Booker had still not been permitted into the processing center, even though their clearances were approved. Without a specific work assignment, they did not yet have a valid 'need to know' entry requirement. Rossy watched the fortified door from near the coffee concession, wondering what was going on in the mysterious computer room. There was, of course, no sound emanating from the totally attenuated space, but at one point he thought he heard a couple of very faint, muffled thumps overhead. He couldn't pinpoint exactly where the noises sourced from, but they were definitely over the restricted area. How could that be? He remembered there was no access to the third floor from any of the stairwells. Was there some kind of way up there from inside the data center? That didn't make any sense, because it would be a breach of the secure perimeter. Then he pondered whether he would give anything away by inquiring about the unaccessible third floor. After all, that enigma was pretty obvious. Anyone seeing a three story building with only a two story stairwell would be inclined to find out what was up (or not) with that. *No! Stick with the plan. For right now, no questions.*

In due course, the four emerged from the data center and floor stacked the containers on the unclassified side of the red tape line. Larry disappeared into his office, redeye returned to his party chief desk in the back and the new guys went downstairs for a beer break. The two techs from Green's section soon showed up with a dolly and removed the orange boxes to their shop at the other end of the floor. There was virtually no conversation among any of the mission orientated participants during the entire process with the containers. They seemed to be executing a well choreographed procedure, that had immediate priority over anything else they would be involved in first thing this morning. But it was a much different temperament the box boys brought back from break. They were loud, jovial and interactive as they entered the engineering room and plopped down behind their home office cad desks.

"Hey, rocko, you miss us, man?" jested Willie "wokker" Mooie, a Chinese-American from Santa Barbara, where his immigrant parents owned and operated a successful restaurant. Wokker grew up over and in the restaurant and learned much about the business, as well as wokking the Mandarin cuisine, though he had not done much west coasting after graduating from Maryland with a civil engineering degree. NAVOSUR was his first job out of college and he had basically been on TDY for the three plus years since.

"What's to miss?" countered a motionless rocko from somewhere behind his magazine and shades.

"Welcome back, mothafrackers," offered bt.

"Well, it's just peachy-creamy dope to *be* back," joined wokker's partner, a short, stocky lumberjack look alike, with longish dark hair and a full beard. Vinnie "the towster" Kallen was from Long Island and a graduate of NYU. A mechanical engineer. He worked his way through school by studying in a scanner-equipped tow truck parked along the expressway. In five years, he rarely missed rewarding first tow on the scene of any accident within ten minutes.

"Bill Rossy and Ken Booker," respectively pointed wokker at the new engineers. "Welcome aboard! Hope you're ready to roll, 'cause some of us need a break!" Rossy was unconcerned about wokker's seemingly knowing them. He had become inured to identification before intro and didn't think anything about it. It was a widespread digital recognition thing. But he would, at some point, think about the different educational backgrounds NAVOSUR employees had. All the varied engineering disciplines represented to do the same work, which did not really seem to require an engineering degree at all. Or any degree, for that matter. As far as Rossy could tell, this job could probably be performed by unskilled dropouts. Maybe, in real life, but that wasn't going to happen here. The official job classification was 'engineer', requiring an engineering degree. He was going to rack up some valuable engineering resume experience, get professionally paid and not really have to do anything. *Not a bad deal! Hit me again!* The returnees shot the gab for a short while, never mentioning a word relating to any aspect of their highly classified field work, and then were off to the Pentagon to file their travel vouchers directly with the Navy's disbursement office. Like taxes, it was generally more cost effective to do this early and in person, rather than delayed and electronically. They would all hook up later at the Mashup.

***

The eagle flew on Friday. The new sailors were ecstatic to receive e-statements of deposits into their accounts, noticing that, as expected, base pay was considerably lower than their PWA salary, but so were deductions. Except for the United Way contribution, which would presumably be the same for the rest of their working lives, or at least as long as the UTG CEO sat in the national fund drive chair. There was a deduct, in lieu of social security, for the federal government retirement program, which was less than the normal FICA amount. Ditto health insurance co-pay share. So, on balance, net pay was not as much less than the base pay difference from PWA and was enough to cover bills and costs. That's all Rossy cared about, because, when the TDY overtime and differentials kicked in, it would be sugartime.

First thing the following Monday, esuper Whittberg corralled Booker and Rossy and instructed a special assignment. They were to drive down to Quantico Marine Base, in Virginia, and report to the firing range, where they would spend the next couple of days in weapons training. *Weapons training! Nobody ever said anything about weapons!* Whittberg explained they sometimes were authorized to carry, if they were going to a very remote area, harsh climate zone, near a region of political instability or if they were transporting classified material or equipment. In actuality, they infrequently packed, mainly because the required paperwork for each spent cartridge was impossibly comprehensive and, if they strapped a gun, they would probably fire it. Regardless, they were all required to maintain qualification in the use, maintenance and storage of firearms. The Quantico MP guard had their names at the main gate and would have them escorted to the range. There was no shuttle or Metro to QMB, so the rookies had to go back to AGA to pick up Rossy's car. Groob advised they could put in for reimbursement, at a half-george per mile plus lunch. They needed daily odometer readings and receipts and he would show them the forms when they returned.

Driving to Quantico was not as easy as it should have been, at least not for the Connecticut turnips. They made the mistake of taking I-95 from Maryland and got caught in a forty five minute delay at the complicated Woodrow Wilson drawbridge interplex. Traffic on the beltway and south from Springfield was horrendous - extreme, rush-hour volume the whole way to Quantico. They encountered about four different types of restricted travel lanes that were difficult to get onto and even harder to exit. Rossy heard the bray of angry horns more than once trying to negotiate the un-familiar tangle of highway configurations in search of the elusive through routes. It was quite a relief to enter the contrast of the tranquil military base from the vehicular war zone of the interstate. The gate guard checked their IDs against the schedule of visitors and directed how to get to the remote firing range HQ, where CMSgt. Iwasi met them at the reception desk and led them through the building to a small open office area overlooking the expansive outdoor shooting facility. Incessantly intermittent shot pops were audible from the range, though the noise was effectively muffled by the sound insulated building. Following introductions and a few general questions revealing the novice naivety of the engineers regarding firearms, the sergeant suggested they break for lunch. The main base mess hall was, not surprisingly, another contract operated franchise of Golden Paddock. Over sterno-warmed, pre-cooked burgers, the marine and his civilian gun neophytes briefed their severely dissimilar backgrounds.

John Iwasi was a career military man, a total marine through every cell of his being. His father and grandfather had both served in the marine corps, as well as a sister. He had marine camo tatts from shoulder to wrist on both arms. Upon graduation from basic training, directly out of high school, he immediately volunteered for the most elite programs available. His proudest moment was induction into a fast-strike mobile SEAL unit, from which he continued sniper development as a sharpshooter weapons specialist. All he ever wanted was extreme combat duty, but the higher-ups recognized his extraordinary shooting skills and mapped a different career plan for him. For certain, he was deployed to Afghanistan, though he spent his entire tour in the mailroom of a buffered rear substation in Kabul. Following return from 'combat', Sgt. Iwasi was assigned to the MC competitive shooting team, where he won the national inter-service championship five years in a row. From there, he settled into a permanent post as chief range instructor at Quantico. Not a bad calling, by any measure, but lacking the glorious combat record he had always dreamed about. Christ, even his sister had a purple heart from an IED shrapnel wound in Kandahar. But the sergeant was good with his station and looked forward to training the civilian rookies in basic weaponry.

Rossy didn't know of anyone in his family who had served in the military. Maybe some distant Indian kin fought with the French against the British. He had never even considered the military as a viable option for what he wanted to do. Not that he had anything in particular against the armed forces, it was just that he always knew a regimented life of following orders was not in his capacity to fulfill. Likewise, Booker had no military role models in his background and he was so radically apolitical that he could never give anywhere near a hundred to a policy driven military mission. No doubt it was best for all concerned that he stayed as far out of the service as possible.

After lunch, the sharpshooter led his students directly to the range. He started by reviewing in more detail what, if any, specific firearms and shooting experience they had. Rossy thought it inappropriate to mention his junior high bb gun battles or thousands of hours of video game havoc and annihilation, but remembered busting a groundhog while working on the farm. The animals were excavating and tunneling under valuable growing land in one section of a prime field and his uncle gave him a .22 rifle and a box of bullets and told him to go out there and take the destructive offenders down. He got one by waiting hidden, for hours, beside a hole, until the poorly sighted digger returned, shooting it right in the nose from about a foot away. It was not exactly a skill shot to be proud of, but evidently was effective, as the remaining groundhogs soon vacated the premises. And then there was the 16 gauge shotgun his dental uncle gave him in hopes of turning him into a Red Bear Lodge hunter. A beautiful, custom-made piece, with specially engraved stock and single barrel, that held six shells. Rossy never had much interest in hunting, though he always enjoyed being in the wilderness. But a shoulder gun was a lot heavier and harder to carry than a fly rod and he decided early on to stick to fishing. In recent years he had not gotten out in the woods much at all, even to hike, and he eventually gave the blaster to his cousin without ever having fired a shot. He wasn't sure how much this all added up to experience, but could tell by the forlorn way the sergeant looked at him that it was not significant. Booker's record was even less extensive. He had never discharged or handled any type of firearm in his life. "How long are you boys assigned for this training?" inquired the marine. "I don't know," shrugged Rossy, "I guess as long as it takes." "Well, that's fortunate, hoss, 'cause this could take a long, long time."

Subsequent to a rather extensive overview of the basic features and operating principles of firearms, they fired 12g shotguns to get used to the feeling of a hard discharge kick. Rossy found this particularly painful to his upper right arm still sore from the recent barrage of inoculations. From shotguns they went to unscoped 30.06 rifles, learning how to steadily squeeze the trigger through the firmly held shot, while slowly exhaling, to directionally stay on target against the reaction. At first they couldn't hit any part of a target circle within a stone's throw away. Gradually, they were able to start seeing shot dots on the target and, at some point, could approximately place the shots with a smidgeon of regularity. Of course, the fledgling shootists never came close to the expert's marking of ten dead center hits in ten seconds from a quarter mile, but over the next three days they actually began to develop a low level of proficiency. Through the week, they each fired close to five thousand rounds using a variety of single action and semi-automatic handguns and rifles. They shot indoors and out, at still targets and movers, from close range to intermediate, in sitting, standing and prone positions, with and without support props and even spent an hour on long range sniper shooting. There was a special session on the complete breakdown, cleaning and reassembly of a Glock 9S handgun, assumed to be the NAVOSUR weapon of issue, or at least the same class of issue. On the last training morning, as a special reward for improved performance and progress, they were permitted to fire a portable rocket launcher and fully automatic rifles and handguns, all seriously illegal armaments among the general populace.

The sergeant then demonstrated a new, highly classified technology. It was a sniper unit called MA 1000, a master assassin's weapon for a range greater than a thousand yards. The featherweight unit unfolded from a pocket-sized transport configuration, including a single projectile and adjustable focus scope to 200x. The 12 mm smart cartridge held an optic microchip that would guide the hit from a selected target lock. Sergeant Iwasi set up on a target 1,500 yards out. He focused the cross on the center, clicked a button with his left index finger and immediately triggered with his right. Absolute silence. They rode out to the target and found a 12 mm hole in the center, but did not find any evidence of the projectile in the backcatch. It had completely disintegrated and vaporized after impact. This weapon could kill with untraceable, 100% accuracy from a distance far beyond any feasible reach of personal security. It was capable of remotely taking out a select human target with no collateral damage and no detection of attack. The prototype MA 1000, developed by a multi-contract weapons research program, cost almost $5B and the field cost for each production model strike was more than $100K. Rossy wondered what kind of paperwork Sgt. Iwasi would have to do for that demo shot.

The grand finale was a tour of the FBI arsenal, which held nearly a million units representing thousands of different types of firearms, including many of high historical value. A significant portion of the pieces consisted of confiscations from raids on criminals, drug gangs, political insurgents, enemy forces and even organized hostile domestics. There was one section containing arms collected from the Grenada coup intervention in the 1980s. From the arsenal, the sergeant took the freshly trained gunsters back to the range office, where he ordained them each with a certificate of completion and qualification for the firearms training program, and then to the NCO club for a farewell brew. He felt a little wistful in knowing he did everything he could with the time he had to bring his two civilians up to a certain passable degree of competence in basic firearms use, but he knew he could advance them so much further, develop a lethal skill, if he only had them for another few weeks. Such was the conflict of a perfectionist, a national champion, a true specialist, a marine. *Semper Fi.*

The shooting engineers were not unhappy to leave Quantico. It had been a difficult week. At the end of each training day, when they removed the protective ear gear, everything seemed acutely loud and at a high pitched frequency, until sounds gradually normalized at some point during the drive home. There was no permanent hearing damage, but it was annoyingly disruptive to their sense of stability. They both had very sore and bruised shoulders from the endless rifle butt recoils, despite wearing padded harnesses. And their eyes were kablooie from straining to sight targets. No doubt it had been a physically demanding and mentally exhausting ordeal, about which, as he thought about it, Rossy had mixed feelings. He was proud of himself for accomplishing something he had never done before and actually enjoyed firing all the different types of weapons. It was really fun, especially when there were reasonably close hits on target. But he remembered all the problems and tragedy associated with firearms. They say 10,000 people a year are murdered by gunshot in the U.S. Who could ever forget all the terrifying, lunatic massacres, the worst where a whole class of little first-graders was obliterated, right before Christmas, by one of the very kinds of weapon he had just spent a week playing with? Sure, he enjoyed the controlled and instructed shooting, but not enough to go out and buy his own piece. He would still be in favor of any effective control lawmakers were able to enact and he found it thoroughly baffling that anyone in America would be against protection from random death by gun. The newly certified gunman also thought about Sgt. Iwasi. He felt a lot of respect for the marine dude and his unbelievable shooting skill, which was nothing other than awesome. But, with some ambivalence, he wondered about the MA 1000. What the hell was that about? Did the government actually assassinate people so often they needed to spend a hi-tech fortune to develop a super sniper rifle? Jesus, maybe he was finding out more than he wanted to know since being cleared. No problem for Booker, though, who was snore-fast asleep within five miles of leaving the base.

***

Training activities continued the ensuing week. The rookie engineering shooting sailors were assigned to Mickey Green's techs to learn how to operate and calibrate a theodolite and a laser tape, both basic autodigital instruments used for geodetic field work. Several of the equipment units had just been brought in by wokker and the towster returning from TDY and they had to be serviced in preparation for the next assignment. Last week the components were broken down, cleaned, inspected and reassembled with new battery packs, processors and hard drives installed in the internal micro computers. All information had been downloaded from the computers and they had to be certified swept of any residual classified data. This week the instruments would be field calibrated and repacked for travel. Green watched in poorly disguised scorn as the four got everything together to go out to the calibration range along the Suitland Parkway, not far from the South Capitol Street bridge. He was becoming increasingly frustrated by the way everyone in the organization ignored him like he didn't exist. His own techs, his subordinates, went about their business with virtually no interaction. They never conferred with him or kept him informed of their comings and goings. And the others, the *oh-so-special, clownass engineers*, never even took the courtesy to coordinate their use of his techs with him. They just called the techs directly. Green was seriously considering filing another suit for harassment, hostile workplace, or something along those lines. As a matter of fact he was keeping book on everybody in documentation of potential evidence to support a suit. With luck, he might be able to score a big enough settlement payday that he wouldn't have to wait until early retirement to get the frack out of here.

Rossy later asked, while helping to load the equipment containers into the agency utility truck, why Green seemed so constantly pissed off. Every time he saw the tech super, the guy came across like he was in a slow burn. "What's up with that?"

"He feels like he's discriminated against," explained Almer "shorty" Vonsbergis, one of the techs, who appeared almost dwarfish at not much, if anything, over five feet tall.

"How come?"

"I think 'cause he's Arab, or maybe Jewish....., whatever, but I can relate, 'cause I'm discriminated against, too."

"Why's that?" pressed the rookie engineer, assuming the guy probably took a lot of slop over his height.

"Cause I'm Lithuanian. At least my parents are."

Huh? Why would you be discriminated against for being Lithuanian? That doesn't make any sense. Rossy concluded the conversation was going nowhere and tended to completion of loading the instrument boxes in silence. The workgroup then boarded the truck for the short ride to the parkway, with the engineers outside in the haul bed along side the cargo, shorty at shotgun and bunny driving. John "bunny" Porter was an interesting dude. Rossy had a chance to talk to him one happy time at the Mashup. He was a native-born and loosely raised Washingtonian, as were his three kids with three women, though he was only twenty two years old. Bunny had quit high school to enroll in the Job Corps program, where he received a GED and some training in computer technology. The program was instrumental in getting him a job at NAVOSUR, which he appreciated, but his real passion was playing bass in a local dancehall band. The OffBeats, as they called themselves, had been working up a repertoire of Bob Marley covers and bunny was talking to Marcie about gigging the Mashup. He thought he only needed a little more time at NAVOSUR to be able to quit the day thing and devote full time to his music. It wasn't real clear how the boy, as a low GS tech, could set himself up financially and retire in his early twenties. The numbers just weren't there, even if he got double TDY overtime on a full-time basis and every base pay differential in the book. Possibly, they taught phone company math at Job Corps.

Bj had never developed a musical talent. Most likely, he never had one to develop. His only experience with organized music was in ninth grade, when the music teacher, a friend and horoscope client of his mom, convinced him to volunteer as a ringer in the marching band. They were looking for a second tuba to balance the other end of the row during parade events. The tuba, or sousaphone, was the bubba of brass horn instruments. Other than in a New Orleans social club band, where the bubba horn was actually played as an integral part of the ensemble, the tuba was a forty pound load that could hold up to a quart of spit if the carrier decided to blow into the silver dollar sized mouthpiece. It was also a target receptacle for anything that could be thrown into the big brass bell while marching down the boulevard past your jeering friends and peers. The ad hoc bassist served for about five parades, calling it quits after a New Year's Day event when his lips froze to the mouthpiece while trying to contribute some bass to the dissonant clash of trumpets, trombones, clarinets, saxophones, flutes, drums and countless other components comprising the marching musical mayhem. They probably needed more cowbell to pull it all together. Despite his best attempts, Rossy concluded the mighty tuba would never sound like anything different from a loud elephant boomfart and he decided it just wasn't worth the pain and aggravation. So, following his final street performance, he broke the bubba brass behemoth down, emptied it out - finding an edible apple - and turned it in for the last time. If bj's participatory musical acumen was limited, he always enjoyed listening to good music, the more off beat, avant-garde the better. And as a fellow bassman, he particularly looked forward to hearing bunny and his OBs play their Marley arrangements at the Mashup.

The instrument calibration ambit was laid out on a long, flat expanse of maintained grass turf directly adjacent to the paved shoulder of the west bound Suitland Parkway into the city. Bunny pulled the truck into the lawn area and parked between two decorative maple trees below a steep, trash filled rise from further off the roadway. The engineers and techs unloaded the containers and removed the instruments. The range field consisted of a network of geodetic markers, inlaid on permanent concrete pads, each defining a point elevation and geographic position. The primary task, today, was to measure distances and angles between markers and compare readings with pre-determined values of record to assure the first-order accuracy and function of the instruments. The secondary intent was to train the greenhorn engineers in the set-up and use of the instruments. Since the computer operated equipment was digitally controlled, there wasn't much to learning how to use it. Everything was automated. The most difficult aspect of retrieving the field data was lugging the fairly heavy units around from one point to another and that also didn't require a lot of training. The engineers were certified experts within less than twenty minutes and the techs let them practice their new skills for the next couple of hours, as they carried out the complex calibration protocols. Bunny and shorty supervised from the shade of the truck while sipping coldies they had retrieved from the breakroom before leaving the Yard.

Late in the morning, the parkway objective was successfully accomplished and the crew worked to repack the instruments into the travel boxes. Rossy noticed bunny frequently glancing over to the high bluff rising behind them. At one point he actually turned and was facing the bluff. The trainee followed the tech's upward gaze and saw the distant silhouettes of three men and a dog on top of the hill looking down at them. The biggest man watched through binoculars. *This could not be!* It was, unmistakingly and without a doubt, the graduate, a couple of the Mule Hillsters and mad dog Clinton!! Bunny raised his right hand and cupped it above his eyes for a moment and then abruptly extended his arm and quickly flashed three fingers, the index, middle and pinkie, before reversing around and resuming the work duty. Rossy looked back up to the bluff top and the gangsters were gone. *What the hell was this?!?* He asked bunny what was going on and bunny said he noticed those dudes watching and waved to let them know he saw they were there. He said they sometimes got harassed out on the calibration range, here, and they had to be alert to make sure nobody tried to rip them off. Under D.C. street law, anything not well guarded was stolen and there would be hell to pay if they lost any of the expensive, classified equipment. But Rossy clearly saw bunny *signaling* to the graduate, not defiantly waving at him. *The fracking graduate!* Not some random parkway bandit! He knew what he saw. And he knew what the graduate had to have seen - his new patsy pal, robin!! And probably batman, too! *Goddam!!* He looked over to see if Booker had picked up on any of this, but shiner was sitting in the truck drinking beer with shorty and missed the whole interlude.

On the return ride to the Yard, Rossy tried to figure out in his head some sort of rational solution to his mounting malaise over what was going on in NAVOSUR. Today, he learned Larry was not alone in secret complicity with the graduate and it was still not feasible to ask anyone for explanations, not only because of his prior reasoning, but because they would lie, as bunny just proved at the calibration range. Since it was impossible to learn truth from professors of lies, or from those who didn't know anything, Rossy had no choice but to maintain radio silence and keep his frustrations to himself. *Ask me no questions and I'll tell you no lies.* Sort of a pseudo-truth approach, but all he had, for now. If his new coworkers were involved in some kind of illegal shit, which would seem to be the case if they were up with the graduate, it did not include him and he would do everything he could to keep it that way. And the graduate would obviously not want it revealed to the

NAVOSUR folks how he knew Rossy and Booker, anymore than Rossy and Booker, or at least Rossy, did not want it revealed to the same people how they knew the graduate. A perfect, mutually exclusive circle. So, DWBH, be quiet and get paid!

***

Dick Whittberg had suspected early on that Rossy was different from the other engineers. He could tell this one was conscientious, wanted to to do a good job, and was not the natural born frack-off that could describe the usual hoi polloi they had to contend with. Kids coming out of school today had a way overblown sense of self worth and entitlement and no concept of what is expected in developing a proper work ethic. They lacked basic cognitive skills and couldn't focus on one assigned task long enough to make significant progress in anything. Unfortunately, NAVOSUR had to take what it could get, otherwise they wouldn't be able to fill enough slots to keep the operation going. But this boy seemed almost old school in his attention to detail and objective. As far as Whittberg knew, the new recruit was the only employee in the history of the agency to completely read the entire Bowditch manual, including the obsolete trig function data tables. And he carried out several menial little sludge jobs without question or complaint. His running buddy, Booker, fell more into the typical category for incoming engineers, exhibiting a traditional 'That's clown shit - why should I have to do that!?' attitude toward intentionally ambiguous assignments. The deciding factor, though, in Rossy's characterization, was, without a doubt, his manifest performance during and following the DIS interview. He demonstrated an innate ability to adapt to bizarrely changing conditions and, more importantly, a willingness to follow specific instructions. As ordered, he did not breathe a word to anyone, except Blackburn, regarding the interview, despite heavy pressure from coworkers to explain the obvious. Whittberg was certain: Rossy was the best candidate - and it was time to execute the initiation procedure.

The next morning, after everyone arrived at work and the director was gone to meetings, the engineering supervisor got up from his desk and went down to the break porch. He took out a new disposable cell phone, replaced the memory chip and disabled the auto locator. He then called the Pentagon public information office and, speaking through a handkerchief, calmly and quickly stated that "a high yield explosive device has been placed and will detonate at the Bowditch Building, in the WNY federal center, at precisely 0847 local, today. Allahu akhbar!" He immediately turned the phone off, removed the memory chip and ground it and the original chip into electronic dust with his shoe heel. He gathered up the debris with his kerchief, put it in his pocket with the shell phone and went back upstairs to his desk. He had not been gone any longer than it would have taken to go to the restroom. In less than five minutes, the approaching wail of a chorus of emergency sirens erupted, as admin Tom came running out of his office howling for everyone to evacuate the building, like, "**before NOW!!!**" This was not a problem for most of the engineers and techs, as they were almost getting ready for break and could easily slip into evacuation mode. Not so much for dps Lockbark, who had his checklist of security protocol to implement in defaulting the data processing center entry mechanisms to no override superlock. First he had to go into the center and clear the computers into deep sleep de-access. He had just completed the secure lock and shutdown procedures and was entering the stairwell to leave the building, when he ran into a boisterous contingent of heavily outfitted military and metro police specialists with bomb dogs and explosive suppression equipment rushing up the steps from below. The lead uniform blocked Larry's departure, pushing him back against the wall on the landing. "Sir, this building is under evacuation order. I must ask you to vacate the premises immediately."

"Yes, I understand. That is what I'm trying to do if you will let me by." The officer's massive German Shepard began sniffing all over the outside of the battered, government issue briefcase that Larry pulled back and up in protective custody.

"What is in the briefcase? Sir, I must ask you to open the briefcase."

"I can't do that. It has classified information." The dog was wildly wagging its tail and squealing with mounting excitement, like an overslopped hog.

"Sir, please open the case, now!"

"That's not going to happen. You don't have statute authority to view these contents. Now let me by, please." Just then someone called out loudly from inside the NAVOSUR office area for the unit leader to come and take a look at something, and the officer abruptly turned and exited the stairwell, dragging his yelping, resistant dog along. Lockbark continued down the steps and into the first floor entrance hallway.

Outside, civil servants were streaming from every occupied structure and facility in the federal center amid the increasing accumulation of emergency vehicles and special response police presence. Red, orange, white and blue strobes flashed everywhere, while a constant, overbearing blare of dueling 'OOGA' horns broadcasted the urgent, non-drill reality of the situation. Whittberg spotted Rossy lagging toward the parking lot behind the group of NAVOSUR sailors and caught up with him without being seen by the others. He tapped his target on the shoulder and motioned for him to follow around to the back of the Bowditch Building, where the utility truck was parked, and directed the young engineer to get in. "We've got something to do," explained the supervisor, as he started the engine and backed out of the small lot. Whittberg knew the evacuation would last hours, if not days, before the experts cleared the area for reentry. Plenty of time to accomplish his mission during the tumult without being missed. He turned into a narrow access lane running through the federal center to an auxiliary gate onto M Street. The passenger looked over at the Bowditch Building as they passed and saw dps Larry coming out of the little used door on the west side. He thought it odd that the dps would be using the exit on the opposite face of the building from the regular NAVOSUR egress, but what really struck him was what Larry was carrying. The same, or similar looking, worn-out old briefcase he had received in the exchange with the graduate, down near The Beecher, a few weeks ago. And it appeared Lockbark was again headed in that direction! Did he have another rendezvous planned? Rossy almost was on the verge of asking Whittberg about these strange goings on he was observing, but checked himself in silent realization that he still didn't have enough information on the issue to format an intelligent question. Besides, where was *he* going right now? Whittberg hadn't said anything since they got in the truck and he seemed sort of tight, like whatever they were doing was not routine, maybe not official business. The hijacked rookie decided to just wait and see, evidently the standard modus operandi for working in this whackhouse. Anyway, he was only doing what his supervisor told him to do. If they were headed toward some kind of unauthorized bullshit, that was SEP and not his wheeze.

The evacuated NAVOSUR techs and engineers sauntered toward the parking lot trying to decide what to do. Several recalled an incident like this happening once before and knew it would be quite a while before they would be allowed back in the building. They decided to go over to the Chiefs' Club for a few brews and consider their options for the rest of the day. As far as they were concerned, this was free time. No one noticed Mickey Green sitting at a remote picnic table near the fence line under the shadow of the bridge, closely watching, government issue pen in hand, carefully chronicling everything he saw his agency colleagues doing into a bound legal journal.

Whittberg was forced straight coming out of the Yard, as M Street was blocked with special response activity. He took 'L' down to an intersecting alley on the left, from which he turned into a driveway and drove far enough behind the Mashup that the blue Navy truck could not be seen from the street. He got out and shouted, "C'mon, let's go!" to a hesitant Rossy, still in the truck. They walked around to the doorway and entered the dark, empty establishment that was in the process of opening up for the day. The only echo of life was from the TV over the bar, tuned to *Washington Wake-up Call*, a local morning news show that was already reporting the breaking story of a bomb threat at the Navy Yard. The esuper led the way across the room to the nearest stools at the end of the bar. **"Anybody home?!"** he called toward the back. The kitchen doors swung open and a tall, frizzy headed white dude, with thick, dark rimmed glasses and a full-length apron, emerged. Junebug, Marcie's first shifter and head jerk man, strode down behind the bar to his inaugural customers of the day. "Yeah, man, we here. What can I do for ya?"

"How 'bout a couple of cold Stripes?"

"You got it, my man."

"Mr. Whittberg, I dunno. It's, like, not even eight-thirty. It's really a little early for me."

"Dick," said Dick. "Call me Dick. And I'm your supervisor. So if you're on duty and I buy you a beer, you'll have a beer - no matter what time it is. Capisce?"

"Yeah, I guess so," conceded the junior engineer, wondering if the out-of-college, real world was actually as universally screwed up as he was beginning to believe it was. He had no idea what was going on here and was starting to sense a grimly bad vibe. The Mashup was much different early in the morning than at afternoon happy time. Colder, darker, quieter. It didn't seem like the usual fun place he knew. Right now, it felt more menacing than anything.

"Mr. Rossy, do you love your country?" inquired Dick, pouring sudsy beer into both glasses in front of the two.

Whoa! What does that mean? Careful. "Uh, sure, of course I do. Why do you ask?"

"Well, America is under siege these days. There's people and organizations all around the world who would like nothing better than to see the U S of A crumble into a pile of dog shit at the bottom of the compost heap of history. Hell, there's even a lot of our own so-called citizens that want to bring this great country down. Truth is, there's a diminishing number of folks admitting they love America and even fewer actually willing to do something about it. Would you do something special to help your country, Mr. Rossy?"

This is getting a little creepy. "Uh... yeah, probably. Guess it depends what it was. I mean, I don't think I would do anything crazy, or illegal, or anything like that. But, yeah, I would do something positive to look out for America. Are you talking about a work assignment?"

"Yes, sort of. Son, there's someone I would like you to talk to who could give you an unusual opportunity to serve your country. Are you interested in meeting with this individual?"

"Uh.........Ok......... What do you want me to do?"

"Let me make a call and I can take you to him this morning." Dick got up from the stool and went over to a darkened area of the room, cell phone in hand. Rossy tried to digest what was going down, but couldn't make anything out of it. He only knew he was just as curious as afraid, which might be a dangerous combo. He remembered mom warning his celestial alignments were all fracked up and wondered if that was coming into play with this newest zany turn of events. If so, he was facing much more of a challenge than he was willing to take on.

JOINT BASE ANDREWS

Randolph Patton Clement was a big man, in a lot of ways. At six-three and two forty, big in stature and size. Big in presence, by the way he filled a space, no matter how small or large, with uncompromising authority. Big in rank - a retired two star in the Army Reserves. And big in status. Very big. He was the highest graded and tenured career professional in the Consolidated Intelligence Administration. GS-18, with a permanent secure delta rating equal to only a handful of elected and appointed officials at the top echelons of government, including the POTUS and the director. Arguably, there was no one else on earth who knew more about the black world of ultra-classified U.S. operations and programs than the general, R. P. Clement. But he had no public sphere and essentially, for all practical purposes, did not exist. Currently monitoring development of a new stealth weapons system, he worked out of a sublevel suite in the ASC headquarters building at Joint Base Andrews and had not even set foot in his own organization's well known Virginia headquarters in nearly two years. And despite all this surreptitious power and influence, here he was, about to meet with some nobody rookie engineer from NAVOSUR to set up the improvised wrap of an alleged developing circumstance before it bloomed. Time was when he would covertly assign a highly trained field agent to undermine the situation and make it disappear as if it never even existed, before anyone on the outside was ever aware of it. Time was when he commanded the largest and most powerful and far-reaching, lethal network of professional neutralizers in the history of organized intelligence. But no more. Extreme funding cuts in recent years had decimated his resources to the extent he could no longer place a viable force of his own investigative analysts in the field. Most of his best and highest paid operatives resigned before they were riffed to take positions with private security contractors, typically doing much the same thing as when they were with the CIA, but for much more money. He now had to rely heavily on intel retrieved from a transient web

of unhandled foreign nationals working as multiple moles, inform-
ants, runners and couriers, through a myriad of underworld
sources, locales and cultures, over whom he basically had no influence other than to pay them. Not nearly as much as he used to
pay his own pros, but much more than they could ever legitimately
earn in their respective broken down, little countries. And he
didn't have to pay per diem, travel, expense and benefit costs,
which were previously, quite literally, breaking the company bank.
Surprisingly, this mish-mash of untrained confusion was somewhat effective, because any asset relaying bad info, or trying to
sell good info to the highest bidder, would be immediately exposed to and dropped by all users. It was a self-policing system
that reasonably often produced actionable material.

To mitigate the gap in on-site field coordination, Clement devised a clandestine program utilizing low-graded civilian government employees in other departments and agencies, normally and
frequently assigned for classified duty abroad in their jobs, to simultaneously act as in-country operatives for the CIA. He enticed
these people with off-the-books, tax-free compensation, usually
some fraction of their base pay, and appeal for a higher service to
the greater good. This, of course, was all totally illegal and, if ever
unraveled, would result in the biggest internal government ops
scandal since the Iran-Contra gun running scheme of the 1980's.
But Clement was confident his 'operation double duty' was failsafe. There would be no whistleblowing expose, because the only
ones who could toot would grossly incriminate themselves by so
doing. If any prospective recruit got wet feet and decided to raise a
righteous holler between petition and enlistment, RPC would
simply deny any knowledge of whatever allegations were made.
Who could prove otherwise? There was no paper trail. No employment records. Payments were made by electronic transfer
from accounts of established enterprise shells - nothing to arouse
the suspicions of anyone privy to the transactions. The main problem was where to find his little 'chipmoles', as he liked to call
them. He needed supervisory coordinators in agencies of potential
interest, who could select candidates as well as influence their
overseas assignments. There were about 150,000 civil service job
slots, in close to 200 separate federal organizations, that required
routine travel and duty abroad. At any given time, there was a civilian U.S. government worker in every country in the world. But

not all were chipmole material. The general shied away from agencies involved in ambivalent social or community development work, like Peace Corps, USAID and even the diplomatic wings of the State Department. Hell, everybody thought all those people were CIA implants anyway, so why feed the myth? No, he found the best sources were the more technically orientated arrows of DoD, Energy, EPA, NOAA - places like that, with clearly defined missions the nationals could see and believe and, therefore, not suspect of unknown ulterior motives.

This was the third recruit from NAVOSUR. The first one collected information, while participating in hydrographic surveys along the east horn of Africa, pertaining to the identification of marauding sea gangsters who were disrupting regional shipping lanes around the continent. The data was critical in the successful elimination of several pirate leaders by U.S. special forces, though, obviously, the intel source was never revealed. Unfortunately, the chipmole was a hopeless alcoholic and died in a coma after falling out of a bus in Mombasa. Another project miscarried before it was born. Clement purposely didn't know much about this newest candidate - only what Whittberg and DIS had reported to him. He preferred to reserve his expert judgement until after, or probably during, the interview, but knew he couldn't be overly selective. This would be the last chipmole in the ODD program, the *grand finale*, and time was of the essence.

***

Since police had closed the 11th Street Bridge in response to the Navy Yard security emergency, Dick took Potomac over to Pennsylvania. They rode out beyond the Washington beltway onto Upper Marlboro Pike and entered the east side of Andrews via the remote Dower House Road gate. The guard looked at Whittberg's credentials and waved them past without even a glance at the younger passenger on the other side of the truck. Rossy felt like the invisible man, but was happy to be able to get into somewhere, for a change, without showing ID. They rode through the industrial complexes of facility plant support and the air national guard and naval air reserve operational districts, staying on Perimeter Road around the desolate south end of the base. In passing the runway end zones the new engineer could see the air traffic pavements stretching more than two miles into the distance and seemingly hundreds of yards wide. This was a huge base. The esuper said there were probably ten thousand people living and working on site, making Andrews a sizable suburb of D.C. As they approached the west side, it looked like nothing but superbly manicured golf course, on both sides of the road, as far as the eye could see. Rossy didn't know anything about golf, but thought this course looked way too big. Whittberg explained there were actually three full-sized courses, two of which were built by Nazi POW slave labor during the War. He claimed many a policy decision, affecting the whole country, often the world, had been secretly formed on these courses over the decades, because Andrews was like a golfing president's personal military playground, as well as home to the legendary Air Force One fleet.

HQASC was a strange looking building in the middle of the congested west base. It resembled a massive half wheel with five spoked wings extending from the center hub to the rim. Not a visibly high structure, only three floors above grade, it was, by far, the largest facility on base, in terms of total square footage, including the three full sublevels below grade. There was a secure perimeter around the premises, maintained by armed guard, variable lethal laser fencing and full scan video surveillance. Underground audio and infrared heat detectors could sense any unauthorized subsurface activity within the perimeter and the building was completely shielded against random microwave propagation. Over the years, nearly $20 billion had been spent on security enhancement for HQASC, which was nothing compared to the trillions spent on the development of secret weapon and defense systems managed within its walls. The only more secure area at JBA was the AF1 compound.

There was just a single entry pass for headquarters visitors and no vehicle parking within the secper. Whittberg parked the truck in the nearby Officers' Club lot and they walked over to the check point. Only cleared personnel were permitted through the check and Dick had pre-coordinated their arrival, but they still had to provide security photo ID, pass metal scan and log digital sign-in. This only got them over the perimeter line. To get into the building they entered a sallyport, where an electronic voice ordered keypad input of the destination code. Handprint ID was required to activate the keypad. Dick successfully performed the procedure resulting in a facial identification scan from the point of destination, after which they were instructed to wait for escort. The sallyport was only long enough to preclude a single person from simultaneously holding both doors open, should the synchronized locking defaults fail, and it was not as wide. Rossy had recently developed an aversion to confined spaces in unknown places and hoped the wait for escort would be short. It was, as a stocky young lady, with about six laminated ID, security and special pass card loops draped around her neck, arrived within minutes and opened the port door into the lobby area of the building hub.

The heavily secured escort led the visitors across the floor to the elevator portals, where they entered an open cab and descended to 'Sub 2'. During the short ride, she removed two temporary pass and locator card necklaces from her stock of IDs and gave one to each of the guests. They exited the elevator into what looked like an unfinished basement and walked over to the middle pair of five double glass door sets. The leader placed her left hand on a print ID pad and, three seconds after a single green flash, key punched an entry code with her right index finger. The doors clicked to unlock and they passed through into a long, narrow concrete corridor, dimly lit with low wattage incandescent fixtures mounted on the walls about two feet below the ceiling. The shadowy hued tunnel sort of looked like a medieval castle passageway. Rossy absently thought he probably wouldn't be surprised to see a detachment of knights appear in full-dress mail and armor panoply. Would they, perchance, be on their way to court with Arthur Pendragon? *Quit abstracting and pay attention! This is serious!* The trio moved noisily on the uncarpeted floor into the abyss, stopping at a wide oaken door about two thirds of the way through the length of the wing. The guide entered another keypad code and opened the thick door into a huge, square-shaped conference room. A monstrous round table, at least twenty feet in diameter, sat in the center of the room, circled by thirteen evenly spaced, high-backed arm chairs. The decor was dark stained ironwood and black leather, above plush, un-patterned carpet, all of which gobbled up the sole area lighting from a fairly elaborate lamp candelabra hanging low over the center of the table. The chair nearest the only other door in the room, in the opposite wall from the access to the wing hallway, was at least a third larger than the rest and slightly higher. The aura of the room was oppressive, gloomy and foreboding and not what any first-time visitor would reasonably expect to encounter at a modern air force base. The escort offered chairs on either side of the master throne and left the room through the adjacent door. The young sailor looked questioningly at Dick, who shrugged 'no comment', preferring to let the general speak for himself and run his own show without prejudice.

***

Rossy was on the brink of verbalizing his bewilderment about what was happening here, when the throne door opened to the forceful entrance of the incontrovertible man in charge. A big and tall, skinhead mr. clean, wearing round, rimless glasses, starched white shirt, gold cufflinks, solid red tie, sharply pressed cotton slacks and spit-shined Gucci points, R. P. Clement strode quickly to his chair between the visitors, blowing billows of thick, bluish-gray smoke ahead of him from an Habanos Limitadas Supreme. The Cuban delicacy cost more than a grant in the bootleg counter economy and burned very aromatically pleasing. Clement threw a quick acknowledging nod to Whittberg and then turned to his potential chipmole, staring intently into the boy's eyes, without blinking or speaking, for a good five or six seconds. The new engineer did not waver his return focus, gazing fixedly right back into the magnified steely grays of the host, like a mirror, waiting to respond to whatever was offered. *That's good. The kid's got some resolve.* The general drew in a long, measured toke from the cigar, held it a moment and exhaled an even line of sweet smog directly into the face of his object of attention. "Mr. Rossy, do you love your country?" intoned the big man.

"Y-yes, sir, I do," choked the candidate, his eyes tearing up from the unexpected effluvial assault. *What the hell? That's the same line that Dick pitched.*

"And would you like to prove it?"

"Prove it? To who? I don't have to prove if I love America." Rossy was becoming irritated. This big dude was way weird.

Hmm....the youngster's got a little game. I like that. "No, son, you don't, but if you had the chance would you go above and beyond to serve our great nation?"

"Well, like I told Mr. Whittberg earlier, it depends what it is. He said you would explain an opportunity for a special assignment in my job."

"Yes, yes. That's true. I do have a proposal for you."

"OK...?"

"Mr. Rossy, I assume you are aware of the long and on-going war against extremist terrorism around the world?"

"Yes, sir."

The general then proceeded into a lengthy, convoluted dissertation about the state of the war. It had very little to do with religion. There were about seven plus billion people on earth and, at any given time, maybe three fifths of them were reasonably happy and content with their lives. The other forty percent was pissed off about something. There might be three billion reasons why they were angry, very few rooted in religious beliefs, because truly religious people were inherently happy. Of upwards of three billion angry people, not more than a thousandth of one percent would be statistically inclined to act out on their anger, which means we've got about thirty thousand potential bombers roaming the earth. Ninety percent of these are isolated loners and not members of any organized terrorist group. The remaining three thousand are organized and we know approximately who and where they are. None of these people officially represent any sovereign state or nation, so, if they do something randomly and massively destructive, they are essentially outlaws, like Jessie James, or Al Capone. The unorganized gene pool of terrorists could be anywhere and they get all their information from the internet. They don't need to go to a nondescript rubble country or uninhabitable territory in the middle east to do push-ups out in a rock field and train under the tutelage of some rabid, has-been mullah. They can go to a neighborhood farm supply store, gas station and pharmacy to pick up whatever they need to build a bomb big enough to kill hundreds. Or, they can hack into an encrypted network and destabilize any automated mass service system on the planet from the comfort of their parents' basement. The organized terrorists are generally pissed off about the same thing and come from the same locale. Those who have actually committed, or abetted, acts of criminal radicalism realize they are, more or less, like fish in a barrel and susceptible to being droned out. They can't just quit being outlaws and go be a plumber, or sell betel nuts, or become a respected citizen. They are condemned insurgents for life. So, there is increasing evidence that an active movement is underway, within the organized terrorist community, to enlist recruits from the unhappy, unorganized, loner, would-be extremists around the world. This effectively makes the terrorism industry non-ideological and infinitely more dangerous. The big guy paused, for effect, and looked hard at his own recruit.

"Well, how can I help with any of that? That all has nothing to do with my job."

"As a matter of fact," continued RPC, "we are aware of one particular individual who is moving from country to country in the emerging economies and, like a Mormon seeking converts, making contact and establishing networks with severely disenfranchised young people about leaving their angry misery behind to board a glory train to hell. We believe this missionary of terror is attempting to build an international supercell of educated, tech skilled malcontents, organized to heavily disrupt, or take down, economy supporting infrastructures around the world. We don't know much about the person, other than he, or she, is charismatic and operates quickly - never staying in one place very long and never leaving any digital trail. And that is where you, Mr. Rossy, can help. In the course of your assigned duties abroad for NAVOSUR, you will covertly interface with our local, in-country assets for information pertaining to the identification, activities and movements of the unsub. You can do this without suspicion, because anyone watching will know who you are and why you are legitimately there. If you are able to obtain good intel such that we can connect the dots and neutralize this dangerous target, you will have served your country greatly and nobly, my friend. Are you interested?"

"Uh,.... I don't know. I, I think I have a lot of questions that I don't even know what they are. I guess I'm interested, but,......like,... who are you? And, what?... are you with the air force? I don't even know where I am right now."

"I understand your confusion, son, but you have no need to know who I am. As a matter of fact this conversation never occurred and you will have no further interaction with me. As far as you are concerned, neither I, nor this place, exist. Any questions you have regarding our discussion can be directed to Mr. Whittberg....Dick, here, who will also give you explicit mission instructions and preparation should you agree to participate. If you do participate, a biweekly, non-reportable deposit, equal to half your biweekly base salary, will be placed in an account you should set up as a traditional IRA. If you violate any terms of this discussion, your security classification will be revoked and your federal service will be terminated. You have until COB today to advise Dick of your decision. I will take the liberty in advance and on behalf of America to thank you for your special service. Have a nice day, Mr. Rossy." And with that, the general arose from the big chair and departed the room as resolutely as he had entered, closing the auxiliary door harshly behind him.

***

Likewise, Dick rose from his chair and started toward the wing corridor doorway. "C'mon, Rossy, we're done here," he commanded to his still seated and befuddled subordinate. They retraced their steps back through the dreary hallway, stopping at a single steel door alcove on the left, before they got to the double doors into the elevator foyer. Whittberg punched four digits on a keypad and the door lock opened. They entered a small, short passageway that spurred into a wide utilidor containing a large matrix of various sized, color-coded pipes, tubes, mains, conduits, ducts and bundled cables running through wall sleeves from a cavernous mechanical room at the juncture. The visitors followed the utilidor for about a hundred yards to a secper cross and check-out point. They turned in their temp passes to the armed guard, digitally signed-out of HQASC and continued through the subterranean utility tunnel. At a certain convergence another utilidor intersected from the left, but the navy yardsmen, at the esuper's direction, kept straight into a gradual upward ascent. This led to a closed, unlocked utility door that opened to the lowest level of a concrete stairwell. They followed the steps up two landings and went through another keypad controlled door into an obscure corner of the lobby of the Officers' Club.

It was still only mid-morning and the O Club was in sort of a neap lull between breakfast and lunch services. There was some traffic of comings and goings of morning breaksters, but the facility was relatively empty. The two approached the reception area at the main entrance, where an attractive oriental woman pleasantly asked for ID. Dick showed his membership card and Rossy his NAVOSUR security pass. She wouldn't accept the security pass, but allowed bj in as a guest of his member boss. With his charge in tow, the senior engineer walked briskly past the cafe recess, through the dining room and into the lounge at the far end of the club. Glancing quickly around, he went over to the bar and found two seats seemingly out of the scope of any noticeable surveillance optics. Most O Club bars around the world had no video monitoring, for obvious, but unstated, reasons, and this was especially the case at Andrews. Dick ordered two drafts as he sat down and motioned for Rossy to likewise have a seat. "So, do you understand what was said to you this morning?" began the esuper, in a low voice, almost a monotone whisper.

"I think I understand, but in all honesty, Dick, I don't know if I'm qualified to do what that whoever he was big guy was talking about. And I'm pretty sure I can't decide by the end of today whether or not to get involved in this."

Whittberg stared down at his icy mug on the bar and said nothing for a few moments. He finally continued in the same subdued, but Rossy thought mildly threatening, tone. "Let me clarify something, son. You do not have a choice in this matter and you do not have until the end of the day. You will either agree to what has been proposed for you or your federal employment will be terminated, effective immediately."

Say,... whaat?! No way - NO WAY!! I don't think so! "What do you mean? I don't remember anything like that assignment in my job description. There's no way I could be fired for not accepting that duty! **I've got rights!"**

"Keep your voice down, please. And, Mr. Rossy, you apparently don't recall the clause in your PD, that alludes to 'other duties as assigned'. Now that covers a lot of leeway and would certainly be applicable to what we're talking about here. You are a new employee, still on probationary status. You might not have all the rights you think you have. Be very careful, son. Don't throw away an opportunity. If you're fired from federal employment, you'll have a very difficult time finding another professional job..... *anywhere.*"

Rossy couldn't believe this was happening to him. "Who the hell are you, Dick? What's your job? Are you with the same group as the other dude? And how come you're all giving me such a hard time?"

"My job is the same as yours. I work for NAVOSUR and, yes, I help the 'other dude', whose code name, by the way, is 'tophead', but, remember - he doesn't exist and you should not make any more references to him, or ever try to contact him. For your information, and just so you won't waste time trying to figure it out, tophead is CIA. That's *all* you need to know. No one is giving you a hard time. You are being given a special chance to serve your country in a way that very few citizens could ever dream of doing, because you have the ability and integrity to do so. Can we, can your nation, count on you, son?"

C..I..fracking..A??!! Jesus fracking christ!! Rossy felt thoroughly trapped, like a beaver in a vice snare. He was holding a pair of twos against four aces. There was nowhere to go. He slowly surrendered a nodded affirmation and took a long draw of beer from his melting mug.

"Excellent! You are making the right decision - one you'll never regret. We'll start briefing your field assignment tomorrow. Now I don't need to remind you, Mr. Rossy, that everything, and I mean *everything*, you heard and participated in this morning is classified. You are not to discuss any of this with anyone, including director Blackburn. If you compromise on this, you will not only lose your job, but you could face felony indictment for violations under provisions of the Patriot and Espionage Acts. Do you understand?" The chipmole recruit meekly nodded through another hefty slug of frosty mug juice. "Good! Now let's get out of here." Whittberg abruptly got up from the bar and headed back toward the lobby. Rossy, feeling like he was about to throw, lagged a bit behind and the two exited the club into the brilliant sunshine of a new day. Not a cloud in the sky.

***

The sailor agents departed Andrews through the main gate onto Suitland Road. Whittberg drove to AGA in Suitland and dropped bj off at his apartment, telling him to take the afternoon and prepare for TDY and get some rest, because he was going to need it. He then returned to the WNY, finding the federal center still crawling with special response forces and the media. The police seemed to be expending more effort trying to keep the media at bay than clearing the buildings, which all remained evacuated and closed. After returning the truck to its concealed space behind Bowditch, Dick walked down to the parking lot, got into his custom, black Escalade EXT and left the Yard. He did not see any other NAVOSUR employees and didn't really care where they were. His mission for the day was accomplished.

But not Mickey Green's. The tech super would sit at his secluded vantage point until quitting time, meticulously recording
any and all observations of the movements of NAVOSUR personnel throughout this evacuation snafu. He saw the engineers and his
techs all headed over toward the Chiefs' Club. Whittberg left in
the company truck with one of the new boys, came back alone and
drove out in his own ride. Simple Larry Lockbark walked down to
the river and looked like he had a brief discussion with some jum-
bo-big navy dude, but then he couldn't see where he went, only
that he never came back to the federal center. He didn't know
what happened to McCarven, other than he was gone - no doubt
somewhere drinking himself into oblivion. Date, names and times.
It was all in the book. Every last one of them away from the premises without authorization. Hell, for all he knew, one of the dickhead engineers called in a bogus bomb threat to get the day off.
Time would tell. Green was satisfied he had documented some
very useful information to build his emerging case. A year from
now he might be sipping rum mojitos on the island beach of his
choice. Hotdamm!!

THE APARTMENT

He knew it was a death chase. The fuddheaded gargoyle was herding him toward an indiscernible dimension of terror. It was like a Cat 5 hurricane over a sheer cliff earthquake shimmering in a bubble of radioactive dust. He called 911 for help and immediately saw a cavalcade of unmarked vehicles string across in front of him. The doors flew open and out jumped a regiment of ninja commandos in long, black flak jackets with **C I A** *conspicuously lettered on both front and back. The unit captain approached him and bellowed in his face,* **"SIR,... YOU WERE TOLD NEVER TO CONTACT THIS NUMBER!! NOW YOU MUST PAY THE PRICE!!"** *The beast in pursuit was closing in. The horror ahead was expanding. All sound yielded to a deafening, tocsinic screech as the air filled with unbreathable fumes.* Rossy sat bolt upright in the bed, sweat streaming from his pores, and, somewhere in the twilight zone between sleep and consciousness, realized something was terribly wrong. He heard Booker thrashing around in the kitchen, shrieking a run-on string of random obscenities. A woman was screaming at an even higher pitch than the head-splitting smoke detector whistle and, outside, the hideously loud building fire alarm system clanged continuously. From a distance came the rapidly nearing cacophony of wailing sirens and blaring firetruck powerhorns. Rossy jerked on a pair of jeans and thrust open his bedroom door. Smoke was everywhere, but he didn't see any flames. He ran through the living room to the kitchen, where Booker was frantically discharging the last contents of the fire extinguisher into the gaping mouth of the oven, out of which copious plumes of smoke belched. Rossy turned and sprinted to open the patio door and adjacent windows for fresh air. The screaming girl was retreating to the front door, furiously denouncing shiner as a total schlub who should never **"ever bother to bother me again!!"**

The last of the Building C occupants were outing themselves to the exterior, as emergency vehicles arrived in the nearby parking lot. The firefighters were able to respond very rapidly, because the apartment smoke detectors were interlocked with a dedicated master alarm display at department headquarters. This was a new county regulation for all multi-unit rental facilities, following a recent tragedy in which several residents died in an apartment fire that the department was slow in getting to because of an emergency dispatch system malfunction. The instant direct annunciation undoubtedly provided a valuable edge for real-time fire response, but also resulted in a lot of non-threatening, false alarm type calls that added a significant burden to the already strained fire emergency resources. And so the chief was not too happy when he discovered this was apparently a dummy run. A smoke blowing kitchen frack-up by some inept, clownass kid cook. DCA Security's Donald Trevair, was, likewise, not very understanding in discovering who was at the epicenter of this 'emergency'. He assured the engineers they would be liable for the front door destruction caused by the firefighters' forced entry into the apartment, as well as any repair costs associated with smoke damage. This would all be in his incident report to AGA management. Trevair told the squatter tenants, in no uncertain terms, that their out-of-state asses would be out-on-the-street if they caused any more trouble, adding he should never have let them into Smith's apartment in the first place. Several other tenants, angered by the disruption of their evening, applauded the security rep's vociferous reprimand of the instigators, as they shuffled by, glaring at the sailors, in returning to their own units.

When the apartment and surroundings were finally cleared of emergency personnel, onlookers, neighboring residents, security and smoke, Rossy asked Booker, "What the hell happened?"

"Aw, dude, I can't believe it. I CAN'T BELIEVE THIS SHIT!! I met this sick chick at the Mashup and we really hit it off big time. We had a couple of Stripes and I got the brilliant idea to invite her to the apartment for dinner. I figured I could pick up some Delmonicos at Morton Meats, over near Iverson, whip up a nice salad and bunt her into scoring position. So everything's frosty, I put the steaks in the oven to broil, shut the door and popped a coldie. Next thing I know, I see through the window the frackin' oven is filled up with flames. So I open the door and throw a pot of water in and the whole thing, like, explodes, man!! Shit!! Then I grabbed the extinguisher and got the fire out, but everything smoked up like a goddam pig barbecue. Jesus christ! What a barge of crap!!"

"Well, why did the steaks catch fire? Did you put them too close to the element?"

"I dunno, man, maybe. I put 'em as close as possible, on the top rack."

"Jesus, Booker, that's way too close. If they hadn't caught fire, they would have burned into tar balls. And you never throw water on a grease fire. Didn't you know that?"

"I'm sorry, dawg. I forgot how to think. Look, I'll pay for the front door. It's my bad."

"No, that's OK. We'll split it. No problem."

"Thanks, bro. Appreciate it."

The roomies surveyed the apartment for collateral damage and cleaned up the kitchen as best they could. They looked into the smoldering black hole that used to be a functioning oven and decided more extensive, probably professional, attention would be needed to bring the appliance back to life. Then they propped what was left of the front door up against the broken jamb and secured it with bed spring slats, duct taped across the opening on both sides. This effort qualified for Miller time, after which they went to McDonald's for a happy meal.

Upon returning, Rossy announced he was done for the day and retreated to his room. Fortunately, he had closed the door and the bedroom was relatively smoke free. Though he was mentally and physically tapped out, sleep did not come quickly. All he could think about was **CIA**. *Good lord almighty! I'm going to work for the mothafracking C-I-A!!* He knew he should be really angry and really, really scared at what went down today, but he seemed to be more excited than anything. Why was that?? Anticipation of living a James Bond intrigue fantasy? Or, maybe potential recognition as an international hero, followed by interviews, books, movies, all leading to unfathomable good fortune? *Stop it!!* In reality, he was, in all likelihood, being set up for big time failure, possibly even fatal failure, and there was no way out, other than to just flat out resign. And he wasn't ready to do that yet. He could bail anytime, so he might as well give it a run and see what happens. *But wasn't simultaneously working for two government agencies, and secretly being paid by one off the books, basically illegal?* He wasn't a lawyer, but the concept certainly seemed illegal. If it wasn't, what would keep people from having as many government jobs as they wanted? Nobody was doing that, so it must be illegal. *Which means if I'm caught, it's check-in time at Hotel California. And, for sure, there would be no back-up from that tophead dude, who claimed he didn't even exist. Or maybe he did exist as Topremica in WarpRove and now I'm going to be his fracking avatar. How would that work for me in court? 'I'm sorry, your honor, but invisible tophead the Topremica made me do it.' Aaargh! I am so screwed!* At least shiner, being overtaken by events such as he was, didn't wonder what happened after the evacuation, so there was no immediate worry about how to not spill the classified activities of his day. *But how could anything classified be illegal? And if it was, why would telling somebody also be illegal? Christ, there must be plenty of illegal classified stuff, so the whole classification system is probably nothing more than a giant cover-up scam! What the hell am I being forced into??* The chipmole engineer eventually wafted to a troubled drowse, if not restful sleep. Tomorrow's another day. Who ever knows what the new rotation will bring? Just take 'em as they roll, one at a time. Boom!

***

In the morning, on the way to work, the engineers stopped by the AGA management office to advise the status of their front door, which was, for all illicit purposes, unclosable. The manager said he was aware of the situation and that a contractor was scheduled to install the repairs as soon as possible. He would instruct DCA Security to make sure the premises were protected during the interim. This was not entirely reassuring to the outbound tenants, who feared the door might be open for a complete loot of the apartment by the end of the day. But there was absolutely nothing they could do about it, other than DWBH and go to work.

THE NAVY YARD

There was still a heavy presence of special investigation and enforcement at the Yard, but the federal center buildings were open for reoccupation by the mostly civilian employees. No explosive device was found, nor any evidence of unauthorized entry, at the Bowditch Building, or any other facility in the vicinity. The police were preparing to individually interview each worker, more as a formality than expecting to discover any useful information. They had already written the incident off as a false hit. At NAVOSUR, only about half the evacuated staff showed up at clock-in time, not undocumented by the vigilant tech super. Rossy and Booker were hooked by Whittberg, as soon as they were on the floor and coffeed up, and rounded into the front office. Blackburn was already gone to meetings and the room was empty.

"OK, gentlemen, I have your first field assignment", began the esuper. "You'll be going to Patuxent Naval Air Station, way down in southern Maryland. Your duty will be to train an incoming class of foreign national naval officers in basic hydrography. The program is scheduled for three weeks and you will stay on site in the same visitors' quarters as the allied officers."

Booker, looking like a pop quiz had just been announced, responded wide-eyed. "How the hell can we do that!? We don't know anything about hydrography! We just got here, for chrissakes!"

"Well, Booker, maybe you should have studied Bowditch a little more, like Rossy, here. But don't worry. You'll be under Robyn Ryder, the resident PNAS party chief for NAVOSUR. She'll train and supervise you in training the clients. It's not rocket science. You'll be leaving tomorrow, so take the rest of the day to prep. Of course, and I don't need to remind you - but I will - all aspects of this assignment are classified. **Do not, I repeat do not, discuss any of your activities with anyone not related to the program.** OK, Tom has your TDY orders, which you'll carry with you to get on base. You also need orders to get your advance on per diem and to file your vouchers when you return. So don't lose 'em, capishe?"

The engineers nodded acknowledgement of the instructions and looked at each other with a certain degree of excited anticipation as they turned to leave. "Hold up, Mr. Rossy, we have some other issues to discuss." Bj checked his departure behind Booker with sinkheart dismay. He had hoped that yesterday's weirdness was dissipated into the purview of a bad dream. *No such luck! Now the real nightmare begins - the one where I'm fracked tighter than Custer at LBH.* Booker walked on, bound up in the aura of his first TDY glow and oblivious to his co-trainer's detention by the esuper. Dick motioned for the remaining subordinate sailor to sit at the worktable in the far corner of the front office, out of the sightline of anyone entering or leaving the short hallway to or from admin Tom's room or the stairwell. He sat on the table and looked down at the new CIA operative, who stared blankly at nothing in particular on the floor, waiting for....whatever.

"Are you still on board, son, with what we talked about yesterday?"

"Yes, sir, I'm good."

"No reservations? No rewinds?"

"Nope." *Except I reserve the right to quit. There's no dishonor in strategic loss and retreat!*

"Great. OK, one of the allied naval officers you will meet next week is a CIA asset. We don't know which one, but she, or he, knows your name and will initiate discrete contact. You must carefully listen for the phrase *'What's in it for me?'*, spoken in either English, or the officer's native language. You will then respond, in kind, with *'I don't know. You tell me.'* It is important that you hear and say these words precisely. Any deviation will abort the contact, so write it down - now. When dialogue is opened you will retrieve whatever information the asset provides regarding the target you were briefed on yesterday. At this point we are looking for the who, what, where, when and how basics. For our internal purposes, the unsub has been coded *'special bean'* and that is the reference you should use from here on in. Questions?"

"Yeah.....how can I recognize the code phrase if I don't know the language? I don't know any foreign languages."

"Could be a problem, so I suggest you talk to Ryder as soon as you check in at PNAS and look up translations to all the official national languages represented by the incoming class. You should also research any common dialects that might be used. Don't think this will be an issue, though, because all the officers speak English and the assets are always ordered to use English in dialoging contacts, unless, of course, their cover is at risk. But you should be prepared for any case as a course of procedure. We don't want to lose any info to poor prep, right?"

"Yeah, OK.....I'll do my best, but, really, I'm not good at languages. But I have another question. How come the asset doesn't just phone or e-mail whatever info he has? Why do we have to go through all this contact code stuff?"

"Alright...that's a fair question. It's because any incoming hard intel pertaining to any ops, anywhere, is never transmitted electronically from the source. It is always a personal transfer. A couple of reasons. One, our assets want to be certain their info is correctly received, so there are no disputes leading to non-payment on delivery. And, likewise, we want to be certain the data is correctly and securely received. The best way to do this, in spite of all our grand technology, is face-to-face contact. Now, you should limit field communication on this operation to the relay of information, which must be sent asap, as you receive it. Use only public facilities, like at libraries, schools, hotels or cafes. No phones. No federal or personal devices. Also, and this is extremely important, no web cams. You must block out the web cam on any device you use. Send your report through the 'contact us' page on the CIA recruitment website and include the target code name somewhere in the transmission. The *special bean* reference will autoroute your message via instantaneously encrypted upload to a dark net, with total webtrack scramble, for the singular 'eyes only' recipient with classified authority to receive and act on your data. Be aware, that this action could include your immediate reassignment, so be ready for anything. Do you understand?"

"I guess. I hope it all works out."

"Don't worry, Mr. Rossy, I have confidence in you and your ability to be successful, otherwise I wouldn't have tagged you for this mission. What could go wrong? Nothing - as long as you keep your wits, pay attention and be ready for anything. Don't be conspicuous so that you stand out in a crowd. Try to look like your in-country TDY colleagues and above all - the most important thing you can remember - do not discuss any of this with anyone. *'Op-*

eration Special Bean' is highly classified and you must be guard-edly discreet at all times. The project will probably send you all over the world during the next several months and it will not be easy, but if we can interdict before *special bean* mobilizes, the payoff will be incalculable. Unfortunately, no one in the general public will ever know of you and your role in possibly saving their way of life, because this entire effort is designated CRAP....."

"Crap? What do you mean, crap? That doesn't sound too cool."

"No, C-R-A-P - classification reduction authorization prohib-ited, meaning it is perpetually exempt from declassification under provisions of the Freedom of Information Act. No, son, you'll never be rich and famous over this, but you'll always have the per-sonal satisfaction of knowing you have served your country well. Above and beyond."

***

Rossy secured his orders from admin Tom and caught up with Booker just as the engineers were filing out for break. Over morning coldies on the porch, groob reminded the rookies to log their mileage to and from PNAS for reimbursement on their vouchers. He also warned them to be careful in Lexington Park, where the unemployed locals liked to play 'gimme your money' with anyone coming off base. Later, bj and shiner took the shuttle to Navy disbursing at the Pentagon to get their advance. They were flabbergasted to receive nearly ten bens each, cash, for what, they had no clear idea. So far, this job was paying out quite nicely and Rossy was starting to forget the inexplicable oddities he had been wrestling with for weeks, essentially going back to hour one of the first day on the job. Since the newsters were departing for duty before Friday, there would be no happy time KOKK party in Georgetown. Instead, they all went to the Chiefs' Club for an ex-tended lunch.

PATUXENT NAVAL AIR STATION

Rossy knew he might not be staying the entire three weeks at PNAS and talked Booker into taking his bike separately, rather than both riding in the Civic. This would give them greater flexibility and keep more options open. Booker agreed and they proceeded to get ready for TDY at their own much different paces. Neither had ever been to southern Maryland before and, looking at the map, they saw there were two different ways to get to PNAS. One followed Maryland Route 4 down the north side of the Patuxent River to Solomon's Island and across the bridge to the base. The other took Maryland Route 5 south of the river, through Waldorf and St. Charles. The distances of the two ways from AGA were about the same, so they decided to make it interesting and have a rally race to the main base gate, using both routes. They each put up a ben - winner take all - and RPS'd for choice. Booker won and chose Route 4.

The next morning, Rossy sat in parking lot traffic between Waldorf and St. Charles and realized he was going to lose the rally ben. There was no way he could beat Booker giving up this fracking handicap of a road mess. He might not even get to PNAS until tomorrow. This area was unbelievable! Endless, continuous strips of shopping malls and commercial outlets on both sides of the dual highway and a five minute traffic light at every single big-box retail entrance. He had never seen so many vehicles on one roadway. Why weren't all these people at work? The recession was over, for chrissakes. It took nearly two hours to nudge through the clusterclog and Rossy vowed he would never again drive anywhere near Waldorf, in southern Maryland.

It was going on one o'clock when bj finally arrived at the PNAS gate. As he showed his orders and ID to the guard, he spotted shiner sitting on the curb beside his parked bike in a pullover alcove inside the gate. Bye-bye benny boy! The two were running more than reasonably late. They were supposed to meet Ryder at the training center at noon and neither had thought to call to advise their status. Not a good start! They were harshly accosted by the party chief as soon as they entered the TC. **"Where have you frack-offs been?! I've been waiting here for more than an hour. Is this the dreck they're sending me now? Christ, it gets worse every session!"** Robyn "red" Ryder established an immediate formidable dominance, leaving no doubt who was the boss. A few years older than the rookies, she struck a memorable, but pleasing, appearance with her above average height, freckled face and shock-bright red hair. Following mumbled excusatory apologies and rudimentary introductions, the engineers trailed their latest superior back outside and, at her direction, got in passenger seats of a double-cab Navy pick-up. A few minutes later they pulled up to the main dining facility and went inside for lunch. Rossy was amazed and bummed to see another Golden Paddock mega-buffet strung out along the far wall and was instantly unappetized, despite not having any breakfast. Booker was elated and ready to spend part of his new ben on as much as he could eat in whatever time allowed. Over lunch with domestic tap beer, the red bosslady laid out the parameters of what she expected during the upcoming training program. The engineers were to conduct themselves in a highly professional manner at all times. She would not tolerate any bad behavior either on or off the base and fraternization with the client officers was to be limited to normal social interaction in the course of their living arrangements and training exercises. Under no circumstances were they to 'party' with the officers in any of the off-site clubs in town. If there was any hint of unacceptable conduct by either subordinate, both their orders would be suspended and they would be dispatched back to NAVOSUR for appropriate disciplinary action. Given their probationary status, such action would doubtless be termination. Did they understand? "Yes, ma'am."

After lunch, the TDYsters checked into the visitor's dormitory and returned to the center for an afternoon of vigorous briefing on the training curriculum and schedule. There would be a mix of classroom instruction and fieldwork, providing a comprehensive introduction to basic hydrographic techniques. Booker was terrified, in that he didn't feel he was qualified to do this with zero experience in the subject matter they were to teach. Rossy was unconcerned, thinking red Ryder would micro-manage everything and he and Booker would just be her step-and-fetch-it boys. The visiting officers were scheduled to arrive over the week-end and the assistants were instructed to spend the rest of the work week in preparation. Near the end of the afternoon, Rossy inquired about the national make-up of the client officers comprising the incoming class. Red provided a roster listing an Indonesian, an Indian, a Nicaraguan, two South Koreans, a Bolivian and a Brazilian - all men. *A Bolivian?? Bolivia was landlocked, so why would they send a naval officer to learn hydrography? How could they even have a navy?? Maybe this was the secret asset. Or, maybe they were planning to invade an ocean front neighbor.* He would have to learn to hear and phrase his special bean contact code into at least six different translations. Not a comfortably easy task, but, hopefully, he could download an interactive phone app for languages and get it done without too much of a problem. At quitting time, red ordered the engineers into the truck and they rode to a large boat pier off the tidal basin on the north side of the base. She lived on Solomon's, across the river, and commuted by pedestrian ferry. She told the engineers to take the truck to the dormitory and pick her up at the pier in the morning, at 0815. The sailors were left alone - their first TDY evening in a strange environment, with three vehicles and a couple of grand in cash. What could possibly go wrong?

***

Later in the evening, the trainee trainers decided to walk into town to look around and get something to eat. They didn't want to drive in a place they didn't know, especially since it would likely get dark while they were still out. It wasn't that far to walk - a couple of miles, at most, from the dorm. They followed Patuxent Boulevard directly from the PNAS gate into town center, where they found a surprising amount of activity. A two or three square block grid of restaurants, stores, shops, bars, clubs and what apparently looked like nudie joints, or casinos, or both, comprised a district reminiscent of a baby Las Vegas strip. Gaudily flashing and highly colorful neon lights, signs and marquees beckoned passersby, who were also lured by sleazy sidewalk barkers urging any and all to come in and see the most beautiful girls in the world. 'ALL NUDE - ALL NIGHT! WE ALWAYS TREAT YOU RIGHT!!' Live music could be heard spilling from the open fronts of several establishments and people were drinking and eating at outside tables everywhere. It looked like a good time scene and the sailors strolled around through Arcade Park, as they determined the district was called, trying to decide where to go.

They finally settled on a huge, pastel pink Victorian structure, called Brass Balls Bar, out of which Lynyrd Skynyrd-style Texas blues overflowed resoundingly to the street. Inside, the bar area to the right was crammed with happily noisy revelers standing and seated into the room behind the small bandstand in an open-windowed front corner, from where a trio of longhairs, the Noble Hats, amped their rockin' notes into the party sphere. To the left of the entrance foyer was a dining room and straight ahead was a rickety looking wooden staircase to a second floor casino. A sign pointing to the stairs, boasting 'Best Payout in the Arcade', enticed them to try their luck and up they went. The large open room held about fifty slot machines of varying designs, shapes, sounds and themes. More than half the units were occupied, sending an hypnotic, pachinko lilt through the room. They found a couple of adjacent empties and sat down to invest some of their per diem advance. Feeding his machine a ben, Rossy self-instructed to cash out as soon as he got up or down by a jack. That took only 32 plays at a george per. He never reached more than one abe up. Booker, however, hit for solid gold treasure chests worth two bens on the third spin, but lost it all, including his original stake, within a half-hour. He figured he was still even, though, since he had played with Rossy's rally ben.

Returning downstairs, the grumbling gamblers found a dark booth in the far back of the bar room area and sat down to relax and enjoy the moment. Their first evening out on official TDY business, as bona fide reps of the United States government. Rossy felt an extra unspoken rush as a classified secret agent of the CIA. They weren't doing too badly for themselves - a far cry from the dead-end doldrums they left behind at PWA in Connecticut. It definitely seemed like they had made an upwardly mobile move. A Hooters looking waitress soon appeared at their boothside and promptly asked for ID when they ordered a couple of Dos Equis's, the most interesting beer in the world. *James Bond never got carded,* thought the chipmole, as he turned over his driver's license. The waitress said nothing about their out-of-state IDs and disappeared to retrieve the drinks. Not long after they were into their second round of brews, a very attractive dark-haired woman, in an abbreviated facsimile of a mini-dress, slid stealthily onto the booth bench tightly next to a rapidly mellowing Rossy and threw a long, lithe leg over his lap. *Hoi! What is this?!* wondered the baffled and boxed-in junior g-man, as the intruder pressed closer, her delicate hands brushing expertly over areas of weakness. She warmly nuzzled the side of his neck and thrust her tongue deep into his ear, hot breath melting whatever defensive resolve the mismatched minion could muster. *"What's in it for me, hon?"* she throatily whispered, barely audible through the clatter of the room. *Whoa!!! Is this my special bean contact?? That couldn't be!! She's not an allied navy officer. They're all men! But what if she is? Dick said be ready for anything!* "uh...uh...I don't know. You tell me."

"Five bens'll get you anything you want, sweetie, all night long. Tosha will not disappoint."

This isn't my contact!! She's a fracking hooker, for chrissakes! Agent bj tried to shift away, but was blocked in all directions except down. He wormed his way under the fixed booth table and came up on shiner's side, leaving Tosha sprawled out on the opposite bench. "C'mon, Booker, she's a hooker! Let's get the hell outta here!" Rossy remembered what pc red said about bad conduct consequences and did not want to lose his job over a circumstantial ambuscade. The engineers hastily made their way to the front without looking back and departed BBB into the dusky evening.

The hungry hoofers ambled through the Park, looking for somewhere to eat, and finally decided to give Perry's Pulled Pig Pen a try. They were drawn by a huge sign in the window, boasting 'World's Best BBQ'. Rossy often saw such *world's best* signs in restaurants, for burgers, gumbo, fried chicken, or whatever, and wondered how anyone could seriously make such a claim. Usually it caused elevated expectations leading to letdown, when the delivery fell far short of world class, let alone best. If a place actually had world's best, there would certainly be no need for a sign - everyone would know it and you would have to score reservations a year in advance to get in. So, in reality, there probably was no such thing as world's best, but they were starving and didn't really give a dreg what the quality ranking was.

After filling up on adequate BBQ dinner platters, the satisfied sailors figured it was about time to return to the dorm. It was dark, but the weather was clear and balmy and it would be a nice walk back. They started out along Patuxent Boulevard, finding it rather dimly lighted, and got well over halfway to the base gate when they saw a group of hoodied youths spread across the sidewalk shuffling toward them from the opposite direction. Under one of the widely spaced streetlights, the approaching hoody dudes looked Latino and Rossy reflexively remembered groob's warning about mugsters outside the base. He hoped that he normally wouldn't clutch up at such an encounter on a darkened sidewalk, but both he and Booker were carrying their per diem cash, which was a lot more than cab fare, rather than leaving it at the dorm. He didn't feel like getting punked on their first TDY night out, so he went into rapid think to devise a strategy for passing safely through the would-be coyotes ahead. *"Booker, when we get about fifteen yards from these guys, on my mark, start running as fast as you can right for them. That should get us past them before they can react, turn around and chase us. After that it's not that far to the gate,"* whispered Rossy. Booker, also apprehensive, nodded in agreement. The outlanders continued walking toward the locals at a normal pace, nervously noticing their attention seemed to be focused intently on the nearing duo. At the prescribed distance, Rossy yelled, **"PUNCH!!"** and the engineers both broke into a full sprint forward. When they realized the charging twosome was not going to yield, the Latinos scattered off the sidewalk, spilling out into the street. Simultaneously, a motorcycle was accelerating out of a curve toward this same point of contention. The biker had to brake hard to avoid throttling through the people appearing in his lane, from out of nowhere, and lost control. The bike went down, as the driver flew off and rolled into the gutter, and skidded screechingly across the boulevard to the curb on the far side. Rossy and Booker kept churning as fast as they possibly could, never slowing to see what was happening out on the street, but they could hear angry shouting behind them as the cyclist picked himself up and confronted the instigators of his wipeout. The hoodies glared after the receding runners with shaking fists and fingers, but didn't pursue. "¿CE PASA CE CONŌ?? PENDEJO LOCO GRINGOS!!!" Up ahead appeared the PNAS gate and the gasping g-men downshifted to catch their breath. Neither could remember the last time he ran that fast and furious, but apparently the breakout strategy worked. They were successfully back at base without loss or injury and, most importantly, had not fallen into any adverse situations involving the police that could jeopardize their jobs. It was sort of a fun night out, but they didn't think they would risk going off base again any time soon.

***

The next morning, the training assistants waited dutifully on the tidal basin pier at 0815, as the pedestrian ferry approached from the other side of the river. A large collection of commuters was amassed near the front end gangway section of the barge-like vessel. Nearly all were African American, save one in the forward middle of the crowd, who stood out like a white pope in a black pizza. Red Ryder's hair and complexion contrasted sharply with the dark faces all around her. She looked straight ahead, as did her fellow passengers, blankly watching their arrival to work. "I honestly didn't think you jack-offs would be here this morning," greeted the disembarked pc. "I guess wonders never cease. C'mon, let's move - we've got a lot to do today." The technical trio jumped into the pick-up and red drove directly to the TC. She ordered Rossy to fire up the coffee and then explained that one of her helpers' responsibilities during the upcoming training program was to manage the break amenities. This would involve daily procurement, in town, of fresh doughnuts and pastries from Derick's Delectable Donuts, retrieval of sandwiches and snacks from GP at the dining hall and all day tending of the cold and hot drinks concession. They would set-up each day in the training center with fresh linens, ice, tableware, condiments and continuous maintenance and clean-up to provide a welcome and pleasing support environment for the client officers. Following a detailed, step-by-step review of the logistical requirements and procedures, red stressed this duty was an important part of their assignment and if they fracked it up, it would be reflected in their TDY performance assessment. She further advised that she only signed off on overtime for good work. Poor work - no OT, no matter how many hours it took to mangle the mission. Rossy thought he had correctly guessed their role here as mindless gophers and was not surprised, nor unhappy, with this service assignment. Booker, forgetting he didn't know anything about teaching hydrography, thought he didn't spend four years and a fortune at engineering school to wait on a bunch of clownass foreign navy dudes. He was not happy with the assignment.

Red then went into an overview of the program introductory session. They would be conducting a series of exercises designed to promote teamwork and familiarity. Breaking the ice, so to speak, allowing these people from different countries, different cultures, to work well together and get as much benefit as possible from the overall training agenda. One of the exercises was called the 'trust fall'. Red explained this involved the standing participants to form a circle, with one person in the middle, who closes his eyes, relaxes and allows his body to be angularly pivoted around his planted feet by the others until the facilitator called 'FALL'. Then everyone lets go and the subject starts dropping to the floor. Before he hits, he is caught by the ringed spotters and returned to an intact upright position. Everybody takes a turn in the middle and the idea is to instill a feeling of trust among the program colleagues - a feeling no one will let anyone drop or fall, so that all can be successful.

The pc then directed they perform a demo trust fall among themselves, to give the training aides a sense for the nature of the exercise. She positioned herself standing face away about four feet in front of the two and, at the count of three, fell stiffly backwards, like a diver off the high platform, toward her trusted assistants and the hard tiled floor. The engineers froze, realizing they would have to grab and hold her in possibly inappropriate places in order to keep her from crashing. They waited too long to react with a clean catch, but managed to dive down under the falling pc right before she made contact, resulting in them all ending up in a tangled heap on the floor. **"YOU FRACKING IDIOTS!!! WHAT THE HELL ARE YOU DOING??! JESUS CHRIST!! IF THIS HAPPENS WITH THE CLASS IT WILL BE A TOTAL DISASTER. NOW LET'S DO THIS AGAIN!! AND DON'T FRACK IT UP OR I SWEAR I'LL SEND YOUR ROOKIE BUTTS BACK TO WASHINGTON.....TODAY!!"** On the second take, the idiots reached out and seized red tightly around the chest well before she was in any danger of a hard landing and lifted her back to standing position without anyone falling out. It was a good trust fall. "OK, that's more like it," smiled the pc.

Another exercise pc red planned to use was the reverse introduction partnership skit, where the class separates into randomly assigned pairs, who are given ten minutes to talk with one another and learn enough for each person to give an introduction of their paired partner to the group. The rip skit allows participants to get to know a little about a new colleague on a personal basis and project their own first impressions into the introduction. Hopefully, this would provide more memorable info on each group member than if they just went around the room and everybody introduced themselves in sequence. It had to be assumed that participants were professional and courteous enough to refrain from negative or insulting remarks in playing the rips, though there was always the risk that someone would take the opportunity, for whatever reason, to ripslam their partner and start the whole program off on a bad note.

Red wanted to practice a little rips with her assistants, because they would all be included in the exercise with the incoming class. They would each give a short summary autobio and then draw names to see who would intro whom. The pc started with her own background brief. She grew up in southern Florida, with four older brothers and her divorced mom. Two of her brothers played in the NFL and one was an investment banker. The fourth was in prison for mail fraud. She went to Georgia Tech, where she earned a degree in surveillance engineering, a relatively new discipline spawned by the explosive growth of robotic drone and digitized information technology. Her employment with NAVOSUR was offered during an interview at a campus job fair her senior year. Because of a poor relationship with her family, she was not interested enough in men to seek marriage and was even less interested in having children. She lived alone on Solomon's Island, with a dog and two cats. Her favorite color was sugarplum red, same as her prized Tesla X. Rossy was next. He related how he spent his formative years in Lancaster County, Pennsylvania, with his mom and two sisters. His dad died before he could remember much about him. Growing up, he spent a lot of time on farms and never had extensive experience with sports. His degree was in chemical engineering and out of school he worked for Peck & Watts Aeronautics for about a year and a half. He got the job at NAVOSUR, without interviewing, or applying, through a friend of Booker's. Right now the three of them shared an apartment in Suitland. Booker then told of his childhood in a small mountain town in southwest Virgina, where most people were unemployed, but made a living running oxy, meth, tea and shine. His parents owned and operated the local post office. He went to school on an Accent

Appalachia scholarship, but some of the funding fell through and he had to borrow considerable money to complete his chemical engineering degree. He met Rossy at PWA, from where they both recently departed at the same time to work at NAVOSUR.

Rossy drew Booker for introduction. He said Booker was an amazing person who had overcome problems with poverty, drugs and alcohol to go to college and get an engineering degree. He was an inspiration and a good friend. Shiner indignantly objected that he was never in poverty and had not been involved with drugs and alcohol before college. He then introduced pc red as probably the smartest lady he ever met, whom he looked up to both professionally and as a person to admire and pattern his own life after. Finally, red introduced Rossy and Booker as apparent losers for majoring in chemical engineering and not making the big fat at a petrochemical processing refinery somewhere. They all had a good laugh over the contrived deviations between bios and intros and the pc pointed out such levity should be very helpful in establishing a pleasant and interesting atmosphere to open the upcoming training event. She then, feeling some unusual stirrings of positive vibes about the program prep, announced break-time. As they headed off to the nco club, Rossy was thinking possibly they were making some leeway into red Ryder's approval fortress. Maybe this could be a very worthwhile overtime venture, *if I don't get shipped out too early by special bean. I still have to learn my contact translations. Oh god, where am I going with all this CIA blarp??*

***

The rest of the week was spent in continuing overview of the technical aspects of the hydrographic training program and briefings of equipment to be used in conducting the field exercises. The 'state of the art' equipment inventory, including geodetic instruments, digital sensors and recorders of tidal, current, thermal and water characteristic data, transponders, side scan sonar, satellite, circular and hyperbolic positioning systems, computers and portable 3D plotting units, was valued at more than ten million dollars and capable of producing the most advanced and comprehensive hydrographic products in the world. These tech resources would be used to conduct an actual survey on the river, demonstrating all facets of the classroom discussions in a real time application of navigational hydrography. The survey would complete the program. Booker wondered why they couldn't just locate depth soundings with a phone app, which would be a lot easier than hassling with all this specialized positioning equipment. Pc red asked if he had ever heard of the Costa Concordia? No, he had not. *Of course, you haven't, you ignorant screwball,* thought red. "Costa Concordia was a super cruise ship that wrecked off the Italian island of Giglio a few years back," she explained. "A lot of passengers died. The captain claimed his navcharts were wrong and a submerged rock formation was not where it was shown. Maybe true, maybe not, but he was prosecuted for negligent homicide. The point is that if the formation was indicated even a few feet off in accuracy, it could take down a mega ship. The GPS is only good to within three to five feet and *that's* why it is not used to position hydrographic data. OK?" Booker nodded his understanding. The pc had her doubts.

The program's training and utility craft was a 24-foot whaler class boat, powered by a 35 horsepower, 4-stroke Coleman inboard motor. Across the midsection was a custom built wooden structure with a pitched sheet metal roof, resembling an oversized outhouse, within which was a flat bed work table, several stools, a wireless data router, a communications system and a lithium battery power pack. The entire ensemble was painted navy gray. It was a strange and rather comical looking little vessel, named the **USNS INVINCIBLE**, as was lettered on both sides of the bow. But it was sturdy and functional for the purposes it served in the program. Red led the assistants aboard at the tidal basin moor, adjacent to a fueling station, and showed them where everything was, including the very important float vests that were mandatory attire for all embarking, outbound personnel and safety flares to be fired only as a last resort in cases of extreme emergency. She went over how the boat and its support systems were used and operated in the training exercises. They then took a few spins around the basin, with each of the rookies assigned a turn as captain to become familiar with start-up, navigation, docking and shut-down procedures of the small, but surprisingly heavy and difficult handling, utility vessel. To the uninitiated and inexperienced men at sea, the **INVINCIBLE** seemed like it should be just that. But in reality, red knew from experience, shit on the water could, and probably would, happen. By the time they refueled, secured and debarked from the work boat, it was quitting time. The pc told the rookies they could have the next day, Saturday, off, but were to report to the TC on Sunday afternoon to help orientate the arrival of the incoming officers. They should be advised that tomorrow would be their only down time during the whole program, so "use it well and take care of any personal issues, because no other leave will be authorized." Red left them standing at the gas pump and walked over to the ferry pier to wait for her ride home. The assistant sailors climbed into the truck and drove to the dorm. They later got carry out pizza and a six pack of Iron City, at the nco club and commissary, and went back to the dorm to watch *WWE* and hit the hay early.

THE APARTMENT

The engineering roomies decided to spend their day off returning to AGA to check on the status of the apartment and the door repair work, which had not yet started when they left earlier in the week. They took Rossy's car and followed Route 4 to Silver Hill Road into Suitland. Traffic was unexpectedly light and they made even better time than Booker, when he won the rally ben. Walking toward building 'C' from the parking lot, they saw no evidence of any work going on and wordlessly assumed nothing had been done and the apartment was converted into an empty crackhouse. When they got to the stairwell, they were joyfully stunned to see a brand new door assembly installed at their entrance and no evidence of mass removal of stuff. Elation soon turned to sullen frustration, though, upon discovering their keys didn't work. The door job included new locks and there was no way in, since Smith had not sent a patio door key. They went directly to the manager's office where the weekend duty person informed them he knew nothing of the project, nor the submittal, to management, of any new keys for C-14. The temp called the regular manager, who said the contractor had the keys and would not turn them over until he was paid. The invoice was in the 'action items' desk tray along with another invoice for oven repair. The temp was instructed to coordinate delivery of the keys for payment directly to the contractor by the tenants and release of the keys to the tenants upon receipt of payment for the oven repair. The total cost was $1,586.74, or $793.37 each, most of the amount they had received for advance on per diem. They now knew what the per diem cash would be spent for, quickly surmising this could not be claimed as a reimbursable expense on their TDY vouchers. Any valid expenses incurred during the rest of their PNAS service would have to be paid out of pocket, meaning it was time to burn the plastic and run up their credit card balances. Rossy felt a downer coming on, knowing his finances had just been dumped into the toilet. Without realizing it, he turned to Booker and blurted, "Guess that would have to be filed as some expensive date you had the other night, huh, man?" Shiner stared back without responding. Bj recanted, "I'm sorry, dude, that was uncalled for. At least we weren't street shanked. Hate when that happens!" They both had a good laugh and went outside to wait for the contractor.

It was not a short wait. They couldn't leave and go do something else, because they had no idea when the contractor would be there, so they sat in the Civic in the parking lot, adjusting the seats to a comfortable recline. Rossy looked out the window and saw they were headed into a mudslide that sloped sharply down into the deep tidal rip of the river below. He ran to the front of the bus to get off before it went down, but found the folding doorway was locked. He tried to force it open to no avail. The vehicle was starting to pitch and roll at violently dangerous angles as it entered the slide. While the panicking passenger continued working desperately to open the door, the driver calmly offered an out. *"If you give me all your money, I'll open the door."* Rossy slowly turned to the source of this incredibly outrageous offer and looked directly into the angrily contorted face of DCA's Donald Trevair, who was methodically rocking the little car back and forth to waken the transient derelicts inside. **"What are you useless dicks doing sleeping here? You can't be out here like this?!?"** Rossy lowered the window and attempted to explain the situation, but the security officer didn't want to hear it. He said the real tenants got nervous when they saw squatter assheads they didn't know sleeping in a car in the parking lot and he didn't like nervous tenants. **"So, either drive the hell outta here, or get outta the car and go someplace else, but you can't stay here!!"** The locked out sailors obediently exited their vehicle and went back to the manager's office, where they sat on an outside bench in the sun for several more hours until the contractor eventually showed up late in the afternoon.

When the returning residents finally got back into their apartment, they noticed two things. Nothing seemed to be missing, allaying their fears of a complete lootout. But the smell!! OMG, the stench was beyond overwhelming! A nasty mixture of paint, smoke and industrial solvent, magnified to near explosive concentration by lack of ventilation, almost knocked the entering engineers back out into the stairwell portico. They immediately opened everything possible to bring in fresh air, but it was obvious the noxious condition was not going away anytime soon. While taking a more thorough inventory to verify all possessions were intact, they found a note on the sparkling clean oven, that the appliance was not to be used for at least ten days, to allow the toxic cleaning materials to dissipate. It should then be wiped down with a damp cloth before turning on. The roomies concluded the apartment was presently uninhabitable. They decided there was no choice, but to return to PNAS this evening. After ventilating for another hour, or so, they set out on the return leg of their journey, satisfied that the trip had been necessary to avoid probable complications in resolving the issues at a later date. Booker said he would send gameboy the new keys and explain how a neighbor almost burned the building down, but everything was good. Bj suggested shiner set himself free and tell the truth.

PATUXENT NAVAL AIR STATION

Once again on Route 4, retracing the morning ride, the traveling trainers planned to stop for dinner at Cap'n Charlie's Crabhouse, near Bristol. They had seen the digital billboard sign on the highway, featuring the unbelievable claim of 'World's Best Crabcakes', and figured it should be decent, since they were, in fact, in deep crab country. How bad could it be? The sign said to follow Rt. 238 for 4.7 miles to Whipper's Landing, as they did. Nearing the directed distance, traffic started to pick-up considerably and they were astonished to find, out here in the middle of nowhere, a massive gravel parking lot, around a huge ramshackle wooden structure, built on pilings along a wide pier extending into a narrow finger inlet from the Chesapeake Bay. A shucking house and kitchen stood behind the restaurant and its attached rear deck, beyond which several work boats were tied down at the end of the pier. Soggy marshland, overgrown with cattails and towering thickets of phragmites swampgrass, flanked both sides of the inlet clearing and a great blue heron was flying overhead to its favorite evening fishing spot. It was an idyllic Chesapeake scene awash in the autumn evening reflections of a setting sun and rising moon, punctuated by somewhat garish colored lights strung from crooked poles around the site. But what was really breathtaking was the overflowing parking lot. They would have to park out along the road and walk about a quarter mile to the entrance, during which the din of the diners got louder and louder as they approached. Inside the clamorous front foyer, decorated with all sorts of decaying marine artifacts and mounted seafood specimens, the wayfaring sailors were loudly asked by a short, gruffled woman, in a tie-dyed Cap'n Charlie's Crabhouse tee-shirt, faded jeans and white rubber waterman boots, if they had reservations? No, they did not. **"Well, we're booked up through the end of the season. Next opening is Juneteenth. You want it?"** *Seriously?? This dumpy place in extreme outer nullsville is filled up and we need reservations?? Do they actually have the world's best crabcakes?? For* *real?!?* Thinking he should check CCC on internet, Rossy shook his head no, they didn't want to make a way future reservation. The rejected roadrunners retreated to the Civic and backtracked to Route 4. They later stopped at a McDonald's, where they were served the world's only, and best by default, 'happy meal' and everyone was welcome at anytime, twenty-four seven, without reservations. It was south of ten when they passed through the PNAS gate. At the dorm, Booker went to his room, ready to flop. The chipmole, however, had some work to do. He would sleep later. One obvious benefit of returning tonight was they would not be late tomorrow.

***

The student officers started arriving mid-afternoon. Most were in expensive civilian attire, but a couple wore their military uniforms, including the Nicaraguan, Lt. Carlos Matas, whose tunic held more ribbons, pins and decorations than a four star admiral. They each had their own rental vehicle, typically, a dark colored, high-end suv, and several of the visitors were heavy smokers. Once they determined who was in charge, the officers paid little attention to the assistants. The pc assigned her helpers to work essentially as bellhops in getting the guests situated into their rooms, after which they were instructed to wait in the dayroom to be available for anything they might be able to assist with in orientating the newcomers to the PNAS facilities. As it turned out, the entrants were more interested in going into town than staying on base and they departed quickly following a cursory on-site tour. Red told the engineers to remain at the dormitory and make sure everyone returned OK and had everything they needed. She then left for the day and said not to call her at home unless there was blood.

The visitors began homing back to the dorm around 2100. First, was the Bolivian, Capt. Emilio Cortez, who stayed in the lounge and seemed absorbed in talking to his younger patrons, asking a lot of questions pertaining to American culture, politics and cuisine that the rookie concierges did not, themselves, know much about. He said he hoped, one day, he, too, would be an American. Rossy found that a somewhat odd, if not slightly uncomfortable, thing to say, wondering what was wrong with being a Bolivian? It was like if a dude was talking to a lady he didn't know and said he wanted to be a lady someday. What would that be about? But he responded with a question of his own, asking, "Why does Bolivia have a navy?" The captain laughed and acknowledged that was a legitimate question, adding he got it a lot when traveling on official business abroad. He leaned back in the lazy-boy easy chair and lit up a cigarette before beginning his answer. There was no smoking allowed in the dormitory and Rossy didn't know exactly what to do. He didn't want to antagonize the guest, but neither did he want him smoking. He ended up going over to the coffee corner and bringing back a container for the ashes. The Bolivian explained that many people in his country were of Aymaran descent, particularly in the ancient region of Tiwanaku, where contemporary Chile, Peru and Bolivia join borders. The Aymaran had always believed the gods would, at some point, reveal an easy access to the sea through secret subterranean channels from the rugged high plateau country, so the people could reap the bounty of the ocean during times of hardship on their native land. Such beliefs were still held in present times, which the government officially sanctioned during the cold war era by establishing a ceremonial navy to prepare for the glorious day when Bolivia would have a contiguous marine connection. The navy was tiny - one admiral, a captain, a junior officer and three yeomen sailors. They had no sea going vessels and were based at a small office building and museum in Sucre, making them, at about 9,000 feet elevation, the highest naval headquarters in the world.

Rossy had quite a few patent follow-up questions about the remarkable Bolivian navy, but was distracted by a noisy disturbance in the entrance lobby. Two military guards were dragging a disheveled and visibly tanked Lt. Matas through the doorway from the outside, where the lights from a police jeep flashed beside the Nicaraguan's parked rental vehicle. The Lexington Park police had stopped the lieutenant on the boulevard for weaving over the lane lines and delivered him to the base gate, when he produced diplomatic immunity ID. After some discussion, the guards released the obliterated officer and his car key to the custodial engineers and departed, happy to have unloaded the foreign bad boy on someone else, though they weren't entirely sure who the two civilians were, or what authority their TDY orders implied. But *el drunko* was SEP, now, and they could get back to watching Sunday Night Football in the gate shack. Rossy and Booker, with Capt. Cortez's assistance, managed to maneuver the fast fading tippler to his room. They got him to the bed, pulled off his boots and left him snoring in uniform, like a useless sentry on forgotten watch. Booker was furious and blew into a snit. It had been simmering all day from when they had to carry the incomers' luggage to the rooms, as if they were some kind of hotel hired help. "We *are* hired help, dawg," offered Rossy, "and being paid some sweet overtime to do really easy stuff. Relax, man." But Booker was inconsolable. He had not gone to college to be a nursemaid to some alien military hoochhead. Rossy thought about the 'other duties as assigned' clause, but did't say anything. They went back downstairs to the dayroom to wait for the return of the rest of the officers. Within an hour, all were accounted for and everyone soon retired to their rooms. The rookie stewards had to be at work early to set up the TC concession. *Mo' OT, please.*

***

Time passed quickly as they got into the classroom agenda of the training program. The subordinate engineers were impressed with not only how well the pc knew and understood the material, but also her talent in conveying understanding to the students. Red seemed to be a natural teacher, but she did not have an easy audience. The Koreans and the Indonesian took copious notes and recorded every lecture. The Indian slouched back in his chair and glared at the instructor, as if to say "when are you going to tell me something I don't know?" The Latinos acted like they had about as much interest in the subject matter as they did sitting in class all day. They had gotten over their indelicate slurs against each other during the introductory exercises, reflecting long standing national differences. Nicaragua felt Brazil was too economically autonomous and did not do enough to promote Latin American trade initiatives. Brazil thought Bolivia's history of drug trafficking and political instability had corrupted the Amazon outback, making it unmanageable in some areas. South Korea was often upset over perceived violations by Indonesia of international fishing regulations. India considered itself the powerhouse of the future and looked down on elfin nations around the world that used to be known as 'third world' countries, but were now called 'emerging'. Despite the differences the international group of officers soon gelled as a class and functioned well together on a personal level. They all wanted to Americanize themselves and by the third day were wearing tee-shirts, low-rider jeans and unlaced Nikes. In class, the most experienced students in the room were the engineers and Rossy found himself paying close attention to the subject matter. He was probably getting more out of the seminars than anyone. Booker also showed some interest, but was easily distracted, just as he had been throughout his educational career. The two quickly adopted an efficient routine for their support responsibilities and found they had more down time than not. They knew this would change when the field work started.

***

Near the end of the week, Rossy was sitting alone in the lounge after dinner, reading some of the class handouts, when he was approached by Aadi Doshi, the Indian officer. Doshi asked 'if he played?', gesturing toward a chess board set up on the far side of the room. The training assistant said, "a little," and the guest officer demanded a game, eager to express his mental superiority over the American underling. Not really feeling like chess, but wondering if this was his contact initiation, the reluctant agent said, "OK," and the two crossed over and sat down at the game table. They flipped a coin for white and Doshi won. He opened 'pg4'. The engineer moved 'pe6'. His opponent emphatically planted 'pf3'. Rossy looked at the board incredulously. The smarty Indian had set himself up for a fracking 'fool's mate'! He waited a moment to politely allow a retraction, then placed 'Qh4', for check and mate. But the challenger didn't concede, nor acknowledge, defeat. He sat staring at the board for minute after minute. Finally, the American pointed out the game was over - there was no escape, no counter - but the Indian dismissively waved his hand and continued studying the impossible configuration before him. Rossy thought the dude was either a poor loser or delusional, maybe both, and went back over to the easy chair to resume his notes review. Later, as everyone started vacating the dayroom to go to their rooms for the night, Doshi remained motionless at the chess table, elbow propped hands under forehead, trying desperately to turn lead into gold. No one else ever knew how long he sat there. The blitzing chesster concluded the Hindustani national was not his *special bean* contact.

***

The weather was beautiful - the only time of year when Chesapeake temperatures and humidity were comfortable, air quality was good and there were no mosquitos. Conditions were benignly optimum for instructional survey ops on the Patuxent River and no adverse fronts or systems were threatening for the foreseeable future. On the first morning of outside activities, red assigned Rossy to take the Brazilian officer, Lt. Alberto Machado, in the **INVINCIBLE** and go check the tide gauges on the river at each bound of the planned survey area. The tidal data was used to correct survey soundings, on a real time basis, to the mean sea level datum. The training assistant and his charge went first to the dining hall to pick up box lunches and then to the tidal basin to prep the little boat for sea duty. After topping off the fuel tank, checking the radio and donning the mandatory vests, the officer loosened the fore and aft mooring ropes and the NAVO operator pulled away from the bulkhead. As they puttered to the basin breakwall, the engineer wondered briefly about the tinge odor of gasoline following them, but figured it was just the lingering fumes from the fuel-up. He headed out onto the river and turned downstream, tracing the channel buoys, toward the lower gauge station. The lieutenant was sitting on the bow bench gazing ahead at the spectacular vista before them and the wheelman was also facing forward in bearing their course. Neither noticed the rainbow colored wake aft of the direction of the boat. When they reached Drum Point, the helmsman began laying to starboard in toward the off-shore, buoy-mounted tide gauge. Without warning, the engine sputtered, coughed a few times and died. The assistant-in-charge couldn't believe it! This was insane! How could the motor just stop?!? It was running fine and they hadn't hit anything. What the hell's going on?? He knew nothing about boats, their motors, or how to fix them, especially when they were out on the water and far away from anyone with such expertise. He glanced at the Brazilian, who shrugged his own 'dunno'. They both looked around and immediately noticed the petro sheen on the water surrounding the boat and back through the wake trail. This would be the source of the gas smell that had been dogging them since leaving the basin. The junior skipper checked the fuel gauge and confirmed his growing suspicion of a tank leak. The needle was pegged out below 'E'. *Now what?* They were two miles from home, dead in the water, in the middle of the river and the tide was receding. In other words, the apparently helpless **INVINCIBLE** was drifting out into the bay. Their search for manual power aids yielded only the realization they were down the river without a paddle. The acting captain then picked up the radio mike and, depressing the speak button, called in their ID, location and a 'MAYDAY SOS'. He had no idea where the call would land, or who would hear it, but there was no response. Confirming the radio was, indeed, on, he tried again. Again, no response. After several more futile attempts, over different frequencies, he concluded they would not be saved by radio, today. Then he remembered red explaining that regional radio communications were frequently disrupted during ongoing wave distortion research activities being conducted by the navy in the lower Chesapeake area. *OK, I'll just call Booker on cell!* The stranded sailor pulled out his phone and flipped it open. No service. *Damn!* There was only one option left, other than abandoning boat and swimming to shore. The last resort option - flares. Cap'n Rossy opened the cabin supply bin and retrieved a gun and several flares. He fired them high into the cloudless sky at three minute intervals and joined the lieutenant forward to break out the happy box lunches and wait for rescue.

"O que está mele para mim?" Rossy stared hard at Machado, mentally registering what the officer had just said, out of the blue, breaking a five minute silence between the free floating castaways. *Holy christ! This is it! This is the special bean asset dude! Game on!!* "Eu não sei. Você me diz."

"You're supposed to speak English."

"Well, *you* didn't."

"That is my prerogative. I wanted to be sure you are my contact."

"OK, what do you have?"

"Not much, but maybe something. We believe your subject was recently active in Recife. As you might know, there is social unrest in my country over recent massive government spending for the Olympics and World Cup. Many people feel funding for these prestigious sporting events has been at the long-term expense of education, anti-poverty and employment programs. Young people, in particular, are struggling with making their way in a tough economy. The've honed in on Recife as the venue of their discontent. This impoverished city has been historically ignored by the national government and offers a good stage for protest without much danger of official retaliation. It has become a mecca, of sorts, for people to congregate and network, while expressing themselves in opposition to government policies, much like the 'occupy' protests in America. There are a lot of disgruntled university graduates in Recife, from all over Brazil, who are well qualified, but cannot find good jobs. It is fertile ground to grow the seeds of agitation."

"Is there anything specific known about the subject in question?"

"Not a lot, except it is confirmed the person is a man. He evidently does not stand out in a Brazilian crowd, possibly because of non-European, ethnic features, or maybe headwear and glasses hide his appearance, especially from public surveillance systems. He is probably of average build and stature. This is my speculation, since we don't have any video or definitive description."

"Any info on where he's going?"

"The word is he might be headed, probably already gone, to Ascension Island."

"Where?"

"Ascension Island, in the middle of the south Atlantic. We have no information on why or how he would go there. So, Mr. Rossy, that's about all I have for you. Could you please record for me, that you have received this intel?" The officer held a device out and the chipmole started to speak into it, when a little top secret bird chirped 'danger' from the far recesses of the back of his mind. "Uh... no, I don't think I can do that, Lieutenant."

"Why not? I need your affirmation of data transfer to protect my payment."

"I'm sorry, but this is all classified and I can't talk about it." The drifters fell silent and continued to await rescue, as the expansive waters of the Chesapeake Bay loomed in front of them.

Pc red saw the orange flare streams arcing across the lower empyrean to the northeast. She didn't need a skycam to tell her from where the signals originated. Yes, indeed, if you send idiots alone with each other into the field, bad shit invariably happens and now she was going to lose at least a day cleaning up whatever mess they made. But there was no way she would take any kind of a hit on this, because she had no control over the meatballs assigned to the program. It is what it is.

The workday was waning at going on 1700 when the **INVINCIBLE** was unceremoniously towed back into the PNAS basin by a smaller, aluminum patrol skiff, used by the base police for minor marine emergencies. They found the hydrographic utility vessel nearly aground in the western tidal flats of the bay, about a quarter mile below Cedar Point at the southern extent of the wide Patuxent River outfall. There was a bit of a hassle in pulling the heavier craft to deeper water, but once they maneuvered into position, it was smooth, but slow, sailing back to the point of origin. Captain Rossy briefed red, stating over and over that he was "sorry, but I just didn't notice the fuel leak until the engine conked out." The tank had evidently corroded through and chose this particular moment in time to fail completely. No equipment was lost or damaged and no one was injured, but approximately twenty five gallons of navgas was spilled into the river and bay. An incident report would have to be filed with EPA's National Response Center and Maryland's Department of Environment, followed by interviews, coordinated site inspections and follow-up mitigation reports. It might involve an hour of paperwork for each gallon of fuel spilled. The primary mission, checking and calibrating the tide gauges, was not accomplished and the boat would have to be repaired before any further survey ops could resume. All things considered, they might lose a week.

But agent bj couldn't lose another minute. He had to go in town to upload his *special bean* report. Though the public library was open for a few more hours, he really didn't want to dawdle much longer with the **INVINCIBLE** fiasco. Finally, pc red decided there was nothing further to be presently done on the issue and she had to get home to feed her animals, so she abruptly dismissed everyone and went to catch the last ferry of the day. Booker started in with questions about what happened out there and Rossy said they passed all their gas and got stuck in the mud. "What does that mean? Hey! Where're ya going??" cried Booker after his colleague, who headed directly for the Civic in exiting the truck at the dorm lot. Little did either engineer know this would be the last time they would see each other for quite a while.

***

The library, located a few blocks off the boulevard away from the Arcade, was a fairly new facility and evidently a popular place. The parking lot was more than half filled. Inside, an extensive media center with at least fifty computer work stations occupied the middle of a large, open space decorated in an attractive, contemporary motif. Lighting was a mix of overhead and lateral, providing a comfortable, non-harsh glow from the many high-efficiency LED fixtures contributing to the overall effect. The room seemed to be a hangout of sorts, as most of the patrons could be categorized as adult youth - same as the visiting sailor - and younger. Rossy approached the check-in counter and was advised he would have to join the library in order to use the media center. The fee was one hamilton - non-reimbursable, he was sure, since it wasn't a NAVOSUR expense. Upon receipt of a membership card, he shambled over to the MC and found his assigned workstation. *This shouldn't take long,* he hoped, sitting down in front of a fixed office tablet unit. After placing a square of black electrician tape over the web cam eye, he googled 'CIA' and clicked to the recruitment site home, then to the contact page. Just as he started to type up the info brief, there was a tap on his elbow from the guy to the left, a thirtyish looking white dude, with severely mottled teeth, who gave a strong first impression of being unemployed. "Scuse me, sir, but could you help me out a sec?"

"I'm sort of wrapped up here, but,......well, OK, what's the problem?" *Damn! I don't need to be bothered right now!*

"I need to send an e-mail."

"OK, go ahead and do it. What's that got to do with me?"

"I don't know exactly what to do."

Oh, god! He doesn't know anything about e-mail. I don't have time for this! "Look, man, I'm not really qualified to show you anything on these systems, but if you ask the attendant over there, I'm sure she'll help you out."

"What, are you just blowin' me off, like I'm nothin'? Like you're better than me, 'cause you can use a computer and I can't? **Is that what it is?** YOU ALL THINK YOU'RE FRACKING BETTER THAN ME?" The man jumped up from his chair, knocking it over backwards and reached under his tee-shirt to the side of his jean's waist. *Jesus christ!! He can't be going for a gun! He would never have gotten through the entrance detector with a gun!?* But the guy whipped out a plastic water pistol and began spraying everyone within range, including the chipmole, while ranting incoherently about whatever was tweaking his troubled psyche. People immediately started screaming and diving for cover all around the room, assuming another fruitcake was opening fire in public. Within seconds the library security guard was on the scene to quickly subdue the obviously disturbed, but apparently harmless individual and escort him safely out of the building. People slowly quieted down and returned to their tasks, though several were sufficiently unsettled by the incident to leave. While Rossy tried to dry himself off and refocus, he overheard someone nearby mutter angrily, "fracking methhead!"

The covert engineer took nearly forty-five minutes to type up his status report, reflecting exactly what the Brazilian asset told him out on the water. He tagged the *special bean* operation reference very early in the report, to make sure it flew quickly. When he was satisfied, he pressed 'send' and all hell broke loose on the pad screen. First, there was a flashing white light with a clanging train horn audio. Then the entire screen was covered with the repetitive phrase 'you can't see me', written in green script on a black background. Finally, the 'blue screen of death'. The classified uploader stared at the little blue rectangle in bewilderment. A young girl at the station to the right said, "Wow, dude, looks like you crashed it good." He wondered how long she had been watching. In a few seconds, the St. Mary's County homepage appeared and the secret agent man assumed his work was done here. *Let me go find something to eat and get on back to the dorm.*

***

Between exiting the library and reaching the Civic in the parking lot, Rossy's phone purred, since he had ring 'off' for being in the library quiet zone. It was esuper Dick. "Good evening, Mr. Rossy. Your message has been received. You are to return immediately to your Suitland apartment and prepare for travel. I will pick you up at 2230. Be ready."

"Jesus, where am I going? What am I going to be doing?"

"I will brief you on the way to JBA. Meantime, not a word to anyone."

"Shouldn't I advise pc Ryder, or inform Booker?"

"What did I just say? Not a word to anyone! Do you understand?"

"Yes, sir."

"OK, see you soon. Drive safely, Mr. Rossy. Do not do anything to attract the attention of the highway police."

The called-to-duty man sat in the car for a few minutes trying to absorb these latest twists in his increasingly bizarre life. He knew he couldn't just start driving back to Suitland. He had to return to the dorm, first, to get his things. Otherwise, he wouldn't have travel bags or enough clothes and necessities to take for whatever trip he was going on. But how could he do this without seeing, or being seen, by anyone? And if he ran into any of the officers or Booker, he would have to talk to them, even though Dick said 'no talking allowed'. *Oh, well. Just have to take my chances, 'cause I've got to get my stuff. No choice! If I talk to somebody, so be it. That doesn't mean I have to discuss any classified special bean intel.* With this mindset, the secret sailor headed back to the base. He parked as near to the front entrance of the dorm as possible and walked boldly in, not trying to hide or sneak. There was no one in the lounge and he encountered no one on the way up to his room. It didn't take long to pack and he was on his way back out in a matter of minutes. Still no sign of anyone. He made it to the Civic undetected, threw the bags in the trunk and proceeded to the gate and out of the PNAS, likely forever. He figured Booker and the officers were either at the club or in town, but probably not together. Red had said no fraternizing. Shiner was on his own now and would have to carry the full training assistant load by himself. As he disappeared stealthily into the cover of darkness, the departing co-assistant felt bad to be abandoning his friend and colleague, but there was absolutely nothing he could do about it. He was once again being 'overtaken by events' totally out of his control.

Rossy did not like to drive at night. There were too many unseen variables. And it seemed trucksters increased their speed by twenty or thirty percent at night, making the road that much more dangerous. As it turned out, there wasn't really a whole lot of traffic past the bridge and it looked like the run up Route 4 would be stress free and uneventful. Time to process the situation and its ramifications on his life and future. He felt lonely. Like he was in classified solitary confinement. There was no one, except Dick, whom he could talk to about anything related to what could only be perceived by others as his increasingly strange and unusual work conduct. And there were still all the open questions pertaining to the equally weird goings on he had observed at NAVOSUR before he was forced into the CIA. He couldn't even talk to *Dick* about those issues. So, yeah, he was starting to feel a bit isolated. But he always had the 'quit' option. *Slip out the back, Jack. Jump on the bus, Gus. Get yourself free.* Easy for Paul Simon to say - he always had another gig. *If I get myself free, I'll be left with nothing, or maybe negative nothing.* What a mess! A lot of new *big unknowns* developing, here, which could only make his head hurt. He turned on the radio and found a replay of the final Atlanta Braves game of the season, as the only static free transmission available. The background crowd buzz, between and through the monotoned, intermittent pitch narratives by the announcer, had sort of a hypnotic effect and the driving engineer zeked out to a certain extent, though not in an unsafe way.

With the light traffic, bj was making excellent time and he anticipated arriving at AGA and being ready to go well before the instructed pick-up time. He didn't want to stop anywhere and jeopardize the schedule, so he would have to postpone dinner until whenever. Cruise control, passive weather and good road conditions allowed the Civic to roll along almost on autodrive. Just when the coasting darkrunner started to congratulate himself for an apparently flawless covert getaway, he saw ground motion on the right shoulder, directly ahead of the car. Then he felt a severe bump, as the right front tire hit whatever ran out onto the roadway. Immediately, there was a loud, cyclic thumping sound emanating from the fore of the engine. *Oh, no, what the hell is this??* panicked the sailor, abruptly losing all wind from his sails. He pulled over onto the shoulder, cut the engine, retrieved the flashlight from the glove compartment, popped the hood and slowly got out. Half afraid to check out the problem, he walked around and carefully lifted the cover panel. A horrible smell greeted him from below. Shining the light down into the black abyss, he saw a thoroughly mangled skunk wedged between the pulley and belt of the coolant fan. He would obviously have to remove the thankfully dead animal and was fortunately able to do so by manually jockeying the belt. The skunk stink was unbearably overwhelming and promptly permeated into the car after he restarted the engine. Resuming the drive with no evident mechanical damage, Rossy soon felt rather nauseous and wondered if he would have to stop at some point to hurl. Good thing he hadn't eaten anything. Luckily, he eventually acclimated somewhat and was able to continue forward progress with little loss of time.

Later, after arriving at the apartment and showering with intense soaping scrub for at least half an hour, the skunkster was dismayed to conclude the stench was still with him. At least his bags and clothes were good, because they had traveled in the trunk, but he had to do something about his person. Looking through the bathroom and lavatory storage areas, he found a bottle of Monte Carlo 'Nighthawk' cologne, which he assumed was gameboy's, since he didn't recall Booker ever wearing such stuff. Without hesitation, he splashed the grossly sweet-scented, oily liquid all over, even rubbing it into his hair and scalp. The result was sort of a hybrid odor, but at least, he thought, not a distinctive, dead polecat aroma. By the time he dressed and repacked, it was still a half hour before liftoff. He was starting to get really hungry and went into the kitchen to see if anything was available. After snarfing about thirty peanut butter and jelly crackers and feeling much better, he cleaned up the kitchen, brushed his teeth and sat down in the living room to wait for his ride to........wherever.

JOINT BASE ANDREWS

The chipmole's handler knocked on the portico door at precisely the prescribed time. They grabbed the travel bags and secured the apartment, then walked wordlessly out to the esuper's suv, got quickly in and drove back out the access to Suitland Road - all observed by Donald Trevair on remote monitor for the concealed parking lot surveillance cams. It looked like one of Smith's idiot squatter buddies was going away for an extended period with some dude he did not recognize. *In a black Escalade! Could be drug related.* Trevair stood up from behind the small desk in his tiny office and went out to take a look at the squatter's ride, parked right in the middle of the lot. As he approached the Civic, he detected the skunk funk from about twenty yards away. By the time he got to the car, the smell was overpowering. *Jesus christ!! What the hell is this!?!* The security rep slowly circled the offensive vehicle and unilaterally decided it could not stay in the lot, for any period of time, in its present condition. It posed a serious nuisance that all the tenants would soon be complaining about. He would have it towed out asap to the AGA impoundment area down at the lower end of the property by the cemetery. This cost plus an accumulative storage fee would be liened against the apartment deposit account. *Ha!! Score one for the good guys!!*

Before they reached the AGA entranceway, esuper Dick started coughing and vigorously clearing his throat. "Holy shit, boy, what the hell's that hideous smell?" Rossy apologized, explaining how he had run over a skunk on the way up from PNAS and the fumes had drawn into his car and all over him, but there was nothing he could do to stop it, even with opening all the windows and turning on the AC. He said he showered long and hard at the apartment, but couldn't seem to wash the skunk off. It was like the super glue of odors.

"No, no, that's not what I smell. I know a skunk smell and this isn't it."

"Well, I did put some cologne on, when I still smelled the skunk after my shower."

"Cologne?! That's what it is! Jesus frack! Cheap cologne is a helluva lot worse than any goddam skunk! You're gonna have to wash that shit off before you fly tonight! As soon as we get to the terminal, get your ass in the restroom and clean up. Christ! Remember what I told you about not being conspicuous? Well, this is no way to keep a low profile! Use some sense, son!"

"Yes, sir."

They rode in silence the rest of the way to Andrews. Rossy was bursting with questions, but was afraid to ask anything, assuming Dick would explain all in due time. They passed through the main gate with whatever ID the esuper showed the guard, who did not even glance at the passenger, while immediately waving them on. It was a short drive to the airfield terminal, where Dick parked next to an empty handicap space beside the entrance. He snatched a thin, rigid briefcase from the console as they departed the truck. The facility seemed deserted, as would be expected at eleven o'clock at night. Going inside to a sizable, rectangular lobby area, the supervisor looked at his charge and pointed to the restroom. Rossy nodded and went in to wash out the cologne, hoping he could make himself normally inconspicuous again.

Returning to the lobby, the freshly re-sanitized engineer joined his superior in a far corner, slumping into an adjacent waiting room chair. He noticed one other person he hadn't seen coming in, a uniformed, one star AF general, stoically watching the civilian twosome from his seat at the other end of the room. Dick opened the briefcase and began his instruction brief to the subordinate operative. Speaking in a low tone and keeping the briefcase lid angled, in deference to any hidden surveillance devices that might pick-up their classified discourse, he explained the *special bean* initiative was shifting to Ascension Island. *No surprise there, from what Lt. Machado reported.* This was a minuscule, British owned outpost, eight degrees south of the equator, about midway between South America and Africa. America had established a NASA down range tracking base on AI, during the first phases of the space program, and continued to maintain the base, supporting a variety of high-tech, telemetric relay activities, under military contract with Global Orbital Dynamics, a subsidiary of UTG. *What?! UTG??! That fracking company is everywhere!!* thought the former UTG affiliate employee. Early on, the US built a full-service airfield to accommodate the logistical needs of the base, since AI had no in-shore, deep port facilities. The British more or less seized control of the airfield, during their brief 1980s skirmish with Argentina, and tore the asphalt pavement up in deploying their long-range warplanes retrofitted with ultra-high pressured tires. Ever since, there has been strained relations between the Brits and the Yanks over who should pay for upgrading and modernizing the AI field. "Your NAVOSUR cover job, Mr. Rossy, will be to plan a hydrographic survey for an off-shore shipping lane to deliver equipment and materials needed for the airfield overhaul. Mr. Ed Richardson is the civilian base superintendent for GOD and he will be your on-site supervisor, as well as your supplier of whatever support you need in planning the survey. Yes?"

Rossy was confused and had his hand up in question. "How can I plan a survey by myself? I don't know enough about either airfield construction or hydrography to do what you're talking about."

"Don't worry about it. Just lay out a preliminary work area, to, say, a hundred feet depth, based on visual landmarks in the vicinity of the airfield. Richardson, who, by the way, is dumber than crushed stone, knows even less than you, in that I'm telling you the actual survey will never be done. It's just to give you a temporary reason to be there, until you can contact our asset and receive a *special bean* update. That's your *real* mission, the only thing that counts. Stay on game and don't get lost in peripherals!"

"Right, so how do I contact the asset?"

"OK, everybody on AI is there on official business, working for either the Americans or the Brits, or both. No one actually lives there permanently and there are no tourists. There is a large contingent of Saints, migrant workers from St. Helena, the next nearest populated island, who do the shit service work, like cleaning, cooking and maintenance, for the American and British employers. Our asset is a Saint, placed to gather intel on what the Brits are doing at their tech facilities. He works on the American base, in the dining hall, I think, and stays in Georgetown, the only real town on the island. I don't know his name, but he has been briefed on you. You will open dialogue with the same verbal code as before. Everybody speaks English there, so you don't have to worry about translations. He will initiate contact as he sees appropriate, so stay alert and make yourself visible and accessible. Again, our objective is to compile basic info on *special bean.* You got a good start at PNAS, so keep the ball rolling. We are looking for a man, probably of average height and build, and possibly other than northern European, Asian or lower African features. That narrows it down to maybe thirty percent of the world's population. Not much, but more than what we had a few days ago. If he has either an American or British passport, which there's a ninety percent chance he would have in going to Ascension, that narrows it down even more. It's a puzzle, Mr. Rossy, to which every little piece counts toward the big picture. We will follow this dissident, assembling all the pieces, until he is neutralized."

"Well, Dick, I have a question. Do I get different TDY orders to go to Ascension? And, if I do, what about my PNAS orders? How can I file a voucher on that?"

"Yes, yes. I've got all the paperwork in here," said Dick, opening the case a little wider, while checking his watch. "Your new orders, your passport with Ascension and other major visas, your shot record and your advance. It's all here, including a micro flash with back-up of everything. By the way, you might have to get the rest of your shots at AI. Check with the medical unit at the American base. Read through all this material, so you know what you have. You'll notice the orders are more, or less, open ended. That, with your official passport, allows you to basically go anywhere. You can just take the case and you'll be all set. As far as your DD-1351 goes, you can file that anytime. There's no expiration, or deadline, on voucher submittals. Keep good records on yourself, though, so you don't glop it up - that could be a nasty felony. For example, your PNAS voucher is going to have to reflect repayment of most of the advance you got, since you are being reassigned after only a fraction of the TDY time period upon which the advance was based. Now, if you need extended advance funding, different visas, airline tickets, whatever, you can go to any U.S. military travel or disbursement post in the world, or any American embassy or consulate, for assistance. You have extensive resources, Mr. Rossy, learn to use them. They will help you to move more efficiently through whatever maze you are entering. And remember to code send all new intel as you receive it, again, through public devices only. Clear?"

"Yeah, OK. So how am I traveling? Do I fly from here?"

"Of course. Why else would we *be* here? Your flight to Patrick leaves at 0015, in about forty minutes. From there you will board a C-17 for Ascension, where you'll arrive at about 1800, local. Richardson is expecting you and will meet you at the AI terminal. It's about a ten hour flight from Patrick, so make sure you get some sleep. Your itinerary is confirmed. Just check in with orders and ID."

"Patrick?"

"Yes, Patrick Air Force Base, in Florida. Just south of Cape Canaveral."

"Never been there. But then again, I've never been anywhere. At least out of the country."

"Well, son, I believe that is about to soon change for you. You might come out of this as one of the most traveled engineers ever at NAVOSUR. But no one will ever know that,...... why?"

"Because it's all highly classified and I can't discuss it with anyone."

"Bingo. And don't you ever forget that, capisce?"

"OK, Dick, but I've got a problem. I know you keep saying not a word to anybody about what I'm doing, but I've got to talk to Booker about the apartment and my car. I have to coordinate paying my bills and I wanted him to use my car while I'm gone, so I have to tell him where the keys are."

"Alright, that's understandable. Here's what you can do. Use a burn phone, not your regular phone, for any extraneous communication. And destroy the chip after each use. No social media correspondence. I've provided two bp's and a bunch of sims in the case. You may call me on your personal phone, which would not raise any flags anywhere if it is traced or intercepted, because you have NAVO orders to be wherever you go. But don't call unless it's absolutely necessary, or an emergency. And don't contact me on the burners. I wouldn't answer and you couldn't even message. I will call you with instructions as conditions and events dictate. Keep your phone close at all times. I cannot put anything on voice mail. OK?"

"Yep."

"Attaboy. Let's go." The airfield door opened and the duty dispatcher advised the plane was ready to board. Rossy showed his orders and NAVOSUR ID. He shook hands with Dick, picked up his bags along with the briefcase and stepped toward the Honda HA-420 compact light jet, waiting on the tarmac.

***

While the apprentice agent was settling into his plush transport seat and starting to go through the paperwork Dick had given him, the military man boarded and sat down diagonally across the narrow aisle, so that the two passengers were facing each other. Rossy glanced up and confirmed his sense that the dude was staring at him. The officer did not look away. The small plane's engines soon fired up and they began taxiing swiftly toward the end of the runway. Within minutes, the shuttle craft was airborne and moving into its flight pattern to Patrick AFB. The nightflier resumed reviewing the contents of the briefcase. He was astounded to find $5,000 in bens included - his new advance. *Well, shit! My finances are back! Is this a great country, or what?!* He checked his 'Request and Authorization for TDY Travel of DoD Personnel Form DD 1610', stamped with a boldly oversized **'TS CLASSIFIED'** across the top. Under *Purpose of TDY*, the form read "Report to various specific sites as ordered to conduct duties as assigned iaw mission objectives in support of authorized operational activities of NAVOSUR." Under *Itinerary*, the form listed Washington D.C., as point of origin, and "points of destination as necessary to conduct assigned duties iaw this authorization, as specified herein, including return to poo", as destination. Travel and per diem were authorized "iaw the joint travel regulations and as required to perform the stated duties as identified herein." The form was signed, with today's date, by an undecipherable scribble, printed underneath as L. A. Wyles, CDR, Acting Deputy Comptroller, USN. Dick was right. It appeared these orders pretty much allowed the rambling rookie to go anywhere to do anything, with a blank check to pay for it. It was like money in the bank.

"So what takes you to Patrick?" Rossy looked up, slightly startled by his co-passenger's inquiry, and did not immediately respond. "What's your business? Why are you going to Patrick?" repeated the officer.

"Uh....it's classified. I can't talk about it."

"That's OK, I'm cleared. Who are you with?"

"I'm sorry, sir, I can't discuss that."

"Look, boy, do you know who you're talking to? I'm a general in the United States Air Force. Even if you *are* a civilian, I suggest you show proper respect. Now, who are you with and why are you on this flag status flight?"

The insubordinate civilian knew the officer wasn't a general. A general had four stars. This uniform only had one, like the asshole he apparently was. "With all due respect, sir, if you are cleared you should know you can only have access to classified information you have the need to know about. You have no need to know anything about me, so please don't ask me anything, OK?" The officer glared at his upstart cabinmate and turned away in 'hrumphing' disgust. The younger traveler, likewise, closed the briefcase and shifted to look out the port. It was pitch black outside. They were already into a high cloud cover and there was nothing to see except the blinking tip lights at the end of the wing. Rossy recalled an old show he had seen during a recent *Twilight Zone* marathon on TV, where William Shatner, before he was Captain Kirk of the Starship Enterprise, looked out the window of a plane he was flying on and saw a clown trying to sabotage the engine. Of course, there was no seditious clown out on the wing here, thought the jetster, because the clown was inside, across the aisle from him, trying to sabotage his security. Soon the lateness of the hour, the drone of the turbos and the gentle yawing of the aircraft lulled the passengers into doze, where they remained until thumpdown on Patrick's northwest auxiliary runway.

***

The terminal building at Patrick AFB did not look much different from the one at Andrews, especially in the dark of deep night. Therein would be at least an hour's detention before the flight to Ascension. The tiring TDYman went inside, knowing this would be all he would see of PAFB, but not caring. He idled into the most comfortable chair he could find and stretched out to await departure.

At approximately 0345, an enlisted airman popped his head in the door and called for Mr. Rossy to "please come with me, sir." The sailor promptly got his things together and went outside to an open jeep, where he and the bags were thoroughly scanned with a handheld detection device and the briefcase was opened and inspected. *Uh-oh....is this a security violation?* It was about a ten minute, slow drive to the end of the seemingly boundless main runway, where sat the unquestionably largest aircraft the infrequent flyer had ever seen. A C-17 cargo carrier. In the shadowy darkness, it looked like a small mountain parked across the airfield. The gargantuan loading access was open to a cavernous, dimly lit bay area partially filled with countless pallets of tarp covered consumable supplies for GOD's base at AI. The airman pulled his passenger's bags from the jeep, except the briefcase, which Rossy was not about to let loose from his own grasp under any circumstance. They entered the loading bay and walked forward to a small compartment wherein several demountable rope net seats were assembled along the bulkhead. A tall officer in blue fatigues stood waiting, coffee cup in hand. He introduced himself as the flight crew navigator and proceeded to brief the sole assigned 'rider of opportunity' on procedures and facilities of the oversized aircraft. He then secured the bags and instructed the roo to strap into one of the passenger seats. Before turning to go up front for preparation for take-off, the navigator asked the guest if he had ever flown over the equator? "No, sir. This is as far south as I've ever been in my life." And Rossy soon found himself alone in a small, nearly dark, windowless confinement, totally at the mercy of unseen persons to deliver him safely to an essentially unknown destination. It felt like surreal entrapment in a virtual environment, as the slightly over-pressurized air dulled his perceptions. He was further assuaged by the rumbling engines, idling somewhere within the mass of the structure, and a sequenced overhead blower, regularly delivering blasts of heated air to the enclosed passenger space. At some point he sensed motion, but could not orientate to speed, direction or position. He never detected the transition from pavement to air. Without sensory references, shutdown came quickly and the airborne agent fell into a near comatose state of dreamless sleep.

CHINATOWN

General 'tophead' Randolph Patton Clement was a creature of structured habit. For years, every Friday at precisely 1900, he entered the narrow doorway on the sidewalk off 9th Street to the upstairs entrance of the Fa Foo restaurant in Washington's Chinatown. An exquisitely decorated establishment in the ancient Qing tradition, Fa Foo's was critically recognized as the best purveyor of authentic Hunan cuisine in the capitol area. RPC had a long standing reservation and he always went alone. But this time was different. He was going there on Monday, because he couldn't return to his home in Chevy Chase. Yesterday, his wife had been granted an emergency court order barring him from within a thousand feet of the house. This, after a vicious argument over finances, compatibility, irreconcilable differences and abuse issues culminated with the general forcefully blowing a lungful of cigar smoke into her face from short range. She had charged him with second degree behavioral assault and now he was released on his own recognizance, staying in the Marriot District Deluxe Hotel, at two bens a night. The inevitable separation was a long time coming and he was not entirely surprised, but what he couldn't get wrapped around was his lack of control. He was being told what he could and couldn't do and it was driving him nuts. Almost as bad as the congressional bureaucrats axing nearly fifty per cent of his operating budget, with no knowledgable consideration of the adverse impact on national security. He had protested long and mightily, but was finally ordered by the featherweight director to "deal with it!!" When his impending divorce finalized he would lose another fifty per cent of his funding, so he was intrinsically facing loss of everything. Idiots!! So tired of shlepping against total idiots, who had no concept of how the real world worked!

Stepping into the Fa Foo stairwell, tophead was instantly pacified by the soft, staccato lilt of the cultural lute emanating from above. He loved this place. It was like a sanctuary, where all the stresses, the impossible problems and misunderstandings and the masses of unappreciative clods were unequivocally barred from entry. And the fare was, simply, unearthly good. Climbing to the small foyer, he was greeted by Vin Lu, the Chinese-Italian maitre'd, who expressed some surprise to see the general on a Monday. Unfortunately, he could not be seated at his regular table overlooking the colorful and busy street below, but was placed at a small drink table near the kitchen passage. He ordered his usual Tsing Tao and hot green tea and began perusing the familiar menu.

The special tonight was duck with tamarind sauce and that would be his choice. The general leaned back to relax and enjoy his solitude. He was sick of people. They all caused him nothing but trouble.

***

The tall, impeccably dressed and groomed Chinese man carefully watched the general from across the dining room. He could tell from his body language that the big man was agitated. And understandably so. Both his professional and private lives were falling apart. Was it time yet? Should he make his bid this evening? If the timing was wrong, everything could fail miserably. But Americans were funny. They were always vulnerable to the trappings of alchemy, no matter what the timing. *Walk narrowly in the wrong direction and you will be forever lost.* Yes, the time was now. The Chinese man ordered another Tsing Tao for the CIA kingpin and waited for his response. When the recipient turned to scope the source of his unordered drink, the noticeably handsome Chinese man beckoned him over to his larger table by the front window.

RPC did not know what to think. He had never socialized with anyone here. No one knew who he was and it was vitally important that his anonymity remain intact. Was this some sort of random homosexual hit? He didn't think so. The man looked like a Chinese national, someone of status. And then his mind clicked. It was Jiang Cheng, the reclusive executive managing officer and majority share holder of the China Petroleum and Provisional Utility Corporation, a quasi-private distribution company supplying a large portion of the imported oil demand for the People's Republic of China. *Jesus christ!! What's he doing in America? In D.C.?? I've received no intel on that! And if he's calling me over, he knows who I am!! How can that be?!? I'm invisible!!* No choice, now. He had to respond to the invitation to find out what the cripe was going on here. Tophead picked up the fresh beer and glass and carefully made his way through the maze of tables toward the front of the room, never taking his eyes off the equally attentive Chinese man seated *at my table by the window.*

"Good evening, General Clement. So nice of you to join me. No need to introduce myself, correct? I'm sure you know more about me than I do myself. Please, please, sit down." Tophead felt a sinking sensation in the pit of his stomach that threatened to ruin his appetite. *How much did Jiang know about him? About what he did? Best thing right now is to not reveal anything more. Say as little as possible. Learn as much as possible.* "Thank you, Mr. Jiang. Good evening," An awkward silence ensued, with the seating of the adjoining diner. Both parties were on full, code-red mental alert and neither knew exactly how to proceed. Finally, Jiang commented on what a fine restaurant Fa Foo's was. It was one of his favorites, anywhere in the world. The general heartily agreed, allowing he had been coming here for years and thinking, *but you obviously already know that.* The two exchanged meaningless niceties about the weather, the traffic, their respective soon-to-arrive dinner orders, like boxers cautiously pushing each other around before the real bout began. Then RPC threw a jab to the head. "So, Mr. Jiang, what is your reason for inviting me to your table? I am certain you are interested in more than my fondness for Fa Foo fare."

"Yes, General Clement, of course. You know, we have something in common, you and I. We both must constantly work with impossibly frustrating bureaucracies that have no basis in reality. They live in their own fantasy world."

Does he know about my budget cuts? "OK?"

"But while our respective bureaucracies each present us with constant challenges, they are vastly different. China wants to move forward at impossibly unachievable speed, without the corresponding resources to meet its unrealistic goals. But America wants to reverse her trajectory and cut back a bit in status and initiative. Take care of problems at home. Reduce spending and the national debt. We seem destined to pass each other going up and down, like two ships at sea in the storm of global macronomics."

China is like America in the 1920s. Been there, done that. They will never pass us in anything, anywhere, or anyhow! "OK?"

"I see you are reluctant to engage, sir. Most of what you do is not open for discussion. Fair enough. I will lead. I have a potential proposition that could be of mutual benefit to each of our stations in life. I do not wish to discuss this proposition this evening, but would rather meet again at your regular time here on Friday. Is that possible for you?"

He knows about my Fa Foo Fridays? Jesus, does he have an asset in here, or something? Vin Lu? There is no one more paranoid than an uncovered intelligence specialist and tophead was feeling very exposed. Despite the goddam 'no smoking' reg, he wanted to light up a Limitados, of which he carried five in his inside jacket pocket. But he prudently refrained. This was no time to draw further attention to himself. He did not say anything in response to Jiang's question.

"Fine. Under the circumstances, I understand and respect your reticence. I will be here on Friday. You can think about what I said and make your own discreet decision between now and then. I hope you will hear me out. I think I can offer you something of momentous interest and import. Meanwhile, let's enjoy our dinner together." The waiter was approaching with a huge silver serving tray perched on his shoulder. Mr. Jiang had ordered tamarind duck, same as his table guest.

ASCENSION ISLAND

At some point after more than eight hours in the air, accounting for passed time zones, the groggy g-man decided to go up front to use the toilet and get a coffee and snack. As he went forward the incessant mechanical hum of the massive fanjets became louder and more vibrationally prevalent. Without windows, he assumed it was just as dark outside as in, like a permanent omniscient nightfall, but was pleasantly surprised to see daylight gleaming through from the cockpit area. He stepped closer to get a better look, maybe a glimpse of where they were and what they were flying over, and saw the navigator stretched out on a bunk, fast asleep. Cautiously moving further into the cockpit, he was shocked to find the pilot and copilot likewise racked out on bunks beside the instrument consoles. Jesus god! Not only was he the only person on the aircraft who knew nothing about flying, he was the only one awake!! *What the hell is this?*

"Autopilot." The passenger spun around to face the navigator standing right behind him. "We're on FIAC in case you were wondering who's watching the store."

"Fiack?"

"Yeah, fully integrated automatic control. And you are in a restricted area, Mr. Rossy. I must ask you to return to your seat. We will be landing in less than two hours."

"Yes, sir." The curious roo took another quick look out of the wraparound cockpit ports and saw nothing but massive billows of cotton cumulus all the way to the space blue horizon. It appeared the sun was slightly behind them, at the lowering angle of mid afternoon. He refilled his coffee styrocup and went back to the darkened passenger compartment, feeling like he, too, was on FIAC, because his life was certainly under extraneous control.

***

Walking slowly across the tarmac to the small stucco and red-tiled admin building situated near the airfield midpoint, the landed sailor studied the palm-sized canvas patch the navigator had just signed, dated and given to him. *'Eternal Order Of The Shellback'* was stitched across the top of the colorful peltate patch, over a formidable, trident wielding King Neptune battling a ferocious sea serpent rising from the deep blue. The patch was in recognition of his first crossing of latitude zero, aka the equator, and he knew he would keep it for the rest of his life as a valuable, personal achievement memento. Right there in the permanently stored artifacts shoebox with his National Honor Society pin, high school ring, Rolen home run ball and varsity wrestling letter. He stuffed the patch in a pocket and looked up to see a middle aged man in an unpressed gray suit with narrow black tie moving briskly toward him from the structure. The man's trouser cuffs, open jacket, tie and grayish-brown hair were flapping in the stiff breeze, reminding the young incomer of a 1950's business parody he had seen on the TV show *Madmen*. Ed Richardson, GOD's Ascension Island base superintendent, briefly introduced himself and directed the bag bogged sojourner to follow, offering no assistance with the luggage. They entered the Wideawake Field terminal, processed the TDYster through arrival and proceeded to the super's office at the end of a short corridor from a corner of the public ops area. New man was ordered to take a seat in front of the oversized, executive oaken desk dominating the room, while GOD's super glided around behind the desk and slouched into a lavishly stuffed, blue leather swivel chair. Sitting up and rolling forward, with hands folded on the uncluttered desktop, superintendent Richardson silently studied his new charge a moment and then, "Mr. Rossy, listen very carefully, because I'm only going to tell you this one time. This is my island. I set the rules here. I enforce the rules here. If you violate my rules I will have you flown out stateside faster than a greased dolphin on speed. No appeals. No second chances. The main rule is no fracking trouble. If you cause any trouble, any disturbance, piss anybody off, for any reason, then you are automatically breaking all the rules and your ass is gone. Got it?"

"Yes, sir, Ed."

"No, no, no. *Mr. Richardson*. I'm *Mr.* Richardson."

"Yes, sir, Mr. Richardson."

"OK. Now, you're gonna need a truck to get around and do your job here. And for that you need an international driver's license with an AI special permit. Tomorrow, I'll pick you up at barracks at 0700 and we'll field test you out for your license. Remember, this is England - drive on the left. Got it?"

"Yes, sir, Mr. Richardson."

"Good. OK, let me give you a quick tour around and get you registered into the visitor's barracks. The dining hall is open for another hour or so, if you want something to eat. First, though, I'm going to need you to sign this." Mr. Richardson removed a multipage form document from a nearby file drawer and handed it across to his guest. Rossy had a personal policy to never sign anything without reading it, rooted in his horrible experience with the vo-tech auto shop and boarding house brothers in Connecticut, so he started reading the document. "No need to read it," protested the super. "Just sign on the last page. It's a standard waivers, releasing GOD of any liability for anything you think you don't like that might happen to you while on GOD's premises here at AI. Not signing is a rules violation, whether you read it or not, so, really, there's no need to read it, at least not now. C'mon...let's go! It's getting late!" The engineer with many bosses, concluding he had no choice, reluctantly signed and passed the form back to his host superior. The two exited the office, through a private door to the facility parking lot, as the outsider again struggled with humping his baggage alone.

The inbounder did not get a chance to see much of his new environment, as it was quickly too dark for a meaningful drive-by tour when they left the airfield, so Mr. Richardson headed directly to the base barracks, about two miles northwest of the Wideawake terminal. The nearby dining facility was still barely open for lamp-warmed, leftover sandwiches and the newest lodger was happily lucky to score a burger and a brew, which he carried back to his room without seeing or encountering anyone. The extraordinarily long and over pressurized flight had taken its toll and he was ready to crash. Unfortunately, he did not sleep well. The room next door was occupied by two men, drunk and drunker, who alternately fought and argued pretty much all night long. They yelled at each other in Dutch-English accents, that could possibly be guessed as South African. Eventually, they passed out, as did their weary neighbor.

***

Next morning, the semi-rested agent was good to go well before 0700. Mr. Richardson was right on time, just as night darkness was rapidly turning to daylight. The new shellback remembered twelve hours ago, when day had just as quickly yielded to night. No dusk or dawn, only uniform periods of daylight and nighttime. It was an equatorial zone thing. The superintendent, still dressed in a wrinkled suit with breeze mussed hair, was all business. Without a 'good morning', or 'how did you sleep?', or any other courtesy greeting, he commanded the prospective international driver to get behind the wheel of the wide bodied pick-up and directed them east, toward the center highlands of the island. Fortunately, the rookie AI motorist remembered to stay to the left, though it might not have made much difference, since there were no other vehicles on the road. AI did not play 'rush hour'. Even more fortunately, Rossy's teenage farm work experience gave him the ability to operate the truck's manual trans, which likely put him in the nintieth percentile of the driving test right from the start.

The landscape was stark, as only a geologically recent volcanic formation could be. Tiny Ascension, a roughly inverted cone-shaped island about eight miles in diameter, was just fifteen thousand years old and too remote to have evolved indigenous flora. The only large botanical growth was on top of Green Mountain, the highest point within thousands of miles of the desolate mid-south Atlantic, where imported hardwoods flourished in a planted rain forest milieu. Off the well-graded and semi-paved gravel roadway, original lava flows were solidified into expanses of javelin sharp spires and upturned fluted blades of metallic igneous, through which it looked like it would be impossible to walk, even a short distance, without incurring serious injury, or worse. Rounding a wide curve, they approached a tee intersection with another road on the right. Mr. Richardson thumbed at the new road and his trainee made the turn and accelerated through a short straightaway toward a rather tight swerve around a crested rise on the left. Suddenly, the superintendent leaned forward, pounded his fists on the dash and screamed, **"STOP!!!"** Rossy reflexively jammed the brake and the truck lurched to a halt, the engine stalling.

"DO YOU SEE THAT SIGN BACK THERE!!? WHAT DOES THAT SIGN SAY??!"

The startled operator looked in the mirror and saw the back of a rectangular shaped sign about a hundred feet behind them. "I don't know, sir. I can only see the back of the sign. I don't know what it says."

"WELL BACK UP SO YOU *CAN* SEE IT AND TELL ME WHAT IT SAYS!!"

Shit! Did I just bomb this fracking field test? The worried wheelman started the engine and reversed slowly backwards to the front of the sign. **"NOW!! WHAT DOES THAT SIGN SAY!??!"** barked Mr. Richardson.

"CAUTION STEEP DECLINE ALL VEHICLES TO LOW GEAR," read the IDL candidate, in a high, stammering voice.

"I CAN'T HEAR YOU!!! WHAT DOES THAT SIGN SAY??!"

"CAUTION STEEP DECLINE ALL VEHICLES TO LOW GEAR," repeated the freaking driver.

"OK, WHAT DO YOU THINK THAT MEANS??"

"Downshift to a low gear?"

"WHICH GEAR??"

"Second?"

"TRY FIRST!! DO IT, NOW!!"

"Yes, sir." Rossy shifted into first and was ordered to proceed. Again, they approached the curve, but at turtle speed. Around the rise, the road disappeared. It was almost a total drop off down into some kind of blind abyss, because it was virtually impossible to see where the falling road went. "Now, do you see the importance of paying attention to the signs? They are not put there to frack up the beautiful landscape. They're there to maybe save lives of unobservant idiot drivers, like you, and keep GOD from losing valuable vehicles. Got it?" lectured the island boss.

"Yes, sir, I understand." The nervous truckster followed the narrow, marble chute configured road down from the steep lava crest for about a mile, before leveling out into a wide flat area, about a thousand yards across. "This is Devil's Riding School Crater, from an old volcano," explained super man. "Pull over. I want to show you something." The student AI driver obediently maneuvered the truck to the edge of the road and stopped. The crater circle looked like an Arizona desert, complete with stony, umber hued sand, tumble weed scrub bushes and tall sauaro cacti waving their thick spiny arms in sentinel greeting. A few yards off the road, a huge jackrabbit, overlong ears twitching, hopped leisurely between the cactus trunks, paying no heed to the newly arrived vehicle sitting nearby. Not much further in, a reflective spot of red in the sand caught the eye. Rossy looked closer and identified a Budweiser beer can partially buried under a sparse shrub. He pondered this, remembering seeing Budweiser cans in other places, other times. In the watershed of Pine Creek, way up beyond human habitation in the Allegheny wilderness, a Budweiser can lying in the creek. At an abandoned homestead, far into the inaccessible terrain of Maine's national forestland, a Budweiser can in the ancient, overgrown yard clearing. On the tidal flat off the undeveloped coast of the lower Chesapeake, a Budweiser can stuck in the slimy muck. Along almost any highway, road or lane, anywhere he had ever been, Budweiser cans in the ditches. And now here, at one of the most remote places on the face of the earth, a Budweiser can in the sand of a dormant volcanic crater. Distinctive red and white Budweiser cans were literally everywhere. Where did they all come from and how did they get so widely distributed? Still another *big unknown* to consider. It was as if there was some kind of mythical 'Bobby Budweiser' figure planting beer cans all over the world, akin to the legendary 'Johnny Appleseed' and his apple tree project.

"Over there," said Mr. Richardson, pointing to an area much further off the road than the daydreaming driver had been focussing on. Following the super's point, maybe two hundred yards distant, he saw a row of about ten charcoal gray donkeys, standing statue-like among the thick, towering cactus plants, all facing and silently watching the parked vehicle that had just noisily invaded their domain.

"Are those donkeys?" asked the newcomer.

"Yes, they are. Obviously, not native to AI, but feral. And extremely dangerous. I wanted you to see them so you are aware of their presence and avoid them. There are maybe six, or seven, herds roaming the island and they will kill you if given the chance. So stay the hell away from them. I don't need any goddam donkey death reports to have to deal with."

"If they're so dangerous, how come you don't just shoot them?"

"Because they're protected by the British Ministry of Environmental Affairs. An endangered species, which is bloody crockwash, since at one time there were zero donkeys here. Sometime in the late 1800's they brought them in to haul materials to build a prison in Georgetown and then set them free after they were done, because they didn't want to take care of them. They've been running wild ever since. The Brits shoot 'em if they get to over a hundred, but we're not allowed to unless we're being attacked and then we would have to do about a year's worth of justification paperwork. The reason they're dangerous is because they're carnivores and that's because there's no free range grass here. They've learned to work together to kill any unlucky animal they can surround and stomp to death. Mostly large land crabs down closer to the water. So keep your eyes open at all times and stay alert."

The engineer didn't know what to think. He never heard of a meat eating donkey. Maybe Mr. Richardson was just having some fun with the new guy, like some kind of island initiation hazing thing. But then he remembered Dick telling him the super was inherently stupid, so it could be he actually believed the donkey bull. Or, maybe the story was true. *Jesus, that would be pretty fracking scary!* Best bet - leave all options open and quietly avoid the donkeys. That way he could stay safe without making an ass out of himself.

The super directed his driving protege to continue on the cross crater road. After about a half mile, Rossy slowed and stopped, with no shrieking prompt from the passenger boss, before another large sign.

"CAUTION STEEP INCLINE - AWD VEHICLES ONLY," studiously read the safety conscious operator aloud.

"OK, what do you think that means?"

"Only authorized work detail vehicles allowed up the hill?"

"WHAT?? ARE YOU CRAZY?!? *ALL WHEEL DRIVE*, SON, *ALL WHEEL DRIVE* !! DO YOU HAVE ALL WHEEL DRIVE??"

"Uh.....yeah. Here it is," found the one-wheel-drive Civic owner. He depressed the dash panel button to activate the green 'on' led light for the AWD control and inched forward. The feel of the drive train was different - heavier, more grinding, and the steering more sensitive. The road rapidly changed texture, becoming gravelly rutted and potholed as it graded upward. The driver instinctively accelerated through second against the backward pull of gravity from the steepening slope. The wheels started to shed traction and spin in the loose surface material and Rossy down-

shifted back to first as he jacked the gas trying to force more acceleration. Mr. Richardson expelled a fearful **"Holy Shit!!"** and,
ripping off his seat belt, opened the shotgun door and jumped out.
The incredulous ex-physics student immediately knew this loss of
dead weight necessitated nearly flooring the accelerator to maintain inertia through the frictional angle of incidence that was
threatening to bring him down. The truck, engine screaming in
protest, wobbled slightly in a back and forth fishtail, as the slipping tires spewed a plume of stones, dirt and dust behind. But forward motion was sustained and, as the grade decreased somewhat
in approaching the top, the former farmhand eased off the pedal.
With a sigh of relief he drove over the crest and parked on the
once again and welcome level road. *Thank you, jesus.* He looked
in the mirror and saw his leader standing, unsteadily, about halfway down the hill waving his arms back and forth over his head.
He was yelling something that could not be heard from inside the
cab. The roadrunner got out and walked back to the edge and
looked down. Mr. Richardson cupped his hands around his mouth
and megaphoned the truckster to back down and pick him up. *Seriously?? This dude is dumber than Dick knows*, thought the perennial subordinate, returning to the driver's seat in the truck to
wait for his bailed boss.

GOD's superintendent, after much huffing exertion, finally
made it up the crater wall road to the truck and flopped back into
the passenger seat. He was a mess. His frazzled hair and sweat
streaked face were encrusted in dust and his suit was totally rumpled, soiled and torn in several places. A bloody knee protruded
through one of the rips. He took a few moments to regain his
breath and then, **"Why the hell didn't you come back down for
me? I'm in charge here, boy, and I don't walk for anybody!
You got that!?"** Rossy had no response to this inanity, not even a
generic 'yes, sir', and sat wordlessly, staring blankly straight
ahead through the grimy windshield, awaiting orders from his
ship-abandoning captain. **"Let's go!! We're done here!"** They
rode silently back to the Wideawake Field office, where the visiting junior fed had to endure a rabid lecture on insubordination,
warning he was less than a hair's width away from deportation,
before receiving his IDL and AI operator's permit. The conde-
scending counsel to de-chip his shoulder conjured unpleasant
memories. He was then told to wash and clean the truck in return

for it's key and use while on the island. Mr. Richardson reminded the engineer to keep him advised of progress and to coordinate all application of GOD's support resources in advance. Dismissed.

***

After lunch, the planted operative began to wonder where his contact was. He had been in-country for almost twenty-four hours, and nothing. There was no one at the dining hall, or anywhere else he had been, who resembled anything like an asset Saint. He knew he had to get a *special bean* fix soon, or he would lose track of the target and probably be fired. But he also had some engineering cover work to do, so he decided to go back out to his assigned work station in a small tech office at the Wideawake terminal building. In looking at an island topo map, it appeared the optimum location for in-skiffing airfield repair materials would be South West Bay, between McArthur and Portland Points. The project would require barging some 40,000 tons of asphalt, sand, aggregate and oil from an anchored, off-shore freighter. Conveyors would need to be set up to off-load the barges and move the materials to a staging area at the airfield. Temporary power and water utilities would have to be designed and installed to accommodate the logistical support operations. Any heavy equipment needed to perform the repair work could be brought in by air. It would definitely be a major, complicated exercise and not an undertaking in which he, nor his limited, unqualified background, should have anything to do with. But since the project was bogus, there was no way he could screw it up.

The most obvious first thing to do was make a visual survey of the site in the field. This shouldn't be too difficult, in that the small bay was within short walking distance of the west end of the airfield. The engineer filled a water bottle from a lobby cooler, noticing there was no beer machine *(GOD must not have a sunshine fund)*, and headed out the door. The weather was spectacular - clear, dry, 72 - as it typically was most days here, from what he had been told. He found a drainage arroyo running from the end corner of the tarmac down to the sea. The bed of the swale was worn, fairly smooth and easily walkable, unlike the adjacent sidewalls, which rose up in precipitous scarps of rugged, uneven lava configurations. He figured the bay beach to be roughly half a kilometer away, as the crow flies, but maybe not as the water runs.

About ten minutes into the trek, the hikester saw movement in the path ahead and slowed to observe what he was coming up on. In reaching closer range, he was astonished to see four monstrous crabs across his passage way, haunched back on hind leg sets with clapping pincers waving in front. The orange, pie-sized land crustaceans stood nearly half a foot off the ground and were not intimidated by the approach of the bipod intruder. Something told the stranger it would probably be unwise to try walking through these creatures and it was out of the question to skirt the roadblock off the walkway, so he picked up and threw rocks at them. The island homies scattered quickly into small cave fissures in the swale walls and the engineer hustled by. Looking back, he saw the crabs re-emerge to monitor his divergence down the slope. Only now, there were more than four. He counted at least ten. *Holy christ!! Do they communicate with each other?! This place is crazy!! Did my flight go into the twilight zone and warp out on a different planet?!?* Rossy knew he had to retrace through this area on the way back and made a mental note to arm himself with a stick or something. Then he remembered the meat donkeys. What if they came down to do a little crab stomping and found him boxed up in the lower arroyo? *Oh, god, please don't let that happen!!*

Expelling such terrifying images from his thought cache, the exploring engineer continued down the gully and soon stepped out onto a narrow, crescent shaped expanse of green obsidian sand. Sunlight reflected off the smooth beach surface into a twinkling array of pale color, slightly suggestive of a ground bound auroral effect. It was a beautifully unusual scene, almost moonscape like, provoking the visitor to reach for his phone cam. Rimming the high side of the beach was a network of randomly shaped tidal pools carved into the cascading lava rock, some holding several feet of crystal clear water containing autonomous ecosystems of aquatic vegetation and animal life. Curiously peering into one of the larger pools, the beach boy saw what looked like a thick, brown and white snake partially submerged on the jagged side-wall. It was perfectly unmoving and appeared to be lifeless. Glancing around and spotting an old wooden broom handle wedged into a nearby pile of debris along the tidal reach, he retrieved the stick, which he would thankfully keep for crab defense, and reached over the edge of the pool to test the snake. Nothing, but it felt rather firm, not dead and decaying mushy. He poked again, near the facing head. Instantaneously, the mottled serpent lashed toward its antagonist with lightning speed. The inquisitive prodder recoiled just as fast, losing his footing and falling backwards. A cranium bounce off the compacted sand, less than a foot from a protrusion of sharp rock, ignited an explosion of stars through his consciousness. He stood up, shakily, and staggered back to the pool to get another look at the again motionless sea snake. Thorough visual scrutiny led to the tentative conclusion he was dealing with *muraena helena*, a species of moray eel. And a big one, too, he thought, trapped forever in this little natural aquarium. Should he try to set it free? It belonged in the ocean, but it could never get out of the deep sided pool on its own. Lacking the means to assist the eel without getting bitten, the pragmatic one decided to let it be and tend to his own problem of evaluating the area for suitability in supporting the fake airfield retrofit project.

The bay appeared clear of promontory rocks and the surf was relatively subdued in what would naturally be the optimum operational zone between the beach and an off-shore anchorage site. The water abruptly changed color from pastel teal to a darker aqua hue several hundred yards out, indicating a drop-off in depth. There was apparent line-of-sight between the two points forming the bay and the barging area of interest, that should easily serve siting for the navaids control stations. He would have to solicit GOD's tech support in tracking the century sounding contour, after which the hydrographic survey plan could be easily sketched. So, without a great deal of effort, or time, he should be able to generate enough info to prepare a project brief that would convince Mr. Richardson his cover mission was real. By then, sometime tomorrow, his *special bean* contact should be made and he would be able to file an update to CIA. The engineering agent was proud of himself. *I'm out here doing it, man!* **This** *is what I'm talking about!* It occurred to him that his short stint of PNAS duty had provided valuable experience to perform solo here in the field and he was thankful to red Ryder for that. He wondered how Booker was doing. He should call tonight.

The field planner pulled a pen and small pad from his backpack and made some notes on his observations and recorded an accompanying video scan. He then took a swig of water, picked up the broom stick and prepared to hike back up the swale. After snapping several still shots of the stationary eel, he started toward the rise, marveling how the creature could remain that consciously inanimate for so long. He knew, for certain, he couldn't do it, especially if trapped in a pit of saltwater, filled with spiny sea urchins and possibly dangerous tropical fish and poisonous microbes. Gradually, he heard the high, distant drone of an approaching aircraft. The Dopplered sound increased in intensity behind the nearing plane, which gave no indication of preparation to land. The former roo watched the assumed C-17 fly far overhead, across the island and off into the troposphere to the southeast. He continued to watch until the diminishing engine rumble faded away and nothing remained but the dissipating contrail. *That's odd*, he thought. *Wonder where the hell they're going? There's nothing out there.* Redirecting his concentration to backtracking up to the airfield without being attacked by crabs, or crab hunting donkeys, the wayfarer picked a careful route, stick in hand poised to strike anything that moved, while keeping an acute eye all around, ahead and behind. He went on high alert in nearing the point of earlier skirmish, but saw nothing in this return passthrough. They must be watching, though, from their hidden bunkers, like crusty little guerrillas, because there's no way they're gone. Onward and upward. Above and beyond. Soon he was safely on the tarmac and walking toward the terminal.

Mr. Richardson looked up from paperwork on his desk upon hearing the timid tap on the open office door. He scowled at the sight of the insubordinate federal kid standing in the corridor. "What is it, Rossy? Better be good. I'm really busy, right now."

"Yes, sir, Mr. Richardson," began the insubordinate subordinate, distracted in noticing his AI driver's ed teacher had not straightened up from this morning's debacle on the crater road. He was still dust coated in the same bedraggled and torn suit. He hadn't even washed his face! "Uh...I was just wondering, I have to locate the hundred foot depth line along South West Bay and I'll need a small boat with a portable transponder and someone to ride me out there. It shouldn't take more than a couple hours."

"OK, be down at the pedestrian landing, in Georgetown, at 0900 tomorrow. GOD's welder, Wilson, will meet you there and he'll take care of whatever you need. Now, if you'll excuse me, I really don't have any more time to be interrupted."

"Thank you, sir." Rossy retreated back down the hallway and went outside to his sparkling clean truck. He had worked on it more than an hour to finally pass the super's inspection and get the key. This, after several failures for insignificant deficiencies like a few stones on the floor mats, or smudged sideview mirrors. He had felt like a contestant on the *Amazing Race* reality show, trying to do some impossible cultural chore over and over for approval to receive a clue. But that was behind him and he was now free to move around the island and take care of business. First, back to the barracks, take a shower and go to dinner. Hopefully, the contact would manifest and he could advance on *special bean*. Whatever, he still needed to check in with Booker this evening.

The free agent was on the sidewalk to his room from the barracks parking lot, when he detected the faraway rolling rumble of distant jets. He looked up and saw the large cargo craft descending from the southeast sky toward Wideawake. With reflection of the afternoon sun, it looked like a giant meteor drifting in slo-mo to landfall. He watched until it went below the sightline and soon heard the deafening roar of the reverse thrust on the runway, before the silence of a successful landing. This had to be the plane he had seen fly past the island earlier. That was, like, two hours ago?? They must have been on total auto-sleep and overflown by at least an hour. Talk about a major FIAC-up. How far would they have gone if they hadn't awakened and found out they were lost in space? Past Africa to Antarctica? *Ground Control To Major Tom!!* Rossy considered that this was the second flight into Ascension in two days. Did they run daily flights here? Seemed like a lot, but if they overflew into oblivion with any frequency, maybe not.

Another *special bean* contact blank at the dining hall, though the chipmole enjoyed about the best Beef Wellington he had ever tasted. The food prep here was five-star, arguably world class and not contracted out to a franchise. There was no Golden Paddock buffet within probably five thousand miles. GOD's master chefs and kitchen specialists provided a true culinary reward for company employees willing to live and work in such extreme isolation. Definitely a valuable job perk. But where the hell was the dining hall asset? There were a lot of Saints on staff here and one of them was supposed to make contact. The visiting operative couldn't go around and code prompt them all to find his guy. It had to be the other way around. He thought about calling esuper Dick to get some direction, but decided to wait one more day. Instead, he called Booker.

"Hey, man, what's happenin'?"

"Who's this?"

"Booker, it's me, dawg, your roomie."

"Seve?? Where are you? Are you in town, yet?"

"No, man, it's **Rossy**. Don't you recognize my voice??"

"Rossy!! Jesus christ, where the hell are **you**, bro?! You fracking disappeared. Did you quit or get kidnapped, or something?? What the hell's going on?"

"What d'ya mean? Didn't Dick explain I was reassigned?"

"Hell, no! Nobody told us anything. Red was so pissed she called Blackburn to have you terminated. He said he would check into it, but never called back. Then she thought something happened to you, so she reported you missing to the PNAS police. So, you've been reassigned? Where to?"

"Can't talk about it. It's classified. You might think I'm out of the country, but you didn't hear that from me. Nobody told red anything?"

"No, man. She just wrote you off as the frack-off she says she had you pegged for right from the start. Now she's busting my ass to take up the slack. I'm puttin' in about fifteen hour days, man. It really sucks. Why the hell did you stick me like this??"

"I'm sorry, dude, but it wasn't my call. Hey, you said something about Smith in town? What's going on there?"

"Yeah, he's on his way back. Change in his orders. He should be here anytime. He didn't know when he's going back out, so maybe it's good you're gone so we don't stack up in the apartment."

"Cool. So what's going on at PNAS? How's the program going?"

"It's OK. Like I said, a lot of work, but everything's going OK. We had a problem with Matas, the Nicaraguan dude. He got in a fight with some Mexican guy in a bar in town and was arrested. He claimed immunity again and the police complained to the PNAS commander, who then put in a complaint to SECNAV. Then the state department got involved and, all of a sudden, Matas is gone. No loss. He wasn't doing anything anyway. He was a waste of time. Red's been tied up a lot with environmental paperwork over the gas spill, but we got the **INVINCIBLE** fixed. I took it out today to check the tide gauges with Lt. Machado, the Brazilian dude you got stranded with? It's funny, he didn't seem to wonder where you were. It was sort of like he knew, but I didn't press him, because he's kinda hard to talk to. I think he's self conscious about his English. I don't know. So how long are you going to be out, man? Anything you need me to do on the home front, here?"

Bj explained he didn't know how long he would be gone. He asked shiner to remit his loan payments, because he hadn't gotten around to setting up auto-payment on the phone. The payment slips and checkbook were in a box in a corner of gameboy's room. Booker could just copy his signature on the checks. Nobody would ever know the difference. He also told him the car keys were in the box and said he should use the Civic as much as he wanted. The federal sailors closed out by promising to stay in touch. Rossy started to feel familiar pangs of worry. His party chief wanted to fire him and the NAVOSUR director didn't seem to know where he was. It was like nobody was talking to each other and he was getting lost in the shuffle. How could this possibly end well?

***

Morning erupted into yet another blue sky day. If AI wasn't so far away from everything else on earth, it would be unaffordable to live here. Skipping breakfast, the nascent hydrographer drove into Georgetown, on the west coast, about two miles north of the base. The town's hub was centered around a long structure of steps chiseled into the lava stone down to a large concrete platform a few feet above the water. The pedestrian landing. He parked the truck in a small side lot almost at cliff's edge and walked over toward the steps, where a blue jumpsuited workman was busy welding a steel frame assembly together. Approaching this activity, Rossy noticed the red-bordered, oval white patch sewn on the upper left front of the welder's suit, with **'WILSON'** embroidered in the middle. This was GOD's tech support and he was better than right on time. The engineer stood watching as Wilson finished the piece he was working on, turned off the arc and lifted his mask. "How ya doing? I'm Rossy, from NAVOSUR. Mr. Richardson told me to meet you here."

"Yeah, Wilson. How's it going?"

The two shook introductory hands and Wilson explained he was fabricating a frame to hold the transponder over the water from the side of the Boston whaler they would be using to collect the field data. The small outboard craft was tied up down at the landing platform. He had already loaded a battery, cables, clamps and the portable sounding instrumentation on the boat. All they needed to do was pick up some lunch sandwiches and they would be good to go. Rossy was impressed. Wilson seemed to know much more about what they were going to do than he did. After moving the welding equipment to Wilson's nearby truck, they went over to a ramshackle structure on the far side of the town square plaza. Cecil's Center Cafe was an open front affair, featuring a sizable, tarp-covered patio furnished with several mismatched plastic table and chair sets. Lucky Dube's *Remember Me* wafted out comfortably from inside, where a group of off-duty Saints sat playing dominoes and drinking John Bull ale. Looking around, the newtimer noticed a battered pool table and a couple video games at one end of the room and three old desktop pc's on metal work stands at the other. A narrow, formica bar-counter paralleled the back wall, behind which was a small kitchen. Evidently, the establishment was an all in one restaurant, pub, arcade and internet cafe. On the sand colored, wood plank floor, guarding the back bar access, lay a sleeping dingo dog, that no doubt would tear apart any unauthorized patron trying to get past. The engineer followed the welder to the end of the counter where a chubby, ruddy-faced man, wearing an underwear tee-shirt, khaki cargo shorts and a badly soiled waist apron, sat reading a week old issue of The Daily Star. "What's up, Cecil?" greeted GOD's welder.

"Well, I say, if it isn't my good chap, Wilson! How are you this fine work-a-day, sir?" smiled the accommodating Brit proprietor.

"Doing well, Cec, doing well. Look, my friend, what are the chances of getting a couple sausage egg biscuits and pints to go?"

"I would say quite good, sir, quite good, indeed. I am at your service." Cecil rose from his stool and lumbered into the kitchen. The dog stirred, flapping a sinewy tail on the floor. The carry-outers sat at the counter to wait. Rossy was curious how long Wilson had worked for GOD, on AI. The thirties-something welder disclosed he had been here six years, ever since getting out of the company trade school as an apprentice. Before that he served two tours with the army, in Yemen and Afghanistan, but couldn't find a job back in the world. So he signed on with GOD, who was always looking for overseas workers. He loved it. They paid incredibly well, all tax free, and he had no cost of living. He figured he could pretty much set himself up, financially, in three more years. Afterwards, he didn't know where he would end up. There wasn't much for him in the states, no family or commitments. He might go to Europe, or maybe Africa. The younger, non-vet wondered if it got boring on the island, so far out in the middle of the ocean? Not a problem, continued the welder, who seemed more than eager to talk about his situation. He got free, round trip transport, plus expenses, to either Nigeria, or Brazil, for a week off every two months. They didn't have to take leave, but were strongly urged to do so by the human resources people. It occurred to the junior fedster that the dude had been gone so long he might have actually lost his place in American culture. Possibly, not a bad thing, considering the reverse evolvement of the homeland in recent years. *Jesus, maybe I could work for GOD, if the CIA gig gets too hot, or I'm fired from NAVOSUR. That would be a good way to pay off my loans. Hell, I can learn how to weld.* In short span, Cecil returned with the order. Wilson paid with American currency and the survey duo sauntered back out onto the plaza.

While walking toward the landing steps, the engineer gazed out on the ocean fanning infinitely before them. He was surprised in seeing an enormous, gray ship, quiet in the water, about a half mile off-shore. Wilson said it was a British Royal Navy warship that had come in overnight. He said Mr. Richardson and the island governor had gone out to greet and receive the BRN captain and ship's crew. They pushed off earlier, around 0815, on a flat decked shuttle barge from the landing pad below. The welder was chuckling out loud as he offered this info and his new associate, not hearing anything particularly humorous in the story, asked what was so funny? Wilson said he was thinking of the last time a navy ship came in, about three years ago, when the big guy had gone out to officially meet and greet, just like this morning. A large swell passed as he was trying to climb up the gunwale cargo netting to the high deck above and he lost his hold and fell back into the drink. Then he had gone through the welcoming protocol soaking, dripping wet, giving the assembled visiting sailors a good laugh. Rossy, imagining Mr. Richardson pompously extolling his role as an important local dignitary in an ocean drenched suit, acting as though nothing was out of the ordinary, also snickered at the welder's recollection.

The two workers made their way down the steep steps carrying the still welded-warm instrument frame. They lifted it onto the whaler and Wilson began the task of mounting the transponder on the frame before securing the assembly to the bulwark. Then they would connect the power pack and calibrate the unit through a wireless, handheld display, against the visual pole gauge installed on the landing. This would take at least a half hour and there was nothing for the engineer to do other than follow the orders of his tech support. After paying close attention to the progress for about twenty minutes, Rossy looked out toward the anchored ship. "What is that?!" he immediately blurted out, as much to himself as to his companion. Wilson turned away from the task detail and followed his client's gaze seaward. "Oh my god," exclaimed the welder. "I don't believe this." They goggled at the approaching shuttle barge, loaded with BRN sailors dressed in shore leave whites. Most wore long pants, but some were in shorts and knee socks and all sported their cockney round hats and precisely tied navy neckerchiefs. They looked like a boatload of large little kids being conveyed to church. Mr. Richardson was perched at the front of the barge, alongside the governor, staring stoically ahead as the shuttle rose and fell on ground swells in its advance toward the landing. *In his dark suit, he stands out like a black pope in a white pizza*, thought the former assistant trainer, reminded of red Ryder on the Solomon's ferry to PNAS.

"Those swabbies are going to frack this town up before the end of the day," Wilson cynically predicted.

"Why do you say that?" queried his task mate.

"Because I've seen it before. You never let a boatload of Brit sailors, who've been confined in close quarters for an extended period of time, go loose anywhere, especially where they can get alcohol. They'll spend three hours getting monkeyass drunk and another three hours beating the British crap out of each other. There could be a couple that don't make it out alive. I don't think Cec knows they're coming in."

"Think we should tell him?"

"Nah. He'll be good. He's got his own Saint mafia to protect the cafe. He'll probably sell out and take a month off."

"Maybe the donkeys'll get 'em."

"Donkeys? What the hell does that mean?"

"I don't know. Nothing. Just a joke." The young standby was instantly embarrassed for mentioning the donkeys. Wilson didn't seem to know what he was talking about, so maybe Mr. Richardson had played his naive visitor, big time. For what? Laughs? The super never even gave a hint of a smirk in warning about the donkeys and had left the whole whacky issue open ended. So where was the 'gotcha' fun? Besides, GOD's island boss took himself way too seriously to goof about anything. As far as the butt-end rookie was concerned, joke, or no joke, he would be watching his back against the killer donkeys for as long as he was on AI, which, hopefully, wouldn't be much longer.

The whaler crew was finishing up the prep work and getting ready to head out, just as the shuttle barge pulled in. They watched the pilot secure the moorings, while Mr. Richardson skipped onto the landing pad ahead of everyone else. He walked sternly past the smaller craft toward the steps, without a glance, nod, or word of acknowledgement to his subordinates. Wilson quickly turned his head away, trying desperately to stifle a roaring gut laugh, upon seeing that the superintendent was thoroughly waterlogged from head to toe. His leather wingtips made a squeaky squishy sound with each step and he had a wide strand of soggy kelp stuck to the back shoulder of his jacket. Rossy choked on his own erupting guffaw, concluding, without any trace of doubt, that Mr. Richardson truly *was* boardinghouse dumb. The following sailors were more affable in shambling past the two Americans. "Hey, mates. Can ya kindly point us to the nearest pub?" The welder smiled and gestured in the direction of the steps. Let the mayhem begin.

***

Conditions could not have been better for the mission at hand. Essentially no wind, calm surf and a totally cloudless sky. The sun might be the only problem. It was surely going to be hot out on the water. The NAVO swabbie thought if his mom was here he would not be allowed to do this without first applying about half a tube of sunscreen to all bare skin. He hated the greasy, noxious stuff, because, growing up, he, like most white children of his generation, was never permitted to be in the sun without protection. There had been a highly successful marketing blitz by the sunscreen industry convincing parents their kids would suffer a lifelong risk of melanoma with only ten minutes unshielded exposure to natural radiation. If you didn't lather the defenseless youngsters with copious amounts of their expensive product, you were an irresponsible parent. Then reports came out that adolescents were developing vitamin D deficiencies, because the screening lotion blocked the catalytic role of sunlight in absorption of vital nutrients. The consumer was left dangling with the dilemma of negating the evolution of human physiology to avoid the Big C. The answer, of course, at least as far as the adult, logically trained Rossy was concerned, was move to shade before od'ing on sun and forget the screen. The problem here, though, was no shade on the little boat. And there was no sunscreen. He would probably get a good vitamin D bump today, hopefully, without cancer.

It was about a four mile run to the survey area, taking almost an hour. The cove in and out from South West Bay looked the same as yesterday. They were able to easily locate the century depth and set about tracking it in both directions across the bay opening. The engineer noted the position of the contour relative to adjacent landmarks, completing the information needed to sketch the project planning area. It only took a little over forty-five minutes to finish the task, after which they dismantled the transponder assembly and brought it back into the boat.

Lunchtime. They broke out the cafe carryouts while adrift on the gentle swells. There was no sound other than the quiet lapping of water against the side hull of the boat. Looking outward, the sea spread like a vast gray blanket of nothing to the distant edge, as the BRN ship was not visible beyond the curvature of the coast. The mainlander observed there were no birds. Every time he could ever recall having a saltwater picnic, the gulls converged like flying ants to pick up any edible morsel that might fall free. Wilson remarked that ratbirds had not yet reached Ascension. Maybe in another ten millennia. But they were not alone. Countless dark colored fish, about the size of large bluegills, swirled all around the boat. Noticing his crew mate eyeing the fish, the welder said, "Watch this!" and threw a piece of sandwich into the water. The surface went into an instant boil, as fish darted in from all directions to get a share of the discarded sliver of food. He reached in and grabbed one of the frenzied feeders and lifted it easily into the boat. It was all black with a small red circle on the gill, reminiscent of a blackbird. In fact it was called a blackfish and was endemic to Ascension. They were in the shallows encircling the island. The former fly fisherman had never heard of a fish quite like this and wondered what would happen if you got in the water with them? Would they rip you up into a bloody soup like piranha? "No," explained the AI veteran, "they only go after dead stuff, and they don't have sharp teeth. Take a look." He opened the mouth of the blackfish, revealing two protruding rows of small, flat-edged incisor-like teeth, that seemed relatively harmless. This made them impossible to catch, because a hook would just slide off. Not that anyone would want to catch them - they weren't really edible.

Wilson threw the blackfish back in the froth and turned to start the motor. Feeling a bit like an eco-tour guide, he said he wanted to show his visitor something special. They churned slowly southward in the direction of McArthur Point. Passing the jagged promontory, the welder maneuvered the craft coastward, where another beach area was visible. About halfway in, he cut the motor and they again drifted with the soft swells. The water was spectacularly clear and they could easily see the rugged bed of the island shelf. After wordlessly peering all around into the turquoise shoal for several minutes, the welder guide emphatically pointed down off the leeward side of the boat. The tourist followed the cue and fixed instantly on the pale form of a giant green sea turtle moving slowly shoreward through the water at least ten feet down. With flipper feet extended from under the massive shell, it was almost ghostlike in its graceful motion and very big, maybe four feet across. Wilson expounded on the life and times of the mighty turtle and Ascension's important function in its migratory and reproductive patterns. He said this area of the island was where they seemed to like to hang out, probably for favorable temperature and current conditions, and they were lucky to see one. The tourist fed reached for his phone cam, having never witnessed a live sea turtle in its natural habitat before. They watched until the swimming shellback faded from view, like a mystical illusion, then started back around the point for return to Georgetown.

About halfway home, the sailor agent, sitting on the prow bench of the whaler and lazily watching the island coastline go slowly by from left to right, noticed what looked like a long shadow following in the water off the starboard side. He leaned over to get a better look when a sudden surface eruption revealed the head of a porpoise arcing into the air. They made brief eye contact, before the huge mammal fish re-submerged. It continued swimming alongside the boat, with its dorsal fin exposed less than an arm's length away! Impulsively, the enraptured passenger reached over and grabbed onto the fin. It felt sort of slimy rough and very strong. The human sensed the immense power of this familiar denizen of the sea and thought it could easily flip their boat if it wanted to. But he doubted that would happen, because there didn't seem to be any hostility related to the big boy's behavior. It actually seemed more playful than anything. Looking further out around the boat and its wake the coast runners realized they were surrounded by a sizable pod of the acrobatic surf riders. The entire ensemble of people and porpoises was swimming and motoring along in formation at the same speed. The fringe podsters dipped in and out of the wet in smooth, seemingly effortless crescents, while the incredible insider stayed close to the boat, allowing the alien to keep a hold on its fin. Rossy was almost in tears from excitement. This was the largest wild animal he had ever touched! In a few moments, the congenial aquameister broke loose with a very dynamic 360 alligator roll and accelerated forward. About one length ahead, it raised a wide, T-shaped tail web high into the air and slapped the water with sufficient force to shower its new friend with cold brine. As the mini-whale veered away from the boat track with another leaping air dive, the slack-jawed hydrographer swore it looked back and smiled. And then they were all gone. As quickly as they first appeared, they vanished. The crew mates high-fived over this unique experience, declaring it a lifetime highlight and the morning mission, therefore, a mega success. The remainder of the run back to the Georgetown quay was unremarkable.

***

The pedestrian landing was not the same as when the whalers had pushed off earlier. There were a number of BRN sailors slumped on the stone steps and several others sprawled on the pad. A few were prone still on the shuttle barge deck. One matelot was laid out on the concrete with his head over the bulkhead, hurling into the water. Their uniforms were dirty, ripped and bloodied and broken glass was everywhere. A few of the goodtimers appeared to be seriously injured, their faces looking like they did punching bag duty in an unequipped fight gym. The ex-Connecticutian remembered the brutal Chickenfeets brawl, in Hartford, and thought this might be worse, though probably with less property damage.

With only their fists, there wasn't much the debarked sailors could do to damage the stone and concrete appurtenances. The surveyors locked the outboard and the mooring chain and hoisted the equipment to carry out of the lower PL area. Making their way up the steps among the wasted swabs was no easy task and they had to strategically place every step to avoid tripping off the unrailed edge. Near the top, one of the bloodied seaman looked up, both eyes almost shut in swollen contusion, and blankly smirked, "Thanks, yanks. We found yer pubs, alright. Nice isle ye got here."

The plaza square above was likewise littered with grayshippers in varying states of alcoholic destruction. The techsters moved quickly to their fortunately intact trucks and drove directly back to the base, where, thankfully, no BRN sailors had infiltrated. In departing Georgetown, the Americans noticed CCC was closed and shuttered. Later in the afternoon, the battered shore leavers were efficiently rounded up by BRN police, with no ICU casualties and all hands accounted for, and barged back out to the warship. Once the crew was reembarked, the vessel cut ties with the anchor buoy and left the island, well under twenty-four hours post arrival. Apparently their brief layover had been solely therapeutic and the mission was accomplished in not much longer than it took a fifteen stone bloke to get monkeyass drunk.

***

Upon return to the barracks room, Rossy noticed, while showering and cleaning up, that he had not gotten too sunburned out on the water. His arms and legs were a little red, but nothing was blistering burnt. He then took a light nap, awakening in time for dinner. He was somewhat nervous about going to the dining hall, because he had decided this would be the last time to come up empty on making *special bean* contact, before calling esuper Dick for supplementary instructions. Calling the handler meant complications and that could only result in life being more difficult, if not more dangerous.

To the sailor agent's dismay, there was again no dining hall asset manifestation, though he enjoyed an exquisite blackened sea bass entree, featuring grilled red potatoes and asparagus tips in a mellow peanut sauce. Being particularly hungry, he topped off with a full monte banana split sundae. Afterwards, he decided to go to the nearby base club and movie theater, for a few brews to help prepare for the Dick call. He hadn't been to this facility yet, though he was aware of it's existence. His focus had been the dining hall. The club bar was a large horseshoe shaped structure of heavy hardwood construction. It sat in the middle of a spacious room that seemed comfortably cozy, despite it's size. The forward walls were covered with NASA and air force space memorabilia, dating back to the early days of the Gemini program. The usual barroom furnishings, accessories and amenities were present, except the far back wall of the facility held a nearly IMAX sized movie screen. GOD obtained all box office flicks, within a week of release, for the entertainment of base employees and stationed military personnel. They ran two showings daily in full hi-def, with the latest digital 3D display equipment. Another AI employment perk. The club was essentially empty, just a couple people at a remote table away from the bar zone. Most patrons came in later, at showtime. The worried agent sat down at the bulge of the bar and ordered a draft Yuengling. He was surprised they had such an obscure American discount beer and confirmed its authenticity with the first gagging taste. It was not his intention to drink much before the call. He noticed the Saint tender looking at him rather intently from down at the open end of the bar, but didn't think much about it as he planned how he would phrase his queries to the esuper. *How do I find the asset contact? If I can't find the contact, where do I go? Back to Washington? Should I ask anyone else about special bean? If so, who? And how do I approach them if they don't know the contact code?* And on and on. The questions are complicated, each one having the potential to send him in a different direction. Ambiguous covert activity is not easy, especially for an engineer trained in reason and fact.

Not long after the chipmole became lost in thought diagramming his mission status and future, two men came in and sat down at the bar on adjacent stools to his right. The agent was a little annoyed they sat in such close proximity, when the whole fracking bar was open, but quickly recognized, in hearing their voices, his previously unseen barracks neighbors. Drunk and drunker. Still here and still arguing with each other. He tried to ignore them, after their drinks were served, and went back to his mental prep work. Soon, a conspicuous silence shook him into realizing the two were not speaking and were looking at him. Evidently, one had asked him a question and they were waiting for a response. "I'm sorry, what did you say?"

"I ask why you yanks are so duppy downpress on Afrikaners?"

So they are South African. "I don't know what you mean. I've got nothing against South Africa."

"I don't think so. You see Afrikaans as always apartheid. We have killed apartheid!"

"Hey, no problem, man. I don't know anything about that. I've never been to Africa, but I'm sure it's beautiful, OK?"

"You patronize me!! Do you think your American apartheid - what is it, John Crow? - was not so bad as Afrikaans apartheid, and that makes you superior to us? You are a pingo, yank, you are a filthy American pingo!!"

Rossy didn't know what to say. He had never encountered a situation where somebody he'd never seen before was pissed off at him just because he was an American. *Oh, god! Is this a rules violation?? Am I going to be thrown off the island? Be very careful, here. This dude is way drunk.* "Look, every country has issues, but no country is better than another because of issues."

"Well, maybe I will solve the issue by whippin' your pingo American ass!"

"**Hey! That's enough!**" shouted the tender, stepping quickly forward to address the developing confrontation at his bar. "You two caused trouble in here last night and you're not going to do it again tonight! Now get out, before I call security!"

Drunk and drunker rose slowly from their seats, glaring at the tender. "You stupid Saint!!You are a bigger pingo than any American, because you are slave for the Americans! You are nothing!! I should spit in your face!! The Afrikaners moved slowly away from the bar and turned to leave. By the time they staggered to the door, they were, once again, yelling at each other. The American thought it would probably be another long night of noise at the barracks room. He looked at the Saint. "Thanks, sir, I appreciate it. I think that guy really wanted to fight, or something. I don't know what that was all about, but you really bailed me. Thanks again."

"No problem. They are South African air force pilots. They come here on training maneuvers every couple of months, get drunk for a few days and fly back. So.....what's in it for me?"

"Uh, gees, OK,.....can I buy you a drink?"

"No, listen carefully....what's in it for me?"

Agent Rossy felt a clanging bell go off in his head. *Jesus christ!! This is my ops asset!! Why isn't he in the dining hall, like Dick told me?!?* "I don't know. You tell me."

"Yes, Mr. Rossy, we finally meet. I thought we would contact sooner, but you did not come in here until now."

"I was told you worked in the dining hall. I was looking for you there."

"I understand. My job changed. Saints are shifted around all the time here, but everybody coming to the island usually ends up in this place within half a day. We have lost valuable time."

"OK, make it rain. What do you have?" The operative was totally relieved to have made his contact. Now he would not have to call Dick. He could get the update, file the report and move on. But the esuper was going to have to give him better intel. He just lost two days and almost got some more unwanted dental work, while trying to find something he had no way of looking for. *Bummer,* he thought.

"Yes, well, the crazy Afrikaner spoke a little bit of truth. Saints here *are* treated like slaves, by both the Americans and the Brits. Long hours, low wage and no chance at any of the high paying tech jobs, for which some of us are well qualified for. We have good schools on St. Helena and many people advance their learning through on-line education programs, particularly in computer and information technology. Could our geographic isolation produce world class cyber hacks? I don't know, but maybe your target of interest thinks so. Maybe. Word is he talked to some people here in Georgetown and then moved on to St. Helena."

"Is he still there?"

"I don't know. There are daily shuttle flights, but he would have to come back here to leave the dependency."

"Is there any video?"

"No, they say he insists on no video, no cams, no devices of any kind in his meetings. He only speaks to a few people at a time and he leaves specific instructions to protect anonymity."

"Well, what is he talking to people about?"

"Freedom. A new world alliance. Equality. Tearing down and rebuilding. He would have a good audience in St. Helena. There are no jobs there. That's why people come to Ascension. They leave their families for extended periods of time to work here, but we are like contract workers. They deduct our pay for transport and cost of living and there is not much left to take home and support our people. Yes, Mr. Rossy, there is discontent in this unknown, forgotten part of the world, and like I said, the Saints have hidden skills, ripe to be exploited by a clever organizer."

"Where would he go from here?"

"It is thought he was interested in Greece, but I cannot confirm that."

"Anything else? Anything at all that works toward identifying this guy?"

"No, that is all I have for you and I cannot be seen talking with you any longer. People are starting to come in and you should leave. Say 'hi' to your uncle for me and tell him to send money!"

***

The contacted agent wanted to go directly into town and upfile an ops report. He figured he could use a computer at Cecil's, but remembered the cafe was closed after the BRN drunksters went through. He would go first thing in the morning. Tonight should be spent in working up the airfield project. Even if the project was pretend, he had managed to collect enough rudimentary data to prepare a summary overview for programming purposes, in case anyone ever decided to actually pursue the effort. He hated open ends and this would be a total incomplete if he didn't pull something together to submit to GOD's superintendent. Besides, if he just left without some kind of tangible result, Mr. Richardson would probably wonder what he was *really* doing here and that could lead to security issues. Yes, a concept submittal was imperative to protect his cover, even though it hadn't been specifically directed by esuper Dick. As the planning engineer started organizing the field notes, he thought of his development work at PWA, remembering how the subgroup leader dick stole his test study. More than likely, that would happen again here, if the airfield rehab project did, in fact, materialize. He might as well just sign Mr. Richardson's name on it right up front. It surprisingly occurred to the pursuer that he had a major similarity with *special bean*. They both were highly anonymous, maybe even ambiguous.

***

The next morning, Rossy was up and running before sunrise, which was somewhat dulled by a high cloud cover. He was hungry after stressing through three days of hide and seek in finding the AI asset and decided to heavy up on breakfast at the dining hall. The kitchen eggman delivered a beautiful custom omelet, served with baked Texas toast and tabasco sauce, that could coax an atheist to baptism. On the way out of his room to the walkway crossing in front of other rooms in his barracks block, he was aware of the silence. There was no noise, or loud voices, no sound at all, coming from any of the adjacent rooms, including that of the fighting Afrikaners. As a matter of fact, as he thought about it, there hadn't been a peep from their room all night long and it looked like they were gone. Did they go back to South Africa after they were thrown out of the club? How could that be? They were too plastered to walk, let alone fly! Maybe they turned the plane over to FIAC and let the computer worry about the pilot stuff while they both flew off into the lost horizon together. Whatever, the yank was good with the apartheid pilot dudes gone, because if they were still here, they would probably beat him up at some point - just for being an American.

Upon arriving at Georgetown's plaza square, the *special bean* operative was relieved to find CCC's front shutters open and people inside. He parked the truck and walked through the plaza into the cafe, noticing the same static activity as when he and the welder were here before. A group of Saints sat at a table drinking stout and playing dominos and Cecil was plopped on a stool at the end of the counter, reading the paper. The dog was asleep on the floor. A *Groundhog Day* rerun scenerio, except all was quiet - no music, TV, video - nothing. The secret agent man approached the proprietor, feeling the eyes of the Saints on his back, and sat down on an adjacent bar stool. An almost imperceptible *grrr* from the floor mutt. "Good morning, Mr. Cecil, how are you today?"

"Well, if it isn't Wilson's apprentice chap? I am quite fine, thank you, and top of the morn to you, sir. How might I be of your service today, me lad?"

"Yes, I was wondering if I could use one of your computers, there, to send an e-mail. It's too long to text out on my phone and I remembered from yesterday seeing you had an internet cafe here, so, could that be a go?"

"Yessir, no problem. Your homeland jackson's good for thirty minutes, payable in front."

Whew! A little steep, but no choice. "OK, any particular unit you want me to use?" Rossy laid the bill out on the counter.

"No, any one will do. The password is 'jumperdog'." Cecil pocketed the jack without looking up from his paper.

Jumperdog?! Must be for some other dingo. This one never jumped a day in its life, surmised the webseeker, glancing at the sleeping mongrel as he made his way over to the computers. In passing by the domino table, one of the Saints called out, a little above softly, "Hey, man, thought you already left the island." The mission man stopped short and turned to face the source of the question statement. The Saints were all looking back at him. "No, not yet, but soon," he offered, continuing quickly across the room.

I don't know any of those dudes. Why do they seem to know me? Do they have me confused with someone else? Like special bean, maybe?!? Jesus fracking christ!! Okay, if that's true, they must know special bean as an American, because they know I'm American and if they have me mixed up with him, then he must be American, too!! And he must already be gone! Wow! This is big!! A breakthrough that has to be highlighted in the update. But wait, could it be the Saint was talking about a third party, like a GOD employee he knew was leaving, or, presumably, had already left? But if that's the case, how could he mistake a guy he knew, for me? Besides, the way he spoke was like he was thinking about somebody he heard of from somebody else, but didn't know personally. A recent arrival. Not a longtimer. That's just me and the bean, because nobody else flew in with me and I haven't heard about another newbie coming in within the last week, or so, other than the Afrikaners, and no way either of them is the man. And it sure ain't me, babe. But shouldn't I talk to the domino Saints to find out what they know? What if I can get some more info on IDing my unknown pal? Isn't it my duty to try? No, I don't think so. If any of them do know the dude, or have been recruited by him, they will send an alert that I'm asking about him and that will be all she wrote. I'll never get anything else, anywhere. I should stick with my contacts and nobody else. But, no doubt in my mind - special bean is American and he's on his way to Greece. That's my report.

The uploader sat down at one of the small work tables. He shifted the monitor away from the room, taped the cam eye, turned off the audio and entered the password. Good to go. It didn't take long to type up the message and, after carefully proofing his work, he took a long deep breath of anticipation. He knew as soon as he pressed 'send', his life would change dramatically within a very short timeframe. *Almost like detonating a bomb,* he thought wryly, pushing the activation control. The screen immediately went through the scrambling sequence he had seen last time and when it returned to the desktop display, the operative realigned the monitor, removed the tape patch and turned the audio back on. He then rose from the table and headed toward the outside, ejecting, "See ya, Mr. Cecil. Thanks much!" as he left the premises.

Walking back to the truck, Rossy expected his phone to ring at any second. He checked its status to make sure it was ready and climbed into the cab. Nothing yet. Christ, he felt like his heart was tripping in the anaerobic zone. Deciding to return to the barracks, rather than wait for the call in Georgetown, he started the engine and eased onto the road out of town. About half way back to base, the jittery g-man jumped at the loud rap of his ringtone, GrandMaster Flash's *The Message.* He immediately pulled over onto the shoulder and parked, while reaching for the phone.

As expected, it was esuper Dick. "Where have you been, Mr. Rossy? We were looking for your input at least thirty-six hours ago."

"Well, maybe if I had better contact intel, I could be faster." The agent sensed heat rising up through his face.

"You must learn to make your own efficiency, son. Dependency is the foundation of failure. Enough small talk. You are to proceed immediately to Greece. Report to the NAVOSUR pc on board the USNS Harknet. That's one of our survey ships presently in port at Piraeus, just west of Athens. You will receive a classified shipboard message with instructions regarding contacting your in-country asset. Use your full name, all caps and no spaces, as ID and 'special bean', one word, all caps, as your access password. Hurry, Mr. Rossy, hurry. Time is of the essence. And remember, not a word! Stay anonymous! Capisce?"

"Yes, but....."

"One more thing. You called Booker on your personal device. You were instructed to use a burner for that. Do *not* make that mistake again! This conversation is over."

Rossy blinked at the sound of the disconnect. He felt like more than the phone was disconnected. It was like his whole life was being detached. *They're following my calls? Jesus, what kind of a bubble am I wrapped in?* So, what next? Probably the travel office to coordinate a flight out. He had seen a sign for this on base, not far from the club. Then he would have to check out with Mr. Richardson. The future Greecer restarted the engine and began to pull back onto the roadway. In checking the empty lanes for oncoming traffic, he saw motion in his peripheral vision. Not far off the road was a line of donkeys, all staring at him and sidling slowly forward in his direction. *Holy frack!* With a burst of instant fear, almost terror, he jammed the accelerator and spun onto the road, nearly rip wheeling through the opposite lane. He throttled past the donkeys without looking directly at them and did not slow down until reaching the reduced speed limit sign on the base perimeter.

***

The air force travel and disbursing office was located in the same central base building as the commissary. Rossy went through a compact, unoccupied waiting area off the hallway, directly to the service counter. He had his briefcase, holding the most important possessions he owned right now - his passport, authorization paperwork and cash. If he lost any of these things, he would be dead in the world, because, though no one had actually said it, he knew any official knowledge of his classified existence would be disavowed if he turned up out here in TDYland without identity. And, yes, cash was part of the identity package, because without it you are nothing, especially if your credit card expires at the end of the month and you can't receive mail.

The civilian clerk glanced up from his desk in a small office on the other side of the window partition and directed the traveling agent to take a number and a seat. The floorsider saw a ticket dispenser on the counter, beside a call bell, and pulled out '001', which simultaneously flashed in digital red on top of the little machine. *What the hell do I have to take a number for? I'm the only one here!* He retreated to a hardback chair, thinking his wait should be very short. He also thought his number indicated he was the first client here today, which meant he was at least a day behind *special bean*, providing the target out-processed through this office. It was a good ten minutes before the clerk appeared at the window and called out, "Oh-oh-one!" Rossy popped up immediately and went over to the service port, placing his ticket on the counter. "May I help you?" asked the clerk.

The road to Greece out of Ascension went through Brize Norton, a Royal Air Force station sixty-five miles northwest of London. From there to Heathrow and then to Athens, with a brief stopover in Rome. There was a daily flight departing Wideawake, via Meridian Air Service, at 1415, arriving BNRAFS 2145, local. A British Airways flight departed Heathrow at 0530, with eta 1500, at Athens International. So, barring unforeseen roadblocks, or airlocks, the international jetster figured he should be able to report to the Harknet by dinnertime, tomorrow. The travel clerk asked a few questions pertaining to the sailor agent's ambiguous schedule, took his passport, shot record and orders back into the office and began scanning, stamping, typing, printing and stapling, while in constant whispered communication with remote tech support through a tiny wireless earpiece. The client returned to his seat, still the only one in the room, wondering if he was willingly participating in a security violation. Dick said 'not a word to anyone' and here he was turning all his classified paperwork over to a total stranger. But what choice was there? He sure as hell couldn't issue himself air tickets.

After what seemed like an hour, but was really only about twenty minutes, the clerk reappeared at the window and repeated, "Oh-oh-one!" Rossy again approached the bench and was asked to sign several highlighted signature lines. He complied without reading anything over the signatures and, following another round of compilation, shuffling and stapling, was handed a thick packet containing all his old and new documentation. The clerk advised the oneway flight tickets, complete with boarding passes, and adjusted per diem advance were inside the packet. The passenger was also advised to go to the clinic and get the missing inoculations he didn't have room for when he first got travel jabs at Bethesda. The European Union required the full contingent of shots for all incoming personnel. Before leaving the AFTAD office, the flyboy sat down to verify he got everything back and had what he needed to proceed with the mission. As far as he could tell, all was in order, though if it wasn't, he probably wouldn't know the difference. Incredibly, he was given another thirty bens in per diem advance, including a differential for entering an official, state department designated 'politically unstable corridor'. He shoved it all in the briefcase, now holding almost eight grand in cash, and walked out into the hallway. Before three steps, he remembered something and turned back into the waiting room. The clerk, standing up from his desk, was preparing to go on break. He glared at the client he was certain he was done with, but waited to hear what the problem was.

"Excuse me, sir, I have a question."

"Yes, what is it? Make it quick!" *Why would he have a question? I gave him everything he needs!*

"I was wondering, was there anyone else you recently processed to leave Ascension, or, more specifically, go to Athens from here, say, within the last two weeks, or so?"

"I can't answer that. All personnel travel arrangements are confidential."

"So, there was someone?"

"That's not what I said. I said I can't discuss anyone's itinerary with you, other than your own, because it's classified. Now, if you don't have anything related to your situation, I've got something else to tend to. Have a nice day." The clerk closed the window and spun around toward an exit in the back of the office. The completed client watched him disappear through the rear door, firing a cigarette, and pondered whether or not he had just been blown off. Why would basic travel info be classified? Is everything in the world fracking classified??

***

Before leaving the building, the cash heavy operative stopped into the commissary to pick up some incidental sundries for his trip. He passed by a souvenir alcove, featuring duty-free diamonds from Angola. He didn't know much about diamonds, but thought the rocks on display seemed really big for the price. "Perhaps a beautiful piece for someone special?" The attractive, young Angolan? woman smiled broadly from behind the display bar. "Oh, no, I'm just looking. Thanks." He wasn't about to spend anything for a gem diamond and couldn't understand why anyone else would, either. It did nothing, had no function and was only valuable because people, for some arbitrary reason, were willing to pay a lot of money for them. If everyone decided to, they could do the same thing with balsa wood. Besides, he heard about the 'blood diamonds' from Africa and had seen the DiCaprio movie on TV. Terrible things happened in the name of the dirty diamond dollar and he wanted no part of it. He moved on into the store to purchase his necessities, which, he was happily surprised to find, cost well less than at Dollar General.

The medical clinic was a white, rapid-built quonset structure, with a huge red cross across the top, situated on the other side of the dining hall from the club theater. The timid traveler anxiously awaited his turn to be summoned to torture. He hated medical facilities. Nothing pleasant ever happened in them, at least not to him. With shot record in hand, he went behind the curtain to receive the anticipated pain and tight discomfort forthcoming from completing his immunization schedule. He had already decided to take one hit in each extremity, rather than multiples at a single site. The good news was rabies was scratched. But meningitis, cholera and encephalitis were still required. Sure enough, he was hurting and sore as he exited the building, but at least now he was fully inoculated and could probably not be medically detained or quarantined anywhere on earth. Almost as good as a free lunch.

The microbe resistant mole was logistically ready to depart. All that remained to do was check out of the barracks and brief Mr. Richardson. Then he was local history! Plenty of time - the flight didn't leave for another three hours.

***

"This is your report?" Mr. Richardson leaned far back in his swivel and thumbed through the thin document the engineer had just handed to him.

"Yes, sir. Remember, it's not a design. It's only a sketch summary for planning and programming purposes. If you do the project, you still have to do all the technical evaluation and engineering. It's not a simple deal."

"What, do you think I don't know that? Do you think I'm stupid? Look, boy, you don't get to be GOD's Ascension Island superintendent-in-charge by being stupid. You haven't shown me any respect since you've been here and, frankly, you're lucky I didn't ditch your insubordinate ass! I heard about your fight with the South Africans and I've been debating all day whether or not to skid you outta here. But since you're leaving the question is moot. By the way, how come you're not going back to America?"

Rossy was stunned. He hadn't said where he was going and there was also a cargo flight to Patrick departing this afternoon. The AFTAD clerk had said his itinerary was classified, so how did the dimbo super know anything about his travel plans? "I'm sorry, sir, I can't discuss that."

"What do you mean you can't discuss that? Why are you going to Athens?"

"It's classified, sir." *This is getting uncomfortable.*

"Classified?! You know, I'm getting sick of your shit, boy. If you weren't booked on Meridian, you sure as hell would be on that C-17. I have half-a-mind to file an incident complaint on you to NAVOSUR. Let them deal with your disrespectful crap! Now, give me your driving permits."

"What do you mean? Why do I have to turn those in? They have my name on them and are useless to anyone else!" The island driver worked hard for the IDL and AI permit and wanted to keep them as souvenirs. Also, the IDL might come in handy in Greece.

"Just shuddup and give 'em here!" *Good! Got something to squeeze this little turd with!* "And, oh yeah, you owe me a ben for truck gas. Give it up!"

"What?? I didn't even drive ten miles! What are you talking about??" Mr. Richardson tilted his head, looking sardonically at the insubordinate, saying nothing. The departing undercover man couldn't argue anymore and didn't want to risk inciting an adverse action from GOD's half-a-mind idiot, here, back to NAVO. It seemed like everywhere he went on TDY, the field boss wanted to jack him up! He opened the briefcase and slipped a benny out of the cash envelope, pushing it carefully across the desk with one hand, while closing and standing the case on the floor with the other. "Can I get a receipt for this, so I can claim it on my travel voucher?"

"A receipt?! Are you kidding me? You would claim ten miles gas money? What a rip off! No wonder the government's in debt!" The super snatched the bill and announced, "We're done here!" ordering the extorted insubordinate to "get the hell out of my office!" *Let the goddam little frackhead keep the licenses, but he sure as hell isn't getting a receipt to pad his expense account with! Who's stupid now? Hell, I'm gonna write his clownshit engineering ass up anyhow. Why not? I'm the boss!!*

***

The secret agent sat about halfway back in the cabin of the modified Boeing 737 watching passengers board. There weren't many and none that he recognized. A woman with two small children, three older, but not elderly, business-looking men, a very tall middle-aged man and several British military uniforms. He didn't see anyone resembling what he imagined *special bean* would look like, based on what was known, and guessed all these people probably booked through the British sector travel agency. He wondered if that's what the *bean* did for a previous flight, because there didn't seem to be any Americans using this air service via the AFTAD office.

It wasn't long before they started the taxi to the pavement end zone, where, after a brief pause, began the classified departure of invisible tophead's last chipmole from his first overseas assignment. The takeoff was a rather bumpy acceleration down the runway, prompting the engineer to wonder whether the phony airfield project might be more valid than he thought. Watching through the port as Ascension Island became a dark round pad on the sea, the ascending shellback was pretty sure he would never see that rock again.

Rossy knew he would be traveling all night and should get as much sleep as possible on this leg of the journey. Fortunately, there were so few passengers it was possible to stretch out across three seats, like being in a bunk, which he did as soon as they rose above the clouds. He didn't think much about planning what to do at his destinations, because he had never been there and didn't know anything about them. He would have to find his way later, in the moment of arrival. The flying sailor was actually getting used to not knowing much about where he was or what he was supposed to be doing, so unknown factors were becoming more a familiar status quo than a nervous threat. And no matter what, if it all became unmanageable, there was always the nuclear option to quit. *Odd that should be such a comforting recurring thought.*

CHINATOWN

The general carefully centered his high-performance Jaguar XK over the line between two spaces in the H Street parking garage. He couldn't tolerate door dings from the inconsiderate jollyriders he was forced to share the facility with. If this upset anyone, let *them* make payments on the $150,000 custom automobile that was his personal pride and joy. He didn't care if he lost everything else in the divorce, this baby was going with him! But that could be worried about later. First, was the matter of Jiang Cheng. He had not been able to think about anything else since Monday. How, in the name of America, had Jiang tapped into his impenetrable domain? Despite super rank, he was not a government celeb. The media didn't know who he was or anything about him. How did Jiang? *Why* Jiang was interested in him was irrelevant. That would be revealed this evening. But how? **How**? HOW?? That was the question. He could not leave this meeting without an answer. *The very security of the nation depended on it!*

RPC had spent the whole week reviewing everything the CIA knew about his unexpected Chinese nemesis. The oilman was born to Communist aristocracy, an only child of high party loyalists. He was an engineering graduate of Stanford University, as well as an honors graduate of Yale Law School. He was perfectly positioned to ride the crest of China's economic awakening, but had universally remained silent on policy issues. As provider of roughly 40% of his nation's energy needs, he was like a major utility line. Not in the spotlight of attention unless he broke. And he was not prone to breaking. He had built a very efficient and productive bureaucratic enterprise through super secretive management practices and, much like the general, was essentially unknown as a public figure. There was not really any information available to indicate how he could possibly know anything about the ultra-classified American intelligence hierarchy. Also, disturbingly, there was no record anywhere of Jiang's present entry into the U.S., or his in-country movements. The focus for tonight was very clear. *Find out what I know I don't know, about Jiang, and for how long and why*

I didn't know it. Anything else the hidden Chinese tiger wanted to consider was distractive and off target.

Fa Foo's was typical Friday evening busy, though no one would usurp the sacred reservation, of this the unwilling center of attention was certain. At the stairtop entrance foyer, he was well greeted, as usual, by Vin Lu, though in an uncharacteristically subdued manner. Upon entering the dining room, the longtime regular saw why. Jiang Cheng was seated *at my table, at my time!!* This was unacceptable! The general looked to the maitre'd for an explanation, but the visibly embarrassed concierge turned away. In being ushered to the table, tophead knew he was engaging the subject from a position of weakness - as a guest, not a host. Big difference in protocol. It was like he had lost home field advantage, making the game at hand that much more difficult.

Jiang Cheng smiled inwardly when he saw the CIA baron enter the dining room at precisely 7:00 p.m. He knew the spy man would be here and in very punctual time. That's why he arrived earlier. The general would be seated at *his* table, rather than he being seated at the general's table. A small detail, but very important in the context of the discussions he had planned for the evening. If he made progress, this date could be marked as a truly momentous occasion in the unrecorded annals of history. It might well be the origin of a major shift in the world's balance of power! *Careful! Do not get ahead of yourself. One can eat more, taking smaller bites.* The Chinese mogul was prepared to stay in Washington for as long as it took to seduce the target and achieve his objective. He had the tools and policy directives in place to effectively manage his energy empire from remote. Besides, he loved this city. It was much more pleasant than the smog smothered megopolis he called home.

"General Clement, welcome to my table," said the businessman, offering a greeting handshake, but not rising. He wanted to strike a preemptive aura of dominance.

'My table', indeed. "Good evening, Mr. Jiang." Tophead accepted the greeting gesture and sat down, his back to the foyer archway, across from the self-assumed host.

"I took the liberty of ordering a bottle of *Placidia def Grande*, one of your country's finest estate zinfandels, I believe. Here's to our collaborative success and prosperity." The oilman poured and raised a glass toward his tablemate, who really didn't like wine, but accommodated the toast. "General, when we met a few days ago, I said I have a proposal for you. I would like to talk about that this evening."

"OK, but first, I respectfully ask for an explanation as to how you have been able to specifically contact me? Obviously, our meetings, here, are not by chance."

He is defensive. My advantage. It is the offense that scores. "How I have been able to approach you is not important. What *is* important, is how we can mutually benefit each other. That is what I want to present."

He's on point. I have to hear him out in order to get what I need. "Alright, let's hear it. What do you have?"

"General Clement, I am aware you are overseeing the development of a revolutionary weapon system that could change the face of nuclear proliferation, as well as the track of international relationships." *I will lay it on the table. He looks like he has been hit with a hammer!* "I believe you call it the stealth accurate fast evaporation bomb, or the SAFE bomb. As I understand it, this is a non-nuclear device, capable of being delivered with surgical satellite controlled precision via portable launcher and undetectable carrier missile to and from anywhere, that detonates on target impact such that all components immediately vaporize. In short, this weapon can destroy any mark on earth with no detection of attack and no trace of origin. It can make a building appear to simply explode, without warning, from within. It is, indeed, from the user's perspective, a safe bomb and it makes nukes obsolete."

What the hell?!? Tophead was speechless. The SAFE program is probably the most highly classified systems development project in the history of the ASC. It is a macro application of the MA 1000 sniper technology and is darker than the Manhattan Project ever was. Its maximum security was his responsibility. Everything Jiang said is correct. *And since I have no idea how he knows this, I am totally screwed.* "What do you want?"

"It's not just what I want, Mr. Clement, it's what we both want. Like I said, a mutually beneficial proposal. I am prepared to pay you one billion U.S. dollars for a high capacity thumbnail flash containing the complete SAFE bomb system design with full development plans, schematics and specifications, including all operational control and sequence codes, as well as a schedule of encryption unlocks."

There was a long silence between the two, during which the big man gazed blankly through the window into the city evening and drank a full glass of the piss tasting wine. Jesus, he could use a cigar! "How about if I have you arrested for attempted bribery of a federal official in a conspiracy to commit terrorism against the United States of America? How would that work to your mutual benefit?" RPC was feeling raw, hot anger coursing through his being and wanted to destroy this oversure, arrogant communist bastard. *Yes, arrest him, detain him in some obscure maxsec facility and maybe try his ass in about five years, by which time whatever he knows about me will be useless information.*

"Oh, please, sir. Let's think this through." *Not good. Not good. If he goes highroad, I lose everything.* "If you call your authorities, I will vaporize, like your SAFE bomb. Look where we are - Chinatown. I can disappear in seconds. Nobody knows me. No one overheard our conversations. Trust me, there is no video of us together, no phone links of us talking, no internet communication between us and, as I'm sure you know, there is no documentation of me being in your country. Also, as I'm sure you have discovered, any covert recording devices you have employed have been compromised. You hold an empty bag. I can snap any line you think you have me hooked with. If you choose to personally detain me until your arresting officers arrive, you will be forced to become a public figure and lose your cover, forever. Are you prepared to do that? Throw your professional effectiveness away? Let's go back. By accepting my proposal, our transaction will not be apparent for some time, perhaps never. Meanwhile, you can retire with honor, in far greater prosperity than anything your lifetime salary and pension can ever provide for you. What will it be, general?"

Jiang knows who I am, but he doesn't have my project specifics. His infiltration is incomplete. I can walk away, change some encryption codes, re-build firewalls and shut him out. But.... jesus god! A billion dollars?! "What would you do with the SAFE bomb?"

Come on back! "That is not what I can tell you. I have my purposes and they are peaceful, but they must remain confidential." Jiang was a paradox, even to himself - the ultimate capitalist wrapped as a devout communist. He wanted to make as much money as he could, but he wanted to enable his government to advance China as the world's greatest economic superpower. The river to cross was energy demand. The bridge was energy supply. The energy vehicle was oil, because China had no other feasible alternative. Specifically, imported oil, of which current market supply was starting to lag. Iran sat on one of the world's largest oil reserves, but had ruined its market by pursuing nuclear weapons capability. They could not have their nuclear cake and sell oil to pay for it. The Chinese entrepreneur saw a gigantic opportunity. If he could offer the SAFE technology to Iran in exchange for unquantified, underpriced crude, he could flip the oil to Chinese refiners at slightly under market cost and make a virtually unlimited profit. Much, much more than the paltry billion for the key to start this massive money machine! He had not yet approached the Iranians with this proposition, but was confident they would be eager to play. They were weary of being an ostracized semi-nuclear bad boy, forced by the U.S. to endlessly stand in an economic corner. They wanted to assume their rightful status as the preeminent Middle East force, to which their neighbors, including Israel - especially Israel, must pay due homage and respect. Yes, he was certain Iran would be all in. And the SAFE bomb would allow them to win the pot. If that didn't pan out, he could easily sell the technology, well over cost, on the competitive world market. It was a no lose venture, beautiful in its classic simplicity. The only hurdle was Clement. "General, I suggest you think about what we have talked about this evening and we can meet again next Friday. What do you say?" *Maybe a mistake? Possibly, but I don't think so. There aren't many Americans who would turn down a billion dollars on principle. And this one isn't among the most intellectually principled.*

Another long silence. *How can his interest in an offensive weapon system be peaceful?* Finally, tophead rose from his chair and quietly said, "Thanks for the drink. I'll see you next week." He turned abruptly and walked briskly out of the dining room, glaring at Vin Lu in passing to the stairway. On the street he felt ravenously hungry and stopped into Cho's Chinese Carryout, ordering *#124 - Moo Shu Chicken w/white rice*, on the way back to the garage.

GREECE

British Airways Flight 865 to Athens was on the tarmac, more than three hundred meters from the nearest terminal gate, at Leonardo da Vinci International Airport. The overbooked Boeing 757 had been on the ground for more than two hours surrounded by polizia, carabinieri, military and special security vehicles, including several armored tanks. A large number of heavily weaponed uniformed and suited personnel shuffled among the vehicles, looking furtively about as they constantly communicated with remote command and support. No one had been allowed on or off the plane for the scheduled four hour stopover, not even those disembarking in Rome. There had been no explanation for this kumbaya for nearly an hour, when word finally spread through the underclass seats that a brutal terrorist suspect was being held in first class. The individual had been arrested in London, in connection with a recent mall attack in Istanbul, during which more than a hundred people were killed, or injured. He was being extradited to Turkey and everyone in and around the aircraft was awaiting the late arrival of the Turkish authorities to take custody. The transfer was too high profile and dangerous to execute anywhere except in a completely controlled environment, hence the lockdown of BA 865 well away from the terminals.

Rossy couldn't look out the port anymore. All he saw was the round black opening of the end of a tank cannon, pointed directly at him, that seemed to get larger and more pervasive as time dragged on. He wanted to go to the rest room, but didn't feel like trying to wiggle by the heavyweights wedged in the seats between him and the aisle. Besides, it looked like the attendants were setting up a rest room sequence procedure, allowing one row at a time to go. He would have to wait his turn. At first there was a lot of murmuring, though everyone was subdued and orderly. But after considerable time elapsed and the drink cart made several laps up and down the aisle, people were starting to get restless. Then a yell from further up in the cabin, followed by a man leaping out of his seat and charging forward. He was restrained by attendants before reaching another man, whose oblivious head was slowly drooping toward the open tray in front of him. The droophead had nonchalantly backtossed his last miniature bourbon empty over a shoulder and hit the charging bull dude in the face. The small glass container had drawn blood and the victim, already near breakpoint from the stressful circumstances, went off. He wanted to press charges and sue. He wanted his unwitting assailant arrested and taken off the plane. He eventually calmed down and was reinstated in his seat and medically tended to. The perpetrator sat unmoving, barely conscious with a stupid, uncomprehending grin on his face, while his wife instructed him, in a whispering attorney's tone, to not say a word to anyone.

There was not going to be an opportunity to view much of Rome, just as England had been a figment of the night. A blind shuttle ride from Oxfordshire to the airport and a three hour wait in a secure terminal gate area. Everything clicked right on schedule, but it was all very unrevealing. The novice rover had, of course, never been to Europe and felt like he was passing through in a tunnel. It didn't seem like his travels so far, since leaving Ascension, qualified as being anywhere. He looked forward to actually seeing Greece.

***

Due to the peculiar delay in Rome, it was darkfall by the time the struggling BA 865 allegedly touched down at AIA. In his limited flying experience, the jet lagged mission man concluded all urban airports looked alike at night from a few thousand feet overhead. Structured rows of operational airfield visuals amid the random lights of the surrounding city. Black holes of nothing between countless points of luminosity. For all he knew they were re-approaching London. Once inside the terminal, however, it was all Greek to him and he had to rely on graphics and a translation app to hunt down baggage claim and customs. He chuckled, thinking of the senseless old adage, 'Russia got Hungary and fried Turkey in Greece'. Probably a cold war leftover, that *could* make a comeback, given the increasingly unpredictable metrics of world affairs. Rossy didn't really follow current events very closely, but he knew Greece was in turmoil, a 'politically unstable corridor'. As a member of the European Union, the un-savvy republic had availed of massive loans to support crazy-high public employee pension and benefit plans. It was an inverted pyramid economy that was in the process of toppling under its own imbalanced weight. Fertile ground for a *special bean* to grow.

When in Greece do as the Romans do. And the French, the Swiss, the Germans, the Spanish, even the Greeks. Spend the currency of the eurozone. The shrewd sojourner decided to exchange five bens' worth, before setting out through the intricate terminal complex to locate a taxi exit. He found the airport to be a uniquely interesting place. It was modern, super shiny clean and full of restaurants, shops, banks and boutiques, all engulfed within the aggressive promotion of the topical decor for tourism in the ancient Athinai homeland. Spotting a narrow, somewhat obscure McDonald's, tucked in tightly between a high, muraled wall and a souvlaki stand, the young American soon got down with a happy meal, which, amazingly, was just as samo' here in Greece as in Maryland. From the vantage of an open court table, it seemed perfectly feasible that a homeless Greecer could easily live in this airport, with only a briefcase full of cash. *Must be at least twenty-one years of age, or accompanied by an adult. Do not try this at home.*

Taxi drivers roll with the pulse of the city. They know what is happening, who's coming and going and where everything is. The sailor agent had only to say, "USNS Harknet, Piraeus," and the cabbie nodded and bolted like a bullet bat out of the airport departure circle. It was a wild trip through the metroplex of south Athens and the port district of Piraeus, not necessarily because everyone drove like acid-luped maniacs, but because they drove without lights. It was fracking nighttime and they were all driving with no lights!! The petrified passenger had never seen anything quite like this and got no response when he asked the driver, 'what the hell?' He guessed it was some kind of Greek austerity thing, like cars run more efficiently with the lights off. *And they probably are totally efficient when they wreck in the dark.*

In contrast, Piraeus was not efficient at all. It was lit up like Times Square on NYE, with commercial lights of all colors and pulsating intensities. A fairly busy place. Groups of sidewalk people shuffling about through a tight array of narrow streets lined with tawdry themed nightclubs, bars and theaters. Reminiscent of Lexington Park, only about ten times bigger, thought the onlooker. He wondered what it was about seaports that brought out the bawdiness in folks. Airports didn't project the lascivious mercantile environment that seaside burgs did, and neither, for the most part, did inland cities. It seemed like ships, or harbored waters, inspired smut, but there was likely no definitive data to support such an observation. After about ten minutes of weaving the labyrinth of center P-town, the taxi entered the much dimmer port sector, where deep water vessels silently bobbed in shadowed berths at long, wide piers like sleeping rows of monstrous metallic whales. The driver followed the waterfront boulevard, between the perpendicular pier accesses and a maze of warehouses, drydocks, freight box depositories and fuel tank clusters, for nearly a kilometer, finally approaching a white ship moored alone on the seaward bulkhead of the last pier. *The USNS Harknet.*

A sleek, three hundred foot survey craft, The Harknet stood out among its bulky, rusted neighbors, many of which were freighters under flags of tax free sovereigns with minimum maritime standards. There was one cruise liner in port, a Norwegian seven decker parked near the front of the pier grid, in town for the Dafni Wine Festival. The NAVO vessel was named for Samuel Harknet, the billionaire founder of HoloMark, a publicly owned internet company that transmitted custom holograms and holophots. Harknet's girlfriend was a free diver, who got him interested in all things ocean. He became obsessed with how little was actually known about most of the earth's surface and bought the manufacture of a fully equipped, state-of-the-art, oceanographic survey ship for the navy. After proper christening, the Harknet was assigned to NAVOSUR, with a permanently reserved luxury stateroom for its benefactor. Samuel, cleared for top secret security, showed up several times a year to stay on his namesake a week, or so, relaxing and observing operational activities, but never interfering. This unique, highly unorthodox and possibly illegal arrangement allowed him open access to a six hundred million dollar yacht, that he could ride for free and had no responsibility for. It also provided the navy with a much needed, updated survey and research unit, that it would not have otherwise been able to procure under the new reality of serious military funding cuts. Both parties privately considered it a high-fiver.

The embarking engineer paid the taximan and struggled with his bags and briefcase up the narrow aluminum gangway to a watch officer on duty at the egress deck. An electronic status screen indicated the NMS master was ashore and the NAVOSUR party chief was aboard. The officer checked the scheduled arriver's name with his orders and passport ID and directed him to the main lab in the center of this same deck level. The officer couldn't leave the duty post, so the inboarder had to lug his own way to the lab. The hardest part of this effort was getting through a number of passageways, separated by tight, heavy steel doors equipped with very strong hydraulic closers. He dutifully fought his way to the ported lab ingress that was protected by a large 'RESTRICTED ENTRY' sign and keypad lock. Without the access code, he could only look through the port, tap on the wire-meshed security glass and wait. Several times. Finally, a door on the far side of the unoccupied lab opened and pc Philip "captain kool" Morris emerged from his office, looking scowl-faced across at the tapping passage port. Captain kool was civilian in body, but military in mind and spirit. He was above average height, with crew-cropped, graying hair, and wore what appeared to be a naval officer's work uniform, but was actually Walmart issue khaki pants and an epauleted khaki bwana shirt. The boots and belt were genuine navy surplus. The pc strode quickly over to the entry hatch and, looking through the round port, recognized Rossy from the transmitted brief he had received on the unexpected assignment to the Harknet field group. It wasn't really clear why he was getting another body - he certainly hadn't requested it, because there was no need. But there was also no choice. Orders were orders and his were to immediately assign the new engineer to the Kolpos Megaron project, near Nea Peramos. *Fine. If they wanted to control everything by remote, makes my job easier.* Kool opened the secure access and waved the unnecessary arrival in.

The main lab was impressively expansive. It's most obvious component was the large observation pit in the center of the room, that allowed direct visual of the sea beneath the ship's keel. The pit also contained several dive locks and a matrix of interface links for connecting a comprehensive variety of data collection devices to the computers above. On the lab deck, along one side of the OP, was a row of I/O monitor equipped flatbed plotters for hardcopy production of processed data. The computers were on the other side of the OP, as well as shielded transmission and receiver equipment serving satellite, navigation and mobile communications systems. A biochem lab occupied one end of the room, facilitated with a mass spectrometer and an electron microscope. Adjacent to the pc office was a library containing a complete inventory of technical reports and manuals pertinent to all mission operations, including the most recently abridged copy of Bowditch's *American Practical Navigator*. The lab provided as sophisticated an oceanographic and survey data collection, analysis and processing resource as was available anywhere. It would certainly be the envy of all ocean researchers if it wasn't so highly classified. In fact, other than the fabricator and a few thousand subcontracted vendors, no one knew of its state-of-the-art existence, except a limited number of navy personnel with 'the need', NAVOSUR, NMS and, of course, tophead and Sam Harknet. And, unfortunately but unavoidably, perhaps some of Sam's occasional, uncleared guests, who were often too drunk or high to see anything they shouldn't.

Rossy plopped his stuff, except for the briefcase, on the lab floor and followed captain kool into the office. He was directed to take a seat in front of the desk, while the pc sat in his ergonomic, executive swivel, behind. "Welcome aboard, Mr. Rossy. My name is Phil Morris and I'm the current party chief for NAVO operations in Greece."

"Thank you, sir. Glad to be here." The two shook hands across the desk. *Jesus christ!! Let the frack go already!* The pc's prolonged, crushing grip nearly evoked an audible wince from his new subordinate.

"The question is, *why* are you here? I didn't request any additional or replacement personnel, so what's going on?"

"I don't know, sir. I'm just following my orders."

"Well, my orders are to get you out to Megaron Bay, asap. And that's where you'll go, first thing tomorrow morning. Now, I happen to be good friends with Robyn Ryder. We talk. A lot. Not about anything classified, but about general management issues. She tells me you recently bolted out of your assignment in her shop and caused a bunch of shit to back up. What the hell was that about?"

"I'm sorry, sir, I can't discuss that."

"OK, here's something you *can* discuss. If you try any of that clownshit here, you *will* be quick and recent history at NAVOSUR. I guarantee it. Are we straight on this?"

"Yes, sir." *God, I'm never gonna make it past probation on this job.*

"One more thing. You have a classified message in cache. What is that?"

"I don't know. It's classified."

"Yeah, OK. We're done here. There's something funny going on with you, son. I don't know what it is, but I'll be watching. Remember what I said. C'mon. I'll show you your state and around the boat. First, let's stop by classcom so you can clear your message."

The classified communications closet was behind the computers in the lab. Anyone with a cached message had to pass facial recognition and a handprint scan to gain entry. The secret receptor processed through screening, proceeded into the tiny room and sat in front of the message monitor. He typed in 'WILLIAMARLOROSSY' and 'SPECIALBEAN', in the respective ID and password fields, and waited. The message came up instantly, with a '**FOR YOUR EYES ONLY - TS CLASSIFIED**' emblazoned across the top. There was not much to it after that. Just instruction that his asset would contact him in Nea Peramos. In ten seconds, the message scrambled and the screen blanked out. Rossy exited classcom and rejoined his pc in the lab. There was no further mention of the message.

***

A little while later, after somewhat settling in aboard the impressive vessel, the finally bona fide sailor relaxed in the wardroom over a cup of thick black Turkish coffee. He had never been on a real ship before. In thinking about it, mostly everything happening these days was something he had never done at somewhere he had never been. If nothing else, working for NAVO was a perpetual learning curve, but it really didn't seem to arc into anything resembling a viable professional career. Actually, he had no idea what he was doing and almost all the people he dealt with were, more or less, jerks. He didn't even know if he was still getting paid. But none of this mattered as long as he had his briefcase, which was seated reassuringly beside him. As he drifted deeper into random ponderation approaching sleep, the wardroom door flew open and two dudes boisterously entered, snapping the wayfarer back to real time. They immediately focussed on the lone occupant of the lounge and plunked down at the same table, eager to interact with their newest colleague. They, of course, knew who bj Rossy was, but he knew nothing about them. He listened carefully as Mason "fourpoint" Hunter revealed he was a corrosion engineer out of Ohio State University, from which he graduated with a 4.0 cumulative gpa. Hence, his moniker - ha! His father was a sixth district federal judge and fourpoint sort of grew up in a courtroom, learning early on how everything had to be complete and accurate. The other one, Halad "al-jersey" Najjar, was a native of Atlantic City, where his Egyptian descent family had prospered over many generations selling soft ice cream. He claimed his multi-great grandfather invented the ice cream cone at the 1904 World's Fair, in St. Louis. Al-jersey was a food processing engineer, with an accredited on-line degree from the New Jersey server site of University of Phoenix. The engineers chatted a while, talking about nothing very specific. The Harknet vets could describe their work activities in Greece, because new man was obviously there to do the same thing, but new man had to be super careful to not say anything about *his* real mission, that was classified in a whole different ops zone. Despite the security dancing, it looked like he might be a fit in this work group and the cautious one started to feel more comfortable. And so he said, "Yeah, why not?", when invited to go into Piraeus for a few coldies. *What could go wrong?*

The town was much more active than when the new assignee initially passed through earlier. The evening was well underway and people were everywhere. It was almost like a themeless Mardi Gras crowd. Loud, laughing drinkers in the street. Music gushing from open doorways. Horn beeping cars, cabs and mopeds trying to inch through the unyielding, meandering foot traffic. Many of the funtimers looked like the freight ship crewmen in a rough and tumble, eastern European port city that they, in fact, were. Among them wandered equally identifiable cruise tourists, in full-flowered, island resort motif, timidly gawking at the revelry with cameras in hand. The diverse engineers sported their own look of neither crew sailor, nor tourist, but more like off-duty government workers. The chipmole wondered if he was the only CIA operative with eyes on these streets tonight. *Probably not.*

Rossy knew nothing about Piraeus and could only follow his Harknet cohorts. They were moving toward a large, masonry block building with a brightly lit marquee over the wide, columned entrance portico. The *Gothic Apollo.* Evidently a popular place, because patrons were streaming in as fast as they could cram through the glass doors. Inside, a chaotic line was formed in the concourse to pay the ten euro cover. A makeshift portable sign by the fee taker indicated *Delores and Demetrius* were appearing tonight for 'one show only'. The lobby emptied to a vast, high ceilinged room with a bare theater stage in front. It was like a dingy auditorium with no seats, just a huge open area. A long bar stretched across the back of the room, opposite the spotlighted stage. Nothing was happening except a few hundred people, mostly men, were milling about drinking and yelling conversation over the babel. The air was blue with smoke and cigarette butts covered the grimy concrete floor. A thumping backbeat of muffled rock music was being amped from somewhere. As the trio made their way to the bar, they had to grapple the tide of the room moving frantically toward the stage. They each got a longneck Marathon Lager and followed the far edge of the crowd forward.

All at once everyone hushed and the room went relatively still when a man appeared on the stage and set up a large pedestal fan on each wing and a two step ladder stool in the center. This evoked wild applause. The speakers croaked and crackled before a booming voice demanded a *Gothic Apollo* welcome for 'the unique   erotics   of   **DELORES   AND DAY....MEEEEE.......TREEEE......US!!!!**' The intro was almost Las Vegas fight-like and the spectators broke into hootamania as the curtain parted and presented, without a doubt, the strangest duo most people would ever pay to see. Delores couldn't have been more than three feet tall and Demetrius was nearly eight. A dwarf and a giant. They both wore white terrycloth robes, were barefooted and had bleached blonde hair down to their waists. They pranced around the stage until the applause died down and then the giant took a position behind the ladder, while the dwarf climbed up in front of him. They both removed their robes and stood naked, facing each other. The high speed fans came on, gusting their hair in all directions and the audio began blasting an acoustic Bob Dylan, singing *Blowin' In The Wind*. And Delores reached up and started playing the titanic oboe stretching above her. For Rossy, this was the new weirdest thing he had ever witnessed, surpassing, by far, the graduate knocking out dog Clinton. The audience was clapping in cadence, increasing the tempo with the sexual frenzy on stage. The crescendo built toward the climax like a Beethoven sonata and when Demetrius ejected a bellow worthy of any wild elephant in rut, the crowd went bonkers. The performers quickly disappeared from the stage leaving many paying customers wondering, 'is that all there is?' *The answer, my friend, is blowin'.....*

Actually, there *was* more. A developing sideshow, subsequent to the main event, was drawing attention on the floor directly below the stage. Two men were in heated argument over a wager booked before the start of the show, pertaining to how long the show would last. One claimed he had bet the exact time and the bookie said he was five seconds short and the winning gamester was good within two seconds. At stake was half the pot, more than a thousand euros. The dispute was dividing the room. It wasn't long before some pushing and shoving ensued, followed quickly by alcohol powered fisticuffs. And then a breakout riot. The Harknet engineers had no skin in this game and unanimously decided to get the hell out of Dodge, and fast. As they sprinted across the floor for the lobby exit, a blood curdling scream trumpeted from the scrum of the brawl. One of the combatants had buried a blade in another's gut and the bedlam turned dangerously ugly. The three runners reached the out just as a brigade of police was bulldozing in. They were clotheslined against the adjacent wall and signaled to stay. The *astynomia* efficiently stabilized the situation and medics soon arrived to tend to the injured and take the knifing victim to the hospital. A senior officer ambled over to the wallflowers and, one by one, looked them hard in the eye. "Parakaló, ID," he commanded in a soft, yet unmistakably authoritative, voice. The sailors obediently reached for their passports. "Hmm.....Amerikanoi. Government workers on official business, I presume, from your passport status. You should tend to your business and stay out of trouble places like this. Kalispéra, gentlemen." The American g-workers departed the *Gothic Apollo* and walked leisurely, but directly, back to the ship.

***

The garden engineer carefully poured from a watering can on the mound where the special beans had just been planted. These were supposed to be magically fast growers, as promised by the urban elf from whom he had purchased the seeds for ten bens. Almost immediately, the top of the mound crumbled like a minia-

ture volcano and several bright green shoots emerged. The inter-
twined stalks rose rapidly, forming a rugged vertical spire beside
an insurmountably high wall, that stretched endlessly, as far as the
eye could see, in obverse directions. The engineer had always
wondered what was on the other side of the wall, but had not been
able to devise a way to scale its height. But now, he could climb
the woven beanstalk and learn what he had never known. With
anxious excitement he started up the rigid bine, easily finding
holds on the knotty growth to support his weight. Nearing the top,
there was a rush of air from the other side and the feeling of anticipation was almost overwhelming. Finally, with eyes over the
apex, surprise quickly faded to letdown, for there was virtually
nothing. Just flat, empty, colorless ground stretching away like the
open sea to the distant horizon. Nothing. He scrambled onto the
narrow parapet of the wall and stood gazing outward, trying desperately to find some detail, something finite, anything to make all
the time of not knowing worthwhile. And then he saw a figure
walking out of the vacant distance toward the wall. As the figure
got closer, he saw it was a man, and as the man got closer, he recognized Larry Lockbark, the dp super. *What the hell?!?* Larry had
both arms wrapped tightly around a briefcase, holding it securely
to his chest. He looked up at the gardener on the wall and, without
saying anything, extended the case upward. The engineer panicked
in identifying it as his own, and, for a split moment, thought about
scrambling back down the beanstalk and running to check if his
briefcase was, in fact, safe and Larry just had one that was similar.
Or, should he jump down from the wall and take what appeared to
be his from Larry? But then how would he get back over the wall?
He decided he couldn't take the chance of being without his briefcase, no matter which side of the wall he was on. The case held
everything important and, if it was gone from where it was supposed to be, he absolutely had to get it back. He jumped. While
free falling the interminable way down to the other side, the leaper
was horrified to see a grotesque giant appear out of nowhere and
snatch the attaché from Larry's still uplifted hands. He watched
helplessly as the ogre loped away, diminishing toward the horizon
with his most valuable possession. Sudden impact made the world
go red.

Rossy awakened abruptly, gingerly feeling a sore spot where
his head had struck a metallic corner of the briefcase tucked under

his pillow. He turned on a light and opened the prized satchel to verify its vital contents. All was intact and, with a huge sigh, he lay back down on the bunk, head on hard vinyl. The deeply internal vibration of the generators and almost imperceptible oscillation of the ship's mass in the water were highly sedating and he was soon back in the merciless REM province of a constantly worried subconscious.

***

Morning broke with a seasonable chill, bringing the usual, warming sun, and the sailor agent got his first look at Greece in daylight. The port district appeared to be grubbier and more trash filled than he had seen in the dark, but the vistas around Saronic Gulf were spectacular. The sharp, rugged slopes rising from the water were covered with chalk white structures stacked like little blocks in a Lego model. Colorful planter rimmed balconies and windows promised someone's story within every concrete facade. Streets between the distant buildings and houses were too narrow and non-linear to see ground level activity and there was a noticeable scarcity of trees, so much of the copious sunlight was reflected. The overall projected effect was a warm, bright and cheery scene, where everyone was deliriously happy. *Probably not,* thought the observer, who also thought he wouldn't mind touristing Athens for a day rather than relocating to Megaron Bay, wherever that was. He hadn't asked anything about where he was going, assuming it was classified and nothing could be revealed until he got there and had a realtime need to know. The immediate question was whether, or not, to take all his stuff? He was sick of scarfing it around and he would have to return through Piraeus to leave Greece, no doubt within the next few days. But if he didn't take everything, others, mainly Phil Morris, would wonder why, which would add to the pc's 'something funny' perception of his new charge. Not wanting to aggravate any more field bosses, he hauled the full travel load up to the egress deck to report for duty.

Captain kool was in a much better mood than yesterday. He realized the surprise TDYster could actually serve a useful purpose. One of the navy enlisted at Megaron recently went on emergency leave and had driven the field vehicle to the Harknet. Since no one was available to ride along and drive back, the van was still on the pier. Rossy could provide a twofer and drive himself out to Megaron, while getting the vehicle back on site. *Sweet.*

It was a tentative situation. The assignee had never driven in Greece, but had witnessed others doing so, and it was not pretty. The Greecers were all over the road, trying to pass in a single lane. Cutting each other off, honking horns, squealing brakes. No signals. Tailgating. Speeding. Screaming out the window. It wouldn't even qualify as controlled confusion and the engineer-in-need-of-transportation really wanted no part of it. But, as with most only options, he had no choice and was soon behind the wheel of the rented Toyota Sienna, on the way to Megaron Bay.

The national road west from Athens was a two lane highway with narrow shoulders. It followed a shelf above the coast and had many blind curves, grade dips and rises and unprotected drop-offs. It carried heavy traffic, including a wild variation of cars, trucks, busses and motorcycles. There was even a significant number of crazy bicyclists and putt-putting mopeders trying to find their way in the malformed mix, as well as an occasional mule pulled wagon filled with salable consumables. The stranger was relieved the Greek driving protocol was to the right, just like he was used to, but found many oncoming motorists favored the center. This meant he often had to go way right, onto the shoulder, to avoid a collision. On curves, everyone went inside, away from the sea cliff, regardless of which direction they were going. The speed limit was 80 kph, but most tried to exceed that as much as possible. Consequently, there was a lot of impossibly savage, unsighted passing going on. In short, though it was an incredibly beautiful and postcard scenic route sidewinding an idyllic Mediterranean coastline, this thoroughfare was a virtual nightmare, a grim reaper of horrible driving abuse. Colorful, elaborate shrines were everywhere along the way, at which friends and relatives were frequently stopped to offer religious trinkets and food in living testament to perished victims of the road. Such visitors presented additional obstacles that only added to the hazard. It was going to be a very long, difficult seventy kilometers to reach the village of Nea Peramos, where the valet vanster had been instructed to locate the hotel at town center. Captain kool said this was the field team's quarters and he could probably move into the vacated sailor's room.

The harried highwayman finally arrived at his destination in mid-afternoon. The trip was as hellishly punishing as could be reasonably expected. Not only did he barely escape mash-up on several pin curves, he actually thought, a few times, he was going to get shot. In America, maybe, but not here. Greek road-ragers, fortunately, did not carry arsenals in their vehicles, so the only heat for slowness and not clearing out of the way fast enough was obscene hand gestures and trills of unintelligible obscenities. But slow trumps dead and there was no way he was going to drive faster than he was comfortable with.

Pulling into the outskirts of town, Rossy approached a petrol station and decided to fuel up. The tank was below a fourth full and it would be a good ice breaker with the field team to deliver a topped off van. The Haas station was very large and extravagant. The monstrous, fully canopied fueling plaza fronted what looked like a mini-mall and the whole complex was awash with bright lights and colorful, flapping banners. He carefully maneuvered to an empty pump and found the service to be cash-only prepay. Since Greecers didn't have cash, they didn't have credit, and, looking at the prices, the stunned fueler understood why. Over one-fifty a liter for regular! *Jesus frack! That's like nine georges a gallon!!* He had never seen that kind of gas price and was still head shaking and muttering internally as he drew two eurobens from the briefcase and went inside to prepay. There was considerable activity at the cashier window and many people in line curiously watched him buy eighty liters of gas. Outside, other fuelers were staring at him as he pumped for a good five minutes. He noticed most people were done within seconds indicating they were only taking a liter, or two. *That's odd,* he thought, but quickly deduced that's all they could afford. And here he was *filling up right in front of the whole goddam town!! Sorry, Dick - not being very inconspicuous today, am I?* This has got to be an unforced tactical error, he concluded, wondering if he would last until sundown before being jacked. With eyes on all mirrors, he carefully scanned for trailers in departing the station and heading toward town center.

***

Xenodocheio tis Néas Perámou stood out as the most prominent building on the center square quad. It was situated on the high end of a grassed park that sloped gently down to a narrow, pebbled beach. Clearly visible from the shallow harbor was the panoramic Isle of Salamis, jewel of the Saronic Gulf. The hotel looked like a white concrete Quality Inn, with three story wings fanning lateral-ly from the ground floor entrance in the center. A small, fenced balcony cantilevered from the door window of each room, some of which were adorned with flowering potted plants, suggesting not all occupants were touring overnighters. The paranoid pumper drove into a tiny parking lot near the front entry. There were only six spaces, but just one car, so he took the second closest spot. In-side, a dreary foyer led to a corridor that transected to the rear door on the first floor level. Alcoved off the corridor was the check-in counter and manager's office, beside a stairwell to the upper floors. There was no elevator. Past the guest room hallways and near the back door, an archway in the concrete corridor wall opened to a fairly large dining room and bar area. No one was at the service desk or in the office. The prospective guest waited sev-eral minutes, finally deciding checking in was not going to happen at this particular time. He picked up his briefcase and followed the sounds of happy time emanating from beyond the arch.

There were two groups of people seated at separate tables in the bar lounge. At one table, drinking cheap draught beer from plastic tumblers, were three U.S. Navy personnel. A lieutenant, a petty officer and a seaman, all men, wearing their non-dress work khakis and denims. The other table was occupied by five incredi-bly attractive young women, dressed in revealing cabana wear, though no pool or swimming beach was anywhere nearby. The women were drinking ouzo and soda from long stem crystal glass-es and seemed to be having a much better time than the sailors. There was no interaction between the two groups. Rossy assessed the situation and walked over to the navy table. The women never gave him a glimpse. He introduced himself as a NAVO engineer assigned to the Harknet, with orders to report to their field station. The noncom heartily invited him to sit down and sent the enlisted dude to the bar to refill the pitcher and bring another cup.

The sailors knew who he was and that he was returning the van from Piraeus. They thought he would have arrived much sooner and were surprised he wasn't at the hotel when they came in from survey ops. No matter, they were glad their transportation was back and, in that respect, were happy to see him. The po asked for the van keys, holding out a palmed-up hand, and the newster readily complied. He didn't care if he never drove in Greece again. But then the noncom, thinking this guy could be a chauffeuring gopher for them and run errands while they were out on the water, gave the keys back. He had nothing else for the new engineer to do, because they didn't need another body on the boat, even without the other enlisted. It was obvious to Rossy the noncom seemed to be in lead of this crew. Maybe because he was the oldest? That couldn't be right. A lieutenant outranks a po. But the lieutenant was pretty quiet and looked kind of glum, or, perhaps a bit menacing? *Best I don't say much and let them talk to me. Something's out of joint, here.*

The team's highly classified mission was to conduct a fine grain hydrographic survey, comprehensive current study and high resolution sonar scan in the central Megaron Bay waterway. This was in support of development of an anchorage site for an American naval war group to augment rapid response in the Levant of the perpetually troubled middle east envelope. NAVOSUR was using military personnel to do this work, because they didn't have enough available civilians to fill the required slots. It was tasking out well, because the lieutenant had a very utile degree in ocean engineering from the University of Nebraska. He felt he was much better qualified than the NAVO civilians with their clown degrees, who were paid three times as much for knowing nothing about what they were supposed to be doing. But he couldn't work for NAVO as a civilian engineer, because he had an ROTC commission and had to languish in the goddam navy for three more fracking years!! Technically, the looie was in charge of this survey team, but if the po wanted to be the boss, who the hell cared? The lieutenant looked at Rossy. "So, what's your degree in?"

Nebraska?! How could Nebraska have an ocean engineering program? "Uh, chemical engineering."

"Yeah, that's just great. What the frack does that have to do with anything?"

A sudden eruption of laughter from the women's table changed the focus of attention and both groups glanced at each other. The gopher wondered if they were hookers, prompting sardonic chuckles from his fellow sailors. The po explained, "No, man, they are what's known as 'áthiktos', or 'untouchable'."

"Untouchable? What does that mean?"

"It means you stay away from them. They're concubines kept here in large style by fat dudes from Athens, who come out on weekends and holidays to get away from their wives and kids. If they hear anyone is so much as talking to their babes, they will find you and kill you. Believe it!"

"Sounds like they're hookers to me."

"Just forget about 'em, dawg, for real. I'm telling you."

Attention was again redirected when the Americans were approached by a stocky middle-aged woman, with medium length, dyed black hair and sequined red glasses on a necklace tether, wearing a white, long-sleeved blouse, black midi-skirt and low-heeled pumps. She walked in slowly from the corridor, eyes glued on the stranger seated with the navy boys. "Uh-oh. What did we do now?" whispered the noncom, trained like a Pavlov dog to expect only retribution and angry debasement from Diantha Baros, the hotel manager and part owner, for anything from loud music, messy rooms, mud in the hallway, using too much water, to whatever she could conjure in harassing her least favorite guests. It wasn't always this way. Initially, she received them with warm Greek hospitality, anticipating their full cooperation in giving her *all* their business. Not just room rental, but also meals at her dining room. Unfortunately, Kleo, nasty, underhanded Kleo, got to the military outlanders early, and persuaded them to eat only at his filthy little cafe down alongside the park, nearer the water. She had, so far, lost possibly upwards of a kiloeuro over this abominable defection and would never forgive either the foreign disloyalists, or Kleo.

But Diantha wasn't thinking about any of this right now. She was interested in booking the new boy into the room vacated by one of the sailors, who had left with two weeks rent balance due. She stopped short of the table, pointed at Rossy and motioned for him to follow her back toward the office. He picked up his case and dutifully rose to obey her beckon. "Be careful, son," warned the po, with an amused smirk on his face. In the cramped, dark office, the manager waved her, hopefully, newest client to a stiff, unarmed chair in front of the desk, as she clutched around to her loudly squeaking swivel across from him. In somewhat broken English, she confirmed he needed a room and offered the only option she had available. The departed sailor's room, with the balance and two weeks minimum advance up front. *Jesus christ!!*

That's like a month's rent for a room I'm only going to be in probably a day, or two! Feeling like he was, indeed, being jacked before sundown, the toasted traveler opened his case and hesitantly, almost tearfully, pulled eight bens. He didn't have enough euros to cover the extortion. Diantha smiled agreeably in taking the favored U.S. currency and handed him a receipt and the key for #36, on the third floor. With no further conference and head down in a posture of dejected defeat, he returned to the lounge and fell back into his table seat, while reaching for the beer pitcher. "She whipped ya good, didn't she?" chortled the po. "Don't worry about it. Our rich uncle should reimburse the damage."

Later, after a little more happy time transition and a final, cup-draining chug, the noncom announced, "C'mon, people, let's pick up. We're gonna be late for chow." The hotelier watched in disgust as the foursome filed down the corridor and out the front lobby. Obviously, the new boy had already been corrupted. They sauntered across the spalling driveway and down through the grass park toward Kafe Kleió, situated about a hundred meters from the hotel. The Kafe was a small, dilapidated concrete box with step-up entrance through a half-open dutch door. A picture window beside the doorway was fringed with blinking blue lights. A well rusted car, two mopeds and several bicycles were parked in the dirt pad adjacent to the structure. Inside, the group was immediately greeted by Kleo, a short, balding man with a thick nose-to-lip mustache over a wide, warm smile of welcome. "Gelá sou, Amerikanios navy filous, kalosórisma."

"Hey, how you doing, Kleo? Good to see you!"

"Yes, yes, parakaló," bubbled the host, ushering the sailors to their usual corner table. Kleo's smile broadened a bit in noticing a new face with his American regulars. The po introduced Rossy as their replacement 'nuclear gunnery technician', knowing the friendly restauranteur understood essentially nothing he said. "Yes, yes, drink?" responded the still beaming proprietor. They ordered beer. There was no problem in selecting dinner, because Kleo only offered one item daily and when he sold out, he closed up shop and went home to his tiny house directly behind the Kafe. That's why it was crucial to arrive promptly at, or before, six, when he started serving. Tonight, the fare was curried lamb over rice pasta pilaf, baked mango and pita flatbread with olives and feta. Excellent, by any standard, and, to the cost conscious navy crew, cheap. Dinner was under a eurohamilton, which was a lot less than at Diantha's hotel dining room. Accordingly, becoming steadfast Kleo clients was a logical no brainer.

There were other Kleo clients, mostly locals, it seemed, in looking around the room. None of the hotel women were here and there was no one who appeared very touristy. A twosome at a small table on the far wall caught the gunnery tech's gaze. A man and a boy, maybe father and son, were seated with two bottles of beer in front of them! *What is this?!* The kid couldn't be any more than ten years old. And it wasn't like the dad had two beers, because the boy was slurping it up from one of the bottles, just like the old man from the other! Don't they have liquor laws here?? In America, the dad dude and Kleo would be locked up, the boy would be sent to state-paid foster care and the Kafe would lose its license and shut down. Plus, there would be media video with the youngster's head blurred out. But this wasn't America and the special observer shifted to taking stock of the other patrons, relative to whether any of them might be his *special bean* contact. He had been in town for several hours, now, and it was time to go on alert. Like at Ascension, he had no definitive info on identifying the asset, meaning the asset would have to approach *him*. He had to be constantly ready for contact. No one in the Kafe was eye-signaling him, so he went back to enjoying the fine, cheap dinner and the new found alliance with his navy compatriots.

Before leaving the Kafe, the sea surveyors were excitedly summoned by Kleo to follow him into the kitchen. He led them to an auxiliary refrigerator right inside the back door, wherein were stacks of cardboard boxes and plastic plate packages. In very difficult, fractured English and animated mime, the noticeably agitated culinary man somehow managed to convey that, tomorrow, he had to go to the north for a nephew's wedding and would be gone about five days. He had prepared box lunches and microwaveable dinners for the Americans, which they could retrieve with a key under a mat outside the door. "Doreán, for free, no charge!" he shouted, but repeatedly demanded they "no go to Diantha!!" Apparently, the rivalry between Kleo and Diantha was so complete and hostile, he was willing to give away forty meals rather than risk losing customers to the hated hotel owner. The sailors saw no downside to this proposal and readily assured their grateful Kafe benefactor they would never go anywhere near Diantha's devil kitchen during his absence, or any other time. The soon to be free-fed Kafe clients each gave Kleo a tight hug and, after bidding a heartfelt 'sas efcharistó', made their way in the dark out the kitchen door, around the Kafe building and back up through the park to the hotel.

***

The next morning, agent Rossy decided to jettison his excess stuff. Yesterday, he had forgotten about it in the van and had to go down last night after everyone retired to their rooms and lug everything up to the third floor by himself. He was tired of carrying all this paraphernalia around, most of which he really didn't need and wasn't using. He had way overpacked. No one ever saw James Bond weighed down, like a pack burro, with his travel bags trying to get through, in and out of the logistical supports of his assignments. It was a total hassle and not cool. From now on he would just go with a small overnight bag and, of course, his briefcase. These could be easily toted on a plane, bypassing both baggage check and claim. He had enough cash to purchase whatever he needed, wherever he went. There was no point in messing with this crap anymore. So, how to get rid of it? He couldn't just leave it in the room when he moved out, because that would be too conspicuous. The best solution would be to rid the overload at a neutral, public disposal resource, like a landfill, or transfer station. First, though, he had to go through the whole inventory and remove any identifiers that could be linked to him. Then he had to scruff it all back down to the van.

It was mid-morning, break time, when the clean-up man was finally ready to roll, but he had no idea where to go. The navy crew was long gone out at the bay survey site. He went to the lounge searching for someone to ask and found the place deserted. There was a bowl of oranges sitting at the end of the bar and he picked one up and sat down at the same table he happy timed at yesterday. The orange was almost as big as a volleyball, with a half-inch thick skin and very juicy. Sweet. "That is cost three euro," said Diantha, appearing with no warning from out of the kitchen to behind the bar. The startled agent looked up and spontaneously, with a hint of irritation, retorted, "Put it on my room bill." He then inquired about a facility where he could take some things he wanted to throw away. Diantha advised of a 'free-zone' outside of town, along the old road to Korinthos, that everybody used to dump rubbish in. She added that if he took her kitchen refuse container with him, the orange was 'doreán', gratis. *Will haul garbage for food*, he thought. *Is this what I've come to?* "OK, deal." He followed her into the kitchen and she pointed to a heavy rubber bin almost five feet tall and at least half as wide in diameter. It was packed full and overflowing with putrid kitchen waste. In giving it a tug, the can proved to be every bit as heavy as it looked. He would have to bring the van around back to load it.

While driving through town from the backside of the hotel, the clandestine visitor noticed an abundance of trash, literally everywhere. Along and in the streets, between buildings, in piles at every drainage ditch. It was almost as bad as in Piraeus. He really hadn't thought about it before, but now he was in a solid waste frame of mind. He remembered seeing a recent news feature on TV highlighting fallout of fiscal problems in the eurozone. Accumulation of uncollected trash was a symptom of financial distress and there was video of Athens looking about like what he was observing here in Nea Peramos. The reluctant garbage man soon found the way to Korinthos and was relieved to discover it much less traveled, straighter and easier than the harrowing coastal 'scareway'. Diantha said the free-zone was about two kilometers beyond the town limits. He couldn't miss it. He actually saw it well before reaching it. Less than halfway there, a column of black smoke was visible, rising from the flatland beside the road. Shortly afterward, a strong stench filled the air with gagging fumes that were almost unbreathable. The FZ was an untended disaster. It looked like about five acres of environmental violation. Trash and garbage were randomly thrown all over the place, much of it unbagged. The flameless burning was from a massive heap of smoldering old tires, plastic debris and general rubble that seemed invincibly timeless in its continuous, polluting emission.

The appalled engineer, who had once taken an elective course in solid waste best management practices, pulled off the road into a makeshift lane that meandered through the so-called 'free-zone'. Aptly tagged, he considered, certain no regulations were applicable, nor enforced, for this blight. He didn't want to drive very far back into the site, so he decided to off-load up front and drag the stuff further in. It would take a couple trips. Obviously, there was no recycling going on here, so he didn't have to worry about separation and designated placement. When he had finished the deposits, he started walking back to the van, about fifty meters away, and stopped dead in his tracks. Just ahead, directly between him and the truck, were six dogs. Skinny, wild dogs, with heads down, ears back, tails straight and standing still in a row, staring at him with blank, yellow eyes! He could hear the faint rasping of their low throat growls. They looked like a pack of starving hyenas and there was no way he was going to walk safely through them to his ride. There was a quick mind flash of the Ascension land crabs. Not being a canine aficionado, the trapped trashster didn't know exactly what to do, except he didn't think he should make any sudden moves. And then he remembered chucking a mass of rotting pig bone and carcass from the kitchen can. He eased slowly backwards to the disposal spot, as the dogs inched forward in front of him. Reaching down, without taking his eyes off the ever nearing peril, he grabbed a huge, stinking ham hock and winged it toward the curs, off to one side of the path. They did not immediately respond, but seemed interested. He threw another bunch of putrid glop and the mongrels definitely started to break rank. With the toss of a couple more offerings, the animals forgot about their potential human live-prey and became completely absorbed in scuffling for the dead meat diversion. Given this opening, the once doomed free-zoner was able to sneak past his possibly final predicament and run hell-bent for leather back to the vehicular haven. He leaped up into the driver's seat and slammed the door. The starving dingos never even looked away from their new-found feast. Rossy sat motionless for a moment, gasping for air through a gradually receding panic. *Thank you, jesus. Thank you, lord. And a special shout out for Diantha!*

Upon calming down sufficiently to drive, the trashrunner fired the engine and started reversing out onto the road. The noxious odor from the empty kitchen container had permeated the interior van space to the extent there was no trace of the toxic free-zone smoke. In glancing all around for traffic, the habitually careful driver spotted something he hadn't noticed before. On a plateaued foothill to a significant distant knoll ridge, stood the crumbled ruins of what looked like an ancient acropolis style citadel. He could see what was left of the old Corinthian columns fronting the structure and the raveled stone deck beyond. At one time, thousands of years ago, this fortress proudly overlooked what was now a degenerate, contaminating dump. *What did it see then?*, the musing onlooker wondered, thinking it must have been better than this helpless mess. *What is progress?* Another big unknown to ponder. But later. For now, he had to get back into town and make himself visibly available for the asset contact. An engineering cover agent's work is never done. Twenty-four seven.

***

After reinstating the empty refuse bin in the hotel kitchen and cleaning up from his solid waste adventure, it was lunchtime. The lightened traveler was content with the morning's accomplishment. He figured he would return the van to the front lot and go down to the Kafe for a box lunch. In getting out of the parked vehicle, he was confronted by an elderly woman, wearing a long, full-skirted lavender dress, heavy wool cardigan sweater and black head shawl, carrying a large, covered basket. She began pointing at herself, him and the truck, while urgently explaining something in Greek. The non-Greeker had no idea what she was saying, but reasoned she wanted him to take her somewhere in the van. *Whoa! Think this through, cap! Once she gets in, you've got a completely unknown situation that you will have no control over. But if I refuse, I'll have the scorn of the town against me, because, I can tell by looking at her, for sure, she knows everybody.* Not wanting to be an 'ugly American', or worse, a conspicuous pariah, he thought, *'oh, why the hell not?'* , and consented for the lady to board, while unlocking the doors. *What could go wrong?*

The somewhat heavyset woman needed assistance in climbing up into the shotgun seat and getting her seatbelt fastened. She held the basket firmly in her lap while the good driver went around and got in on the other side. He turned the key, backed out of the lot and looked at the passenger for direction. She pointed and off they went, approximately in the same orientation he had taken earlier. But they didn't go out of town. She quickly gestured to a narrow side street and then to a small concrete house on the right, a short distance in. He pulled over and stopped. The woman struggled out of the van and walked up to the front door of the house and entered without knocking. He waited like an obedient cabbie for what began to seem like a long time. Just as he was thinking of peeking in the basket she had left on the seat, the house door opened and his passenger emerged, followed by another, similar looking woman, also carrying a covered basket. He went around and assisted them both in getting properly seated and strapped and got back in operating position to await instruction. The shotgun woman again indicated the way and he drove accordingly, having no idea where they were going, or why. They picked up another basket woman at another small house, and then another and another, until he had a van full of old women and baskets, with every seat occupied. He was seriously curious, at this point, as to what the end game was.

Whatever the baskets contained was sweet, because the van filled with a blend of fresh, hungering aromas. Almost like a morning bakery. The chauffeur felt his empty gut churn and hoped they might give him something to eat for his service. *Will drive for food!* He followed shotgun's directions and they were soon on the road he had originally come into town on from the coastal highway. They passed the Haas station and he concluded, with sinking dismay, they were headed for the dreaded route he never intended to drive on again! *OMG!!* He really wasn't sure he could do this! No choice, now - they were on the entrance ramp! Rossy tried to look unconcerned while feeling sweat prickling out all over. Hopefully, his face wasn't going scarlet scared. He didn't want to alarm anyone. *Just drive, dawg. At least you know what to expect! Yes, you **can** do this. Other duties as assigned.*

The national road eastbound toward Athens was not much different from westbound to Nea Peramos, except going onto the shoulder to avoid centerline oncoming could flirt with an open drop to the sea. In deference to his passengers, the van runner put an extra dose of caution into his driving, resulting in a greater frequency of adverse reaction from fellow motorists. Not a concern, though, as he was preoccupied with wondering where they were going and how much further. *Could it be the whole way to Athens? Jesus, if that's the case, we'll be riding in the dark coming back!* No way did he want to drive after sundown in Greece! Past a little more than ten kilometers, they went over a rise and approached a particularly sharp curve that nearly doubled back on itself around a narrow coastal promontory. Rossy thought he remembered this coil from yesterday and slowed drastically to safely negotiate the grade of the roadway. The shotgun navigator began pointing emphatically at a shrine, positioned just off the pavement at the outermost protuberance of curvature, and made a waving motion that could only mean she wanted him to stop. But there was hardly any time or room! He signaled right and immediately pulled over toward the monument, within less than a meter of the travel lane on one side and an un-railed limestone steep on the other. The left rear corner of the van was almost sticking out on the road. The traumatized operator heard a cacophony of vehicle horns as he cut the engine, put on the emergency blinkers and set the parking brake. It was not clear how the hell they were going to get out of this alive.

The women needed assistance in removing themselves and their baskets from the vehicle without falling over the cliff. It took about ten minutes for everyone to disembark and maneuver toward the rather sizable and elaborate structure at the edge of the escarpment. The ceramic cenotaph looked like a colorful, tinsel and ribbon clad little bandshell, about four feet tall, sheltering a framed photo of a young man, a newspaper article in a plastic bag, a thin journal book, a tiny oil lamp, several Jesus statuettes and an orthodox bible. A small cord of battery-operated, multi-colored lights framed the saran protected front. One of the women, a bit younger than the others, shuffled over next to the apparent memorial and sat down alone beside the opening. She lowered her face into her hands and wept softly for a moment. The others, standing away, watched silently as she carefully lit the lamp, scribed a journal entry and placed a string of smooth black beads, a silver crucifix and small servings of delectable snacks in the alcove of the open shell. Another of the women, waiting with the American outlier in the back of the group, whispered in fairly good English barely audible above the rumble of the traffic, that the grieving woman was the mother of the young man for whom she mourned. The son had gone off the road and over the adjacent precipice on his motorcycle about a week ago. The funeral was yesterday and they were here at his point of death, or at least as close as possible to the exact location, to lay beads of redemption, crucifixes of passage and sustenance for the journey, all to help the deceased soul transport safely into the afterlife. The other women, one by one, approached the first and laid offerings from their baskets in support. Soon the little roadside sanctum was littered with plates of baklava, almond butter cookies, moussaka, cheese rolls, flatbread wraps, pastitsio, broiled figs and king kong oranges. Someone even placed a bottle of Retsina next to the edible treats.

Rossy stared wistfully at the collation of wonderful, home-made specialities, clinging to the hope they would offer him a bite. He was, really, very hungry. The English speaker whispered for him not to worry, the food would not go to waste. When the soul took what he needed, poor passersby would stop and help themselves, as would ground animals and night birds. The palatable alms would be quickly consumed. So was the will of God. *What about the will of my stomach?? I'm going to need some sustenance, too, for **my** journey out of this fracking deathstop!*

The sympathizers gathered closely around the mourner and, led by the woman who had originally coordinated transportation for this event, prayed a continuous litany of poetic epiphany lasting more than forty-five minutes. Unaccustomed to orthodox proceedings, the starving wheelman sat on a rock off to the side, resigned to being marooned at this remote highway curve for the rest of the day. Finally, the group began to break up and the women retrieved their empty baskets and moved slowly back toward the van. It seemed to take longer to get everyone properly situated back in than it had taken to get out, but eventually they were ready to spin.

Re-entry onto the highway was not going to be any easy task, as they were positioned on a blind spot from both directions. Turning left was out of the question. The wary driver made an operational decision to go right and hang a 'youie' where the road was straighter. The women all promptly protested he was going the wrong way, when he saw, in the mirror, a large tanker truck bearing down around the bend from behind. The truck's blast horn barely overrode the screams of the passengers, as he accelerated forward to the rear bumper of the car in front. There was nowhere to go and it appeared they were all going to pile up on the eastbound lane, probably in an apocalyptic fireball of exploded fuel worthy of the grand finale of any *Fast and Furious* chase scene. The mind is a quirky thing and for some strange reason the terrified chauffeur thought, on this seeming verge of destruction, that at least he would get something to eat in the aftermath. Then the truck veered to the center and started to pass. Everyone in both directions scattered to the shoulder and the tanker roared on by to open road ahead.

Later, after returning to Nea Peramos without further incident, off-loading all the women at their respective homes and re-parking the vehicle in the hotel lot, the shaken, fatigued, but still famished sailor decided to go directly to the Kafe for something to eat. Despite the near fatal road experience, he was satisfied he had done the right thing in conveying the ladies to their mission. It should serve him well for however longer he would be in town, even if it was another conspicuous exposure. He felt he was not blending in very anonymously with the environment, but hoped the notoriety would flush his *special bean* contact. It was becoming more and more evident that secret cover work was a job of many facets and he absolutely had to be ready to do anything.

***

The Kafe kitchen door was unlocked and the sound of muffled voices issued forth from within. *What the hell?* Rossy slowly opened the door and found his sailor colleagues gathered around the main prep table eating dinner. It was early for them to be back in from surveying and he wondered what was going on. They told him to get a plate and showed him where the microwave, utensil drawer and beer cooler were. When he got situated at the table, the po explained they had to break ops ahead of schedule, because of an accident. The Greek coast guard had been practicing search and rescue maneuvers near the Megaron survey grid, involving rapid deployment from overflying aircraft. They were jumping from flybys a couple thousand meters up, carrying raft packs designed to inflate on impact. One individual free fell for a long time after release, drifting over near the survey work zone. The sailors had watched in horror as the flier fell way past the point his chute should have opened. They saw the splash as he plunked into the water several hundred meters from the survey craft. The chute never opened and the raft didn't inflate. The coast guard recovery skiff was much further from the downed jumper than the Americans, who immediately set a fast course for the strike point. They found the distressed rescuer face down in the water, partially submerged and sinking. With extreme, untrained effort they were able to snare the unmoving dude using a life-float and rope and wrangle him, like a two hundred pound, deadweight tuna, up into the aft of the boat. The man was unconscious, not breathing and appeared to be severely injured. The looie started CPR, continuing for almost ten unresponsive minutes, until the coast guard vessel arrived. The Greeks took over, working another fifteen minutes before finally conceding their countryman was gone. They transferred the body to their own boat and interviewed the hydrographers, who had to contact the Harknet for the coast guard OIC, to verify their authorization to be conducting whatever it was they were doing in the bay. Fortunately, sufficiently ambiguous explanations were provided, referencing documented permission from the ministry of waterways and port affairs, and the Greeks left without compromising any classified information.

The sailors were too unsettled by the incident to do any more work and headed back in to the small fishing marina in the cove below the hotel, where they secured the boat during off-ops. The po asked the new engineer what *he* did today and the gopher replied, "Not much. Just hung out and got some rest from my flight. Walked around a little." He didn't see the need to relate he had almost been killed, twice.

The navy crew made a mutual decision to take tomorrow off. They assumed there would be coast guard specialists in and around the survey area investigating the training accident. No doubt, the media would be there, too, swarming in helicopters, boats, or both. It would not be prudent to add themselves to the jumble, engaged in classified activity and exposed to news interrogation. The po suggested they have a party to relieve tension and readjust from the unexpected stress of the day. He had a case of Cold Duck in his room that had been given to him some time ago by the embassy commissary manager in Athens, because they couldn't sell it and it was taking up valuable storage space. "What's cold duck?" asked the covert engineer, having never heard that term before.

"It's sort of a carbonated red wine drink, with a high alcohol content. Kinda tastes like sugar shit, but it's great for a fast buzz. It's supposed to be cold, but, since we don't have ice, we'll have to drink it warm. That'll probably make it worse, but, hey, what the duck? A party's a party, right? Love the one you're with! We can bring the folding chairs from the rooms down to the gazebo in the park. Score a couple bags of chewies, set up speakers, stream some tunes and we're good to go! Maybe we can get a few townies to join in. It'll be a blast!!"

The others were somewhat leery of the noncom's ambitious party plan, but soon acquiesced, and the group departed the Kafe to set up in the park before it got dark. Weather-wise, there was no

problem. It would be a mild, clear evening and pleasant to be outside. Why *not* have a party, relax a bit and enjoy the ambience of
the setting? Nea Peramos actually was a picturesque little village.
And, if they interacted with the locals, it was good public relations, which never hurts. By the time they were seated in the gazebo, plugged into a cache of classic country rock and unscrewing
the first bottles of 'duck', the Americans were convinced the party
was a *great* idea and they were about to have a memorable time.

***

Agent Rossy tried to open his eyes, but they felt glued shut.
His head amplified the beat of his heart like a kettle drum in an
echo chamber and he had no recollection of who, or where, he
was. The only proof of consciousness was overwhelming pain and
nausea. He tried to move something, anything, but couldn't verify
success. It seemed like bright, hot sunlight was filtering through
his eyelids, so it must be daytime. *Jesus god!! What it is!?*! He lay
in the bed for a long time, trying to develop a coherent strategy for
what to think about next. It was not happening and he drifted back
into darkness. Something in the deep sub-psyche knew better and
prodded another attempt at awakening. This time he was able to
partially open an eye, albeit painfully. Everything looked red. Realizing there was no waking up without sight, he concentrated on
getting the eyeballs energized. With visibility came verification of
daylight and awareness of surroundings. He was in the hotel room.
#36. Next task - sit up... without throwing. Check. Stand
up.....without falling. OK. Simon says - walk over to the table and
see what time it is. No way!!! He couldn't believe his clock! The
phone said it was morning, obviously, but *the day after the day
after the last day he remembered!!* So he was waking up *two days*
after the cold ducking, and still had a cracked head hangover??!
How could this be?? He had been out for, what? Thirty-six
hours?? *Holy lord christ in heaven!!*

What the duck happened?? *Think, agent, think!!* The last co-
gent thing he recalled was tipping the bottle up for another slash of
juice and he kept tipping and tipping, but was not able to get it to
where he could drink, because his head was falling backwards and
away at the same rate. Next thing he knew he was on the ground
covered with cold duck. And then the screen went blank and he
woke up here in the room, with no intel on yesterday. This was a

scary sensation. He had never lost a whole day before, nor been this ducked up! He wondered where everyone else was? Did we have a good time at the party? Lots of questions, but first he had to shower, dress and regain some semblance of stability. What a ducking bust!!

There was no hot water and the cold shower actually aggravated the tentative condition of the duckster. By the time he sufficiently got it together to leave the building, it was almost noon and he was overcome, once again, with a feeling of overbearing hunger. It seemed he really wasn't getting enough to eat in Greece, like he had been hungry ever since arriving. Not that there wasn't any food - there was plenty of great stuff to eat here - it's just that he was always being overtaken by events and missing a lot of meals. However, right now was different and he intended to go right to the Kafe for a box lunch. On the way out he checked the rooms of his colleagues. They were all locked and empty. Outside, while walking down along the grassy mall, he found the room chairs still in and around the gazebo, along with twelve empty duck bottles and other debris and trash from the party. There didn't appear to be any signs of damage or anything gone terribly wrong, suggesting the po's little soiree might have proceeded reasonably well. He decided to police the park area after lunch. Looking toward the marina, he noticed the survey craft was gone, meaning the navy crew must be out working. He wondered what time they got underway this morning and, if they felt anywhere near as ducked up as he did, how in god's hell could they function on a rocking little boat? Even such a thought summoned the hurls, so he put it out of mind and walked over to the Kafe. The lunch was excellent - a couple beef, tomato and hot pepper wraps, cheese, fruit and raw figs. He felt much better after partaking, energized, perhaps even optimistic, though about what, he had no clue.

Back in his room, following execution of the self-assigned task to straighten up the park gazebo, Rossy considered the mission status. If there was no *OPSB* contact by this evening, he would be in the red zone, facing a Dick call for supplemental instructions - a situation he wanted to avoid at all costs. It occurred to him he had not yet seen another person today. Certainly an oddity in itself, but a privation in context with going forward in this phase of the operation. How could an asset be contacted, if there

were no people?? Where was everybody? It wasn't that he, himself, had been incognito. Christ, by now, everyone for miles
around had to know who he was and where he could be found. If
the asset was here, there should have been contact by now. He
went out on the balcony to clear his mind and think through a
structured strategy.

The view was stand alone spectacular and even more so as
enhanced by the brilliant sunlight and pure clarity of the air. He
could see the gulf islands and even the mainland beyond, all entic-
ing as the alluring vacation destinations they proudly were. The
calm, blue waters were dotted with a variety of recreational, fishing and commercial vessels, moving silently among each other,
seemingly with an orderly singularity of purpose to enjoy the day.
The secret sailor stepped forward to the balcony rail in hopes of
possibly spotting the NAVO survey boat working in Kolpos
Megaron, but the bay was out of scope of observation from this
vantage point. He looked down from the railing to the balcony
directly below and reflexively lurched away, almost stumbling
backwards into the room! He couldn't believe what he saw!! There
was a nude woman down there, lying face down on a chaise
lounge in the sun!! He waited a few minutes and stealthily approached the railing again. She was still there, in the same position, maybe asleep. She was young, exquisite, with classic Mediterranean features, à la the legendary Sophia Loren. Her olive
brown skin glistened in the luminous light, reflecting an oiled
smoothness and perfection any Hollywood producer would kill
for. The transfixed voyeur could not take his eyes off the mesmerizing Greek goddess, when suddenly, "Ti einai afló gia ména?"

What?!? Is she coding me? Is this the contact asset?? The as-
tute agent didn't believe it. He thought it far more likely she was a
concubine babe, an áthiktos, who was trying to hook him, because
there was no doubt in his mind that these hotel dudettes were nothing other than high-end hookers. "Five hundred euros," he answered, smugly playing along with what had to be a bad joke.

"You think I am poutána? Amerikanoi men are all the same -
vlima kolotripas! Say the code response, William, say it in
Greek!!"

Holy frack!! She's for real! My contact! "Den xéro. Esý tha
mou peis."

"OK. Meet me in the lounge in fifteen minutes. There's no one there during rest time. We can talk freely with no bother."

***

The star-quality beauty poured herself an ouzo and grabbed a Marathon, before returning to the table from the untended bar. The seated operative thought she looked even more stunning, upright and minimally clad, than as he first saw her a few minutes ago. She sat down across from her payday, placing the beer in front of him. He pushed it to the side, not even wanting to see anything alcoholic. "So, what's up?", he blurted, not knowing how to begin the interview. His fogged head and her forceful presence boggled his good sense and he was involuntarily breaking foolish.

"Gelá sou, William. I believe you are seeking information regarding your CIA's suspected cyber terrorist, are you not?"

"Yes, I am. What can you tell me?"

"He has recently been in this country. He has been in contact with several people in Athens. My ears tell me he was very quietly maneuvering in the Plaka district, where technically inclined men and women interact hoping to find or form employment opportunities. It is almost like a continuous, unofficial job matrix for highly trained engineers and technicians looking for work. As you might know, Greece has many problems, caused by long-time inept, perhaps corrupt, government policies. This has resulted in a very severe cutback in public spending and loss of jobs by many engineers serving infrastructure initiatives. They call it austerity. It sounds positive, but in reality there is very little systemic improvement or upgrade happening anymore in Greece and many professionals see nothing but deterioration and decline. They see only a future of frustration, especially young engineers just out of school, with little prospect for employment in their field. There is much sadness and discontent. Perhaps growing anger."

"Is there any info on what he talks about?"

"Not really. There was maybe a focus on infrastructure systems, but nothing specific."

"Has anyone you know identified or taken video of the subject?"

"Óchi. There has been no information pertaining to ID. No video. The people he talks with are very secretive. It is difficult to hear anything definitive about your target, and what we get is second or third tier. I think, though, it was fairly reliably disclosed that he is, himself, an engineer, trained and educated in some aspect of an energy related or applied field."

"Is he still in Greece?"

"Óchi. It is much certain that he left the country at least a week ago."

"Anything on where he went?"

"Naí. We hear South Korea. The southern part of the peninsula, in the Busan area. This was triangulated from multiple sources, so it should be good."

"Anything else?"

"Óchi. That's is all I can tell. I must go, now. Do you want the beer?"

William shook his head. "Good luck, glýka." The unlikely asset grabbed the bottle and sashayed out of the room. He still didn't believe she wasn't a hooker, a very intelligent and well educated hooker.

***

The pensive pointman remained alone at the lounge table trying to collect his thoughts and plan the next move. He felt great relief that the contact had been made and new reportable intel was secured. Another piece of the puzzle. *Special bean* is an engineer. He is scouting and recruiting disconnected infrastructure engineers and he has relocated to South Korea. *Now I have to find a device to send this in on. And then I'll be done with Greece! Praise jesus!* It wasn't that Rossy disliked Greece for any particular reason. He just felt on edge here, sort of like being weighted with a premonition of....what? Not doom, exactly, but closer to, like....trouble, unpredictable trouble. It was more uncomfortable than scary, and he would be glad to be rid of it, hopefully, upon migration to Korea. First things first. He remembered a computer on Diantha's desk in her miserable, cubbyhole little office. Surely, she would let him use it a few minutes to transmit the *OPSB* update. He stood up and strode briskly toward the corridor.

No one was in the office. God, this was getting spooky. Really, where the hell *is* everybody? Did we drive all the people out with our party!? Apparently, yes, except for the hooker asset. CIAsters are tough and not afraid of anything. The guest agent saw the computer and sat down before it on the squeaky swivel. It was on. The desktop backdrop was a photo, in front of the hotel, of Diantha and the concubines. The *SB* asset wasn't among them. He didn't know what that meant, but was more interested in noticing there was no password field and no screen cam. This was all he needed to get it done. Just after sending the report and as the scrambling sequence began, the ambient room light darkened. Startled, the unauthorized user looked up to see Diantha standing in the doorway, with a threatening scowl on her face. "What are you doing? You cannot be in here!" she nearly screamed, moving quickly around the desk to block his escape. Before he could respond, the scramble went into its audio effects, followed by the blue screen, and the manager freaked out. "What have you done to my computer?" she wailed, certain the American idiot had crashed her machine, for what reason she did not know.

"I'm sorry, Diantha. I needed a computer and didn't know where you were. It's OK, there's nothing wrong, see?" He pointed to the screen that had returned to desktop.

The skeptical owner checked recent items and couldn't find anything she didn't recognize. She glared at the intruder and said, in a much more composed tone, "You will pay one hundred euros."

"What? You're kidding!! I only used it for a few minutes! I'll pay, but a hundred euros? C'mon! That's not fair!!"

"One hundred euros."

Rossy was in departure mode. He expected a Dick call at any moment and didn't have time to argue. Whatever the cost, he planned to bolt without checkout, because his advance payment more than covered all charges, contrived, or otherwise. "OK, put it on my room bill," he conceded, while exiting the office to run back up upstairs and wait for the call.

***

There was no call. Instead he received a text within a few minutes of returning to the room. This was odd, in that Dick had said he would only communicate by voice call. He wasn't going to use text, for security reasons, because the chipmole's phone was not a remote user verified device. The message was brief, ordering the operative to proceed immediately for Busan, South Korea, and report to the NAVO pc on the USNS Wyeth, a survey unit currently in port at the restricted military sector of the city's commercial shipping district. There was nothing regarding making an asset, meaning the contact had to be in the vicinity of the port zone and would, like before, eventually pop up somewhere, unexpectedly and from out of nowhere. The agent engineer was learning the drill and had no concern over the opacity of the orders. He had enough to move on and that's all he needed. The message closed with a reminder to not coordinate anything therein, or any subsequent movements, with anyone. Go dark or go deep. Precisely five minutes after the text was opened, it disappeared, vanished from the phone with no trace it had ever existed.

The secret opster was ready to roll. He was short on clothes, since dumping the excess baggage and ducking himself the other day, and briefly considered going back out to the free-zone and pulling an outfit from his thrown aways. Then, remembering the wild dogs, he rejected that notion in favor of buying whatever was needed at the airport. He called a taxi, left his room open with the keycard on the dresser and walked into the hallway. After sliding the van keys under the po's door he headed for the stairwell, jauntily carrying only his overnight tote and the briefcase. Unburdened by the extra luggage, he felt like a free and classy traveler. Outside, a small, Renault wreck-of-a-cab showed up at the front entrance within minutes and off he bolted without checkout. Not exactly Bondesque, but effectively iaw plan. The ex-chauffeur gopher would be well on the way to Korea before anyone concluded he was missing.

**

Rossy did not want to ride up front, knowing they would be taking the dreadful national road back to the city, but there was no choice. The cab was too damn small to sit in the back for anyone of average size or larger. The driver, who resembled Kleo, was happy to get such a good fare and wanted to talk, even though his English skills were less than lacking. The non-Greeking American could only nod and concur and hope nothing was said requiring a negative response. Eventually, conversation tapered and the visitor became engrossed with the remarkable scenery sweeping by as they sped on down the highway. The only previous times he had been on this road, he was driving and couldn't look at anything other than straight ahead. He wondered how the wee car could go so fast. When they approached a familiar curve, the front man pointed to the visible off-road shrine and asked the driver to go slow. He was interested to see if the food was gone, like the funeral lady said it would be. The driver thought he wanted to stop and whipped off into the curve pullover. "No, no, don't stop!! I just said to slow down so I could see something!" Too late. They were already parked where the Sienna had spent considerable time a few days ago. Since they were there, the rider got out and walked over to the miniature mourning shell.

"Nickola, filos?" asked the driver, apparently thinking his fare was a friend of the ill-fated biker, whom he seemingly knew.

"No...well, maybe a little." After all, spending an afternoon at the boy's death marker counted for some degree of connection. The edible offerings were completely gone. All that remained were a few plastic plates. The question was, *how were they taken?* Did people actually stop from the roadway to share? Did wildlife scavenge the site? Or, did the soul of Nickola.......? These were unanswerable wonderings. *I gotta get out of here!* The faux friend looked at the driver and motioned toward the rusty Renault. "Let's go, man!"

The cab driver faced the same blind turn that had recently terrorized the former van driver. Cabman, however, had no fear and pulled right out in front of a ready-mix concrete truck barreling around the curve. The truckster laid on his ear-numbing pressure horn in furious protest, as he thundered the behemoth machine all but through the defenseless little go-cart daring to throw up a forward block! **"Ilithíos!!"** The good fare felt like a gnat on a dragon's nose. He cupped his hands across his ears and leaned over, head in knees, expecting, momentarily, to follow Nickola into the magic kingdom. *Can I make it there OK without food?* The cabbie accelerated as much as possible, while trying to avoid running up on the car ahead. And then he slued left over the centerline and began passing. The truck followed suit, closely pressing directly behind. Other motorists scrambled to make way for the lane hogging lunatics, some sailing off the road altogether. As soon as there was clearance, the cabster careened back to the right and the truck exploded past, horn blaring, to the now vacated highway beyond. The petrified passenger felt a strong sense of dejá vu, except now he rode in a Greecer vehicle that was part of the problem. *These people are all fracking nuts!!* He had never seen roadwork quite like this, not even in New England, and only wanted to be at the airport, where he could fly out of this crazy country in a nice, safe airbus.

The rest of the trip on the coastal highway was way too fast, but uneventful. They approached the northern limits of Athens in much less time than it had taken the novice international driver to cover the same route going out. In speeding around the bypass and looking down on the main metropolitan area of the capital city, the Parthenon temple ruin, perched high on the Atheni Acropolis, was clearly visible in the distance. This was the iconic symbol of Greece, one of the biggest and most famous tourist attractions in the world. Who travels to Greece and doesn't go see the Parthenon? It would be like touring Arizona and not stopping by the Grand Canyon. The agent engineer thought he would probably never pass this way again. He should make a diversion and go take a look at the remarkable structure, walk in the footsteps of Plato and his ancient contemporaries and get some pics. It wouldn't be that far out of the way and he did not yet have a flight time, so why not? What could it hurt? He tapped the driver's shoulder and pointed at the Acropolis. "Naí! Naí! Acropolis!" beamed the happy Greecer, obviously proud of his national treasure. The tourist indicated through signs and one word explications that he wanted to go see the historical preservation. "Naí! Naí! No problem, OK!" finally comprehended the cabbie, exiting sharply right onto a connector entering a downtown freeway.

The Acropolis loomed mountainously large as they approached the entrance kiosk and concession pavilions from Theorias. The driver parked in a taxi zone. The excited outlander opened the door and asked the cabmaster to wait for him. "Periméne mé, OK?" he said in phone app Greek. The driver held out one hand, pointing to the battered meter with the other. *He wanted to be paid!* Uh-oh. This could mean he's not going to wait. Rossy reached for his case and paid the fare, repeating the request for the smiling driver to wait. "Naí! Naí! No problem!" The dubious passenger disembarked, carrying the crucial case with him. He was not about to risk losing the paper equivalent of his life over a runaway cab. It cost a substantial admission fee to enter, which gave one the immediate authority to climb up about a hundred stone steps to the crest of the mesa-like formation. On top were many separate, crumbling structures, dominated by the big boy ruin, the Parthenon. It was impressive, with its colonnades of massive doric columns and classical architectural style. By far, it was the oldest public building the young tripper had ever seen, originally constructed almost twenty-five centuries ago and evidently re-constructed much more recently. Up close, the restoration work contrasted sharply with the original remains and it actually looked a little bogus, sort of like a movie set. There was probably an optimum distance from which to view the Parthenon, where it would, indeed, appear to be an indestructible temple of the ages. But none of that mattered right now. The real time mission was to click a bunch of quality photo shots, as quickly as possible, and get back down to the taxi zone before the cabman snagged another fare. In doing so, the would-be tourist discovered the scene of the surrounding city, from this elevated perch, was just as spectacular as the ancient buildings. He could see the Olympic stadium and competition complex, a huge park area with an historic outdoor theater and wide expanses of the city. In less than five minutes, he took pictures of the Parthenon from all sides and the view from the Acropolis in all directions, at least twenty-five or thirty photos, and then literally ran back down the steps to find his ride.

The cab, of course, was gone and with it, the overnight tote bag. All the disgusted sightseer had left was his goddam briefcase and a phone cam full of amateur photos. If he hadn't acted on the brilliant idea to detour to the Acropolis, he would be at the airport by this time, with all his stuff intact. Now he had to find and buy new things to replace what was lost. He sat down on a bench and checked the cam cache, finding about half the new shots were unfocussed blurs! So basically, he had virtually nothing to show for this fiasco and it was getting late in the afternoon. Another bucking bust! World traveling was not nearly as easy as portrayed on TV!

It was past 1800 when the weary sojourner finally made it to the international terminal at AIA. The next available flight to Busan was on Korean Air, departing 2015 tomorrow. It arrived 1300, local, the next day. He would have to spend *over twenty-four hours awaiting departure!!* Oh, well, that gave plenty of time to go shopping. He had more than enough resources to weather the wait, even after paying cash, including his balance of euros, for the airline ticket. It would be fun and he could test his theory about surviving in the airport with nothing but money. At least he was forever safely removed from the barbarity of the Greek highway system. And it provided a little free time to think, review and re-group. Maybe fabricate some answers to nagging issues he really hadn't been able to wrap his head around. Like, exactly what was he doing and who was he chasing all over the world? Was *Special Bean* actually a real person? It just didn't seem anyone could cover this much territory without being seen or showing up on video somewhere. *The DIS agent, Mr. SPAM, found me on the road in Pennsylvania, before he ever even heard of me!!* Conversely, plenty of people have evidently heard of *SB*, but no one has seen him! What's up with that?? Another question. *Do I still have a real job? Pc kool said if I disappeared on him, I was NAVO toast. Well......?*

CHINATOWN

It was raining in Washington, an early autumn shower starting to carry the chill of the changing season. Randolph Patton Clement stepped briskly from the Metro station in walking through the weather to his appointment. Friday evening traffic was heavy with people making their weekend moves. The general did not want to risk a fender bender in these conditions and left the Jag at the hotel. He approached the Fa Foo restaurant, within five minutes of his reservation, carrying both a sense of anticipation and angst. It had been a particularly trying week for the CIA kingpin and he knew, at this point, his decision was irreversible. There were two issues he had wanted to address. Did the SAFE project development team have a mole? Short answer, no. They had been hacked, but not totally. The Chinese had not been able to crack into any separately protected technical files. They only got to planning and programming documents, which didn't contain any 'how to' development information. They were still locked out of the good stuff and that's why he was being offered the billibuck. The other thing he had wanted to investigate was where Jiang was staying in D.C. A simple task, but, disturbingly, he couldn't find out. With all the resources of the greatest intelligence organization in the world, he couldn't locate one of the most covertly influential people on the planet. This made the super agent doubt his own effectiveness, his professional purpose. What was the point of continuing in a job he was hamstrung on? And things were only going to get worse. It was time to get out and he had decided to take the money and run. This evening's business should be very interesting.

Vin Lu was not at his usual station at the top of the steps. Instead the general was wordlessly greeted by a minatory looking Chinese host, whom the long-time regular guest had never seen before. The tall, martially fit, maitre'd led the big man directly to his regular table by the front window, at exactly 1900, where Mr. Jiang was comfortably seated, reading the China Business News.

"Good evening, General Clement. So good to see you again," welcomed the oilman, neither rising, nor looking up from his paper. Clement sat down without saying anything. Jiang continued reading, in silence, for a few seconds and then folded the paper and looked hard at the expected ontimer. "Tell me, sir, have you come to a decision?"

"Yes, Mr. Jiang, I have decided to accept your proposal."

"Excellent, excellent. A decision you shall not regret, I am certain. If you can bring the merchandise with you next week, I will be prepared to transfer payment and we can make a simultaneous exchange. Details of the mechanics and conditions of the transaction will be stipulated at that time to our mutual satisfaction. Is this agreeable?"

"Yes."

"Good. Now, if you will excuse me, I have another appointment." Jiang held his gaze without rising. He was dismissing the usually favored patron from his *own table* without having even been served.

Tophead departed Fa Foo's feeling like he had just made a deal with the devil. But, as far as he was concerned, it was a great deal. He didn't care about service and integrity anymore. Everyone was trying to screw him, so why not screw back? It was time to contact Whittberg, at NAVOSUR, and line up a chipmole. At least he had sufficient resources left to go out with a high profile, deflective win. Whether it was real or not was of no consequence, because, in this business, perception was everything. The general stopped in CCC's and ordered #82 - Lo Mein Pork and a double serving of shrimp egg rolls. He then returned to the Marriot and settled in for the night, watching *WWE Smackdown* reruns.

SOUTH KOREA

The flight to Gimhae International Airport, west of Busan, was extremely long and not entirely smooth. There were stops in Qatar and Bangkok, requiring change of plane for the last leg. The crescent shaped route was dictated by China not allowing non-stop through flights in its airspace, forcing a southern vector over the Himalayas. The high mountains were experiencing a fairly strong pre-winter storm system that generated considerable turbulence during the flyover. At one point the craft rapidly tanked a few hundred feet, prompting gasps and isolated screams from the properly seatbelted passengers. Rossy had mental images of crashing on a steep, snow-covered slope and sliding down the mountain with an avalanche, eventually coming to a crunching stop buried in an impossibly deep drift. The rest of the movie would be a tale of unlikely survival against the elements and an onslaught of ten feet tall yetis, interjected with irrelevant power struggles, love trysts and untimely deaths. In the end, only the stars would remain standing to be escorted to safety by the uniformed, rescuing authorities. Would he be among the lucky? If so, would he have conducted himself well? No way of knowing, because they made it through the disturbances with no further pitch falls and descended quietly into the still air of Bangkok. Applause.

Surprisingly on schedule, the Asian incomer made it to the ground side of Gimhae's international terminal by early afternoon. He was losing account of time and instinctively pulled out his phone to verify the date. No service!?! What is this??! He had activated and paid for expensive international calling through the GSM network before leaving the states and now there is no service? At the goddam airport, for chrissake?! Through inquiry at an information kiosk, he learned it was mandatory to register his mobile phone with the government, in order to use it in South Korea, and that cost ₩50,000. He didn't have any ₩ and wasn't sure he *should* register. That would certainly breach his anonymity and possibly create a security soft spot. But then, if his phone wasn't

active, how could he communicate with handler Dick? Maybe
through classcom on the Wyeth. He elected to wait and determine
all options before engaging a procedure as conspicuous as phone
registration. After all, he was supposed to be traveling dark, like a
shark in the deep, even though they had thoroughly processed his
classified identifying paperwork, a few minutes ago, at arrival.
The ever alert agent felt a headache coming on in trying to continuously coordinate the many complicated parameters of the mission. He decided to buy a few bens' worth of ₩ and get something
to eat at the super Mac he had spotted across the terminal. Then he
could take the monorail into the city and cab his way to the NAVO
survey ship.

***

Pc Merlin "hitman" Plough looked somewhat bemusedly at
his newest subordinate. He was actually happy to get an unexpected engineer delivery, having had one of his navaid site leaders
abruptly reassigned last week with no specific replacement stipulated. All he had was a tech on the site, a violation of protocol
prohibiting 'lone rangers' at field stations. But then that particular
site was off-line and scheduled to be broken down in the next day,
or so, and it might not be worth it to send a greenie out there.
Maybe he would wait and see. Talk to the rook and find out if he's
useful for anything. Most of the new engineers TDYed to the field
didn't know their ears from their ass flaps and there had been no
advisement as to where this one was coming from, or how he was
to be utilized. There wasn't even an official communication he
was being assigned to the Wyeth. The boy's orders were unintelligible gibberish and the pc found it a little comical how ineffective-
ly random and unpredictable NAVO's management moves often
transpired. So, no, pc Plough was not overly concerned that some
dude he had never seen before shows up for whatever, saying this
was where he was supposed to be.

Hitman was normally one of the most easy going and popular
party chiefs on the agency's staff. His sobriquet originated at
UTEP, where he football scholarshipped as a particularly ferocious corner. More than a jock, though, he graduated with a degree
in social engineering and joined NAVO after failing an NFL draft
and a subsequent walk-on tryout with the Dallas Cowboys. The
'hitman' moniker occasionally manifested itself in off-duty set-

tings, most recently at a club bar in Cheat, West Virginia, where the ex-Miner was trying to relax after a brutal day of whitewater rafting. One of the local patrons, in town for the day from Deliverance Mountain, took a liking to Merlin's leather outback hat and alpaca poncho to the extent he thought the rafter should either give them to him or buy him and his wasted buds a round of drinks. Hitman thought neither would happen. He calmly removed the items in question, carefully placed them on his barstool, and proceeded to mop the floor with the helpless homies. A security bouncer completed the task by sweeping them out the door. The hitster returned to his seat, reinstated the accessories and continued enjoyment of the evening with his associates. So, while everyone got along well with the incumbent Wyeth pc, no one ever pressed him on anything.

"OK, Mr. Rossy, welcome aboard, I guess. Tell me, what brings you to us at this particular point in time?"

"Uh...., I'm afraid I can't talk about that, sir. My assignment is classified."

"Really? Classified, huh? Hmm....... OK, so what am I supposed to do with you?"

Jesus! This dude was not informed of me coming here. Have I been cut loose? Or, am I completely off the grid?? "Well, I'm willing to do whatever you need me to do. That's about all I can say."

"Yes, well, I'm sure we can find something for you to help out with. Do you know anything about what's going on, here, son?"

"No, not really. I assume you're involved with some kind of hydrographic project, somewhere in the area?"

"Yes, that's true. And since your orders are classified TS, I will assume you're cleared to be briefed on our operations, which are also level three." Pc hitman then gave the phantom newcomer a mission overview of the Wyeth team task in the southeastern coastal region of the Republic of Korea. It was actually a double faceted effort to develop new technology in the process of collecting practical data. The Busan port basin and shipping channel were silting in and a major dredging project was in the planning stages. The Wyeth was assigned to complete a thorough hydrographic survey of the entire inner harbor and outside the breakwater narrows to the East China Sea. The survey would be analyzed to quantify the amount of material to be dredged. The NAVO work scope also included comprehensive current studies and bottom sample analysis to evaluate dredge spoil disposal requirements, as well as any mitigation construction needed to protect the improvements. It was a mammoth undertaking, that could take several years, but was entirely necessary as a vital component to both the ROK export economy and national security. In the course of performing the hydrography, NAVOSUR was field testing new robotic survey technology, featuring drone hydrofoils, computer controlled from the ship's lab through autonav integration with the remote positioning systems. The DHs were cam equipped to provide visuals and controls for surveying in active shipping waters. All sounding and fixed-point tidal data was instantaneously transmitted to shipboard processors that plotted real-time mapping products. Basically, the operation was like a video game, except there was no catastrophic, full-screen fire and destruction going on, at least not yet. Though the work was intense, requiring close monitoring and continuous attention to all interfaces, the NAVO engineers much preferred robotic survey ops, in the comfort of the lab, to being on the water in the sucky little boats. The ultimate payoff, like any automated procedure, was better efficiency in time and cost, at greater quality of result. Riding the cutting edge can be fun, even while your job is possibly being sliced away.

There were currently three engineers and two techs in the lab and an engineer and tech at each of two navaid sites, though one site engineer was gone. Survey ops were presently suspended in order to break down and relocate the positioning site of the missing engineer. Maybe Mr. Rossy could take his place at the new remote site. *Don't think I'll be here long enough and I can't go remote, but it sounds interesting.* Maybe.

The labsters were lounging around in the duty room, exerting minimum effort, since field ops were down. They were in Navy Yard mode, except now they were copping at least sixty hours OT a pay period, on a base rate adjusted for night, sea and area differentials. Korea was considered a combat zone, because, technically, the war with the north had never ended. Chaching! Twenty-five percent. They were working shipboard, so, technically, they were at sea, even though the ship was in port. Chaching! Ten percent. Survey ops went 24/7, all through the night. Chaching! Fifteen percent. Overtime. Chaching! Chaching! It all added up to at least triplepay, not including per diem and expenses, which was a whole separate bag of feed. Obviously, money was the primary incentive NAVOSUR had to offer to attract duty bodies, though there were other unquantifiable benefits and opportunities available to those who were creatively ambitious. Probationary Rossy was not yet privy to the art of settling travel claims and was not fully cognizant of what being a NAVO sailor was all about. All he knew was that he had not really seen anyone, including himself, do much of anything since he started working for the agency. Pc Plough introduced the new engineer to his Wyeth shipmates.

Sean "doc" Misenor was the most senior of the professional shipboard subordinates. He was a bio engineer, from East Tennessee State, who had flunked out of med school at an offshore college on the Caribbean island of Saba. He claimed his Saba bomb was precipitated by a false 'eff' in the final exam of an elective course in ethics, for which he had retained an attorney to dispute before the school's board of chancellors. If he could get the grading of just one exam question reversed, it would elevate his gpa sufficiently to be reinstated. Doc was confident his rep could convince the board members it was in their best financial interest to approve the upgrade. He was ready and eager to continue his quest of becoming a doctor, because health care was where the big bucks were stacked in America.

Please put your hands together for Hasken "farmer" Hess, on middle flatbed plotter. Hess was an agricultural engineer out of the University of Iowa, whose family farm dried up in a seemingly endless drought most assumed was associated with climate change. Hess had been living on federal subsidies to not grow ethanol corn, in deference to the strong shale oil lobby, but finally opted to get out of farming and take a job with uncle government.

How about Jerry "talker" Wolff, a graduate of Northern South Carolina State in general engineering, on correctional data processor? *What the hell is a general engineer?? I never heard of any degree like that.* It was a curriculum targeted to remedial students having the interest, but not the aptitude, to pursue a rigorous engineering major. South Carolina had a critical dropout problem and was experimenting with alternative educational programs to get more people into and through college. As a general engineer, talker could expound on almost any tech topic, but was never more than a question, or two, away from, 'I don't know, dawg'.

The techs were sitting at a work table reading the latest issue of *Stars and Stripes,* the DoD contracted newspaper for military personnel abroad, consisting mostly of wire service stories, blog reprints and commissary exchange ads. Marvin "flu" Prescott was the longest serving field employee at NAVOSUR. He had almost thirty years service and found himself frequently thinking retirement. Especially since 'the incident', a few years ago, when he was tentatively pinpointed as the source of introducing an unusually vile strain of flu to the Washington D.C. area following return from TDY in Taiwan. The AF329 virus had almost killed him, as it subsequently did scores of others, and he was interviewed by CDC specialists from Atlanta, as the first reported case in the mid-Atlantic region. On the upside, the ordeal might have left him permanently immune to everything, because Prescott had not been even remotely sick since. His tech partner, Gus "flo" Walls, looked like the reincarnation of a Black Panther street soldier, with his block-out afro and gold chains. Flo (for ladies only) had a serious jones for seaport hookers and had been treated numerous times for a variety of stds. He boasted it was entirely possible there was a small legion of little flos running around in several major Asian cities.

The agent noticed his new colleagues were not exactly GQ ad ready, as their physical appearance was probably a little rough. Long hair, beard, torn jeans and soiled sweat shirt would, more or less, be a typical witness description of any of them. Actually, bj was not that much in contrast, but quickly ruled against straightening up, in lieu of becoming conspicuous. Besides, it was easier and more comfortable to be unkempt, though he would still maintain basic cleanliness and hygiene. Blending in, melding with the crowd, swallowing into the center, just like *special bean.* You must become what you pursue.

Rossy sat down at the table and glanced at the front page section of the paper in front of him. A minor header with a *Washington Post* byline caught his eye: ***Navy Scraps Greece Site***. Reading on, the article reported that, due to budget cuts, the Senate Armed Forces Committee abandoned consideration of the proposed plan to develop an offshore group anchorage site in the Saronic Gulf, west of Athens. The SECNAV subsequently withdrew request for the program approval and preliminary development work in progress was terminated. *Holy christ!! This can't be true!!!* It had to be about the Harknet survey going on in Megaron Bay, but the story was dated, like, a month ago. They're still working on it now! Why would they continue working on something that was shitcanned?! And how could it be in the newspaper if it was classified? The puzzled sailor didn't know what this meant! He wanted to ask pc hitman about it, but realized he couldn't, because that would reveal his secret itinerary. Another NAVOSUR inconsistency he would have to file under 'say what?!?' and worry about it whenever.

***

A short time later, the Wyeth subordinates decided to punch out and head over to the Seamen's Service Club, a privately operated establishment owned by the International Merchant Marine Association. The iconic landmark was located right outside the secure naval compound along a busy waterfront thoroughfare. It was always a popular gathering spot for all types of crewmen from the many vessels using the civilian and military port facilities. Normally, the old watering hole never closed, but a daily curfew recently in effect required everyone off the streets between midnight and 0600. The national curfew was temporarily enacted for general public safety considerations, due to heightened tensions with the north through a period of scheduled joint U.S. - ROK military maneuvers. This meant the club was typically more crowded than usual, because the seamen had to compress what they normally drank in twenty-four hours, into eighteen. There was only one table open when the NAVO sailors arrived, located in a high traffic space in front of the bar and between a wall row of slot machines and the restrooms. A Korean band, evidently called 'THE BETLES', as magic-marked on their bass drum, offered unsynchronized western pop covers from a dark corner in the far recess of the dining room. Fortunately, the terribly played, outdated musical renderings were hardly audible over the din of the ignoring crush of drinking shipsters. If there were any listeners, they would be doubly annoyed by the band's irritating practice of immediately repeating each butchered number.

The club crashers ordered cheeseburgers with fries and Oriental Brewery beer. The burgers were prepared using ground Kobe beef imported from Japan and carried a reputation of being quite good. While awaiting the order, the neo-Korean operative watched the slot players. He remembered the rapid destruction of a jackson at the Lexington Park casino and wondered how long these dudes had been throwing their money away. There *were* a few payoffs, but the machines didn't dispense a noisy, exciting reward for bonanzas over a certain amount. If a big hit lined up, the lucky pigger had to fetch the club cashier, who verified and separately paid the prize, before cranking it away. One of the participants seemed to be almost hypnotic in his rhythmic motion from coin trough to slot to lever arm, apparently so used to losing he was nearly asleep. The sideliner watched in fascination when the wheels spun a row of gold treasure chests, worth more than a dollar grand, and the clueless player robotically reached for another coin. The unbelieving observer shot up from his chair, yowling, **"NOOO!!"**, as he dove across the table to grab the fist of the startled slotster before he unconsciously pulled the jackpot off. The instantly defensive seaman thought he was being waylaid and reflexively smacked his assailant back across the table from whence he came. All the Wyeth OB beers smashed to the floor, like a bowling alley strike, and pandemonium was on the verge of breaking bad. The game saver, holding a napkin to a bleeding lip, pointed frantically to the jackpotted machine and everyone realized what had gone down. The unlikely winner was so ecstatic he bought all the broken bottlers a new round and went immediately back to his slot work. Within an hour the wily mechanical bandit took its payout back.

Following happy meal time, the NAVO locals elected to shift for the evening to 'Texas Street', a nearby backwash of the city where ported seafarers could find anything they wanted. Hookers, drugs, booze, inkers, gambling, music. Even a few genuine Korean restaurants and culturally correct wagon vendors. The sailors gathered outside on the SSC sidewalk and waited for a traffic break to cross the wide, heavily traveled avenue. Pedestrians had no rights in South Korea, so they had to be sure they could make it over before committing. On the other side, they single-filed on a narrow dirt path for several hundred meters leading downslope into a tunnel under a railway yard. New man warily followed the others into the unlit underpass, stooping beneath the low concrete overhead. The air was dankly moist with a strong odor of sewer and the puddled walkway paralleled a water filled trough. Countless droplets seeping from the ceiling echoed upon hitting the floor and channel surfaces, so it almost felt and sounded like amplified rainfall. Wet, algae slicked sidewalls were barely visible in the fading endpoint daylight. The mucky tunnel was long enough that the first-timer did not want to be there as soon as he entered, but knowing there was really no choice he dutifully plodded on behind the entourage. At one point, he thought there was some extraneous lateral motion as he passed by, but couldn't make out anything in the darkened shadows. About two-thirds of the way through, with no warning, the lagger felt a sharp, viselike clamp on his shoulder and the presence of a short body jammed up right behind him. *Jesus frack!!! Am I getting punked??! What the hell is this??* Too shocked to say anything, he kept moving forward, sort of dragging whatever was attached to him from the back. When they emerged out of the abyss, the Wyeth regulars broke into laughter in seeing their terrified new colleague besieged by a familiar figure. "Johnny!! How's it going, man??" Rossy slowly turned his head to look into the grinning, toothless face of a small, middle-aged Korean man, whose chin was still firmly implanted in his shoulder. "How ya doing?" he croaked and the little guy broke away, giggling like a ghoulish leprechaun. The freed one was stunned to see his unexpected 'backpacker' was armless, having only minimal flesh nubs protruding from the sleeves of a filthy, white tee-shirt. "This is our pal, Johnny noarms," introduced doc. "He's a thalidomide baby. Also, he's our slickey-boy and takes care of us on the street. I suggest you give him a donation. Like, right now." The rookie retrieved a grand₩ from his wallet and stuffed it into the jeans pocket of the still guffawing hustler, who turned abruptly and ran back into the tunnel. "He'll be back. Just going to get your welcome gift."

"Welcome gift?"

"Yeah, you'll find out. Just make sure you pay him. Cool?"

"Yeah, right. OK, I guess."

Texas Street was more an alley walkway than a street. There were rarely any vehicles in its not-more-than two block confines. It was gloomy, in the early evening, despite the glittering, oversized neon signs above the doorways of six, maybe seven, working nightclubs and several other shops and eateries. Many of the colored lights were in some stage of disrepair, or blinking malfunction, and the mostly two and three story structures lining the uneven pavement looked to be in generally dilapidated condition. The ground level clubs had names that seemingly reflected the spirit of the old American west. 'Sidewinder Saloon'. 'Painted Pony'. 'Riverboat Room'. 'Blue Buffalo'. 'Pearl's Pink Pistol'. They each beckoned any and all wayward seamen for restful relaxation and good enjoyment in many ways. *Give us your time and money and we will make you happy.* The Wyeth crew homed directly to their regular dive, The Golden Gate, where everyone knew each other. Except for the secret agent man.

The music immediately changed as the NAVO crew entered the club, switching from a Celtic bag and flute set, for the Irish sailors already planted, to contemporary hip-hop for the arriving Americans. This was standard practice in all the Texas Street establishments. They had incredible play lists of tunes accommodating any nationality of clients walking through the door. They also had efficient procedures for quickly deploying female companions to fracture the camaraderie of the men in favor of employing the women, either for the evening, the night, or both. It was all expertly directed by a semi-visible, club mamasan, who was unequivocally the boss, if not always the owner. When a new dude came in, he would be covered by at least two hooks and physically separated from his friends in a different part of the room. An effective move to execute the age old divide and conquer objective. It would be no mistake to see these tactics as akin to military strategy, because, as far as the mamasans were concerned, they *were* at war - to get as many incoming W as possible, as fast as possible, out of the corrupt, loose-walleted foreigners. This was not about cultural exchange, it was all about funds transfer. And the managing generals were very good at what they did. They supported the curfew as a sound business tool, because it trapped drunken shipmen in place for the night, sending them upstairs with their respective hooks of choice to keep the revenue stream flowing strong.

Before he could even sit down, Rossy was dogied by three attendants and boxed in at a small corner table completely removed from the Wyeths. This was an unusual scenario for the relatively inexperienced ladies' man. He could not remember ever being alone with three reasonably attractive women in a nightclub. It was all a bit overwhelming, even if they couldn't communicate very well and he knew they were only doing their job trying to redirect his money. The stranger drank OB, while his table mates sipped what he assumed was water, very expensive water. He was drifting into the moment, feeling only slightly out of control, when jarringly and again from undetected obscurity, Johnny noarms appeared. The girls scowled at the skinny slickster and slid their chairs away from the table. Johnny eased in close to his new port buddy and eye-pointed at his jeans. The curious clubber reached into the streetman's pocket and pulled out what seemed to be a slightly crushed pack of Newport cigarettes. He looked at Johnny, who grinned and nodded at the little green and white container, indicating the recipient should open it. The non-smoker complied and flipped the lid, finding what looked like a normal box full of cigarettes. But it didn't smell like cigarettes. Upon closer examination, he discovered they were actually hee-hee spliffs. The tobacco had been carefully removed and the wrappers tightly repacked with shredded cannabis. The non-toker's first thought was *how the hell did he do this?* Fabrication of the modified smokes would have required considerable dexterity. There was no way the boy could have done it without arms, so he must have an accomplice somewhere. Surmising this was his 'welcome gift', bj remembered doc instructing him to pay, but he had no idea how much. He turned over a ten-grand₩ and the NAVO slickey-boy seemed very pleased, perhaps overpaid pleased. The entire transaction was furtively scrutinized by mamasan. She came trunging out through a silk curtained opening from a private back room, grabbed the little Korean by the nape of his neck and harshly steered him through the door onto the street. After replacing the sailor's payment in noarm's pocket with half the amount, she returned to the club, while Johnny vanished into the darkness. Yes, indeed, it was all about funds transfer.

The comparatively unviced agent was not much of a get high guy. At least he didn't used to be. He might now be drinking more beer than in college, probably since it was more affordable, but he still didn't particularly like to be high or drunk. He only had one experience with labeled liquor and that was during a fraternity rush party, resulting in a situation almost as bad as the recent cold duck-up. He hadn't been knocked out as long, but was sick longer. It had been sufficiently disagreeable to know he would not do whiskey again, as a drink of choice. As for drugs, he had only tried stoning once - in school, again at a frat event. And, again, it did not go well. The grass was laced with hash and animal tranquilizer and he was nearly paralyzed on the floor for about six hours. Also, as a lifelong non-smoker, the acrid fumes really irritated his throat and lungs. He always figured weed as a carcinogen, just like tobacco, because the late, great Bob Marley, who might have smoked more ganja than anyone ever, died way prematurely of a malignant brain tumor. Despite all this, he intended to hang onto the 'welcome gift'. Marijuana was essentially legal, or at least not totally illegal, and maybe the potentially future toker would give it another draw sometime.

During the commotion of noarms being bumrushed out of the club, the latest T-Street patron rejoined his colleagues at their table, accompanied by one of his greeters, who anticipated trying to work him for an overnight. A couple other girls sat with the diminished group, earning their 'drinks'. Flo had already gone upstairs for the night and talker was off to the PP to see a special friend. The evening had settled into mellow monotony with not much going on, when a severely bedraggled white dude peeped his head in the doorway and timidly scanned the room. Espying the Americans he quickly entered the club and slipped over to their table, like a rodent running along the wall. Pulling up a chair beside doc, he was not approached by any of the idle hooks. They all made 'eeeww' faces of disgust, while watching mamasan make her way out of the back room.

"It's OK, mama," pre-empted doc, holding up a hand. "We've got him covered. No problem." Mamasan stopped and glared hard at the seated sailors, saying nothing, then turned slowly around and returned to the back. "Hey, insect, 'sup?? Long time no see. Where you been, man?"

"Oh, man, doc, it's been a rough stretch. I was up top to find if maybe I could score a job somewhere around Seoul and I got picked up by these dudes that said I could work their farm for a couple weeks picking cabbage. They put me in the back of their truck and took me over the fracking line, man!! The mothas were from the north and they were gonna slave my white ass, dawg. I got away, but it took me a week in the boons to make it back over. I thought I was fracking going down."

"Jesus, man, that's sounds like a hard way to go. Why don't you just turn yourself in and take your shit? At least you'd be shipped back stateside." Daryl "insect" Dawkins was a fugitive, a wanted man. He arrived in Korea, about six months ago, as a U.S. Army pfc logistics specialist, stationed at Camp Walker. One night, he got into a card game with a bunch of soldiers, including his boss, captain dickhead, as it turned out, and cleaned the table. He took a huge pot with an all in bet on a pair of fives. Cap wanted DD to keep playing, give him a chance to recover his loss, but the pfc cashed out. Not long afterwards, Daryl heard the captain was putting in paperwork to falsely charge him with stealing from supply and selling government issue goods on the blackmarket, a serious offense that would bring hard time, if convicted in court marshal. The pfc panicked, feeling *this* game the cards were shuffled against him, and went awol. He had been on the run ever since, trapped in-country with no way out. The Koreans dubbed him 'gonchung', because he was always flitting around, never staying in one place very long, like a flying insect.

"No, doc, can't do that. You don't know the army. They'll fry my innocent ass just to wrap the paperwork and there's no way I'm going to the cooler! That's not gonna happen! But, look, man, can ya help me out? Like ya'll did before? I just need one more push and I promise.....I *promise*, big dawg.....I won't lean on you anymore. OK?"

Doc looked thoughtfully at insect. The boy was hurting and needed help from somewhere, no doubt about that. What he wanted was for them to sneak him on the ship so he could take a shower and clean up, get something to eat and rest a day, or so, and then he would also want some cash before they smuggled him back onto the street. It was really no big deal to do this, as the Wyeth survey was a civilian operation under no military propriety. Christ, they could probably bring hookers on board and no one would know the difference! "OK, Daryl, but this is the last time. You're on your own after this, hear what I'm sayin'?"

"Yeah, solid, I hear you. No problem. Look, man, I really appreciate it. For real, dude."

"OK, let's go. We gotta get back before curfew." Doc stood up, along with the other NAVO sailors and insect, and they all headed for the door. Rossy was again bringing up the rear and didn't know what to do when two of the greeter girls grabbed his arm and yanked him back into the club as he tried to leave. His colleagues were already outside. He yelled for help and the Wyeth team responded, seizing the other arm and pulling him toward the street. The disbelieving middle man was like the rope in a tug-of-war. A third hook joined the golden gaters and the object of dispute found himself being drawn back and forth over the entrance threshold. Finally, the club siders let go and the government workers tumbled away, falling into a noisy, chaotic pile in the middle of the alley. To anyone watching from the outside, they looked like the short end of a saloon brawl, being tossed en masse through the front. The latecomer's would-be escort stood in the doorway screaming first language obscenities and shaking an angry, three-fingered fist high in the air, knowing her failed hustle would not go without consequences. The surveyors of the evening collected themselves and shambled slowly off into return to the ship, hiding the hapless insect in their midst.

***

Early in the morning, hitman located his bonus engineer in the wardroom, sipping post breakfast coffee. Pc Plough wanted to send the inexperienced rookie to Yeongdo, to help the resident tech break down the positioning site for relocation further out in the survey zone. It should be about a half day job. The secret subordinate was directed to report to the navy support helicopter, on the Wyeth fantail, scheduled for lift-off in thirty minutes. The young g-man dutifully complied, looking forward to riding on a helicopter, something he had never done before, while helping with a technically useful mission, which he also had not really done yet since climbing aboard NAVOSUR. He found the SH-60 utilicraft idling on the red and white helipad, as its military crew performed checklist preparations for flight. The pilot stood on the deck by the cab ladder, eyeing the approaching civilian suspiciously. The assigned rider identified himself, saying he was a NAVO engineer ordered to report for duty ops. Lt. Cmdr. Carson didn't particularly like civilians, especially those really looking the part, or worse. Hair, sweat hoodie, jeans, sneakers. *Oh yeah, sneakers.* "I'm sorry, sir, but I can't let you on my aircraft with that footwear."

"Excuse me?"

"The sneakers. Not allowed. You gotta have steel-toed safety boots in order to board."

"What? I don't have safety boots!"

"Then you can't board. It's regulation."

"Well, what am I supposed to do? My boss told me to fly out with you."

"I don't know, sir, that is not my problem."

The obstructed civilian felt frustration anger rising. He sensed the pointless military aversion and knew he was being arbitrarily booted. *Frack it!! I'll just go back to my room and let somebody else sort it out. I don't want to fly with this meathead, anyway!* And so he did. A short time later, as he was starting to drift away on the comfortable stateroom bunk, the flight-blocked engineer heard a sharp rap on the door. "Open," he called out and hitman entered. The obviously irritated pc wanted to know what was going on and, after receiving a brief of the situation, ordered the un-booted underling to follow him aft. Within fifteen minutes the Seahawk was airborne carrying its sole, sneaker-clad passenger.

First stop was the red navaid site in the north central part of the island, on a remote highpoint overlooking the inner survey area. Though less than five straight-line miles from the pier bound ship, the site was inaccessible by vehicle. The flight time was only about ten minutes, so the helicopter never developed much altitude after lift. The support ops schedule was to drop the engineer off at red, load equipment and gear, zip across the harbor to the green site in the Nam-gu district to deliver supplies, stop by the ship to offload red's inventory, then go back to red to pickup the engineer and tech, who by that time were supposed to have policed and restored the locale to it's original condition of pristine, inhospitable boonieland. NAVOSUR's policy for remote site use and abandonment was the same as the Sierra Club's: 'take only memories, leave only footprints'. The red positioning point would then be relocated further south on Yeongdo after the equipment was checked out and re-calibrated for return to field service.

The red tech, a navy enlisted sailor, was very well organized. He had packed all the electronic geonavigational equipment to be lifted back to the ship in floatable, watertight containers, secured for transport. The camp was broken down and high value reusables were neatly and tightly crated to avoid any shifting in flight. The adjacent area had been cleared of loose flotsam and debris that might rebound into the aircraft's rotor draft. R-tech started carrying boxes to the cargo bay immediately after the helicopter touched and idled down and the engineer disembarked to help out. The co-pilot came back to properly place and strap everything, while the pilot remained up front in the big boy's seat.

Working together, the upload was completed in about twenty minutes and the Seahawk was gone.

There was a small collection of miscellaneous things, including some canvas tarps, a carton of MREs, several worn, but usable, hand tools and a couple twelve volt batteries, huddled at the perimeter of the now defunct campsite. Bj asked what the stuff was for, since it obviously wasn't going back to the ship. Rt explained it was a bunch of expendables they had plenty of in supply and it was easier to give the shit away to the locals than haul it around. The tech had recently told visitors from below that he was leaving today and would have some surplus for them, if they were interested. He figured someone would probably be showing up anytime, having, no doubt, heard the copter, and they should move the stack over to the head of a path that led down off the hill. To start the task they each picked up one of the heavy batteries and began the more than hundred meter trek over uneven, rocky terrain toward the small opening in the downslope bush. Car batteries are not easy to carry around, even on a nice level surface, and the engineer found himself struggling a bit with the load, while watching each step. Near the end of the run, he skidded on some loose stones and the lead weight slipped from his grip, falling directly on top of his right big toe. The flimsy, non-regulation sneaker offered no protection and the NAVO sherpa yelped in pain, wondering if the sockless toe was broken. The tech was more concerned with whether the battery was broken and angrily told his helper to be careful, because they didn't want to distribute useless, damaged goods. Fortunately, nothing was broken and the re-staging of giveaways was completed.

The two were just finishing final clean-up of the site, when they saw a small party of Koreans making their way single file up the hill from below. There was a man and a woman in the lead, each pushing a battered wheelbarrow, followed by two other women and several children. The Americans met the villagers as they emerged on the bald from the top of the pathway. After exchange of bowed greetings, rt pointed to the free pile and gestured for them to take it away. The man went right to the batteries and loaded them both into his barrow. The lead woman, evidently not his wife, screamed, "ani ! ani ! ani !" and snatched one of the units out of his barrow, to place in her own. Without a word he took it back and she went off. **"dangsin-eun kkoim eul buckethead !**

**dangsin-eun geu baeteoli leul modu gajil su eobs-seubnida !
dangsin-eun dangsin-i nugu leul saeng-gag habnikka?"** She
then got physical, smacking him repeatedly across the face and
pummeling her fists into his stomach and chest. The man just
stood there, stoically guarding his wheelbarrow and absorbing the
abuse without retaliation. The enraged woman ran over to the left-
overs and grabbed a hammer from the assortment of tools. She
turned and charged back toward the target of her wrath, wielding
the ball peen with possible intent to kill. The navy seaman stepped
swiftly forward and disarmed the anger crazed lady before any
regrettable and irreversible harm could be done. He knew if she
whacked the dude on this duty site, the ensuing investigation and
paperwork could dog him out of the military, maybe even with a
DD. Upon the thwarting of her attack, the woman instantly calmed
and the rest of the items were peacefully loaded evenly into the
little carts. Bowing profusely, the Koreans repeatedly muttered,
"gamsah abnida, annyeong," as they slowly reversed into the narrow and treacherous trail down the hill. Bj mused about what he
had just witnessed, marveling that such an explosive situation
could defuse so quickly. "Oh, it's not over, believe me," asserted
the culturally canny field man. "He'll deal with her later, in private
when there're no foreigners around."

The red stationeers were done here on the hill. All they had to
do was wait for their ride. They sat down on a large rock and the
bivouac man broke out a couple MREs and beers he had saved
from the camp stash. The meals were split pea soup with ham,
mashed banana and rice and a package of whole wheat cheese
crackers. Red tech opened the olive brown cans with a little pocket
tool called a P-38 and they scooped out the can-colored mush with
plastic spoons included in each box. Meals Ready to Eat had no
expiration date and no content information, other than the generic
name of what was in the cans. They could have been manufactured
by anyone, anywhere, at anytime. No one knew, or particularly
cared, because when you ate MREs, you were seriously isolated
and had more important things to worry about. As the afternoon
wore on to the later hours, it became apparent the helicopter was
getting to be way overdue.

Weather was moving in, the temperature was dropping and
daylight was fading away. The Americans on the rock had nothing. All the site equipage was gone. The only communication was

the tech's phone with a nearly dead battery and no service. No food. Nothing to drink. Lightweight clothes. They couldn't have been more ill prepared to be remotely stranded had they carefully pre-planned it. When the wind started to pick up, a cold rain slashed down and the castaways looked around for anything usable to shelter themselves. They found a few dead bush branches to prop against the lee of the rock, forming a makeshift lean-to through which rainwater quickly leaked, soaking the cloistered duo beneath. For sure, it was going to be a long, wretched holdout.

At some point after night black was fully established under a heavily clouded sky, after the washed out sailors inured to their predicament and settled in for a hard time, the greenie heard a rising tide of chirping sounds emanating from the dense scrub thicket all around them below the crest of the butte. It was like the uncoordinated trill of a million canaries and was quite mesmerizing, if specifically listened to. He thought it must be some kind of nocturnal frogs, but the resident rep said, "no, man, they're bush rats." *Rats!! Holy shit! We're surrounded by rats!??* Yes, Yeongdo was inhabited by untold numbers of wild wood rats that, over the eons, migrated and proliferated from the nearby port facilities. They weren't really a problem, though, as they generally stayed under vegetative cover and didn't like to come out in the open. However, to be safe, rt wanted to move the debris from the earlier lunch away from the shelter rock. It was too dark to walk anywhere, so the trapped twosome threw the stuff as far out as they could into the blank. It was good to stretch a little from the cramped position they had been sitting in, but a steady rain still fell and they soon crawled back under the saturated foliage, that at least softened, if not deflected, the water's impact. *Oh, god, this really licks!* The lost operative had never felt so covert, so dark.

Time was, more or less, in limbo. There was no way of knowing how long the partially dazed maroons sat up against the rock, contemplating hypothermia, when they heard the extraneous crunch of someone approaching. They could see the flittering flare of a flashlight ahead of the increasingly discernible footfalls. Within seconds, the light was directly in their faces and they had to shield their eyes against the harsh white glare. The young Korean man lowered the beam and made a hand motion resembling, to the culturally illiterate professional, 'get out', or 'get away'. "Does he want us to leave? Are we trespassing on his property, or something?"

"No, you idiot. He wants us to follow him. C'mon, let's go." The navy man jumped up and hustled after the light man, who was already walking away back toward the off hill path. The clueless agent scrambled to bring up the post, hobbled by his painful toe. The way down was not easy, a winding, mud rutted and sometimes steep convolution through the tangled, waist-high gorsey growth. Rossy had to stay close to the tech ahead of him, because in this, probably the blackest night he had ever been out in, he couldn't see a damned thing. Plus, the continuous, much louder than before, clangor of the chirruping rats was distracting in its proximity. They were slopping right through where the furry little frackers lived, for chrissakes! No doubt, his partner was good with this - just like the shit they trained for in the military. But *he* was a goddam engineer. The only tough field condition he was trained to face was an empty coffee pot in the office concession. Finally, the trail started to level out and broaden some and they emerged onto a flat, open terrace containing a number of small, clustered structures. Their guide led them to one of the buildings where loud voices of a group of people could be heard from within.

The very warm interior of the hooch was an open, unfurnished space about the size of a DIS interrogation room. A fired kerosene lamp sat on the sheet linoleum floor right beside the entrance, casting shadowed light off the faces of the squatted men around the inside perimeter. They all looked up at the arriving weather refugees and scrunched in closer together to make room for the guests. Light man invited the Americans to sit down, handing them each a plastic smurf cup. He also indicated they should remove their shoes, which they did before settling in cross-legged at the assigned openings on the floor. The men broke into ludicrous laughter upon seeing the oversized, discolored big toe of the one stranger. A wide and deep ceramic bowl rested on bricks in the middle of the floor, with a long, steel ladle handle protruding from its lip. One of the men reached for the ladle, as the others held their drinking vessels forward. Ladle man slowly emptied a dirty milk looking liquid from the bowl into each cup. Makoli, a fermented rice, wheat and soy concoction, is the Korean national home brew and they imbibed it with proud impunity. Koreans do not drink to socialize, they drink in toastless unison to get collectively drunk, like college shooters, and this effort was well on its way to success.

All eyes were on the visitors, waiting for their containers to be filled so another round could proceed. The uninitiated fed looked at the marbly swill being poured into his cup and wasn't sure he could participate. There was some sort of slimy, oatmeal colored material, either in suspension or phased out dissolution, swirling in the murky liquid and it all smelled like rotting vegetables. He thought there was a good possibility of hurling if he slugged this mix and, under the circumstances, that would not be cool. Feeling the crushing reality of a *fear factor* moment, he decided to go for the gold. Up with the mug, down with the mash and exhale.... easy... long...slow. Do not cough! *Sweet jesus!* It felt like the chug was a keeper! The Koreans watched with curious amusement and voided their own cups in slurping approval. "Well played, boss," whispered rt, lifting to throw back his contribution for completing the round.

Before the novice makoli man could savor his accomplishment, he found the ladle in his hand and, still, all eyes in his direction. They wanted him to serve for the next round! Looking at the circle of extended cups, he thought it much too soon to take in this horrible slop again. A glance at his colleague found only a noncommittal shrug. *Oh well, let's get 'er done!* He reached into the bowl and began refilling clockwise from the left. In doing so, he got a better look at the individual men, his newfound drinking buddies. Most were dressed in knee shorts, tees, ball caps and flip-flops. Many of the shirts and hats exhibited logos and images of American sports and pop culture. For some reason the Chicago Cubs were represented. *What's going on there?? Why would there be CC fans in Korea?* One face was strikingly familiar and the ladler pegged the man on the hill, the one who was beaten up by the woman over the battery dispute. He seemed a lot happier and more relaxed now than then. Actually, it felt like a long time since the sailors were freezing and soaked in the pitch dark of the abandoned camp. Their fortune was much better now, but the survivor agent did not think he could handle any more brew. He decided to discretely chuck his refill out the door when the others raised theirs to drink and couldn't see what he was doing. The navy rep grinned and nodded, in following suit. High five.

One of the binging Koreans knew fairly good English and, once the novelty of the unexpected presence of the outliers had subsided, was eager to engage the youngsters in their own speak. The man was at least as old as grandpap Rossy, with a long, braided gray beard, under a severely frayed and faded *Grateful Dead ContinuanceTour* cap. The man said he first learned English in Viet Nam, where he served, during the long ago war, with an ROK army division assigned to an American command near the Cambodian border. Their mission was to keep a specified zone clear of enemy infiltration. "I kill many cong gooks for America," boasted the old vet, proudly. The civilian visitor didn't know where to go with that, as he didn't know much about the Viet Nam war, but he thought it odd that a Korean would refer to fellow Asians in a nasty slur, using the g-word. "Thank you for your service," he murmured, feeling a somewhat awkward uneasiness.

It wasn't long afterward that the party started to disintegrate under the weight of its achieved intoxication. One by one, the locals struggled to their feet and staggered out of the hooch, guiding hands along the top of the corrugated fiber glass walls to keep from keeling over. The empty makoli bowl remained in place on the center floor. Two of the drunksters stayed inside, the old soldier and a younger dude, maybe his son. Soon a procession of others entered from outside, a grandmotherly woman, a younger woman and three small children. The women were carrying rolled bamboo mats, which they unfurled and carefully placed around the room on the floor, including two for the guests. The older woman looked at the standing hilltoppers and pointed to their designated places by the door, while everyone else laid out on their own respective pads. Grandmamasan extinguished the lamp, leaving the room in total, absolute blackness. It was bedtime.

The engineer couldn't sleep. There were at least two heavy snorers somewhere in the hut, whose erratic, croaking grunts easily overrode the distant cheeping of the rats. The linoleum deck was hard, he had no pillow and he was still damp from sitting in the rain. Also, he had to pee really bad, but couldn't make out a hand in front of his face, let alone find a way outside to make water. But, thankfully, it was not cold. The floor radiated warmth from fire-heated rocks heaped beneath, creating a sauna-like effect that was quite cozy against the nighttime chill. Resigning to the reality that he must lie here for the next several hours, being about sixty percent miserable, the situation analyst concluded this was a helluva lot better than hoveling in the weather on the hill, being *totally* miserable. But, he had to get some sleep, because tomorrow was a work day. Not that he looked forward to going to work, he just needed the job, even though it really sucked, bigtime, like a fracking modified hoover. First thing would be to gather the eggs. There were a hundred thousand rats in his house, each one in its own tiny cage, churning out an egg every two days. So he had about fifty thousand rat eggs to collect daily. They tried to bite when he grabbed their produce off the collection tray, so he had to wear gloves. This reduced deftness and led to frequent drops. To avoid breaks, he had to wear soft sneakers to cushion fallers with his feet. He would have much preferred his safety boots in this environment, but management wouldn't allow it. They pay-deducted a ben₩ for each break. The noise of the chirruping rats was insufferable, taking several hours each day to acclimate against. When the hideous racket mentally faded to background, the egg drop rate declined. After collection, he would water the rats. This involved pressurizing the distribution lines from a supply hose and for some reason it wasn't happening. The pressure was there, actually much higher than normal, but water wasn't flowing. Just as he was about to go outside to check on the water problem he felt a sharp tapping on his shoulder. Christ, it was probably his supervisor, the headless Korean, wanting him to do some other duty chore, like stocking the beer machine.

"Rossy, Rossy, c'mon, man, wakeup, we gotta go!" The egg catcher opened his eyes and didn't immediately tune to where he was. He slowly recalled the enclosed makoli room, now awash in sunlight streaming through the open door. Red tech was already stepping outside and the last sleeper in the house rolled over to push himself off the floor mat to a shaky upright position. Wincing from the severe pressure pain of an urgent head call, his first priority was getting to a bathroom, *afap*. The single minded potty seeker wobbled out to join his countryman, asking where to go to go, without even offering a social 'annyeonghaseyo'. Rt pointed to a minuscule shed, peeping over the bushes well beyond the other buildings. Bj made a binjo beeline, hoping he could reach it without an involuntary pipe burst. Nearing the outhouse, he was dismayed to see the form of a sleeping dog, lying right in the doorway. *Damn! Please don't be crazy!* But the mongrel jerked its head up with a protective growl in detecting the stranger's thrashing approach. There was no time to finesse this canine obstruction to gain entry. The panicked pisster ran around to the back of the latrine shack and relieved himself outside, hoping no one was watching this, undoubtedly, major social faux pas. He couldn't remember a more satisfying bladder drain and was grateful there wasn't a corresponding solid waste disposal emergency on the other side of the plant. That was probably because he hadn't eaten much in the past twenty-four hours. In thinking about it, he was starving hungry. Surely, they would get back to the Wyeth this morning.

Returning to the village center in front of the party house, Rossy found his colleague sitting on a shallow stone wall talking on a cell phone. The resourceful navy man had borrowed the phone from light man, who was sitting beside him on the wall, and made contact with the ship. As it turned out, the helicopter had developed a split rear rotor blade and they were unable to come back to red station yesterday, as the repair took the rest of the afternoon and into the evening. By that time, unauthorized air traffic was restricted and they were grounded. Since rt's phone was dead, this status couldn't be advised. Sorry about any inconvenience, red. Expect revised eta today, at 1030. *Roger, copy that.* Out.

It was only 0730, so the strandees had plenty of time to get back up the hill for pick-up. They looked around for the hooch hosts to thank them for their hospitality and, hearing a calling voice behind them, spotted grandma in the doorway of another place across the small common. She was making the same wave away signal that light man beckoned with last evening and the red station boys responded accordingly. Upon reaching the entrance stoop, grandmamasan ushered them inside and prodded them to sit on the floor at a low table. They removed shoes and complied. She then brought them each a plate of kimchi, topped with dried fish and a runny fried egg. The unaccustomed visitor couldn't help but catch her dreadful halitosis as she leaned close in to serve the food, smiling and talking all the while. "It's the kimchi," explained rt, "and the only defense is to eat a lot of the shit yourself, so go for it!" Yes, it was the kimchi, a decaying pickled cabbage and spice dish, that smelled just like the woman's horrendous breath. The tourist agent was too hungry to desist and he dug to, though the sticks were a struggle. Old mamasan laughed heartily in watching from the side.

After breakfast, the sailors thought it would be best to return immediately topside, in case the copter was early. They were both ready to leave and offered a refrain of bowing thanks and good-byes to their benefactors, in the process of proper departure. Finally walking out of the hamlet toward the rising path into the bush, they passed a woman moving slowly in the opposite direction. She was barely recognizable as the wheelbarrow lady encountered yesterday up by the camp. One eye was swollen shut and a massive bruise marred the cheek below. A gash on her lower lip oozed watery blood. Her left arm dangled at an unnatural angle from a makeshift rag sling. She faltered by looking down and away, obviously in considerable pain. The foreigners were silently shocked in remembering red tech's dire prediction of her fate. It was a cultural thing.

The parted pair barely made it back to the rock on the hill, when they heard the distinct clopping chop of the helicopter approaching from the northwest. It was a few moments before they could actually get a visual and confirm that, yes, this was their transport, arriving almost two hours early! If they had dawdled any longer down below, they would be left for dead again! What the hell kind of fracked up coordination was this?!? The chopper made a wide circle around the butte bald before noisily settling down at the same level spot it had landed on before. The groundsmen ran from the rock, heads lowered through the dusty downdraft, and scrambled up into the open cargo bay. The pilot immediately started his lift-off, maybe even slightly before the two pick-up passengers were completely in, and off they went. Moving rapidly away from their isolated point of desertion, the always observant agent looked down and saw the red and white glint of the Budweiser beer cans the drenched darksiders had thrown to the bush line last night. So this is how it happens?! There is no mystical 'Bobby Budweiser'. It's just a never ending sequence of unlikely, innocent circumstances responsible for the wide distribution of KOB empties to remote places around the world.

During the brief return ride across the harbor, the co-pilot informed they had to run ahead of schedule, because they had been ordered to Chinhae Navy Base for stand-by duty in support of a visiting ASSDEF, assistant secretary of defense, who was in-country to monitor progress of the joint-milman ops. The weary engineer didn't care. He just wanted to get back to the ship, shower, do some laundry, get something to eat, possibly take a nap and reorganize. He had to start thinking about his local *SB* contact. It shouldn't be difficult for the asset to find him - he didn't exactly meld blindly into a country full of Koreans. Now *that* was a paradox. How could he be inconspicuous in an atmosphere where he stood out like a squirrel in a bird cage? *Time to get my head back in the game!*

***

Later in the morning, pc hitman told the rook engineer to go with techs flu and flo out along the pier access to recalibrate the red station positioning equipment. They sent the new man down course carrying a lightweight point rod, equipped with a laser target and solar powered mini-receiver, and a two-way communicator. All he had to do was set the rod up through extension of retractible stabilizers on a level surface about three kilometers away, as far as he could go while maintaining line of sight with the techs. It was a nice day for a walk along the inner bulkhead and the agent set out, on the mindless task, feeling pretty good. He was really happy to be off the navaid island and doing something useful, even if it was a simple assignment that could be carried out by a grade school dropout. *Whatever it takes, as long as I'm getting paid.* One by one, he passed by a series of humongous pier structures that extended at least a half mile out into the harbor from the access way. Intimidating navy warships, mostly ROK, some US, occupied the parallel berthing slots along the piers. Past the mooring zone was a massive drydock facility, featuring water locks and elevated hydraulic lift tracks. At the end of the active operational sectors the access widened into a large paved field, like a giant cul-de-sac, surrounded by ominous looking warehouse structures without doors or windows. He crossed over a broad red line painted on the pavement and looked back to make sure he was still sight aligned with the techs. Walking to the center of the round, he found a stable surface tract and started to set up the rod. All of a sudden and seemingly from out of nowhere, running bootfalls and excited, urgent shouts. The civilian sailor found himself quickly encircled by camoed ROK military men, with extended, bayonet tipped M16A4 auto-rifles all leveled at the monkey in the middle.

"jeongji ! jeongji ! yeogi e ol su eobs-seubnida ! igeos-eun jehandoebnida !"

The monkey had no idea what was being screamed at him, but intuitively suspected it was more of a demand than a greeting. He didn't know what to do, other than to stay passive. Very slowly, he raised his arms and clasped hands behind his neck, while slumping to his knees on the pavement, like a captured prisoner of war. *What the hell?!? I'm a fracking American! We're all on the same side, here!!* He closed his eyes and waited for whatever would happen, because, incredibly and yet again, he had fallen hard into an OBE situation.

"You are in a restricted area. May I see your ID, please?"

The inadvertent intruder looked up into the face of a Korean navy lieutenant, standing over him as the obvious officer in charge. *Oh, god, no! I don't have any ID.* "My name's Bill Rossy and I'm an engineer from the USNS Wyeth."

"I need to see your ID."

"I'm sorry, sir, I don't have ID with me, but I can get it back on the ship."

"What are you doing here?"

Rod man explained how he was setting up a calibration point for equipment they were using to survey the harbor and it would only take a few minutes for his distant colleagues to take readings and then he would be gone, no problem. The lieutenant was familiar with the survey project. "OK, but you cannot be in here. You must be on the other side of the secure perimeter." He pointed at the red ground stripe about fifty meters behind them.

"Yes, yes, of course, sir, no problem."

"Your country and mine are close allies, but that doesn't mean you can go anywhere you please in Korea. You must respect our boundaries and be very careful. We are always at war."

"Yes, sir, I understand." The American rose slowly from his passive position, picking up the rod beside him. He started retreating toward the secper marker, followed by the contingent of armed guards. Right before they reached the line, the OIC ordered 'halt!' and pulled a clipboard from under his arm. He wrote date and time on two fields of a form, along with some brief notes, and handed the board and attached pen to the unscheduled visitor, directing him to sign twice. It was a record of his entry and departure from the controlled area. The unauthorized calibrater was then allowed to recross the red pavement stripe and continue his task. The guards remained on the secure side, with weapons ominously trained on the nearby American, fingers on live triggers, watching his every move. The moving target had never had so many close-range, allegedly friendly guns simultaneously aimed at him. He nervously proceeded to reset the instrument rod and, following coordination of status and position with the techs, the calibration readings were completed. The down range lackey began his return trek up the pier access road, stopping every five hundred meters, or so, as instructed, to set up an interim target point. Periodically glancing behind to where he was withdrawing from, he noticed the security soldiers held their position at the critical red power line, like robocops stuck in neutral, through his entire way back. He was damned sure earning the war zone pay differential.

***

After lunch, the Wyeth engineers and techs were gathered in the dp lab working up some final mapping products and planning the next phase of survey ops. The junior engineer found the procedures very interesting and asked a constant stream of questions. He was hopeful that maybe there actually *was* some technically challenging aspects to NAVO sailor work. The longertimers accommodated their new colleague's inquisitiveness without complaint, seeming happy to find anyone who gave a shit about what they were doing. Soon it was break time, and they all went down to talker's state for beer. During the course of the break gabble, bj asked talker if they had to make any adjustments on drone data for time variations related to frequency differences between sonar and positioning wave propogations? "I don't know, dawg, the info is automatically plotted. Whatever's in the program, I guess. I don't do code." *Jesus, this guy's useless!*

Shortly following break, they were all back in the lab, when there was a loud, muffled *THUMP* and the entire ship lurched like it had been broadsided by a rogue wave. Power spiked out for a microsecond, a moment of silence, and then an uproar of sirens, alarms and emergency alerts filled both the onboard and adjacent pier ranges of sensored vigilance. People emerged from everywhere, running in all directions, yelling random commands and inquiries. For a brief time hysteria prevailed, until confusion quickly yielded to structure as crisis protocol activated. ROK soldiers appeared in full force, seemingly from thin air, directing initiation of a full evacuation of the pier and port sector, including the Wyeth. "**EVERYBODY IMMEDIATELY OUT, NO EXCEPTIONS!! NOW!!**" But the sailors had to secure the lab first, because all the data and equipment were classified. They had never really drilled for this scenario and the hitman had to almost get physical in moving his OB buzzed surveyors to rapid response mode. Before debarking, they were able to run back to their rooms and grab props for a possible off-site overnight.

The NAVO crew finally regrouped on the pier access, remote from the evacuation zone, along with a multitude of military, civilian and merchant personnel. In talking with others, the scuttlebutt was an underwater explosive device had detonated near the vacated berthing slot of a ROK non-nuclear submarine, that had set to earlier in the day for scheduled rendezvous and readiness maneuvers associated with the joint ops program. There was no official confirmation, denial, or accusation of attempted sabotage by the north, but this, of course, was the overriding presumption. *Christ, almighty!! They could have blown our fracking ship up!!! The sub slot was not far from the Wyeth! That means there were fracking terrorist scuba dudes swimming around out there last night to lay the device. This place is crazy dangerous and I gotta get outta here!!* The secret servant did not want to operate anymore in Korea, if guns and bombs were in play. He had to somehow contact the *SB* asset for his transfer itinerary, like tonight!

***

The Seamen's Club was thoroughly mobbed. There was barely room to even stand on the front sidewalk outside the door. Despite the early hour, the Wyetheers opted to steer directly to T-Street, rather than fight the port evacuation crowd. There was no word on when, or if, the ship's pier would be cleared for reentry. They could go native for dinner at the Busan BarBQ, a decent eatery on the strip. First, though, a couple of rounds at the Gate. Nearing their home club, the distinct rap of Big Kik spilled out from inside. There must be Americans in the house, surmised the approaching regulars, but they found only a bunch of outdowner Aussies, as they later found out, who liked hip-hop. The sidelined surveyors screechingly pulled a couple tables together and sat down to await service. They were not immediately besieged, as usual, but actually had to wait a few minutes before any of the girls came over from their hub behind the bar. Apparently there were still some hard feelings over the departure spectacle the other night. But the chill thawed quickly and their tables were soon littered with OB bottles and designer water glasses, with several gaters nestled among the goodtimers, laughing lustily at the bantering conversation.

Flo was his usual nightclub self, bragging on and on how he could outlast any fox on the street and how he was so legendary fly that hookers paid him to pick them, just so they could learn technique and excel in their profession. The other sailors were tired of hearing the junior tech's swaggering crow and wished he would go ahead upstairs and let them relax in peace. Unfortunately, it was a little too early, even for the teacher, but before long he *did* excuse himself for a binjo call. Right after the mythical hookmeister left the room, doc reached into his b-pack and removed a vial of blue powder, which he quickly poured into the flo man's beer. "What's that?" asked farmer, maybe not quite wanting to know.

"Ciagra," smirked doc. "I got it from a corpsman over at Chinhae sickbay."

"Ciagra? What's Ciagra?"

"It's that shit for old dudes that can't frack. Didn't you ever see their smutty ads on TV? Christ, they run 'em all the time. You pop one of these and BOOM! Your stick puffs up like a birthday balloon and you're good to go the rest of the day. You be chasing the lady all around the house and yard like a cat after a bluebird. And then after all that they show 'em falling out in some clownass tub. It's sick, man."

"It looked like you put more than one in there."

"Yeah, that was from about ten capsules. I been waitin' to prank this a while. See if lover boy can frack his way out of this!"

"Whoa, I think I saw that ad. Don't they have a lot of disclaimers about all kinds of bad shit that can happen?"

"Not to flo, bro. He's the man! Didn't you hear him? Shit, he's about to find hookerfest nirvana, the holy grail of frack!"

A few minutes later, binjo boy came bouncing back from the alley, spouting additional self superlatives he evidently thought of while making room for more beer. Not only was he the undisputed ladies' choice in Busan, he was an international all star known and wanted throughout the east. He was a lifetime pro-baller. In plopping down and resuming his drink, the high tech screwed up his face, saying, "This shit tastes kinda funny. Y'all put somethin' in there while I was out?"

"No, man, you know how OB is. It never tastes the same twice."

"Yeah, you right about that," grinned super flo, draining the bottle and sending his gater aide for another. As GG happy time rolled merrily on, the Wyeth family forgot about the serious downer of their ship being nearly blown away - *while they were all aboard!* - and started to cool out with the mood. Except for the floster, who had ceased toasting himself and was fidgeting unnaturally on his chair, in obvious discomfort. No one said anything, though everyone noticed. Doc looked away, stifling a cynical chortle. Finally, the manliest man in town rose unsteadily to a not fully standing position and, tying his jacket around his waist, sidled around the table to where Doc was sitting. "Doc, I don't feel too good," whispered the sidestepper. "It's like my whole body's turned into a woody and li'l herc, he's tryin' to bust out on his own. Jesus, even my *brain* feels hard... and I don't think my heart's runnin', man."

"Don't worry about it. Go upstairs and ice up, son. You'll be fine." The walking woody waddled toward the stairs between the bar and the back room. His main attendant followed in tow, going with the flo, who was moving quite slow, but was good for the go, at least through the night, though somethin' ain't right! *Ask your doc if Ciagra is right for you.*

***

As afternoon yielded to early evening and waning daylight, the sailors broke into a dinner frame of mind and rose up from their tables to move on to the BBBQ. The secret coverman remained seated, saying he wanted to finish his beer and would catch up with them. The departing diners snidely figured the rook planned to make arrangements for the night and left him sitting alone. Actually, the shifty operative was looking to isolate himself from the group and give his *SB* asset a chance to connect in relative seclusion. He was confident the country contact knew exactly who and where he was. Experience dictated that's how this game was played.

Within five minutes Johnny noarms materialized like a ghost-
ly vision from somewhere other than the present and, standing before the solitary agent man, chinned at the familiar pocket. The
watched one apprehensively glanced around and reached into the
slickster's jeans. He pulled out a small folded paper, opened it and
read, '**folrow me**', in unsteady hand print. Looking up, he was
startled to find Johnny already at the door, waiting for his 'client'
to join him. There seemed to be a degree of urgency in noarm's
demeanor, and the engineer understood why. He saw a scowling
mamasan slowly emerging from the back room, like a giant spider
crawling in on a web snare.

Outside, Johnny took off at a frenzied fast pace, almost trotting, down the street in the opposite direction from where the sailors normally came and went on the strip. With some difficulty in
keeping up, the curious client 'folrowed' behind as they headed
uptown. Busan was a big city. They reached a long commercial
broadway that was heavy with activity, both vehicular and pedestrian, and lined with an endless variety of shops, stores, open markets, restaurants, business buildings and night spots. Mobile vendors were everywhere, with bicycle powered carts full of food and
salable consumables, much of it unidentifiable to the fast stepping
visitor. There was a constant, uneven blaring of car and truck
horns, mixed with squealing brakes and jammed traffic noise, as
drivers competed with leggers for the same space. At first take, it
might have seemed like overcrowded chaos, but in reality there
was an ordered cadence to the dense bustle. No one yelled, or displayed any degree of verbal or physical anger, against anyone perceived to be wrongly in the way. It was like road rage wasn't an
option, even if justified. The mission man remembered the delayed
reaction he witnessed on the island and wondered if that's what
happened in the city. You cut somebody off on the street, they
wouldn't protest in public, but would find you and mess you up in
private. Actually, the scene was reminiscent of Anacostia, in
Washington, D.C., except here the people and signage were all
Korean. Among the obvious fruits of capitalism was a significant
number of global economy indicators, including Coca Cola, Dun-
kin' Donuts, Pizza Hut, Apple Computers, Banana Republic, Bank
of America and countless other neon logos of familiar products
and services. There was even an old Lehman Brothers Investments
sign fading away over a small, shuttered office suite. No Walmart,

though. Koreans probably wouldn't buy the cheap other-Asian products pedaled by the Big W.

The odd couple stayed on the busy thoroughfare for sometime, then turned into a very narrow alley that was essentially deserted and very dark compared to where they had just been. There was only one lighted front in the alley block, about midway between the larger, more congested avenues it connected. As they neared the white florescent light, the apprehensive stranger saw motion behind the shop style display window from where the illumination shone. Upon reaching the window, the American slowed to look inside and was horrified to see a cluster of young girls pressed up against the uncurtained glass, dressed only in scanty underwear. They couldn't have been more than twelve or thirteen years old! They taunted the outside passersby in muffled shouts, vigorously trying to lure them in with pseudo seductive movements. *Jesus Christ!! What the hell is this?!? They must be child hookers! This has got to be totally illegal! But how can they be out in the open like this? Where's the police?* While mentally asking himself these unanswerable questions, the shocked onlooker had inadvertently stopped walking. Soon realizing he was standing alone gawking at a grossly bizarre setting he wanted no part of, the follower ran to catch up with his leader, who was almost at the end of the alleyway.

The twosome emerged onto another active commercial boulevard, though not quite as busy as the one they had shortcutted from through the disconcerting alley. They walked past a park square across the way and on for several more blocks. The operative was beginning to feel pangs of concern about where the hell they were going, countered with a certain trust he would soon meet the *sbean* program contact, when they came to a single structure, on a large, fenced lot. The attractive building was of pagoda architecture amid exquisitely landscaped surroundings, softly lit with an orderly array of hand-painted, rice paper lanterns. The elevated entrance was from a wide, full-length hardwood deck, over which the tiled roof extended with graceful precision. The transom above the oversized double doors held a huge mahogany sign, decorated with elaborate border carvings, identifying *Chasjib Choa*. Noarms stopped at the gate and nodded for his charge to go in. This was the endpoint and the Wyeth slickey-boy was done here. With a grand₩ tip pocketed, Johnny was gone, leaving the possibly lost-in-the-city *bean* stalker on his own.

***

"I solry, sir, but this teahouse for Korean only." The American did not understand. If the contact had made the elaborate arrangements for him to come here, how could he not be permitted inside? He looked at the bow headed host, who had intercepted him immediately after he had stepped through the doorway, and could tell the exclusion was nonnegotiable. *What the hell do I do now??*

"geuga nawa hamkke , gwang ju-won OK ibnida . kkeul-eo ollyeo ." The voice on the other side of the alcove partition sounded vaguely familiar. Ju-won obediently led the unKorean into a private service nook adjacent to the portico entrance, where the summoned newcomer was dumbfounded to see pfc insect sitting cross-legged on a floor mat behind the low tea table. "Welcome, Mr. Rossy, please sit down."

The astonished agent removed his Reeboks and carefully lowered himself to the floor across from his...what? Host? Contact? Fellow American? He was thoroughly confused. Insect didn't look anything like his first impression. The dude was clean, dressed in nice, expensive casual wear, and didn't even speak the same. He sounded professional, with no slangy street jargon. So what was going on? Who *was* this guy? "Thanks."

"Good to see you again. I suppose you're wondering why I'm here and why I called *you* here? For openers, let's just say I'm not entirely what you might think I am from when you first saw me. Nothing is ever really as it seems, wouldn't you agree?" A server entered the alcove with a tray of kimchi, kimbap, and sun-dried squid appetizers, as well as a large ceramic pot of house specialty cha. She placed drink bowls and plates, with paper sealed sets of confounding chopsticks, and whisked silently away like a light breeze.

"Uh,....yeah, I guess so." *I have no idea what is happening here, but if he's my contact, he's got to open the code. I can't ask him out cold, without blowing my cover. He's got to speak correctly to me!*

"OK, my name *is* Daryl Dawkins, as introduced to you the other day, but I'm not a military fugitive, nor a homeless dick. I'm the East Asian resident representative of Unit Systems Engineering. Normally I'm in Seoul, but as a USER, I travel all over."

"Well.....how come you're awol insect? What is that?"

"You know, compadre, the tech industry is so unbelievably competitive and tough, especially in Asia, you need an edge, some kind of unique angle to ever make it to the inside rail. If I'm just a USER, living the high circuit, I don't know what's happening out in the world. But if I can get my eyes and ears on the pavement, that's when I feel the pulse of the consuming public and learn what the mass economy wants. Insect is my edge. Korea is a small, rapidly developing country and if you don't know what you're doing here, somebody else does."

"So, why am *I* here? What's in it for me?"

"I don't know. You tell me."

"How the hell do I know? I don't even know where I am right now."

"Pay attention, Mr. Rossy. *I-don't-know. You-tell-me!*"

"Oh, shit! Damn!! Are you my asset?"

"Yes, I am. Now let's talk business."

Jesus christ!! Why do I keep missing these codes? But this one was out of sequence. I initiated, by mistake, and he responded correctly. So is he good? Has to be, because he knew the whole dialogue. Let's get it on! "Ok, what can you tell me about the target in Busan?"

"Well, he was probably never in Busan. He came in through Gimhae and apparently went directly to Seoul via ground transportation. Don't know whether it was bus, train, or cab. Definitely not a rental. We just think we know he was verified to be in Seoul the same day he allegedly arrived in-country."

"When was that?"

"Don't know for sure, but circa a week ago."

Christ, why is everything so gray about this motha? Nobody ever knows anything for sure about him!! "So, what did he do in Seoul?"

"As I said, Mr. Rossy, the South Korean economy is booming, while, of course, the neighbors to the north have no economy. It's not really well known, or publicized, that the DMZ border is as porous as a rotted sprinkler hose. There are undocumented people moving back and forth all the time across the line. Increasingly, they are moving forth and not going back. This makes competition for jobs, including professional class jobs, a growing hassle, and the homies are getting restless. The government doesn't seem interested in addressing the problem, because they don't want to agitate the unstable, hotheaded, nuclear north. Many young people coming out of ROK colleges are having a tough time competing with unregulated illegals, who might be equally educated, but debt free and willing to work for salaries far less than the nationals can afford. There's a lot of discontent and disillusionment, especially among engineers, who have been taught since grade school to excel in their studies and be securely rewarded in their profession. It's not happening and they feel they are being undercut. These are the people the dude is talking to, those interested and willing to rock the status quo, which is not rocking them."

"Are there any identifiers, anything to help nail this guy down?"

"Nothing physical. But as we know, he's American, and we think he might have connections with Pennsylvania. Indirect recaps of his clandestine contacts say he frequently referenced that state as an example of hardship in a destabilized economy. And by 'indirect' I mean several times removed, because we just couldn't get that close to receive definitive info. Christ, the reference could have been from another American. There certainly is no shortage of Americans in Seoul!"

"So is he still in Seoul? If not, where did he go and when?"

"We're pretty sure he's gone from Korea and the scoop is he was interested in the Philippines, specifically in an area devastated by the recent mega typhoon through Mindoro."

"You don't know when he left Korea?"

"No. Sorry."

The operative went into a side-to-side stretching motion. He still wasn't used to sitting on the floor and could feel some back stiffness creeping in. Also, he needed to extend his knees. It was probably a good time to leave the teahouse, since this *OPSB* mission phase was accomplished and he had managed something to eat, despite the mess of stick droppings on his side of the table. But there were a couple questions nagging. "That's Ok, I've got enough to update. But let me ask you, so, you're like, what, three different people here in Korea? How do you keep it all together?"

"Well, I gotta say, it's not always easy. You're the only person who knows all three of me, and I hope I don't need to remind you to keep this info to yourself. As CIA kin, you should consider my secrets classified. Are you good with that?"

"Absolutely, no problem. But how did you get to be an asset? I thought assets were country nationals."

"I'm in the air force reserves. A major. I do my annual active at JB Andrews, in Maryland, specifically in the program development group overseen by General Clements. Tophead, whom I assume you know. He covertly recruited me for this special service a while back, which has worked well for me here as a USER, along with paying some sweet, tax-free tea. All in the righteous cause of freedom, son, above and beyond for truth, justice and the American way. Now, I've got a question for you."

"Sure."

"How would you like to change course and work for me, for USE, here in Korea? I can pay a lot more than you're making as a junior fed, plus living costs. I'm going under, here, and really need some help."

What!? Didn't see that coming! "Are you serious? I really don't think I qualify. I'm a chem e, not a computer guy. I don't think I would be much use to you."

"If you're an engineer, you've got an analytical head, and that's what I need. Don't worry, I could get you up and running in no time."

"Well, why don't you hire a Korean?"

"In all honesty, I don't trust them. There's a lot of Koreans who are fed up with the forever American presence here and would not hesitate to sabotage a global American company if given the chance. It's too risky to hire them for anything other than manufacturing, low labor jobs. Anyway, think it over. It's a standing offer. Give me a call if you want to do something bankable and out of the ordinary." The CIA asset handed the CIA operative his card. If the junior g-man called, it wouldn't be until he was out of Korea.

Rossy had one more issue that was tripping his sense of conscience. He told asset insect about the little girls he had seen in the alley window on the way over to the teahouse and wondered, "What the hell's going on with that?"

"A bad, sorry situation. There's extensive, organized trafficking happening as fall out from China's 'one child' policy. Many couples prefer a son to a daughter and some sell girls away at birth. These kids are raised into prostitution, finding a big market in Korea, because the police and overseeing agencies are easily bribed away. It's a clear violation of Korean and international law, but there's so much money and so many people, influential people, involved, they can't clean it up. Best thing you can do is forget about it. Sounds hard, but there's nothing any outsider can do. Koreans have to take this down by themselves and they probably eventually will, but not today."

The engineer didn't know if he wanted to work in a country that sandheaded such an atrocity. America had perpetual problems itself, but was always trying to do something about them. At least talk and argue the issues to death, if nothing else. He left the teahouse after USER Dawkins called a cab for him. It was two hours before curfew, when he arrived back at the Wyeth pier, which was, fortunately, reopened for authorized personnel. They were verifying IDs at a newly established port entry checkpoint. It was good to be out of the city and into the cocoon of the ship. The agent wanted to get some sleep before cranking into mover mode. His mind went stone cold blank as soon as he laid out on the bunk. Too much had happened today to replay. *Tomorrow....*

***

.......yesterday's future, a new now. Got to get going. There's tons to do and no time to tarry. The short-timer bolted updeck to the wardroom for breakfast, mentally assembling a task plan for the day. He needed to go to the travel office at Chinhae Base for flight tickets. Before that, though, the *SB* update must be sent. But, without a phone, he would only be able to receive authorization instructions through classcom on the ship. This meant there was no going to the base ahead of the messaging. He hadn't seen any internet cafes near the port zone and couldn't borrow anyone's web access, so there was no way to upload on a non-government device! It looked like he would have to use a lab computer, which would be really hard to do without being watched. What a crock! Why does everything have to be so gnarly difficult??

No one was in the wardroom. Perchance the others all stayed in town for the night and wouldn't be back until later. That would work! The stewart retreated to the galley with his only patron's order for raisin oatmeal, strawberries and skimmed yogurt, while the loner went over to the concession for coffee. With his back to the entry passage, the caffeinator nearly spilled it upon hearing, "You still here, Rossy? Thought you would be long gone by now."

What the hell?? The startled sailor turned to face pc hitman, standing on the far side of the room. "What's that mean? Of course, I'm here. Where else would I be?"

"C'mon, man, don't jive me. I did a little collaborative research and found you don't stay very long in one place. So what's your game, son? Who, exactly, are you?"

"Look, Mr. Plough, like I told you before, I've got some classification issues I can't discuss, but, other than that, I'm just a NAVO engineer, following my orders."

"That's about as clear as the mud in your cup. Can you help me out a little here?"

Bj liked hitman. He was a little different from the other field pcs and supervisors, more reasonable, less domineering. Maybe someone to trust over a level table. Maybe there was no choice. The latest *SB* ops work had to be done on board the Wyeth. The agent called an audible and decided to bring hitman under the cover a tad. "OK, yeah, I'm involved in another mission outside of NAVOSUR. It's a special intelligence assignment supporting national security. But I really am a new engineer at NAVO and my orders are good. I got them from Tom and Dick."

"Intelligence? Like with the CIA?"

Uh-oh. I'm boxed. He won't believe anything other than the truth. "Yes, sir, that is correct." *This is a total security breach. I'm fracked!!*

"Well, hell, why didn't you say so!? Are you working for tophead, I'm probably sure? I was routed for a special ops with him a couple years ago, but the project crashed before it started. We were prepped for riverine surveys supporting inland, deep port development in Suriname, South America, and I was supposed to contact an in-country asset for intel on two-way drug and gun running out of there through points U.S. But then Suriname elected a notorious international criminal for president and the U.S. cut off diplomatic relations. Both the planned survey and my ops were burned. So, how's the big guy doing? Still blowing smoke?"

Wow! Two separate darkmen knowing non-existent tophead within twenty-four hours. That's not very invisible. This could be good or bad, or both. I need hitman to help me use the Wyeth comm resources, but can't do that without conceding something

about what I'm doing. A thin row to hoe, here, son. Stay in line!
"Yeah, guess he's about the same. I only met him once. He's a
force. Look, Mr. Plough, I need your help. I've got some messaging to do and I need to use a lab computer and classcom. Can you
set me up?"

"Sure thing. Let's do it before anyone else gets back from the
beach."

"Great! Appreciate it."

***

The classcom special instructions did not come through for
three hours after transmission of the *SB* update. Most of the message was a severe admonishment for using a government computer
to upload the report. After wading through the useless bunk of reprimand, the opster found his authorization. He was to report to the
USNS Trader, currently ported in Subic Bay, on Luzon, near Manila. He would then be assigned to field ops on the small island of
Caluya, off the southeast coast of Mindoro. His official cover
work was to assist in recovery of ferry routes through the Mindoro
Strait, that were disrupted by the typhoon storm surge. The asset, a
Philippine government employee, would contact him on Caluya.
Click! The agent had everything he needed to move out, but was
struggling with a growing parcel of puzzlement that had settled
into an off shore recess of his mind. *How come everywhere I update the whereabouts of special bean, NAVO has a project in progress?* He knew NAVOSUR was a big organization. Gameboy
said they traveled all over the place, but the world is bigger. How
could they be randomly everywhere the *beanster* was? It almost
seemed like something was rigged, being controlled by remote.
But the missions were completely unrelated, so what gives??
Maybe, hopefully, just a coincidence. If not, he was being played
like a puppet. But why? Without answers, or any way to get them,
he knew there was no choice, other than to stay in motion. It was
time to go to Chinhae.

***

With tote and briefcase in hand, the chipmole departed the
Wyeth in early afternoon. No one saw him leave and he didn't talk
to anyone. He was not coming back. First stop was the Seamen's
Club, for a burger and beer, and then a cab to Chinhae. The ride

was about an hour, through a nearly continuous industrialized nexus that was not nearly as scenic as the Greek coastal highway, but a testament to Korea's much superior prosperity. The non-English speaking driver played ear numbingly loud Metallica, in deference to the young American fare, for the entire trip. The head rattled passenger would have much preferred some nice, soft K-pop, but, not to be.

Chinhae Navy Base was a strange place. It had everything a military installation normally facilitated, including an exchange, medical clinic, billeting office, admin center, commissary, mess hall, restaurants, school, library, housing, chapel, clubs, operations hub, barber and beauty shop and even a bowling alley. But it did not have a mission. No one assigned there did anything other than support the existence of the purposeless base. There were no ships, or naval port facilities. ROK had its own navy bases and the functional U.S. naval forces in Korea operated out of Japan. CNB was commanded by a one star admiral, whose sole responsibility was to fight ceaseless initiatives to close the base, like Monty Python's legendary last knight. It was almost a sea level compeer to the world famous Bolivian navy headquarters, high in the central Andes.

The arriving under cover boy didn't care about base politics. All he wanted was a ticket to fly. He easily located the travel office in the admin center and submitted his classified documents for process. It always seemed like an inherent security violation that some miscellaneous clerk, with no need to know, could see his TS orders. Such a potential compromise was quickly forgotten, though, when the disbursement officer handed the secret fed another hefty cash advance on per diem, along with a flight ticket package and return of the authorization docs. The officer's closing suggestion to 'have a nice day' was considered doable by the recipient. The flight to Manila, again on Korean Air, departed from GIA early the next morning, so there was time to pick up a few things at the base exchange and grab something to eat somewhere before heading back. He planned to layover near the airport, despite not remembering seeing any hotels above flophouse grade. For only one night, and as long as they had TV, how bad could it be?

The CNB exchange was enormous, as big as any retail superstore in the states. After basketing some new clothes, a back pack to replace his tote and other necessary travel items, including a pair of aviator sunglasses for the tropical Philippines, the shopping sailor worked his way into the extensive electronics department, where he was amazed to find prices for trendy brand products at a mere fraction, almost in the stolen goods range, of what would be expected in the U.S. Plus there was free, insured military shipping, with no sales, or duty tax. What a benefit perk for assigned base personnel! Enlisted navy birds could get some really great stuff here, that they would never be able to afford at home as unemployed, loser civilians. And then the bankrolled browser saw it! The indisputable, authentic, highly contagious *solar phad*! Probably the currently most sought after personal device in the world. He immediately checked the sticker tag. *Are you kidding me?* **$379.95!!!** This was unreal crazy. Could it possibly be true?? Upon verification of the price with a meandering Korean floor staffer, the excited engineer snatched one of the packages with no further thought. This was the deal of a lifetime and there was no need to ponder a decision to buy. He was gonna be a phad man, sitting right over there with the fortunate few in the cutting edge section of technology! *Thank you, jesus. I promise I'll be good!*

While standing in a checkout line to pay, Rossy could not help noticing the contemptuous glares of two middle-aged women behind him. He overheard their loud, agitated whispers wondering how he, an unauthorized, redneck hippy civilian could be allowed in *their* exchange. It was unconscionable and they were going to complain to the manager as soon as they got through checkout. The women did not appear to be military, and the object of their disdain figured them to be senior officers' wives. Of the worst sort - entitled and exclusionary, with a serious 'I've got mine and the hell with you' attitude. Never mind that whatever they thought was their's was earned by their husbands and paid for by taxpayers, this was private turf and they did not like unwanted intruders. The imminent phadster knew his orders allowed him TDY access to base facilities, but he had no intention of engaging the obnoxious SOWs. After payment he departed the premises quickly and disappeared away from the retail zone, wondering, at this point, if there was anywhere in Korea, or any place else, that he could inconspicuously fuse into. Probably not, if he was one of a kind.

With travel prep errands accomplished, the base bum thought he would check out the o club for a few coldies and dinner. Dick had told him his orders were also good for officer service clubs around the world, even without membership. Dick said the ocs generally had the best food on foreign DoD installations. On the way to the club, he passed by an on-site restaurant, Tongin Treats, that appeared to be in the throes of some kind of special event. The place was packed and others were thronged around outside the open door looking in. Easing through the mix of uniformed and civvie clad onlookers, the secret stranger was able to gain a vantage for seeing inside. Across the small dining room a special table was set up against the wall, at which sat a lone dude, wearing a Captain America tee shirt, who seemed to be the focus of everyone's attention. A huge timing clock sat in the corner. There was nothing obviously extraordinary in this scenario, until the former Wyetheer recognized his ex-island colleague, red tech! *What the hell's going on here??* In short order, the gallery broke into wild, cheering applause with the appearance of a grinning, white-jacketed Korean emerging from the kitchen carrying a massive steel serving tray. The chef removed a plate, at least two feet in diameter, from the tray and placed it on the table in front of rt. Carefully stacked high on the plate were four pounds of specially prepared Tongin kimchi, topped with two pounds of North Carolina mac and cheese, all garnished with seven, runny-yolked fried eggs arranged in a happy face configuration. This was the Big Lunch Treat. The weekly challenge. TT's owner offered one U.S. ben to anyone able to successfully consume the BLT in forty minutes. It had never been done and, apparently, the Wyeth navtech was set to give it a shot. *Good god, the boy's gonna kill himself,* thought the unnoticed onlooker, wondering if he should intervene and give red t a ben, if the sailor was this desperate for cash.

Before he could act on this notion, a loud bell gonged, the timer hand jumped and the race was on. Without use of utensils, the contestant scooped globs of the gooey mess into his mouth by hand. It was a gross spectacle to watch, but the crowd loved it. Chants of 'U...S...A, U...S...A' broke out every few seconds and, after five minutes, it looked like the challenger was well ahead of pace. The problem was, the initial effort concentrated on the mac and cheese, which would expand in the stomach and block space for the follow-up main event. A poor strategy resulting in a near shutdown at fifteen minutes in. After at least three, long minutes break, the teetering tech continued, though at a much slower pace, trying frantically to whittle down the formidable mound of misery remaining before him. The fans were riveted, sensing a growing pressure, and collectively gasped when the front man nearly exploded at the twenty-five minute mark. Now sweating profusely, he again took several minutes off. The challenge was at a critical point. There was nothing but kimchi left, almost two pounds of it, and less than ten minutes to go. With trembling hands, the gamester resumed shoveling the putrescent, habanera-laced cabbage concoction into his trancelike face, seemingly resolved to either finish the plate, or die trying. The room was silent, except for the gurgled slurping of the gobbling kimchi killer. At thirty seconds, everyone started counting down with the clock. It was going to be a photo finish. Incredibly, the last morsel was mouthed simultaneously with the end gong, like a winning three pointer at the buzzer, and Captain America's ashen head slammed facedown onto the empty plate. He had given more than all, well over a hundred, and there was less than nothing left. The witnesses to this historic performance busted nuts and all beer taps flowed full open in celebratory exuberance. TT would recover its paid prize stake in minutes and red tech would probably have bad breath the rest of his life.

The visiting watchman considered whether, or not, to check on the new eating champion's condition. The distended diner did not look well, as he had not yet moved from his meltdown at the bell. *No, stay on plan! Get some dinner at the club and go on back to Gimhae. Tomorrow's moving day. No time for complications. If rt needs help, there's plenty of people here to take care of it. It's clearly SEP, so, let's go!* The agent clandestinely resumed the way to the officers' club, where he found a much more structured and sedate atmosphere.

***

During the relaxing enjoyment of his second Kalyani, a fine Indian lager, the mellowed missioneer detected peripheral movement from further down the bar. Glancing in the direction of the disturbance, he saw Lt. Cmdr. Carson, the Wyeth chopper pilot, making his way clumsily toward him. *Oh, no.....incoming! The pilot dude is lubed and he's got a problem.* Carson stumbled up next to the non-compliant, wiseass engineer he was forced to fly against regulations and glowered in hard-on disbelief at what he saw. *What the hell was this clownfrack civilian doing in the offic- ers' club??* **"How'd jew get in here? You don't look like an of- ficer of the United States military!!"**

"No, sir, I'm not. I'm a civilian."

"Well, get the hell outta here, then! This is an o club!"

Oh, christ! "Look, commander, I don't want trouble. I'm on TDY for the navy and I have as much right as you to be in here."

"Not looking like a goddam freak hippy, you don't!! C'mon! Let's go see what rights you got!" Carson turned toward the adjacent dining room, signaling the civilian to follow. *Jesus, I might as well humor this bozo, otherwise he'll create a scene put- ting me in a spotlight I don't need to be in.* The aggravated agent grabbed his backpack and briefcase and trailed the crazy com- mander into the dining room. They walked over to a secluded ta- ble, where a party of suits sat in conversation with a uniformed admiral, the base CO. "Excuse me, sir, but do you think this indi- vidual looks like an officer of the United States military?" inter- rupted the pilot, pointing rudely at the hippy freak behind him.

The admiral turned slowly and peered up at the disrupters of his private confab with the visiting ASSDEF, an accompanying congressional representative and their respective chief aides. He scanned the individual in question and said, "No."

"Well, then, shouldn't he be not allowed in our club, or may- be not even allowed on base?"

"What's your point, commander? Maybe he's *not* an officer of the United States military. Are you, son?"

"No, sir, I'm not. I'm a civilian."

"Civilians are allowed here," said the CO, gesturing at his ta- ble mates with a sweeping arm motion, "so what the hell's your issue, commander?"

"His appearance, sir. He doesn't even look like a civilian."

"For chrissake, man, civilians don't have a dress regulation. They can look anyway they want." *That didn't sound right,* thought the admiral, hoping not to insult his special, appropria- tions-connected guests. To the unlikely covert civilian, "Look, son, you're entirely welcome here. Why don't you pull up a chair and join us?" And then, sharply, to the disgruntled, subordinate officer, "That will be all, commander. Dismissed."

Seriously?? Sure. Why not? The incredulous interloper snagged a chair from another table and sat down with the presently highest ranked and profiled group of people on base. The tippled navy pilot retreated angrily to the bar and ordered another cherry gin fizz, while contemplating the sorry state of America in decline.

Later, over an outstanding dinner of skewered broiled shrimp and scallops on a thin house pasta in white sauce, with a side of lightly steamed garden spinach, the young club crasher answered all questions the curious dignitaries directed at him. He revealed he was an engineer, working for NAVOSUR, currently assigned to the Wyeth for an ongoing harbor survey in Busan. Before that, he worked in Greece and Ascension Island. "Ascension Island?? Really?" One of the aides mentioned what seemed like a significant coincidence in that he had just reviewed a preliminary programming request for a major project to upgrade the airfield at Ascension. "Like, who ever knows anything about Ascension Island?" He wondered what the place was like, as he had never been. The engineer was careful not to allude to anything close to his real reason for being there, here, or anywhere else. He was asked about his background before NAVO, and was astounded to learn the other aide used to work for a major insurance corporation in Hartford. He knew most of the Connecticut places the ex-PWAster did. They marveled at how strangers in the mix could have so much in common. All in all, it was an unexpectedly enjoyable evening, but soon after coffee and ice cream dessert, the roving operative took leave of the pleasant conclave, lying that he had to get back to the ship to complete some planning work for tomorrow's survey support. The high rankers, impressed by the young man's poise and service dedication, thanked him for his company and wished him well. As a final touch of affable appreciation, the admiral picked up his dinner tab. On the way out of the club, the nonconforming civilian spotted Lt. Cmdr. Carson, in a semi-passed out posture, at the end of the bar. He gave the incognizant officer a tight military salute and strode through the lobby concourse into the eve of a new direction.

CHINATOWN

The conspiring adversaries sat tensely at the window table, each staring icily into the other's eyes. Fa Foo's was strangely empty, even devoid of staff, though one tall servant stood on duty behind the kitchen passage. He had just locked the street entrance door behind the punctual arrival and seating of the big man at Mr. Jiang's table. A small, sealed envelope lay untouched between the two. After a moment of studying the American's demeanor and detecting no trace of anything but cold resolve, the Chinaman reached slowly for the package, feeling the rigid outline of the small thumb drives contained therein. "Very good, General Clement. I guarantee you shall not regret this transaction." He then went on to explain how his side of the deal worked. An account had been established at an ultra secret and secure digital institution, accessible only through formatted password and facial recognition scan, which they would set up this evening via a darknet phone access. The account held one billion $US. As a test of the validity of the activated account, the general was permitted one free transaction, to transfer any amount within the balance to any destination. Every subsequent account access, for any reason, would deduct a fee of ten grand from the balance. The cost of doing unofficial business with black money. He elected to place $100,000 in the corporate account of one of the front companies used to support CIA basement ops, which only he had knowledge of, or access to, and which were federally pre-cleared for any amount of funds traffic. He planned to use these company accounts to fence his monster payday. Upon satisfactory completion of the logistics of the exchange, the parties relaxed over a final drink together. Tsing Tao for the seller, a vintage Sancerre Blanc for the buyer.

"A word of simple caution, my friend," said the Chinese enigma, lifting his glass in toast. "If your merchandise is not precisely as agreed to, or if you choose to default in any way, you will be killed and your account dissolved. The sun never sets on treachery. Do you understand?"

The insurgent spy king reached into his inside jacket pocket and withdrew an HL Supreme. He fired the rich cigar, inhaling deeply, and touched his bottle to the waiting glass. Exhaling a long stream of sweet reek directly into the face of his instantly gagging and disbelieving counterpart, the general curtly replied, "Yessir, Mr. Jiang, I understand perfectly." Totally unfazed by the finality of the somber warning, he was pretty sure he would probably ZAP the thumbs as soon as he cleared the new account and laundered its contents through a complex series of untraceable washing machines. The zero application protocol could be satellite activated anytime to subtly neuter the drive data on any device it was uploaded to from the mother main frame at Andrews. RPC was done here. He stood up to leave, offering a handshake to the still hacking wine connoisseur. "Good-bye, Mr. Jiang. It's been a pleasure." The oil executive waved him away in another fit of coughing, thinking he might whack the big ass dummy, anyway.

While descending the stairs behind the key carrying martial maitre'd and waiting for the door to be unlocked, releasing him from the temporarily closed restaurant he would never patronize again, the invisible CIA superstar sensed a developing outrage. Who the hell did the arrogant communist think he was dealing with?? Did he really believe he could willfully take out the world's most accomplished and experienced cover master? The ultimate self-handler had remained deeply incognito for thirty plus years. He had a dozen identities he could disappear into, all ready to spring to life with the choice of a wallet and portfolio. Christ, he could make a small country vanish. Besides, if he turned up murdered, or inexplicably gone, all kinds of internal darts would fly, activating all sorts of investigations. Could Charlie Chan be sure nothing would find its way to him? No, of course not. Jiang's threat was a hollow cry of weakness and the general decided for certain to ZAP the devices when the time was right. Until then, there was no danger of hardcopy production, because the thumb drive deal did not include the custom printer and plotter needed for output. He wasn't about to let the Chinese, or anyone else they wanted to dance with, touch his baby. Not for any amount of money. But for a substantial amount of money, he would let them try.

Feeling much better, the world's newest billionaire veered into the carryout and ordered #13, the White Tiger Special. While waiting, he thought of his complementary parallel project. The end game. People like tophead did not retire on neutral terms. There was either a scandal or high achievement preceding service departure and he intended to leave with the highest internal accolades. Maybe even a non-publicized Presidential MOF award in the Oval Office. But definitely a kick in the face of those pinhead congressional cretins who slashed budgets with no clue of the impact. He would show all of them, including the idiot director, how good he really was. How his genius innovation for intelligence could overcome any obstacle they put in his way. Soon he would be meeting with the last ODD chipmole. Whittberg assured him there was a viable candidate in his sights. Then there would be considerable background coordination to be established among the field assets. Not a difficult issue, because when you were the very best at what you did, it simply all came together. Winning takes care of everything. That was a given.

THE PHILIPPINES

Ninoy Aquino is one of the busiest airports in Asia. There were always hordes of people covering the open expanse of Terminal 3, despite the destruction from a chemical bomb blast that recently closed a significant portion of the facility. Public speculation was that the attack was the result of a long running dispute between the terminal building contractor and the national government's airport authority. Or, it might have been the work of the radical Philippine Statehood Association, al-Qaeda in Polynesia, Philippine Christian Service Organization, or any number of militant right and left extremist political and religious groups roaming the seven thousand islands comprising the republic. The Philippines was a volatile place, historically rife with corruption and regional self-interest. Rossy, obviously, had never been here and didn't really know much about the country, except that it seemed to be very hot. The bombing had knocked out the AC and it must have been close to a fahrenheit hundred on the terminal floor. It looked even hotter outside, where a mass of sweating cabbies pressed against the glass doors awaiting ground fares departing the airport.

Following phone check, money exchange and a Bo Jangles lunch, there was no putting it off any longer. It was time to move. The nervous outheader didn't need a tour guide to know he was about to enter a cauldron of heated, hands-on hustle. He could tell by observing other arrivers, who had ventured out, that this would be a physical ordeal. The goal was to get situated in a vehicle as quickly as possible, because the fare fighting seemed to subside after lock-in. And he had to be very careful to keep control of his stuff. The cabbies' first target was loose travel satchels and luggage. If they separated you from your belongings, they had you. Pity the fools with a bag wagon - they had no chance. Approaching the exit doors, the wary wayfarer could see the outsiders watching him coming, like crocs at a waterhole. He tensed for the onslaught, gripping his backpack and attaché as tightly as possible.

No one knew it, but this undercover, millennium hippy with a briefcase was carrying almost ten grand cash plus a brand new phad. *Sweet jesus lord, please give me the strength to make it through this gauntlet without losing anything. I'll be even gooder than before!*

The heat hit him like a propane fire flare, but before he could wonder how it would be possible to survive in this climate, he was yanked in three different directions. The cabbies were screaming at him and each other, as the odd little group, guided by the opposing forces of the wrenching coercion, started dancing in a wobbly spiral in the middle of the adjacent through lane. Desperately holding on to his vital possessions, the secret agent felt his shirt being pulled up over his head, so that he couldn't see anything. He staggered blindly about as if playing 'find the piñata', because it wasn't an option to free a hand to uncover his face. He was not about to let go of either the backpack, or the case. *I am so not James Bond,* he thought, and then, a loud, booming voice, different from the others, and he was slowly released. Someone yanked his shirt down and he faced a fourth cabbie, who stood at least a foot taller than the original three. Big hack summoned the frowsy fare over to an old, beat-up green Mercedes, that idled in line behind three yellows in front. He opened a rear door and the engineer shuttled into the back. The big boy went around and got in at shotgun. Another dude sat low in the driver's seat, sipping warm beer from a 500 ml can of Red Horse.

"Good afternoon, sir, and welcome to The Philippine Islands, *The Land of Enchanted Dreams.* My name is Rodrigo and I'll be your mechanic today. And this is Felix, your driver. How may we be of service for you?"

Oh, god, this is it. My time is up! Jesus, who the hell ever heard of a ride-along cab mechanic?! "Uh, yeah, well, I need to go to the USNS Trader in Subic Bay. That's about all I know."

"Yes, yes, we know exactly where that is. It will be about three hours and I must tell you we have to pass a few district checks. They are sometimes unknown cost to go through, OK?"

So I'll be repeatedly robbed before I get to the ship? Beautiful. As long as they don't kill me and they leave me enough for cab fare back to the airport. "Yeah, whatever. Just don't drive too fast, please."

"Oh, no, sir. We are very safe. No problem." Felix whipped the wheel left, jammed the gas and shot out of the cab queue lane directly into the path of an oncoming tram. Under barrage of a blaring horn and squealing tires, they sped away. The horrified back seater didn't raise up from crash brace position until they were well clear of the airport access.

The first 'district check' was encountered within five kilometers from the airport, just before reaching the sprawling squalor of south Manila. There was a small, open-sided gazebo along the road, occupied by two militia types, heavily armed with automatic rifles, belt-holstered sidearms and vested grenades. They were not stopping all vehicles, but when the Mercedes cab approached, one of the road guards stepped out of the shelter and extended his lowered arm in a detention gesture. Felix pulled up to a slow stop and Rodrigo got out to talk to the man with the guns. After a few minutes of muffled conversation, the mechanic returned to the car and looked through the window at the passenger. "Sir, I'm afraid we must pay a cash toll fee to continue through this point. It will be five thousand pesos, preferably in U.S. currency." *Holy shit, that's like a ben plus six hundred pesos! What the hell!?* The dumbfounded rider reluctantly opened his briefcase away from the watchdog and withdrew the money. He asked if he could get a receipt, in handing the 'fee' over the front seat back, to which there was no response. The big siderider sauntered back to the waiting uniform, turned over the U.S. ben and pocketed the pesos. *Wow! So the cabsters are in negotiated collusion with the checksters to rip me off!? What a fracking racket! How many of these do I have to go through??* The confused backseater felt skimmed. But what could he do? He was at the mercy of his transporters. He wondered if the armed toll takers were government soldiers, or police. They looked official, except they were wearing scruffy, pink plastic flip flops, which seemed rather out of code for approved issue. So, if they weren't real military, or something, who the hell were they? Professional racketeers? *Jesus, what a crockopile of crud!!*

Manila appeared to be an infinite compression of ground shacks aligned along narrow sand lanes littered with people, unconfined animals and slum debris. The hovels were loosely constructed with any scavenged material remnants available to shelter adaptation. Far in the smoggy dim of the distance, the high rise structures of the center city were visible in sharp contrast to the wretched poverty of the outlying ghettos. The American thought this was a much different look from any suburban housing development he had ever seen at home and wondered what the inhabitants did to make it work under such adverse living conditions. Probably their best asset was the temperature never going much below hot. They could not exist like this in cold weather. Straight ahead, his attention was diverted to the incredible hulk of a ship looming on the seaward side of the highway. At first, It might have been mistaken for a vessel riding the coast in a parallel course to port. But as they got closer, it was obvious the old and rusting hull was a permanent fixture on the beach, the remains of a large freighter washed ashore during a typhoon more than twenty years ago, so explained the shotgunner. At some point the density of the city subsided somewhat and the road became more open, through increasingly agricultural surroundings. When it finally seemed possible to speed up a little and make better time, Felix slowed, for no apparent reason, drifted over to the side and stopped. *Oh, christ, what now?* There was nothing here, except a roadside produce stand a short distance away. The driver got out and pissed, in plain sight of the young girl at the stand, who gave no reaction of affront. *Damn! That would be a misdemeanor sex offense in the states*, thought the westerner, remembering when he had to go outside in Korea, but at least not right in front of anyone.

Underway again, Rodrigo sparked a big fat roll, filling the car with whacky weed fog. After pulling a deep, long toke, he passed the joint blindly over his shoulder to the back, waiting for the hippy fare to take it. When that didn't happen, the mechanic turned around to see what it was. The probationary g-man waggled a hand in refusal, thinking he had enough to deal with and didn't need to be doing illegal smoke as an added complication, although he would probably soon get an unavoidable contact high, regardless.

"C'mon, sir, this is the best. *Sagada Gold*. It will make you relax."

"No, Rodrigo, I can't. I'm on duty. Thanks for the offer, though, I appreciate it."

There were two, maybe three, more district checks before they reached Olongapo, near Subic Bay. The slightly sillied sailor wasn't sure and just paid whatever he was told. By the time they arrived at the Trader, piered at the old naval facility with about twenty other, mostly commercial, ships, the cab charge from NAIA totaled over eight bens. It was easily the most expensive transportation, in terms of cost per unit distance, the novice traveler had ever taken. But he was just happy to be where he was trying to go, with all his stuff, most of his cash and, above all, his life. He also had the taxi team's card, with parting instructions to call when he needed a ride back to the airport.

At one time, Subic Bay harbored the largest navy base in the world. The USN had scores of warships, including two carrier groups, operating out of the Subic Naval District, which was the keystone of the American defense comportment in southeast Asia. Then a nearby volcano erupted and Philippine sentiment shifted, covering SBNB in ash and political fallout. The base was closed and its hundred million dollar payroll evaporated. The local economy was devastated. In time, the bay recovered as an excellent port, hoped by many, on all sides of the table, to be eventually re-established as a strategic American naval stronghold in the region. The future probably depended on how threatened the Philippines felt by a body building China. For now, the U.S. was permitted access for non-military ops, such as the NMS's Trader recovery mission. The Trader was an old navy supply ship, retrofitted, painted white and recommissioned as a NAVO survey vessel. Not very large, less than two hundred feet, it carried good tech capability. Agent Rossy stood alone before the gangway wondering what kind of bunkum he was about to be throttled through here.

***

"Well, I'll be damned, if it isn't new man bj, just like the classified directive said. Last I heard, you were at PNAS. Not a real long time, no see! Wassup, dude?"

Redeye Bergle. God, what's he doing here? Is he the pc? "Hey, Trent. How's it going? Nothing much. Reportin' for duty as assigned."

"So, where you been, if you're not down the river?"

"I was relocated on special assignment and now I'm here. Just following orders."

"Alright, sounds bureaucratically well stated. You must be a good government worker. And I need some help. We got ourselves a crazyass mess of shit and not enough bodies to clean it up, so I hope you're ready to work."

"Who all's here?"

"Groob, the towster, shorty and one other sailor I don't think you met. Murry Cohen. Plus some navy clods. We just got here yesterday. We were over at Quy Nhon, in Nam, getting ready to start some shipping lane surveys, and the NMS cap took us out before the storm came in. I spent two days rolling back and forth on the lab deck in fracking thirty foot seas. You ever ride a ty-phoon?"

"No."

"Well, it ain't happy time, I'll tell ya that. Anyway, then we got orders to divert here to help reestablish storm damaged ferry routes between Panay and Mindoro. Storm *Josuer* was a total bitch, man. They say it was one of the worst ever. Christ, we got some shit to do."

"Well, what's the schedule?"

"We're supplying up here through tomorrow and then we head for Caluya, which'll be about a one day steam. We'll do some ocean track on the way around western Mindoro. I'll put you with Cohen and two navy techs on Caluya and Silvera, Kallen and shorty on Semirara. All y'all have to do is set up camp and moni-tor a doppler transceiver for about fifty satellite passes of data to iterate into a class one gp. Then you set a permanent geodetic marker and we'll be good to go in the Strait. Simple, no?"

"I guess, if you say so."

"Super! Hey, let's go into town and grab a few brews, maybe get something to eat and relax a little. Next to last chance to chill before we have to earn our overpay. I think the others are already gone. You ever been to Olongapo?"

***

The way from Subic into the adjacent burg bridged over an open sewer canal that was fairly deep. Murky, olive gray water roiled by at least two meters below the bridge deck. A group of children, boys and girls seemingly ranging in age from about eight to fifteen, sat on the un-railed edge of the deck trying to compel passersby to throw coins into the water for which they would dive in to retrieve. The pc flipped a peso piece into the drink and sever-al kids immediately followed, like dogs after a stick. A few se-conds later one beaming boy surfaced holding the coin high over his head and everyone watching applauded loudly in whistling approval. The divers climbed out of the mucky swill and returned to the bridge to await the next offering. Bj thought that this whole scene was pathetic and couldn't believe his new field boss abetted such a degrading activity. "Hey, they're making honest money," defended redeye, "which is a lot better than sucking government welfare that American taxpayers probably pay for in foreign aid." *Honest money? Why would anybody jump into a sewer for, what, less than three cents? God almighty! That's insane!* But, then again, as the objecting observer thought about it, it was actually pretty amazing that anybody could find anything in that crappy water! How did they do that? A minor unknown that would remain in question, as the Trader twosome moved quickly on.

Just before entering the fringe of the downtown commerce and entertainment district, the sailors passed through a snarl of sidewalk moneychangers, who accepted all major credit cards and electronic bit-money, in illegally buying any currency at way undervalued rates. Their operation was a total ripoff and anyone dealing with them was either waffled drunk or hopelessly desperate, or both. Consequently, the MCs had to be aggressive in trying to snare the business of anyone carousing in proximity to their tables. An irritating reminder, for the enchanted dreamer, of the airport cabbie hassle. At least the Olongapo changers were not about to leave their cash wares to physically grab potential clients, so it was possible to get by them without bodily assault. Further on in town, the city was noisy with musical, bell-ringing 'jeepneys', garishly decorated open-sided vehicles for hire, roaming the streets like tasseled clown cars. They were everywhere, in full primary-colored splendor, blaring screech horns at foreign pedestrians, sometimes all but running them over, trying to hustle the fare. It was a psychedelic jungle, perhaps not all that conducive to safe passage for the unsuspecting visitor, because, in his personal punctilio for awareness of surroundings, the covert engineer astutely observed that every jeepney looked like it carried a 'mechanic'. That could very well mean 'wrong way' for the defenseless, non-native rider.

No need for a potentially dangerous jeepney to go where redeye was leading. They were within easy foot distance of an extempore sign, over a rathole opening between a couple of undignified street-front structures, reading simply, *'PEOPLE'S MARKET'*. Ducking into the claustrophobic space, they followed a slender, dark passageway to the back edge of the buildings, where a bewildering jumble of shoebox stores, shops, stands, eateries and impromptu enterprises of almost anything imaginable fanned out in all directions. Random, non-linear walkways meandered through the makeshift mall, which, once inside, gave the impression of boundless horizontal dimension. Nothing in the PM was of permanent construction and everything was tinder dry flammable. The place was a cat five fire disaster waiting to happen. Exposed electrical wires were everywhere, including on the ground over the graveled paths. The open-fronted business cells were separated by cardboard, or burlap, partitions under a low canopy of patched waterproof tarps and polyethylene sheeting. Conflicting music resonated in consonant, indistinguishable rhythms, mixed with the whirr of countless fans and probably thousands of voices. The strange, but fascinating, spontaneous bazaar was perpetually crowded and never closed. And it was thoroughly, irreversibly permeated with the sweet, pungent redolence of *Sagada Gold*.

The junior engineer followed his supervisor through a disorienting imbroglio deep into the complex of the highly animated and confining galleria. Redeye advised his minion to 'keep centered on the walkway and watch your pockets', while hucksters from both sides groped and yelled at the fast stepping out-of-towners. The attentive agent was confident there was no way he could find his way out of this morass by himself. So he stayed close, maybe too close, to the pc ahead. When Bergle abruptly stopped at a tiny 'cafe', no bigger than a tailgate cookout, bj almost collided right into the leader's back. Savoy Sis's Snacks was well known as serving the best Filipino street food in the market and redeye had been here, at the direction of a knowledgeable Trader crewman, last evening. Sis looked up from the portable kitchen at the back of the cubicle and, recognizing the returning red-eyed American, warmly welcomed him and his friend to take a seat anywhere. There were just three small tables and two were occupied, so they sat at the only available place. An adorable little girl, Sis's daughter, took their order for lamb adobo, sisig, turon rolls and San Miguel beer. Same as last night, all very good, and cheap. The PM's best.

Upon getting settled with food and drink, Rossy asked what was happening 'back in the world', as he had heard overseas military people refer to homeland America. "Not much. Same 'ole', same 'ole'. Except bunny retired."

"Bunny's gone?"

"Yeah, it was classic. We had a going away lunch for him at a Chinese place downtown. It started off as a pretty small party, but then bunny's relatives, kids and exes showed up and all of a sudden there were about forty people. The old Chinese mamasan and papasan didn't know what to do with so many unexpected customers and they froze up in confusion. So wokker went into the kitchen and took charge. He broke into the dialect and was ordering everybody around like an ambushed field general. He even directed the wait staff and the old owner couple. We could hear him constantly yelling and there was a lot of banging metal sounds, but he pulled it off and everybody was served and happy. The boy should open his own place. He knows how to run a restaurant."

"Well, how in the hell can bunny retire? He's what, twenty-two? A GS-3? There's no financial way he could retire!"

Redeye looked hard at the new sailor and ordered another round of San Migs. He didn't speak until well after the refills came, gazing thoughtfully into a personal cyberspace, as if trying to carefully formulate his next words to say something he didn't really want to. The younger g-man waited nervously for a response, thinking the senior sailor might have slipped into some kind of beer trance. Finally, "We have a little side gig going on at NAVO. It makes bucoo big bucks for those of us that play. Bunny was a player."

Wow! What is this? Do I really want to go there? "What does that mean?"

Should I tell him? Hell, I've already opened the lid. No closing back now. We're gonna need a replacement for the rabbit. Rossy's smart and a liberal. If he's in, he'll be a plus. If not, well, shit, the kid's got his own scam going,'cause he's disappeared from three TDYs already. What the frack's up with that?? No, he's good either way. "Drugs, man. We're running narcs back to D.C. from all over the world. High quality demand stuff we get cheap from the sources. We send it back in the equipment containers, which are secured and classified. Everybody along the way recognizes them, but no one has the legal authority, or special tools and codes, to open them up. They know the boxes are gps tagged and if there's any type of forced entry, an embedded plastique device will detonate with sufficient implosive force to destroy all the contents. That's never actually happened, by the way, but it could. The whole unit is designed to protect the classified integrity of the equipment technology, but it also gives us a systemically failsafe vehicle for getting our product home, where we can sell it for ten to fifty times cost. Bunny's been in the program for three years. Trust me, dude, he's made enough to retire. So, you wanna play? We have an opening." Another round of San Migs........

God, I can't believe this!! My job and career and life are all sitting on ground fault zero. My whole future's about to blow. What the hell do I do now?! "Well, how do you sell the stuff when it gets back?"

"We have a street man, who takes as much as we can bring. Lockbark has known the dude since he was a kid in a city mentoring program. Larry volunteered in the program as a math tutor and kept in contact with the boy, almost like an adopted godson. He tried to get him a job at NAVO, when he got out of school, but the guy didn't have an engineering degree and all he could qualify for was tech. Apparently, he turned gang-related and somehow the two of them worked up a scheme to set us up in our little operation, that we like to unofficially call DAFT, or, 'drugs are for trips'. Get it? Trips are TDY, where we get the drugs, which are for tripping. Cool, huh?" Another round.......

Yeah, cool, alright. Cool, like we're all gonna be frozen so deep in prison we won't even thaw out with a thousand years of global warming. The graduate. This answers a lot of questions, but I'm not revealing any of my shit and I don't need to know any more of theirs. Best thing I should do is get the hell outta here as quickly as possible. But then if I go off bean, tophead and the CIA would probably ice me down. Oh, god, why didn't I listen to mom about this job?!? "Yeah, that's pretty good. Looks like you have everything covered."

"Thass right. DAFT is 'bout as airtight as it gets, while we do our gitimate, ficial bidness as gummit engineers. So, lemme ass you again, son, you want in? Believe me, iss worth it and we can sure use 'nother player. Jus doan spect ta use our produck on the job, though, 'cause we gotta stay alert!" Round......

Oh, no. Redeye's going down. He must have been swilling all day! "I'll have to think about it, Trent. Sounds good, but there's lots to consider." *Like, who would do me first, the police, the CIA, or the daftmen? Don't forget the graduate! Or maybe some loco Filipino hustler. Jesus, I wish I would have stayed in Connecticut!* The probie watched in horror as his pc's head sunk slowly onto the little table, arms dangling to the floor. Sis soon came over and said they would have to leave. No sleeping allowed and she needed the table. The also feeling not-so-good, but at least awake, subordinate paid the tab and wrestled the wasted lead rep to his feet. Now what? He had no clue how to get out of the PM and Bergle was like a blind, dead-weight zombie! Rossy slung his incapacitated colleague's arm around his neck and started dragging him away, like hobbling an injured ball player off the field. They started back the way they came in, but the first-timer soon lost any perception as to where they were, relative to where they needed to be. At some juncture along the shuffle, an unsolicited marketeer man lifted redeye's other arm, making the load a little lighter. This help would surely not be gratis. *Christ, I might as well just take all the money left on me and throw it up in the air. They're gonna get it one way or another!* The unlikely trio finally emerged from the market onto a different street from where the two Traders had entered. It was very night and the now attentively worried bj felt dangerously lost. Redeye continued to nod in mumbling submission and the Filipino helper let out an ear piercing whistle. Within seconds a jeepney crept silently and lightless into sight from around a corner and slowed to stop in front of the three. The assistant pushed the engineers into the back, took his seat at shotgun and the jeepney immediately sped away from the curb. *Goddam it! This is a set-up and we've been scoped! Everything just keeps getting worse!*

Incredibly, the driver headed directly to the Subic Bay port zone and delivered the sailors to the Trader. Before they could move to scramble out of the vehicle, the mechanic turned around, brandishing a machete that ominously gleamed a finely sharpened edge in the dim pier light. In a low, deadly voice, he ordered the passengers to give up all the paper they had, or he would cut them well and throw their American pieces into the harbor. The pier was shadowy dark, no one was around and the air evoked heavy silence. There was no option but to get punked, right in front of their ship, under the homeland flag. Following the forced cash transfer and rapid departure of the jeepney, the sailors stood alone on the concrete deck, trying to process exactly what had just happened.

At least bj did. Redeye was still outsourced. They lost about a half ben, but that wasn't the issue. They were still alive, and that, though obviously important, wasn't the issue, either. The question in the junior rough rider's mind was, *how in hell did the jeepney driver know where to take them!?* It was like they had been marked as soon as they entered the PM, or maybe even before. What kind of conspiracy of corruption are they ensnarled in here? Is the whole Philippines linked in? The airport cabbers certainly seemed to be on the same team as the armed road stoppers. Did they all communicate with the creepy jeepney robbers? What defense is there against this?? *Tall up, man. You're CIA! You've got resources, assets. Use them!!* The concerned chipmole calmed a bit in remembering his alter role. The CIA was a helluva lot bigger and more powerful than any rinkydink Filipino crime net. Then he remembered the NAVO drug cartel. *Holy son of jesus, I'm fracked!!*

***

The next day was just as hot as most of the other Philippine days. Following breakfast, the NAVO sailors were congregated in the air conditioned lab, hanging out with no pressing work related items to do during ship's resupply. It was sort of like a day off, except they would still draw overtime and adverse climate differential. Groob and the towster sat at opposite ends of a work station playing hand football. Shorty was logged on to a *Doomsday Battle Dragons* internet game and Murry "(the) rabbi" Cohen sat in a far corner reading the Talmud, looking slightly orthodox, in his black trilby hat, horned rim glasses, white tee and suspended 'shucker' jeans. Redeye was not yet on deck. Rabbi had been introduced at breakfast, to the Philippine joiner, as a graduate of Columbia University, in traffic engineering, with a minor in Jewish studies. He had started as a religion major, intending to transfer to seminary in Jerusalem to become a Chasidic rabbi, just like his Brooklyn father. But one thing led to another, goals and finances didn't pan out and the young Jewish student redirected his ambitions to the easiest route available. Cohen was a good friend of Kallen, who towed his car, at their first encounter, from a minor mishap on the LIE. They kept in contact after the wreck and hung out from time to time through school. The towster actually recruited his highway pal to NAVO, when the Columbia grad found his education to be unmarketable. Rabbi maintained an interest in Judaism and loved to study the ancient scriptures.

The street slapped market runner still felt a little woozy from last night's beering and wondered who of these Traders was daft. He figured the towster as in, remembering the episode with the containers that he and wokker delivered to Larry at the Yard. And if rabbi was a friend of the towster's, *he* was probably a player. Shorty, too, because he was tight with bunny when they apparently signaled incoming product to the graduate out along the parkway. Groob? Hard to tell. Don't know much about the dude, except he's good at vouchers and a rabid New England sports fan. *How about me? Go to hell, man! Homey don't play dat!* Since nothing was happening and the boss was below, the fifth wheel decided to return to his room and check in with Booker. It'd been a while since he talked to his roomie and he wanted to make sure everything was good at the apartment. One less thing to worry about. He'd use a burner to call, to keep Dick happy.

"Booker, how's it going?"

"Who's this?"

"Rossy, man! What the hell?!"

"Oh, yeah, Rossy. Where *are* you?"

"You know I can't say. Just that I'm not where I was last time I called."

"OK, whatever. Look, about your car, it's gone, dawg."

"WHAT?! WHAT ARE YOU TALKING ABOUT?? WHADUYA MEAN MY CAR'S *GONE*??"

"Gone. Evidently stolen. I went out in the lot at the apartment to run it, like you asked, and I couldn't find it anywhere. I looked all over. Nada. So, I called the police and said I think somebody stole your car. They showed up and asked a million questions and I explained the situation, like a hundred times. In their investigation they checked the AGA security surveillance records and saw the doofus DCA guard, Trevair, having your car towed away. When they asked him about it, he said the car smelled bad and he had it towed down to the apartment storage yard so tenants wouldn't complain. Problem is, it wasn't in the storage yard, either. So, Trevair gets busted for grand theft auto and fired. He's gone and so is your car. Haven't heard anything more from the police, but I reported everything to your insurance. Haven't heard back from them either, because they said they couldn't do anything until the police report is final. That's it. Now you know everything I do."

"Holy shit! I can't believe this! I'm still making payments on the goddam thing!! What the frack?!!"

"That's right. I sent one in the other day for you, just like you told me."

"Armmmph!"

"Oh, yeah, and gameboy got married."

"What?! How did that happen?"

"Well, he decided to have a homecoming party at the apartment and he called up the Swedish embassy and invited all the single women that worked there. You know, like a blind shot in the dark thing? And, unbelievably, a carload of them showed up! So he started dating one of them, Svelda something, and next thing you know they take off for Vegas to get married. She moved into the apartment, but I don't think it's going to last. Seve told me he's not sure he can go through with it. Apparently, they planned to go to Sweden at some point for a real wedding with her relatives there, so he thinks he's not completely married yet. I told him, 'dude, you be married!' but he doesn't believe it! Anyway, now he's trying to go back out on TDY, which will be pretty awkward here with gamegirl Svelda. Guess we'll have to move out. I dunno, man, it's a real mess."

No car. No apartment. I've lost everything!! Why the hell did I make this call?! "OK, Booker, you got any other happy stuff to tell me? Otherwise, I gotta go!"

"No, man, that's about it. Nothin' else happenin' here. Seeya."

The unexpectantly homeless homie felt as though he had mind-slushing trouble exploding everywhere. He went up to the waterside lateral deck, smashed the burner into smithereens, probably with much more vehemence than necessary, and threw it over the rail. There were too many issues to deal with in a rational manner. So, rather than deal with them irrationally, he decided to not deal with them at all. Once again, he would not worry, be happy, and try to enjoy being in the dreamy Philippines. After all, he carried official authorization, had plenty to eat and friends, as they were, to associate with, at least until they got bumped for drug running. All the basics of human exigency. Hell, just go with the flow, as he had forced himself to do so many times before during this era of frustrating uncertainty, no left turns during rush hour and play it as it lies. Chances are, things might turn out for the best, ...or not. He returned to the lab to rejoin his colleagues in hanging out, doing nothing. The loll before the storm.

***

Leaving port on a large, sea-going vessel was a special new experience for the unsailed globe trotter. He stood to starboard on the forward deck, just below the bridge, enjoying the passage of the lavish scenery, feeling a warm brush of motion against the steamy tropical air and thinking how fortunate he was to have such an unusual job that sends him to all these places he would never even consider going to on his own. He was engulfed by one of those lucky moods where you just felt euphorically glad to be here. Forget all the crabble crap he was slugging through and take in the moment. His placid frame of mind actually began last evening when the Traders grouped into town for some final nightclubbing. The live music had been incredible. Filipino bands could cover any song ever recorded better than the original artist. They sat in one place, Tina's Terrace, and raptly listened to a U2 impressionist group flawlessly play the entire *Joshua Tree* album, while drinking only one round of beer. The performance was *that* good. And now, here he was, sailing off into what might be the waters of Lethe, for all he knew, without a conscious care in the world.

Pc Bergle had set up a work schedule for monitoring ocean track, the record of geo-positioned sounding data for the en route course to Caluya. This was easy lab duty, since there was no bearing direction involved and the data collection and process were completely automated. All the duty person had to do was make sure satellite locks were occurring correctly. Rossy was assigned newbie midnight watch, meaning night differential, although everyone drew ND, no matter what the scheduled shift. Conditions were beautiful, with flat sea, cloudless sky and no storm in the forecast. Once sure he was not susceptible to seasickness, the rook wanted to stay awake and enjoy the ride, but knew he should get some sleep before his duty shift. Maybe after dinner.

At some time around mid-afternoon, emergency alert honkers shattered the relative ambient silence with head jerking force. The maiden voyager followed everyone else on the ship running toward the main deck midsection, where they lined up under the life rafts. A loudspeakered voice of authority started reading names in roll call sequence, separated by a bellow of 'HERE' from each called body in presence. After all assemblers were accounted for, a simulated raft deployment exercise ensued, during which all hands, except the confused NAVO neophyte, seemed to have and know something to do. At the end of the drill, the big voice commanded dismissal and then ordered **'William A. Rossy'** to the bridge.

The publicly addressed detainee nervously made his way into the surprisingly small control cabin, facing a rotund, khaki-clad man seated at the helm panel. The NMS master was a semi-Santa looking oldster, with bushy white mustache sans beard and rimless, undersized bifocals. He was not ho-ho smiling. No, he was scowling. At the new engineer from the client agency. "Mr. Rossy, do you know what a boat drill is?"

"Uh, yes, sir, I think so."

"You think so. What did we just exercise on deck?"

"A boat drill?"

"Are you sure? Because, if you know what a boat drill is, why did you show up with no head cover, no long sleeve shirt, no flotation vest and no proper footwear?"

Oh, god. Here we go again. Is he going to put me off the ship? Make me walk the plank? "Uh, well, no one told me the boat drill dress code, sir. I'm sorry."

"You're sorry. Do you think sorry counts during a real abandonment event? Do you think sorry counts when others have to use critical time and resources to accommodate your unpreparedness?"

"Uh, no, sir, but..."

"Shuddup! I don't want to hear your excuses! You so-called engineers are all alike. You think you're above the rules. Well, you're not! This is my ship and while aboard you follow my protocol. Now, if this happens again, I guarantee you will be disembarked, no matter where we are. *Do you copy!?*"

"Yes, sir."

"OK, that's all. Now get off my bridge!"

Are you kidding me?? This fracking flipper is barging all kinds of illegal drugs through international waters and he's worried whether I have a long sleeve shirt?!? Who the frack has a long sleeve shirt in the deep fried Philippines?! The non-compliant, so-called so-and-so would have to see pc redeye asap to get what he needed to pass boat drill. There was no way he could be disenfranchised out here in the middle of crime nation nowhere.

***

The midnight lab wasn't much different than the lab at noon. There were no ports to the exterior, so the artificially lighted interior was constantly the same. The nightshifter sat alone observing the automated data components do their work. With no input or control sequences required, he was essentially just a token bystander. This was by far the easiest work he had ever done. All he had to do was monitor satellite locks with scheduled passes to make sure gps data was being properly received and coordinated by the network logic. Sounding positions would not be as accurate as with planned mission surveys, but it was close enough for unclassified ocean track, or, as the private sector liked to say, for government work. After several hours of listening to the soft whir of the AC fans, the deeper, internal rumble of the ship's drive and the intermittent mechanical clicking of the data process and output, the ocean tracker started duping out. The gentle, almost imperceptible, yawling of the ship in the stilly sea didn't help. No, he did *not* want to doze off on his initial shipboard solo watch as a NAVO sailor, but he was really feeling muzzy, like being road mesmerized while driving. All of a sudden he snapped to, sensing a radical change. Near total silence and the only visible room light emitted from faint, nicad emergency fixtures over the hatchways. The ship was dead in the water, in the dead of night, all systems down. *What the hell is this!?* The computer processes were still running, on internal battery source, but red LED alerts indicated automatic shutdown had begun, during which procedure called for the operator to disengage from any satellite lock in progress to avoid indeterminate iteration and loss of the entire current data cache. The inexperienced operator, of course, had no knowledge of this and watched helplessly as all information collected on his first watch went *poof* down the power drain. *Shit!!* Rossy concluded there was nothing more to not do in the lab and decided to go outside.

It was approaching pre-dawn, but still pitch black, and the Trader was wafting aimlessly on the quiet water, like a massive piece of driftwood. Or maybe like the **INVINCIBLE** on the Chesapeake, as the aggravated agent recalled his PNAS misadventure. He was not logging a record of good productivity at sea. The sky was clear and lushly filled with neighboring stars of the hometown galaxy. It actually looked alive in displaying the varying intensities and sparkling shades of unknown billions of pulsating cosmic bodies scattered across nature's overhead IMAX screen. But the duty man didn't have the time nor inclination to revisit the wonders of the universe. He thought he would try to find the darkened way to the wardroom for a cup of coffee and figure out how to fix his broken watch while enjoying the upcoming rising sun. After all, he had not had a break all night.

During the arduous backtrack from the galley, the sleeping floater lurched to life. Lights came on, turbines roared and the shafted props churned. As the vessel returned to speed and course, daylight was dawning and a spectacular sunrise was developing to the port side. While sipping cooled, age-thickened coffee and taking in the scene of the moment, the breakster heard a heavy splashing in the water at some distance off the stern. A taut nylon filament line, nearly thin rope thick, stretched from the fantail deck to the visible disturbance in the middle of the wake, about fifty yards out. Forgetting his watch woes, the sunrise and everything else that had been occupying his unsettled thoughts, the distracted loner grabbed the line and started handing it in. He was not only fighting the source of the surface swash, but also the drag of the wake and it was quickly obvious this would not be an easy task. Without gloves, the rope dug into his un-calloused palms, tending to slow the progress even more. Once started, quitting was not an option. He had to see what was on the end of the line. After almost half an hour and the equivalent of a decent morning workout, he had the object of interest directly below the deck railing. It was definitely a fish, though he couldn't yet tell what kind. Hoisting it up out of the water, he saw the snag was a bull-nosed dolphin, at least a meter long and probably thirty pounds. It was rainbow beautiful and the biggest fish the former fly trouter had ever dealt with. He grappled it onto the deck and sat on a nearby mooring capstan to rest and admire his accomplishment. What a great break! The best he had taken since joining NAVO. Rejuvenated, the sailor went back into the still empty lab to try and see if it was possible to angle any useful results from the closing hour of his watch. A short time later, the galley sous chef appeared on the fandeck, slapped the dead dolphin over his shoulder and took it back to the kitchen for use in prepping a special seafood quiche. No one would ever know who reeled in the catch of the day, because the midnight rookie was not about to reveal he had gone fishing, while his workplace crashed.

***

Fortunately, there was little fallout from the overnight data drop. Ocean track was a policy requirement and not mission orientated, so few field teams took it seriously. But redeye still seemed a little distant to his new charge, who worried whether the pc was waiting to see if he would go daft, or not. Of course, that wasn't going to happen, and he would probably have to convey this sooner than later, but at the same time he wanted to assure the bizarro secret was good with him. Otherwise, he could be lost at sea, or anywhere in the Philippines, in a hurry. It was a dangerous situation and not one to easily DWBH his way through. Maybe, hopefully, he could make contact with the country asset and *bean* out before the issue red flagged.

The rest of the trip around southern Mindoro was uneventful and the Trader reached Caluya in early afternoon. Then began a physical ordeal the new timer was not really prepared for. The port town, though relatively undamaged by the typhoon, had no facilities to accommodate the ship, which had no helicopter unit, meaning all site logistics had to be transacted via small boat and by foot. They loaded up an onboard utility skiff with everything needed to establish a geodetic satellite point and navaids survey site, including a high caliber, semi-rifle placed among the equipment and supplies by the rabbi. *Really? A rifle?? What the hell do we need a rifle for?!* Bj inquired about the weapon and rabbi, in a rather short, perhaps threatening temper, said, "Don't ever touch that. It's signed out to *me* and is *my* responsibility! Just stay away from it, OK??"

"OK, OK, hey, no problem!! What the frack, man??!" *What the hell is that all about?? This rabbi dude seems a little paranoid neurotic, so they give him a gun? Phew, boy! Like livin' in America! It keeps getting better all the time!* The laded craft was lowered by hydraulic crane, with the NMS driver and the navy techs, and the two engineers followed in a personnel basket. The agent, his backpack already aboard, insisted on carrying his vital briefcase with him. Not prudent, as it turned out, because he nearly fell in the water when the case got tangled in the basket webbing as he tried to step out, in tandem with a wave crest, into the boat. Everyone watching, above and below, snickered and called him a greenassed idiot. He felt like dumb Mr. Richardson, at Ascension, but at least he knew where all his personal effects were. If necessary, he could leave from Caluya, without returning to the ship. Agent's operative rule: always keep all options open.

The boatload of support had to be moved, by hand and back, to the selected site way above the town. Plus they had to procure some necessities at the village general store, primarily several cases of beer and ice. The winding footpath to the destination stretched through the jungle more than three kilometers, rising at least two thousand feet. It was godawful, steaming hot and there was no way the Americans could do this by themselves, so they hired about seven of the onlookers from the small crowd of people who had been following them around ever since they docked at the public pier. It took a good three hours to reach the top of the hill, after which they all, including the hired carriers, enjoyed a San Mig break. The navy techs then set to in making camp, while the engineers continued gazing at the stunning island vista overlooking the Tablas Strait.

Rossy was not much of a camper. When traveling, he preferred to stay in a choice group hotel, with all the modern comforts and conveniences of the road and a continental breakfast. The bulk of his camping experience was during a brief stint in the Boy Scouts at age thirteen and, later, a few forgettable times at the juvie correctional wilderness in New York. Also, a couple weekend recreational jaunts as an adult. He had been dragooned into the BSA by a friend, whose older brother was a heavily decorated, overachieving eagle scout. As he remembered it, camping often meant spending squalid nights on cold, wet ground, with water falling on your head through leaks in the tent and soggy, stale granola bars as the only food. The Boy Scouts came across to him as a somewhat specious organization that forced you to do a whole lot of things you really had no interest in, or need to know how to do. Like precision marching, which his troop spent ninety per cent of its time practicing, at the direction of the scoutmaster, a retired ceremonial infantry lineman. In the scouts, he was constantly being cajoled to work on merit badges, of which he never earned enough to get past the rank of second class. They were vapid exercises in pointlessness, as far as he was concerned. He had one in tying knots. Another in how to mark your way so you wouldn't get lost in the woods, an unlikely scenario if you stayed on the trail. How to make a hiking stick, like there was a shortage of them laying around in the forest. The environmental art of picking up trash. Purifying water, as if boiling was a difficult concept. The last one he worked on was first aid. At a troop meeting they were receiving instruction on bandaging wounds and one boy started wrapping another in gauze to the extent the demo kid took on the visage of a mummy. Young teener Rossy and his pal began laughing so hard the leader called them immature disrupters and angrily ordered them to get out. They staggered out of the clubhouse and fell down in the yard, rolling around in uncontrollable fits of giggles. When they finally were able to regain sufficient composure to stand up, they walked off the premises, still chuckling heartily, and never went back. That was the end of their second class scouting careers and any dormant desire to consciously pursue camping as a future, free-time activity.

But now the ex-scout had to camp out, in a no-choice work predicament. Though never in danger of being confused with an expert on camping materials and procedure, the engineer could see the shelter being erected by the techs might prove to be the wrong solution for the conditions they were stuck in. The military issue tent, a heavy, dark green, fully enclosed canvas structure, was a thermal sink that would absorb and hold the heat of the tropical sun. It would probably reach unlivable interior temperatures, way out of range of the acceptable operating conditions for the microwave transceiver and computer appurtenances to be housed within. If the equipment broke down, the mission would be a bust. Fortunately, the tent was on raised, wooden platform slats that might allow sufficient air circulation to keep the hardware functioning. Only time would tell.

By early evening, the site had been settled, an antenna point established and satellite locks were in progress. So far, so good. The NAVO crew had fired up propane stoves for heating MRE tins of corned beef hash and cut beans and carrots, augmented by apple sauce and crackers. Not much different from a baby food meal, except for the beer. The locals, who had been coming and going at the hilltop in varying numbers ever since the Traders arrived, continued to meander around and among the new hilltoppers, closely inspecting everything that had been brought up from the big white ship anchored offshore. Most of the people had never seen, in real life, anyone other than Filipinos. Americans were a novelty and the blond bearded, blue-eyed navy techs were a complete wonder. Rossy looked the least interesting, as he was the least different, with his dark hair and eyes and off-pale skin tone. Indian heritage, according to crazy, old grandpap. *Maybe it can work to my plus, here, in some unfigured, inconspicuous way.* As curiosity evolved to familiarity, the site visitors, especially the younger ones, began to ask for selfies with the surprise guests and some even showed up bearing coconuts to trade for family portraits alongside the strange outliers. The activity subsided quickly as darkness descended and the native Caluyans went home. They knew better than to be out in the jungle in the black of night. The Americans continued San Migging for some time, before bagging in, except for one of the techs, who took first satellite watch. The covert camper couldn't help but notice rabbi laid out with his rifle tucked up close beside him, his arm wrapped loosely around the open metal stock, like he was embracing a teddy bear. Bj had no doubt, if need be, the traffic engineer could assume ready-to-fire attitude in a split second, just like they were taught by the marine sniper specialist at Quantico. After all, there were many bad actors in the Philippines and a NAVO rifleman had to be always alert. He stifled an horrific premonition that rabbi was actually a daft hitman, assigned to make the non-player problem disappear. *Sweet dreams aren't made of these!*

***

The un-camper awakened from a sleepless doze in a dawning sweat, feeling about as uncomfortably stationed as possible under the circumstances. It had to be over ninety degrees in the airless enclosure and the sun wasn't even fully fired yet! The second tech was on satellite duty, reading a pulp fiction vampire novel, and the others were snoozing noisily. *OK, then, so what are the voices I'm hearing right outside the tent?* Emerging to the very slightly cooler exterior, the early riser found a large family of island homies gathered around the now sizable heap of coconuts mounded up nearby. The parents and six children, all dressed in their best Catholic Sunday attire, converged on the groggy g-man to request a photograph with the Americans. Not fully awake and about as scruffily unkempt as he had been on this TDY tour, the vagrant visitor posed in stark contrast with the smiling, clean-cut group, as the father's tripod mounted digital camera auto-clicked a series of memorable shots. The agent, realizing he really couldn't be any more conspicuous, wondered inwardly whether this family photo op could be construed as a security violation. Probably not. As messed up as he knew he looked, no one would be able to recognize him without comprehensive facial scanning analysis. And that couldn't happen unless the pics were up-posted and went viral. *What are the chances?* The family did not immediately leave, as they wanted to wait for the other campers to record pictures of themselves with all the aliens.

The poster boy left the locals sitting quietly by the coconut pile, to seek the utility of the latrine the navy techs had excavated some distance from the shelter. On the way back, he missed treading on a little, yellow green snake by a mere few centimeters. A green mamba. The two step. One of the most poisonous snakes in the world. Get bitten, take two steps and die. They had warned caution about this tiny viper on the ship and now here he was - less than one step away from a two step death, or three steps from the edge. Funny how events, in a momentary instant, can turn the arrow away from everything that matters to the only thing that counts. The bush walker had to pause and catch his breath, vowing to be more careful and watch his feet placement at all times. *Still good, thanks to my man, jesus! Thank you, lord!*

Later on in the morning, as the sun came up full bore, the reluctant tentman got so wretchedly hot he decided to trek down over the hill, find a beach and go in the ocean to cool off. None of the other Traders thought that was a good idea, so the sweating sailor agent set out on his own. It took about an hour to get to the water, where he found a party of young girls rollicking in the waves, laughing loudly as they chased and splashed each other through the surf. The beach was a beautiful strip of smooth, white sand that shelved out under the break line, forming an ideal place to swim and enjoy the tranquility of the soothing sea. He picked a spot some distance from the group bathers, kicked off his sandals and waded into the water. In resurfacing from diving under a wave crest, he heard a chorus of screams and saw the girls scrambling out of the water and running away down the beach. *OMG, they must have seen a shark,* he panicked, looking freakishly around for a telltale jaws fin. Seeing nothing, he decided to get out of the water anyway, since there had to have been something in there that spooked the others. While drying off, feeling, at least temporarily, much cooler and more comfortable than before, he saw a woman, wrapped in a colorful, patterned sari, walking rapidly toward him from where the girls had run. As she got closer, it was evident she was not enjoying a happy stroll on the beach. In fact, she looked angry, zooming in directly at him! *What the hell's this!?* He stood in the sand, waiting her approach, anxious to find out what was going on here. The woman marched right up to him, clearly very agitated, initially saying nothing. And then, "You were swimming with the girls?"

"Uh, not really. I went in the water up the beach from where they were. I wasn't with them. What's the problem?"

"You cannot go swimming with the girls! It is forbidden!"

"No. Like I said, I wasn't with them. What are you saying?"

"I'm saying you were in the watra with the girls. And now you must marry Ina, the eldest. She is only fourteen."

"What?? No way! That's not true! I'm not marrying *anyone*!"

"It is our custom. If man and unmarried woman go into the watra together, they must wed. It is the way. You will marry Ina."

"Nooo! I didn't go in the water with anybody! I was by myself! This is totally bogus!"

"I will bring the matter to council." The woman turned abruptly and returned down the beach from where she had come. The again perspiring sailor remained motionless, dumbstruck, wondering what the hell had just happened.

***

By the time the secret swimmer climbed back up the terrain to the work site, he was sweatier, dirtier and hotter than when he originally left for the beach to cool off. A thin film of grainy salt from the sea covered his skin like a moist, itching powder. He was nearing a state of catatonic misery and went directly to the supply bin for a coldie. But the ice was long gone and the San Migs were as hot as everything else on this godforsaken little peak of hell on earth. Upon unsealing the cap, the heated beer exploded in a volley of coffee-looking foam, leaving only a fraction of the inert beverage intact in the container. The latent beer lover took a swig of the barley gag and spit it forcefully into the weeds, dumping the rest and disgustingly throwing the empty back into the bin. He opted for a plastic bottle of hot water, featuring a label picture of an ice cold mountain stream gushing through snow covered boulders. It was almost time for his turn at monitoring satellite passes in the sauna tent and he stared balefully at the cartons of MREs, knowing he would have to eat something before going on watch. How 'bout dumplings in gravy paste, baked beans and pears? *Yeah, that'll do it! Gimme two!*

The afternoon was peculiar and somewhat awkward, at best. The navy techs had gone down to the pier center to retrieve more ice and cold beer, leaving the engineers alone on the duty hill. Other than a latrine call, rabbi had not been out of the tent all day. He laid on his cot alongside the rifle, finger caressing the trigger, reading his scriptures, not saying a word. Bj couldn't figure the dude out. It almost seemed like he was plotting some kind of Jewish jihad, or something. The tension between the two became palpable when the watchman discovered the transceiver battery pack apparently suffering a heat stroke. It was bubbling over in smoking, acrid liquid and making ominous popping sounds. The inexperienced operator didn't know exactly what to do, but concluded the power pack should be quickly taken off line before it exploded, or caught fire. He called to the reticent rabbi for help, who responded curtly that it was not his problem, because he wasn't on watch. *Jesus christ!! What's wrong with this clownhead?! Are we a team, here, or what??* Realizing he was on his own, the dayshifter proceeded to shut the system down, trying to remember the proper sequences and controls that had been overviewed by the techs during startup. The equipment inventory included spare battery packs, so replacement and restart should be the reverse of shutdown and removal. *You would think.* Nope, there were different codes involved to lock receptors back on to satellite transmission frequencies that the addled agent either couldn't recall, or never knew. He would have to contact the techs for remedial instructions on how to get the system rebooted and operational. A quick cell call found their phones off and it would probably be at least another two hours before they were back on site. Likewise there was no radio response from the Trader. Consequently, a significant data block would be lost, which could affect the chronological iteration process in determining the point position, depending on the weighted classification of the satellite propagation streams missed during the outage. In other words, another data drop.

The new NAVO engineer's TDY performance results were oh for three, due, in plenteous part and no large consolation, to events beyond his control. Why couldn't he execute with easy efficacy what, for all practical purposes, seemed to be the simplest work assignments in the world?? Christ, under normal conditions, *no one* on watch would beat his dismal record. It was embarrassing. He was better than this, but it might not matter if he got poor probationary evaluations from the field supers, especially redeye. *What the hell difference did that make? Are you seriously going to continue working in an organization that's running drugs??! Best thing is to play out the Special Bean assignment, so tophead and the CIA are happy, and get the hell out of government service. But what then?? Who the hell knew?! Oh, sweet god jesus help me!!*

The sullied surveyor went outside to wait for tech support, leaving the gunner asleep in his rack. Maybe the lazy lummox would die-in-place in the over hundred heat of the tent. Or, he might have DIPped already. Who cared? It wasn't much better outside, but at least there was a slight breeze. Sitting by the coconuts and gazing seaward, the mind of the duty downer started drifting vicariously further into restricted areas it shouldn't be. Nothing was going right and he had serious problems on more fronts than he could juggle. Forget being happy, it was time to worry, meaning it was time to *bean* up to the safety of jumping ship and flying the hell outta here. Where was the *SB* asset? He had been on Caluya Island for a day, now, and no sign of contact. Not terribly unusual, but he needed a high speed escape avenue and fast. *Marry whoever Ina?? I'll be damned!*

Sounds of moving brush down in the hillside diverted the doleful daydreamer's attention away from the seascape. It was too early for the techs to be returning from below. He stared at the disturbance, biding the manifestation of its persona. After some preface of presence, a young island local burst into the site clearing and glanced obliquely around in all directions. Espying the American he trotted over to the coconut amassment and offered a burlap rice bag full of yet more coconuts. His name was Mayi and he was from Sabang, a small barangay on the mountainous south end of the island. With great and obvious excitement, Mayi asked if the big ship onlanders would come to his barrio in the evening to be honored as the first Americans to ever visit his home. The cloistered chipmole had an immediate thought flash that he might be facing the elusive asset. He must speak carefully, leaving a clear opening for the verifying coded exchange. "I would very much like to visit and hear what you will say."

"And your compatriots?"

Not what I'm looking for. "Well, they're not all here, right now, but I'll ask when they come back."

"I would be very happy. First, I must meet a friend, then I come back to guide you to our village."

Before leaving, Mayi unsheathed his machete and showed the honored stranger how to open a coconut, an activity the campsters had obviously not been pursuing. Gently hacking the wooden shell downward around the narrow end, while slowly rotating the fruit on the ground, he formed a long point, which he lopped off, exposing the interior. He then tipped the big nut so a cloudy liquid poured out and handed it to the impromptu student, indicating he should drink. Rossy took a sip and was amazed at how sweet and cool the juice was. As a matter of fact, it did not seem thermodynamically possible the cocomilk could be that cool, considering the husk had been baking in the sun and was Philippine hot. Was it some kind of super insulator? This was worth investigating. And learning how to crack coconuts should be worth a BSA merit badge. The erstwhile scoutsman practiced on several more units after Mayi departed and soon became quite adept at his newfound skill. A satisfying feeling of accomplishment displaced the disappointment in concluding the soon-to-be islander guide and host was not his *SB* contact.

***

Only two of the stationed newtimers followed the course down the hill path to the dirt road leading to Sabang. The rabbi had watch and the midnight tech didn't feel like walking anymore and remained on site to drink the new beer while it was still reasonably chilled. The trek behind Mayi turned rapidly difficult upon exiting the road onto a bush trail. They tracked a ridge that steeply rose and fell like a natural roller coaster. The footing was often wet, mossy rock, upon which any slipped step could result in a death drop over the clifflike escarpments on either side. Falling off to the west would send you to the sea and to the east, your body would bounce down into a lush valley below the interior, central mountains. The ridge route gradually descended toward the valley and it was a good forty-five minutes of tedious hike before the terrain started to level out. As they approached a partially open tract ahead, the host guide suggested his guests stay close behind him and not speak, look around or make eye contact with anyone. *What the hell does that mean??* It was soon evident they were passing through the perimeter of an organized agricultural operation, maybe ten acres in area, that was striking in its complexity and well managed appearance. Straight-rowed plantings grew in mounded, black soil plots, segregated by size. Irrigation piping was distributed between the planted rows and high, pole mounted fans rotated silently throughout the network of plots. Overhead, was a lattice of rainproof, ultraviolet light fixtures providing essential radiation to replace the sunlight blocked by the strategically remaining tree canopy. A large greenhouse on the far other side nurtured seedlings for sustaining regrowth of harvested produce, which was dried and processed in a nearby camouflaged outbuilding. Several workers stood up from their toil and stared harshly at the American strangers moving through the concealed and private district. They said nothing, as the outsiders were with a known friend and neighbor, but silently telegraphed their displeasure at the unadvised intrusion. The only audible sound was from a muffled generator, running at some unseen place in the distance.

Peeking peripherally, the furtive follower quickly realized the hidden valley spread was an illegal cannabis factory and the only thing keeping the tech and him alive was the accompaniment of their local guide. If they were here by themselves, they would be dead meat before getting half way across the exposed through trail section. Just before re-entering the bush, the wide-eyed nutcracker glanced over toward the greenhouse and saw three people, shielded in-part by the corner of the structure, standing in ardent discussion. Without hesitation and sensing an immediate wave of angst, he recognized redeye and groob, with an illicit looking Filipino farmer. Illicit, because he had an automatic weapon slung on his shoulder and farmer by the way he was dressed in cargo shorts, tee shirt and work boots, under a wide, straw *saklat*. Probably the owner, or manager, of this jungle market garden. And the Tradermates were most likely trying to work a daft deal. Yes, angst, from confirming groob was a player and now knowing he, Rossy, the embedded CIA operative, was the only straight civilian member of this NAVO survey crew. Odd, he should feel like the fugitive in this surreal scenario, when he, alone, has done nothing extraneously wrong in dutifully following his orders.

Shortly past the doob farm, the trio broke into another clearing that was far less ominous than the last. A number of family *nipa* huts, featuring raised bamboo floors, awning sides and palm frond roofs, circled a common open space on the brow of a shallow knoll. In the middle of the central yard was a huge pit, where several whole chickens were slowly roasting on spit sticks over wood fire coals below. Children ran noisily around the fire pit chasing a football, aggressively pushing and shoving one another away to get in a kick. Behind the houses, some distance from the village social circle, a group of men was crowded around another pit, also with chickens, but these birds were very much alive and trying to rip each other from gullet to gut. The men were aggressively pushing and shoving one another away to get in a frontal glimpse of how their *tupada* wagers were doing. A company of women sat near a gas stove, laughing their gabbing gossip, while cooking a massive pot of rice for the *liang* dish they were preparing. A typical domestic evening scene, on a remote rural island in the dreamy land of enchantment. Mayi led his prized entrants to a small, unbacked bench, partly removed from the activity, and told them to rest. He then disappeared, leaving them alone to ponder their surroundings. The seat only held about one-and-a-half adult sized people, so the two soon became somewhat uncomfortable. No one seemed to pay them any attention and after more than fifteen minutes of benign indifference, as they started to wonder *'what's happening?!'*, the spirited host guide reappeared and said they were almost ready to begin. He then darted away again into a nearby hut. *Begin what??*

The nervous visitors noticed the village people slowly congregating on the common, some bringing plastic chairs, some sitting on the grass, some standing, all eyes fixed directly ahead to the strange twosome in their midst. Mayi and another young man stepped out of the house, struggling with a folded vinyl card table,

12v battery, small phonograph machine and a tangle of wires. They set the ensemble up between the benched honorees and the gathered onlookers. The hard working host then addressed his peers in their native Tagalog dialect, introducing the bedraggled Americans as scientists from the big white ship, here to install satellite TV for the island. This evoked loud, enthusiastic applause, to which the noncomprehending scientists responded with waves and smiles. The excited deejay yelled, **"It is the time to dance!!"**, and proceeded to energize the phonograph, placing an ancient, slightly warped forty-five platter on the turntable. After a few, cyclic crackles, a tinny squawk of King Elvis choked forth, belting the timeless, moronic lyrics of *Hound Dog* into the burgeoning festivities. Mayi turned to his surprised charges and called for them to get up and dance. *Whaat?? Dance?! I don't dance!! That's not gonna happen!* The unwilling hoofer didn't budge from the bench, but the tech immediately leapt up and commenced his rendition of the funky wildboy, flailing about in total dissonance to the scratchy backbeat of the record. He grabbed his civilian partner and pulled him up by the arm to join in. The villagers continued their approving applause, but did not, themselves, participate. They just watched and laughed at the loco guests of distinction. Rossy closed his eyes in embarrassment and tried to sway with the music, weakly snapping his fingers in time.

At the end of the interminable record, the host handed warm brews to the dancing duo and offered them chicken from a plate that had been placed on the table. Before they could enjoy much of the refreshment, the turntable was reactivated and *Hound Dog* again barked into the eve of the rising moon. And the Americans of honor were again emphatically wheedled into dancing to the pleasure of their adoring audience. So it went. They danced for their beer and chicken until the battery began to fade, along with the remaining daylight. Ex-bassman was certain he had never listened to one song so many times in succession. The experience was a unique first for both, on many levels, and the humiliated professional just wanted to get drunk and disappear. In contrast, the younger tech thoroughly enjoyed the ordeal, having ended his performance with an athletic execution of 'the worm' and a running high five through the screaming new fan base, who had never witnessed anything like what had transpired this hot, tropical evening, right in their own front yard. Mayi was an instant hero for bringing the unexpected and immensely entertaining show to his people and now, **"It is the time to eat!!"**

A hellish realization perforated the hazy thought process of the food and beer sated sailor. He had just finished choking down, at the willful urging of one of the mother cooks, a sample of the ancient Philippine delicacy known as *balut*. This was basically a rotten bird embryo boiled in the egg and it was a heaver, a deal breaker. After the *balut*, he didn't want to stay in the barrio another minute. No more ethnic food, no more stinky hot beer. They had fulfilled their obligation as honorary Americans and now, **"It is the time to go!!"** But jesus god! The partial moon was clouded over and it was ink black dark in the jungle bush! How could they make it back over the death ridge to camp under these conditions?? A failed scout is never prepared and the second classer, of course, had no flashlight, and neither did the navy tech. They would need help in walking out of here. Mayi told them to wait on the bench and he would make arrangements for guiding their return trip. A few minutes later, he presented a small girl, who couldn't have been more than ten years old and four feet tall, carrying a glass beer empty filled with kerosene. A cotton wick, stuffed into the bottle neck, burned dimly on the open end. This is it? This is our ticket home? The midnight rambler was crestfallen. There was no way this child could safely backtrack them through that horrendous trace, at night, with barely more than a match light. And what about the pot plantation? How could they pass through there unscathed? At this hour, it was probably laser booby-trapped and patrolled by meat-starved demon dogs. This was going to be a dead-end disaster.

Nighttime in the island wilderness was an altered world. Sound traveled differently. A small branch falling out of a distant tree could resemble a nearby footfall. Heavily shadowed vegetation shifting in the breeze might be easily discerned as purposeful movement. Virtually invisible light dispersions cast forth as threatening infrared eyes. Daytime wildlife was strangely silent, while the nocturnal denizens of the thick made unfamiliar noises. But perhaps the biggest contrast was how the night mind distorted input from the senses, inducing the imagination to possibly false conclusions. Rossy was terrified. Not just from the illusions he perceived, but because he flat out couldn't see where he was going! Here he was, out in the middle of Philippine nowhere, totally dependent on jamming right up the back of a molotov cocktail toting little girl for any hope of making it through this treacherous slog alive. On the menacing ridge, it felt like they were walking a tightrope, blindfolded, across the Grand Canyon. Even the legendary Wallenda stunt devils wouldn't try this at home.

At some unmeasured point, the darktrekkers followed their tiny lifeline out onto the sandy Sabang road. The girl's assignment was done and, with a silent wave to her American trail wards, she ducked back into the rough to go home. Gone was the little bit of light they had been relying on and the party pair stood alone in the pitch, with some distance remaining to camp. But at least the final leg was less than halfway and not particularly perilous. The footing was solid and If they veered off course into the copse, it likely wouldn't be fatal, unless there was a coincidental encounter with the deadly mamba. Such an unlucky happenstance for one, or the other, would probably make the 'two-step' his last dance.

It was close to midnight when the tested trailmongers stumbled out of cover into the station camp overlook. Their ecstatic relief in safely reaching the hard-hiked terminus fell to immediate dismay when they looked up into the barrel hole of the rifle pointed directly at their tapped out, scratch bitten faces. **"What the hell you doing, man?? Are you crazy? Get that thing away!!"** screamed the instantly infuriated junior engineer, pushing the offending weapon bore to the side.

"I'm doing my job...*man*....protecting this site against unauthorized personnel. That's more than your sorry ass self is doing, off drinking somewhere all night. How the hell do I know who's busting through here at this hour?? Shit, bitch, you're lucky I didn't blow you away. Maybe I should've. Count on it, if you touch my piece again."

Bj was thunderstruck. He couldn't believe rabbi was such a dick. A dick with a gun - not a winning combo. He had no idea why his alleged colleague was so hostile, but the dirty rabbi dude was evidently looking for a reason to shoot. *Go ahead, bitch, make my day!* Best thing to do is stay low. And so he did, by going into the tent and crashing onto his floor cot. While too enervated to be scared, he was able to definitively conclude this as his worst camping experience ever, before slipping into a deep, pass-out sleep.

***

The next day dawned with continued incinerator level heat and the NAVO nighthawk purported to find a fresh water bath before his duty watch at noon. The techs said they didn't know but they were told of a spring head located near a spur off the port path a little over halfway down the hill from camp. Probably about a forty minute march. Sound off. Noon man packed a few things in an empty coconut sack and departed without eating. Hunger was not panging, as it felt like the specialties ingested last evening at the barrio bash were still in his stomach. That would save having to choose between bad and worse from the MRE fare.

With minimal recon, the weary water seeker located the spring pretty much as described. It was at the crutch of a small woodland canyon. A pool, formed under the spring fall by a stone dam bridging sloped, gravelly side embankments, was totally shaded by the forest canopy, like an oasis in the desert. To the sweat encrusted, hung over, camped out, secret sorry ass it looked like an exotic spa in the Garden of Eden. Except for the water buffalo ensconced in the deep end against the dam. The animal must have weighed a metric ton and had wrap around horns a half-foot thick. A large steel ring through its nose septum indicated it was domesticated, though no people were in sight anywhere. The wretchedly squalid g-man didn't care if he shared the little pond with a buffalo, he just had to get wet and cool, or lose control...whatever that meant. He was in unzoned terrain for being physically miserable. The monster bovine stared blankly as the pervasive hominoid, that it didn't recognize because they all looked alike, eased into the shallows at the spring outfall. The water felt like seductively soothing, liquid velvet, so wonderfully cold on his overheated skin he quickly stripped down for maximum exposure. Why not? There was no one around. After rinsing the duds and tossing them to the bank he leaned back and let the therapeutic flow cascade down over his head and face. With eyes closed, the only conscious thought was how much better it felt in the pool than not. The meditated chillster never wanted to leave. This could be his permanent venue of existence for the rest of his natural life. And then he heard the unmistakeable sound of sandal steps on loose pebbles. Snapping to, he saw a middle-aged woman gathering his garb and makeshift tote into a basket. **"Hoi! What are you doing? Those are my mine! Please, NO!!"** squawked the barebacked bather, promptly panicking in realizing he was about to be stranded in the woods with no clothes.

"Do not worry, American satellite TV man. I will wash for you and bring back clean in one hour. No problem, OK?"

Rossy watched as the woman disappeared downstream, taking everything he owned out here in boonatoria. Now there was no choice. He had to stay in the spring pond. It was his only veil, but he no longer had any desire to remain there forever. Strange, how shifting circumstances can reverse your priorities in a Manila minute. He glanced at the buffalo, which was still gaping passively at him, and reclined in the water to begin waiting for what would surely be a very long hour. There was no consideration of contingency, should the wash lady not return with his stuff, since there simply was no Plan B available, other than to bite the bullet and run butt-naked back to camp. Such an escapade could well result in arrest for the Philippine equivalent of indecent exposure. The sometime agent, under procedural standing orders from his handler to stay inconspicuous, had to chuckle at the irony.

The buffed waterman had no way of knowing how much time had elapsed, thinking it much more than an hour, when he finally saw the wash woman making her way slowly up along the stream bed to the pond. In addition to the laundry, she carried several large buckets and a coil of heavy rope. But what mostly caught the sideliner's notice was that she was wearing his aviator sunglasses. He had left them in his pants pocket, because the spring head area was so well shaded, and now they were apparently serving the eyes of a new owner. She moved methodically along the bank to the high end of the pool and carefully laid the folded clothes packet down on the ground, maintaining a constant hawk at the submerged foreigner. When she reluctantly started to remove the glasses to place them with the returned items, he waved her off, saying to keep them for the wash service. This brought a huge brown-toothed smile of gratitude and "Ina will marry a good man!", as the woman turned to tend to her other chores.

What?? She knows about the 'Ina' thing? Holy frack!! The whole goddam island must be in on it, like some kind of mass conspiracy against me!! "No, no, no! Ina will *not* marry a good man! She's not marrying anybody and neither am I!!"

The spa lounger, now waterlogged and ready to get out and put his clothes back on, had to remain in shielded place while the hard working islander filled the buckets with water and sidled across the dam to the massive buffalo head. She gently threaded the rope through the nose ring and retreated to the rim, where began the task of tugging the behemoth out of the drink. This was no easy endeavor, as the beast of burden did not want to leave the comfort of the spring cool to haul water in the sun. There was a lot of thrashing and splashing resistance, but the goaded animal eventually relented and the buckets were loaded. The visitor, highly relieved he wouldn't have to play Tarzan in the raw, waited until the buffalo and its mistress were out of sight downstream before rising from the sanctuary of the pool to redress. He felt vastly refreshed in setting forth on the backrun to satellite camp, but worried anew about Ina. There was no clear tilt on how real the phantom 'Ina' threat was, or what it actually meant. It reminded him of the boarding house daughter. *Why do I have all these problems with fourteen year old girls?!? I don't give a damn about fourteen year old girls!*

***

By the time the afternoon duty man arrived back on point, he was all sweated out again, as if the spring skinny dip never happened. At least there was no seawater salt film on his skin, a condition he had learned through the scientific method to be intolerable in this climate. Approaching the front tent flap, the returning authorized person yanked short in sighting a dog curled up on the entrance pad. The medium-sized canine appeared to be asleep, but leapt to life with the next forward footfall of the surprised oncomer. This was not a pet dog. It was a dangerous looking growler and it wasn't about to yield an inch to what it obviously considered an invader of its newly claimed territory. There was no way to ease past the animal to enter the tent without being mauled and evidently no one was inside. Where the hell was everybody? If dirty rabbi is in there with his precious piece, why doesn't he come out here and blow this bitch away? A frustrated shout to anyone found no response. The mongrel crouched down, eyes on the prize, continuing with a guttural, pre-attack rumbling noise. Rossy wanted no part of the snarling stray. He had no idea where the others were and was not about to risk his well being trying to pound through such a portentous obstacle to go on work duty. *God, I hate dogs!! They're totally useless and nothing but trouble! And now I have another busted watch! Dammit!*

The obstructed inzoner would need help in clearing the tent access. He remembered passing, on the way back from the spring, a small field where a worker was building a hut. It was only a few minutes from the station camp. The free range dog watched its antagonizer retreat down the incline, content that the challenge to its assumed post had been rebuffed. The hut raiser was busy cutting bamboo floor dowels with a machete when the harried sailor ambled in from the hill path. He halted his activity and waited for the young American's advance. After exchange of greetings, the boy explained his impasse with the uninvited wolfer and asked for assistance. Grabbing a long dowel and the machete, the worker accompanied his not too distant neighbor back to the hilltop tent. Sure enough, the cur was still flayed out in front of the entrance flap and, as predicted, rose up growling with the advent of the returning encroachers. The offsite mercenary moved in quickly toward the offending impostor, yelling for it to get out, but the infuriated fourlegger stood its ground, spewing loud, throaty snarls through viciously bared, slightly foaming teeth. It was ready for war. The equally engaged enforcer raised the long pole and sharply jabbed the maniac mutt in its face and side. The animal countered with bites and claws on the end of the prod, but didn't move from its spot. Stickman wasted no time in escalating the initial spur into a savage beat down, through which the wild pest endured at least a full minute of horrendous, bloody thrashing before limping off in a wail of angry agony. A small pile of wormy turds was all that remained where the vanquished furry infiltrator had blocked egress to the tent.

The insentient sitekeeper was wholly thankful the offending little monster was removed from the station and wanted to show his gratitude to the helpful stranger for the timely assistance. All he had to offer was hot beer, of which the mere thought spawned upper gut churns. The native fiend fighter instead chose a coconut from the pile, deftly hacking it open in seconds to release the refreshing liquid within. The de facto host asked if his benefactor was a professional builder, learning that, no, he is actually a government rep from the Philippine Ports Authority, in the region to inspect and evaluate damage at remote marine facilities related to the recent typhoon. PPA man said, while here, he was helping his elderly aunt reconstruct her flimsy old place that had been flattened in the peripheral winds of the storm. He revealed he used to work for the U.S. Navy in Guam, but took a job last year with the Philippine government to be closer to home. He wasn't sure he made the right change, financially. "Sometimes I second guess my move and think....what's in it for me?" mused the rep, looking directly at his breaktime companion.

"Yeah, I know what you mean. I flipped jobs not long ago myself and I'm wondering, too, whether or not it was the best thing. Funny, you quit the navy and I start with them. Guess it all evens out."

"No, but really.....*what's in it for me?*"

"I don't know, man. You'll just have to figure it out."

"Agent Rossy, are you tuned in to what I'm saying to you? Now, one more time, *what's in it for me?*"

Oh my god. I missed the fracking asset cue again!! "Uh, yeah, sorry....I don't know. You tell me."

"Alright now, good to meet you. I've been waiting for a chance to catch you alone, but you've been mostly closed in. Maybe the doofy dog had a purpose."

"I hear you. OK, so what is the Philippines brief on our mark? I need to know info on his ID, his in-country activities and his destination, including travel itinerary."

"Wow, that's a lot. I don't know if I have enough to fill all that in."

"Well, I need at least enough to get my orders out of here. Give me what you got."

"OK, the dude of interest spent most of his time on the UM campus in Quezon City. That's where the main facilities are for the engineering school. He met with students on campus and recent graduates at the Ocean Park in Manila. He had no trouble finding people to talk to, because the engineering community in the Philippines is highly dissatisfied."

"What's the problem?"

"The PI is a strange place. In a lot of ways it is ungovernable from a central, unifying institution and relies on local, autonomous systems of abject anarchy to hold it together as a nation. As I assume you might know, several other countries have tried their hand at PI management and all have failed. They bailed through aid agreements with either their successors, or directly with the titular officer in charge. So there's always been considerable outside money coming in, resulting in corrupt distributions to block bosses, who dole out tidbits of insignificant benefits to the people, in return for delivery of votes. The divisions of competing factions are geographic, political and religious, but there's not much danger of civil war, because the Philippine people, collectively, aren't very aggressive. Maybe they've been Americanized in that you would be hard pressed to find any two Filipinos agreeing on much of anything, so they do nothing. In due course, the issues are forgotten and the problems evaporate. Anyway, in recent years we've suffered some unusually devastating typhoons, many say related to worldwide patterns of climate change. Huge amounts of emergency monetary aid have come in from the world community, and little has gone to assist the stricken areas. Engineering associations have been screaming that rebuilding of critical infrastructure destruction is going unfunded, while the government uses aid money to line the pockets of its corrupt puppeteers. The dead response to typhoon Josuer might create a last straw situation that could lead to radicalization. I'm seeing many vital rural ports in almost unusable condition due to lack of funding. Where does the money go? Who is benefitting? Why isn't the necessary work being done? I think that might be what your special friend is telling engineers to ask themselves. The answers could lead to the dangerous reactions you suspect him of promoting."

"Do you know anyone who has had direct contact with the subject?"

"No. His methods of communication are impeccably quiet. No way to get an inside bead on him. There was some indication his persuasive discussions could have transpired while playing billiards at the university student center or a park arcade in the city, where he would be almost unnoticeable, because, apparently, he looks very similar to the people he associates with. That's the feedback I received from my eyes, and I assume that means he has at least passable, or partial, Filipino, or Polynesian features.

"Any photos, even from a distance?"

"No, but one source heard he speaks with a photogenic smile, one that instills confidence and trust in his confidantes. He's generated an invisible aura of loyalty that can't be penetrated to obtain any definitive information relating to his activities or contacts. It's unbelievable how specifically vague this guy operates."

"Anything on where he's going, or when?"

"We heard he's gone from TPI, maybe two days ago, and that he's very probably headed for America. Don't know where, but most likely through Hawaii."

"That's all?

"That's it. All I can tell you."

Jesus, where does this get me? No doubt Hawaii's just a stop in a through flight. Where would the bean go from there? I've got nothing to report, but an open-ended lead!! How's Dick gonna get me off with this?? "OK, thanks. Not much, but I guess it is what it is. Oh, one other thing......" The chipmole went on to explain his dilemma with the 'Ina' affair, wondering if there was a real situation there, or if it was something he could just ignore and it would go away?

"Well, yes and no," advised the contact rep. "The cultural council the beach lady spoke about has no political or legal power, but it can influence those who do have such authority. Of course, no one can force you to marry the girl, but a small gift payment, maybe a couple hundred American, could show respect for the cultural mores and smooth the whole thing out. If you want, give me the token and I'll take care of it for you."

"What happens if I don't pay?"

"Hmm..., unless you went through with the wedding, they could make it very difficult for you to depart the country."

"I never heard of anything like this. It's crazy talk! What the hell?!"

"Local traditions go back a long way and are very consequential, even if they don't always make sense in the modern world."

"OK, I guess there's no choice. There's no way I'm getting married and I sure as hell can't stay here. Hold on, I'll be right back." The agent ducked into the tent and retrieved his briefcase from under the cot. He opened the carrier, pulled two bens from the cash stash, closed up and returned the vital belonging to hiding, all in one quick motion. With a glance at the transceiver, wondering how many satellite passes were missed so far on his watch because of the goddam, frackheaded dog, the delinquent duty man slipped back outside to the waiting asset, who left immediately upon receiving the cultural correction money.

Before tending to tech duty, the solitary sitester cleaned up the entrance mat where the extermination transpired. He did not

feel very well. The more he thought about it, the more he concluded he had just been royally ripped by the asset, who was supposed
to be an ally, a brother darkman, but was actually as non-linear as
everyone else in this fruitloop country. Dejected, the worrying
watchman went back into the tent to track satellites.

Sometime later, during afternoon break, Rossy sat outside between data passes and followed the slow pace of the returning rabbi up from the hill path to camp. The testy tentmate was alone and
looked like some kind of war abandoned trencher, in his recently
donned camo fatigues with shoulder slung weapon. *How the hell
can he juke around the island with a rifle?? What is that? And I
get ballbusted for swimming in the ocean!?* The eccentric site boss
sat down on an equipment container and, without a word to his
colleague, popped a San Mig hottie. *The dude lets the tech blow
off watch, leaves the site unattended and he's got nothing to say??*
The junior engineer couldn't let it be. "Where the hell you been,
man? How come you walked off with nobody here?"

"It's all righteous, son. You partied last night, so now I can,
too. What's your problem? Besides, we got all the data we need to
set a point. We're done here."

"So nobody tells me? What is *your* problem, dude?"

"I got no problem," smiled rabbi, tapping his piece. "FYI, the
techs went downstairs to get help. We have to pour a marker,
breakdown and be on the pier for pick-up by 1800. Lot of shit to
do. Stay close."

The apparently off-watch shifter was upset about being mushroomed by his so-called station superior, but really happy with the
prospect of leaving the island and going back to the ship. He refo-
cussed his thoughts on how to submit the *special bean* update as
the next step in escaping TPI.

It was well into the evening before everyone was successfully
collected from the field. Despite the hour, the surveyors were
treated to a fine wardroom dinner of stir fried bami noodles,
sambal calamari and an unusual salad prepared from the leftover
dolphin fish on shoots of fresh canal cress. Pc redeye then called
his team into the lab for a rare staff meeting to announce the invitation and mandatory attendance of all NAVO personnel to a special event sponsored by officials of the Antique provincial government. The event was a cookout party, featuring a whole pig
BBQ and endless beer, for everyone on the Trader. It was a wel-

coming and thank you commencement gesture for the buoy restoration effort, considered a much needed assistance service supporting critical ferry operations in the central Philippines. TPI did not
have the resources to perform the required route surveys and could
not afford to lose any vessels to grounding in uncharted, storm-
shifted shoal patterns. The fest would take place tomorrow afternoon on Panagatan Reef, a tiny, isolated sandbar of an island in
the Caluya municipality. The shuttle skiff would leave at noon and
anyone not on board would be docked overtime and all differentials for one pay period. The meeting adjourned to the wardroom
lounge for bingo and a special showing of Clint Eastwood's legendary spaghetti western trilogy.

Agent Rossy skipped the movies and went to his state. There
was coverworld work to do. He had decided there was no way he
could access either a private or commercial internet device for up-
loading the *SB* brief and there was even less way he could use a
lab unit. The remaining burner he had left did not have an internet
chip, so the only option was his regular phone, which the handler
had said not to use unless it was absolutely necessary, or an emergency. OK, so this was necessary, but it was going to be a long,
tedious process, as he had no keyboard. Transmittal over the ship's
non-secure service wifi wouldn't be a problem, since the upload
would be scrambled, the same as if he used an unprotected commercial resource. Time to get to work.

It took more than an hour to punch out the report in text. He
debated whether, or not, to include a request for classcom to the
Trader pc explaining whatever change of orders was forthcoming,
feeling it was becoming increasingly risky to just disappear from
an assignment with no local coordination. There were at least two
pcs, so far in this TDY, who wanted his professional head and he
did not want to add to the list. But, then again, he for sure wasn't
going to stay in this job when he got back to the world and redeye
was probably already gunning for him as a daft evader. So, what
difference did it make if he bolted into the blue from the Trader?
Forget the classcom. He punched send and watched the scramble
sequence blow his little screen back home. Now all he had to do
was wait for the response call from super Dick.

***

Panagatan Reef was less than an isolated sandbar. It was a caricature of the proverbial deserted island. There were no inhabitants and the only structure was a wee shed, used by the caretaker as shelter during visiting work details and to store a few tools and provisions. The only vegetation was a stand of a dozen, or so, king palms growing through the dune grass on the central highpoint of the roughly circular cay. A narrow band of white sand beach encircled the spit, from which no other land was visible on the ocean horizon except the peaks of the Caluya island group, about ten klicks to the hazy east. It was hard not to feel more exiled than welcomed, in arriving on the Trader skiff, and the sailors wondered what the hell they were going to do all day on this god forgotten dot of sea-swallowed wasteland. The BBQ pits were already fired and cooking and a stack of iced coolers stood in the shade of the limited tree cover. The custodian and two assistants were working the pigs. As the shuttle departed for return to the ship, the honored Traders began to drink.

Enough beer had been stockpiled in the coolers for everyone to get puking drunk and this was well in progress, at some point in the early afternoon, when groob and a NMS machinist decided to take the caretaker's catamaran out for a spin. The antsy chipmole happened to be sitting nearby and they invited him to come along. Feeling a bit like a sequestered outcast, the secret loner accepted, thinking it might be fun to ride in the small sailcraft. What could go wrong? The three maneuvered the boat into the water, pushed out past the wavebreak and climbed up on the hulls. It was quickly obvious that none of the impromptu seafarers knew anything about sailing. A stiff prevailing breeze started sweeping them due west away from the beach at a fairly hefty clip and, when they decided they had gone far enough, the machinist yanked the rudder with no one on tack. The sail turned broadside into the wind and the boat immediately began to capsize. There wasn't enough expertise on board to stop the ill-fated flip and the crew of fools soon found themselves clinging to the undersides of the overturned hulls. There was no danger of sinking, but the submerged mast and sail was now a keel, making righting the vessel very difficult, especially if they were orientated perpendicular to the current, as they unfortunately were. It did not take a sailing genius to realize they were drifting out into the Sulu Sea and no one knew where they were.

Several issues begged consideration. They had not asked permission to use the boat, so it was essentially stolen. If they could not get the craft back, intact, to the rapidly disappearing party reef, they would be liable for damages, that could be thousands, or whatever the caretaker owner dude wanted to claim. Maybe tens of thousands. Of course, if they didn't get the boat back, they wouldn't be coming back themselves, in which case the damages claim wouldn't matter, at least not to them personally. They were dangling in shark infested waters that was well below body temperature, making hypothermia a real threat, if they weren't first devoured in place. The direct and reflected sunlight was blindingly brutal and yesterday's buffalo poolster sorely missed the sunglasses he would now gladly re-trade his clothes for. But then he would be without a long sleeved shirt and in continued violation of the master's SOS policy. It was unanimously decided the first priority was to get the boat right side up, because if they worked it into shallow water upside down, the mast would break. In order to turn the thing over, they had to align it parallel with the swirling, omnidirectional current. Not an impossible task, but close enough. They soon realized it was important to work in conjunction with each other to avoid fatigue. No one panicked, though it was a tedious, patience demanding process, and they were finally able to put the sail back in the air. Bad news was they were considerably further away from the now barely visible locus of focus.

There was no feasible way for these anti-sailors to ride the boat home. They had to kick swim it holding onto the hull tubes, like trainees for a triathlon. Against the wind, progress was slow, but steady, as long as each kept up his share of the propulsion. If anyone stopped kicking, they would lose bearing and meander off course, again, away from the still distant islet. Eventually, the synchronized swimmers had to take a collective break to rest their numbing legs. Groob reached into his pocket and pulled out a sealed plastic bag holding a Bic lighter and several joints of *Sagada Gold*. He lit one up and passed the bag to the machinist, who did likewise and passed it to the come alonger. This was no time to not be a Roman and the non-smoker, following the lead of his crew mates, fired a jay. After a sputtering start, he was able to inhale a little and soon feel the magic puff's rubberhead effect. They all did.

They're stonin' when they're driftin' out to sea....

They're stonin' while they wonder where they be....
They would not float so all alone....
Elvrybody love to git stoned....

The toke break served well to relax the troubled trio and they were able to resume swimming the clumsy craft toward the target without really remembering being in, quite literally, a tangible life or death quandary. If they were knocking on heaven's door, there was seemingly no one home, because the door didn't open and nobody noticed. They just kept kicking along without a care in the world. It was late afternoon when their feet finally felt the beach head rising out of the water. The lost, now found, joyriders scuffled the undamaged little dinghy up past the tidal reach and staggered through the dune to the picnic area on the other side of the trees. It was Miller time.

Many of the Trader goodtimers were either passed out or asleep in the vicinity of the coolers. The mostly unconsumed pig carcasses remained in the cooking pits, covered with flies, over the waning embers. The nodding caretaker sat in a broken plastic chair below the wet line, surf fishing with a medium sized spinning rig that had definitely seen better days. His helpers lay in the nearby dry sand, arms flopped over faces against the sun. It appeared everyone in the beach party was oblivious to the sea roamers' reemergence from a vanished fate, since, apparently, no one had ever been aware of their absence. There was no indication that anyone was looking for lost bodies, or was relieved to see the overdue colleagues. The three adventurers decided to leave it that way and agreed to keep the account of their near disaster to themselves. What happens off Panagatan stays off Panagatan.

***

It was not until all the reef revelers were safely reversed to shipboard that the special operative redirected attention to the business of his secret assignment. He had not heard anything from Dick following the *SB* upload brief. This was highly unusual, in that the esuper typically responded within minutes, or, at the most, hours, of a mission update. Reaching into a soggy wet pants pocket, and before confirming, a second later, what he instantly suspected and feared, he withdrew his saturated, still dripping, ruined phone. He had completely forgotten about the device, as well as the under ops it linked to, in the excitement of risking it all for a stupid, hijacked-boat ride. Dick had specifically instructed not to call home on anything other than the drowned cell and now his only connection with his only contact to authorized reality was irrevocably gone. There was no point in using the remaining burner, as the call would be deflected by the super's security settings without record of contact. The new phad was inert, because it wasn't activated, he hadn't purchased a local SIM card and the bp's SIM was incompatible. Hold on! Maybe Dick sent a classcom! The disconnected darkster made a beeline for the lab to check the message queue. Nothing. He was severed, alone in spyspace, like an EVA astronaut without tether.

Rossy knew it was time to leave the Trader and TPI, if he was to stay on *bean*, but he didn't know how. And he didn't have *OSB* orders. He would be freelancing. The first issue was figuring out a travel itinerary, which, in plotting it through, was not quite as complicated as it seemed. Simply break down the sequence, one step at a time, starting with getting off the ship. Tomorrow morning, they would begin provisioning and equipping the navaid site they had just finished setting the control mark on. That would put him in port on Caluya. From there, catch the ferry to Semirara, where he could take a domestic flight to Manila. Then on to Hawaii. Simple, as long as he had the resource briefcase. Without this most critical component, he would dry up like a raisin in the sun and go dead in the water with no way out. In that unthinkable case, he would probably end up marrying Ina and live ever after on Caluya as a perpetual alien offender, the swimmer of girls. Conversely, with the briefcase, he could easily go anywhere from anywhere. The table was set and the hungry-to-fly man was ready to eat.

There would have to be some kind of collaboration with pc redeye. At this strange point and under these loopy circumstances, it was not feasible to bolt, as previously schemed. That was before the phone link was blown and while forthcoming special orders were expected. It was a different game now and, from here on in, tophead's nearly solo chipmole would have to handle himself, call his own shots. Meaning, he would have to watch his own back. To do this, he should keep the daft field boss close and in sight. No surprises, no sudden moves. Same as dealing with an enemy, or a dangerous dog. He would confide he was covertly immersed in highly classified special ops involving national security and had to immediately relocate out of country.

***

"But why haven't I received advisement of a replacement? We've got a really difficult job, here, and I can't be shorthanded!" Redeye whined his protest from the early morning Trader foredeck while helping to load the skiff with navaids site supplies. The soon-to-depart subordinate said he didn't know, suggesting, perhaps unwisely, the pc contact NAVO. Not knowing how such inquiry could impact his precarious status, the opster wanted to come off as an advocate, not an adversary. He was playing both ends against the middle, but such was the modus of a CIA field agent. Dick had told him to learn to be resourceful, cut his own openings and be ready for anything.

"Oh, the hell with them! I've got more important things to worry about. Look, bj, I hate to lose you like this, but can you do me a favor?"

Careful. He's being way too nice. "Sure, what do you need?"

"Yeah, I've got an equipment unit that needs to go back to the office, but I don't want to send it from here. Pilipinas Postal will either steal it, or destroy it trying, and I'm on thin ice with SECNAV after losing that stuff in Palau. Also, we're not allowed to ship classified material. So, could you carry it out with you?"

Jesus shit!! He wants me to mule drugs back to D.C.!! No way!! I didn't sign on for anything like that! But, christ, if I don't, I might not leave here alive! Wincing with the horrible mental flash of daft rabbi raising the rifle to blow him away, the terrified anti-terrorist quickly concluded there was no choice. "Uh, OK, sure...I think I can do that."

"Super! It's not the largest container, so it shouldn't be too much trouble for you. I really appreciate it." The two went down to the lab to retrieve the item for loading on the skiff to shore. It was a distinctive, bright-orange, fiberglass hardbox, clearly labeled 'USN CLASSIFIED' and secured against unauthorized tampering, or attempted opening. Fortunately, redeye didn't give his delivery boy the access keypad code and the reluctant courier didn't want it. He had no desire to open the container, wishing to believe, however unlikely, the box held only an innocent, very expensive piece of classified surveying equipment. In his gut, he was ninety-nine positive it was crammed with *Sagada Gold*. Whatever, this was going to be a fifty pound albatross for the rest of his TDY, at least to Hawaii, where he planned to UPS it the rest of the way. So what if that would, technically, be a violation of protocol? He wasn't going to run illegal product half way around the world for nobody, even if they fired him. Besides, he was quitting and nothing really mattered anymore.

***

The local ferry ran twice daily between Panay and Mindoro, stopping at all ported points in the straits. The morning carry to Semirara was long gone by the time the bulky box bearer made his way to the ferry pier. He bought an order of chicken inasal over garlic rice, available from a close-by warung serving the port traffic. It would be a long tarry before afternoon transport and the ex-Trader began the wait at the head of the pier, along with a number of other outbounders, on a hard bench edging a canopied wooden deck. Mostly everyone had some sort of carry-on belongings, but nothing as conspicuous as the prominently orange container all eyes seemed absently fixated on. *God, they would freak if they could x-ray see what was no doubt inside,* worried the tender, wondering if he was the only departing ferry fare possibly carting such contraband. All of a sudden a monstrous Malaysian flat roach climbed up through a rotted deck opening and lumbered around in front of the gathered commuters. Sightlines shifted to the nearly decimeter long jurassic insect, but no one moved to eradicate it. Finally, the American, not able to any longer stand watching the repulsive arthropod strutting aimlessly about in such close proximity, rose up, walked over and savagely stomped on it. With an audible crunch, bile looking liquid spurted out from under the Reebok. He lifted his foot and the mighty roach continued to crawl! Another slamdown and still it moved. It took two more thwacks to finish the thing off, resulting in a mushy mess in the middle of the deck. Everyone stared blankly at the manic foreigner, wondering why he reacted so violently to a simple bug. It was a cultural thing.

The ferry finally arrived, though at least two hours behind the published schedule. It was slower than normal due to the washed out route buoys, requiring extra cautious passage through the unmarked channels. The run to Semirara was about ten miles, at least an hour's ride. With his sun-baked skin tone and somewhat indigenous features, the solitary sailor blended in fairly well with his fellow passengers, like a brown pope in a brown pizza, except he was the only one with a big orange box full of dope. In this respect, he felt like he stood out like coal on snow and nervously avoided eye contact with any of the security types stationed at several points on deck. This was going to be a long, hard schlep, even without the box, and with it would be that much more difficult. He decided to mail the damn thing asap. After all, he only told redeye he would carry it 'out'. It was never discussed where 'out' was. As far as he was concerned, it meant out of Caluya. He couldn't be covertly effective lugging this thing around, so, yes, he would ship it, probably from the airport in Manila. If a signature was required, he would sign Bergle's name. He sure as hell wasn't about to put his own ID on this ticket to Leavenworth.

At the small airport on the largest island in the Caluya municipality, the disconnected agent booked a flight to Manilla, as well as to Honolulu. Finding his credit card had expired, he had to pay cash, putting a sizeable dent in the advance reserves, but that much less to worry about getting stolen. ETA Hawaii was about three days. Ground time between flights would be spent at airports, where the globe runner was becoming quite skilled at living in terminals. While awaiting transit he intended to activate the phad, using the burner, and make some calls. He wanted to try contacting Dick and, also, he had been thinking about Narpcomming grandpap. Not only to check in like he promised, but he wanted to see if the old guy could get up with his narpnet correspondence buddy, Bobby Waintrow, and see if the retired general knew anything about tophead. After all, if he was AFS commander while the CIA was working with his people, he should have something on the big bald dude. Rossy was feeling increasingly uneasy about his under role, but he didn't know exactly why. There was too much not adding up, too many ambiguities, too many inexplicable coincidences. And now there was no direction. He really didn't know what to do next. It was, in two words, *fracking frightening*.

***

The serious-faced departure uniform reiterated the requirement. The young American, even though he was in the Philippines on official business, must pay the cultural heritage enforcement and transit fee for an ethical violation in Caluya. The CHEAT fee, in the amount of five hundred $US, was due, in cash, as requisite to out-processing through NAIA. There was no choice. The man held his passport and wouldn't give it back without receipt of this bogus scam charge, just like the crooked asset warned. This country was incredible! If not for anything constructive, other than its musical cover bands, then for the effective organization of its corruption. The violator slowly withdrew another five bens from his attaché, calculating he was starting to go low on funds. If he ever got *OSB* orders, he should probably locate a military travel and disbursement office somewhere for another advance. Maybe in Hawaii. The worried, unhappy airfarer found his way to the boarding gate. Paalam, Republika Ng Pilipinas,*The Land of Enchanted Schemes*!

HAWAII

At least an hour prior to the attendant's general instruction to 'fasten seatbelts and prepare for descent into Honolulu International Airport', passenger W. A. Rossy, in seat 48A, had seriously considered going to the rear of the underclass cabin of the Boeing 777 and kicking out an emergency door. At ten thousand meters, such an act might have brought the aircraft down. If not, it would have caused severe turmoil and stress, maybe a few deaths, or some serious injuries. But at least it would have created a diversion and escape from the torture of being trapped in the port-side, row 48 seat group. The flight was sold out, every seat occupied. The window man's pot-luck companions were a heavily pregnant woman and her four-year-old daughter. The very sick mother had been steadily gagging, snargling, spitting, coughing and hurling into a bag, and the child alternately sobbing and screaming, for the entire flight, now in its sixth hour. The normally forbearing g-traveler thought he had never been so thoroughly uncomfortable, for so long, in his whole, relatively short life. The only thing that kept him straight was knowing he was not the most miserable person on board. That would be the poor, disconsolate woman next to him. Human nature allowed tolerance of almost anything, as long as there was someone worse off. *If I'm not the last one, the most unfortunate, I'm good.* And so he maintained, held on and outlasted the situation he was ensnared in, like a chicken stuffed in a perimeter cage on a flatbed truck, until the plane thumped down and came to a complete stop at the terminal arrival gate. When it was his turn, he literally ran through the accordion egress tunnel to freedom. He was back in the USA!

The customs officer rapidly stamped the returning homeland citizen in with no detainment nor special inspection of the accompanying items. His only comment, upon seeing the government service passport, was a curt 'welcome home, sir'. A nice gesture, reflected the arriver, feeling a little more official, but not really considering Hawaii home. He had never been to Hawaii and, of course, always knew it as a state, but sort of subconsciously imagined it more Asian than whatever part of America he was familiar with. It occurred to the homecomer that he had traveled nearly the whole way around the world and had no souvenirs to show for it. And he shouldn't, because collecting mementos was not what TS classified special field operatives do. But then again, maybe he wasn't as much of an agent as he thought. There had been no response from Dick on the activated phad.

Rossy decided to go in town, find a hotel room and chill for a few days. He needed to rest and recuperate and try to figure out exactly what his status was. What better place to regenerate than Honolulu? Especially following the hideous flight from TPI. After cashing out all his foreign currency, the weary journeyman ventured outside to flag a cab, which conjured a strong sense of dread in remembering the last taxi experience, when he easily could have gone missing. But this was America, where cabs were regulated and operated in a safe, orderly manner. The Olympus-Kalihi Hotel, off I-H1 about five miles from the airport, was located in a not great part of town, nowhere near the beach, but was listed on the internet as a four star value. The unreserved chiller arrived well before the earliest check-in time and had to wait in the lobby for a few hours before getting into a room. There was a small problem with the expired credit card that was trumped by the official passport and a cash deposit. Following a shower and short nap, he sat down to e-mail grandpap. He extended the phad screen, went to Narpcom, entered name and ID and proceeded to give the old guy a mundane account of how he was having a good time in his new job, traveling to a lot of neat places he had never seen and generally really enjoying what was turning out to be an excellent career decision. It read sort of like a September school narrative of how he spent an awesome summer vacation. Then he waxed serious and related how he was also working another duty as assigned for a guy at Andrews, who was involved with a classified ASC project. Randolph Patton Clement. Could grandpap please contact Bobby Waintrow and see if the former ASC commander had any book on Clement, aka tophead? *Thanks, grandpap! Love ya and see ya soon.* Grandboy Billy felt good about contacting the old man. Not just in fulfilling what he had promised to do, but because he had genuine confidence the correspondence was secure.

The next morning brought renowned Hawaiian sunshine, after an early cloud burst, and a well rested Pacific airbounder. He was famished from not eating through the last barf blasted day and went outside to seek a suitable drifter's dive. Within a block of the hotel he had to sidestep a large puddle of red liquid oozing over the curb and down the gutter. It looked like coagulated blood thinned by the rain, an image the overstayer had an immediate problem with, because it implied someone might have been murdered last night, way too close to his room. He rather hoped it was a harmless accident, like maybe a cherry Kool-Aid spill. Further down the street was a place that looked benignly interesting. *Renny's Reefer.* There were no vehicles in the small lot, but a green 'OPEN' light flashed in the window. The hungry drifter coined an Honobserver from the dispenser by the door and entered into a wide, shallow room, featuring wall-to-wall bar at the back and a few tables scattered around the floor in front. A trophy sized swordfish, arched in it's final pose of defiance, was mounted over the mirror behind the bar. The joint was about as clean as a reefer dive should be and the likely first patron of the day took a stool seat at bar central. Presumably Renny pored over a charter fishing trade magazine at the end near the kitchen port. Hawaiian uke music intoned from some concealed source, otherwise, a peaceful, easy ambience. The tall, thin, bespectacled, short-haired, stubble-bearded haole proprietor moved toward his earlybird customer without much noticeable enthusiasm. He looked like a university professor who had lost tenure and opened a beer hole for the non-tourist locals. The non-local tourist ordered a Honoburger and draft Kona and Renny disappeared into the kitchen after pouring the beer.

A short while later, as one worked on the sandwich and read the paper, the other returned to post at the end of the bar with his magazine. There was no conversation between the two. The quiet was soon shattered by the front door bursting open to the entrance of three menacing looking kanaka dudes, who strode directly to the bar and straddled the sole occupant in the middle. Two sat on one side, one on the other. Renny looked up slowly and carefully spoke in a loud, slightly wavering voice, "I'm sorry, gentlemen, but I can't serve you in those jackets." The gentlemen were clad in well-worn, black leather biker jackets, emblazoned with the distinctive colors, symbols and lettering of HAHI, ***Hell's Angels***

Hawaii, Inc. This was a feared, outlaw maoli organization, included on Homeland Security's terrorist watchlist, that was prohibited service by any public establishment licensed under city zoning regulations. The HAHIsters stood up and away from the bar, clustered closely behind the lone, legal customer, and glowered at the owner. Silence, except for the ridiculous uke picking, dragged on second by agonizing second, as the terrorist Angels telepathically calculated their response. The boxed bysitter froze up like a coiled grub worm, head down, eyes tightly closed, and tried to be inconspicuous amidst the stare down. All at once, the gangsters wheeled sharply and clomped swiftly out, leaving the door widely ajar behind them.

Professor Renny shuffled over to close the door and returned behind the bar to pour himself a drink. With shaking hands, he lifted the four ounce glassful of bourbon and drained it faster than a junkie's needle plunge. "Don't know if I should've done that, but the law's the law," he choked. The still paralyzed guest said nothing. "God, sometimes I don't think any of this is worth it. I mean, really, what the hell's in it for me?"

Hello!! The agent couldn't believe his ears! *Is this guy an asset trying to code me? How could that be? No one knows I'm here. I don't have orders. I'm freejacking.* "Uh, I don't know, man, I'm new here, a nobody just passing through."

"No you're not, Mr. Rossy, you're a special ops agent for the CIA. And you're not just passing through. You are hunting. Like all agents, you're hunting a target."

Whhaaat? Holy god!! What's going on here? The dumbfounded operative didn't know how to react, or even what to say! How the hell could this guy know him? He hadn't coordinated his travel itinerary with anyone. "Well, OK, so what do you have for me?"

"You're being called in. You're supposed to return directly to Washington, asap."

"Huh?? Well, what about *special bean*? Is he in Honolulu? Do you have anything on his movements, or activities? I have to file an update to get my travel authorization."

"Don't know anything about that. I had one message to get to you and I have, so we're done here. I suggest you mobilize. Beerger's on the house. Have a good one." Renny abruptly went back to bar's end and vamoosed into the kitchen, leaving the stunned agent by himself. He was not only alone in some deserted bar, but felt alone in the world, in his own reductive shell, everywhere. As he walked back to the hotel, one eight hundred pound gorilla thought dominated his mindscape. *How the hell could they possibly set up with an asset to contact me at Renny's Reefer, if I had no idea where I was going when I left the hotel a few minutes before???* There was no rational explanation, but if there was it would answer all questions pertaining to this uncanny, scary run of events. Sort of like if we knew where the space of the universe came from, we would have all answers to the great unknowns of the cosmos.

***

Despite the asset's apparently valid message of order to go home immediately, the addled agent had to clear his head. He decided to go to the beach and relax a few hours, while formulating a plan of action. After all, how could he 'pass through' Hawaii and not go to the beach? The bus ride to Sand Island Park took about twenty minutes through heavy traffic. The public area was not as crowded as expected and the visiting sand seeker easily located a relatively secluded spot to sit and ponder. Though the visuals of the ocean scene were pleasantly mesmerizing, the constant noise of commerce emanating from the proximate airport and shipping districts was a bit distracting, and the unsettled fed soon got up and started walking along the shoreline through the breaker wash. Spotting some young girls out in the waves, he abandoned all notion of going deeper into the surf. He did not want any trouble, not today. Further down the way was a group of adult people, standing in about waist high water, appearing to be methodically dunking each other. *What the hell?* He stood and watched a few moments, noticing they were moving closer. Seemingly in a moment's blink, he was surrounded and a man sloshed forward and looked him dead in the eye. "I see a sinnah. A puhson in **neeed** of the Lawd. Come, my son, let us give you the gift of **Reee**-born Life. Let us wash you **cleeen** for *Jay-zuz*!" The circle tightened and the sinnah felt an onslaught of panic. He turned and broke through their perimeter, stepping quickly away to the high, dry dunes. Fortunately, the washers didn't pursue. Rossy had enough of the beach. It was the time to go. Without really thinking it through, he figured to check out of the hotel, taxi to the nearby Pearl Harbor-Hickam military base and see if he could find a travel and disbursing office to get a flight ticket to D.C. and a cash advance on per diem.

***

"I'm sorry, sir, but I can't authorize any advance for direct travel to your poo. It's regulation." The personnel support officer at the PHH Moanalua Service Center gathered the travel documents, passport and flight pass items together into a packet and handed it through the window tray to the rather disheveled appearing civilian client before him. The homebounder was a little stressed he would have to spend another night in an airport, but there wasn't much alternative. His credit card was out of service and he was low on cash, so he had to take whatever the military travel guy gave him. He would depart Honolulu at 1000 tomorrow and arrive D.C. at 0700 the following day. There was a one hour layover in Los Angeles, where he had to change planes for the redeye to Washington.

***

Settling into his seat, the terminal man was happy to be done with the extended wait at the airport, but not exactly looking forward to being in a plane again. Experience revealed the skies were not always all that friendly. Though he had managed to sleep some in the terminal, he was drained. Hopefully, this flight would be smooth, quiet and uneventful. He had checked his phone. Still no word from Dick. Not much point in trying to figure out what the communication blackout meant, because there was insufficient information to even speculate a question. At best, it meant nothing and he was on course, doing the right thing, executing operational security. At worst, he had been cut loose and was being set up for failure, which didn't make any sense, since he had done nothing wrong and followed all *special bean* protocol, as instructed. Except maybe a few minor, unavoidable times of no consequence. But he couldn't have been expatriated, because they were tracking him. They knew where he was in Honolulu and when he was there, meaning he was still in play. So his status was somewhere between the best and worst and he would just have to wait to find out.

The narptext from grandpap wasn't as succinct as the no-call from Dick. General Waintrow did not know General R. P. Clement as invisible tophead. He knew him as an arrogant, dangerous program manager, who would crush anybody that got too close to his ultra-classified weapon system development project. The secret CIA highrider exercised total control over assigned ASC personnel and facilities to the exclusion of the commander, who only ever had a single one-on-one with Clement. Waintrow remembered the meeting ended in disagreement over security cost issues and the big man blowing cigar smoke in his face, while accusing him of being unAmerican. *UnAmerican?* A four star USAF general, unAmerican?? There was nothing the then highest ranking military officer at Andrews could do about it, because RPC's autonomous authority came from a higher directive. Bottom line, tophead Clement was possibly unstable, and not to be trusted. See, Billy Boy, I told you the government is a big scam. You best get out of there and come on home!

Wow!! The drifting darkrunner didn't know what to think. He felt like he was ensnared in a rubicon of confusion where the only way out was through the back door of ignorance. He no longer thought he was doing something special, above and beyond, to help his country. Actually, he really didn't know what he was doing, other than flying to LA. Reclining into the empty seat space behind, the only present tense thing to do was relax and enjoy the trip.

***

The flight from Hawaii arrived a few minutes behind ETA and snuggled up to Gate 35 of Terminal 3, at the unbelievably vast Los Angeles International Airport. The incoming agent had fifty-two minutes to transfer to his Washington D.C. connection. He figured this would be an easy maneuver, because the boarding pass indicated he only had to go to Gate 38, in the same terminal. Inside and glancing up at the schedule screen, a complication was evident. The departure had been relocated to Terminal 5, Gate 53B, same time. Electing to wait for the shuttle, it took nearly twenty minutes to get to the new gate, where another look at the jumbotron found, shockingly, his departure flight had been re-relocated to Terminal 1, Gate 12, still at the same time. He had less than half an hour to find the phantom plane. Rather than wait for the shuttle again, the anxious flyer opted to walk, finding no time savings in taking another twenty minutes to reach the revised boarding point. But, no! Astoundingly, the gate was changed yet again! Back to the original Terminal 3, Gate 38! *Is this some kind of telekinetic jape?* The frantic gateseeker realized he would have to run to make the scheduled time. He noticed he was not unique. Everyone seemed to be running. LAX was like a repressive qualifier for world class air travelers. Reaching the elusive gate with no time to spare, the breathless sailor was the last to board and the aircraft started reversing out to the taxiway almost immediately.

Sometime after the reassuringly smooth takeoff and rise to altitude, the nearly stranded connecting flighter had a chance to look around the cabin to see with whom he would be incapsulated for the next five hours. He checked to see if anyone might fit the limited description of the *beanster,* wondering what he would do if there actually was a dude that matched the ops target knowns? Follow him in Washington? Hell, no! He didn't know anything about visually tailing a mark. But the question was moot, because he found the boarded manifest to be typically ordinary in appearance. Except,.... wait a minute! Who was that sitting in the last row in the back?! The two in the aisle seats looked.....no way! It couldn't be! Bergle and Cohen?!? How the frack could they be here?? Discretely watching as redeye poured a drink and the rabbi read, probably, something akin to the Pentateuch scriptures, the former Traderman couldn't help but notice the large orange box strapped into the seat beside the pc and the rifle propped between the knees of the senior site engineer. How could he get on the plane with a firearm?? Oh, gees!! This was too much to figure. It was just getting weirder all the time! And the box? Did they intercept it from shipment in Manila and were smuggling the drugs directly back themselves? *Which means they'll kill me if they see me! Oh, god!! Dirty rabbi is looking right at me! I've been made!!* The defunct agent spun quickly in his seat and faced ahead, trying desperately to be inconspicuous. With hands over eyes in a daze of total fear, he sensed the approach of his rabid ex-colleague and then felt the repeated jab of the cold steel muzzle in his chest. **"No! No! No! Please, don't! Don't shoot me!! I'll play! I'll play! Don't shoot!!"**

The horrified victim of circumstances opened his eyes and saw not daft rabbi, but the concerned features of the Transportation Security Agent, who was urgently tapping the distraught final boarder to rouse him from an apparent nightmare. "Sir, wake up, wake up. You are disturbing the other passengers. Is everything OK? Are you alright?"

"Uh, yeah. OK, yeah, I'm fine. Sorry. I was thinking about something else. I'm good. No problem." The embarrassed ill dreamer took a water offered by the attendant and leaned heavily back in the seat. When the in-flight service people were convinced they did not have a terrorist situation, or a bad tripper, on their hands, they returned to their stations, leaving the baffled disrupter to his own demons. He was sweating and trembling, not really sure he was, in fact, good. Carefully twisting around, he looked to the rear of the cabin. Ignoring all the unsmiling, marginally irritated faces sneering towards him, he focussed on the most distant seat row, where a single man, of average build and dark hair and complexion under a gray hoodie, sat studying a minicomp screen. All other seats in the row were empty. Though vaguely familiar, it was nobody the abstracted g-ster recognized and he fronted forward to tolerate the remainder of the flight in shambolic solitude.

WASHINGTON D.C.

It was nice to be home, to be done with flying and the hassles of inconvenient schedules. Reagan National AP was a mess at this early morning hour, jammed with people hustling about everywhere. The returning rep did not have to hurry, because there was no place he needed to immediately be. As a matter of fact, he didn't exactly know where he should go from here. He had half expected to be met at arrival by esuper Dick, in that the special ops eyes obviously knew his position at all times, but so far, no one. After visiting a restroom to freshen up, he decided to find a MacDonald's for breakfast and then catch a cab out to the apartment. No way was he going to the Navy Yard, today, or maybe any other day. He needed to think.

As the apprehensive globerunner made his way down the wide terminal corridor toward the main concourse, he alerted to the sudden presence of two suits, one on each side, who were way into his space. They simultaneously flashed FBI agent IDs and one asked, no, commanded, "Mr. Rossy, please come with us."

"What's going on? What's this about? I didn't do anything wrong!" The agents each grabbed an elbow of their subject and wordlessly guided him to an unmarked wall door leading to an exterior, non-public delivery area behind the central building. They went down a short flight of concrete steps adjacent to a loading dock and approached a black SUV parked at the foot of the ramp. The clueless chipmole was placed in the back of the vehicle with one of the agents, while the other got up front to drive, and away they went. There was no conversation, as the FBI gophers were completely unresponsive. Rossy gave up asking questions and rationalized, for his own peace of mind, that he was being intercepted and taken to *OSB* debrief. This was all part of the security protocol for his classified CIA mission. It's what happened when you were called in from the deep. Like decompression before you could resurface. *But why was the FBI involved?* He looked absently out the tinted window as they passed through the muddle of the capital city's morning rush, not really paying attention to where they were going. The sight of holiday decorations reminded him it was almost Christmas, though the weather was unseasonably warm. He had to start planning the always distressing annual shopping ritual. Maybe this year he could turn Buddhist and skip the whole senseless spectacle.

Following more than a half-hour of congested, stop-and-go gridlock across Capital Hill, they approached a large, stark concrete structure, off Pennsylvania Avenue, in Northwest. The Hoover Building, FBI Headquarters. The driver agent whisked the SUV into a narrow service alley to the rear and, again, parked in the pit of a loading zone. The three got out, climbed the steps to the platform and entered a keypadded utility portal. Inside, they trundled down a basement-like passageway to an elevator and rose to Level 3. Exiting into a typically bureaucratic office building element, the agents hustled their assignment through a warren of muted hallways to a tiny square room, featuring a card table, two folding chairs and a black window. The hijacked homecomer, instantly recognizing an interrogation cubicle, was directed to enter and sit. The agents took his backpack and briefcase, returned to the hall and closed the door, locking it from the outside. One of the agents was already on the phone. "We have WAR at HQ."

"Good. Keep him isolated and secure. I'll be there in forty-five."

***

"Good morning, Mr. Rossy, how are you, today?"

What the frack?!? Impeccably dressed Mr. SPAM, from DIS?? What the hell's he doing here?! "I don't know. You tell me."

"Very clever, son, but I'm not your asset. I might be your liability, though, if you don't cooperate. Now, I understand you have been involved in a special mission, tracking information on an individual of great interest to our intelligence community?"

Goddam! Nobody ever told me about anybody else knowing anything about OSB. Dick and tophead said never talk about this with any unauthorized personnel! "I'm sorry, I can't discuss that. It's classified."

"Of course, it's classified, but I have a need to know what I'm asking you. So, again, have you been involved in an operation, known as 'special bean', to gain information on an individual possibly planning international cyberterrorist activities?"

No way! I'm not going to do it!! "I can't talk about it."

"OK, very well, Mr. Rossy. But let me explain something to you. We have your passport. We know where you've been. We also have sworn affidavits from CIA field assets affirming the active presence of an individual possibly inciting certain foreign nationals to intra-global subversive action. And guess what? The loci of activity of the individual in question matches your travel itinerary. Guess what, again? The description of the individual in question received from the field assets is a young male, average size, dark features, probably American - maybe native American - with ties to Pennsylvania, probably a tech-savvy engineer, likes to shoot pool, engaging personality with a nice smile, meaning, I suppose, good teeth. Sound familiar? Maybe the hunter is one and the same with the hunted. It would certainly make good mutual cover. *Now* is there anything you want to tell me?"

Jesus christ!!! Am I being set up?!? What the hell's going on here?!! The cornered chipmole had seen enough TV shows to know precisely what to say in a situation like this. "I want a lawyer!"

SPAM was willing to begin moving into enhanced interviewing techniques, but he was under clear and direct orders to play this strictly by the book. There was not yet enough hard evidence to seriously charge the young subversive, but he could be held almost indefinitely, under provisions of the Patriot Act, for investigation of reasonable suspicion of conspiracy to engage in terrorist activity. He also could be charged with misdemeanor possession of more than two ounces of a banned, controlled substance, for which bail process would take at least twenty-four hours. They found a pack of marijuana reefers in his briefcase. OK, he could lawyer up. Fine. But they sure as hell weren't going to release the traitor, terrorist bastard. For now, he would be detained in a downstairs holding cell, here at FBI. The special agent knew he had been right about his former clearance file. The original intel on his photo integration comparison analysis did not lie. This boy is bad news! Gotta hand it to CIA - they facilitated a big league hit, here! Out of the park!! "OK, Mr. Rossy, as you wish. Is there any rep in particular you want to call? Otherwise, we can get an appointment for you from the District's Public Defender Service."

The detainee didn't know any attorneys and he didn't have much cash, but he was so innocent of any wrongdoing he was sure even a pre-law student could get him out of here. "Public Defender is fine."

"Alright, so be it."

***

"Mr. Rossy, I can't help you if you won't tell me anything about your activities and reasons for being where you were. Quite frankly, it doesn't look good." The PDS paralegal was becoming frustrated. This had the preliminary characteristics of a high profile case, but the client wasn't talking. "And what's with the funny smokes? That certainly doesn't help the situation."

"I got them as a gift in Korea. I put them in my briefcase to get rid of later, but forgot. They can't hold me on that. It's just a fine."

"Maybe, depending on the exact amount in your possession, but they can use it to stay your release, without cause, and the longer they hold you, the harder it is to get you out. If you can just give me anything to work with, it would be a lot easier."

"Look, my orders are classified, and I can't discuss them specifically, but they are not inconsistent with my travel record. I was supposed to be where I was. Everything I did on TDY was official business. You must talk to my supervisor at NAVOSUR, Dick Whittberg. He can verify my schedule and activities. If some terrorist was operating where I was, so what? It didn't have anything to do with me. If a terrorist does something in D.C. while the President is here, does that make the President complicit? There're terrorists everywhere, for chrissakes." The young detainee was getting irritated. They had been holding him for over three hours and he never did get breakfast. Now it was almost lunchtime. He asked the paralegal if maybe he could get a Big Mac box meal.

The paralegal didn't know exactly how to proceed, because he didn't know what the FBI was going to do. The initial goal was getting the boy out of the cooler. This was complicated by the marijuana possession. They could use that to override a lot of other issues, at least temporarily. It bought them time to solidify a position. But, barring anything definitive under provisions of national security, they still had to charge him within seventy-two hours, or yield to a rights violation. The first thing would be to contact the supervisor. Then he should make sure his client got some lunch. This case could be very interesting, if not frustrating.

***

Esuper Dick was not in the office when the call came, so the paralegal asked to talk to the director. Blackburn was at the Pentagon and the call was transferred to dpsuper Lockbark. The paralegal briefed Larry on the situation with Rossy and advised it was imperative he meet with someone holding authority over his client's movements in the field. This had to happen really soon to clear the matter before whatever charges being contemplated by the FBI were filed, likely at some point in the next three days. After charges, it was a whole different ball game and the case would probably go viral in the media. The FBI, a perennial hammer in search of nails, loved to play up it's own catches, whether they were valid or not, and any publicity was good for image. Larry panicked. He really didn't know anything about the rookie engineer's classified TDY itinerary, because he didn't have the need. But christ god!! He also didn't need any kind of mass media scrutiny of NAVOSUR, which is what would happen if one of its engineers was indicted for terrorist espionage. No, that wouldn't work with ten kilos of daft product stored above the dpc ceiling, more on the way from the Philippines and over $500K cash in the old Beecher vault safe. There was no way he could clear all that in three days. He had to make code red emergency contact with his street man, his godson. Lockbark assured the legal rep he would have Whittberg get back to him asap.

***

The graduate said very little during the conversation with his old mentor and present day business partner. He remembered the locked up engineer as one of the goofy white dudes that stumbled down Mule Circle a while back, the same one he had later seen out along the parkway with a couple of Larry's crewmen. Yeah, he didn't mind helping out here. He could probably move the inventory, even though he was trying to phase out of drug operations. It just wasn't the biggest moneymaker anymore. Too much competition, falling revenues and now governments at all levels wanting a piece of the pie, as they preempted each other trying to legalize and tax all kinds of stuff that had always been lucratively outlawed forever. Times were changing. The orange man formulated a plan as he listened. He would meet the godfather at the Yard later today for a cash and goods exchange, but he couldn't pay as much as before on such short notice. Meantime, he would hack the FBI to see what they were up to regarding the NAVO engineer. Directly following this phone meeting, the dpsuper destroyed his burner and disposed of the remains in the Anacostia, not far from the Beecher. The graduate rose from the front stoop rocker and went back into the sophisticated computer center he had established in one of the small cottages bordering the cul-de-sac. Clinton dozed nearby in the dirt, oblivious to the strange events about to unfold.

***

Incarceration is not a condition normally contemplated until it is reality. To a claustrophobic, forced confinement in a small space is akin to suffocation, or drowning. Fortunately, the suspect engineer did not suffer phobic effects from being in jail, but he was having a critical problem trying to come up with an explanation for his predicament. Evidently, grandpap's pen pal general was correct in assessing tophead as dangerous and the last ODD chipmole sensed his invisible CIA boss was calling the shots in what was going down here. He was also certain the non-existent ops manager would not intervene on behalf of his specially recruited and assigned agent, now perp. That would require exposure and loss of cover and simply would never happen. But what about visible Dick? He had no reason to not support his engineer, unless tophead had total control over the esuper. What kind of manipulation would supersede doing the right thing? Rossy remembered being told by both tophead and Dick that if he compromised the *special bean* mission in any way, he would lose his job and could be prosecuted as a traitor and threat to national security. And once you got swallowed into the black hole of national security, you could easily disappear, indefinitely, without a trace. Obviously, there was no danger of such consequence, in his case, because there had been no mission compromise. Everybody knew this. Didn't they?? But still, why the hell was this happening?? There were no answers. All the locked up patriot could do was trust his legal advocate and wait. Alone in the cell. Just he and the video monitor cam. Alone.

The cyberpath into classified FBI priority ops was not difficult and well worn. The graduate had developed and utilized the code sequences many times before. He routinely checked the bureau's hidden agenda in planning his own ventures and business initiatives. But this time his foray into secret FBI world was coming up empty. There was no chatter pertaining to the arrest and procedural intent regarding the NAVO robin boy. This was potentially their highest profile case in quite a while and there was complete digital silence behind the lines? Not typical. They must be under some kind of gag. The innovative hackmaster decided to go higher. He would take it to the top and crack the director, requiring a little extra time, since new codework was necessary. When he finally got in, surprisingly, there was still no indication of anything pertaining to the engineer. However, there was some unfiled codetrack to a non-government hard drive, which the IT intruder did not hesitate to follow. What he found brought a smile to his face. *God bless America!* A large cache of doubly protected files linked with several illegal web sites and live feeds on a dark net sector. *Oh, my!* It looked like the esteemed FBI director was heavily involved in child pornography, both solicitation and distribution. This should be worth at least triple snake eyes in forcing their hand. The Mule Hill boss made a sourcing and content record of the encrypted gold, and backwormed out of the hack, leaving no trace of electronic infiltration. It was time to go meet the godfather.

***

The paralegal was ecstatic. While waiting for a return call from his client's supervisor, he was contacted by the DIS interviewer and advised to come back to FBI HQ right away. Upon arriving, he found the NAVO engineer out of detention and in process for unconditional release, with all pending charges expunged. There was no explanation for this unexpected action proffered by the FBI. This would be a clean resolution to what had been shaping up to be a protracted, highly publicized ordeal and would leave the young fedster clear, with no record of apprehension and arrest. No other agency had arresting authority or jurisdiction on this matter, so the case was closed. This was a major victory for the PDS. The legal rep had no idea what happened, but he had learned through his career to take all credit available for any victory, even if he was clueless how he won. The law was an unpredictable science. He took the similarly confused, but happy client across the street to a barristers' bar and bought him a celebratory micro-brewed specialty draft. In going through his belongings, the free agent found everything was intact, except the reefer pack was gone. He no longer felt classified.

***

It was late afternoon and nearing seasonal early twilight. After the paralegal departed, the liberated sailor enjoyed another designer strawberry lager with some happy time hors d'oeuvres and then asked the barkeep to call him a cab. It was time to go 'home' to Suitland. He was slightly uneasy about returning to AGA, as he had never really experienced anything memorably positive happen there. At least the whacked out security guard was gone, so there shouldn't be any harassment in getting to the apartment. But what about *in* the apartment? What would he find there? It could be anything. As it turned out, the place was empty. Seve was evidently gone back out on TDY and maybe Booker was, too, though he hadn't heard anything on that. Maybe Booker had already moved. What about Svelda? Was he going to be here alone with gameboy's bride? *Oh, god! Please don't let that happen!* But no! He found a note on the message board by the kitchen. Svelda was gone!! She wrote to Seve the marriage had been annulled and she was going back to Sweden. "Thanks for ruining my life, you pucko American äckel. Get ready to pay!! Do not call me, my advokat will call you, if you have not already been burned in helvetet!!" *Whoa! There's some major wrath going on here!* Rossy was glad he wasn't Smith, though he had his own problems that might be worse than the tilted gamester's. Like no car, no job, maybe no life, if tophead was still in pursuit.

The lone, soon to be former, fedman returned from triple G with a pizza and a six pack and stretched down on the front room sofa to go through his mail. Booker had piled it up in a box in the small bedroom, along with his checks and other paper records and the stolen Civic key. Among the deluge of junk, including a disconcerting number of NARP solicitations, he found a thin, white legal envelope with his typed name and address and no return. It was stamped and postmarked from Abbingdon, Virginia. He didn't know anyone there, or even where that was. Inside was a single letter sheet. As he read the typed, unsourced correspondence, his hand went numb and the Heineken bottle slipped through his fingers, spilling beer all over the carpeting around his feet. *Jesus god in the devil's den!! Was this for real?!?* He reread the missive, slowly, a word at a time, piecing it together, trying to form the unfathomable message he couldn't get a handle on. Was the note *actually* saying one million U.S. dollars had been deposited in the tax exempt IRA account he had previously set up for his biweekly, off-the-book CIA payments?! Was this money *really* paid to him as special ops bounty for information leading to the identification, apprehension and arrest of a highly sought subject suspected of conspiracy to commit international acts of terror threatening the homeland security of the United States of America? Was he *truly* being congratulated on behalf of the POTUS for exemplary civil service 'above and beyond' the normal oath of duty to 'protect and defend'? *Seriously?? SERIOUSLY??? Oh, WOW!!* There was no signature, no letterhead, no referenced names. An untraceable, unidentified communiqué telling him he was a net millionaire. This had to be a joke, some kind of prank. But, OK, hey! Let's check it out. The disbelieving defender reached for the phad and apped up his Credit Union account transactions. And there it was, just like the letter said. A one mil deposit, ten days ago. But that was before he was captured by the FBI, and, he was never arrested. He was released before arrest. So what the hell's going on?!? If the notification was from tophead, as access to the special account and pre-knowledge of the FBI score would indicate, the mighty darkman was either blindsided by the bureau, or ordered a reversal. Neither made any sense. This was all totally incomprehensible. He didn't know what to do, other than flip another beer, and another, and another....

***

Suitland's newest millionaire slept in. He was emotionally drained when he finally crashed sometime during the small hours. Awakening in somewhat of a midmorning brume, he remembered it was a weekday and he should probably go to the office. Though not feeling up to it, he assumed they knew he was in town and would be looking for him. But what was the point? He was going to resign anyway. Oh well, might as well do the right thing and try to keep as many bridges intact as possible. He was still reeling from the freakish events of the past twenty-four. There was no way he would be doing any straight thinking in the near future.

Admin Tom watched Rossy's approach to the Bowditch Building on the new entrance surveillance monitor, installed in response to the bogus bomb threat incident. He was waiting as the still newest NAVO engineer arrived at the top stair landing. After exchanging greetings, the administrative super directed the return-ee to sit at the hallway table for the uncleared and wait for Director Blackburn, who wanted to see him. It occurred to the weary wayfarer that he was being treated in a restrictively stiff manner and he started to feel a little uncomfortable. Maybe he should've just e-mailed his resignation and gone on down the road. *Slip out the back, Jack.* Right before lunch, Paul appeared from the stairwell and motioned for the salient subordinate to follow him into his office. "Please have a seat, Mr. Rossy," gestured the NAVO leader to the chair in front of the desk, as he settled into his executive swivel behind. "Ken, we have a problem....."

"No, I'm Bill, sir."

"Yes,....Bill....,we have a problem."

Bill looked at the solemn faced director and didn't know what to say. "Uh, OK. What's up?"

"Well, I've received substantial negative feedback from the field regarding your performance on TDY and, quite frankly, I don't know what to make of it."

"Like what?"

"OK. Robyn Ryder reported you grounded a work boat during PNAS training ops and shortly afterwards disappeared from the assignment. Mr. Richardson, at GOD's base in Ascension, complained you were non-compliant with local driving regs and disrespectful to his authority. Phillip Morris said you were non-communicative to requests for information and disappeared from your assigned survey support post in Greece. Merlin Plough indicated you created a security breach in Busan port, that might have encouraged an ineffective mine attack on port facilities. He also said you refused to comply with flight support ops protocol. Trent Bergle says you lost a large block of ocean track data around Mindoro, failed to follow shipboard emergency safety procedures and violated equipment transport policy. He also stated you departed the Philippines assignment without authorization. And yesterday, we received notification that you had been detained by the FBI, here in Washington. For what, we don't know, but it's not good business at the Pentagon for our employees to be held by the FBI. So what was that about?"

"I'm sorry, sir, I'm not at liberty to say."

"Well, that's unacceptable and, I might add, disrespectful of me. This all adds up to a pretty disappointing performance record, which is rather surprising, son, because we were expecting good things from you. What do you have to say to all this?"

"Well, gees, sir, I don't know. I think a lot of of the perceived problem is circumstantial, or open to interpretation, and I don't think anyone can say I did not follow my orders. I thought that's all I can, or should, do, is follow my official TDY orders."

"Hmm...., maybe, but there's just too much here to ignore. You know, you're still on probationary status and I hate to have to say this, but there's really no choice. I'm going to have to let you go."

"Really? Well, I'm disappointed, too. I thought working for the federal government would give me a special opportunity to go above and beyond to serve my country. I'm totally sorry it turned out this way, but thanks anyway." *Should I tell him he's presiding over a major drug running operation and a CIA black cover program? How would that play for good business at the Pentagon? Nah, let it rest. He'll find out the hard way. I'm outta here.*

"OK, well, good luck to you and I'm also sorry it didn't work out. Please check with Tom to out-process your separation paperwork." The director stood and extended a hand across the desk. The terminated engineer hesitated, remembering the crushing wrench of welcome on his first day aboard, then accepted his punishment of pain in leaving, this last day of federal service.

***

The asuper was head down asleep, hands folded on top of his watermelon belly, when the sacked sailor walked in the admin office to separate. Tom awakened with a start upon hearing the rustling of the newspaper from the other side of his desk. "Oh..., how you doing, Bill? I didn't hear you come in."

"Yeah, I'm pretty stealth. Look, I'm leaving NAVO and Paul said to see you to close out. So, here I am. Let's do it!" After filling out some forms regarding termination of benefits, protection of classified material, forwarding of personal data and waivers of right to claim, the outbounder had to complete a DD1351 travel voucher for his TDY service. This took some time, as he had to compile and reference all the accumulated receipts, notes and logs he had stuffed into the magic briefcase during his official globe trot. Also, there were questions pertaining to statements of nonavailability, transportation authorizations, certified receipts, deductible reimbursables, disbursement accountability and nonclassified expenses. He had no idea what any of these things were and needed considerable help from admin Tom to complete the form. The bottom line, including subtraction of advance payments received, computed to an additional allowance due, in the amount of $1,323.68. He could receive this payment, as well as cash-in of his accumulated retirement pension, $1,791.42, at the Navy's Pentagon disbursing office. Tom would electronically submit all the paperwork, so the money should be ready for pick-up by the time the closer got there. Rossy was thinking he had a million bucks in the bank and why hassle with going over to the Big P for a piddlin' three grand? But then the pragmatic side of his character interceded, arguing he could use the cash for walking around costs through the immediate future, in lieu of having to transfer withdrawal funds at the credit union. Besides, if he didn't sign for and receive the amounts due, there would forever be an 'open issue' flag under his name, and he always preferred anonymity, given the option.

As the new clownass engineer left the office, probably for a three hour beer lunch, tech super Green logged that the rooker had come in two hours and forty eight minutes late for work this morning. The journal was really shaping up. The main infraction of all these jerks was unauthorized absence from work. So far, he had documented almost two thousand hours that his so-called colleagues had stolen from the government, which extrapolated to an annual rate of about ten thousand hours. Assuming an average salary and labor burden of thirty dollars per hour, these dicks were wasting three hundred grand a year of taxpayers money! And who knows what the hell they did on TDY? His FWA payback for blowing the whistle on this zoo should work very well, indeed. Better than any goddam retirement pension he would probably have to die in place for. Yep, Margaritaville's gettin' closer all the time, as long as these assheads keep fracking off.

In exiting to depart the Bowditch Building for the final time, the unemployee again wondered about the missing third floor steps. Maybe it was something simple, like a specification typo ordering 'block third floor access', rather than 'lock third floor access', in some old contract project that nobody monitored. *Who knows? Guess it will always be a mystery.* Just like the NMS office on the first floor. He had passed by the dingy hallway entrance to NAVO's support agency countless times and had never seen anyone coming or going through that door. He had tried it a couple times and it was always locked and the office seemed perpetually closed and empty. There wasn't even anyone coming out of there during the bomb threat evacuation. And nobody ever said anything about the shadow suite below, like it didn't exist. A shell company - probably an invisible tophead Navy Yard branch office. Nothing was a surprise anymore.

It occurred to the last timer that he had said far fewer 'goodbyes' in leaving NAVO, than 'hellos' in arriving. Actually, he had not seen, nor did he look for, anyone to say 'so long' to, because, since he no longer held a security clearance, he couldn't wander around the floor unescorted. Just as well - he didn't particularly want to talk to anyone right now anyway, especially Dick, if he was in. That mummer was supposed to cover him in the field, but instead, cut him cold. What the hell kind of handler was that? Oh, well. It's all history, now.

***

It took the rest of the day to cash out at the Pentagon. On the return through D.C., the former civil servant thought he might stop in at the Mashup and see if any NAVO happy timers were there. It would be nice to kick back and relax a little with no particular point in mind. He was starting to feel aimlessly easy. Nowhere to go and nothing to do. A special freedom associated with being fired. Approaching the familiar doorway, the sounds of live music pulsated from the other side. Upon entering, it took a moment to adjust to the dimmed down atmosphere before looking around to assess who and what were where. Suddenly two arms slithered around his waist from behind, like twin black snakes, and a soft voice in his ear, "Oooh, dis bwoi, him not come see Marcie for some long time! How you are, bj, mon?"

"Hey, Marcie, great to see you! I'm good. How're you doin'?" Wow! She looked as fabulous as ever and it appeared she was doing very well. The place was packed. He glanced toward the back, from where the vibes shook, and there was bunny, front strutting on the floor, bassing out the core riff of Marley's *Rebel Music*. The self-retired tech was surrounded by his Off Beats and seemed to be thoroughly enjoying himself. *Oh, yeah, the boy was a player!* Over in the usual corner was the sailor table, at which sat wokker, rocko, blacktongue and shiner, who was pulling in another chair as he excitedly motioned for bj to come and join them.

"Hey, dawg, what's happenin'? Heard you were recruited by the FBI. Waddup wit dat??"

"Aw, nothing. Just a misunderstanding. Mistaken identity thing."

"So what's going on in the mothafrackin' outside world? Where the frack you been, anyhow? You see groob out there? You tell the dickface he took off owing me three frackin' bens?"

"No, bt, I had no intel on that, but everything's cool. Groob said to say 'hi'."

"I believe bj need to buy a round of troggs for the table! Ain't that right, bj?"

"Yeah, sure, why not? How's it goin', rocko? Hey, wokker!"

"MARCIE!"

The sailors settled in for an amiable happy time. It was evident no one yet knew of bj's axing, and he wasn't about to tell them. This evening could well be the last time this particular fivesome toasted together, making it sort of like a secret going away party privy only to the unknown guest of honor. He didn't anticipate any gross BO pranks. The gab centered around insignificant smalltalk and trifling banter, often erupting in raucous laughter. But they weren't any louder than anyone else. The Mashup was really rockin', despite it being a work night for those that were employed.

Booker filled his ex-roomie in on home front changes. Smith was gone on extended TDY to Diego Garcia, a strategic military research atoll in the Indian Ocean. Svelda was gone, returned to Sweden in a fit of blond rage. And he, himself, was gone, run out by the crazy jinks of the incompatible newly half-weds. Booker had moved into a one bedroom at AGA. He stored all Rossy's stuff in the smaller br at Smith's, where he had been stockpiling the mail. So, the fallout boy had the gamester's whole big apartment to himself. *Sweet!* But what about the car? "Gone, man, like the rest of us. No new info from what I told you before, so you'll have to get up with your good hands people. Good luck with that." *Goddam it! Now I have to buy another car?!*

Shiner then eagerly spilled he was leaving tomorrow on TDY. He had to pick up an equipment container that had been stranded at Honolulu IA, for insufficient payment of shipping fees, and carry it home to the Yard. Then he would turn right around and go back through Hawaii to the Trader in the Philippines. "Is this a great job, or what?" *Yeah, Booker, this job is a real trip!* The Trader vet saw no point in telling the unwitting new daft mule the truth. Let him find out for himself. NAVO was not his problem anymore and he had no official business with them, or anyone else. He was unemployed! It was starting to sink in. Out of work. On the street. All the fears and insecurities endured and suppressed over the past year were starting to rush from hiding into this lonely void of joblessness. And there was no one to talk to about it. He had to bear it all by himself. Just he and his ten thousand bens in the bank. *Oh, sweet lord, yes, Booker, this was for sure a **super** job!* "Hey, rocko! Another round on me, my brother!"

The incognito farewell party continued into later evening. Bunny hip-hopped by on a break, updating his former workmates on the progress of his new career. The band was booming. They had started work on a studio album and had offers for other gigs around town, but, for now, were staying put as Marcie's housies. They had incorporated a tuba into their repertoire and bunny, remembering bj was a fellow bassman, invited him to sit in for a set. The purist demurred, protesting a bass bubba 'oompah' horn was to roots reggae, as drums were to bluegrass - an outsider that didn't belong. Bunny argued it was innovation, a must in the business.

Eventually, before too long, before it got too late and as the conversation started to drag, the severed sailor decided he was happy enough and asked Marcie to call him a cab. Pursuant to a boisterous round of departure homilies, the tuckered freelancer headed over the river and up the hill to AGA. He didn't feel vulnerable riding through the ghetto with a briefcase full of new cash, because he was already in a cab and certainly had enough for the fare. It had been a long day. He thought he might sleep through tomorrow and start fresh on his redirection the next day. But, sitting in the apartment by himself, thinking about everything outré beyond his wildest dreams that had happened in his recent past, the lost-in-service agent, for some unchanneled reason from nowhere, brainstormed he should text his old PWA subgroup colleague and ask if his job slot had been filled. And then he laid down and slept until the day after tomorrow.

***

As he retroverted sufficiently from unconsciousness to hear the phone message beep, the well rested rouser reached for his phad on the floor beside the bed. *Omigod!* It was from doo-wop engineer at PWA! The long text response was a veritable game changer. Shortly following the dynamic duo's now legendary exit, the company hired a young lady engineer, freshly returned from a post-graduation missionary service in South America, and assigned her to their subgroup at FCPRF. Through the ensuing weeks the sg leader made increasingly hostile advances on the new hire, especially during contrived, after hours assignments when the two of them were alone in an empty office confinement. This resulted in her filing a very detailed and well documented harassment complaint, complete with compcam video, which bordered on a charge of sexual assault and subsequently led to his dismissal. The dude was there one day and cleared-out gone the next. Doo-wop was then promoted to sgl and there were again two slots to fill in the group. So, yeah, Rossy's job was still open and it was his if he wanted to come back. They were starting to get really busy and could sure use the help. Please let him know asap!

Damn!! What a totally unexpected development! The door of opportunity had opened so fast it rapped him right between the running lights! OK, a lot to analyze, so think it through. First, it's pretty clear this is a one and done, take it or leave it offer. No time to find, check and compare other options and then return to re-PWA as a default. He had to decide now on a stand alone basis. Actually, there were no other options. Work on the funny uncle's farm for R and B and a george?? Or be a sub-tech salesman for gonzo insect in Korea? Maybe a welder on GOD's forsaken island?? *I don't think so!* Second, he wasn't sure he wanted to go to work right away. He needed some time to clear his badly scrambled head. Maybe after the holidays and a mandatory trip home to let his relatives pound out their gloating rubs on a colossal career mistake they had all seen coming from the future like a runaway locomotive from government hell. That difficult reunion would no doubt straighten him out and jump start a corrective course. Third, it didn't seem Booker's vacant job was available to Booker. The text didn't mention that at all. But it didn't matter. Booker was good with his mistake. Fourth, under the new surprise financial circumstances, *do I really want to ever go back to work?* Well, the big mil pays for a lot of non-workdays. But not for life! It's not enough to support retirement for the next fifty years. Probably less than daft bunny quit on and he's looking to keep working a long time in his new performance career. So, yeah, *I gotta keep pushing.* OK, this is easy. All things considered, lets do it, but not before the new year. The lucky backtracker decided to get up and go out for a MacDonald's happy breakfast before returning his affirmative text answer to doo-wop's fortuitous offer.

***

Preparation for rebound to Connecticut was not easily simple. It wasn't like the well grounded engineer could just pack up the car and head out. There was no car. The former Civic owner had to try and coordinate the status of his allegedly stolen vehicle between the police and the insurance company. For whatever reason, but probably mainly because Booker was involved, neither had any record of followup in the investigation, nor the claim. There was no new information beyond the original statement of the non-owner complainant, who failed to document anything. It was a cold case. Rekindling the fire of justice proved a difficult undertaking and Rossy spent the better part of several days fighting the machine. In the end, he walked away with a check for one third the book resale value of the missing car, payable after remittance of the insurance premium balance due. It then took several hours at DMV, with no tags to turn in, to unregister the lost vehicle. The frazzled bureaucracy mazer thought it could be a lot smoother if all you did was pay a corrupt fee for what you needed, like in the Philippines, but, unfortunately, that was not the accountable American way.

Buying a new car was another exercise in provoked befuddlement. The aspiring repeat auto consumer didn't know anything more about cars than the first time he bought one, so he selected another Civic. This one was brand new and had a lot more features than what he was used to, including adaptable controls. *Sweet.* The least ugly color of the available, on-lot selection was an ecru beige, that was, by any standard, not very attractive, but would likely not present a primetime target for theftmeisters. The hard part of the purchase came in paying. The sales dude started to write up the bill of sale and adjoining paperwork as a fully financed manufacturer's loan, meaning the young client would ride out with almost nothing down and make monthly payments for years, eventually totaling nearly twice the sticker price of the car! No, no! He was paying all in, lump sum, up front. No monthly payments. Cash and own. The salesman's demeanor shifted from cheery to irritated. He tried to justify the financing plan, but the math didn't compute. OK, how about an extended warranty? An annual two grand takes care of everything. Maintenance, repairs, replacement, parts, labor. Everything. 'Nope, not interested.' Well, how about a super special undercoating treatment? Lifetime corrosion protection guarantee for only nine bens. 'No, don't think so.' Finally realizing he had a goddam pay-as-you-go thrift-spender on his hands, the rep relented and accepted full payment for the agreed to price with no add-ons. By the time the administrative ordeal was over, the new Civic was prepped and road ready to roll. It was nice to drive out into the world over your own wheels, and the revitalized highwayman felt a blast of zestful freedom in his acquisition.

One of the most satisfying issues on the to-do board was erasing the debt. *Amen for tophead, my non-extant million dollar man!* In preparing the final checks for payment of all the student loan account balances, the educated paperworker felt like an eternal boulder of doom was lifted from his future. Payment of the stolen car loan balance was a different story. Writing *that* check felt like crap! But to be debt free at his early post-college age was the *accomplir complét.* Now he knew the same buoyancy as the ghetto gang graduate in cutting the anchor of debt weight. But, unlike the graduate, *his* special funding resource was legal.......*wasn't it?*

And, lastly, the least favorite task on the list. The dreaded Christmas shopping. Oh, god, how the neo-Buddhist hated Christmas. Maybe the socializing and reconnection with friends and relatives was positive, at least in theory, and helping the needy and unfortunate was good, but the obtuse spending for gifts no-body really wanted, or had any use for, was insane. Worse, though, was the ruination of families trying to get way overpriced, artificially limited, specialty toys for children who wouldn't understand the negative impacts of the unaffordable purchases until they were adults. Every year people actually died, desperately trying to get a copy of the latest new thing for their kid. And the strangest facet of the sad story was how much the national economy relied on the retail sales of Christmas. The U.S. didn't manufacture and export much anymore, so internal, personal spending was the fuel driving the economic engine. The hype tried to condemn anyone, not buying their share, as an unpatriotic leper. An unAmerican under consumer. An economic non-conformist. So, what would Jesus do?

Jesus would probably go to the mall like everyone else. Where the manic crowds were compressed to panicky density, trying to find Santa Claus. So what if you trampled your neighbor? At least you got ahead in the line. And who could avoid the endless, continuous canned replay of about ten classic, seasonal songs? Over and over and over and.... The same tired old songs, for weeks, months, sometimes shrilled at a maddening degree of irritation by Alvin and the fracking Chipmunks. *Oh, please, dear Christmas, let my people go!*

The reluctant shopper had no idea what to buy. He had his mom, sisters, bros-in-law, aunt, uncle, grandpap, a cousin and a couple miscellaneous others to cover and really didn't know what to get any of them. Hopefully, the mystical mall would talk to him and reveal the secrets of successful speed shopping. In the end, he elected to buy each either a copy of *Company Business*, the current NYT's best seller by some first-time author, golf balls, or a scarf. The scarf was dubious, since it was almost hot outside, but surely it would be cold again sometime. He took all his purchases to a gift wrapping kiosk, and headed to a nearby open front bar for a Christmas coldie while he waited. Before leaving the hectic mall, he went through a Techways hub store to check the price of phads. $755.99. **Yes!!** It would *never* be lower here than what he paid in Korea! Elated, he subconsciously whistled along with *Deck the Halls* as he exited to the overflowing, four hundred acre parking lot. The high mood quickly collapsed when he arrived at his new ride and discovered a very visible one inch gash in the center of the driver's door. *Merry fracking Christmas!!*

***

Packing for departure was an exercise in rapid efficiency. The anti-consumer actually had less stuff now than when he first arrived in the D.C. area. He would have to go clothes shopping before returning to the work force, but that could be worried about later. Once ready, there was no lingering, no one to coordinate with, no need to sign out. Leaving the keys on the dining room table, he left the apartment, got in his little tan car and drove away. It had been a short-lived government career, here, in the storied capital of the free world. He had made a few new friends, maybe just as many enemies, and got to experience lots of different places and cultures. There was a multitude of memories, many of which he wasn't sure he would ever understand. It wasn't clear what, if anything, he learned through this page of his resumé, except he was done with civil service and would probably never pass this way again.

CUBA

The scene was striking in its empty beauty. Pure white sand, sun-spilled sky, aqua clear sea, a hint of breeze, like a zephyr of peace from the satisfied gods. The beach fronting Las Brisas Hotel, in Playa Ancon, on Cuba's south coast, would normally be, not really crowded, but well populated with a variety of international tourists seeking the quiet mystique of the forgotten island nation. Not today. Today, as of early afternoon, the beach was closed. The *Policía Nacional Revolucionaria*, Cuba's national law enforcement agency, had taken over and restricted the premises, following receipt of an unidentified call describing a curious situation on the beach. There was a man in a low folding chair facing the sea, legs extended and crossed at the ankles and arms splayed out in the sand, who had not moved from the same position for several hours. Guests had started to complain that something didn't seem right down below the dunes and the hotel desk manager called the PNR without directly investigating. In Cuba, the best thing to do, always, was not get involved. The less you knew about anything, the better you could conduct your affairs with minimum hassle.

A cadre of uniformed and suited men made their way slowly toward the motionless figure from the hotel deck cabana. Their boots and hard leather shoes were not well adapted to walking through the loose, fine sand. As they neared the target, the official in charge did not like the look of the unnatural, uptilted angle of the head, lolling against the back of the chair. They were going to find a body, not a passed out tourist. And sure enough, they found a *big* body, maybe almost two meters and well over a hundred kilos. The dead man was clad only in a pair of black Nike knee shorts and military sun glasses and there was no phone, wallet, nor any form of paper ID in his pockets, or anywhere in the vicinity of the remains. His exposed, bald head was grayish pink and severely blistered. A pair of Ralph Lauren strap sandals lay in the sand by his feet. Near the chair was a teak carton of Habanos Limitadas Supreme cigars and a monogrammed platinum lighter, worth well more than the PNR official made in three months. He hated these rich outsiders, who came to Cuba to flaunt their money and gawk at its residents as though they were some inferior race of underclassers, existing only to serve the lazy vacationers. One of the cigars was held in the body's right hand, tightly pinched between the index and middle finger, where it had burned down to a stub and singed the adjacent flesh. But the most significant observance was the condition of the forehead, featuring a 12 mm hole in the middle that had oozed a thin stream of dried, cauterized blood, like a punctured third eye. There was no evidence of any projectile or foreign material embedded in the wound and there was no exit opening. While it looked like some sort of gunshot, nothing could be concluded until autopsy, except it appeared the man died instantaneously, with no premonition of demise. The body had not moved from a position of relaxing leisure before death to the exact same position after. The victim never saw what was coming and never knew what hit him. The official field noted it was his preliminary opinion the man had been assassinated by a single shot, from an unidentified weapon fired from far off shore. He called for medical and criminal investigation specialists to come down from ministry headquarters in Havana and ordered his subordinates to secure and protect the site. He then went back to the hotel to interview the manager and any guests who might have information pertinent to what was shaping up to be a rather spectacular murder case.

The manager identified the deceased as Johann Lijsenraad, a Dutch business agent traveling under a Canadian passport. The Hollander had been a registered guest at the hotel for almost a week and his documentation indicated he was in Cuba to promote resort development along the south coast on behalf of an unnamed American venture capitalist. Search of the businessman's room found nothing unusual. A wallet with a small amount of cash, a few credit cards, an international driver's license and other miscellaneous IDs. Also, a typical visitor's wardrobe and accessories, another box of expensive cigars, a phad and a travelcomp. The PNR investigator would have the devices analyzed by tech services. Without any obvious clues the official speculated the Dutchman could have been zapped by someone, could be anybody, opposed to further development of Cuban resources for the benefit and profit of foreigners. There was a growing sentiment in

Cuba that the people had waited long enough for their own prosperity and they didn't want to be hijacked by recent enemies of the state.

The next step in this preliminary evaluation would be questioning of other guests who were on the beach this morning. This was a tedious task failing to reveal anything substantive, except it was rather uncommonly agreed that no one heard anything resembling a gunshot and no one remembered seeing any type of vessel off coast that could have facilitated a waterside sniper. The PNR super went back out to the body site on the sand. He re-instructed the others to wait for the support investigators and make sure no one disturbed anything. He then confiscated the cigar box as 'special evidence' and departed the resort in his government assigned, twenty-two year old Land Rover, feeling fairly certain this case would soon freeze. There just wasn't enough to follow up on. One thing nagged, though, from some incomplete memory chip in his mind. The Dutchman looked vaguely familiar, in a photographic way. The police official thought he had seen a picture of Lijsenraad somewhere, quite a while ago, but he couldn't remember the context. He would have to check it out further when he returned to district headquarters.

INTERSTATE

The road back to Connecticut could be taken many ways. Rossy decided to run the urban route, Interstate 95 from Baltimore, through Wilmington, Philadelphia, New York and New Haven. This was, arguably, the most heavily travelled stretch of highway in the world. There was not a day went by without a sensational mashup, usually involving one or more trucks, occurring at some point along the reach of I-95. And any accident in this mid-Atlantic corridor, even if it only blocked one lane, invariably resulted in several hours delay to through traffic. As the so-stalled northbounder sat in an elongated field of stationary vehicles between Newark and Wilmington, he checked the local status on an advisory app. The wreck was seven miles ahead and closed most lanes in both directions. A bus had crossed the median and sideswiped a tractor trailer, which then jackknifed sideways and overturned. Several cars crashed trying to get out of the way. It was going to be a long day on the big road, going nowhere.

Civic man didn't really care. He didn't have to be at his new, old job for another week and had planned a slow paced trip, with frequent stops to sightsee in areas he had never been to before. Presently, he was getting a good first look at the six lane parking lot he was trapped in, wondering why those in the other five lanes were moving forward at a slightly faster creep than he. He reminisced about the past holiday week spent in Pennsylvania. It had been a predictable tribulation, but it was over now and he was glad he had dutifully made the family connection. There was a comfortable freedom in retracing his future with the blessing of everyone knowing best what he should do with his life. But he had to endure a lot of 'told you sos' in the process. He learned a sister was expecting his first nephew, which was cool. Mom was fine, doing the same loony astro-clairvoyant stuff she was obsessed with. She had been upset by his lack of contact, but he told her, and everyone else, he couldn't talk about the Washington job, because it was tightly classified. They soon forgot about trying to find out what he did during his gross mistake with the government and focussed on how lucky he was to be able to return to a real job. *OK, whatever, already.* Grandpap was doing well, after they had to clear his apartment again. Most of his collected dross ended up in the landfill and he was already making plans to acquire new things he had looked at, but never had room for.

Fortunately, the holiday reveler was able to break from family for an evening and hook up with the Camster. They met at the Inn, because uncle Billy refused to go to Millton, where Cam related big changes were underway. Evidently, the night they were thrown out of town, there was a near street riot, resulting from a tense confrontation between the police and the citizenry. The unrest continued for several days and a joint task force was set up to identify issues of dispute and points of resolution. A major contention was that the police force, more than ninety percent white, did not reflect the demographics of the community. It was agreed the department would actively recruit a more balanced representation. Out of this initiative, two things happened quickly. Officer Henke, the drunken false arrester and civil rights abuser, was fired. And guess what? Shelby was hired as his replacement! Yep, Shelb was in training right now to become a member of the Millton Public Safety Force. A twofer on the borough's path to redemption. Unbelievable! Also, during the disturbances, the Lounge burned down and Leonard claimed insurance as a victim of the riot. He's gone to Florida, retired in the sun. So now, Cam spends his Saturdays at the track, where he holds part interest in a harness racing horse. A lot of changes. The ex-fed had nothing to report. His recent experience was classified.

The family gift exchanges offered no surprises. Mostly everyone was unimpressed with what they got, but expressed bogus gratitude for something they had always wanted. There was one lighthearted moment when Billy and his cousin gave each other the same book. They signed their respective copies, so they wouldn't get them mixed up. Mom gave her only begotten son underwear and socks. *Underwear and socks!* Like he was five years old, for chrissakes! But what the hell, they were on his list of things he needed to buy, so it was a good gift. The scarves prompted a discussion about global warming and climate change that ended up in a heated argument split along party lines. There was peaceful agreement to disagree agreeably, though, by the time they met their reservation at Abel's Amish Almshouse for a Christmas dinner buffet. The clever Amishman was open on the extreme holiday, knowing anyone showing up would be willing to pay any price he charged. But he put out a damned good fare, that allowed everyone to watch football the rest of the day without guilt. All things considered, it wasn't a bad Christmas gathering.

***

New York was the main event of the trip. The Big Bad Apple. Farmer boy had never been to the king of cities and planned to stay a few days visiting highlights and maybe doing some shopping. The last image of NYC that stuck in his mind was a recent sci-fi movie on TV about some kind of super, polar vortex, tsunami storm causing Manhattan to ice up over the head of the Statue of Liberty. But, of course, that was not the case in reality. It was still unseasonably warm, in the mid-sixties, with plenty of clear sky and high pressure sunshine. Not a typical winter weather pattern, but perfect for sightseeing. The road warrior pulled into the Midtown Motor Manor, where he had made internet reservations, in late afternoon. The drive from the interstate was against the rush and not difficult to engage. He planned to park the car at the hotel and use cabs, subway and feets to get around everywhere he wanted to see. After check-in, he went out into the spectacular early evening lights of the city. Iconic Times Square was still bubbling over from holiday fervor and the small towner soon found himself standing on the sidewalk, under a pigeon smitten soup cafe awning, just taking it all in. People of all makes and models were everywhere, fast stepping in every direction as though they knew exactly where they were going and were late. One young woman, of obvious high fashion, shoved an abe into the hand of the startled bystander as she bustled by without even looking at him. *What the hell?!* She must have thought he was a homeless panhandler! He tried to thank her, but she was gone, melded into the pedestrian mesh, a hit and run samaritan. Glancing at his reflection in a window, the man on the street decided that, yes, he *did* look homeless. And actually, for the moment, he *was* homeless, but he had means. Tomorrow he would dehippify himself, get some decent clothes and reset. It was time to prepare for reentry into the work force. But first, he slipped into the nearest pub to buy a free, New York happy time brew.

The interstater thoroughly enjoyed his tourist time in the BA. He visited a number of world famous attractions and savored ethnic New York cuisine in a variety of site characteristic eateries. He got his head straight in a regionally renowned barber shop on Broadway, across from legendary Central Park. After touring uptown Harlem by subway, he returned to the landmark East Side Macy's to pick up several new, working casual outfits. By the time he was ready to leave, it was like he had gone through a personal metamorphosis, from declassified, loser ops agent to metropolitan professional. It was with high spirits the NY vet crossed over the turbid river into Brooklyn, retraced to I-95 and continued on toward the Connecticut endpoint, his special destination of second chances.

CONNECTICUT

Rossy couldn't imagine he was once again walking through the lackluster FCPRF entrance. It felt like he was receding in time, sort of a 'back to the future' scenario. Doo-wop engineer met his past associate in the tiny lobby with glad-handed greetings and escorted him through the building to the familiar sg cubicle in the development section, where he found his old desk and workstation essentially intact. The same pens and random office items were still in the shallow supply tray, just as when he departed, seemingly many moons ago. There was even an ancient credit card receipt he had forgotten. Booker's desk was empty, but the new engineer, Nonny Jones, sat at doo-wop's previous place, as he had moved over to the sgl corner. The returnee plopped down into his subordinate swivel, that still had an irregular thump-up at one point in its rotation. Despite his prior service, he was low on the sg pole, being the most recently hired, but that was fine. He was just grateful to have a job.

Nonny looked conforming in her attire, work casually dressed in khaki slacks, blue oxford shirt and penny loafers with white silk socks. Her long, brownish-blond hair was braided and coiled into a flawless bun and she wore no jewelry, minimal makeup. She introduced herself as an MIT graduate with a master's degree in energy systems engineering. The junior rerook thought she would one day be his boss. Barely after introductions, the subgroup was visited by the recognized former colleagues from another cubicle and the five engineers shifted to the Deli Diner for breakfast break. The ex-admin assistant dater was still ex-status and had no inside company scoop to relay. Then, when everyone accepted the come back man could not talk about what he had done during his hiatus, the garble turned to sports. Nonny was a severe football fan and predicted Super Bowl glory for her precious Patriots. Oh, no, another irrational Boston team sports nut.

***

The administrative supervisor leaned back in his chair and removed his glasses, rubbing his eyes with the heels of his hands. He looked tiredly at the organization's most recent hire, seated before him in the glass corner office, and shook his head in slow dubiety. "Mr. Rossy, I cannot believe you are with us again. You're like a bad bounce and trust me, if it was up to me, you wouldn't even be allowed to drive past this facility on the county road. But, unfortunately, it's not up to me, so here we are and I've got to process you in."

"Yes, sir, it's nice to be back."

"OK, first, the UTG CEO is still national chairman for United Way, so what's it going to be? Please don't give me any crap on this. It's been a long day."

"Yes, sir, I understand. No problem." The rebounder had anticipated this issue and, after much soul searching, had decided what he wanted to do. He reached for his wallet and withdrew a check he had previously written out for the moment. "I want to participate as required and here's my contribution."

The supervisor looked at the check and scrunched his entire face into a warped grimace. "**What the frack is this?!** Do you think this is some kind of a goddam joke? I swear to god I'll take this to the top of corporate headquarters and get your clownass butt thrown out of here for good. I've never had to deal with such unprofessionalism. You should be ashamed."

"No, sir, it's not a joke. It's for real. It's what I want to contribute to United Way as a participating PWA employee."

"*Five...hundred...thousand...dollars??!* Seriously?? How the hell can you do this?"

"I've had some unusual circumstances and, yes, totally seriously. I can give you my account contact information so you can verify the check."

"Well, OK, OK. I guess thanks are in order, then, on behalf of the organization, the chairman, everyone. This is extraordinary. I don't know exactly what to say." The super knew what he would have to do, though. Once this got processed, he would have to award this bozo *'employee of the quarter'*, giving him the parking space by the door during the dead of winter. *Shit!*

"Thank you, sir, I appreciate that. Glad to help out."

***

After work the reunited happy timers convened at Dexter's Drinkery, a new place that opened not long after they had been permanently exiled from the Grill, during the way-back-when farewell caper. A few rounds into the homecoming HT, someone asked Nonny what her missionary work before she started at PWA was all about, because she didn't come across as being particularly religious. She revealed her full name was 'Anonymous Jones', deriving from an administrative error in her infancy. As a new-born, she was abandoned with no ID at the gate of a children's home in Cambridge. She was taken to the hospital for observation and examination, during which someone copied her impromptu anklet tag onto a birth certificate, so she could be issued a SSN and receive medicaid. She never found out anything about her birth family and grew up in the church sponsored home. There was an arrangement with MIT, that residents at the home who qualified academically could attend the university on a full scholarship, as long as they maintained their grades. The only caveat was they had to give six months' missionary service to the church upon gradua-tion. But it was worth it to get a free education. Even though it was hard growing up without a real family, she felt it all turned out for the best and she was ahead of the game.

Rossy felt the same way. Even though, since graduation, he had gone through the strangest period of his life, enduring an un-accountable series of ups and downs and wild experiences and occurrences he would never be able to interpret, or possibly re-member in a straight line, it apparently was all turning out for the best. And he, too, was definitely ahead of the game. It was good to be here, good to be back in the world, back with a real job. This time for keeps.

◆ ◆ ◆ ◆ ◆

Meet our Author

Bill Runyan is originally from Pennsylvania, where he spent his formative and educative years. Upon graduation from Bucknell University's engineering school, Mr. Runyan was fortunate to be confronted with several comparable opportunities, of which each was a path to a different life. Literally dartboarding a selection, he began an excursion leading to a stint in the mashhouse world of large corporate employment, a quarter million miles of travel around the world with federal civil service, a foray into the crockpot of local politics as a county engineer and nearly four years volunteer service in Peace Corps. This varied career has provided experience in working with others, working alone and living on three gallons of water a day. It also developed a macro view based on respect for others, respect for the natural milieu and optimism for the future. After residing in several different locales and cultures, Mr. Runyan doesn't make the distinction of a favorite place to be, believing everyplace has unique and memorable qualities to offer anyone taking the time to learn them. He is currently in Newland, North Carolina, in the middle of Appalachia high country, enjoying the retirement pleasures of fly fishing, golf, blue grass music and, finally, writing. And, always, the special privilege of life with Jayne and the never ending quest to coordinate live connections with three distant daughters and eight grandchildren. Peace.